BY JAMES ALDRIDGE

Signed with Their Honour

The Sea Eagle

Of Many Men

The Diplomat

The Diplomat

JAMES ALDRIDGE

The
Diplomat

Boston

LITTLE, BROWN AND COMPANY

1950

1

Published simultaneously
in Canada by McClelland and Stewart Limited

PRINTED IN THE UNITED STATES OF AMERICA
BY THE HADDON CRAFTSMEN, INC., SCRANTON, PA.

Author's Note

All the characters and incidents in this book are fictitious.

At the same time, not even a fictitious mission cast in the present can escape the existence of living historical figures. In certain parts of this book I have pictured particular living statesmen in their own rôle and by their own names, and like any historical novelist I have given them words to say. Yet all incidents and conversations around them are mere images.

The mission itself is an image; and though it might very well have happened, its only possible claim to fact is in the historical parallels of the last few years.

BOOK I
Lord Essex

Chapter 1

Lord Essex sat in the Douglas aeroplane and smoked his pipe and waited for another conveyance to come and take him away. The plane had force-landed in the darkness after running into a snowstorm which had frozen its controls. It rested now on its belly in a bleak white Russian field, washed quietly by the snow and the wind. Looking out of the small window at the snowing darkness, Lord Essex was sorry that he was not a younger man so that he could have gone with MacGregor and the Russian crew to look for a farmhouse and some transport.

At fifty-eight Essex was too old to be anything but the man left behind, even though he looked ten years younger. Essex was deliberately healthy and strongly opposed to growing old. His face was pink and calm and adult; he had confident eyes and a solid noble broken nose. As he leaned on his elbows in the cushioned seat he was relaxed and even sleepy and he showed no reaction to the dangerous landing they had just made. He was more concerned about the snoring of the Russian passenger behind him, and by the fact that his arrival in Moscow would be one day delayed. One day's delay could be unfortunate on a mission that had to be done-with as quickly as possible. Apart from that he was glad of this interruption. He was one of those gifted men to whom adventure always happens. He could expect something like a forced landing to come along at the right time and give him romance. The more that happened to Essex at fifty-eight the more he liked it, so long as it did not destroy him. The pity of it was that he could not go with MacGregor across that dark wash of snow.

MacGregor had gone off with the Russians without asking Essex's permission. Though he had never seen MacGregor before meeting him on the London airfield, Essex felt that the young man might have asked his permission before going. MacGregor was his chosen assistant on this mission and MacGregor owed him the courtesy of some deference. MacGregor had not been impolite, but he was unusually independent and brainy-looking for an India Office expert. Essex had undertaken this mission at a few hours' notice and he had chosen MacGregor on paper as the best man he could get on Iranian affairs. Since leaving London Essex had not succeeded in thawing him out. Even the forced

3

landing had not broken MacGregor's restraint and he had behaved in the worst moment of the crash as unnervously as Essex himself. Nevertheless, in their short and broken conversations Essex had already detected a slight and unexplainable reluctance in MacGregor, a careful withdrawal or a discontent. Essex did not like it. On a mission like this he had to have the quick co-operation of his assistant: success or failure could depend upon it. It was time that he took MacGregor in hand, because MacGregor would have to be straightened out by the time they reached Moscow.

The Russian behind Essex snored again and Essex leaned back and touched the man to stop it. Then he bundled up in his fur-lined coat and tried to sleep with his mind upon the first meeting with Molotov. He would make sly jokes with Molotov about their forced landing in a Russian plane. They would be English jokes which Molotov might not fully appreciate. No doubt Molotov would smile with his flat face and think up a reply which would come rattling off his sharp tongue. It would be something clever, humorous enough, but political because the Russians behaved that way even in their humour. They were always half serious and half proud, and always politically single-minded.

When Essex awakened, MacGregor was sitting beside him. They were alone in the plane. "Well, MacGregor," Essex said. "Any luck at all? Did you find a village?"

"We found a farmhouse," MacGregor said. "Apparently there is a village across the far north end of this field. The pilot is bringing a sled, and we can ride in."

"How about transport to Moscow?"

"We'll have to do what we can at the village. One of the crew has gone to a Red Army camp somewhere about, and with a little luck we may get a car." MacGregor spoke with this care which Essex did not like.

"How far are we from Moscow?" Essex asked him.

"About forty miles."

"What about that sled to take us to the village?" Essex would have to ask the questions because MacGregor would not volunteer much information.

"It will be here any minute."

"Well that's something," Essex grunted.

MacGregor added nothing and they sat quietly in the cold plane. Essex lit his pipe again, and MacGregor sat still as if he did not want to disturb Essex or remind Essex of his presence, but Lord Essex stretched again with calm laziness.

"I suppose we will miss Molotov to-morrow," he said to MacGregor.

"Yes."

4

"Of course no definite meeting had been arranged with him but I was counting on seeing him to-morrow so that we could start quickly."

MacGregor listened with dull silence.

"Are you all set to go to work?" Essex asked him.

"I am not sure," MacGregor said. "I was just given a bundle of documents and a very brief outline by Sir Rowland Smith. I don't even know the agenda."

"There isn't any agenda," Essex said. "The Russians don't want to talk, they don't want to make anything definite, so we will have to work things out as we go along. I hope to God you know your Azerbaijan, MacGregor, because these Russians have to be met with plenty of details. You have been working in London on northern Iran for some time haven't you?"

"Six or seven months."

"How long did you live in Iran?"

"Most of my life."

"Good. Then you know what we are up against there and you will understand the job we have to do in Moscow. All I have is a bare instruction telling me to get the Russians out of Azerbaijan and restore the Teheran Government's authority. Not much to work on, is it?"

"I don't suppose it is."

"It's a tall order for us, MacGregor," Essex said, "because the Foreign Minister failed to shift the Russians at the Moscow Conference barely a week ago. So we are beginning with something of a lost cause. I think we can pull it off if we keep right up to the mark. We're not very well prepared but we know what we want, that is the main thing. What sort of material did Rowland Smith give you?"

"Mostly documents prepared for the Moscow Conference."

"What's it like?"

"I haven't read it all." MacGregor was a calm fellow alright.

"I don't place much store in a lot of documents so don't worry too much about it. I'll be better satisfied if you know your subject. One man who knows his area is a damn sight better than a trunkload of documents. I don't understand why they didn't take you to the Moscow Conference in the first place."

"Sir Rowland went himself," MacGregor said.

"I know that, but he could hardly have your knowledge of the country." It did not sound at all like flattery. Essex smiled. "How do you feel about getting in on this trip, MacGregor?"

"I don't mind," MacGregor said in a friendly way.

"You don't mind!"

"No. But how long will we be in Moscow?" It seemed to be the first question that MacGregor had asked Essex since they had left London.

"Good heavens, I don't know," Essex said. "Do you have something more important to do?"

MacGregor did not reply and Essex guessed that MacGregor was blushing. He should blush, but Essex was sorry that he had caught MacGregor like that, and he laughed a little and cracked MacGregor on the knee.

"We won't be long," Essex said.

"I wanted to catch someone in London, that was all." MacGregor was embarrassed, and this pleased Essex all the more and he did not let this go.

"When?" Essex asked.

"In about two weeks, I think."

"Oh, we should be back by then," Essex said. "If we're not you can probably telephone whoever it is from Moscow. I think the phone is going again. Is it important?"

"It might be." MacGregor had no choice but to explain. "It's a fellow who is coming from Iran, as a matter of fact, and I want to see him about going back there. Back to my job."

"Oh?" Essex lit a match and almost looked at MacGregor's face with it as he lit his pipe. "I remember reading something about it in your file. Geologist weren't you, or something like that, with the English-Persian oil people. In Iran was it?"

"Something like that," MacGregor said.

"What exactly were you?"

"A micro-paleontologist."

"What the devil is that?"

"A paleontologist, but specializing in microscopic fossils."

"I thought you had been a geologist."

"It's part of geology."

"Little more academic eh?"

"In a way."

"And you intend going back to it?"

"If I can."

"You don't intend staying in the India Office at all?"

"No," MacGregor said. "I was more or less drafted into it."

"You seem to be turning down a golden opportunity in leaving the India Office, MacGregor. This particular job you are on will be quite a start for you. What on earth do you want to go back to geology or paleontology for?"

"It's my work," MacGregor said carefully.

"How long have you been away from it?"

"All the war. About six years."

"Then I don't suppose it will be easy for you to go back to it."

"No. It will be quite difficult."

"Oh well. Every man to his own field. But haven't eight months in

6

the India Office convinced you that there is more in diplomacy than in geology?"

"I don't know much about diplomacy." MacGregor had thawed a little. "I was surprised when I was told that I was going with you."

"I picked you myself, my boy."

"I had wondered why." MacGregor hesitated over it.

"Ah, I pick my men for being men MacGregor, not for being good Civil Servants. I like young men, and thirty is a good age for you to begin. You had lived in the country of course and knew the languages, and that pretty well decided me, but I thought you had quite a few extra qualifications. New man in the field, good war record: Military Cross eh?"

"Yessir." It was the last military trace of the man.

"A good war record is a good background to have, particularly in this business." Essex knew what he was talking about because he had a good war record himself: not only a Military Cross but a Distinguished Service Order. Apart from that he looked upon war as a necessary experience, and he had never been sorry for his own experience. He had been in France within the first year of the First War's beginning, and within another year he had been a Captain in the family regiment, the Household Cavalry, and in charge of five hundred yards of line on the Somme. Actually, when he wanted to be honest with himself, Essex admitted that he had not liked the Western Front, and though he had fully enjoyed the liberality of Paris on his rare leaves, he had been very glad to get out of it and move over to the Middle East. He had found in Cairo what he had hoped to find in every other city in the world: leisure, importance, ease, warmth, and wealth, as well as a few moments of really great experience. As a Major and a Staff Officer he had spent some of his time along the Red Sea with Standish and Lawrence, men he had recognized immediately as historic figures. For that alone the war had been worth while. He must remember to tell MacGregor about it because it did these young fellows good to see that their experience in this war was not exclusive, particularly for a fellow like MacGregor whose record showed that he had spent a considerable amount of time in the Long Range Desert Group, which to Essex was the only unit in this war to resemble Lawrence's exceptional men. That had been another reason for choosing MacGregor, but Essex didn't mention it. Instead he told MacGregor that his knowledge of Russian had been a factor in his selection.

"I wouldn't count on my Russian," MacGregor said.

"I never count on anything," Essex told him. "Anyway: how did you get into the India Office? Did Rowland Smith acquire you?"

"I don't know. They just lifted me out of the Army and discharged me on the condition that I went into the India Office for a while. They won't let me get out of it now."

7

"Well, you will just have to put up with this for a few weeks more, MacGregor. I am going to need all the assistance you can give me."

"I don't know much about this work," MacGregor said again.

"And I gather that you are not particularly interested?"

Essex could see that MacGregor did not want to answer that.

"Yes, I'm interested," MacGregor said and got up and stamped his feet on the cold metal floor of the plane and walked up and down away from Essex. Essex got up when someone banged on the metal door from the outside. MacGregor opened it and the snow blew in and Essex could hear the two Russian passengers. He watched them get into the plane again and throw their bundles into a rough sled which had been backed up to the door. The pilot had climbed in against the luggage, and he laughed and said something to MacGregor in Russian and did not wait for MacGregor's reply but went up to the cockpit.

"You can ride," MacGregor said, and jumped down.

Essex told him to move aside as he leapt down into the slush. "I can walk," he said.

"The snow is deep and wet." MacGregor did not know yet that he was saying the wrong thing to this old-young man.

"I prefer to walk," Essex told him. The peasant pulled and kicked his horses. The sled jerked forward and led Essex blindly in the darkness across a rising field, through its timber, and over the snowbanks. It was too much for MacGregor to watch Essex walking, and he got off the sled and walked the rest of the way to the village.

The village was small, a few wooden huts in the surrounding snow, primitive and black, even in the night. The sled stopped at one of the low huts which showed a yellow light in its small window and Essex followed MacGregor into the dim room. Essex saw a tiled stove in the middle of the rough floor and he walked forward with his hands outstretched and said to MacGregor, "What the devil is this place?"

"The post office," MacGregor told him.

It was a dark and warm but dingy hut, with one golden corner of light. This came from a small floating wick in an open cigarette tin of oil standing on an old timbered counter. A round stocky peasant girl leaned on the counter near the light, her hand at her chin and her lips pouted. A small Russian soldier with crossed legs leaned on the side of the counter playing a thirteen-string guitar. These two watched the strangers disinterestedly, as the luggage was brought in and blankets were spread out and their stove surrounded. The soldier went on singing lightly as the pilot of the plane faced the girl and shook the snow off his leather coat and turned the handle of the phone which was hanging precariously on the wall.

"It's a dingy place and damned dark," Essex said, and sat down on one

8

of the blankets near the stove. MacGregor stood near him for a moment taking off his trench coat to hang it on a hooked post.

"What would these people be doing in the post office at two o'clock in the morning?" he said to Essex, avoiding two other Russians, asleep on mailbags around the corner of the stove.

"No home," Essex said and watched MacGregor lean on the counter near the soldier with the guitar. Essex sat with his back to the warm tiles of the stove and he took a good look at MacGregor. It was the first time that Essex had seen him out of his crushed trench coat. Essex found it hard to single out any characteristic by which he could better identify MacGregor. He was lean, and about as tall as Essex himself. His face seemed small but very smooth and very tight. It was set with the expression of a man who did his own thinking all the time, and who kept all his thinking to himself. He had thin straight hair, but it was the sort of hair that suited him. It was the sort of hair that stayed throughout a man's lifetime, a little like Essex's own, but not so well cut or groomed to fit his features. It was the only similarity between the two men. Where Essex's nose was broken, MacGregor's was thin and straight and Scotch. Where Essex's eyes were quick and humorous, MacGregor's were too controlled and patient. Their clothes were different. Essex wore a good flannel suit and MacGregor wore a shaggy herringbone cut too loose. This annoyed Essex because he liked men who had the imagination to dress well, even if they dressed untidily. MacGregor's untidy and dull clothes were something of a contradiction to his careful attitudes and his apparent independence. Essex did not like too many contradictions in his assistants, and he watched MacGregor closely to see from which direction he could charm this fellow into loyalty and co-operation and understanding. He dozed off without getting far, and MacGregor was again sitting on the floor beside him when he awakened.

"Did they phone Moscow?" Essex asked him.

"Yes," MacGregor said. "They eventually got through."

"Did you talk with the Embassy?"

"No. The pilot said that the Embassy would be told about us."

"It may not be wise to leave it to our Russian friends."

"It will be alright if they remember at the other end," MacGregor said.

"Perhaps we ought to insist on a car to Moscow as soon as possible."

"A car will be here in about an hour. If the roads aren't too frozen we can probably reach Moscow by early morning."

Essex eased down on the floor and leaned on his elbow. "I see that fellow is still playing his guitar. Did you find out what he was doing here at this hour of the night?" He mumbled this at MacGregor as the guitarist started to sing again to the plump girl.

"He likes the postmistress," MacGregor said and smiled.

9

Essex looked up at him. "At two o'clock in the morning?"

"Time doesn't seem to mean much here. He told me he has to start cutting timber at five o'clock in the morning — this morning."

"Who are these other people lying about on the floor?"

"Peasants."

Essex took off his shoes and put his stockinged feet back near the stove. He was now fully reclined upon the floor along the stove, his head on his fur-lined coat and his hands beneath his head. "Russia hasn't changed much despite its revolution," he said and looked at the straw-lined ceiling. "Have you been here before, MacGregor?"

"No." MacGregor leaned down on his elbow as if Essex's informality had emboldened him a little. "Have you been here before?"

"Yes," Essex said sleepily. "I was here in 1905 during the first Revolution, when I was sixteen or seventeen. I really came over with my father to present a gold vase to the Czar from the King, to console him for his revolutionary troubles."

"A vase?"

"Yes. I don't know why. But it was quite a beautiful vase as I remember it, even if it was a little baroque. It was etched or engraved with Michelangelo's Seven Apostles and inscribed with goodwill messages in old Russian religious characters. I wasn't allowed to go with my father when he presented it, but I remember him coming back shouting with laughter because the Czar had called in the court jewellers to look at it. They were French, Faubourg people, and the Czar sent for them right there and then and asked them what they thought of such delicate engraving. They had to flatter it of course, but their idea of flattery was to suggest that it must have been done by a Frenchman. My father told them it had been done by a heavy-handed Wilkinson swordsmith, and suggested to the Czar that he get a few good English tradesmen in the palace instead of these French foreigners. As a matter of fact I found out later that the vase had been engraved by a Frenchman specially brought to England from France to do it, and I shall never forget the look on my father's face when I told him. It was the best diplomatic joke he had heard in his life. I believe that the old Czar thought so too, when he found out." Essex sighed. "Ah: those were the days of diplomacy, MacGregor. That was in St. Petersburg of course. I wonder where that vase is now?"

"Perhaps Molotov could tell you," MacGregor said.

"I wouldn't ask him. They don't like to talk about their Czars; remember that, MacGregor. They like to forget everything that happened before their Bolshevik Revolution."

"How do they manage it?"

"I don't know," Essex said, "but they try. How much do you know about this country, since you speak the language?"

"Very little," MacGregor said. "My Russian is an accident of living with a Russian family for many years, and the only thing I know about Russia is from scientific papers, which have nothing to do with politics."

"What about the Russians — scientifically?"

"They're alright."

"Backward?"

"I wouldn't say that," MacGregor replied. "In some of my work they are ahead, but I don't know much about other fields. I believe they are very good in physics and other pure sciences, but they seem to be backward in the techniques."

"They are damned backward politically," Essex said.

"Would you think so?" MacGregor said.

"Wouldn't you?"

"I wouldn't know," MacGregor said carefully, and Essex felt the layman's annoyance at the rationalist's care as to what he did and did not know. "Perhaps they will learn something from us, now that we are all co-operating," MacGregor added.

"Co-operation will not last long," Essex said, annoyed with MacGregor's care.

"Why not?" MacGregor said.

"Friction will wear it out, my boy."

MacGregor said "Oh" and did not carry it any further.

"Look at the United Nations meeting coming up in London," Essex went on. "It hasn't begun yet, and they are already arguing about who is to be President or Secretary General, or who is to sit on the Security Council. They are fighting before they begin to have a United Nations."

"I suppose they have to fight among themselves," MacGregor said, "but can't they get something out of it?"

"What can you see them getting out of it?"

"It seems to be better than the old League of Nations and at least the Russians are in it." MacGregor stopped short, not sure whether he had said too much because of their informal occupancy of the post-office floor.

"The Russians are in it alright, and that means the trouble is already beginning. We argue more than we agree, and the first signs of a split are beginning to show."

"I thought that the Moscow Conference had been fairly successful," MacGregor said, "even if they didn't settle this argument about Azerbaijan."

"Oh they settled a few details about the Balkans, and Clark-Kerr has gone down to Rumania with Harriman to see that the Governments are broadened and expanded and democratized, but these are details, MacGregor. Unsettled issues like Azerbaijan and the Dardanelles are much more important than a few politicians in a Balkan Government. That's

II

why Azerbaijan is not settled. It will not be settled until we show the Russians that we mean to be firm with them, and that is exactly what I intend doing."

"Is it Azerbaijan we are worried about, or Russia?" MacGregor asked.

Essex felt his eyes open a little at such a simple question. "Both," he said.

MacGregor withdrew again and though Essex felt better about him, he did not like this running hint of MacGregor's separation from the mission he was attending. MacGregor appeared reluctant to be personally involved, and that was ridiculous for a man who had to give Essex all his material facts and his expert opinion on a political situation. Having overcome MacGregor's personal barriers, Essex was by no means satisfied that he had settled with this young man.

"I am glad you came along, MacGregor," Essex said. "I like good company and intelligent conversation. I should think we would get on well together."

"Yes," MacGregor said.

"Odd that you don't want to stay with the India Office though."

"Is it?"

"Most young fellows would drop everything to have your job."

"I'm not much good at it." MacGregor had to offer some explanation.

Essex laughed. "I must say that you are an honest fellow, MacGregor. Just hand me that pouch will you."

MacGregor gave Essex the soft tobacco pouch from the floor and waited for him to continue. Talking with Essex had been easier than MacGregor had expected, and he was almost beginning to find it simple. MacGregor did not know what he had expected of Lord Essex and he had taken no chances with him; but now he found that he could relax a little. He knew Essex as any Englishman would know him by reputation, but he had not expected Essex to be a man who could lie on the floor of a Russian hut with his shoes off and his legs stretched out, sleeping and snoring without any thought for his surroundings. MacGregor would have been pleased to do it himself but several years with the English-Persian Oil Company and five years in the army had taught MacGregor care with men who were outside his own scientific environment. Living in the tightly knit English community at Fields in Iran had prepared Mac-Gregor for men like Essex. He had always been outside the pale of these men, because he had always been something of an academic freak, and it was better to ostracize yourself than have others do it for you. He had learned this lesson at Fields where thirty or forty Englishmen and their families lived in a hot compound surrounded by desert and Persian coolies. They had lived their circumscribed English lives among each other, and the man that did not conform had been laughed at. MacGregor had not conformed to it because he had never been part of the life of sport and social gathering; he had simply done his work and let it go at that. The result had been a joke on him — the fellow who bulged with grey matter, but who didn't mean much with his fossils when other men were drilling out the oil, and still others were running the whole show by clever administration and good business sense. Apart from that he had made the mistake of being too well acquainted with the half-dozen Persians who had worked at Fields as doctors or laboratory assistants, and this was unforgivable, even though MacGregor had spent his life in Iran and seemed as Iranian as some of these natives. Two years of Fields had been enough for MacGregor, and despite his work he wondered how he could go back. He had never lost his memory of it. It had even been carried over into his army life, and he had kept himself out of the usual routine of being an officer. The army had not been as bad as Fields, particularly in the early Western Desert days, but he had always been careful as he was being careful with Essex now. He was particularly careful with Essex because his eight months in the India Office had been eight months of not understanding any of the men around him, and Essex could easily be identified with the men of the India Office, with the Fields administrators in Iran, the sport-playing superintendents, the majors and colonels and brigadiers in the army. But by now Lord Essex had become like the colonel one could talk to; the colonel who could step down from his authority to talk with you but who could return quickly to his authority if you went too far. MacGregor knew that he would never go too far with Essex, but he was not sure of what Essex expected of him in this work. Essex did not know much about Azerbaijan; MacGregor had guessed that very quickly. Essex would certainly make his own decisions about Azerbaijan, but MacGregor did not want to feel responsible for them. He had his own ideas on Azerbaijan and they probably did not agree with Essex's; in fact he was certain that they did not agree at all.

Essex rubbed his stockinged feet together.

"What do they call old Rowland Smith's section now?" he asked MacGregor. "I'm not very familiar with the India Office these days."

"Trans-Caucasus and Northern Iran," MacGregor told him.

"How far into Turkey and Russia does that go?"

"Most of the Caucasus as far as Georgia and right across to Turkey, but it doesn't go into Turkey proper. Our section stops at the borders."

"Then you aren't dealing with this argument about the two Turkish provinces which the Russians are claiming, Kars and the other one."

"Ardahan," MacGregor said.

"Yes."

"That's part of the section, but I don't know much about it."

"Don't worry," Essex sat up and smiled and held his elbow while he smoked. "I'm not expecting you to know anything about it, although you might read up on it when we get to Moscow."

"Will Turkey come up for discussion?" MacGregor asked him.

"It might. I have a habit of throwing in everything. We don't like the idea of any Russian claim on Turkey, and we intend scotching that before it begins. But if we can stop the Russians and stop the revolt in Azerbaijan, we will have done enough. Think we can do it, eh?"

"Stop the Russians or stop the revolt?" MacGregor asked.

"It's the same thing isn't it," Essex told him.

"It might not be," MacGregor said.

"Oh! Are you in doubt about it?"

"There have always been revolts in Azerbaijan," MacGregor said.

"Russian-made revolts!" Essex told him.

"Not always."

"We have no doubts about this one being Russian-made," Essex said, "so don't confuse yourself on it. I hope you'll bear that in mind, my boy."

MacGregor nodded and they were interrupted by the pilot who had arrived with the car. As they bundled into it and left the mirage of the post office, Essex settled down for a slippery ride to Moscow. Their diversion was nearly over and he was not sorry. He was sleepy and feeling uncomfortable in his clothes. "I hope that our little delay will not worry anyone," he said to MacGregor. "Are you married?"

"No," MacGregor said.

"Neither am I, thank God," Essex confided. "Newspapers make such a fuss of this sort of thing. I suppose they will have us dead in the snow by now. Ah well, I think I will sleep a little." Essex moved back into the corner of the seat. "Just wake me up when we are coming on Moscow, MacGregor. I like coming into a city in the middle of the night — unless you want to sleep, of course."

"I can't sleep in a car," MacGregor said.

"You don't relax enough," Essex said. He thought again how curious it was that MacGregor should consider returning to some obscure branch of geology. That was a choice that Essex would never understand. His own entrance into the diplomatic corps had not been any different from MacGregor's. Essex's family, for instance, were not a diplomatic family. The Essexes had been Court people as far back as there had been an English Court. They had also been the Earls of Cadiz for a brief period of a hundred years. The title, the first foreign title in England, had been created for them in 1190 when Richard Coeur de Lion had given it to his Master of the Horse, Harold Essex, for a private Crusade upon the Moors at Cadiz, a Crusade which had produced a rich return in un-Christian gold plate. Unfortunately this unusual earldom had been taken away from the Essex family by Queen Elizabeth, in one of her cunning moments of appeasing King Philip of Spain, an act for which the Essexes had never forgiven Elizabeth. Since then they had merely had title to their family name of Essex. Because it was their family name, Essex was tired of explaining to curious Americans and ignorant foreigners that he was *not* the Earl of Essex. He was nothing to do with the Earldom of Essex, no relation and no connection. He would explain that the Essex in his case was the family name, and he liked to add drily that it had existed long before any Earldom of Essex. Furthermore, the Essex family had an illustrious history of its own, a history rich in soldiers and court intriguers. Yet the only diplomat among them — excepting his father's occasional favours for King Edward — had been a later Essex, sent by George the Third to converse with the Turks about having a war with the Russians. He had ended his mission by rotting to his death in the Seven Towers of Istanbul — a fortress kept by the Sultan for suspicious and demanding foreigners. Apart from a deep admiration for this ancestor, Essex had no other leaning toward the diplomatic service, but from his first taste of the life he had desired no other, and he could not see how MacGregor could reject opportunities so casually. Essex went to sleep on that, and MacGregor rubbed the frozen moisture from the window near him and watched the long flat waste of fields and timber go by him until they came to the outskirts of Moscow.

Nothing indicated the city until they were right at the lights and the scattered factories. MacGregor awakened Essex, and they both watched the black outline of Moscow surround them with its dark buildings, its wide streets, its bare and ragged avenues of trees. It was like any other city, but a little wider and darker, until they came into the heart of it. They followed a tram line along a cobbled road and came into a series of traffic lights.

"Quite a large place," Essex said to MacGregor as they looked at a large flat square which was banked with snow.

It was the largest city square that MacGregor had ever seen, and at one side of it was the long brick wall of the Kremlin. MacGregor spoke to the pilot in Russian, asking him if this was the Red Square. The pilot said No, the Red Square came next. By then they had taken a short slope and entered a large stone rectangle.

"This is it," the pilot said. "The Red Square."

As the car bubbled over the cobblestones they had a brief view of the Kremlin towers, crowned with bright red stars. For a moment the dark outline of Lenin's Tomb was haloed by a line of stunted fir trees, and then they dipped down past the compressed curves and domes of Saint Basil's mad little church. They went over a modern bridge and turned along the white river and into the open U-drive of the British Embassy.

As the car stopped beneath an entrance hall, somebody came out in heavy flying boots rubbing his hands.

"Lord Essex?" he said.

"Yes."

"My name is Melby, sir. Sir Francis asked me to apologize for not staying up but we weren't sure when you were arriving. The Russians told us you were on your way but that was all. We have a room ready for you. They said you weren't hurt, is that right?"

"Yes, Melby, we survived it. This is MacGregor." They shook cold hands.

"I have a room in my flat for you, MacGregor," Melby told him.

They unloaded the baggage, and the Russian soldier carried in their three suitcases and a flat tin box of documents while the pilot shook hands with them and apologized in careless Russian for the inconvenience and accident.

Inside the warm panelled hall of the Embassy MacGregor waited while Melby took Essex upstairs.

"Thank you, Melby." Essex said as he looked at the pale blue bedroom. He was also looking at Melby to see what sort of man he was. Melby was forty and finished with youth, and he held himself up by his stomach. He looked back at Essex through thick horned-rimmed glasses and Essex wondered if he was the First Secretary, Second Secretary, or one of the Counsellors.

"The bathroom is behind that door." Melby pointed to it.

"I am sorry you had to wait up," Essex said.

"That's alright, sir. I didn't want Sir Francis to wait up too long."

"I am glad he didn't."

"Is there anything you want?"

"No."

"Then good night, sir."

"Good night, Melby."

"And welcome to Moscow, Lord Essex."

"Thank you."

Melby went out and closed the door very quietly. Essex undid his American suitcase and threw his silk pyjamas on the bed and zipped open the toilet case which his man Evans had obligingly packed on top. He took out his toothbrush and cleaned his teeth and washed his face in hot water, which was another surprise, and then eased pleasantly into the good Bradford sheets and slept.

Chapter 2

Sir Francis Drake had the Moscow Embassy as Special Envoy, with the rank of Ambassador, while Sir Archibald Clark-Kerr was away in Rumania and London. He had invited Essex and MacGregor to lunch, and he was standing silently at the fireplace of the library downstairs waiting for Essex to arrive. MacGregor, looking scrubbed and washed, was already there, and though he sat calmly on a couch near the fire he was not happy about arriving before Essex. It didn't matter very much, but he would have felt better in this very British room if he had arrived with Essex.

This was the first Embassy that MacGregor had ever been in, and this was the sort of room he expected to see within it. The room was large and warm, and lit by two long windows. It contained just enough books to be a library. Its walls were panelled with varnished oak which reached from the carpeted floor to the ceiling, and the ceiling itself was supported by hewn oak beams. The fire-place was also faced with oak, but its inner surface was white marble. On the panelled walls were large paintings of three or four generations of British Royalty, at least they looked like British Royalty to MacGregor. He was not sure about it because his picture of royalty stopped with King George and Queen Mary. He looked at each painting slowly and deliberately, and he knew that Sir Francis Drake was watching him as if he had noticed MacGregor in the room for the first time. Drake had shaken his hand on arrival and had said a few words of greeting but that was all. MacGregor put his eyes on Drake now to see why he was being watched. Drake looked away and stood there neatly in his black coat and striped trousers and butterfly collar. MacGregor was glad when Essex came in.

"Hullo Francis," Essex said vigorously to Drake. "It's very good to see you."

"Good morning Harold," Drake said properly. "How are you?"

They were shaking hands warmly. "Amazingly fit," Essex said.

"You didn't get hurt in any way?"

"Good heavens no."

"I have been expecting one of those planes to crash for some time, the way the Russians fly them. Perhaps now they will allow us to bring in our own planes."

"I doubt it," Essex said. "I see you have met my assistant."

"Yes." Drake hardly noticed MacGregor. "Let's see, Harold? When did we last meet? I suppose it was in Paris, when I was on my way to Munich in 'thirty-eight."

"Did we meet then?" Essex said. "I have forgotten."

MacGregor watched him taking this room away from Drake. Essex was walking about it looking at the pictures and opening the bookcases and shifting the ornaments. Essex wore middle-man worsteds and a small knotted tie and brogue shoes, and there was nothing formal about him. Drake by the fire was a prim grey-haired man with cut-off neatness all over him. He was smaller than Essex, and MacGregor wondered if that was the reason for Drake's stiffly erect posture or whether this was the result of Essex's bold inspection of the room.

"Bit of a horror isn't it?" Essex said of the room.

"Oh, it's not so bad," Drake said.

"What do you think of it, MacGregor? Horrible isn't it?"

"It's English," MacGregor said.

"Nonsense!" Essex told him. "It's a foreigner's idea of being English: in fact it could be a bad copy of the Fifth Room at Castleton before the termites got at it." Castleton was the Essex family seat near Arun in Sussex, a miniature Hampton Court. The Fifth Room had been the "hogs-room," so named because the earlier Essexes had used it for roasting pigs on the flagstone floor, but it had later become the "gun room," when Essex's father had taken to shooting water buffalo in West Africa. Its pan-elled walls were hung with Holland and Holland's and long-barrelled shotguns. Castleton had been sold to a flour miller because no Essex could pay the taxes on it, and when the guns were taken down the long panels of the hogs' room had fallen out in sudden unexpected hollowness, eaten away by generations of termites. Essex wondered how the flour millionaire could live in a cold mediæval place like Castleton. He had been bitter about its loss, but looking back on it he could not help shiver-ing a little. For all its pretence — this was at least a warm room, and it wouldn't have been so bad without the royal portraits on the walls.

"Whose bright idea was it to hang the walls with royalty?" he said to Drake. "I didn't expect to see Queen Charlotte hanging there, I thought she had been forgotten for ever, and old George looks a little forlorn too."

MacGregor felt that Drake was shocked. "They are too large for the room," Drake said loyally. "I believe that when Stalin was here with Churchill he mistook King Edward for the late Czar Nicholas. They had quite a discussion about it."

"I thought they wouldn't discuss their Czars."

"Oh, Stalin will discuss anything."

"What about Molotov?" Essex sat on Drake's neat desk.

"Molotov is too clever for his own good. Sharp, academic sort of fellow."

"MacGregor is a bit of an academic," Essex said and eased off the desk.

"Oh?" Drake said.

"You only have to look at him," Essex waved an open palm at Mac-Gregor.

18

A white-coated houseman brought a tray of drinks and set it on a small table as Melby came in behind him and took over the matter of serving them with whisky. "You met Melby last night of course," Drake said to Essex. "I brought him with me from London."

"Yes," Essex said. "I wondered where he had come from."

MacGregor felt repaid for Drake's subtle way of ignoring him. He took the whisky that Melby gave him, although he didn't like it and seldom drank whisky even in politeness. Melby sat next to him on the striped couch, and now that Essex was here MacGregor stretched his legs to relax a little. Yet he was still anticipating more of Essex's embarrassing remarks. Melby sat properly as Drake would sit properly, and MacGregor thought him a curious imitation of Drake. Even though Melby was stouter and heavier, they had the same primness and the same sweet speech.

"Well Harold," Drake said as they both stood and held their whisky glasses. "What do you expect to achieve on this Azerbaijan business so soon after the Moscow Conference?"

"Perhaps you can tell me that," Essex said. "How do the Russians feel about the Moscow Conference? Do they think they got anything out of it?"

"They seem to think it was very successful."

"Good," Essex said. "They should now be willing to listen to reason."

"That's a slim hope," Drake said.

"Oh I don't know," Essex replied. "We have always misjudged the Russians a little, Francis, and we ought to give them the benefit of the doubt occasionally."

Drake put on pince-nez glasses and looked at Essex. "I wouldn't talk to the Russians in those terms if I were you, Harold."

"Why not? Isn't that the approach now?"

"Perhaps," Drake said. "But you might take that with a pinch of salt."

"Oh?" Essex threw a log on the fire. "I thought the results of the Moscow Conference depended on a certain amount of co-operation. After all they are broadening the Balkan Governments."

"That is simply their tiny concession to our agreement to establish an Atomic Energy Commission in the United Nations. They want the atomic secrets."

"I agree with the scientists," Essex said and sighed. "We might as well give them the details of the bomb and get it over and done with."

"Good heavens!" Drake said.

"Is that how you feel MacGregor — scientifically? Would you give it to them?"

"They'll find out themselves anyway," MacGregor said.

"Of course," Essex said.

19

"I can hardly believe that is our official attitude, and I know that the Americans have no intention of sharing the secret with anyone at the moment, even ourselves."

"They are a child with a new toy," Essex said. "They'll get over it."

"Perhaps. But it's the only real bargaining factor we have with the Russians, Harold. So long as they haven't got it we can force concessions out of them."

"I had hopes of the United Nations doing away with all these differences," Essex said. "After all, we meet there on equal ground."

"Hardly!" Drake argued again. "Not while the Russians insist on all decisions being unanimous. If they don't like something they simply veto it and that's the end of that."

"Of course we can do the same," Essex said.

"True, but we don't want to."

"No. We are not likely to veto our own proposals, are we?"

Drake was shocked again and Essex looked reflectively at the ceiling. "What do they feel about us, Francis?" he asked with half-closed eyes.

"In relation to Iran?"

"In relation to anything — Iran if you like. Do they say anything about us these days?"

"Not directly, but they do by underhand implication in their newspapers. They are always hinting that we are more concerned with oil than we are with the Iranian people."

"Hm!" Essex nodded. "What about Molotov and the Foreign Office? What do they say to us or about us?"

"They don't say anything," Drake told him unhappily. "It's hard to get a word out of them. Haven't you read my summaries to Bertram Cooke?"

"Naturally, but I don't always understand your summaries, Francis."

"You will old chap. A couple days here and you will draw a complete blank."

"That is why I have been sent here, Francis." Essex shifted a medallion and a clock on the mantelpiece. "I am not supposed to draw a blank."

"I'm afraid you might, Harold."

"I don't think so."

Sir Francis Drake came very near to spontaneity. "Listen, Harold," he said. "With all due respect to London, they don't yet understand about Russia. It's alright to have these big conferences and think that you've done well with them, but in reality one never has a case in talking with these people. What is good diplomatic argument in any other part of the world doesn't mean a thing here. They do not understand the common forms of diplomacy, they understand nothing of give-and-take in bargaining. They talk a language of their own, and the whole basis of their argument is their absurd and strict formula of Marxism, a dogmatic assertion of history in economic terms which makes everything they say clumsy and unreal. It will not take you long to realize that the Russian system is irreconcilable with our ideas and our world. There is hardly any use talking to them at all, and you certainly can't argue with them."

"I have MacGregor," Essex said lazily. "We will find good enough arguments."

"There is no such thing here as a good argument," Sir Francis Drake repeated and put his glass upon the mat set near him on a table.

"It's just a matter of knowing how to get at them," Essex told him.

"I wish I had your confidence," Drake said.

"Oh, I'm not awed by the Russians." Essex handed his glass to Mac-Gregor.

Drake did not say anything to that. "We will give you all the help we can, Harold, but we are a little confused here at the moment with the results of the Moscow Conference. We do have one good man, though, who has been looking after Iran for us. He was in our Teheran Embassy for a year and he knows the country well. He was about to go to Finland but I could keep him for you."

Essex looked over at MacGregor. "Don't bother," he said to Drake. "There isn't a better man than MacGregor and we work together rather well, eh MacGregor?"

"Yes." MacGregor was irritated now with Drake's idea that Essex needed somebody more than himself.

"Do you think you will need any assistance?" Essex asked MacGregor.

"No, I don't think so." MacGregor's cheeks were almost pink.

"It was only a suggestion," Drake said flatly. "How is lunch John?" he asked Melby.

"Any time you like, sir."

The lunch was expansive and satisfying, and Essex told himself that any such sensible pleasures in this Embassy originated with Clark-Kerr, rather than with Drake.

"How often do you see Molotov?" he asked Drake.

"Very rarely," Drake said. "You will have to remember that you are not in Washington now. One doesn't have free access to the Foreign Office or the Foreign Minister here. At the moment we are having some difficulty getting hold of Molotov to discuss the Russian land seizures in Eastern Germany. We can't see him because he doesn't want to talk about it with us."

"Why not?"

"Because he knows that parcelling up land among the peasantry is not our idea of solving the political problems of Eastern Germany. We want to stop it."

"That sounds pretty hopeless," Essex said. "The large estates have already been done away with. We can hardly persuade the Russians to give them back to the landowners. We ought to leave those hopeless issues alone and meet the Russians where we have a chance of coping with them."

"As in Azerbaijan?" Drake said and smiled neatly.

"Why not?" Essex ate his lemon meringue. "How are the Russians feeling about Azerbaijan these days, Francis? Still denying everything?"

"Of course." Drake felt on safer ground now. "Their Press keeps talking about the spontaneous Iranians and the corrupt Fascist landlords in Teheran and how the Democratic Party in Azerbaijan has overthrown these feudal beasts. It's simply a ridiculous pattern."

"Oh I don't know," Essex said. "There may be spontaneous Iranians. Isn't it possible that the revolt was partly spontaneous in Azerbaijan, MacGregor? Don't you think it could be so?"

Without knowing it, MacGregor dropped his guard a little, believing that Essex had some objectivity which he had not recognized before. He did not suspect that Essex was using him to shock Drake. "It could be spontaneous," MacGregor said.

"And I suppose the North is, after all, more or less feudal?" Essex added.

"More or less."

"That may be so," Drake ignored MacGregor, "but surely that is not the big issue we are facing in Iran."

"We must take local conditions into account," Essex said wisely. "We can hardly blame our Russian friends for everything, you know."

"You can blame them for all the trouble in Iran," Drake argued.

"I wouldn't say that. What would you say caused the revolt in Azerbaijan, MacGregor — outside any Russian part in it of course?"

"A generally bad situation," MacGregor replied.

"What do you mean a 'bad' situation?" Drake said sharply.

"Azerbaijan has always been badly treated by the Teheran Governments, and there have always been parties of revolt there. The revolt that gave Iran its only constitutional government started in Azerbaijan and most of the leaders were Azerbaijanians."

"You see, there is something to it," Essex said. "Of course the Russians should get out, don't you think?" Essex looked seriously at MacGregor.

"Everybody should get out," MacGregor said.

"And let the Iranians settle their own problems and revolt if they wish, eh?"

"There is no other way of settling the situation," MacGregor said, "whether it's in the north or in the south."

Drake put his hands on the table. "I hardly believe that you are here to

22

arrange our evacuation from Iran, Harold, MacGregor's opinion notwithstanding."

"I hardly think so either," Essex smiled at both of them. "Just pass me the wine will you Melby, the red wine. The truth is, Francis, we have made too many bad mistakes in dealing with the Iranians in the past. Isn't that so, MacGregor?"

"Yes."

"We can't treat them any more as if they were not there," Essex said. "Isn't that what we have been doing in our political policies for fifty years, MacGregor? Have we ever given the Persians a chance to decide their own affairs?"

"Not really," MacGregor said.

"Surely we have done well by them in the south," Drake argued. "I spent a little time in Persia myself some years ago, and I know that at our English-Persian refineries you will find the only decent housing and health facilities for natives in Iran. MacGregor should know about that."

"Is that right MacGregor?" Essex was enjoying this.

"We give the Persians working for us much better treatment than they get anywhere else, that is absolutely true. The oil company gives them some housing and runs clinics and even some schools, but on the other hand we don't give them much say in their own affairs and the little schooling and medical attention they get is of very little use when you consider their general living conditions."

"All that has to be changed," Essex announced.

"By the Russians?" Drake said acidly.

"No." Essex rubbed his chest. "By us. Unless of course the Persians can improve their own conditions on their own account. What chance is there of that MacGregor?"

"None," Drake said. "I know the Persians."

"What do you think MacGregor?" Essex said again. "Can the Persians do anything for themselves at all?"

"They might," MacGregor said. "The reports we get in the India Office show that there is all sorts of trouble in Iran. Strikes for instance. There were never any strikes in Iran before. There were never any real political parties either. Now they are springing up all over the place. I might be exaggerating a little because this is the first time that I have ever had anything to do with what is happening politically in Iran. All the same, there is no doubt that something new is happening. Of course Azerbaijan is different. The Azerbaijanians have always been trying to get some kind of autonomy, and I suppose if they can succeed it will mean that Iran generally could do something on its own account. It's really hard to say."

"Well that's a nice scientific sort of pronouncement, MacGregor," Essex

23

said, "but how much of this new political activity is genuine? Hasn't Iran been so corrupt politically for so long that a few more political parties mean just a few more grafters?" Essex seemed to have forgotten Drake for a moment.

"It might be that," MacGregor said. "I don't know a great deal about the worth of any of the political parties, but there is plenty of other political activity in Iran that has nothing to do with any particular political party."

"An increasing awareness?" Essex suggested knowingly.

"I suppose so," MacGregor said.

"I can hardly believe it," Essex said.

"Neither can I!" Drake said.

Essex remembered Drake. "Ah, but we can't argue with MacGregor, Francis. He is the feller that knows, and we have to listen to him."

Drake said nothing and MacGregor felt that Sir Francis was indicating his intention of never listening to MacGregor. Essex had walked to a large window to see the sun clearing the air of the faint snow-light. The sky had become a hard blue and he looked out at the back of the Embassy where the dry snow was heaped in banks along the fence. He saw a wired-off enclosure at the end of the grounds, and he rubbed the moisture off the window to watch a woman skating there. She was gliding very confidently backwards in a large figure eight, which only English skaters seem to dignify. She was dressed in a skirt which was too tight for skating, and in a red sweater with a white band around it. She wore a tasselled cap which tossed about on her head as she circled around. Essex saw the flashes of a laughing face which even so briefly appeared too confident and beautiful.

"A skating rink," he said, thinking of the woman, as Melby stood beside him.

"That is our tennis court," Melby told him. "Some of the RAF Mission chaps froze it over with water so that they could play ice hockey, but everybody uses it now."

"Why is the young woman alone then?"

"There is some shortage of skates and I suppose she is waiting for some one else to turn up. Some of our Russian staff manage to get skates."

"Is she Russian?"

"Good heavens no," Drake said. "She is English."

Essex turned to look at Drake with undisguised interest.

Drake said they might go to his room, and he walked out.

Melby took this opportunity of leading MacGregor to a large chandeliered room on the ground floor. This, Melby said, was the room for Essex and MacGregor. It was a plush room with red curtains, and small forgotten oil paintings on the pale walls, but it was light from the tall

windows facing the river and warm from the fire in the
were two desks, one large and glass-topped in the center (
and the other smaller and near the windows. The desk und
dows was obviously for MacGregor, and Melby sat on the c
swinging his stout leg.

"Make yourself at home, MacGregor, and if you want anythii
know. I would take you around to some of the other people but
all out to lunch and it will have to wait. Incidentally, Miss Willian
will be Lord Essex's secretary, is very reliable. She's been at Ei
work for years. I don't suppose you know much about Embassy m
and routine."

"Nothing at all," MacGregor said.

"Then depend on Miss Williams or come to me."

"That's very nice of you," MacGregor said.

"Have you seen this view?" Melby leaned back on the desk toward ti
window.

MacGregor left the fire and looked out. Just across a roadway Mac-
Gregor saw the frozen Moscow river. It was not very wide, and by bending down to avoid the roof of the porch outside, MacGregor could see
right across the river and up to a small plateau on the other side. The
small plateau rose up from the river like a hill, and though there was a
red brick wall running its length on the river level, the remainder of the
hill was easily visible. There was a garden on the slope, but higher up it
was scattered with churches and large buildings that looked like cream
palaces. MacGregor knew this place must be the Kremlin.

"I thought the wall would be so high that you couldn't see into the
Kremlin," he said to Melby. "It is the Kremlin, isn't it?"

"Yes. We look right into the heart of it."

"What exactly is the place?" MacGregor said. "I thought it would be
just a building."

Melby looked with MacGregor. "No. It's simply that collection of
palaces and a few churches and a large number of administrative buildings,
all surrounded by a wall. Stalin and most of the Government work in
there, they use the administrative buildings. Stalin lives in there too but
no one quite knows where. No one that we know has ever seen or even
identified the exact place where he lives."

"I suppose it is in one of the palaces," MacGregor said.

"That's doubtful," Melby said and cleaned his glasses as MacGregor
went to the next window where he could see it all without stooping.
"Apparently the old man is rather simple in his habits, and most of the
palaces are used for offices. One of them is used by the Supreme Soviet,
which is the Russian idea of a Parliament." Melby laughed at the idea,
and left MacGregor with the joke still in the air.

25

MacGregor sat down and looked across the white river, feeling rather st until Essex came in, followed by Drake.

"Feeling at home, MacGregor?" Essex said.

"Not exactly," MacGregor replied. "Did you know that we were opposite he Kremlin? If you look out this window you see right into it."

"Well, this is nice," Essex said to Drake. They looked at the Kremlin. "I had forgotten what it looked like. Impressive, eh MacGregor?"

"I was surprised to see right into it like that."

"Don't let that deceive you, MacGregor," Drake warned. "Wall or no wall it is the most secretive place on the face of the earth. We just don't know what is going on in there. Lovely wall though, isn't it, Harold?"

"I don't like the red stars on the spires," Essex said. "But it's well kept."

"Most official buildings in Moscow are well kept and warm," Drake said. "Not at all like some of the houses of the people." Sir Francis held his white collar with his pale thin hands.

"Same the world over," Essex said liberally. "MacGregor," he said, "if you are feeling ready and alert we will get right down to work. Alright?"

"Yes. Alright."

"Francis," Essex said. "I wonder if I could ask Melby to do something."

"Certainly."

"I want MacGregor with me so that we can get right onto our material. Could Melby ring the Protocol people and find out what has been arranged for me? He could ask them when I can see Molotov, and where."

"By heavens you're an optimist, Harold," Drake said. "Don't expect so much."

"I never expect anything but what I get," Essex said. "Molotov will see me, don't worry; and if you don't mind I'd like Melby to get right onto that."

Drake lingered a moment. "I'll tell him for you," he said and watched Essex pulling back the long red curtains to let more light into the room. "Anything you want, Harold, you might let me know. Miss Williams will look after you well because she knows the ropes. There is a buzzer somewhere on that table for her. I'll just go up and see what I can do with Protocol."

"That's jolly nice of you." Essex pushed the button for Miss Williams. "I'll probably be up later to see how we can get around the official Russian."

"Are you well provided for, MacGregor?" Drake asked him from the door.

"Yes thank you," MacGregor said, surprised at that from Drake.

"Then I'll leave you to it," Drake said to them. "And good luck."

He left as Miss Williams came in with a notebook and pencil.

"Have you got enough room in that small office out there?" Essex asked her. She was using the small hall at the entrance to the room as her office.

Miss Williams was short, and almost young. "Oh yes, there's plenty of room." She flushed.

"You can leave our door open if you like and get some of the warmth from the fire," Essex told her. "We don't want you freezing out there."

"I have a radiator," she said with the earnestness of an easy captive.

"Fine," Essex said. "Now I was wondering if you would bring down all the files and the attaché case on the desk in my room upstairs, but first of all where is that small tin box of documents?"

She pointed to a corner of the room. "I have a filing cabinet outside if you want me to file everything there."

"It doesn't matter yet. We will reach that later."

Miss Williams went off with loyal promptness.

"Where is all your stuff, MacGregor?" Essex asked.

"In my room." MacGregor too went promptly.

While he waited for them, Essex walked over to the window and stood there with his hands in his pockets looking at the black painted onion domes of the church in the Kremlin. He knew enough about the Kremlin to know that the church was St. Sophia's. Its domes looked thin and uncertain, and a faint glimmer of transparent gold shone through the black paint. The giant cross of St. Nicholas was mounted on each dome, held up by a complicated array of guys which had become part of the decoration of the cross. Essex had not expected to see the crosses on the domes, and he admitted that their presence was all in the Russians' favour, although it was probably part of their sudden use of religion in Eastern Europe for political purposes. Everything in Russia was done for political purpose, there was no doubt about that.

Miss Williams returned and spread the papers out on the desk, and MacGregor arrived with a square brown paper parcel under his arm, a parcel tied with heavy string.

"That's an odd way to carry important documents," Essex said.

MacGregor did not seem to notice anything unusual as he put the parcel on his desk and undid the string. "I didn't have any case to put them in," he said. He had folded the paper and rolled the string and put it in the drawer of his desk for its re-use in carrying documents. Essex watched, and decided for a moment that he must never part with MacGregor. "What have you got there?" Essex asked him from his desk.

"They are copies of the four summaries from Sir Bertram Cooke to you," MacGregor said. "I read them last night."

"When?"

"In bed, when we got here."

"Well that's certainly getting down to it for a man who appears as disinterested as you are, MacGregor. I hope that you will always surprise me like that. What did you think of them; any good?"

MacGregor could never believe that Essex was serious when he asked these deferential questions. "They seem alright."

"They amount to my instructions, MacGregor. The limits of our compromise."

"Are they the proposals you are going to suggest to the Russians?"

"No. No. You never start out suggesting something on the level of your instructions. You will learn in this business that you retreat to your instructions. We will have to offer something much more demanding."

"What?" MacGregor asked spontaneously, being drawn into it by Essex.

"That is what you and I have to decide on now."

"I see."

"I will have to feel them out and see how they can be influenced to make some changes to satisfy our interests."

"Our interests?" MacGregor asked.

"Well, Iran's interests," Essex said carelessly. "It's never much use talking about your own interests. You'll learn that as we go along." He threw MacGregor a large folio. "Here you are MacGregor, this is our material. It's mainly Foreign Office Information Reports and files on the ambassadorial exchanges in Teheran regarding Azerbaijan, but it should supplement your India Office supply. You might go through these and get the gist of the information and see what we can get out of it."

"I think I read some of these in London."

"Then it should be easy for you to get them in some coherent order. I thought you said you hadn't read much of it."

"I had expected something new."

"There's nothing new," Essex said. "For that matter we will be suggesting very little that is new to the Russians. But it isn't so much what you present to them as how you present it. That is what our Foreign Ministers never learn, whether they are Conservative or Labour. That is where the professional diplomat is a better man, MacGregor."

MacGregor was already sorting the documents and putting them out in piles on his desk. Though he was not yet sure of Essex's intentions, he felt that he was dealing with a reasonable man, and he might as well do the best job he could. While MacGregor worked, Essex leaned back. Essex could see that his own presence had been almost forgotten by MacGregor. Nevertheless Essex enjoyed talking.

"There is a lot of history to this, MacGregor," he said. "In many ways we are picking up where Disraeli and Curzon and Randolph Churchill and Castlereagh left off." Essex folded his arms by holding his elbows. "It is all a matter of our old rivalries. Too much of our Empire is close to Russia and always has been. Now Russia is expanding and we are not in a very good position to prevent her. Yet we will have to do something. In particular we will have to watch the countries which decide our strength in

28

the Mediterranean, India, the Far East, as well as the Middle East." Essex walked to the fire and stood with his back to it. "This even involves our interests in Europe, because the Russians have taken over Eastern Europe just as surely as the Germans did. Our only hope, MacGregor, is to meet the Russians at all points of expansion with political opposition and good alignment. The Russians are trying to come down to the Middle East and break our influence there. If they succeed in establishing an ascendant influence in Azerbaijan they will take hold of all Iran. They will force Iran to look to Russia for political as well as economic and military alignment." It still didn't matter to Essex that MacGregor was taking hardly any notice of him. "If the Russians get a grip on Iran it will affect all the Middle East and all the Arab countries," he went on, "because Russia will not show any respect for our need of influence in the Middle East to protect our lifelines. The Russians don't respect our need for these areas, MacGregor. They never have and they never will. Yet we have always met the Russians half-way in Iran, and we have always stopped them before they got very far. They have tried time and time again to get that hold on Azerbaijan, but we have always weakened it as we must weaken it now. Our people are doing a very good job in Iran, but it looks as if we will have to do quite a job up here. Quite a vital job. Much of our future strength in all the world can depend on what you and I achieve here in Moscow." Essex stood behind MacGregor and put his hand on his shoulder to look over it, and then he returned to the fire. "If we know the import of what we are doing then we will do our job well."

MacGregor had heard none of it and Essex stopped to watch him working. He had methodical hands and his face had become narrow in occupation. Essex wondered if MacGregor understood what he was doing. Not many of these youngsters did understand their rôle, because they were too young to have seen better days. They failed now to see that their life depended on England's right and necessity to Empire, to every crumb of her Empire. He had met plenty of young men in the Foreign Office and in the Diplomatic Service generally who understood the necessities of Empire, but for the most part they were unintelligent about it and too slavish and too conservative. The intelligent men were unfortunately those men who didn't seem to care at all; and though he knew that MacGregor was intelligent, he doubted if MacGregor understood the rôle he was playing at this moment of history. He liked the way MacGregor had gone to work — so easily and so simply. Perhaps MacGregor had more heart in his work than Essex had thought. He must get at MacGregor again, and in the meantime he called in Miss Williams and began dictating his first queries back to London, the queries which he had pondered en route. He kept this up until MacGregor said, "I have sorted them out in some rough order."

"Does any of it make sense to you?" Essex said as Miss Williams left politely.

"Some of it. I have had to divide all this material to give it some workable order, and as a matter of fact it falls naturally into four divisions." Essex was standing near MacGregor's desk looking at the four stacks of papers as MacGregor explained them. "This lot is about what is going on in Azerbaijan, based on our Teheran reports. The second, our complaints about it. The third lot, the basis we have been given for proposals to the Russians. And the fourth is a file of some evidence to support our proposals in argument."

"Excellent," Essex said warmly. "What does it all amount to?"

"Very little," MacGregor said.

"Oh?" Essex leaned forward. "What's the matter?"

"Everything here is based on our Teheran reports over the last ten months, and the trouble is they aren't much good," MacGregor told him.

"I thought they were excellent."

"They may be good Embassy reports but they seem to lack fact. Most of it amounts to interpretation of the situation without any supporting evidence at all."

"What else?" Essex could see that MacGregor was annoyed.

"The whole approach is one to justify our attitude, and though our attitude may be right we would be better supplied if we knew the simple truth and all the details, instead of this mass of speculation. Everything has a ready-made interpretation. Facts are simply offered to support Teheran's ideas. Nothing of it is properly objective."

Essex nodded patiently. "You can't be very scientific about political reports, MacGregor. You have to take another man's understanding as your own at times. The important thing is to have what we need for our job. Have we got it there?"

MacGregor had acquired enough confidence in Essex to feel comparatively safe. "No, we haven't got it," he said. "Of course it depends on what we want to do. If we really want to know what is happening in Iran, we haven't got the proper material here."

"Then send a cable off to Teheran telling them exactly what you want."

MacGregor looked up at Essex to explain himself. "There is nothing exact that we want. We simply need someone who understands the place."

"Well, we can't get bogged down because of a thing like that, MacGregor." Essex had his shoes off again. "Let's go over this stuff just as you've sorted it out. Let's hear about it." Essex stood by the fire in his stockinged feet smoking his pipe and waiting for MacGregor to begin.

"As you say," MacGregor said with a reviving doubt about Essex.

"What have we got about what is going on up in Azerbaijan?"

"These reports give an outline rather than the details; I suppose the details are in the files," MacGregor said. "It's hard to get facts out of this lot, but in general the Teheran reports describe the development of what they call a Russian-planned separatist movement taking over the northern Iranian province of Azerbaijan. The separatists call themselves the Democratic Party, and we have some facts quoted directly from these people themselves. The Democrats say they have established an active government in Azerbaijan, and they have declared themselves autonomous within the scope of the present Iranian constitution, which gives equal rights for all races and proportionate representation by various tribes in district authority. The Azerbaijanian Democrats say that they are giving men and women a vote, and they seem to have established some kind of one-party parliament. Their policy for Azerbaijan at the moment is one of immediate land reform and abolition of absentee-landlordism altogether. There are also a lot of economic reforms which allow for the taking over of industries, mines, and transport facilities. We have a lot of data quoting the Tabriz radio about the organization of unions and the establishment of wage rates, and the abolition of the mukhadil."

"The what?"

"The pyramidic system of bribes. That would be mainly aimed at the civil service, the police, and the army, which they say will be re-organized and paid a living wage. It will also be a crime for civil servants to take a bribe."

Essex chuckled at these impossibilities.

"That's about all, unless you want me to go into Teheran's interpretation of the changes up there. You probably know about that already."

"Yes. I know enough. Go on with the next lot. Our complaints isn't it?"

"Yes."

"What do you think of our complaints then, MacGregor?"

"Some of them are right and some of them seem wrong."

"Go on then. What are they?"

"Mainly that the whole change of power in Azerbaijan was done by force with Russian assistance. The Iranian Government has lost its authority over the biggest wheat and rice and other food-growing areas in the country. The land and economic reforms amount to revolution or to unjust and illegal seizure under Iranian law. We can't get experts into Azerbaijan to observe, and those already up there are restricted by the Democrats and Russians. Several atrocities have been reported, and business men and merchants and landowners who attempted to flee from Azerbaijan have been shot or raided or robbed, and on one occasion killed by the Kurds. The Democratic, or separatist, Government refuses to receive any envoys from the Iranian Government or even the Shah. A Democratic Army is being formed in Azerbaijan, which is considered dangerous within the border of Iran and may lead to civil war similar to that in China." MacGregor paused and looked up. "It goes on." He had been flicking over one document after another and mumbling through some of them by good memory of previous reading.

"Next?" Essex knew that he had made a find in MacGregor. Anyone who could accumulate these details so quickly and effectively and sort them out like this was bound to turn out a good man. Essex knew the details, but he had never planned them out and divided them as Mac-Gregor was doing. "What comes next?" he asked.

"We will propose to the Russians that the Government be allowed to send police, gendarmes, and army units there to establish order. We want some kind of guarantee from the Russians that the Iranian Government will be obeyed by the Azerbaijanian Democrats. In exchange we say we will offer a liberal interpretation of the Democratic Party's aims in Azerbaijan. We insist though, that responsibility for implementing any reform in the province of Azerbaijan must be left to the central authority of the Iranian Government. We also want the Russians to cancel immediately all land and economic reforms, until a five-man committee can be established to investigate the situation."

"Committees to investigate are always a good point," Essex said.

"We suggest it consist of one Russian, one Englishman, one representative from the Iranian Government, one man from the Azerbaijanian Democrats, and possibly one American."

"Yes. Yes. We must have the American in."

"Then we want the withdrawal of all Foreign troops from Iran by next March 2, in line with an American suggestion. Later on we want a British-American-Russian-Iranian Commission set up to investigate the origins and the validity of the Democrats' actions in Azerbaijan." MacGregor moved the papers away. "There are plenty more suggestions and they are mostly along the same lines."

"We need plenty more." Essex had begun to walk up and down to get the full picture of what MacGregor was outlining. "The more proposals we can make the less we will have to retreat."

MacGregor went on. "Then there are our arguments to support whatever proposals we make to the Russians. The most important is the incident of the Russians refusing Iranian Army units entry in Azerbaijan to restore order. We say that this was a violation of the Anglo-Soviet-Iranian Treaty of 1942, in which all parties guaranteed Iran's national sovereignty. We say that Russia has also violated the Teheran and Yalta and Potsdam agreements about no unilateral actions and no violation of the rights of small nations. There are also specific clauses which they have apparently violated, if you want them."

"I know them. Go on."

"We also have various reports of evidence on direct Russian interference

32

in the Azerbaijan revolt, and we quote from assurances of Iranian sovereignty by the Soviet Ambassador in Iran and by Molotov to show that the Russians are breaking their own promises."

"Excellent."

"We believe that this is not a genuine democratic movement in Azerbaijan but a revolutionary movement. We state that Iran is not ready for such drastic political measures and that the people will object and civil war may result. This would threaten the entire peace of the Middle East, and encourage extremists to start upheavals in at-present-peaceful countries. We have plenty about that, and we link it up closely to the Charter of the United Nations."

"That is where we may catch them," Essex said.

"Then we come down to the effect on world opinion and the weakening of international confidence, and the handicap this Russian interference in Azerbaijan will place on the organization of the United Nations. Quite a lot has been said by our Cabinet Ministers about that already, and it seems to be entirely a matter for the imagination."

Essex should have been warned by MacGregor's unusually dry word of conclusion, but he was too pleased with MacGregor's efficient approach to the material to observe any subtle reaction to it. MacGregor had thrown himself into the work quickly and thoroughly. To Essex, that seemed enough assurance of MacGregor's intentions, and he lost his cautious method of handling and winning MacGregor. With one of his quick decisions on a man, Essex decided that his doubts about MacGregor's co-operation had been wrong. MacGregor probably had queer ideas but they were basically sound.

"That's the whole picture?" he said to MacGregor.

MacGregor did not turn around. "Yes," he said.

"With that material as a basis," Essex said, "we have to get the Russians out of Azerbaijan, out of all Iran. That is our job here, MacGregor."

"I don't see how you can do it," MacGregor said.

Essex sat down and pushed on his shoes. They were laceless shoes and they had buckles on the sides with straps, but Essex could get his feet in and out of them very easily. "We will do it," Essex said. "My first proposal to the Russians will be a clear-cut offer to bargain with them if they get out of Iran. We haven't much to bargain with, but we can make a pretty good show of accepting some of their ideas on Iran if they'll only get out."

"Why are we so desperate to get them out?" MacGregor said.

"Good heavens, don't you want the Russians out of Iran?"

"Yes," MacGregor said, "but there are more urgent things we could do in there."

"What is more urgent than that?" Essex said.

33

"The country isn't in very good shape as it is now," MacGregor said. "Since we are not going to get out of Iran I thought we might ask the Russians to co-operate in straightening it up a little."

"At this stage?" Essex said. "What on earth could we do?"

"We could make sure that some real government exists, instead of the collection of bribed men who govern the place now. We could do it quite easily, particularly if we get the Russians to do it with us. We could set the country going properly if we took out the worst men and the worst landowners and got some objective men in there to establish a proper administration. If we get something started like that then we would have a friendly sort of a people there, instead of a whole population that doesn't like us."

"Perhaps we should also abandon our oil concession. Give it to the people?"

"No," MacGregor said. "We could go on getting the oil and stay in the south, but at least we would have given the rest of the country a chance. As it is now," MacGregor said again, "it's no good."

"It's a nice hope, MacGregor," Essex said, "but you don't think that we are here in Moscow to begin reform like that in Iran, do you?"

"I don't know," MacGregor said suspiciously. "I have never been sure of why we are here."

"I will repeat to you very clearly what I have told you before: we are here to get the Russians out of Azerbaijan, MacGregor." He would not be too hard on MacGregor.

"Is that our sole purpose?"

"What else?" Essex said.

"Why don't we consider the needs of the country itself?" MacGregor said.

"We do," Essex said.

"I don't think so." MacGregor felt that he had been cheated by Essex because Essex was contradicting his previous attitude with Drake. MacGregor even guessed that he had been used by Essex as a foil against Drake, and he reddened with the thought of it. "I don't think so at all," he said.

"Wouldn't you think that the best thing for Iran would be the immediate evacuation of the Russians from the north?"

"There are more important things than that to be done in Iran," MacGregor said stubbornly. Committed all the way, he was now stubborn enough to hang on and go as far as Essex.

"That's the trouble with you fellows who live their lives in a foreign country." Essex knew he had made a mistake with MacGregor but he couldn't stop now. "You see the problems too locally. We have to think in terms of our position in the world, MacGregor, and we have to sink our local considerations for the bigger issue. Diplomacy involving our world situation can hardly stop for local problems."

"Then there must be something wrong with diplomacy," MacGregor said.

Essex laughed. "By Jove!" he said. "We're going to have some good arguments about this, I can see that." He sighed. "But we'll have to keep it out of the line of our work. Let's get on with what we have."

MacGregor did not think it amusing and he felt impelled to pin Essex down. "I know that the India Office is opposed to every kind of reform in Iran," he said, "but I thought you might have had something else in mind."

"Oh I'm not opposed to reform," Essex said patiently, "but there is a time for everything, and if we admit any need for reform in Iran at this moment we will be playing right into the Russians' hands. That is their big excuse for doing what they are doing in the north. Reform at the moment is their idea."

"It isn't entirely Russian-made reform," MacGregor said.

"Of course it is," Essex said, impatient now.

"The facts show otherwise," MacGregor told him.

"Facts are relative in a political situation, MacGregor, just as they are relative in certain sciences, you ought to know that."

"I do," MacGregor said, "but facts are also a matter of interpretation."

"And are you interpreting the facts to show that this revolt in Azerbaijan has come from the Azerbaijanians, eh?"

"Partly."

"I have to disagree and correct you then." Essex stood up. He had been foolish not to keep a closer watch on MacGregor, with his efficient mind and his overdeveloped belief in reason or logic or objectivity or whatever it was that the scientists called their attitude. Yet Essex looked at Mac-Gregor and knew that it would be unfortunate to continue this argument, because MacGregor was ready in surprising abandon to argue with Essex until doomsday. MacGregor had settled into a waiting attitude, and his grey eyes did not move from Essex's face. Essex did not like arguing with stubborn men. "I suggest that you investigate your facts again, Mac-Gregor, and if you still think you are right then we will talk more about it. As far as we are concerned officially, however, the revolt in Azerbaijan is Russian-made, and that is how it must stand."

"Is that part of this mission too?" MacGregor asked unhesitatingly. "To resist any kind of reform in Iran or in Azerbaijan?"

"For the moment, yes. We'll get around to reform when we get the Russians out of the country. That should satisfy you."

It obviously didn't, and MacGregor turned back to his work as if there were nothing more he could say to Essex and nothing more he could listen to.

"Of course you know more about the country than I do." Essex did not let his anger with MacGregor take hold of him and he complimented himself on his patience. He was starting all over again. "I am probably too concerned with the vital importance of this situation to our British existence, but that is an understandable error. A few good discussions like this and I will begin to get the whole picture of Iran itself in relation to our own problem, and I'm glad you have a passion for the country, Mac-Gregor. I always like a man who can feel responsible to the situation he is studying. Now let's go up and discuss with Francis Drake the best way of presenting the whole issue to the Russians." Essex gripped MacGregor's arm and they walked out like that through Miss Williams's office.

As they swung into Drake's office, Essex said: "Francis, I want your advice on how to approach the Russians."

"Yes. Just a moment." Drake took off a pair of rimless spectacles and called Melby on the phone and told him to come up here. "Sit down, will you," Drake said to them.

Melby appeared almost immediately and Drake asked him what he had found out from Protocol.

"There was only that rather stupid girl there," Melby said. "She did not know anything about Lord Essex. She said she would tell Antonov to ring when he came in, but that is too much to hope for."

"Who is Antonov?" Essex asked.

"The head of Protocol here," Melby said. "He arranges all contacts."

"Can't we get around Protocol departments?" Essex asked him.

"Not here, Lord Essex," Melby said. "You can't avoid them."

"Can't I!" Essex said boyishly. "Just get Molotov on the phone for me."

"Good heavens," Drake said. "You can't do that."

"Why not?"

Drake smiled faintly. "You just can't do that here, Harold. Anyway Molotov doesn't speak any English or any other known language, so you couldn't talk to him."

"MacGregor can do the talking," Essex said. "Is your Russian good enough to talk to Molotov for me, MacGregor?"

"I think so."

"I wouldn't do that," Drake said and stood up to face Essex adequately.

"Why not? I don't think we would be exactly imposing on Molotov if we telephoned him." Essex was poised to go ahead and order it done.

"You would be imposing on yourself." Drake was worried now. "It would only lead to a very short answer from Molotov and a quick re-buttal, and that would delight the Russians. We can't have that sort of thing happening, Harold."

Essex did not want to go too far in opposition to Francis Drake — although he considered Drake's attitude a mere repetition of all the other advice he had received and rejected in London. He decided to be patient.

"Then who do you usually talk with?" he asked Drake.

"Borodin, the head of Western Europe."

"Don't you get any higher than that?"

"Occasionally the Vice Commissars, Vishinsky as a rule, but we avoid him if we can because he is too argumentative and too ruthless. So is Lozovsky."

"What has happened to Litvinov? Is he in Siberia?"

"No. He is here," Drake said, "but he isn't important any more."

"Out of favour?"

"You can never tell."

"And Maisky? We used to get on well with Maisky."

"He is not much better off than Litvinov. I think those two understand us better, and that is why they are out of a job. Molotov will not let anyone get to Stalin who is friendly to us."

"I suppose there is no hope of getting to Stalin?" Essex said.

"No. No," Drake said.

"They tell me in London, Francis, that you have to go to Stalin if you want anything done. Nobody else will make the decisions."

"That's true," Drake said.

"Then what are we wasting time with Molotov for?"

Drake knew that Essex could start telephoning Stalin to suggest that they get together for a friendly chat. Drake considered it a terrible spectre of diplomatic error. Essex would have all Moscow laughing at him if he did such a thing, and Drake himself would never live down the shame of it.

"We must go through the formal channels," Drake said urgently again. "John," he said to Melby. "Go and phone the Protocol people again, and tell them it is important. Try and get Antonov, wherever he is, and keep at it until you do."

Essex sighed. "I'm in your hands, Francis," he said, "but we are in a hurry you know."

"I know." Drake was sympathetic and relieved. "But we'll manage alright."

"I hope so," Essex said and waited for Melby. He went over to where MacGregor was sitting at the window, and he looked out at the skating rink as MacGregor had. Almost at the same moment the skater herself came into the room, dressed now in a black woollen dress with a white collar.

"Oh," she said tolerantly to Drake. "I didn't know you were busy."

"That's alright, Katherine," Drake said. "What have you got?"

37

"The news summaries and a short cable from Teheran," she said. She had walked to Drake's desk, but she was looking quite calmly at Essex and MacGregor, who faced her from the window. "I thought you would like to have the Teheran cable right away." She put the documents near Drake.

"Thank you," he said. "This is Lord Essex and Mr. MacGregor," he told her. "This is Katherine Clive, Harold."

"Are you the skater?" Essex asked her.

She nodded her head, and looked with straight Saxon eyes at Essex and then at MacGregor, and said: "You are the people that crashed in the plane?"

"Yes," Essex said.

Her head was very still, very composed. "The Russians have been ringing up all day apologizing about it, and I think two men from Intourist have just been down to say they were sorry. I don't suppose you wanted to see them did you?" She spoke with the poise and overconfidence expected of her. She was remotely tight-lipped, and her eyes were too direct, yet she appeared to be a person for whom nothing was important, neither their unfortunate aeroplane crash nor the Russian apologies.

"No," Essex said. "I didn't want to see them."

"Did you?" she said to MacGregor.

MacGregor said No, he didn't want to see them either.

"Good," she said. They both watched her exit.

"Who the devil is that, Francis?" Essex said with pleasure and surprise. "Is she another of the staff you brought here?"

"No." Drake fiddled with the dispatches. "She is doing attaché work and is something of a personal assistant."

"You don't say." Essex was impressed. Close sight had improved Katherine Clive's possibilities and even by Essex's standards she had been well possessed and well presented. This was quite an achievement for any woman, because Essex's standard was his own mother. He always measured the best women alongside his mother. A beautiful young woman always reminded him of her, probably because it was the early picture of his mother that he recalled; always the same picture of himself also — coming home to London from Eton and jumping out of the hansom cab and running up the stone steps of the Georgian house in the spring sunshine and pulling the long door bell and listening for the sound of his mother — knowing it was he — coming to answer the door herself, with the dogs scuffing on the rugs excitedly, and his younger brother hammering at the window near the steps. And then his amazing, charming, gentle mother; stroking his hair and running her fingers on the inside of his starched turned-down collar and laughing at him and half lifting

38

him up the long stairs to his own room. She was the one woman who had never done an inept thing in her life, always possessed and always gently dignified, even when she sat on the floor to play with the younger Richard, folding her legs neatly, sideways, under her long black skirts. Even with her mad husband she had been like that, and Essex had never yet seen a woman who could approximate her gentle beauty. There was nothing very gentle, for instance, about this young Englishwoman who disturbed Drake so; but she was English and full of presence, and Essex was going to ask more about her, but Drake interrupted him.

"Do you want this Teheran dispatch?" Drake asked him.

"After you," Essex told him. "What is in the news summaries?"

Drake was glancing through the foolscap sheets. "There is something here about Ribbentrop. Apparently he has written a letter to Churchill saying that Hitler fought the war so that Britain and Germany could head a flourishing Europe. I never did understand that fellow, and I never did like his cheek."

"He was quite a clever chap really," Essex said good-naturedly, "but he is going to hang for it."

"Do you think so?"

"Popular opinion, Francis."

"Rather hard on a man who was simply doing his job."

"Yes, I don't like this trial business," Essex said.

"You are not going to like this Teheran dispatch either," Drake said.

"What has happened now?" Essex said.

"The Iranian Government is expected to resign and we think that a new and more Leftist cabinet will be formed. That is the result of our failure to shift the Russians at the Moscow Conference! The new Cabinet is expected to re-orientate itself more to Russia, and to a conciliation with Russia." Drake looked up. "We are already losing our race with the Russians down there."

"By heavens we're not," Essex said. "Is there anything else?"

"No."

"If anything more comes in, Francis, would you mind having it sent to MacGregor?" Essex remembered MacGregor sitting quietly by the window: "Although MacGregor here doesn't think much of our reports from Teheran."

"Oh?" Drake said. "What's the matter with them?"

MacGregor felt that he might disagree with these two men on every attitude they took to any subject. They seemed to be so easy in their acceptance of the whole world as their own, their jobs being to play with it and juggle with it. MacGregor had seen plenty of this state of mind in the India Office, in fact it had been the proper attitude in all India Office

39

activities, but he had never been personally a direct part of it before. He did not like it, and now Drake was asking about the Teheran reports. What was the matter with them?

"They are bad," MacGregor said.

"Why are they bad?" Drake said irritably.

"They are inadequate," MacGregor said.

"And inaccurate!" Essex added pleasantly.

"Inaccurate?" Drake's precise voice rose. "How can you say that?"

"They don't show much understanding of the country." MacGregor did not move from his window, though he knew that Drake did not like him sitting there while talking to them.

"That doesn't sound right," Drake said to Essex. Then to MacGregor: "We have excellent people in Teheran, and to suggest that they lack understanding is rather unethical, MacGregor."

MacGregor looked at Essex but Essex wouldn't get him out of that.

"I don't want to be unethical," MacGregor said, "but I did not want Lord Essex to go into this with a false conception of Iran."

"Do your conceptions depend upon MacGregor, Harold?" Drake asked.

"Some of them," Essex said.

"Then I suggest that you have a talk with MacGregor." Drake knew his responsibilities and he could not let this pass. This sort of thing always happened when Essex appeared. He always brought disturbance and dissatisfaction and wild thinking, and no one was safe from his insidious charm. "What sort of work will you do, MacGregor, if you have no faith in our reports?"

"I don't know," MacGregor said honestly.

"You can't place yourself above the Foreign Office."

"I would not like to do that," MacGregor said.

"Good!" Drake was satisfied, although he was not sure of MacGregor. "It's not a very wise thing to criticize other departments or embassies like that, so try and remember it." Drake looked sternly at him.

"I really wasn't criticizing the Embassy, as such," MacGregor said, and as he had fixed his eyes on Essex he did so with Drake now. "I know nothing about the Teheran Embassy. I was really commenting on their information, which is bad."

"How do you know it is bad?" Drake was becoming angry.

Essex interrupted them: "Because it suggests that everything that is happening in Iran now is done by the Russians."

"Is that why, MacGregor?" Drake said.

"One of the reasons," MacGregor said.

"Well, isn't it true that the Russians are inspiring this trouble?"

"No," MacGregor said. "We apparently think that the Iranians are incapable of doing anything for themselves. They have as much interest in

40

their own affairs as anyone, and they are not as stupid as we seem to think."

"Are you defending the Russians, MacGregor?" Drake said.

"I don't care about the Russians," MacGregor said and stopped it there for his own comfort.

"It doesn't matter much," Essex said, "so long as you know what you are talking about. You can think what you like about Teheran, MacGregor, just so long as we get our job done, and it is a job that is becoming more urgent every day."

There was nothing more to be said, and MacGregor sat quietly at his window while Essex talked with Drake. He did not see how he could do an honest job, when he knew that he disagreed so basically with Essex. He hadn't gone far into this problem when Melby returned with a solemn face.

"I found Antonov," he said, "but he didn't seem to know anything about you."

Drake closed his lips tight. "Do we have to go through this again?"

"He said he had no instructions about Lord Essex."

"Did you tell him to ask Molotov for an appointment?"

"He said Molotov was not available."

"Not available!" Essex said. "Great God Almighty."

"That's the way it is." There was almost satisfaction in Drake's voice, but there was hopelessness too. "What else, John?"

"I told him it was important, and he asked me what it was about. I said it involved the talks on Azerbaijan. The idiot asked me what Lord Essex wanted to say about Azerbaijan."

Essex laughed.

"What else?" Drake said.

"That's about all, except that I asked him to let Molotov know that Lord Essex was here in Moscow and waiting to commence talks. He asked me to confirm it with the necessary formalities."

Essex had made up his mind. "I think I'll go down there myself," he said. "If you can spare a car, Francis, I'll go right now."

"It's no use doing that, Harold."

"Why not? I'll simply have to acquaint these people with my own person."

"No, Harold. They wouldn't even let you by the guard."

"Good. That will give me a chance to stir them up."

"They won't see it your way."

"They can see it any way they like," Essex growled. "Can you get me a car?"

"I strongly advise against it, Harold."

"I can't sit here and wait for the Russians to find out who I am, Francis."

41

"I will send them a strong complaint."

"Don't bother," Essex said pleasantly. "I'll complain strongly myself. Come along Mac," he said to MacGregor. "You can do the translating."

Chapter 3

FROM the back seat of the ambassadorial Rolls-Royce, Moscow looked quite different. By daylight it was a mixed city, a city of wide streets and enormous squares, yet it had the appearance of being compact and small. They went over the river behind the Kremlin, and the Russian driver pointed out the long white buildings of the old Imperial stables which were now the Kremlin garages. Beneath the turreted Kremlin wall there was a cold street-garden with rows of black city trees which were bare and very stark against the thick snow beneath them. Across a wide street was the best building that either Essex or MacGregor had seen in Moscow, and the driver told them it was the House of Soviets. It was a straight building with a granite face, about ten stories high, and occupying most of a whole block. It had a plain pale front with plenty of long windows, and it was one building that appeared absolutely new and adequate for the weather. Most of the other buildings were soft-looking and older, and some appeared to be crumbling, although there was never any real sign of decay in them. The city looked like an old house which was kept clean and neat and tidy and bare, an old house that was having its walls and body rebuilt. There were plenty of people on the frozen Moscow streets, and MacGregor saw them all as a hurrying, solid, bundled-up mass of faceless men and women. They were on the wide footpaths and collected at tram stops and hurrying in and out the buildings. The Rolls-Royce with its imperative Union Jack on a nickel-plated flagstaff paddled over the ice-rutted roads, and the people stood aside to let it pass and to look at it curiously. The driver had to honk and evade the black bundles of women who were sweeping the roads with long witch brooms, and who let the car pass without a glance. Then they came to a double square, which Essex recognized.

"There you are MacGregor," he said. "There is the Bolshoi."

The Bolshoi was a noble building with a high frontage of long white columns and a geometrical Greek pediment. Mounted on the pediment was a large bronze shape of four leaping horses drawing a chariot.

"Is that a theatre?" MacGregor asked as it disappeared.

"One of the most famous in the world," Essex said.

"Oh."

42

There did not appear to be any shopping or business district in the city, although there were a few small shops intermingled with the office-fronted buildings. They went up a hill, and the driver turned around and smiled at them and said, "The Lubianka. Our gaol." It was a red brick building with one side under extension. The scaffolding was still on its walls.

"That is the NKVD Building," Essex said, having read of it.

MacGregor had heard of the NKVD.

The policemen were small and dressed in long blue coats, and they blew their whistles at pedestrians (and at boys with flapping ear-caps) who were crossing the road away from the corners.

"The people look pretty black and miserable," Essex said.

MacGregor nodded. "They huddle up too much."

"Dismal city," Essex said as they slowed down, "but there is something about it, MacGregor."

They had arrived at the Foreign Office and it was an inconspicuous and dull place which was simply a door on the street among a lot of other doors. Essex led the way, and they went through an air-lock into a dim and dusty hall with a grey tiled floor. A khaki guard wearing a worker's cap and a pistol stood at the entrance holding out his hand.

As they stood undelivering, he said "*Propusk*." (Passes.)

"Do we have any passes?" MacGregor asked Essex.

"Of course not," Essex said.

"We have no passes," MacGregor told the guard in Russian.

"Well," said the guard, "you must have papers."

"We have only arrived in Moscow this morning," MacGregor said. "We have come here to see Mr. Molotov."

"Is he expecting you?"

"Of course."

"I have no instructions about you. Who are you, please?"

"I am MacGregor from the British Embassy." MacGregor pointed to Essex and wondered about the title. He did not think that Lord (literally) would be a good title to use in Russia, and he did not want to say *Gospodeen,* which meant "Mister." Whatever he was, Essex was not Mister. "This is Comrade Essex," MacGregor said to the guard, "and he has come here to see Mr. Molotov who will know all about him."

"Just a minute." The guard was frowning and unimpressed. He used a small wall phone and asked for an extension number and mumbled that two foreigners, English, named Mahrenker and Isaacs were waiting without papers to see Molotov who apparently was expecting them. He said Yes a few times and hung up and looked at the two of them.

"What does he say?" Essex asked MacGregor.

"Nothing. He is waiting for something."

Essex looked at the stairs. "Did you tell him that we must see Molotov?"

"Yes. He wasn't very impressed."

Essex did not like the appearance of the guard so he did not try the stairs. "We must see Mr. Molotov," Essex said in English. "It is very important and we can't be kept waiting down here."

"I don't understand," the guard said to MacGregor.

"He says that we must see Mr. Molotov."

"Wait." The guard looked sceptically at Essex's fur-collared coat with its black braid. "Someone will come down."

Lord Essex had expected something different. He had expected a more imposing building with a parquet floor and a white marbled staircase. In that atmosphere he could have swept forward and carried out his original plan of simply walking into the place and saying casually that he was Essex. He had not expected an unimpressive building and a silent-mouthed guard who stood like a watchdog making sure that Essex did not storm the place. It wasn't a good beginning.

A dark man in the grey uniform of the Foreign Office came down the steps unhurriedly. He had a thin drawn face which did not break in any way, either with expression or characteristic. He was small and wore black-rimmed glasses, and he nodded his high head impassively as he held out his hand to Essex.

"Good afternoon, Lord Essex," he said in English. "We are very sorry to delay you here but we were not expecting you. Would you come up, please?"

"Thank you for coming down," Essex said. "This is Mr. MacGregor, my assistant."

They walked up the stairs. "I am Korin," the Russian said.

Essex did not offer any explanation of their presence to Korin, because he preferred to wait until he identified the man, his position, and his importance. They walked silently up the dull steps and onto a worn timbered floor. Essex looked unhappily at a large painting of a shipwreck which met them on the landing, but it was mercifully out of sight as they turned into a corridor and entered a carpeted room. Korin gestured to a worn leather couch near a tiled stove. As they sat down he took a box of Russian cigarettes from his desk and offered it to them. Essex took one, squashed the cardboard end, and accepted a match from Korin.

"We were sorry to hear of your accident," Korin said tiredly.

"We survived it alright." Essex was still waiting to identify Korin's position and trying to relate this room to his own conception of a Foreign Office. He could not get the feeling of the place as he looked at the old and irregular furniture and at the wearing carpet and the dull pictures. It was an old place that seemed to have forgotten its history or its tradition, and Essex did not like that.

"Mr. Suchkov will be here in a moment."

"Who is Mr. Suchkov?" Essex began.

"He is the head of this section."

"Is this the Western Europe Section?"

"No. We are part of Mr. Molotov's own office." Korin did not say which part.

"I see." Essex was looking for the proletariat in Korin, but Korin looked more like a sick professor than a worker.

Korin was watching them. "I believe that Mr. Suchkov will be looking after you while you are here. He is in our Iranian Department."

"Ah!" Essex said happily.

Korin sat immobile and silent, waiting for Suchkov to arrive. MacGregor realized that Korin was taking stock of them, just as they were investigating him. MacGregor knew how to sit silently, but Essex was uncomfortable. Fortunately he did not have to wait long. Suchkov came in with the honest appearance of hurrying.

"Lord Essex!" he said in good English. "You are well and here."

Suchkov was a dark, smiling, earnest young man, square and small and healthily (in fact solidly) built, even to his dark forehead which bore an earnest frown above black eyebrows.

Essex stood up and they shook hands. "How do you do, Mr. Suchkov," he said formally. They exchanged some of their good feelings and estimated each other. MacGregor was introduced, and Essex felt his age beside these two. The Russian was no older than MacGregor, but he was more open-faced, and he had none of MacGregor's appearance of control and care. Suchkov was a peasant and an intelligent man, whereas MacGregor was a Highlander with an intellect. Suchkov could not pronounce MacGregor's name and he compromised at MagGre*gor,* putting the accent on the last syllable and rolling the *r.* He said that Gre*gor* was a Russian name, and this made the last part of it easy. MacGregor laughed when Suchkov laughed, and Essex behaved like a father to both of them. Suchkov asked them if they had met Mr. Molotov's messenger to the Embassy.

Essex said: "What messenger?"

"Mr. Molotov sent a messenger to your Embassy some time ago to inquire after your health, and to express regret at the accident to the plane."

"We must have missed him." Essex spread his hands as generous explanation.

"Then he must still be there, at your Embassy."

"We telephoned to Mr. Antonov at Protocol and he knew nothing about us," Essex said. "That is why we came direct. We did not expect any messenger from Mr. Molotov."

"Ah: Comrade Antonov." Suchkov became earnest. "No. He would not have known about you, I am afraid." Suchkov leaned forward and smiled.

45

"It is I who would know about you, because you have arranged everything with us direct in London, and we have not put this through the formal channels of Protocol. You must forgive Antonov for not knowing about you."

To MacGregor this seemed meticulously correct, and he smiled at Essex to see if he would appreciate the humour of it; but Essex said nothing.

"I regret any inconvenience." Suchkov filled their silence.

"Don't worry about it," Essex said quickly. "In view of the informality of our original arrangements, and since we have no agenda, we took the liberty of calling informally to present ourselves. Would you convey my greetings and good wishes to Mr. Molotov?"

"Certainly."

"We would like to present our respects to Mr. Molotov personally of course."

"Of course."

"And naturally we are most anxious to begin our conversations." Suchkov nodded.

Essex waited for him to say something about Molotov, about Molotov not being in, or Molotov anxious to see them, or Molotov willing to see them to-day or to-morrow. Suchkov smiled and said nothing, and Essex began to feel annoyed and tightened up a little.

"Perhaps your Mr. Molotov was not expecting us to arrive in Moscow so soon."

"I believe he expected you, and of course he knew of your plane mishap."

"Then we haven't arrived in Moscow unannounced," Essex said cleverly.

"No, Lord Essex, you haven't." Suchkov pulled down an unruly and unstarched collar and blew his solid nose on a white handkerchief. "I see that you are anxious to get things done," he said. "You are like a Russian."

"Yes," Essex said. "Important issues have to be settled." He was interested in Suchkov's white handkerchief because he had not expected to see such a white hemstitched article among any of them.

Suchkov continued a leisurely and unpointed comparison. "I believe that we Russians and you English are alike in many ways, particularly in our feeling for history. My friend Mr. Korin is an historian and we have discussed this before."

Korin nodded silently.

"I have never been to England," Suchkov went on, "but I have met many Englishmen in Iran, although I missed meeting Mr. MacGregor there." This was pointed.

"We might have met," MacGregor said negatively.

"No," Suchkov said seriously. "I think you left in 1940 didn't you?"

46

"Yes." MacGregor was surprised that Suchkov knew anything about him.

"I wasn't in Iran itself until some time after that."

"Oh?" MacGregor's grey eyes opened a little.

"And you were in the south and I was mostly in the north."

"How do you know about me?" MacGregor asked undiplomatically.

"Your name is very well known in Iran, Mr. MacGregor, because of your father. I believe we have every one of your father's published geological reports in our various scientific archives. I know that our geologists think highly of his researches in the field, and our engineers in the north have actually used some of his surveys since our occupation there. I personally have one of his original sketches of Demavend from the south side, and I think of him always as a very good geographer and artist, as well as being such a remarkable geologist. Perhaps we appreciate him here almost as much as you do in England."

MacGregor enjoyed his own astonishment that anyone here had ever heard of his father's work in Iran. The only time he had ever seen any of it recorded or referred to was in the Imperial College Library where his father's work on physiography had been used occasionally as a supplementary study, but it was little more than a paper on the subject. In this field his father had been occasionally recognized, but very little reference had ever been made to his great geological surveys of Persia, even though they were in the Library under the simple heading of "The Geology of Persia." His father's collection of researches in Persia came nearest to being the only standard work on the geology of the country. MacGregor had never been able to understand why this had not been better recognized, particularly since it covered such a wide field — from the study of the great surface features of the Zagros to the particular study on the petrology of southern Demavend, the work he had been doing in making the sketch which Suchkov possessed. To find someone who had heard of his father was very satisfying to MacGregor, personally as well as scientifically, and it was an influential beginning for him.

"Are you a geologist?" MacGregor asked him.

"No." Suchkov had apparently expected the question. "I have graduated as a mining engineer but I turned away from it during the war. I had thought that you were a geologist, Mr. MacGregor, like your father."

"I'm afraid the war interfered," MacGregor said.

"And you intend to remain in the diplomatic service?"

"I don't think so."

Suchkov nodded. "The sciences are more satisfying," he said, "but I think the world of diplomacy needs a few more men like us with some patient training in objectivity." Suchkov was smiling solidly at both of them.

47

Essex had allowed them long enough, however. "Mr. MacGregor is one of our rising young specialists on Iran, Mr. Suchkov. Don't you think he is a natural man for the work, and don't you agree that we have done well to bring him here?"

"You are lucky to have someone who will understand Iran as well as Mr. MacGregor," Suchkov said to Essex, and then to MacGregor: "A man who knows the country will see Soviet policy there in its true light, and he will understand it."

"Then you will appreciate my intentions in bringing MacGregor."

"I hope we can," Suchkov said.

"Perhaps we could see Mr. Molotov," Essex said.

"Unfortunately he is not in Moscow at the moment," Suchkov said. "He is taking a short holiday after the strenuous work of the Moscow Conference, but he should be back to-morrow or on New Year's day."

Essex wasted no more time. "We are very glad to have had this meeting with you, Mr. Suchkov, and you also Mr. Korin, and you might tell Mr. Molotov that we will be happy to meet him as soon as he returns."

"We will arrange everything and let you know," Suchkov said.

Essex decided he had succeeded. "Then we will hear from you soon?"

"Yes. As soon as I have heard from Mr. Molotov."

"Good." Essex had been standing near a mantelshelf which held a half-dozen English books between two marble ends. He took one of them down. "May I borrow this book from you?" It was Harold Nicolson's *Peacemaking, 1919.* "I haven't had a chance to read it, and I have forgotten my old Paris days."

"Of course you were with the British delegation," Korin said.

"I was rather young then, Mr. Korin. May I borrow it?"

"Please," Korin said with his cold mouth. "We are translating and publishing the book in Russian. It is a revealing work."

Essex was impressed. "You publish it untouched?" he asked spontaneously.

"Absolutely."

"Then I congratulate you," Essex said.

He shook hands quickly with Korin because he did not like sick men. He allowed Suchkov to show them to the door and then to the stairs and then by the guard. Essex never forgot any man, and as he passed the guard he nodded to him and said good-bye and thank you. Suchkov did not come out onto the pavement but he opened the first door for them.

"Good-bye Suchkov," Essex said as they shook hands. "We will meet again of course, and I hope it will be soon. I'll look after your book."

"Good-bye, Lord Essex," Suchkov said. "I will get in touch with you."

MacGregor hesitated for a moment and then he asked Suchkov about Professor Onegin. "He is one of your geologists," MacGregor said. "I

48

would like to get in touch with him and see him, if possible. How could I arrange it?"

"Professor Onegin?"

"Professor Alexander Onegin," MacGregor said.

"I will see if I can arrange it for you, Mr. MacGregor." Suchkov said it with the confidence of promise and good-fellowship for MacGregor, and they shook hands as Essex walked ahead and out the second door. Essex and MacGregor entered the patient Rolls-Royce and returned in the eventide to the Embassy.

Melby heard them come in and he met them as they were hanging up their heavy coats on the pegs in the entrance hall. "Would you go up to Sir Francis, Lord Essex?" Melby said. "There is a Russian up there from the Foreign Office. He is waiting to see you."

MacGregor followed Essex, unasked, into Drake's room. The Russian was there, uncomfortable and official and waiting with an impatient Drake. The Russian stood up and spoke officially of Molotov's sorrow and regret about their accident, and bade them welcome to Moscow. Essex shook his hand and the Russian went away. Essex sat down heavily on the couch and put his feet up.

"That is the first time they have ever sent anybody down here on a mission like that." Drake's surprise was greater than his curiosity about Essex's experience at the Foreign Office. "You never know what they are going to do next."

"Francis: you take these people too seriously," Essex said happily.

"I suppose you walked into Molotov's office." Drake could be humorous.

"Very nearly," Essex said. "We were met and welcomed by a gentleman named Suchkov."

"Never heard of him."

"He is Molotov's Iranian specialist or something like that."

"Did they know about you?"

"Yes. They thought we would handle this direct with Molotov, and that is supposed to be why your friend Antonov didn't know about me. Is that an excuse?"

"Of course it is. We are an Embassy and our official contact is through Antonov. There is nothing so informal here as contacting Molotov's office direct. We don't even know his phone number."

"Well, I just contacted Molotov's office direct," Essex told him peacefully, "so that is a beginning in informality for you. Just march in there sometime yourself, Francis. Do them good."

"Did you arrange your meeting with Molotov?"

"That is hard to say," Essex said. "He is supposed to be out of town."

"They'll take their time," Drake said.

"I shan't let them take their time." Essex was still looking at MacGregor.

"They were very impressed with MacGregor," he told Drake. "They knew all about his father, and thought us fortunate in having a man like him in the diplomatic service and here with me in Moscow." Essex was being paternal about it, but he was thinking that it was a real stroke of luck to have MacGregor with him, a man whom the Russians already respected. Essex could get at them through MacGregor and he did not mind admitting it. MacGregor could become just the medium he needed, if only MacGregor could be persuaded into this a little further. MacGregor seemed to be breaking down slowly, but he was still playing this game of keeping himself outside the spirit of the mission. It was those curious ideas of his. But no man's ideas had ever been a problem to Essex. He knew that anything could change in a man once he had given himself, even for a moment, to the demands of the diplomatic work he was doing. MacGregor was difficult to embroil but not impossible, and Essex could see that he had hit it off with Suchkov. It was falling his way.

"MacGregor," he said. "I wonder if you would read the outline of proposals which I dictated to Miss Williams this afternoon, and then read all our instructions very carefully. Acquaint yourself with the spirit and the intention and the purpose of this mission a little more, but quickly if possible. You may have to do a few meetings on your own with Suchkov to thrash out some of the details. I'll be down after dinner."

"You certainly intend taking chances," Drake said to him when MacGregor had gone.

"On MacGregor?" Essex lay back.

"Yes."

"MacGregor's alright," Essex said. "He just needs a little coaxing."

Drake said nothing.

Essex went on sleepily. "If Molotov doesn't show up by to-morrow night I think I shall tackle Stalin himself. I don't want to do it that way, but I am in a hurry and I am not going to wait on Molotov's whims. I have to be back in London by mid-January, and for the Russians' own sake they ought to see that things are shaping up against them, not only in Iran but everywhere. Yes, if Molotov doesn't come through I think I'll see Stalin."

Chapter 4

Lord Essex told MacGregor that he had been quite impressed with Suchkov, and MacGregor admitted that he also liked the stocky Russian. "Apart from a doctor at Abadan," MacGregor said to

Essex, " he is the only man I have ever met so casually who has heard of my father's work."

"Is that why he impressed you?" Essex chuckled.

"No. I simply liked him," MacGregor said. "But it's an odd change for a man to have made from mining engineer."

"It's the sort of change that can be made," Essex said. "You have made it."

"Not permanently," MacGregor said.

"I would give that some thought if I were you, Mac," Essex said. "You know, there is a certain truth in that heavy joke of Suchkov's about diplomacy needing more men trained scientifically in objectivity. We do need more of you: men who see facts more coldly than people like me who have lived too long in diplomacy. We diplomatists are too inclined simply to find facts to fit our diplomatic requirements, don't you think?"

"You are the only diplomat I know, so I can't commit myself." Mac-Gregor had not been cautious at all, and he was smiling at Essex across the room.

This was one of a number of spasmodic talks since last night's meeting with Suchkov. They had been at their work steadily all day, interrupting it only for their separate lunches and waiting in the meantime to hear from Molotov.

It was the last day of 1945, and it was Essex's limit in waiting for Molotov. It was already late afternoon and Molotov had not called them. By now their work had tapered off into nothing. They could do little more until they actually began the negotiations, and even MacGregor was beginning to feel impatient. On the other hand he didn't mind sitting here on his desk in the darkening room, talking across to Essex, who sat by the fire with his stockinged feet on the hearth.

Essex was pleased with MacGregor's quiet but personal humour. "You are becoming something of a diplomat yourself," Essex said. "Perhaps you should speak more generally and be a little more critical. If you wanted to be critical of the efforts of modern diplomacy, MacGregor, what would you say was wrong with it?"

"Ignorance of common facts, I suppose," MacGregor said after some consideration.

"Is that all?"

"I have never given it much thought," MacGregor said, "but it always appears that most diplomacy is concerned with each nation's own demands, instead of considering all countries in relation to each other. In any science you learn quickly that everything is interrelated and interdependent, but diplomacy seems to operate on the principle that every country is on its own, fighting for what it can get."

"True," Essex said. "But diplomacy is an art, not a science. It's quite simple to understand it if you realize that each nation must use diplomacy to look after its own interests, just as it uses war to protect itself. After all that is just what we have been fighting for."

"Self-protection?" MacGregor said.

"Basically."

"Surely there was more to it than that," MacGregor said.

"What more?"

"Well, we didn't protect ourselves simply to go back to what we were. We don't want to restore all the problems that started the war, because that will certainly take us into another."

"Unfortunately, MacGregor, diplomacy is not simply a means of making peace. Sometimes it is supposed to make war."

"Then that is where I disagree with it," MacGregor said.

"Would you have peace at any price?"

"No," MacGregor said. "I never liked that at all, and I was glad that we fought the war, but I should think it is up to diplomacy to see that there is enough agreement or co-operation to stop wars, particularly now."

"Why now? Is it any different now than ever before?"

"Another war would finish us all off, all of us."

"You are thinking about this atom nonsense!" Essex was chiding him.

"It's something to think about."

"I am weary of hearing about it," Essex sighed. "It's a nice diplomatic weapon, but it's not something to cry peace about. Weapons have always been terrible."

"Not like this one," MacGregor said.

"Perhaps not, but it's hardly our responsibility, MacGregor. We are each concerned with protecting and securing our national interest to our best advantage, and if that involves atomic bombs then we just have to face the fact. Nations cannot get on in any other way but selfishly, and no organization of nations will ever balance common interest against self-interest. Our United Nations friends are trying, but they can hardly succeed."

"They seem to be doing alright," MacGregor argued.

Essex smiled. "Just before we left London I had lunch with a very witty fellow on the American delegation, and he had cleverly reversed Clausewitz's famous dictum to say that 'diplomacy is a continuation of war by other means.' That is your United Nations, my boy."

"Perhaps it is that way at the moment" — MacGregor watched the red stars lighting up on the Kremlin towers — "but sooner or later they will have to organize some kind of arrangement to stop us all fighting. It might be difficult but surely it isn't impossible."

"That may depend on fellows like you." Essex knew when to stop argu-

52

ing and when to bring a man into personal responsibility. "There is not much hope of any organization succeeding unless you young and objective fellows take hold of it and organize it properly. It's up to you clever young men to take your part in these problems: in this Iran problem for instance. It is your job to see that it is properly settled. Don't you feel that this is your responsibility, MacGregor?"

"Not exactly," MacGregor said.

"Then can't you see that this argument on Iran is vital to us?"

"No. I can't see that at all."

Essex wriggled his silk toes over the dying coals and dealt with MacGregor very carefully. "Then what do you see, MacGregor?" he asked. "Don't be afraid of being critical. I am really most anxious to hear your attitude because it can be quite important to me in understanding our rôle better. I can see that you don't like the idea of talking to the Russians about Iran at all."

"I think we should leave the country alone and let it settle its own affairs," he said. "I don't know how Iran could settle its own affairs, but everybody will have to get out before they can try. It's not much use persuading the Russians to get out if we remain, because we will simply replace Russian influence in the north with our influence, and that is no good either. Actually, I don't see what gives us the right to discuss Iran with anyone."

"The right of occupation," Essex said patiently. "By the same right that we exercise occupation rights in Germany and Italy and Japan. We must establish law and order and friendly authority, so that we can feel secure."

"Then why are we dealing in Iran with the very men who fought us there, and who were pro-German during the war?"

"None of these men is in the Government."

"No, but we are trying to get them into the Government and into Azerbaijan. Six of the governors and generals whom the Russians have thrown out of the north were pro-German, and now we are asking the Russians to take four of them back in Azerbaijan."

"Are they on our list?"

"Yes."

"Then strike them off. We don't want that sort of people."

"The trouble is we have a lot more of those people, and not only in Azerbaijan. We have just allotted newsprint to one fellow in Teheran for instance. He was known to have taken money from the Germans for propaganda; in fact he is starting his newspaper with funds he got from the Germans during the war."

"Do you know that definitely?"

"Of course."

"Did you bring it to anyone's attention in the India Office?"

53

"Several times."

"They did nothing?"

"Nothing at all." MacGregor eased off the desk in the darkness. "But that is only one unimportant example," he said. "We are doing that sort of thing all over Iran. We are gradually making the worst men our best friends because we seem to be obsessed with the idea of getting rid of the Russians by any means."

"What else can we do but get rid of them?" Essex asked him.

"I don't know," MacGregor said, "but I would sooner have the Russians there than some of the men we are dealing with."

"Aren't you seeing this a little too much as a local problem, rather than as one which seriously concerns the interests and security of the Empire?" Essex lit his pipe, and the light brightened the room for a moment.

"Perhaps I do," MacGregor said.

"Do you think you are taking the right attitude?" The match went out. MacGregor did not like the question, but now that he couldn't see Essex across the dark room, his answer did not matter. "I know we have to hold the Empire together," he said, "but not the way we are trying to do it in Iran." He smiled a little. "I probably say that because in Iran I am a better Iranian than I am an Englishman."

Essex enjoyed that. "I can see what you mean," he said gently. "Unfortunately I have always been an Englishman. I always will be an Englishman, and I find it hard to be compassionate for any country but my own. I would like to hear more from you about Iran, MacGregor, because I see that you have a feeling for the place; and I am willing to be influenced by any honest man's considerations. Iran is a strange land to me, I have never been there and I know nothing about it, so I depend upon you for a proper understanding of the country. Always tell me what is on your mind in relation to this subject, because I want to see your picture of our job here." Essex felt that he had impressed MacGregor in the right direction. "And of course," he added with jocular good-fellowship, "I am anxious to put you to work wherever possible in these negotiations. If we are going to be dealing with Suchkov I shall leave him to you, for the most part."

"What would that involve?" MacGregor was now sitting opposite Essex before the fire, his leg hooked over the end of the low sofa.

"Oh it might involve some negotiation. Or perhaps settlement of the details to general decisions which Molotov and I might agree on."

"Am I supposed to make any decisions?"

"Some," Essex said.

MacGregor closed one grey-green eye and pulled at his ear. "I doubt if I'm fitted for anything like that," he said. "I know little about our political requirements."

54

"There is nothing complicated to it," Essex said. "As you get the feel of the mission you will find yourself falling naturally into place."

MacGregor did not want to fall naturally into place, but even in the intimacy of this dark room he preferred to keep the thought to himself. For a moment, however, he did not mind being a little more co-operative. MacGregor felt that talking with Suchkov about Iran would not be such a bad thing, whatever Essex intended. And if Essex himself could be influenced, then the whole aspect of the mission might change. It was at least worth a try, and MacGregor decided to watch for the opportunities of showing Essex where he was wrong.

An evening stillness had settled upon the room, and MacGregor could see the ruby reflection from the Kremlin stars caught by the varnished surface of a dusty oil painting over the mantelpiece. It was sensible of Essex to sit here like this in the darkness. It was easy and quiet, and it was not at all peculiar, because Essex simply made it a natural thing to do.

"It looks as if Molotov will not call us to-day," Essex said.

"I suppose not," MacGregor said. "What can you do about it?"

"I'll think on it for a while."

"Must it be Molotov?"

"Molotov is the proper man," Essex told him.

"And Stalin?"

"It will probably be hard to get at Stalin over Molotov's head."

"Is it like this in other parts of the world?"

"Good heavens no. Anywhere else it is a simple matter of a telephone call; and in Washington, for instance, it is less. Any of our chaps there can drop in on the Secretary of State at almost any time about any subject, and by Jove it's thrashed out right then."

"Ah, but we don't argue much with the Americans," MacGregor said.

"True," said Essex, "we are natural partners. It's fortunate that we are, because only our combined efforts will enable us to stop the Russians. America is really the only country strong enough to cope with the Russians these days, and we depend upon her support for much of our policy in Europe and the Middle East. Of course the Yankees are not in this for nothing, MacGregor, as we are finding out in the Middle East. They have just bought a monopoly oil concession in Saudi Arabia, and now they actually have more oil holdings in the Middle East than ourselves. That makes our rôle in Iran doubly important, because the Americans will try to pick up Middle East influence where we drop it. However, it is in our mutual interests to see that Russia is checked in the Middle East. We can always depend on American support for our case." Essex laughed softly. "In fact the Americans are more vigorous about the Russians than we are, because they are between the devil and our deep blue sea. But I like the Americans. I can talk with them and understand them, and I can laugh

55

with them and handle them. Now the Russians are too irascible and unbending, and it is damned difficult to handle them, particularly when they are on their home ground. How did you find them in Iran, Mac-Gregor? The same heavy-handed sort of people? The same unapproachable devils?"

"I don't ever remember seeing any Soviet Russians in Iran," MacGregor said. "There were plenty of White Russians and they were a rather unhappy sort of people who did not want to go back home, and yet did not like Iran. Most of them did go back during the war, particularly those from the Caucasus and Soviet Armenia. I think they were sorry that they ever left home, whatever they thought about the Russian Government."

"A man should never leave his country," Essex said, "no matter what happens. If a man doesn't agree with what is going on in his own country then he should stay and do something about it and not go running off to America or England, like so many of those fellows in Europe did during the war. Thank God there were no English refugees during the war."

"Didn't we send some people off to America and Canada?" MacGregor said.

"Mostly children, but I was strongly opposed to it. I had a poor but noble cousin, a loving mother of three young boys who came and asked me to get her children to Canada before the bombing started. I told her that as far as I was concerned even the Pilgrim Fathers had been cowards, and I sent her to the devil. I last heard that her children were in Canada and did not want to come back to England. Now they will make neither good Canadians nor good Englishmen and you can't be both, can you?"

"No," MacGregor said. "It's quite difficult to be both."

MacGregor knew what he was talking about. He had never been to England until he was seventeen, and he had enjoyed no preliminary life as an Englishman, because his father had ignored the social habits of his fellow countrymen in Iran, most of whom had been English-conscious officials attached to the Iranian Army or to the old Shah. To these people the MacGregors had been a strange, isolated, obscure, scientific Scotch family: an old man with a very young and gentle wife and a quiet self-contained son who did not attend the English schools but went instead to native schools and to other foreign institutions. When MacGregor had finally gone to London to attend the Royal College of Science he had been a foreigner, and in five years there he had remained something of a foreigner. It had been little better on his return to Iran, because English-Persian's oil fields were a provincial English suburb surrounded by hot desert hills. The life there had been more English than in England, and MacGregor had always been outside it.

Miss Williams had opened the door, and she switched on the light. In a moment the ruby darkness had gone and MacGregor and Essex found themselves facing each other very informally, Essex with his feet still in the fire and MacGregor with his leg over the end of the couch. MacGregor unbent his leg and straightened up and pushed back a lock of hair, and Essex bent his head back in annoyance and asked Miss Williams what it was that she wanted.

"I'm sorry," she said. "I didn't know that you were in here. It's just the BBC evening bulletin and the notes you dictated."

MacGregor stood up and took them from her and behaved as kindly as he could, because Miss Williams was blushing and she had dropped one of the sheets. He picked it up and opened the door for her and then came back to Essex. He gave Essex one of the bulletins and the notes, and then took the other bulletin and sat properly at his desk to read it, still a little under the enchantment of Essex's informality.

"By Jove!" Essex said. "Are you reading that Persian Ambassador's statement?"

"Yes." MacGregor read the BBC bulletin through. "How does he know that Russian troops are massing on the northern borders to invade Iran? We haven't had anything about it, and I know that most of the information which the Iranians get about the Russians comes from us. We have had no reports about it at all."

"Oh, he's just playing his hand rather heavily," Essex said and laughed.

"Yes, but he is making a flat statement," MacGregor said.

"Damn fool," Essex muttered. "There is a time for that sort of pressure, but it isn't now. I wish those fellows would keep out of this and leave it to me. That's what we get for giving the Americans a share in this. They always overplay their hand."

"Why should the Russians mass troops on the northern frontiers when they can put all the troops they want into northern occupied Iran? And what have the Americans got to do with it?"

"The Americans love to play diplomacy by making scares. It's a crude method. I suppose this Persian fellow, in London or Paris or Washington, or wherever he is, has fallen for it. Uff!" Essex said. "Don't worry about it."

MacGregor felt so annoyed that he was restless, and he wanted to get outside.

"Do you want me for anything?" he asked Essex.

"No. I think I'll get in touch with the Americans and have a talk with them. Just look in later on, will you?"

MacGregor nodded.

"I believe there will be fireworks to-night for the New Year," Essex said. "Apparently they love fireworks here, salutes and all that sort of thing. I have always wanted to see their salutes. We probably will to-night. Are you going anywhere?"

"I'm still tired," MacGregor said. "I think I shall go to bed early."

"I think I'll do that too, although I have to go to the Americans I suppose," Essex said. "Tell Miss Williams to go will you, Mac, and turn out the light as you go out."

MacGregor turned out the light and left Essex in the darkness.

Miss Williams stopped typing to watch MacGregor, and to envy at a quick glance his transparent skin and his calmly set features. She liked the look of MacGregor's intelligent face and she thought it the proper face for a man to have: quiet and slightly withdrawn and yet well possessed.

"I hope I didn't disturb you in there," she said to him.

"No," he said. "We were just sitting by the fire."

"I thought Lord Essex seemed a little angry at the interruption."

"He's sleepy," he said and wondered why she blushed so much. "There is nothing else for to-night," he told her. "It looks as though Molotov will not get in touch with us."

He needn't have told me that, she thought appreciatively. "I'll just finish this letter," she said. "I'm in no hurry to go. Are you going to wait for the New Year to-night, Mr. MacGregor?"

"No, I don't think so."

"We are all having a party up at *Britansky Suyuznik*, if you would like to come." She pushed a wisp of fair hair away from her pink face.

"At where?" he asked.

"*Britansky Suyuznik*. That is the paper our Ministry of Information prints here for the Russians. Hadn't you heard of it?"

"I think I did somewhere."

"It's really the most popular foreign paper in Russia," she said. "Down at the open market you can get six cigarettes or ten roubles for a copy."

"I didn't think the Russians would allow anyone to publish literature here except themselves," he said.

"Oh the Russians bring a paper out in London, so we publish one here. So do the Americans. They are starting a big coloured Russian magazine here like *Life*, but theirs is only a monthly, ours is a weekly."

"What do we do — tell the Russians about the war?"

"Not now," she said. "It's mostly about reconstruction, or Parliament, or our way of doing things, or the Royal Family and the Empire. I shall get you the next copy."

"I'd like to see it," he said.

"Would you like to come to-night?"

"I don't think so, but thank you all the same. I am still sleepy," he said. "What time will the Russian salute start?"

"At midnight I suppose."

"I might wake up for that," he told her.

"Happy New Year," she said.

"And to you," he replied. "Good night."

He went out through the main doors and across the frozen ground of the Embassy courtyard to Melby's flat. Dinner with Melby was silent, even for MacGregor, and he was glad when Melby brought out a bottle of brandy and finished the meal. He thought of going straight to bed, but he was still restless, and he went out to see something of Moscow.

He was crossing the rutted drive of the Embassy when he stepped aside to avoid someone walking with head down. It was the poised skater, Katherine Clive, and he said good evening to her and helped her over the broken ground to the footpath which ran beside the granite wall of the river. She didn't seem to care whose arm she held or with whom she co-ordinated her warm movements.

"If I had any sense I would wear boots," she said. "All these footpaths are like glaciers." She kept a grip on his arm as they walked. "Where are you going?" she asked him.

"I am just out to see something of Moscow," MacGregor said.

"Have you been here before?"

"No."

"Then you might as well walk through the Red Square, because I am going that way." She lengthened her steps to meet his, and it was not difficult for her to keep up with him because she was almost as tall as MacGregor. "You are MacGregor, aren't you?" she said.

"Yes."

"Are you fed up with Moscow yet?" It was impersonal, but sharp and provocative.

"After two days?" he asked.

"Two days are enough for most people," she said cynically. "Haven't you been told what a terrible place this is?"

"Not yet."

"Then it will come," she said. "When we have finished with you here, Mr. MacGregor, you will be glad to leave Moscow."

"When who is finished with me?" he asked her.

"Perhaps I shouldn't be so unethical," she murmured with deceptive mildness, "but sooner or later someone in the Embassy will tell you the whole truth about Russia. Do you mean to say that no one has been at you?"

"No."

"Then it is something you can expect."

"I'm afraid there will not be time for that. I shall only be here a little while."

"In that case you may survive the ordeal," she said.

"How long have you been here?" he asked her.

"A little over a year."

"Have you survived the ordeal?"

"Barely," she said.

MacGregor did not know whether to take her seriously or not.

"Tell me," she said. "What did the Russians do when you and Lord Essex walked in on the Foreign Office unannounced? Did it shock them?"

"It surprised them."

"I am sure it did," she said. "They need surprising. No one has ever stormed in there before, and no one has ever made such an impression on them as a result. Do you think the Russians objected to it?"

"I didn't think so."

"Then nobody here will ever realize it," she said in her lazy English. She spoke the language as if she liked it, but MacGregor found it hard to connect this soft cynical tongue with the self-possessed beauty he had seen in Drake's room yesterday. Her extreme assurance worried him, until it turned into ease. Then preliminaries were not necessary, so MacGregor was at ease himself. "I suppose the Ambassador was more shocked than the Russians," she said; "in which case you should both do well in Moscow."

"We haven't seen Molotov yet," MacGregor corrected. "We may not see him at all."

"Oh they'll take their time," she said, "just as we take our time when they want something from us. It's an equitable business." She let go his arm and tightened her soft fur coat about her. "We had better walk singly here," she said. "We have to get up that steep bank to the bridge and there is only a rut for a path. I will go ahead of you."

She walked slowly but not at all cautiously, and MacGregor followed her up the ice path to the steps and then up the frozen steps to the bridge itself, where she held his arm again.

"What is it about Moscow that everybody objects to?" he asked her.

"I suppose it's the insular life we lead."

"Not knowing Russians?"

"I thought that no one had been talking to you?"

"I have heard a little," he said.

"It's partly that," she said, "but it's probably ourselves. We are a rather miserable lot, Mr. MacGregor."

"Do you know any Russians?" he persisted.

"Not many."

"Why would Russians be forbidden to know Englishmen?"

"They are not forbidden." She swept snow off the bridge rail and it fell into the frozen river below. "But Russians with any sense keep away from foreigners, because too much intrigue has originated from the Embassies in Moscow. That has kept the Russians away since the purges. It seems ridiculous at times." She gave it no real importance.

"I thought the war would have changed that," he said.

"The war didn't change anybody," she said, "including ourselves or the Russians. In some ways we might as well be at war with them now."

"That is something I don't understand," MacGregor said and it was easy to say it to this satirical woman. "What are we supposed to be fighting about?"

"It shouldn't be difficult to find something to fight about," she said gracefully. "We are angry enough about Iran to start being strong-minded with the Russians, aren't we?"

"Yes, but that is hardly war."

"I suppose not," she said. "It's a silly affair anyway."

"Iran?"

"Yes and everything else. One can never find out what we expect of the Russians or what they expect of us. Can you?"

"Not in Iran anyway," he said.

"Nor here," she said. "People like me will tell you all sorts of things and so will others, but if you have any sense you will ignore us all. We are all reduced to petulance by this crazy life, and if you ignore us all then you might like the place while you are here."

"Do you like it?" He looked at her flashing earrings.

"I might as well say that I don't like it," she said peacefully, "but it's too much like being sorry for oneself. We are all supposed to be so unhappy because we are cut off from the Russian people. We are so wonderful about that sort of thing. If you have been to Cairo or a few other Embassies, then you have probably seen just how much we usually mix with local populations. I don't suppose it matters whether we mix with people or not, but it's hardly worth making such a fuss of our particular isolation here. Most of it depends upon our own habits, and we are just as afraid of contamination as they. So you see, Mr. MacGregor, it begins where it ends. Perhaps Russia is just too much for most people."

"Is it too much for you?" MacGregor enjoyed his own question.

"I deserved that," she said lazily and allowed her gloved hand to tighten on his coat sleeve. MacGregor guessed that she was laughing at herself. "I am just as stupid as anybody, because I never know why the Russians behave as they do. We behave stupidly because we are simply ignorant, and here we can blame the Russians for our ignorance; although anywhere else we are not even conscious of being ignorant."

It was so wise and so sour that MacGregor laughed, and as they came under one of the yellow lamps on the bridge he turned his head to look at Katherine Clive because he wanted to see again what this woman looked like. She apparently had the same intention, and they simply glanced at

61

each other and looked away. To MacGregor she appeared very English in that momentary glimpse. She had such soft and yet such defined features that he saw them as a foreigner sees an Englishman. He liked her narrow straight nose and the firm pronounced crescents of her cheeks over hard bones. Her mouth too was an English mouth, and it was straight and wide and not at all like the tapered mouths of the Persian women.

"At the top of this slope we will come to the Red Square," she told him as they crossed a cobbled road. "It's the only square in Moscow you will like because the others are too bare. They would all be very attractive if someone planted a few trees in them."

"I like these large bare expanses," he said.

"I don't think you will after you have been here awhile."

She was so sure of it that MacGregor did not defend his preference.

"I don't suppose you know anyone in Moscow," she said to him.

They stepped over an exposed pipe to get onto the footpath. "No," MacGregor said, "but I am looking for one man here."

She lengthened her stride again. "Do you know where he lives?"

"I know nothing about him," MacGregor told her, "except that he is probably at one of the universities."

"What is his name?"

"Professor Onegin." MacGregor looked up at St. Basil's concentric domes. "He is a geologist — a sedimentary petrologist, to be exact."

Nothing was outside her casual but sharp interest. "What do you want of him?" she asked.

"I need to have a short discussion with him," MacGregor said, "or perhaps an argument."

"Oh? What about?"

They were now at the real perimeter of the Red Square, and though it was poorly lit, MacGregor could see across it to the Kremlin wall. The large clock on the Kremlin gate-tower showed almost nine o'clock, and MacGregor wondered if the clock chimed. "Professor Onegin doesn't agree with something I said about some rocks in Kermanshah," he said, and added by way of explanation, "Kermanshah is a province in north Iran."

"How could you get involved in a dispute right up there?" she asked, and it made Kermanshah seem very remote, even to MacGregor.

"I have been there off and on," he said. "I used to go over southern Kermanshah with my father, collecting rock samples. I eventually made a study for my Ph.D. of the marine microfossils of Kermanshah."

Apparently this should have explained the whole thing, but Katherine Clive was not quite satisfied. "What did you do? Prove there was oil there?"

"Not exactly," he said. "I tried to show that it was possible, by a study of the environment and deposition of marine fossils, to determine the depth of sea and the temperature of water at any time in geological history."

"What on earth is the use of knowing the depth of seas that have long since been replaced by land?" she said.

A policeman blew his whistle and told them to get back onto the pavement. He watched them until they were over the curb. "By knowing the condition of the water that once existed," MacGregor said, "you know a great deal about how the land was subsequently formed, its structure, and its age. Geology is so much surmise and guesswork that any improved method of identifying the past history of the earth is a great help in finding what you want."

"And Professor Onegin?"

MacGregor was more curious than irritated by her insistent questions, but he went on with deliberate patience. "The dispute with Onegin really began when I went to work for English-Persian. In fact it goes back to an oil well which the Iranian Government drilled before the war at Khush plateau, just outside the British concession boundary in Kermanshah. I never did find out why the Iranians started drilling there: they did very little oil prospecting themselves; but I think they were trying to interest the Americans in the area. Anyway, they put down a trial well at Khush; but the drilling stopped because the Iranian geologist in charge said the oil-bearing bed had been passed through — without there being any oil. I was down at Fields in southern Iran then, and though it wasn't one of our wells, we eventually got all the drilling reports and samples. I was interested in anything from Kermanshah, so I read the material very carefully, and I thought then that they might be wrong. Later on I managed to get back to Kermanshah. With what I read of the paleontologist's reports and what I saw for myself, I was sure that the oil-bearing beds had never been passed through at all."

"Amazing," she said.

"I suppose I was a little too hasty and sure of myself, but I wrote a paper on the oil-bearing beds of the Khush plateau. A friend presented it to the Geological Society for the *Q.J.*"

She looked at him.

"The *Quarterly Journal* of the Geological Society of London," he explained. "I was surprised when they published it, and a little embarrassed, because later on the Iranian geologists published their arguments in the same journal. I didn't have a chance to follow it up because the war came."

"And Onegin?" she said, with nicely balanced exasperation and persistence.

"A few months ago I was given a Russian geological journal in which

63

Professor Alexander Onegin took up my argument and denied it again. He had seen the Iranian reports on the drilling spot. He came to the conclusion that I was wrong and that the geological evidence was right."

"And that is your dispute?"

He nodded. "That is the dispute," he said.

"Then where do your microfossils come in?"

"The microfossils," he said, "are the crux of it. You see the whole thing finally resolves into an argument as to whether certain rocks are deep-water or shallow-water rocks. The geologists say they are shallow-water rocks. As a micropaleontologist I think they are deep-water rocks. Professor Onegin in a petrologist, a specialist in rock formation, and he supports the geological evidence and says they are shallow-water rocks."

"Couldn't they drill deeper and find out once and for all?" she asked.

"Yes, but who will do it? The Iranian Government has lost interest, and the Russians aren't likely to drill the Khush Plateau if one of their petrologists says there is no oil there."

"So you will never really know," she said, as if the irony of it pleased her.

He shrugged a little. "No, I might never know," he said.

"Then why do you want to see Professor Onegin?"

MacGregor held her while five or six Red Army men swept by them. "There is a great deal of personal feeling involved when one man makes a claim and another refutes it. Onegin states, for instance, that I find microfossils where there aren't any."

She looked carefully at this cautious unknown man who had been transformed into a warm-blooded scientist. "Do you think you can find Onegin?"

"I have asked one of the Russians at the Foreign Office to get in touch with him," MacGregor said, "but beyond that I haven't had time to do much about it."

"*Hm,*" she said slyly. "Would you like me to try and find him?"

MacGregor realized that in hurrying through the wind-swept Red Square he had taken little notice of it. Now they were leaving it, and Katherine Clive's soft deceptive voice was reminding him of where he walked. "It doesn't matter," he said. "I ought to be able to find him alright."

"It might be easier for me to do it," she said flatly, "and it's only a matter of being discreet about it."

"Why discreet?" he said. "Surely there need be nothing secret about it."

"Remember," she told him, "you are at the Embassy."

"Does that matter? I simply want to talk to Onegin on this particular subject. No one could object to that."

64

"Perhaps not," she said unconvincingly. "Do you want me to try anyway?"

"Only if it is done openly," he said. Remembering his obligation, he added with some embarrassment: "And if it isn't too much trouble. It's nice of you to suggest it."

"I'm intrigued," she said carelessly. She stopped him and turned around so that they could look back at the square, and at the buildings decorated for the New Year. "Before you leave Moscow," she said, "you ought to walk in a straight line from here right across the square to the main Kremlin gate under the clock. If you do it determinedly enough, you will be stopped somewhere before you reach the gate by one of the police-men or by one of the Kremlin guards. They will ask you for your papers, and then you will have an interesting conversation. I suppose you speak Russian?"

"Some," he said.

"I speak very little," she said, "but it is always a fascinating experience—particularly if you get as far as the gate and then try to walk right through into the Kremlin."

"What happens?" he asked her.

"They just turn you back," she said.

"Can't you get into the Kremlin at all?"

"Not without a pass." She waited for him to look carefully at the shadowy outline of Lenin's tomb against the Kremlin wall. "It used to be quite easy to get in there before someone murdered Kirov ten or fifteen years ago. He was supposed to be a very popular fellow and a close friend of Stalin's. They say his murder really started the purges."

"Is it a fact that they shot so many people?" He watched the clock hand approach the hour and waited to see if it would chime.

"Probably," she said. "They are a little indiscriminate about that sort of thing, but I suppose it is just as well. They didn't seem to have many traitors about during the war. I could never feel very shocked about it, could you?" She added these questions of confirmation so casually that they were really a method of trapping the other man into an opinion, a device which MacGregor failed to recognize.

"It was pretty bad at the time," he said, "but now you can't help wondering how much of it was right, or how much of anything we heard about this place was right. Most people thought the army would collapse, but look what happened. There is something about Russia which makes everybody fall one way or the other, and it's hard to know what to believe about it."

"Are you politically minded, Mr. MacGregor?" she said.

"No. Not particularly."

"That's clever of you," she said. "Are you completely ignorant of Russia?"

"Ignorant," he said, "but curious."

"But surely you would know something of them, scientifically for instance."

"They are the same as anybody else," he said.

"Aren't they terribly secretive about everything?"

"In some fields."

"Isn't that supposed to be bad for you scientific people?"

"Yes, but everybody is being secretive these days, and the Russians are no worse than we are. In fact they are rather free with their scientific information as a rule."

"Couldn't that be clever propaganda?"

"That's impossible," he said. "You can't fool people scientifically."

She laughed and the Kremlin clock began to chime and MacGregor was pleased, even though he realized that Katherine Clive had dragged a provocative opinion out of him. "I like that chime," he told her.

"I do not like any bells," she said, "particularly church bells. They are so sanctimonious and demanding. I don't like them at all."

"I had never heard a church bell until I went to England," he told her.

"Where on earth had you been?"

"Iran."

"Oh yes, of course! Are you part Iranian by any chance?"

"No." He was amused. "Why?"

"You are such a careful sort of man," she said, "that you seem almost too English to be English. I could have guessed that you had lived somewhere else. You went home to study?"

"Yes."

"And then you went back to Iran?"

He nodded. "I have only been in the India Office about eight months." He was apologetic.

"Ah!" she said satisfyingly. "Do you intend to remain there?"

"I don't think so," he said.

"Why not?"

"It's not my work."

"But you have made such a magnificent start," she said, and MacGregor didn't know whether she was being serious or cynical. It sounded as if she did not know herself. "After all," she went on, "coming to Moscow as Lord Essex's assistant is practically the beginning of a magnificent diplomatic future. What would you want to go back to micro-paleontology for, when you have such a wonderful chance in diplomacy? You must be good, for Lord Essex to have chosen you."

"I know nothing about diplomacy," he said solemnly.

"Then you should do well," she said. "Most men of your age in the Service are dullards and idiots; so that any man of intelligence and originality is in a far better position to do well, particularly with Essex I believe. You have a flying start, you would be foolish to waste it."

MacGregor still could not detect her real intentions and so he said nothing.

They lost each other for a moment as they entered a converging centre of people who pushed into a large black-pillared underground entrance which had the approximate shape of a Delphic temple. A giant red M for Metro cast a purple shadow on the ice pavements and on the impolite crowd. They met again off the footpath and as MacGregor stepped down to her he noticed for the first time that Katherine Clive wore a fur cap which fitted on the top of her head and allowed her polished hair to fall properly on her rich collar.

"Does it worry you to see such poorly dressed people?" she asked.

"Not if they look warm," he said.

"They are warm, but they are all dull lumps of padding. It must be depressing after London, although London must be bare these days."

"Not like this," he said. "How long is it since you were there?"

"About two years."

"Were you at the Foreign Office?"

"No. No. The Wrens," she said, "and for all I know," she added reflectively, "I am still a Wren. Did you like army life, Mr. MacGregor?"

"I didn't mind it."

"I would have thought you hated it."

"Did you hate it?" he asked her.

"I never saw much sense to women pretending they were in the Navy," she said. "Spit and polish and decorating various naval headquarters is a waste of anybody's effort, and that's about all it amounted to in the last few years. At the first possible opportunity I got out of it on a temporary transfer to duty with the Foreign Office. That took me as far as Cairo, and it didn't take me long to get out of there."

"Did you want to come here?"

"It was a choice of here or Sweden and I prefer this to Sweden."

"A woman attaché is something new in an Embassy, isn't it?" he asked.

"I'm not an attaché, I am simply doing the work. There is only one woman attaché that I know of. I am simply a temporary acquisition, and I suppose I am doing attaché work because I am no good at anything else. I don't know anything about typing and I make a bad archivist."

"Will you stay in this work?" He repeated her own question.

"If I don't get tired of it," she said. "It's a congenial way of moving about, and it's cheaper and better than going from one resort to another."

She stopped before a revolving door.

67

"This is the Metropole," she said. "I'm going in here to collect a friend."

"Then good-bye," he said and was sorry. "I will see you at the Embassy."

"Can you skate?" she asked him.

"I don't think so," he said.

"You must come out and try. I think I can get you some skates." When she chose, her voice was rich and natural and not edged all the time with satirical raillery. "I would like to see such a careful man skating." The relapse had been brief.

"We watch you from the window of the Ambassador's room," he said.

"Yes I know." She put her gloved hand on her long throat. "Perhaps you would like to come up here with me," she said. "I shan't be long, and then you could come along to the New Year Party at *Britansky Suyuznik*."

"Miss Williams asked me to go there and I said I was going to bed."

"That doesn't matter, you can tell Ella you changed your mind. She is an understanding girl and she won't mind. Come on up and meet Jeb Wills. He is a correspondent, and he would be jolly pleased to see you. Come along." She did not wait for confirmation but pushed through the revolving door.

MacGregor had no choice but to follow.

The hotel was old and dimly lit, and its wide entrance was divided by thick marble pillars. A few runner carpets covered the stone floors, and they walked along one strip by the reception desk where a clerk lifted his head to watch them. He was not dressed for his position, he simply wore a high collar with a crumpled tie, and a woman sitting near him wore a heavy roll-neck sweater. Katherine walked straight by them and past an old grille-work lift to the stairs. They were poorly lit but it didn't matter. Katherine knew how to walk upstairs as if the stairs weren't there, and MacGregor watched her until they came out on the first-floor landing, a large expanse with high-backed sofas along the walls. An elderly woman with a motherly face and small worried eyes sat behind a mahogany desk and watched them as they disappeared into one of the long dark corridors.

At the end of it Katherine Clive shook the handle of a door. "Jeb," she said. "It's me." She had made a good job of walking straight to the room in the dim light. "I have brought somebody with me."

The man who opened the door was a dark thick-haired fellow who looked like an American. MacGregor guessed he was an American now because he wore both braces and belt to hold up his trousers.

"Hullo Kathy," he said. "Stand by the radiator while I put my coat on."

They went into the room which was little bigger than the single bed along one of its walls. "This is Jeb Wills," she said to MacGregor, "and this is Lord Essex's assistant, Jeb. His name is MacGregor." They shook hands and Katherine sat on the edge of the bed before the electric radiator. "Why do you keep this room so bare?" she said to the American. "It's becoming just a place for you to dump your books."

68

Jeb Wills smiled with his dark face and eyes and bushy eyebrows and flat teeth. "I like the dormitory life, Kathy," he said.

"You are becoming a wretched bachelor," Katherine said to him.

"That is not my fault," he said and pulled on galoshes.

"Are you a bachelor, Mr. MacGregor?" she said to him.

"Yes."

"I thought so. You look like it. Jeb is a literary bachelor and you are a scientific bachelor. You both look too sensible to get married."

"Am I supposed to bring anything with me? Vodka?" Jeb Wills asked.

"No," she said and turned off the radiator.

"Then let's go."

They walked with Katherine between them, and she held onto both of them as they went through the crowded decorated streets. In the large square outside the Metropole a dance band was playing from trucks parked in its centre, and already large groups of people were dancing Russianized Vienna waltzes. They did not stop to watch but pushed up the main thoroughfare of Moscow, the Okhotny Riad. Looking up at the buildings MacGregor saw big portraits of Stalin and other important Russians framed in the big windows of the hotel and the building opposite, and long red banners were draped between each picture. Music from the loudspeakers on each corner completely eliminated the pale Vienna waltzes with full-blooded Ukrainian folk songs. They did not have far to walk, and half-way up the hill of Kuznetsky Most they went into a door near a women's frock shop and up a wooden flight of stairs and into the flat occupied by *Britansky Suyuznik,* which in English meant *British Ally.*

It was not a living apartment but a makeshift editorial building, the stomach having been pulled out of the place and plywood divisions supplemented in army style. The wooden floors were bare and worn, and a large brick stove had been built into the entrance hall to heat the building with hot air from galvanized pipes. The main room was a long bare place lined with books in library fashion. Trestle tables were stacked with food and drinks. Men and women were around the tables, and at the far end near a gramophone pick-up some were dancing. There were so many people in the room that their entry was not noticed, and yet it became noticed because of Katherine. They were quickly given drinks from a large punch bowl; and a small rubicund Londoner was introduced to Mac-Gregor as the editor. Then MacGregor was eased around the room by Katherine, and as he went he was introduced to one group after another as a simple act of passing through them. There were a few Russians but most of them were English girls who worked on *Britansky Suyuznik* or at the Embassy, and most of the men were from the paper or from other Embassies or newspaper correspondents or officers from the British Military Mission. They all knew Katherine, although they were more politely careful with her than seemed necessary. MacGregor noticed it and felt that Katherine's arrival had affected the atmosphere of this gathering. MacGregor enjoyed watching her possess this room just as Essex had possessed the Embassy. It was unconsciously hers and she knew it.

"Kathy," an American said to her, "are you still running the Embassy for the old man?" These words came straight out of the American's throat, impudent and open words that made MacGregor look at the man. He had close-cropped hair and thick lips and his eyes were like his voice — open and almost insulting in their unrestrained and personal appraisal. His mouth was set with the overriding honesty of an arrogant man.

"Are you still running the world for your newspaper?" Katherine said to him.

"Honestly Kathy, they should make you the Minister," the American said. He was not fooling. It was clear that he never fooled.

"This is Al Hamber," Katherine told MacGregor. She introduced other newspapermen. "Jackson Steele and Peter Holmes. This is Mr. MacGregor. He came in the other night with Lord Essex."

MacGregor knew Hamber and Steele to be Americans by natural appearance, and Holmes to be an Englishman. Steele was an intent and solidly built fellow with limpid but puzzled eyes, a strong man with deep concern visible on his face in contradistinction to Hamber's detached arrogance. Holmes the Englishman was the most handsome of the three, a tall fair man with poetic features. He smoked a pipe and nodded to MacGregor in a quiet and matter-of-fact gesture. MacGregor nodded back and realized that these people were a familiar group. With his usual care he stood with the gathering without being a part of it, quickly liking or disliking each one of them.

"We were just telling Kathy," the brazen Hamber said as Jeb Wills joined them, "that she ought to at least be Minister, if not Ambassador; although the British don't like women ambassadors, do they? That seems to be an achievement of the Russian women only."

Katherine had not heard it. Having delivered MacGregor to this group of men she had gone away as if she had already heard everything they had to say.

"No Russian woman has ever achieved anything except servitude," Steele said passionately to Hamber. "That is where the Communist Party has been so clever here. They teach the dignity of work; that work in a socialist state is freedom. A Russian woman works like a nigger and she is told that she has achieved equality and liberty. It's a cruel delusion," Steele said unhappily.

"Six months have certainly changed you," Jeb Wills said.

"Of course they've changed me," Steele said. "I came here expecting to see that Russian women had really achieved the utmost freedom and equality, but now I can see that neither woman nor anybody else in Russia is free. Every time I see those women on the streets sweeping the snow I wonder why they don't revolt. It is servitude."

"It doesn't matter a damn whether the women sweep the streets or not, Jackson," Hamber grunted at Steele, "or whether the people are free or not. The thing to worry about is that the Kremlin and the Communist hierarchy try to force their ideas of freedom onto the rest of the world. That is the real danger."

"That may be so," Steele said, "but you just can't ignore the shocking conditions of the Russian people, Al. You just can't ignore it."

"Oh yes I can," Hamber said. "I did not come here expecting a people's paradise, and I haven't suffered your peculiar disillusionment. To me Russia is Russia, and Communism is Communism, and this business about the people doesn't come into it. Just worry about the hierarchy and let the people fall where they may. They are not important to the scheme of things."

"If they are not important," Steele said, "I fought in Spain for nothing."

"Now come down off it," Hamber said with a ruthless good-nature. "You didn't fight in Spain, Jackson, you were a correspondent with a crazy passion for the Republicans; a sentiment incidentally which you had no right to feel. You shouldn't be in this game at all, Jack, good as you are. You let your feelings run away with you. No newspaperman has the right to get involved, people or not."

Hamber went no further because the gramophone was playing a resonant, punching tune, and they stopped to listen to it. "That is the only swing record in Moscow," Hamber said to MacGregor. "I had it brought in by diplomatic bag. It's a Benny Goodman."

"Actually," Steele went on when the record had finished, "no one outside Russia will ever really see the danger of this country clearly because the political understanding of it is always confused by people who say, What about the marvellous theatres? or, What about the Red Army? Well, I say, What about them? What do they prove?"

"You can hardly ignore them," Jeb Wills interrupted.

"Why not?" Steele insisted.

"The Red Army seems to have defeated the German Army," Jeb Wills said.

"Oh nonsense Jeb," Hamber said.

"What if it did?" Steele said. "What does that prove?"

"How could it have fought so well," Jeb Wills said, "if the political structure of the country was so bad? It doesn't make sense."

"The Red Army fought well because it had American equipment," Steele said.

"Bah!" said Jeb Wills.

"Whatever made it fight," Hamber said, "this country is bankrupt after the effort, and it is beginning to expand. It is behaving like all Imperialisms. I have no objection to Empire as such, but this is one that threatens the rest of the world, and it has to be stopped. Communist Imperialism is far too clever and ruthless to let live."

"It isn't Communist Imperialism, Al," Steele said. "It is Fascist Imperialism. I have fought Fascism all my life and I know what Fascism is, and this Red Fascism is the worst I have seen. It is even destroying the mind of its own people. If we have any sense we will do something about saving them from this vicious collection of dictators. The Russians themselves are wonderful people. They are simple and primitive peasants who have been given a little knowledge of politics and mechanics, and that makes them dangerous. Yet they are worth saving and I think they want to be saved."

"Who is going to save them?" Katherine asked as she came back.

"I don't know about saving them," Hamber said, "but it has to be Britain and America who stop them. It is our only hope of survival."

"One battalion of American infantry marching through Moscow would be greeted as saviours," Steele said, "and it wouldn't take long for the people to clean out the Kremlin. It's got to come."

Jeb Wills said, "Why not a division to make sure?"

Holmes took his pipe out of his English mouth. "I doubt if one battalion of Doughboys would be enough," he said, "but it might be a start. I think we might as well drop the bomb and be done with it though."

"Well, that may not be necessary," Steele replied unhappily.

"Of course it's necessary," Hamber said. "Why be squeamish about it?"

"Well, I'm squeamish about it," Katherine said. "If you Americans start dropping your atom bombs about, someone is going to drop one on England sooner or later and nothing much will be left."

"Oh, England is finished anyway," Holmes said.

"Be ashamed of yourself," Katherine said to Holmes.

"It's the unfortunate truth," Holmes said commonsensically. "I have been a Socialist for fifteen years, waiting for England to become Socialist. Now it doesn't mean much. We are too poor to stand on our own feet and too weak to fight our own battles. We are facing a choice of being the junior partner of America or Russia, and for my part I would sooner see England in the dust than a partner of Russia. At least we have common ideals and common forms with the Americans, and if we must go with them, then we might as well. We have no choice, and if the Americans want to drop a bomb on the Russians then let them have it that way and get it over and done with. I have been here for five years and I can't see that it would be a great loss to the world to blow this place up, providing I was out of the way, and providing they couldn't retaliate."

"The Russians might have a bomb of their own," Katherine suggested evilly.

"They might," Holmes agreed wearily.

Hamber laughed, and Steele said: "They haven't got the scientific know-how."

"You don't know if they have or not," Katherine said.

"You always take the contrary side of any argument, Kathy," Steele said. "You know as well as I do that the Russians couldn't possibly make an atomic bomb. They are scientifically and technically incapable of it."

"I don't know any such thing," she said, and looked at MacGregor who was leaning against the bookcases as if there were a curtain between himself and this conversation. He had been watching all of them, Katherine in particular. He had seen enough of her to know that she took part in the conversation only when she could say something apposite, but he failed to see that Katherine had her soft eyes upon him now. "MacGregor is a scientist," she said to Steele. "Ask him if the Russians are capable of producing an atomic bomb."

MacGregor's isolation ended abruptly and they turned upon him as if he had suddenly appeared out of the ground. He saw them all now as people he must cope with in the midst of dance music and other people's laughing conversations and the arrival and dispatch of drinks, punch, and cheese sandwiches.

"I am not a physicist," MacGregor said. "So I know little about the atom bomb."

"You are more scientifically informed than we are," Katherine said.

"But I know nothing about Russia," he replied.

"You don't have to know anything about Russia," Katherine said. "You just have to know whether the Russians are scientifically capable of producing an atomic bomb or not. Are they?"

"Probably," MacGregor murmured.

"Please do not be so scientifically cautious, Mr. MacGregor," Katherine said. "You must have an opinion. Do you imagine that in the matter of physics, for instance, they are behind the rest of the world?"

MacGregor knew that he would have to answer this properly or appear a fool. "Well, the Americans gave their Franklin Medal last year to Kapitza, the Russian physicist, for his work in low temperatures. They are supposed to be very advanced in that particular field and in some other fields of pure physics; but I don't know much about it personally."

"Low temperature is not the atom bomb," Steele said.

"No it isn't," MacGregor said, "but you can't separate it from other physical research. Low temperature investigation is important, for instance, in the study of the behaviour of the hydrogen atom, and one thing always leads to another in science, particularly in physics."

"What has that got to do with the atomic bomb?" Hamber said.

"Nothing at all," MacGregor admitted, "but I should think that any use of atomic energy is largely a matter of research, and the Russians are doing just as much research as anybody else."

"I think you are wrong there, MacGregor," Steele said. "As far as I know the atomic bomb is a matter of technology and production method. Its manufacture requires such an extensive industrial effort and such technological organization that only the United States is capable of it. Russia certainly isn't."

"Producing the first bomb required a tremendous manufacturing effort," MacGregor said, "but that is already outdated by further pure research. It is always a question of research: even physical production depends upon it; and no one has a monopoly on research: no country can call a scientific fact its own."

"Then why haven't the Russians got the bomb?" Steele said.

"How do you know they haven't got it?" Katherine repeated.

"Because they would use it if they had it," Al Hamber said.

"On whom?"

"On us," Jackson Steele said. "The moment they get it they will drop it. I think even MacGregor would agree with that."

"Why should they drop it?" MacGregor said. "They would gain nothing by it."

"They would hope to gain the world by it," Steele said. "Can't you see them heading for Washington at the first opportunity?"

"They might," MacGregor said, "but I don't see any difference between Washington and Hiroshima when it comes to that. The thing should never have been used in the first place, and the destruction of Washington wouldn't be any worse than the destruction of Hiroshima."

"Great God!" Steele said grimly. "Isn't that being a little anti-American and anti-Democratic, to say the least?"

"No it isn't," MacGregor said. "I am simply saying that it should never have been and it should not be used again."

"But it ended the war, man!" Steele said.

"It might have shortened the war," MacGregor argued.

"I think if you had been in the army you might have thought differently."

"Don't be so ridiculously personal, Jackson," Katherine said to Steele. "MacGregor was in the army for five or six years."

"Then weren't you glad when we dropped it on Japan?"

"No," MacGregor said. "I was sorry to hear that they had even made it."

"Great Scott!" Holmes said. "Why?"

"It's a mistake to use science for wiping out whole cities and whole populations."

"You must be a pacifist," Hamber said.

"I am not a pacifist," MacGregor said with unusual insistence, "and I don't think pacifism has anything to do with the question. Dropping atomic bombs is a tragic misuse of any scientific effort, and if we do it again we will start something that can't be stopped."

"But we are being forced into it by the Russians," Hamber said.

"Why?" MacGregor said. "Why should we drop an atomic bomb on the Russians or have them drop one on us? We have nothing to fight about."

"Then what are you here with Essex for?" Hamber said boldly.

"We aren't here to make a war," MacGregor replied with no little astonishment.

"Damn near it," Hamber said. "English and Russian rivalry will use every method of fighting it out in Iran short of war. It is really the beginning of a bigger struggle, and Essex is here to jockey for position. It's all part of the conflict that is developing between Russia and the Anglo-Americans everywhere, not only in Iran but in Eastern Europe, and the Far East, and the Arctic, and even within our own borders. Surely you realize that, MacGregor."

"I don't know anything about that," MacGregor said.

"How can you avoid knowing about it?" Steele said. "Isn't Essex here to manœuvre Iran into a better position against the Russians?"

"I wouldn't say that," MacGregor said.

"Then what is he here for?"

"Iran is in a bad way," MacGregor said. "Lord Essex is trying to straighten out some of the mess."

"Nothing can straighten out the Iranian mess. It's a hopeless place," Jackson Steele said, "and I doubt if Essex cares a damn about it anyway. You should save that nice diplomatic front for the Russians, MacGregor. You don't have to convince us you are here for the good of Iran." They all laughed with Steele.

MacGregor laughed with the rest of them. "I'd hate to convince you of anything," he said to Steele. "Nevertheless we are here about Iran, nothing else."

"Are you trying to convince yourself?" Hamber said.

MacGregor was rescued from Hamber's affronts by the Benny Goodman record which someone was playing again. The noise in the room had increased so much that the music could hardly be heard. MacGregor was beginning to feel that he had enough to worry about without facing men like Hamber and Steele and without attending to such tight and crying

75

music, but when the music had finished Hamber tackled him again.

"Actually, you must admit you are here to get the Russians out of Azerbaijan."

MacGregor shrugged. "Perhaps."

"What if they refuse to get out of Azerbaijan?" Steele suggested.

"I don't know," MacGregor said. "It may not be important."

"Ah, it's vital!" Hamber said.

Jeb Wills and Katherine Clive were talking to other people farther down the room. MacGregor looked at his empty glass and wanted more of the sweet purple sticky mixture, but he could not escape.

"You have no choice," Steele said to MacGregor. "You have to get them out of Azerbaijan, out of all Iran."

"Is it that important?" MacGregor wanted to drift away.

"It means your Empire if you don't get them out," Steele said. "Azerbaijan is the thin edge of the wedge, and if you care about your Empire you have to stop them before they get any farther."

"We don't care much about Empire these days," MacGregor said.

"I'd hardly say that," Holmes interrupted as he came back with a jug of punch. "Empire with us is a matter of necessity," he said, "and if we let it go the Russians will grab it, so we really have no choice but to hang onto it."

"How do you English Socialists believe in Empire like that?" Steele said to Holmes. "Empire is inimical to Democracy and it has no right to exist in a free world."

"Are you suggesting that we give it up?" Holmes puffed on his large pipe.

"No," Steele said. "You can't give it up, because — as you say — the Russians would get it."

"And we will make sure you don't give it up!" Hamber added.

"Thanks Al," Holmes said with lifeless sarcasm and watched MacGregor. "What is the feeling in England these days, MacGregor? Do you think we would fight the Russians?"

MacGregor saw Miss Williams, who smiled at him. "I don't think so," MacGregor said. "Most people seem to admire the Russians."

"It doesn't take long to dispel admiration," Holmes told him.

"I don't think we want any kind of war," MacGregor went on.

"No one ever wants war," Steele said.

Jeb Wills stood beside MacGregor again. "Are you still fighting the next war?" he said to them, and MacGregor guessed that he and Katherine had come back to get him out of this. "Can't you wait until it starts before analysing it?"

"What's the matter Jeb?" Hamber said. "Has Kathy been at you again? Don't you know that peace and goodwill are just a pose with Kathy? She's more war-minded than any of us."

76

"You can have your war if you want it," Katherine said, "and it may teach you a lesson in peacefulness, Alfred. A few Russian raids on continental America will make you see it so differently."

"They could never build a plane to fly that far." Holmes was yawning.

"I wouldn't say that," Steele said. "They are copying some of the B-29's that force-landed in Siberia after the Japan raids. That's why we have to stop them soon. With a B-29 and an atom bomb they'll be over Washington in no time."

"I'll be glad when the war starts," Jeb Wills said, "so that you fellows will stop talking about it."

"By the way, MacGregor," Hamber said before Jeb Wills could interrupt further: "How is Harry?"

"Who?"

"Essex. Harold Essex."

"Oh!" MacGregor said. "Do you know him?"

"Sure. Since pre-war Paris. Marvellous guy, Harry," Hamber said from his throat. "You are lucky to be working with him. Would you tell him I am in town, and that I shall be down to see him to-morrow or the next day? Is he busy?"

"Yes."

"Have you seen Molotov yet?"

MacGregor shook his head.

"I suppose Molotov is trying to avoid him," Steele said. "In fact it will be a miracle if Essex sees Molotov at all."

"Harold will get to Molotov," Hamber said.

"I doubt it," Steele argued.

Hamber went back to MacGregor. "Then who did you see at the Foreign Office the other day? Antonov?"

"No. Suchkov and Korin."

"Korin!" said Holmes. "He is a stupid ass." He had a tray of coffee and cheese and biscuits, enough for them all.

"Korin has stomach ulcers," Hamber said. "You can't expect a man to be perfect when he has stomach ulcers. Take a look at his face someday. That guy is in pain."

"He is too dumb to feel any pain," Jeb Wills said unkindly.

"He isn't dumb," Hamber insisted. "Talk to him about Japan some day."

"What does he know about Japan?" Steele said in disbelief.

"A hell of a lot." Hamber knew what he was talking about and his tone was not argumentative, it was final. "He is quite a guy, I tell you."

"Has he ever been known to say more than two words at a time?" Jeb Wills said.

"You just think that these Russians won't talk," Hamber said. "They'll talk if you get right down to cases with them."

"They are afraid to talk," Steele said. "Particularly men like Korin."

"You can get anyone to talk if you know how to handle them," Hamber insisted, and he returned to MacGregor. "Which one of them is Suchkov, MacGregor? Is he one of the Protocol boys?"

"No. He is in Molotov's office."

Katherine put her arm through MacGregor's. Off and on she had been dutifully attending other people with coffee, but she had been close enough to hear the latter part of this conversation. She seemed to tug gently at MacGregor to take him away. "Do you dance, Mr. MacGregor?" she asked him.

MacGregor shook his head, but she had already taken him into the centre of the room. She faced him with one of her arms on his shoulder. "Then you can walk with me," she said. "Just hold me lightly and move slowly."

MacGregor did as she told him, thankful that the punch had given him confidence but regretting that he could not concentrate on what he was doing. He was too much influenced by Katherine Clive's carelessness with herself. They gave up when Katherine said, "Can you never relax entirely, Mr. MacGregor?"

"I'm not much good at this sort of thing," he told her. "Sorry."

"I haven't been on a dance floor for five or six years, so don't apologize," she said. "All the same, you should relax yourself a little more. It doesn't do any harm to subside and let people get at you. You don't have to be so apprehensive."

"Is it that bad?" he asked calmly.

She looked at him. "I deserved that."

"Deserved what?"

"That imperceptible humour of yours!" she said. "It is very deceiving."

"Is it?" he said as they came to Miss Williams. He bade her good evening and said, "I went out for a walk, but Miss Clive persuaded me to come up here." It seemed to be a full explanation.

"Kathy can persuade anybody to do anything," Miss Williams told him, to make it easy. "You seemed to be having quite an argument with those Americans," she went on, looking at his flushed face, and feeling sorry that he was not as thoroughly withdrawn as usual.

"Yes. They don't seem to need any stimulant to argument," MacGregor said.

"They are all very clever," she told him. "Particularly Peter Holmes. He has written several novels and I think he is writing another one about Russia. He was very pro-Russian for about ten years, but now he despises them."

"What changes a man like that?" MacGregor looked across at Holmes's handsome face and saw in it the expression of a man with an overwhelming appreciation for the common sense in everything. Too much common

78

sense, and common sense where there wasn't any. Nevertheless he rather liked Holmes.

"I think the censors changed him," Miss Williams said. "They are very bad here. Even when he was trying to be friendly they made it impossible for him to write. They should have treated him better than the others, but the Foreign Office here treats all those correspondents the same way, whether they are enemy or friend. They made a big mistake doing that to Peter. When he leaves here he is going to write a book exposing them, and they jolly well deserve it."

"Do you also think we should fight the Russians?" he asked.

"I would hate to see another war," she said, "but I don't think that we should give in to these people. It's rather hard being an Englishman in Moscow at times," she said, "but it's not so bad when Mr. Bevin shows them that we are not finished yet. I didn't vote for Labour, but I'm glad that Mr. Bevin is the Foreign Minister. Aren't you?"

MacGregor watched Katherine Clive talk to an officer. "I think I preferred Eden," he said, "although I voted for the Labour Government."

"Then we are both satisfied," Miss Williams replied and smiled as Katherine brought the officer to them and introduced him as Captain Alexander. She told him MacGregor had been part of the Long Range Desert Group.

"How long were you with them?" Captain Alexander asked.

"Through Africa until the beginning of Italy," MacGregor said. "Then we were broken up and sent to England." He felt like talking about the L.R.D.G., but Kathy took him away, leaving Miss Williams with the soldier.

With Kathy, MacGregor was slowly shunted from one group to the other until Jeb Wills beckoned to them from a smaller room across the hall, and they went into the editorial office of the *Britansky Suyuznik*. There was enough room to sit down on a low table in one of the corners. They had hardly settled there when five or six people around a filing cabinet began to sing a Russian song which MacGregor could guess by the words to be called "*Zhdy Menya*" ("Wait for Me"). MacGregor knew that he would never appreciate the distinctions between good and bad music, but he had a respectful ear for any music that he heard, and it seemed odd to hear English voices singing such a Russian song. It could have been that he was beginning to lose the warmth of the punch, and he knew that it was time that he went back to the Embassy. He told Katherine.

"Must you go?" she said. "You are not expected, are you?"

"Not exactly."

"Then wait awhile," Katherine said. "Jeb has gone to get some more of that terrible vodka mixture, and you might as well go home cheerful."

"I think I'm cheerful enough," he said, glad that the singing had stopped.

"Is Lord Essex one of those men who insist on having people available all the time?" She looked at him as if he were compelled to return but afraid to admit it.

MacGregor watched her unusually brown finger rubbing slowly at her English mouth. "No," he said. "Essex is quite a casual sort of a person."

"He can't be too casual," she said. "He is supposed to be the man that never fails. With that background he must be serious about his diplomacy. Actually I can't imagine how you two could see eye to eye about anything."

"Do you know Lord Essex?" MacGregor asked.

"No. But I know enough about Essex and I know something about you; and I can't reconcile you at all. I'm sure you must disagree about Iran. Do you?"

"On some issues," MacGregor said.

"Don't be so cautious," she said. "You probably think that Essex is all wrong, and you are too ethical to say so."

"No!"

"Then what do you disagree about?"

"If anything — about the purely local situation in Iran," he said.

"I'll bet Essex doesn't see much of the local situation," she said insistently and added: "I accidentally read his first cable. It was mostly about the Russians."

MacGregor felt that he had to recover himself. "It's just a matter of explanation," he said. "He hasn't had time to understand what is happening in Iran, and it is not an easy country to explain to any man."

"Do you think you could change his picture of Iran?"

"Why not?"

"Even if it denied his very purpose in being here?"

"You oversimplify," MacGregor argued.

"Do I?" She was laughing at him.

"Yes," he said seriously. "It takes time for a man to understand a complicated country like Iran, particularly if he hasn't been there."

"It doesn't matter whether Lord Essex understands Iran or not," she said and taunted him further. "He is here to carry out a British policy, and policy never depends upon a knowledge of the country concerned, it depends upon self-interest. All your explanation couldn't change that."

"I don't want to change it," MacGregor began.

"I'm disappointed," she said, still smiling. "I thought you were going to behave like a watchdog for your native land. Are you going to allow Essex and the Russians to parcel it up between them?"

"Now you exaggerate!"

80

"I suppose I do," she said, "but you should be wary of diplomats. They are unconvinceable people, and if you have a disagreement with Essex then you might as well resign yourself to the fact that you will never resolve it; not unless you yourself compromise and give in, and I can't see that happening. Am I embarrassing you?"

"No."

She lifted her head back. "I hope you disagree with Lord Essex, because I should like to see what happens. Do you get on well with him?"

"Very well."

"I suppose I am being too personal."

"Not at all," he said so sardonically that she laughed. He went on less provocatively as he looked about: "Perhaps this isn't the place to go into it."

She ignored that. "When is he going to see Molotov?" she said.

"I don't know."

"Wouldn't you feel better if Molotov ignored Essex and let him go home empty-handed?"

"No — and it isn't likely that Molotov will ignore him."

"It's very likely," Katherine argued.

"Is that your hope?"

"No," she said. "I hope he sees Molotov. We need someone like Essex to cope with Molotov. There's Jeb." They watched Jeb Wills as he looked for them, three glasses of punch in his hands. "Thank heavens for Jeb."

As he approached them MacGregor told her that he was going. "Can you get home?" he asked her. "Or do you want me to wait for you?"

"No," she said. "Jeb will see me back. Perhaps to-morrow you would like to try skating?" She seemed to be suggesting this to stir something out of Jeb Wills, but he simply smiled at MacGregor as a fellow conspirator.

"I might," MacGregor said about the skating, and said good-bye again.

"And make sure that you don't fall a victim to another man's diplomacy," she said after him. "In trying to convince Essex, he might convince you."

MacGregor went out as if he hadn't heard her at all.

The cold Moscow night depressed him and he wished for a moment that he could feel the sanity of a good hot desert day, the sort of Persian day that ate into you with its heat and took away the responsibility of active thinking and active living, and left you dry-mouthed and exhausted and sleepy. This frozen air awakened you and made you responsible. In so much cold sanity, influencing Essex seemed so impossible that MacGregor wanted to forget him, and forget the mission. He did not want to be here in Moscow, and he did not want to be any part of a British-Russian rivalry for Iran. At the Embassy he saw a light in the working room. He went in, and Miss Williams was there.

"I have been waiting for you," she said. "Lord Essex has gone to see Molotov and we have been trying to get in touch with you."

"How long ago did Essex leave?"

"About half an hour. I rang *Britansky Suyuznik* and got hold of Katherine, but she said that you had left. I just missed Lord Essex myself." She was blushing again.

"I suppose it's too late to follow him now," MacGregor said.

"Yes," she said. "Sir Francis would like to see you."

"What for?"

"I don't know, but I'm supposed to go up with you."

"Why would Molotov call Lord Essex at this hour of the night?" MacGregor complained. "It's almost midnight."

"The Russians always do that," Miss Williams said. "They have a habit of ringing up at two o'clock in the morning to make an appointment for three o'clock the next afternoon. Stalin starts work at night and works until the early hours of the morning, so everybody else does it. It's the thing to do, but it's a nuisance because you can never get hold of any of the officials during the day when you want them. You have to wait until late evening or half-way into the night. They love to do what Stalin does, and they all look sick and pale because they don't get enough sleep."

They walked up the stairs. "Why don't we change our hours to fit theirs?" MacGregor said irritably. "At least we wouldn't be surprised like this."

"That would be giving in to the Russians," Miss Williams said.

"I suppose it would."

They went into Drake's office and Drake was sitting at his desk with the chair pushed back. MacGregor wondered if Drake ever left that desk, although he was dressed in a dinner jacket and stiff shirt and had obviously been out.

"You asked me to come up with Mr. MacGregor," Miss Williams said to Drake.

"I just wanted to make sure that he got here," Drake told her. "That's all Miss Williams. You needn't wait up any longer."

As Miss Williams closed the door softly behind her, MacGregor noticed a man he had never seen before. He was sitting on the couch, leaning on one arm, his feet stretched out in a manner that disfigured the leather and seemed disrespectful to Sir Francis Drake. MacGregor had a quick impression of a rather big man, middle-aged, with a drooping face or rather a drooping moustache that turned his entire face downwards. He was smoking a pipe which reclined in his mouth upside-down and he seemed to wink at MacGregor as he came in, but MacGregor didn't believe it. MacGregor passed his gaze right onto Drake who was looking at him sternly and holding the nose-grip in his pince-nez glasses.

"Sit down MacGregor," Drake mumbled.

MacGregor stood for a moment.

"This is the Honourable John Asquith," Drake said. "And as you can see John, this is the young man we have been waiting for. Where have you been, MacGregor?"

"I was at *Britansky Suyuznik* with Miss Clive," MacGregor said.

Asquith looked up at MacGregor and said explosively: "Hah! You haven't done too badly for a couple of days in Moscow, MacGregor. Did you bring Kathy back with you?"

"No. She stayed on with an American friend."

"Ah!" said Asquith in disappointment. "Then you haven't done so well after all."

"Of course you realize that this is awkward for Lord Essex," Drake said.

"Harold may not do so badly on his own," Asquith put in ironically. "How is he, Francis? Still the ageless young man?"

"He's quite well," Drake said, not wishing to be interrupted.

"Healthiest man I have ever known," Asquith said and stood up.

Asquith was as tall as MacGregor expected him to be. With his rich hair and shaggy moustache he was an upsetting man to find in Drake's room. MacGregor realized now that this must be one of the Indian Asquiths; one of the large and famous family of the Viceroy whose wife had been so beautiful that a Deccan Prince had attempted to assassinate her rather than see her the property of another man, an incident which MacGregor remembered in history as part of "the Asquith Reprisals," since it was followed by a series of Indian revolts and British reprisals which had finally resulted in a massacre by both sides, one of the worst in Indian history.

"You should be responsible enough to remain at hand when you are needed," Drake was saying to MacGregor. "You appear to be a casual sort of a fellow, MacGregor, and I don't like that. Every man in this Embassy must realize that he has an extra responsibility in being in Russia, and I would like you to keep that uppermost in your mind and behave accordingly."

MacGregor did not want to argue with Drake because he did not feel up to it: his mind was too warm and diffused, and he did feel a certain guilt in missing Essex. Nevertheless, he did not want to hide his dislike. He felt his own scruffiness beside the white-fringed and proportionate English head of the precise diplomat. Drake had the right amount of hair and the correct-sized ears, amazingly important factors in an Ambassador. MacGregor felt that he should have bought a new suit in London, a grey flannel like Essex's, and he should have worn one of his two stiff collars to-night instead of this unstarched shirt. He knew that his china skin was so thin on his face that his hostility to Drake became obvious. But

MacGregor said nothing, and Asquith suspended the situation by intervening boisterously.

"Perhaps you two gentlemen could straighten this out later on," he said.

Drake was about to reply when the whistles and the bells of midnight sounded. They waited until the noise died down, and then Drake shook Asquith's hand and said "Happy New Year John," and then he shook MacGregor's hand and wished him a happy New Year, and he sat down again. "There is nothing we can straighten out until MacGregor appreciates his position," he said.

MacGregor was beginning to see the humour in the situation, but he was not out of his difficulty yet.

Asquith filled his pipe, nodding his head a little. "You might as well talk about it to-morrow," he said equally and provokingly to both.

MacGregor agreed, and before Drake could say anything further MacGregor said good night. Asquith touched the untouchable Sir Francis on the shoulder and said, "I'll talk to him." In the corridor he shouted loudly: "MacGregor."

MacGregor waited.

"Do you want to wait for Harold to come back?" Asquith asked as they walked.

"I can see him to-morrow," MacGregor replied.

"No. You had better come over and wait a little while with us. My wife is mostly Scotch and she would never forgive me if I didn't take you straight over to her." Asquith was blowing enough smoke from his pipe to hide the ceiling above them.

"It's late," MacGregor said.

"Nonsense. Come on." Asquith took his arm and there was no resisting. MacGregor felt he would not mind anything if he could only get away from here. As they crossed the Embassy courtyard to go to the Asquith flat, the rockets and the star shells (which had been exploding since the midnight chimes) suddenly ceased, and Moscow was now in its New Year.

Chapter 5

Essex was annoyed with MacGregor. Instead of MacGregor's accompanying him, there was this dull fellow Melby, and a complete stranger — an Embassy translator — who knew nothing about Iran. It was almost midnight and it was New Year's Eve, and it was hardly the moment to begin diplomatic business. All the same, Essex was

84

rather pleased with the hour. It implied an urgency and an excitement that had been lost in diplomacy since the war. It had been particularly satisfying to leave the American Embassy (after appearing there as the Essex that all men had waited to see), for when he had left the big room in such a hurry it had been clear to everyone that he was going off to see Stalin, or at least Molotov.

At the Foreign Office there was an official waiting with the guard for them, and though Essex had never seen the official before he was greeted immediately by the Russian and led urgently up the stairs. Essex handed his pouch to Melby and also his topcoat, and he followed the agile Russian.

Essex knew exactly how to run up these stairs. Melby and the translator were two steps behind him, and the Russian was the proper distance ahead of him. Essex took three of the steps quickly and then two slowly and he held his head well up. This was always the real moment of his life — this moment of approach to the great man — and it was almost the reason he loved his job so much. He had lived his life running up the stairs of the chancelleries of Europe to see important men. It not only made Essex great, it made them all great, even those will-o'-the-wisp fellows in the Balkans who had been given greatness by a moment of office. He had seen them big and vital sitting on their thrones of office for a while, and he had seen them small and spent when they were out of office, nothing more than spectators and café habitués. He had a feeling that he was about to see one man who would never be spent and out of office. Of all the important men Essex could quickly imagine, Molotov seemed to have the best hope of keeping his importance, and Essex felt for the first time in twenty-five years that these Bolsheviks were here to stay. It did not worry him, because he knew that he was better equipped to carry off this moment than Molotov. He was bred for this, whereas Molotov was in it by accident. Essex knew how good he could be in the circumstances.

They passed through the old and dusty regions of the Foreign Office and suddenly arrived in bright corridors of clean white walls with modern lighting. They went through a new room with light furniture and then through a conference room with fresh white plastered walls. The chain that supported the light was of modern dull bronze, and the furniture was modern and simple and clean-edged and well kept. Then they stepped into Molotov's carpeted office which had the same white newness about it, a neatness which was like Molotov himself as he stood on the carpet waiting for them: a short poised smiling man with huge cheeks and oval rimless glasses and a square grey moustache which spread with his beaming cheeks across his Russian face.

"Mr. Molotov," Essex said quickly to have the first word. "We are finally met after such a long time in diplomacy; a very happy moment I might say."

Molotov was also speaking as they shook hands, and a Russian in a light grey suit behind him translated it: his apologies for the plane crash, his regret that he had missed Lord Essex yesterday, his hope that Lord Essex would enjoy his brief visit to Moscow, and his wishes for the New Year. He did not speak monosyllabically as Essex expected, yet Essex knew that it was precise and brief, even though he did not understand Russian. When Molotov had finished he introduced his translator as Troika, and Essex introduced Melby and his own translator, Joyce. As Essex returned the New Year greeting Molotov nodded and smiled again.

"Does Mr. Molotov understand English?" Essex said to Troika.

Molotov was already replying in Russian which Troika repeated in English immediately. "I understand enough English to decide to know more," Molotov had said. "In many ways your English language is quite elusive, and the grammar is too cunning for a Russian."

"Cunning?" Essex said as they sat on a low red couch with gold buttons.

"Then let us say concealed!" Molotov added quickly in schoolmasterly Russian. He was holding his blue vest at the lapel and pushing his first finger under his blue silk tie. "It is a language for hiding one's feelings, and that makes it difficult for a Russian." Molotov offered them cigarettes from a silver box.

"Mr. Molotov," Essex said with a flourish. "Nobody has succeeded in hiding their hurt feelings so diplomatically and honourably as the statesmen of the Soviet Union have done in the last twenty-five years."

"Perhaps we have simply been misunderstood," Molotov said.

"Very much misunderstood," Essex emphasized.

"We have always given the world a chance to understand us," Molotov said, and Troika barely caught up with him. "Our attitudes have always been clear and we have publicized our policies in our newspapers without complication of rumour or speculation."

If this was pointed Essex took no notice of it, and he waited for Troika to finish Molotov's rapid sentences. Troika caught Molotov's sharp expression in faithful English, and he wore a self-conscious smile as apology for transferring another man's feelings into a foreign tongue. Troika was a small man with a pointed chin and Essex doubted if this inadequate little man would be able to keep up with the two of them, although he hadn't done badly so far.

There were more formalities: greetings and letters to present. Essex thought it awkward to be sitting on the couch with Molotov. He moved to a leather chair so that he was facing Molotov and Troika. He felt very warm in this overheated room. He wore a dinner jacket with a hard shirt, just a little too stiff for comfort. He was glad, however, that he was

impeccably dressed, because he saw that Molotov was not at all sophisti-
cated in his clothing. Molotov was quite well dressed, but his coat was
cut too short and on the lines of bad Continental tailoring. In that he was
as Russian as Essex expected him to be. Otherwise Essex found it surprising to hear Molotov behaving with a certain diplomatic *forme de rigueur,*
and if Essex wasn't mistaken he could see by Molotov's attitude that he
knew how to handle an Envoy — even a British Envoy. Though Essex
could not imagine Molotov engaging in any diplomatic trivia, he was polite
enough. But it was already clear that everything Molotov said had a
mocking whiplike twist to it, and Essex did not like that. The terrible
wall of language handicapped Essex. He had an idea that much of his
English subtlety would be wasted on this short sharp Russian.

Molotov was in no hurry to get around to business. Since Essex had
come to ask something of the Russians, Molotov did not give him any
lead into the subject of Iran. He sat there laughing, as Essex told him
about the sled journey, but before Molotov could lose his humour Essex
came to the point.

"I suppose I should mention Iran at this stage," Essex said casually,
and paused for a moment to watch Molotov react.

Molotov simply spread his square hands. "*Pojalusta,*" he said.

"It's a pity that we have to worry about Iran so soon after the Moscow
Conference," Essex said in a deep breath of regret, "but we should appre-
ciate a little clarification of certain points of Soviet policy in Iran, Mr.
Molotov."

"Has a new situation arisen which makes Soviet policy suddenly unclear to the British Government?" Molotov said unhesitatingly.

"It's not exactly a new situation," Essex said. "It is the steady deterio-
ration of the political situation in Azerbaijan which concerns us. We are
not happy about the activities of the separatist movement, which has
seized power in that province, and we are anxious to settle this matter
with the Soviet Government and to appreciate the Soviet's point of view."

"Our point of view is very clear," Molotov said, unsmiling as Troika
caught the sentence. He had folded his hands in front of him and his eyes
were wide open behind his pince-nez glasses. "Our attitude is still as we
expressed it in the 1942 agreement on Iran. We do not remain outside
Iranian affairs, since we share the occupation of that country with
our British allies, but we will not interfere in Iranian affairs, nor prevent
the democratic forces of Iran from gathering strength and influencing
Iran's future. The Soviet Government wants a friendly and democratic
Iran, and our relations with that country are based on this premise."

Essex considered that a vague and general statement which amounted
to evasion. "I am afraid I haven't made our interest clear." Essex forgot
the need for translation and spoke directly to Molotov. "My Government

is specifically interested in the situation in Azerbaijan, and the effect it is having on the rest of the country. We have several suggestions to make which could improve the situation, and I would like your permission to present them."

Molotov leaned back and looked at a large grey portrait of Marx, as Troika clipped the words out in Russian, portioning them off neatly with his tongue and using exact phrases to convey Essex's English tone of subdued insistence.

"If the British Government is worried about the situation in Azerbaijan," Molotov said, "it is either misinformed or it does not understand what is happening. The situation in Azerbaijan is normal. A Democratic movement has arisen, which is permitted under the terms of the Anglo-Soviet-Iranian Treaty of 1942. This movement can have nothing but good effect on the rest of Iran and it will strengthen the chances of democracy in Iran."

Essex zipped open his pouch and took out a document and held it firmly in his hand. "We feel by the evidence we have that this movement in Azerbaijan is not democratic but separatist. Its intention is to split Azerbaijan off from Iranian authority and establish a separate state. To allow such a thing would be a breach of the 1942 Treaty, Mr. Molotov."

Molotov remained immobile. "I can only repeat," he said, "that the British Government must be misinformed."

"We agree that we lack information," Essex said. "We have asked the Soviet Government on several occasions for details of developments in their zone of occupation but we have received no replies. Our understanding of Azerbaijan is based on statements of the so-called Azerbaijanian Democratic Party itself. We have evidence that this Party's expressed policy is separatism, revolution, and independent action. We feel this is a danger to the rest of Iran, and we should like to present some suggestions which would lessen the existing tension and restore the unity of Iran."

If Molotov continued to ignore Essex's request to put forward proposals, then Essex knew that he might fail before he had begun. His whole mission depended on getting the Russians to sit down at a table and talk his suggestions over. He watched Molotov rise, a short stocky figure, and go over to his bare desk and come back with a large box of Russian matches.

"Do you smoke at all, Lord Essex?" Molotov pushed the cigarettes forward again.

Essex refused and took out his pipe and said to Troika: "Ask Mr. Molotov if he will forgive me if I smoke my pipe."

"Try some of this cigarette tobacco in your pipe," Molotov told him and pushed the box towards him again after offering it to Melby and

Joyce and Troika. "Comrade Stalin has a habit of breaking these cigarettes into his pipe. He says it is very light tobacco but very sweet." Even in this Molotov was sharp, almost brusque.

Essex broke some of the cigarettes over an ash tray and filled his pipe with the yellow tobacco and wondered if Molotov was avoiding further discussion. Molotov had obviously arranged this meeting as a formal politeness, and these were not the circumstances for serious negotiation. Molotov went on smoking vigorously as if waiting for Essex to take up the discussion, but Essex knew that he should take his time. He was fascinated by Molotov's smoking. He had heard that Molotov was abstemious in everything, and that he was a vegetarian. When Essex thought of a vegetarian he always thought of a thin sickly sort of fellow who swore off all the necessary social habits of life; but Molotov was round and healthy, and he was enjoying his aggressive cigarette-smoking.

"Mr. Molotov," Essex began again. "I believe that the Anglo-Soviet-Iranian Treaty of 1942 made provision for talks between the Soviet and Britain should any situation arise which required mutual consideration. I submit that the seizure of power in Azerbaijan by a minority group is a matter which concerns Britain as well as the Soviet Union. Therefore it is worthy of discussion."

Molotov had transferred his thoughtful look to a large oil portrait of Stalin which occupied the wall beside Marx and Lenin. "Does the British Government consider this issue local or international?" he said.

"At the moment" — Essex was almost warning Molotov — "it is local."

"Then I suggest that any discussion should take place in Iran between the Ambassadors of Great Britain and the Soviet Union. That is the level on which a local issue should be discussed."

Molotov was right and Essex knew it. If this was a local issue it was primarily an affair for the Ambassadors in Teheran. Essex felt that he had been trapped too easily, and he wasted no time in getting out of it.

"Since this is a situation which could eventually affect relations between the Soviet Union and Great Britain," Essex said, "His Majesty's Government feel that it should be settled quickly and on higher levels. We are always concerned in guarding our good relations with the Soviet Union, and we do not want this situation to cause ill-will between us." And by heavens let's see you get out of that, Essex added to himself, knowing now just what to expect of Molotov. This Russian might be polite but he would give no quarter and would obey no diplomatic rules of discussion. Essex decided to throw every biting reply back in the Russian's face.

Molotov sat erect like all small men. He answered with his usual rapid impatient clarity. "The Soviet Government is deeply sorry if the British

Government feel any ill-will over this matter," he said. "We do not feel that ill-will is justified, and we can see no reason why the situation in Iran should affect our relations with Great Britain. Therefore we cannot see any reason for discussions or conferences on the subject. If the British Government have any suspicions they should be brought out into the open and stated clearly."

"Mr. Molotov has misunderstood my meaning," Essex said with grim English patience and common sense as he waved his black pipe with an easy flourish. "The British Government have no suspicions of the Soviet Government. Good heavens no! We are simply concerned with the picture this situation is presenting to the world at a critical stage of historical development. We do not want to encourage suspicions of our joint motives in Iran. That is why we believe the situation in the province of Azerbaijan needs adjustment. That is why we suggest a conference at which the Soviet Union, Britain, the Iranian Government, and the so-called Democratic Party of Azerbaijan be represented. We feel that this could establish a new basis of understanding between all parties in Iran, and it could restore the unity of that unhappy country." Molotov only had to say one word about the composition of the suggested conference and Essex would feel that he was on the way.

But Molotov replied in his sharp political terminology. "Lord Essex," he said, "there is no reason for any nation to be suspicious of the Soviet Union's intentions at this critical stage of historical development. Our policy in Iran is clear and definite: we encourage all new democratic forces and we resist the idea of meddling in Iran's affairs, whatever spurious suspicions exist. There are no grounds for suspicions of our motives. As to our joint motives, I can only speak for the Soviet Government, I cannot answer for the British Government."

Molotov's last remark brought Essex nearer real anger than he had been for many years. His hand was warm where it held his pipe and he did not like the feeling of perspiration that clung to it. He held his pipe in his clenched teeth and wiped his hand with a silk handkerchief. At the moment he didn't care a hang about the mission or about Iran, because he would not take any more of this super-directness from Molotov. If it was not personal it was at least insulting, and he wouldn't take it. He told himself again he wouldn't take it.

"If that is the Soviet's only reply," Essex said, "then I have come to Moscow for nothing, Mr. Molotov."

Essex could see that the Russian was contemplating him. (There was no doubt that Molotov was placing him as a typical example of his class —a handsome man, a man who had enjoyed the benefits of good food and excellent health as a child, a man completely unlike the English workers who were small and ugly by comparison because they lived their lives in black unhealthy cities on bare inadequate diet. A great people, the English, but beware of the Essexes.) It was a look that made Essex uncomfortable and he waited for Molotov's anger, ready to defend himself.

"Nobody comes to Moscow for nothing," Molotov said with precise formality and mildness, "and nobody leaves empty-handed. You must see our city, our theatres, our ballets."

Essex knew that he had risked his whole mission by feeling angry. He took a grip on himself. "I was sent here by my Government to achieve something more than sight-seeing," he said wisely. "Settlement of these vital problems cannot wait while I see the ballet, Mr. Molotov. What must I say to my Government when I return? That Mr. Molotov invited me to see the wonderful theatres?"

Molotov was smiling and he leaned back, still too erect. "It is the sort of disappointment we all suffer at times," he said with no desire to take the conversation back to Iran.

"These Iranian problems are always a disappointment," Essex sighed. "We English and Russians always get involved in them and we always suffer. We are both disappointed. That is why I think we should both talk it out as soon as possible."

Molotov shook his head. "The Soviet Government is not disappointed about anything, Lord Essex, least of all Iran. We feel very encouraged about it. What is there to talk about: your disappointment and our hopes?"

"If you like to put it that way," Essex said: "Yes."

"That would take us in a hopeless circle," Molotov said finally. He rose, and it was so definite that Essex had no choice. Essex stood and accepted the hand which Molotov had suddenly thrust forward.

"You are limiting me to the ballet, Mr. Molotov?" Essex said.

"You are very welcome in Moscow, Lord Essex, and don't be too unhappy about our ballet," Molotov said smiling again. "It is worth while coming to Moscow to see the ballet alone."

"That sort of diplomatic leisure ended with your Empress Elizabeth, Mr. Molotov."

"Elizabeth?" Troika questioned before translating it.

"Yes. Elizabeth," Essex said in reprimand. "She had a habit of asking our English Kings to send only the handsomest diplomats to her Court." Essex looked at a curious Oriental design that had been worked into the moulding around the room and he looked again at Molotov's straight eyes and decided that the Slavs were orientals after all. "Those decorative fellows have gone out of British diplomacy, Mr. Molotov. These days we must achieve results and settle problems. A dull world, Mr. Molotov."

Essex did not hurry. He put on his coat with Melby's help, and he lit his pipe again from the large box of matches on the table.

"However," he said to Molotov, "I can hardly take this as Mr. Molotov's final answer. I hope to see Mr. Molotov again within the next few days."

Molotov said nothing but walked to the door with him, and they shook hands again.

"We will meet again," Essex said as the door opened.

"The world is too small for us diplomats to avoid each other," Molotov said and stood aside for Melby and Joyce to follow Essex. Molotov walked through the secretary's room with them and stood at the outer door beaming upon them.

"Can I expect Mr. Molotov's call?" Essex said casually to Troika.

"Perhaps," Molotov said and bowed a little as they left.

Essex strode along the corridor and he did not slacken his pace until they were right out of the Foreign Office on the cold footpath. Essex rubbed his hands and looked up and around, and then the whole sky burst with noise and streaks of light as the New Year arrived. He stepped into the Rolls-Royce and closed his eyes against the sound and the sight of it.

"Did the Russian translator fellow catch what I was saying correctly?" Essex said to Joyce, the Embassy translator, who had spoken no word. To Essex he was faceless and nonexistent except for this moment.

Joyce gave it some thought. "Troika does extremely well," he said carefully. "He is not only a translator, sir, he is a mimic. He catches the tone of voice in one language and carries it faithfully into the other, and he has a way of picking the exact phrases instantly." Joyce was a naval officer and he was honour bound to moral fairness. "I speak Russian and English equally well," he said, "but Troika has been trained for translating, and he has made an art of it."

Essex grumphed and sat back, unable to avoid himself any longer.

He had been in expert hands and he could not blame that little Russian for it. He could be disgusted, however, with this Embassy translator who had sat dumbly erect during the entire proceeding and given him no assistance. Stupid fellow. Melby too. What the devil was a man like Melby doing in the diplomatic service? He should be a draper. That is the sort of man that Drake would pick. They should be in business together selling men's shirts in Hammersmith.

As for Molotov. There was no doubt that the Russian was cunning and sure of himself, too sure of himself. Under different circumstances this discussion might have gone differently. Molotov would not have had it his own way, if Essex had not been in such an impossible position. To begin with the mission was hopeless so soon after the Moscow Conference. And the Russians had everything on their side because they were confident enough of what they were doing in Iran to send the British and Essex to the devil. Molotov had done it very neatly but quite ruthlessly, and Essex tolerated it only because he did not want to go straight back to London with so little achieved. But this was only the beginning. To Essex the art of diplomacy was the art of sustaining a certain superiority over circumstances and people, even ministers and events. That made a good diplomat. Essex was a good diplomat, and he knew when to attack and when to retreat. He had learned that very successfully in the last twenty years, particularly before the war when half his work had been placating irate dictators and showing them at the same time that Britain would take no nonsense. Yet it was quite clear that Molotov was no blustering dictator. He was cool and undivertible, and this made the mission more difficult than Essex had expected. Essex also felt a little out of diplomatic practice. His last long spell had been in Washington, and four years in Washington persuading the Americans to send twice as much material as they wanted to had not been difficult, particularly with that idealistic chap Roosevelt with whom Essex had got along famously. In Washington he had only to go around being wonderfully and beautifully British, creating good-fellowship for his American friends and terrible envy in his American enemies. His broken nose and three rows of miniature medals and orders had been just about all that was needed, adding of course his natural charm and English humour. But Moscow was not Washington, and Essex hadn't taken the feel of this place yet. He hadn't really come to grips with Molotov. Unfortunately Essex wasn't sure whether Molotov had been final or not. It was an old device to make the first meeting seem like the last, particularly when you were on top, as Molotov seemed to think he was on top. All the same — Molotov had been definite in refusing to discuss Iran. It was confusing for Essex, and though he had met diplomatic rebuffs far worse than this one, he had never before felt so confoundedly stupid about it.

The car swung romantically into the Embassy drive and its lights swept across the front of the Embassy and stopped at the gradient. The driver revved his engine to cope with the ice and the car surged up the gradient to the Embassy hall. Essex waited for the driver to open the door and he threw off the camel's-hair rug and stepped out. He was about to go into the Embassy when someone shouted: "Harold. Is that you?"

Essex looked down the slope and a man without top coat (a tall loose-limbed and gangling fellow) was coming up it. "Harold!" he said again.

"Who's that?" Essex said.

"By heavens, the man doesn't recognize me!"

"Who is it?" Essex said irritably.

The figure was upon him. "John Asquith," the figure said.

"What the devil are you doing here?" Essex and Asquith were gripping each other, and Asquith was hitting Essex on his warmly padded back.

"I have been here for three months," Asquith said. "Heard you were up here old boy, but we just got in from Finland. Couldn't be bothered going out. Come over to my flat."

"Where?"

"At the side here. Come on."

"Always turning up somewhere, in fact everywhere." Essex was so pleased to see Asquith that he forgot Molotov. He told Melby and Joyce that they were through for the night. "By jove it's a long time since I saw you," he said to Asquith. "What a sight you are. This place was beginning to get me down."

"What's the matter?" Asquith said disdainfully. "Aren't you kicking the Russian bear hard enough? Aren't you enjoying yourself?" Asquith laughed heartily, his hands in his jacket pockets. "Where did we meet last?"

"I don't know."

"Probably in one of those stuffy places you think so much of," Asquith said.

They had walked around the corner and they came to a small square building similar to Melby's except that this was two-storied. At the door a spaniel jumped at Essex and Asquith beat him off saying, "Get down Vodka or I'll destroy you."

A woman was standing at the door and she closed it behind them and made a movement of being cold. "Jane," Essex said as he embraced her. "Still Jane. It's marvellous to see you. Good God, fancy seeing you both here."

"It's about time we met somewhere, Harold," the woman said. "You went out without a coat," she told her husband gently.

"Ah!" Asquith waved his hand to dismiss it and lead the way. "We have your factotum here, Harold." Asquith took him into a fire-lit sitting-room.

"MacGregor!" Asquith called and swallowed hard on the word like a Scotchman. "Your lord and master is here, and by Heaven you are in for it now."

Essex smiled briefly at MacGregor but added no word of greeting because he wanted MacGregor to feel his displeasure. Asquith seemed madder than he had been when Essex saw him last. Jane Asquith on the other hand had become even more gentle and charming — if that were possible — and Essex thought again how good it was to see them, although he knew that Asquith would begin his usual attack upon everything. It was already beginning. Asquith was standing before the fire with his arms along the mantelpiece and a fierce look upon his face and his eye on Essex.

"I have been waiting for you to come to Moscow," Asquith said. "I have been saving a particular gem."

"Now nothing complicated, John," Essex said warily.

"Complicated!" Asquith complained dramatically. "There isn't a line of Wordsworth that isn't hopelessly complicated."

"Well go on," Essex said. "What is it?"

"Ah!" Asquith said rather contemptuously. "You will like this if you remember it. It was written for you in Moscow, Harold. Exactly that."

"I'll remember it," Essex said. "What is it?"

"Wordsworth's English complaint on the French Revolution."

"Which particular complaint?"

"This!" Asquith said and waved his arms oratorically. "Portentuous change, when History can appear as the cool advocate of foul device; reckless audacity extol, and jeer at consciences perplexed with scruples nice!... They who bewail not, must abhor the sneer born of Conceit, Power's blind Idolater; or haply sprung from vaunting Cowardice betrayed by mockery of holy fear!" Asquith beat his chest a little and then glared at Essex. "Go on," he said. "Take it up anywhere you like. Let's hear it."

Essex had no difficulty. "Hath it not long been said the wrath of Man works not the righteousness of God? Oh bend, bend — ye Perverse! to judgments from on High, laws that lay under Heaven's perpetual ban, all principles of action that transcend the sacred limits of humanity." He looked down at Asquith. "Well?" he said. "That's it, isn't it?"

Asquith shook his big head impatiently. "Is that all?" he cried. "You are not going to leave out all the best part of it, about *Woe for him who thus deceived shall lend an eager hand to social havoc*! That is the part that should satisfy you," Asquith said. "Go on."

Essex put a hand to his forehead to think of it. "But woe for him who thus deceived shall lend an eager hand to social havoc! Is not Conscience ours, and Truth, whose eye guilt only can make dim; and Will, whose office, by divine command, is to control and check disordered powers?" Essex could have gone on, but Asquith interrupted him.

"Just listen to that," Asquith moaned, "and the rest of it: Long-favoured England! Be not thou misled by monstrous theories of alien growth, lest alien frenzy seize thee, waxing wroth, self-smitten till thy garments reek dyed red with thy own blood, which tears in torrent shed fail to wash out; tears flowing ere thy troth be plighted, not to ease but sullen sloth, or wan despair — the ghost of false hope fled into a shameful grave. Among thy youth, My Country! if such warning be held dear, then shall a veteran's heart be thrilled with joy, one who would gather from eternal truth, for time and season, rules that work to cheer — not scourge, to save the People — not destroy." Asquith had reached something like

95

anger and his wife put down her knitting and called to him to cease.

Essex was laughing and so was MacGregor.

"That is enough John," Jane Asquith said. "It is quite ridiculous."

"Of course it's ridiculous!" Asquith said.

"Please sit down," Jane Asquith told him again and said to MacGregor: "They do this every time they meet. They consider themselves the only two men on earth who know every line of Wordsworth by heart. You will have to forgive them."

"Ah, that was greatness!" Essex said of Wordsworth.

"It's the most shocking nonsense ever written," Asquith said.

"John, don't say that," Mrs. Asquith told him calmly.

"I remember when you considered Wordsworth the only poet in the English language," Essex said to him. "I still think he is."

"The only poet worse than Wordsworth is Swinburne, and he isn't a poet at all." Asquith fell into a chair and stretched out his legs.

"You don't know what you're talking about," Essex said. "Wordsworth shook the English language out of its decay and gave it back some of its Elizabethan beauty. Look at the sonnet to the cuckoo."

"Pah!" Asquith stood up again. "Sonnets to cuckoos and pet lambs and linnets. What sort of a poet is that?"

"The sort of poet an Englishman should be," Essex said. "Nothing like those Irish fellers or that impossible American — Whitman."

"His tastes are impossible," Asquith complained and sat heavily on the chair again, twisting his pipe around in his mouth. "How the devil do you work with a man like that?" he suddenly flung at MacGregor.

"You are embarrassing Mr. MacGregor," his wife said and smiled at MacGregor.

"Nonsense," Asquith said. "Are you embarrassed, MacGregor?"

"No."

"I should think not," Asquith said.

MacGregor was quite embarrassed. Asquith's wild oratory had left him a little dumbfounded. He could not help enjoying it, however, and he had forgotten about Essex's greeting. He had even forgotten his fight with Drake.

As if to quiet Asquith, Essex asked him again what he was doing here.

"I'm wasting my time," Asquith said unhesitatingly. "I've been sent here to anticipate what will happen in Finland and Poland and Rumania and all the other border states, but I am a bad anticipater. I am supposed to go and look in every hole and corner of these miserable countries, but I might as well stay here and be comfortable. This is a marvellous place, Harold, a nice contradictory sort of a place. Did you know that they mobilize dogs in this country?"

"No."

96

"Yes." Asquith pointed a long finger at his dog. "To get my meat allowance for Vodka I have to have him trained by the Army so that they can mobilize him in case of war. Good training and kindness and all that sort of stuff. It finishes up like this." Asquith stood erect and cried "Hoish!" and the spaniel leapt up in amazement from a calm sleep and landed by reflex in Asquith's arms and then looked sheepishly about him. "Ever see anything like that?" Asquith said. "Have you?"

Essex patted the dog's head and pulled its ears and rubbed an expert hand over its sensitive nose, and MacGregor leaned back in the couch to laugh softly.

"I didn't think you had a sense of humour," Asquith said to MacGregor.

"No Englishman should say that to a Scot!" MacGregor said.

"You deserved that," Jane Asquith said to her husband.

"Ah, I am pleased enough to see that he has a little humour in him." Asquith tugged at his long moustache. "He has been fighting with Drake."

Essex said "Oh" and looked at MacGregor.

"Yes," Asquith said. "And two more solemn humourless men you have never heard. If you would let him, he would now go back to London, because he doesn't think much of himself for fooling about in Moscow diplomacy."

MacGregor wondered if anything was sacred to John Asquith. He realized that he had told Asquith a great deal about himself in the half hour of their acquaintance. By his argumentative, provoking questions Asquith had easily drawn him out, and it was startling to hear Asquith talk so casually about him now.

"John," Jane Asquith said. "I'm sure Mr. MacGregor doesn't like your saying such things."

MacGregor found to his own surprise that he didn't mind at all.

"MacGregor is a scientist," Asquith said heatedly, "and he has to put up with the truth. But you will have to watch him Harold. Like so many of these scientific fellows he does not consider himself a part of ordinary human affairs. Soon he'll be attacking you with all sorts of scientific objectivity. He will be telling you where you are right and where you are wrong. But suggest to him that he participate a little in your Iran affair, and he will say that it is nothing to do with him. They are all alike, these scientific men with consciences. They like to be conscience-stricken about the ills of the world, but the thought of taking any part or any side in a political problem horrifies them, and they go on being beatific and indignant and objective and useless. They blame other men when politicians and warriors take their science and blow half humanity off the face of the earth, but they go on giving their science to the devil. Give them a chance to stop it all and they run away. Look at MacGregor!

97

A little direct participation in human affairs is too much for him. He is ready to get out and leave dangerous men like you and Drake to do what you like. I'll never understand it!" Asquith said in despair.

"You are just embarrassing Mr. MacGregor," his wife protested again.

"He should be embarrassed."

"And you exaggerate too much," she said.

"Do I exaggerate, MacGregor?" Asquith demanded agreement from MacGregor.

MacGregor was not so easily pacified. "Why pick on the scientist?" he said. "His scientific problems are enough without adding others."

"If you don't face your other problems," Asquith said, "you won't have any science left. You can no more be let out of political responsibility than we can, although we are no better, MacGregor. Take comfort in that. There never was a more useless group of men than the diplomats, and Harold and I are good examples."

"John," Essex said. "If you are going to start on me . . ."

"I'm not going to spare you," Asquith cried. "There has never been a more wretched line of men in history than the diplomats, Harold, and none has been more blackguardly than the British diplomat because he never dies out. There is always another Essex and another Asquith, and when we go to Hell and Heaven we become legates for God and the Devil and we just go on being diplomats."

"That's blasphemy John. Stop it."

"Then just look at my own family: the most illegitimate family in England: a long line of thieves cheats robbers liars courtiers and strumpets: beginning with Anne Godstone herself who wantonly sacrificed the honest-to-God integrity of the London slum for the few favours she could get from an overfed licentious King. Thus were born the Asquiths and thus we have always been diplomats."

"Now you are being vulgar," Jane Asquith said gently but hopelessly.

"I'm sorry, Jane, but I'm trying to compensate MacGregor for his embarrassment. I am just telling him that the diplomat is worse than the poor liverish scientist. If I can't begin with my own family then I'll begin with the Papal Court. That was the birthplace of modern diplomacy anyway, and it's a better example because never was a profession born more suitably than ours, beginning as it did in the rot and garbage of the Middle Ages."

Essex had to protest. "I haven't seen you for five years, John," he said, "and here you are crying Popery already. What has Popery got to do with diplomacy, and why drag it in like that?"

"Wasn't the legatine system the first diplomatic service?" Asquith said. "And aren't the forms of diplomacy given to us by the papal legates of Rome?"

"That is nonsense," Essex said. "The first great diplomats were writers and philosophers and patriots: Dante, Boccaccio, Petrarch."

"They were hopeless amateurs!" Asquith pronounced. "The real men of the profession were the Borgias and the Medicis. They covered Europe with a net of clerics and papal spies, and that is our origin, Harold. The only man of the time worth a damn was Machiavelli and see how he has been maligned. Even after Machiavelli it was not until the Venetian merchants came along that a drop of honest blood came into the profession."

"Pah!" Essex said. "Merchants."

"They were honourable and well-travelled republicans," Asquith insisted, "and they didn't weigh their decisions and their activities by papal lies and saintly deceit. Their reports to the Venetian Senate were models of clarity and instruction, and not a one among them was a Pope's agent."

"You are Popery mad, John," Essex complained.

"I am diplomat mad!" Asquith stood up and searched for his tobacco pouch until he found it in his wife's work basket. He filled his pipe untidily. "Why! the first diplomat to arrive in England, Dr. Roderigo Gonsalez de Puebla, was a papal spy; but in those days we knew what to do with foreign diplomats. Henry the Seventh set his dogs onto them and clouted them occasionally with the shin-bone of an ox. If there had been more Henry the Sevenths there would never have been an Aix-la-Chapelle and if there had never been an Aix-la-Chapelle three hundred years later there would never have been any legalizing of diplomats as ambassadors and envoys and plenipotentiaries and nuncios and every other cunning title of legal respectability for men who have never been more than dishonourable wretches. Now we are extraterritorial; we are above the land we live in; we are rich, honourable, eloquent, witty, deceitful, cunning, scandalous and rude; and we have settled our consciences with the legality and the title of our activities. Diplomacy! It's a shameful blot on the rest of human affairs."

"If John is finished," Mrs. Asquith said, "I'll make some coffee."

"He is worse than he ever was," Essex said to her.

"He is getting homesick," Jane Asquith told him.

"Go and get the coffee," Asquith said to his wife and lay on his back on the couch puffing smoke straight up into the air.

"How can you put up with him?" Essex called to her.

"She is young enough to have to put up with it," Asquith said. "The ten years' difference between us is a guarantee that she will behave. Why didn't you ever marry, Harold?"

"You are getting out of hand," his wife said to him as she came in with a coffeepot and put it on a small metal stand over the fire. "You will have to excuse him, Mr. MacGregor. I can see that you are a little worried by his tomfoolery and I can't blame you."

"I'm not worried," MacGregor said sleepily.

"Of course he is worried," Asquith said. "Ask him where he was when he should have been with you, Harold. Ask him what he means by fighting with Francis Drake. That's what he is worried about."

"What were you fighting with Drake for, MacGregor?" Essex asked, more for his own curiosity than any obedience to Asquith's command.

"It was a mild dispute, nothing more," MacGregor said.

"Nonsense," Asquith said. "It might have been polite but it was an argument with all sorts of implications. You know, Harold, this fellow MacGregor can be an indignant man, and that is not allowed. Remember, MacGregor, you are not supposed to have any feelings of indignation. It is unscientific and it will force you to take sides."

"What are you talking about?" Essex said.

"I am talking about this young man who is disgusted with himself for meddling in the petty habits of an Embassy when he should be fingering some dead rock in a dirt-fouled laboratory."

MacGregor pushed back his hair and Asquith enjoyed his embarrassment.

"Do you know where he was when he should have been with you, Harold?"

"No."

"He will not tell you but I shall. He was out with Kathy Clive . . . old Sandy Clive's daughter. There is your academic for you."

"So she is old Sandy Clive's daughter," Essex said.

"Yes. Have you seen her? Statuesque sort of a girl?"

"I've seen her."

"So has MacGregor," Asquith said. "As a matter of fact we ought to have her here now. Wonderful gal, Kathy."

Jane Asquith interrupted his move to the telephone. "No John," she said. "Leave Mr. MacGregor and Katherine alone. I won't have her here so that you can tangle these two up in embarrassment."

"Tangle Kathy up?" Asquith said indignantly. "She usually strikes me dumb."

MacGregor was too sleepy to appreciate Jane Asquith's move of defence. His eyes were open, but the last of the warm influence of the punch was overtaking him, and he sat immobile with his legs crossed and his hands gripping each other, struggling to hear what Essex was saying because he wanted to know how Essex felt about him.

Asquith, however, was asking Essex how he had found Molotov.

Essex was raising his hands. "He won't even talk about Iran," Essex said.

"What do you want them to do in Iran?" Asquith asked.

"We just want to even things up a little," Essex said.

"Ho. Ho. You came to the wrong place. What are you going to do now?"

"I think I'll start off with a Note," Essex said, "a nice official Note demanding consideration of our proposals in view of the serious situation which exists in Azerbaijan."

"Give up and go home," Asquith said. "You are wasting your time here."

Jane Asquith served coffee before the argument could develop.

MacGregor revived enough to listen to Essex and Asquith start discussing other men. He then waited to leave with Essex, because he wanted to find out whether Essex was really annoyed.

"So you were fighting with Francis Drake?" Essex said pleasantly to MacGregor when they eventually walked out into the snow.

MacGregor found that he could not explain that particular dispute to Essex. "It was just an argument about where I was and what I was doing," he said.

"You know, MacGregor, Drake is in a rather difficult position here."

MacGregor said nothing.

"Is it a fact that you want to go back to London, or is that one of John's exaggerations?" Essex was not making an important point of it.

"If you have finished with me I wouldn't mind going back," MacGregor said.

"Because of Francis Drake?"

"No," MacGregor said and added nothing more. How could he explain to Essex the sudden feeling of hopelessness which Drake had given him? Oddly enough he had explained quite a lot of it to Asquith, perhaps because Asquith had known how to get it out of him. To Essex, however, he could say nothing. Yet he did not want Essex to be annoyed.

"I could probably get along without you alright, MacGregor," Essex said thoughtfully, as if he had given it careful and fair consideration and was doing MacGregor the favour of letting him go. "I shall be delayed here anyway, so I can easily get another man from London if you want to go back." Essex was thinking that he couldn't get another man from London at all and he didn't want another man from London. He wanted MacGregor and he knew that he would have MacGregor. No man liked to be dismissed so easily as dispensable, and he had no doubts that MacGregor would stay of his own free, desirable will. "You can let me know in the morning," Essex said and added as extra inducement to make sure of MacGregor: "I'll square you with Francis Drake. Good night, my boy."

"Good night!" MacGregor said, no longer sleepy but rather slighted by Essex's willingness to let him go, and ready to blame Essex for the situation he was in.

Chapter 6

THE LATE morning sun lit MacGregor's steam-warmed bedroom and threw sharp golden reflection off the brass fire-irons which stood before the fire-place. Though it was winter sun, it easily penetrated the printed curtains. MacGregor got out of bed and sat for a while in the beam of yellow light at the foot of the bed, reviewing the decisions he had made about himself before and after his heavy sleep. In the clear light of day he decided that he had made no decisions at all, except perhaps one, and he was not sure that he could carry that off.

He bathed and breakfasted, and rang Katherine Clive.

When she answered he said: "This is MacGregor."

"Good morning," she said. "Did they find you last night?"

He told her what had happened.

"Should I tell Sir Francis that I am responsible for your disappearance?"

"I wouldn't do that," he said.

She laughed. "He probably knows it anyway."

He did not want to talk about Drake. "I thought this might be a good day for skating," he said.

"Alright," she said slowly. "How about lunch time? I shan't have any other time."

"What time do you call lunch time?" he asked.

"In about an hour and a half: say one o'clock at the tennis court. Can you skate at all?"

"I have never skated in my life," he said.

"Hm. You are the sort of person who tries anything, I suppose."

He wasn't, but he was pleased that she said so. "Just so long as I don't make too much of a mess of it," he said to her.

"We shall see," she said. "At one o'clock then."

"Right."

It had been so easy that he laughed at the difficulty and the doubt he had made of it. He had really expected her to put it off and say some other time, because he knew that last night had been exceptional for himself as well as for Katherine Clive. But he thought that perhaps he wasn't such a stiff fellow after all. He wanted to explain himself a little more to this woman, but he doubted if he ever could.

He walked out, and the sun caught his eyes and made him homesick again for the dry heat of a good Persian summer day with hard light coming off the rock mountains and sweeping across the bare plains. He turned around for a moment to look back at the city. It seemed to be nothing but the Kremlin from his position, but he could see a little of the low sky-line and the high-tension wires and the curving bridge-tops that gave Moscow its shape from the British Embassy. It was an old and permanent-looking city. The zooming of an aeroplane seemed out of place.

Essex was not in, and Miss Williams was putting coal on the fire.

"Everybody is late this morning," she said. She looked at him to see if he was in better temper. "I was sorry I couldn't get you in time last night." Apparently she had to say it.

"It was my own fault," he told her.

"There is some good news in the cables I put on your desk," she said rapidly. "There is a new Civil Service award. It looks as though we are all to get an increase in basic salary when they do away with the war bonuses. It's a good beginning to the New Year," she said and left him.

MacGregor did not read about the awards. He read some of the cables from Teheran and two from New York via the Foreign Office. The latter reported a speech at Harvard University by one of the Undersecretaries of State. He had made a reference to the situation in Azerbaijan as being the work of un-democratic forces and recalcitrant men who planned to cause revolution in all Iran, thus destroying and defying the legally elected body of parliament in Iran, and preventing the present government from continuing its struggle for democratic reform. Essex came in and asked him what he was looking so sour about.

"This report from New York," MacGregor said.

Essex did not hear him. He was reading the English press summary on his own mission. He read some of the items out loud to MacGregor. Two of them stated authoritatively that Essex had seen Stalin on arrival. A more conservative paper reported that Essex and Stalin had already agreed to establish a group to enquire into the situation in Iran. Another report (from the *Daily Worker*) said that Lord Essex hadn't seen Stalin and added that he was wasting his time in Moscow and suggested that he should go to Iran and see conditions there for himself.

"Nonsense, all of it," Essex said and tossed them in the fire. "What those fellows can write always astounds me," he said.

MacGregor was still waiting for Essex to ask him if he wanted to stay or return to London, but Essex had apparently forgotten all about it and MacGregor felt slighted. "I forgot to tell you last night that I had met a couple of Americans named Hamber and Steele who asked for you," he said to Essex to remind him of last night. "They said that you might be interested to know they are here."

"Ah yes, Hamber and that Steele fellow. They rang me this morning. We will be talking to the newspapermen to-morrow or the next day, MacGregor, depending on what reply we get to the Note. Not much use giving them anything official until we have finished our business here. Too dangerous. These newspaper johnnies give everything such a peculiar twist that you have to watch them. We might have a couple of them down here for dinner to-morrow or the next night; all unofficial; just putting them right on a few things."

"They seem to know everything already," MacGregor said.

"They're odd specimens, particularly that fellow Hamber. I have known him for years. He has a hide like a rhinoceros, but I suppose you have to have it in that profession. Though Steele is a bit more sensitive, an impassioned sort of chap. I remember him in Paris. He annoyed me like the devil. Great believer in the Russians, that fellow."

"He has changed his mind," MacGregor said.

"Is that so? I don't suppose you can ever tell with those cause-seekers. Now a man like Hamber will always be consistent and I always get on well with him, much better than I ever have with those English reporters. Never yet met an English reporter that I really liked. The life seems to have gone out of them, and they are always men from either Bloomsbury or Swiss Cottage. In the old days the *Times* produced some great men, Churchill and Curzon. There are no Churchills among these English reporters to-day, although I wouldn't be surprised if that fellow Hamber became President of the United States one day. That is obviously his intention."

Miss Williams stood at the door and told them that a diplomatic bag was leaving for London at four o'clock this afternoon if they wanted anything to go.

"Is there a plane leaving?" MacGregor asked her.

"At five-thirty," she said.

When she had gone Essex asked MacGregor if he was thinking of going.

MacGregor was satisfied. "No!" he said. "I don't mind staying."

"I thought you would stay," Essex said. "I can see that you don't think much of the type of work you're doing, MacGregor, but you will get over that."

"The trouble is I know nothing about this work," MacGregor said.

"Neither did I when I was a young man. I had my first real opportunity on a job that I knew nothing about at all — that was in Paris with Lloyd George. I am hanged if I knew anything about treaty and peace-making when I started, but I knew a devil of a lot when I had finished. It gave me the initial experience I needed, just as this particular mission will give you valuable experience to begin with, MacGregor. So if you want to disagree with me on anything that I am doing, MacGregor, then go ahead and disagree. No doubt we will both benefit by the experience. Is there anything you want to discuss now, before we go any further?"

MacGregor said "No. There's nothing."

"Are you sure?"

MacGregor was sure. Anything that he said to Essex at this moment about Iran would sound like a quibble. Essex had talked sense out of any argument he could offer about Iran. MacGregor was silent, because he did not want to make an issue of their different opinions, not right now anyway. He wanted to stay in Moscow, and that was enough for the time being, even though he was suspicious of his reasons for staying. He knew it was more than the weather that was keeping him here, but he avoided further self-examination of it.

"Do you want to send your report on Molotov in the bag this afternoon?" MacGregor asked Essex.

"Yes, I suppose so."

"What time will you want me here then?"

Essex was reluctant to think about the report because he had no desire to put into words the fact that his first meeting with Molotov hadn't gone so well. "What time is lunch at Melby's to-day?" he said.

"I don't know," MacGregor said. "I was going to do some skating."

"With our fair skater?"

"Yes."

"Then we can do something about the report after lunch. In the meantime you might get in touch with Melby and the translator chap and get whatever you can from them to supplement my own memory. Get Molotov's exact wording from them, and check one against the other. I always like to have a man's exact statements. I would do it myself, but I want to see Francis about this Note." The truth was he didn't want to go over the details of the Molotov interview with either of those fools: it was bad enough in recollection already.

On the way to Drake's room, Essex caught up with Katherine Clive on the staircase, said how do you do, and stopped to talk with her.

"Good morning, Lord Essex," she said and did not hurry away.

"I hear you are going to do some more skating," Essex said.

She nodded and went on up the stairs.

Essex followed. "I was going to ask you to lunch with me to-day so that we might talk more about that remarkable father of yours."

"Lunch where?" she asked.

"With Francis Drake."

"He may not want his staff lunching with him," she said, so that Essex laughed.

"Then we had better put it on a family-friendship basis," Essex told her.

"I am really supposed to go skating," she reminded him, but added: "I see that the sun is beginning to melt the ice again."

"You can skate any time," Essex said.

As they both arrived at Drake's door she looked at him and said: "I shall wait and see what Sir Francis says."

Essex had a faint suspicion that she was laughing at Drake, or suggesting at least that Drake would be embarrassed by her attendance at lunch. But Essex decided that he was mistaken when he looked at Drake's neat face, and exchanged morning greetings. He waited while Katherine Clive had a short discussion with Drake about four clauses in a Soviet-Polish Commercial Treaty. At one moment it actually became a mild argument when they discussed a wide-gauge railway which the Russians had taken into Poland and kept in operation. Drake said that the odd-guage Russian railway in Poland was obviously for political and infil-tration purposes, an attempt to make Poland more dependent on Rus-sian transport, and Katherine Clive argued that it was being used to shift a lot of urgent materials between both countries and that it was hardly worth objecting to. It was polite, of course, and barely perceptible, but Essex was impressed and amused at the same time.

When they were finished he said to Drake, "Would you mind if Miss Clive came to lunch to-day, Francis? I am an old acquaintance of her father's, and we have quite a lot to talk about."

Drake looked quickly at Katherine but she was expressionless. "Please!" Drake said to Essex. "Katherine is always welcome."

Katherine smiled just a little and left them.

"We are having two other guests for lunch," Drake said quickly to Essex. "They have just arrived on another of these missions from Lon-don: Empire Wheat Pool people. One is a Labour M. P. named Clipp who is on the Wheat Pool Board and the other is some scientist chappie from the Advisory Wheat Board."

"What the devil do they want here?" Essex said.

"Something to do with Russian wheat methods, although I am hanged if I know what we can learn from the Russians about wheat."

"When did they arrive?"

"Last night. They are staying down at the other house."

"I didn't know you had another house."

"Oh yes," Drake said. "We keep the Commercial people in another building down at Arbat. We really need a further building to house some of the Ministry of Information girls living at the Metropole Hotel. I don't like to have our women living there, it's a bad influence on them. The life is loose and unstable, and there are too many of those newspaper reporters there. It's bad for the Embassy."

"Ask the Russians for another house then," Essex said. "Demand it!"

Sir Francis Drake placed the tips of his fingers together and looked at Essex, trying to detect for the hundredth time the exact amount of mock-ery in what Essex said. It always seemed a challenge to Drake, but he was not a man to accept foolish challenges and he ignored it by fussing with his papers.

Essex sighed. "I hear that you and MacGregor had a bit of a toss-in last night," he said. "He is sorry about it, Francis, and so am I. I shall keep him out of your way if you like."

Drake was not sure that Essex was not laughing at him again. "He is a rather rude young man, Harold, and I don't like having people like that in the Embassy. They get into trouble sooner or later and I don't want embarrassment of that sort while I am here." Drake was letting MacGregor off more lightly than he had intended.

"Don't worry about it," Essex said. "He'll be alright."

"I hope so," Drake said and felt that some day he might take issue with Essex's subtlety and put the man in his proper place, but this was neither the time nor the place, because they had a mutual problem with the Russians. The Russians had to be settled first, and he would give Essex all the assistance he was asking for in planning a strong Note to the Russians. "Now what about this Note, Harold?" he said.

It took them almost an hour to finish with the discussion and Drake felt that he had done his duty, even though Essex left him with a casual wave of the hand, showing no sign of urgency about his task. Essex would come a cropper one of these days and that would be something to see.

For the moment Essex had no fears for his future, and he returned to his office and found MacGregor waiting for him with the material he had obtained from Melby and Joyce.

"Do you want to start on the report now?" MacGregor asked him.

"No. Not yet," Essex said and waved it away.

"We had better get an early start after lunch then," MacGregor said, "that is — if you want to catch the bag to London."

"We'll catch it," Essex said impatiently.

The phone on Essex's desk rang and he picked it up and said Hello and then handed it to MacGregor who stood on the opposite side of the desk. He watched MacGregor as he greeted Katherine Clive.

"Ah it's you," MacGregor said in surprise.

She did not waste time on detailed politeness. "I am sorry," she said, "but I can't go skating with you to-day, Mr. MacGregor. I am going to have lunch with your boss and Francis Drake."

MacGregor looked at Essex who was sharpening a long goose-quill and trying it out on a blank sheet of paper with large bold strokes.

"Can't you put off that lunch?" he said.

"I could, but we can go skating to-morrow," she said.

"I suppose we could."

"Anyway, the ice is melting."

"Is it?" he said disbelievingly.

"Yes. I'm sorry. Are you angry?"

"No. We can do it some other time."

"Yes."

"Good-bye," he said.

"Good-bye, Mr. MacGregor," she said, "and don't be angry."

MacGregor put down the phone and sat down at his desk. There was silence except for Essex humming and scratching the paper with his quill. It was a silence that seemed too much for Essex, and he yawned and stretched his arms upward and pushed his feet into his shoes and stood up.

"I'm off to have lunch, MacGregor," he said.

MacGregor did not answer and Essex strolled out and up to Drake, feeling a younger man than he had been since his arrival in this accursed Moscow.

The Member of Parliament and the scientist delighted Essex as they exhibited themselves over an excellent lunch of braised veal cutlets and mashed potatoes. They were men he could enjoy analyzing and provoking, and men that he could easily impress. The M. P. was a small middle-aged man with a croft of black hair and horn-rimmed glasses that hid watchful eyes. He was perky and moved energetically, and he was not at all self-conscious, even though he spoke a broad Yorkshire dialect with a few Cockney expressions thrown in. The scientist was the perfect antithesis, and he looked like a parson to Essex . . . as did most scientists for that matter. This one was a small white-haired man with little interest in Katherine Clive, Lord Essex, Sir Francis Drake, or anybody else, including his M. P. companion. The M. P., however, was delighted to meet Essex, and he laughed heartily at everything that Essex said. He was particularly taken up with Katherine, and every word of his conversation was directed at her. Essex watched this and provoked the situation, although Katherine Clive was not very responsive to his word-playing. She just sat there and allowed it to go on, as if her permission had been given. As a result the M. P. strove more than ever to impress her. He explained his mission to her as they ate apricot and apple dessert.

"We are not worried about Empire wheat, Miss Clive," Walter Clipp said with a finger raised. "We are concerned about our rivals. The Russians claim that they are doing great things with perennial wheats and the transference of spring wheats into hardy winter varieties. We are supposed to be here to exchange planting information, but we can say confidentially in this gathering that we are here to find out just how much truth there is in Russian claims about planting perennial wheats which come up regularly for five years without re-planting. Think of our Empire market if the Russians really produced a seed like that. They could grow enough wheat to swamp us out of the world market, even though there is a shortage at the moment. Think too of our situation if we ourselves had such a seed-wheat. Its possibilities would be unlimited."

"Are you planning to steal it from the Russians?" Essex asked.

Clipp laughed with a roar. "No. That is Shame's job. He is a geneticist and if anybody can get at the two Russians developing this wheat — it will be Shame. He is the best geneticist in England, aren't you Shame?"

Shame said nothing. He ate his apple and wished that Clipp would shut up.

"Are you going to spy on these Russians?" Essex said.

Clipp enjoyed that also. "Oh no," he said. "Shame is going to watch them and study their methods and listen to their explanations and see the results. He will be able to tell in a jiffy if it's the real thing, won't you Shame? We picked him for his knowledge in this sort of thing. He has written papers galore about heredity and environment."

"What has heredity got to do with wheat growing?" Katherine Clive asked.

"Good heavens, young lady," Clipp said. "Everything! To get a perennial wheat you have to change a seed in its environment, overcome its hereditary tendencies. This Russian chap Lysenko, claims that all our laws and knowledge of heredity are wrong. Lysenko claims that almost anything can mix with anything else, I mean among the plant life, providing you give it the right start and the proper environment. Isn't that what you were saying, Shame?"

"Something like that," Shame mumbled.

"How will you investigate this Lysenko?" Essex said. "The Russians will hardly welcome you with open arms, and I can't see them being tricked very easily."

"I don't think anybody is trying to trick them," Drake put in.

"You never know," Clipp said with a cunning smile. "Shame is a scientist and I am something of an expert myself. We are not negotiators. They trust us. Not like you diplomats, Lord Essex." Clipp enjoyed his own joke.

So did Essex. He didn't mind Clipp's heaviness because he guessed that Clipp was probably overcome by the illustrious company. Moreover, Essex knew that the man was not a fool. He knew that Clipp was a Morrison man. He had an excellent reputation for administration and efficiency in the Wheat Board during the war. The bellowing heartiness was probably natural to the man in the circumstances. Essex supposed that Clipp had been hail-fellow-well-met with a few peers of the realm and a couple of conservative M. P.'s on the Wheat Board, and no doubt Clipp had decided that they weren't such bad fellows after all. He had now turned in familiar approach to Drake, and Essex knew that this would be interesting.

"Tell me, Sir Francis," Clipp said. "How are our relations with the Soviet Government these days? Are they good?"

"As good as can be expected," Drake said noncommittally and signalled to the houseman to serve the champagne, hoping to end this before it began.

"Are we satisfied about Poland, for instance?" Clipp said.

"In what way, Mr. Clipp?"

"We hear in London that Mikolajczyk is getting a raw deal and that the Polish Secret Police are terrorizing the place under Russian orders."

"That is really the Warsaw Embassy's problem," Drake said.

"Ah, but it is really an affair of our relations with Russia, since we both put the present Polish Government in power and guaranteed to stick by it. Are the Russians carrying out their agreement faithfully?"

"In their own way," Drake said. "Though we don't agree that their way is always correct of course."

"No we don't," Clipp said, "and there you have the whole problem of our relations with Russia. We don't always agree that their way is correct. In fact we never agree. What are we doing to understand the Russian point of view, Sir Francis? What is the Embassy studying about Russia?"

"We have our usual methods of understanding a country, Mr. Clipp."

"But there is more than that to it, surely," Clipp said. "Russia is a strange country and we should try to see it as it sees itself."

"I believe that an Ambassador did introduce the study of the official Russian history of the Communist Party of the Soviet Union among Embassy secretaries and others among the Embassy staff."

"The Bolshevik history?"

"Yes. You remember that, Katherine. Weren't you here then?"

"I was here," she said, "but I didn't study it."

"Why not?" Clipp asked her.

"I had already read it," she said, "and I didn't see anything in it to study. You only have to read it once to see what it has to say."

"How did you feel about it?" Clipp said.

"I have forgotten," she said.

"And what about the classes, Sir Francis?" Clipp persisted.

"They were something of a joke, so that it was really a waste of time."

"Do you think it's really a joke, Sir Francis? Isn't Bolshevism too dangerous to treat lightly as a joke?" Clipp said.

"Perhaps."

"No 'perhaps' about it. Even in England we are facing a downright dangerous situation from the Communists who are trying to attach themselves to the Labour Party and sabotage it and Bolshevize it."

There was a polite silence because Clipp was the only Labour man present.

"The Prime Minister is quite worried about it," Clipp said informatively. "And so is Mr. Churchill."

"Is Churchill worried about the Labour Party being Bolshevized?" Katherine Clive put down her champagne and did not hide her surprise at the statement.

"Certainly. There are times when we are all above the Party, Miss Clive."

"Oh!" she said.

"You weren't above Party at the General Election," Essex said.

Clipp roared again. "You have me there, Lord Essex. But we had the chance and the right to fight our own battle and we took it, and won mind you. Won magnificently."

Drake gulped his champagne uncomfortably and hoped that this political talk had ended, but he saw that Essex was watching Shame the geneticist.

"What about the world of science?" Essex asked Shame. "Are you also afraid of being Bolshevized?"

Shame inclined his white head. "Science has no politics," he said.

"Couldn't it be Bolshevized?" Essex said again.

"I don't think so," Shame said moderately.

"What about these Russian scientists? Are they dead men or are they men with ideas and men with revolutionary intentions?"

"Some are good and some are poor."

"In what fields?"

"One can never really be sure. Our mathematicians believe that the Russians are well advanced in higher mathematics, pure mathematics, and the physical sciences. On the other hand their biologists are rather primitive."

"And their geneticists?"

"That remains to be seen."

"And Mr. Lysenko?"

"I am sceptical of course."

"And the other fellow?"

"Tsitsin?"

"Yes," Essex nodded. "What about Tsitsin?"

"He is just a peasant," Shame said. "I believe he has had no scientific training. A peasant who has experimented with hybrids and tough grasses."

"He is the perennial-wheat fellow?" Essex asked.

"Yes."

"And the wheat is not perennial?"

"That is what we are here to find out," Walter Clipp interrupted. "Though Shame is sceptical about it all, aren't you Shame?"

"It does seem a little far-fetched at this stage," Shame murmured.

Moderation was the prerogative of the scientist, and Essex could see that Shame had no desire to express himself at all. In fact Shame was probably glad that Clipp had become his mouthpiece, however hopeless the M. P.'s scientific explanations. Anything, rather than tangle himself in politics. Essex tried him once more, however.

"What will be the effect on the world if we get perennial wheat?" he asked.

"I don't know," Shame said.

"Would world wheat-growing be revolutionized?"

"Perhaps."

"That would affect world economy, of course."

"It might."

Essex gave up.

Drake rose and suggested that they take coffee in the small lounge. He escorted Katherine by quietly walking with her. Essex followed and felt again that she and Drake were unnecessarily restrained with each other. As Katherine leaned back into a soft chair, Essex enjoyed a quick moment of excitement, and he decided that he had never seen a woman with such poise. Though Katherine lacked his mother's gentleness, she had a natural presence about her. That could make a woman great. Essex leaned over her and poured cream in her coffee.

"Now that I look at you I can see a very deep likeness to your mother, although I haven't seen her for ten years. You have Sandy's stubborn mouth but you have your mother's soft eyes. Buckingham all over."

She was really annoyed. "I am not a Buckingham at all," she said. "I am a Clive and there is not much use provoking me."

"I am not provoking you, my dear," Essex said mildly and wondered why she was so vehemently opposed to the Buckinghams, a fine family —even though they were all dead from the neck up. "How is your mother anyway?"

"I don't know," Katherine said. "I haven't heard for some time."

"And your father?"

"He is shooting or killing something somewhere," she said.

"Isn't he getting a little old for that?"

"The older he gets the more he likes to destroy," she said. "That is what the Buckinghams have done to him. He would like to shoot all that family, but since the law forbids it he goes out and shoots beasts instead."

"He was always pretty wild," Essex reminded her.

"He was always mad," she said, "but he was never fond of killing."

"Odd thing," Essex said. "What about your brother?"

"Jeff?"

"Yes."

"He was shot down in the Battle of Britain."

"I am sorry to hear it. I didn't know."

"He was mad too," she said, "and so is Alice."

"Are you the only sane member of the family?"

"No," she said, "but I am the most self-disciplined."

She relaxed again, and when she had brought them all to her attention she stood up and left them abruptly, as if she were satisfied that the situation had been as it should be. Essex was tempted to go with her but he could see that she intended to leave them all. He let her go and waited a little while and bade good-bye to Clipp and Shame with promises of seeing them again. He waited awhile, and then left quietly to work on his Molotov report.

Essex did not hurry. He prepared himself properly by opening his long Chinese pen box and taking out two of the quills he had sharpened in the morning. He tried them again and was satisfied with them. Everything was ready, including the thick parchment paper which he used even for first drafts. Parchment and quill were essential to Essex's report writing because they gave him the necessary feeling for the histrionic. Every word that he wrote would go into the archives of the Foreign Office, and some day they would pass to the National Museum as a record of the diplomatic history of the last twenty years, beginning with his first notes on the Peace Conference and ending latterly with his long wrangles with Mussolini, his easy persuasion in getting the remnants of the Spanish Republican Government to leave Madrid, his desperate attempts to keep the French from surrender, and finally the record of his mission to America, a mission which had done so much to keep Britain supplied with arms and equipment, a mission which had practically kept the war going. Now came this — the first of the new struggles with the Russians for world position.

"Are you going to do the Note also?" MacGregor asked him as he sorted his papers to bring over to Essex's desk.

"Yes, we might as well," Essex said. He looked quickly at MacGregor to see if he was angry about the lunch-time diversion of Katherine Clive. MacGregor displayed neither malice nor memory of it, and Essex decided that he could forgive MacGregor almost any sin, providing he was always so intelligent about personal affairs.

"When are you going to hand the Note to the Russians?" MacGregor asked him.

"When we get all-clear from London," Essex said. "When we deliver that Note, MacGregor, I think things will begin to happen."

Chapter 7

LONDON's permission to present the Note to the Russians did not arrive, though Essex waited patiently for it all day. By the next morning he was no longer patient. He ate his breakfast of toast and marmalade and tea with little taste for it. The food was really bad when you came to think of it. It was the same food one had in London or anywhere else, and it was just as well prepared, but in Moscow it seemed tasteless. Only the strong tea satisfied him. He sat in the armchair at the small coffee table, dressed in pyjamas and a velveteen smoking jacket and strong American slippers, reading a two-day-old copy of *The Times* which had arrived from Berlin. He sipped tea from a thin English china cup. When he had finished, he leaned on the mantelpiece, propping up *The Times* so that he could fill his pipe. The stem was blocked, and being alone he stooped over the fireplace and blew through the stem as hard as he could. He straightened up quickly when he heard a step in the corridor and a knock at his door. He wiped his mouth with a serviette and said "Come in" as he fitted his pipe together.

It was Katherine Clive, dressed in skiing pants and a sweater and a short white waistcoat with an angora collar. Her boots made dull thuds on the polished floor as she approached him with a folded paper in her hand.

"Good morning," she said healthily.

"Why good morning!" He showed his pleasure. "Have you been skiing?"

"No, I am about to go skiing," she said. "I've been on early morning duty and I am just going off. I thought you would like to have this cable."

He took it but did not look at it. He was still looking at Katherine Clive, a clean and polished Katherine Clive who wore no lipstick and displayed a face gleaming with morning cleanliness. He liked her scrubbed cheeks and clear eyes, and he liked to see that her figure could be boyish and feminine at the same time. He fingered his soft silk pyjama collar and felt pleased that he had shaved and bathed before breakfast so that he was a youthful sight himself.

"Who are you going skiing with?"

"Jeb Wills. One of the American correspondents."

"Are there good slopes here?"

She shook her head. "There is no real skiing near Moscow, so we go out to one of the small jumps."

"I should think jumping is rather dangerous for a woman."

"Not if you are a reasonably good skiier."

He laughed. "And you are good, I can see that. I can see it by the way you wear those fascinating trousers. Surely they are not Russian?"

"Austrian," she said.

"The trouble with ski-trousers is that they are so unpretentiously masculine and urbane," Essex said. "Don't you think?"

"It depends," she said.

"On what?" he asked.

"On the sort of figure you have. Do I look particularly masculine?"

He pulled his right ear. "Not exactly, Katherine."

She waited then while he read the cable. It was not the permission to present the Note. It was an involved cable from the Foreign Office about MacGregor. It quoted a report in an American newspaper on Essex's mission to Russia, a report under Hamber's name. It also quoted one of Steele's dispatches. Both stories talked about Essex's mission and explained what Essex was doing in Moscow by quoting his assistant: Mr. I. A. MacGregor. This was followed by the Foreign Office comment to Essex that MacGregor's talk to the newspapers was completely unauthorized and quite dangerous at this stage of the mission. Perhaps it had not been wise to permit MacGregor to converse with the Press, in fact measures must be taken to prevent MacGregor's utterances resulting in a serious Russian objection.

"I have just remembered something," Essex said to Katherine, putting annoyance with MacGregor out of his mind for a moment. "Was it you or your sister who made some mad attempt to climb the Matterhorn ten or eleven years ago?"

"It was both of us," Katherine said.

"I recall reading about it," he said. "I must have been in Italy at the time arguing about Albania or something. When I read that Sandy Clive's daughter was involved in it I wasn't surprised, knowing Sandy. Were there just the two of you?"

"And a Swiss girl," Katherine said.

"I thought only an Englishwoman would be mad enough to do such a thing."

"There was nothing mad about it," Katherine told him. "Sooner or later a woman will climb it. It is not really difficult — it's a matter of timing and equipment, and following Whymper's original route. We might have reached the top if the Embassy hadn't interfered and had us stopped. With one attempt we got more than half-way."

"How old were you?"

"Eighteen," she said and added casually: "If I ever get back there I shall try it again."

"You should be saner and wiser by now." Essex rubbed his broken nose. "It surely is a waste of human effort to climb a mountain for no other reason than its physical challenge. There doesn't seem to be anything inspiring about the peak, in fact as I remember it Whymper himself described it as a lump of sugar on the end of a table, a dull thing."

"Nobody climbs it for its beauty," she said to him.

"Then what the devil do you climb it for?"

She stretched because of the warm fire, and her long arms bent outward as she yawned and stood on tiptoe for a moment. "For the physical satisfaction it gives you," she said with her eyes almost closed as she looked at him. She smiled a little and pulled down the sleeves of her jumper and left.

She did not go to her own room. She went over to Melby's apartment and opened the front door and walked in, calling for the housekeeper, Fenya. The old woman came and saw Katherine and smiled happily and started talking in warm Russian to this wonderful daughter who was so healthy and so lovely. Katherine understood very little of it but she liked to hear it and she guessed its meaning. She put her arm through the old lady's and said: "Fenya. Which is Mr. MacGregor's room?"

Fenya did not understand any English, yet she understood Katherine Clive at any time. They went through the main dining room and Fenya smiled and knocked on MacGregor's door.

"Who is it?" MacGregor asked.

"It's me," Katherine said.

He opened the door and she walked in.

"Are you just getting up?" she said.

"No," MacGregor said in surprise. He was in his shirt-sleeves. "I was just getting dressed.

He left the door open and Katherine closed it.

"You will forgive me calling on you unexpectedly," she said, "but you might as well get used to our Moscow informality." She looked around. This was a room in which everything had a place, and though the brass bed was yet unmade there was nothing dishevelled about it. MacGregor's suitcase was in a corner, his clothes were properly hung, a bathrobe and a towel were hanging neatly over the end of the bed, a pair of shoes were before the electric radiator. Some pinned foolscap sheets were on a chair, and a few books were stacked on the mantelpiece. Beyond that it was practically bare, and Katherine had a quick recollection of Essex's room: a room filled with odds and ends. On Essex's mantelpiece there were two pictures and a small Italian clock with a porcelain figure on it. There were also pipes in an ivory rack and a tobacco jar worked in some kind of filigree. On Essex's dressing-table Katherine had noticed a litter of articles: a set of ivory and silver hairbrushes, two rows of miniature medals, a nail set, four quills, some embossed paper, two small Dresden figures, and one or two unmounted cameos. MacGregor's dressing-table was bare—there wasn't even a hairbrush on it. The only litter in the room was the stack of paper-back books on the mantelpiece. Katherine picked up one of the books. It was in Russian and she did not bother to look inside it.

"What are they about?" she said of the books.

"Iran," he said.

He had been leaning restlessly against the bed. He wore no tie and no coat, and his thin hair was unbrushed although he flattened it with hands as he sat down. He put on his shoes and Katherine watched him, knowing that he had other things on his mind beside herself. Katherine looked at the pinned foolscap on the chair and knew that MacGregor had been reading his morning cables. She had read them herself. Much of the material concerned police action by Teheran to prevent the spread of the Azerbaijan revolt to other provinces, and she assumed that this was disturbing MacGregor in some way.

"I suppose you call Iran a police state," she said to him.

"More or less." He looked up to see why she had said that.

"I was reading your cables this morning," she explained.

"Oh!"

"Another one came a little while ago for Essex, and I took it to him myself. I thought it wouldn't be a bad idea if I came over and told you about it. It was actually about you, and in a way I share responsibility for it."

He waited, looking at her.

"It seems that Hamber and Steele have written up your conversation the other night as official comment on Essex's mission. The Foreign Office has just cabled Essex telling him politely that it was indiscreet, to say the least. I thought you would like to know."

"What did those two quote me for?" he said in astonishment.

"You are with Essex aren't you?"

"Yes, but that conversation was informal and they knew it."

"Of course they did," she said, "but I should have warned you that nothing is sacred to either of them, so I feel responsible in a way. I don't know what Essex will do about it but —"

"He just telephoned and asked me to go over there."

"I thought he would. That's why I came over to warn you."

"That's very kind of you." MacGregor ran his hand through his tousled hair. "I must say I'm amazed at those fellows doing a thing like that."

"Never be amazed by anything a newspaperman does," she said to him and went right on. "Why do you put oil on your hair? It looks better loose like that."

He didn't hear her. He was thinking that Hamber and Steele had taken a lot on themselves. They must be fools to quote him as official or informative or anything else, and apart from that it seemed to be a miserable trick and he was suddenly angry.

"It's a pretty poor thing for those fellows to do," he said.

"That's their job," she said philosophically.

He remembered something. "I was talking about Iran just before I left them. Is that why you led me away from them?"

"I have forgotten," she said. "I suppose so."

"Perhaps I should thank you," he said with bare cynicism.

"Oh don't let it worry you," she was smiling at him. "You just have to take those Americans as you find them. Let it go at that and dismiss the whole thing."

"I haven't much choice," he said.

Katherine pushed back her chair because she was too near the radiator. She expected him to look at her but he stared ahead.

"Are you really thinking of going back to London?" she asked him.

"Who told you that?"

"Pooh!" Katherine said. "Everybody knows everything about everybody else here."

"I suppose it was Asquith."

"Yes, it was John," she said. "Do you really want to leave?"

"Yes: if it were possible." He put on his tie.

"Why?" she said.

"This isn't my job," he said. "It's foolish of me to be here."

"You have picked a devil of a time to get fed up," she said. "If you think anything of your native Iran, MacGregor, you are in a good position to do something about it. Why give up now?"

"There is nothing I can do," he told her.

"You can't really believe that," she said. "You are a clever man aren't you—you must be with hair like that. It's very easy and ordinary to get disgusted with a job like this because you happen to disagree with its purpose."

"I like to understand what I am doing," he argued. "There is no understanding of this diplomatic business at all. It has no laws and it has no regulation, and its approach to a problem like Iran is one of set opinion. Facts don't matter."

"You sound contemptuous," she said.

"I probably am."

"Any kind of diplomatic activity is really world-juggling," she said, "but important decisions are also made, MacGregor. Some of them aren't bad decisions."

"I want no part of it," he said.

"Why not?" she said. "Don't judge diplomacy by some of the people

118

you are beginning to dislike. There are bad diplomats just as there are bad scientists."

"Bad scientists don't get very far," he said.

"You may disagree with me, but neither do bad diplomats."

"I do disagree."

"I don't mean that all important diplomats are good." She stood up and smoothed down her long legs in unmasculine gestures. "There are some very bad diplomats, but within the rules of the game most of them are sensible and intelligent and honest men, whatever chicanery they practice."

He shook his head. "I would sooner be out of it," he said.

"You are too anxious to make grim decisions," she said. "Just let things happen to you for a change. It's a marvellous experience and you will enjoy it and see your job a little differently after a while. Just let your decisions wait."

He put on his coat. "I have let them wait too long."

"No you haven't," she said, "and a few more weeks will not matter to you. Just stay here and watch things happening, and if you don't like what is being done then tell Essex so. He won't mind it."

"There is no chance of my leaving," he told her. And as she went off to her skiing, he went up to see Essex.

Essex thought that everybody appeared unnecessarily young this morning. MacGregor's pale skin was frosty-looking, and it made Essex feel too comfortable in his velveteen jacket and slippers. It was an old man's attire, and he walked over to his bed and changed, allowing MacGregor to sit quietly and wait for him. He dressed in worsteds and in a striped shirt, and he brushed his hair and lit his pipe and sat down and folded his arms.

"For such a quiet fellow, MacGregor," he said, "you get into a lot of trouble." Essex was unashamedly inspecting MacGregor as if he had never seen him before.

"What have I done now?" MacGregor was not a good deceiver.

Essex had the cable. "You told the American correspondents that my first task was to get the Russians out of Azerbaijan. They report that we hadn't seen Stalin but that we had seen Suchkov and Korin. Did you tell them the details like that?"

"I suppose I did — without thinking about it," MacGregor said. "But the comments about getting the Russians out of Azerbaijan have been put into my mouth."

"It's their job to put words in your mouth," Essex said sharply.

"It was also a private conversation and they knew it."

"There is no such thing as a private conversation with those fellows, MacGregor, and you should know it. You are an official, and you express

119

no opinion but official opinion every time you open your mouth about your work. They have a lot of other stuff from what they call 'usually reliable sources' — I suppose that is you also."

"I suppose it is," MacGregor said.

"Don't you realize that this can jeopardize our whole mission here?"

"Nothing that I said could do that," MacGregor argued.

"Perhaps not," Essex said, "but that Hamber feller's bald use of your information is enough to finish this mission right off, because the Russians will read it and they will send us packing."

"Well, what on earth did he write?" MacGregor was empty and puzzled and he held out his hand for the cable, but Essex was annoyed enough to read it aloud.

"After a severe shaking in a Russian plane crash," Essex read, "Britain's top negotiator, Lord Essex, arrived here several days ago to talk with the Kremlin about Russian activities in Azerbaijan, the recently revolted province in northern Iran. It is believed that Lord Essex has direct instructions from Premier Attlee to go the limit in his demands for an explanation of Russian support to the Leftist Democratic Party which staged the autonomy revolt. Mr. I. A. MacGregor, Lord Essex's assistant, indicated to this correspondent to-day that Essex's first task would be to get the Russians out of Azerbaijan. This clearly indicates that Britain has new information at her disposal with which she can force a showdown on the whole issue. Usually reliable sources support this contention and say that Lord Essex's presence here indicates the gravity which the British Government feels about the Azerbaijan situation. I have also been informed that Lord Essex has already had conversations with Alexander Suchkov and Vladimir Korin of Mr. Molotov's own office but that these were mere preliminaries to more important talks with Molotov. Talks will take place in the Kremlin and it is understood that Stalin himself will take part in the negotiations."

"That is a whole concoction," MacGregor said angrily.

"You gave him the thread to concoct it with," Essex said.

"But surely it is easily denied."

"Denying it would worsen it. We don't want this mission to become the centre of a newspaper controversy. The Press is dangerous, and you must always look on it as dangerous. It is useful only when you need it, MacGregor, but otherwise it is red-hot fire. Your statement has given Molotov a weapon."

"He must have understood why we were here anyway," MacGregor said.

"Understanding is one thing but written evidence is another. Diplomacy is a matter of never allowing the other fellow to get any kind of trick on you. He can know what you are doing but so long as he hasn't got anything to prove it at a council table then he can never accuse you nor discredit you with your own intentions. The issue is legal, Mac-Gregor, and on a legal issue we have the Russians in a corner. We can accuse them of having broken the 1942 Treaty, which specifies that there must be no interference in Iran's affairs. Now along you come and say that our clear purpose is to get the Russians out — obviously in our own interests. Our own interests are not a legal argument, couldn't you see that?"

"No," MacGregor said. "The legalities seem to be a sham anyway," he said with unexpected discovery. "The Russians must know why we are here and we ourselves know, so why deceive ourselves with legalities?"

"It's no deception," Essex said impatiently. "Legality is the operative law of diplomacy. Without it there is no diplomacy. Our honour in international affairs has always been high because we have always obeyed and respected the utmost letter of legality. We never step outside legality, MacGregor, you will find that in all our history. We are here legally to call the Russians to terms for violating the 1942 Treaty. We are here legally to defend Iranian sovereignty."

"Isn't that camouflaging our real reason for being here?"

"That is what the Russians will say, now that you have told them so. There is nothing much we can do about this incident, but now that the Press has become involved we might as well use it. I think I will have some of those newspapermen down here this afternoon. I want to put them straight, and I may need your help. It must be pointed out to them that our rôle is tied up with the very existence of Iran. I can put them right, but a few words of your expert knowledge would assist."

"What sort of expert knowledge?" MacGregor said suspiciously.

"They must see that we have made a thorough study of conditions in Iran. They are the very devil when they start asking questions, and they are always inclined to know more than you do yourself."

"I can appreciate that," MacGregor said.

Essex laughed. "You look a little morose, my boy," he said. "You don't have to take that newspaper incident too seriously you know." Essex's whole manner had changed and he had closed the incident as he would close a book; he expected MacGregor to do the same thing and to appreciate his good-fellowship.

"I am not taking it too seriously," MacGregor said, "but it should convince you that I am no good at this work."

"Are you trying to run away again, MacGregor? It's too late to change your mind. If you disagree with me about Iran, go ahead and disagree, just so long as it doesn't interfere with the mission. You are not trying to justify the Russians are you?"

"Not at all," MacGregor began.

121

"Then you have nothing to worry about. Now: those newspapermen," Essex said and finished the diversion.

MacGregor wondered if he was being told to get hold of them.

"It's a pity that Katherine Clive has gone skiing," Essex said thoughtfully. "These things need a little stage-setting, and I gather that Katherine knows all the newspapermen in Moscow. She could probably arrange this nicely."

"She will be back at two o'clock." MacGregor surprised Essex by knowing about her.

"Then we might as well wait for her." Essex shifted the two small oil portraits from the mantelpiece to his desk, propping them against a heavy candlestick and blowing soot from their gilt frames. "Have you got anything to do this morning, MacGregor?"

"I was going to write a summary for Sir Rowland Smith on the reports in the Russian papers about Iran. He wanted to know what the Russians were saying."

Essex looked at the empty tennis court. "I should like to see that summary myself, MacGregor," he said. "But before you do it you might write out a short explanation of how you spoke to Hamber. I shall send it on to London with my own comments, and that should end the incident. I doubt if there will be official repercussion if we explain it properly."

MacGregor did not care whether there were repercussions or not. He had a very annoying conscience; but this was the sin of Hamber and Steele and he would not feel guilty about it. "Will you have Hamber and Steele down here with the others?" MacGregor asked.

"Of course."

"Would you mind if I asked them about these stories?"

"Go ahead," Essex said largely. He laughed at MacGregor and sent him away and forgot about him.

Essex left word for Katherine to see him when she returned, and when she came he told her about having the newspapermen down to see him. "I want them this evening if possible, Katherine, and I thought I would ask your help, if it doesn't cut across any of your proper functions here. You seem to be familiar with these men," he went on, "and no doubt you know where they all are. I want them down here for a drink and an informal talk, a very informal talk. How many English and American correspondents are here?"

"Not very many these days, ten or twenty," she told him. "It's very simple to get them. It's just a matter of calling the secretary of their Association. He finds them all, and tells them where and when to come."

"I particularly want those two Americans, Hamburger and Steele."

"You mean Hamber."

"That's right. Could I leave it all to you? If you want Miss Williams to do anything you can take her. I would like the right men and the proper setting."

"You sound as if you are plotting something."

Essex walked with her to the door. "I am just making up for Mac-Gregor's unfortunate meeting with those clever men," he told her.

Essex knew his rôle. They had all arrived by the time he went down-stairs — deliberately late. Drake, Melby, and MacGregor were also there. Drake's attendance was a courtesy, but Essex would have preferred Katherine Clive. She had refused to come, but she had done her job well. The newspapermen were clustered by the fire, the windows, and the drinks table, where four bottles of Scotch whisky were quickly disappearing. When Essex walked in they turned to look at him. Essex had prepared himself for that look. He wore light brown gabardine trousers and a sky blue jumper which was thick and collegiate, as the Americans say. The sleeves were turned back at the cuff and the waistline was long and well fitting. He wore no tie and his white silk shirt lay neatly open. He looked a young man of forty as he strode through the newspapermen to shake hands with the surprised Drake in his striped pants and black coat and butterfly collar. Essex knew delightedly that he could sur-prise Drake every time.

To MacGregor he was very pleasant. "What do you think of this weird collection, MacGregor?" he said quietly. "Have you had a chance to talk to any of them?"

"Not yet," MacGregor told him.

"I don't want to miss your conversation with Hamber," Essex chuckled.

Essex was then taken among the newspapermen by Melby, who knew them all. When Essex came to Hamber and Steele he greeted them by their first names and asked them about Paris and Rome and Bucharest and Prague.

"You look as if you're at a football game," Hamber said about his attire.

"Isn't a convention with the Press something of a football match, old man?" The phrase "old man" was never used by Essex with anybody but Americans. They expected it, and Essex enjoyed burlesquing it for them.

Essex passed on and listened to the names as Melby told him about these men. He remembered their names and their faces because that came as second diplomatic nature to him. It was better to remember a man's name than remember anything else about him, and so these men were easily registered at a glance. He could investigate them better later on.

He was surprised to see three women among them. They had arrived a little late and he saw them standing at the door together. One was tall and dark, and she looked at Essex with immediate and undisguised contempt. She was obviously English and quite attractive, unlike Essex's memory of other newspaperwomen. A smaller woman, blonde and very young, stood near her and she regarded Essex with interest bordering on invitation. The third was entirely different. She was older and obviously American. She was stylishly dressed and slim and wore a hat with flowers on it. She presented a rich and well-groomed American appearance, particularly her face which had been well kept with creams and lotions and beauty parlours and good living so that she looked old and young at the same time. She had sharp features and a chin-lifting sort of independence, and she shook hands firmly with Essex. He greeted them all formally, and treated them no differently than the men. He was telling them in fact that he did not like women newspapermen.

When he had met them all he stood near the fire with a long drink of whisky in his hand, inspecting them before he began. He had seen plenty of these men in his day, and yet they never ceased to interest him. No two groups looked the same at first glance, but after a little observation they all became the same. This particular collection were men in their unpressed best suits. There were English and Australians and Canadians and a New Zealander. More than half of them were Americans who were easily distinguishable as such. These Americans were mostly tall confident young men, men he liked to see: clear faces and good teeth and plenty of hair. They were an obvious contrast to their English colleagues who were a short-middling-and-long collection of nondescripts, including the Australians. These British were poorly dressed too, and their attitude was milder — too mild for Essex. One of them was a little better than the others, the blond and handsome Holmes, but he was too Bloomsbury with his khaki shirt and green tie. A quieter middle-aged Englishman named Allison looked the most impressive of them because he had a composed and diplomatic sort of face, but Essex knew that it might be a deception. The only other Englishman to attract his real attention was a man named Low. He was the kind of Englishman one sees in hundreds going home every night in suburban trains to Acton and Ealing. He was Essex's concession to the existence of the people. The word had been forced on him during the blitz, particularly in reading about it in the Washington newspapers. This was the sort of man who had won the war; one of the great lower middle classes. Essex could easily picture Low with a pair of gum boots on his feet and a tin hat on his head calmly attending bombs with the local ARP. Essex supposed he must thank God for this Low and the other Lows. He had to thank God for somebody among the people and anything beneath the Lows was not quite in scope for heavenly blessing.

For all their divergence, however, all these men looked and behaved like newspapermen. The only deviation from some recognizable pattern was an American named Gaspar Ford. He was over fifty and he sat in a chair drinking strong whiskies in quick gulps and talking in a very loud voice. He was grey-haired and florid and looked more like a successful American salesman than a newspaperman. He reminded Essex of the men who had flocked to Washington during the war looking and lobbying for contracts. Ford was a little out of place here.

As Essex looked around, Hamber and Steele stood each side of him as old and favoured friends, telling him about Greece which they had recently visited. Hamber was supporting the British attitude in Greece entirely. He told Essex that any concession to the EAM would mean a Communist Greece, and that would mean a solid bloc of Communists in the Balkans. British policy must prevent it. Steele said that he didn't like some of the Greeks the British were dealing with, but he could see the necessity for using them to stop the Communistic EAM. He told Essex how the EAM were defacing the lovely Greek villages with huge slogans painted on every wall in red paint. Had Essex read Bill Blue's book on Russia, and read about the shortage of paint in Moscow? Well there it was. The paint had come from Moscow and everybody knew it. So had the EAM.

"Is it really so Communistic?" Essex said to them.

"You can take it from me it is," Steele said.

"Those EAM people did great work during the war you know," Essex told them.

"That was in their own interests," Steele said.

"They expect to clean up for it now," Hamber said.

"But what is the alternative?" Essex said provocatively. "Would you suggest a King for Greece?"

"I'm not suggesting it," Hamber said. "But if you British want to suggest it then I will agree that a monarchy would be better than the Communists."

"And you, Steele?"

"On principle I am opposed to a monarchy," Steele said, "but on principle I believe that a monarchy would be the best thing for Greece to-day. The Greek people are not quite ripe for a full-blooded republican democracy, and if the people want the King, then they should have him — on principle."

"The principle's the thing alright," Essex said seriously. "That is something of our problem in Iran. I suppose that is why I am here in Moscow."

The Americans waited expectantly for the follow-up on Iran. They knew that he hadn't mentioned Iran for nothing. They knew Essex too well.

"I am afraid we are fighting a losing battle on principles there," Essex went on, "but it is always a worth-while fight. We have a responsibility in Iran because of the 1942 Treaty guaranteeing Iranian independence, and we must see that this Treaty is respected. We are trying our hardest to see that our word is not violated by someone else."

"Have you got specific proof that the Russians have designs on all Iran?" Hamber said forcefully. "We know they have such designs, but have you got the proof?"

"That's hard to say." Essex smiled and put down his glass and felt for his pipe in his hip pocket. "I am not qualified to speak about the Russians."

They laughed.

"But I can assure you that *we* haven't designs on Iran. You could hardly accuse the British Government of precipitating this issue because we want northern Iran, for instance." It was so simple it was undeniable, and if these men hadn't written that before they would write it now as Essex intended.

Essex had waited long enough, and since the correct amount of drinking had been done, he inclined his head slightly at Melby and went on filling his pipe as Melby worked around to the fire-place, where Essex told him to go ahead.

Melby spoke a little above everybody. "You might like to sit down for a while," he said. "Lord Essex has asked you here because he thought you would like to hear something of his mission, and no doubt you have some questions you would like to ask him."

They sat down and Essex remained standing, smoking his pipe.

"Now Al," he said to Hamber. "Put that paper away. This is all off-the-record. I know you fellows hate that phrase, but it is unavoidable at this stage."

"Can't you tell us something to print, Harry?" Hamber complained.

"I don't want to give you anything more than background," Essex said. "This isn't an interview, nor is it a conference, Al. It's just a talk, because I know how tough it is for you fellows here, and we always like to help you out when we can. Isn't that so, Francis?" Essex turned to Drake.

"Quite!" Drake said with precise surprise.

Essex then set about describing the background of the Iranian problem and the British concern over the 1942 Treaty, until he was suddenly interrupted.

"I don't suppose oil has anything to do with it," a thin critical voice said.

"Neither the Russians nor ourselves have mentioned oil in relation to this matter," Essex said decisively. He kept his stern eyes upon the small sick-looking fellow who had mentioned oil so provocatively. This was the New Zealander named Henry George, and Essex considered it a minor act of disloyalty for a Briton to be so obviously cynical. "We have no oil concessions in Azerbaijan," Essex went on. "As far as we are concerned oil has no influence on this at all."

"Just what do you hope to achieve here, Lord Essex?" Holmes asked.

"That is a fair question." Essex leaned casually on the mantelpiece and gave the matter some thought. "I hope to achieve a peaceful settlement of the unequal situation in Iran," he said. "I hope to restore the legal authority of the Iranian Government over its northern provinces. Of course it is not as simple as all that. We have some very revealing information about the goings-on in Azerbaijan, and naturally the Russians know it. Therefore, they may be reluctant to talk to us at all, because it's not easy to argue against undeniable facts."

Mrs. Bell, the small young woman, had her inviting eyes upon him. "What sort of facts?" she asked.

"Now that is a feminine question." Essex needed this moment of humour. "That is just a little too inquisitive, my dear Mrs. Bell. Perhaps these facts are for Molotov's ears alone. For the moment anyway."

"Couldn't you release some of them later on?"

Essex knew that the small round Jewish fellow was an agency man. "You agency fellows are always wanting long statements of important facts," he said. "You will just have to realize that there are other organizations in the world now besides your news agencies. Organizations which can act on facts and not just repeat them."

"Does that mean that you will present these facts to the United Nations Organization in some way?" Henry George asked in his sick voice.

"I can't express higher policy than my mission, Mr. George."

"You implied it."

"Then I am sorry," Essex smiled carefully. "Don't look so worried, Mr. George. I can assure you that our relations with New Zealand will not be affected."

The others laughed as Essex had intended; but Henry George looked sour and unembarrassed and he whispered to his neighbour, a short grey-haired Welshman named Jack Tanner who represented the London *Daily Worker*.

Essex went on with his attack. "What about you, Mr. Tanner? Surely you must have something to ask me." Essex had read all of Tanner's dispatches since arriving in Moscow. The Foreign Office had assiduously sent them back as a reflection of Russian opinion, but Essex had found no opinion in them at all.

Tanner had a Welshman's lilt to his voice and he took Essex at his word. "In view of all that you have said about the situation in Iran, is the British Government thinking of demanding satisfaction by some kind of ultimatum to the Soviet Government?"

Essex knew his man and he replied instantly. "No. Our relations with

Soviet Russia are too good to think in terms of ultimatums, Mr. Tanner. That is why I have been sent here. We believe in talking this over with the Soviet Government. I am sure they appreciate our interest in Iranian independence."

"Don't you think they wonder about our interest in Greek and Indonesian independence?" Tanner asked, his blue eyes fixed upon Essex.

"My job is Iran, Mr. Tanner. I can see your point, however, and I agree that all is not well with affairs in Greece and Indonesia. Nobody regrets those unhappy situations more than I. But Iran is a joint responsibility, Mr. Tanner, and that is why we are taking it up with the Soviet Government."

"What is there to take up?" Tanner said and Essex was sorry that he had begun this. "Has the British Government any objections to the democratization of Azerbaijan?"

"Certainly not," Essex replied.

"Has the British Government studied the reforms of the Democratic Party there?"

"We have studied the whole problem. Mr. MacGregor was sent along with me because he knows Iran. He has lived most of his life there and speaks the languages."

"And the reforms?" Tanner said.

"Ask MacGregor," Essex said.

"Are we opposed to reforms in Iran, Mr. MacGregor?"

MacGregor knew that he was speaking officially now, but he only knew how to speak for himself. "No," he said.

"What sort of reform do we think Iran should have?" Tanner asked suspiciously.

"I don't know," MacGregor said, "but I suppose it would include the whole existence of the country: government, police, army, land, industry, education, sanitation. Everything needs reforming and reorganizing in Iran."

"Then what's the matter with the Azerbaijan reforms?"

MacGregor looked at Essex. "Nothing that I can think of," he said.

"So you are not trying to have them cancelled or stopped?" Tanner said.

MacGregor paused and then said, "You had better ask Lord Essex about that."

Essex had decided to take it up anyway because he couldn't trust MacGregor any further. "Certain aspects of the reforms in Azerbaijan are nominally acceptable as improvements," he said, "but the British Government must take exception to the methods used in implementing these reforms. Revolution and force are not legitimate methods of changing a situation."

"We recognize America and France and Russia," Tanner said.

128

"That is historical revolution. To-day revolution is not a legitimate act of history, and we must take exception to it. We encourage democracy in all nations in which we have responsibility, our record shows that. Unfortunately you cannot press these things too hard. People aren't ready for democracy."

"Is that why we are so anxious to prevent it in Iran and Greece?"

Essex ignored Henry George who had made this last comment, deciding that he had been patient enough. He was about to deal drastically with both Tanner and George but the famous Lisa Cort, the stylish American, saved him the necessity by addressing him in a confident voice. "Lord Essex!" she said.

Essex waited for her pronouncement, wondering what this prima donna was doing here. She was the wife of one of America's biggest publishers, David Aintree, as well as being one of the richest women in America in her own right. Aintree published a weekly fiction magazine that found its way into every American home and influenced the thinking of the entire nation, and this had become Lisa Cort's outlet for political expression. She had been a well-known writer before marrying Aintree and now she had taken to writing long editorials for him from all parts of the distant world, editorials which were renowned for their sense of responsibility to America and the American way of life.

Her voice was almost English. "I wanted to ask you whether you realized the danger of World Communism, Lord Essex, and whether you understood Russia's imperial policies in Iran, and therefore acted upon them and against them."

This was a politician's question and it should have been made in Congress as far as Essex was concerned. He treated it carefully. "As I said before, Mrs. Aintree, I can't claim to understand Russia's foreign policy." He refused to call the woman by her maiden name.

"This is not just her foreign policy," she said. "This is her world policy."

"Is there any difference?" Essex asked simply.

"If you are concerned with Iran you should think in terms of what Russia wants in the world and how she threatens to get it," Mrs. Aintree told him. "Your rôle is one of preventing a catastrophe, Lord Essex."

"I should be inclined to put it a little more modestly," Essex said.

"Can you say that the British Labour Government is giving you full support?"

"Certainly. They sent me here."

"Then it's safe to assume that the Labour Government is conscious of the danger of Russian imperialism and the threat of Communism in Europe and England?"

"I am sure the Labour Government has its own opinions about the Communists in England, Mrs. Aintree."

"We are getting away from the subject," said Allison, the diplomatic-looking Englishman. "Could Mr. MacGregor give us a fuller picture of the situation in Iran?"

"You have read enough to know what the situation is like in Iran," Essex said without giving MacGregor a chance. "All you have to remember is that the Russians have been propagandizing the Azerbaijanians since the occupation, and remember also that the Democratic Party of Azerbaijan is created in the likeness of its Bolshevik neighbours."

"Will you demand the dissolution of the Democratic Party and the Autonomous Government of Azerbaijan, Harry?" Hamber asked.

"We want the sovereignty of the Iranian Government restored in Azerbaijan," Essex said. "Such sovereignty can't exist while sections of the country are in the hands of revolutionists who declare themselves separate."

"Would you tell us how many shares the British Government has in the Anglo-Iranian oil fields in southern Iran?" Henry George said in sudden interruption.

"I can't say off hand," Essex said, "and I don't see what that has to do with the subject we are discussing at the moment."

"Can your expert answer it, Lord Essex?"

"MacGregor?" Essex turned around.

MacGregor knew that Essex wanted that question and subject evaded but MacGregor thought it appropriate enough to warrant an answer. "The British Government owns 52.55 per cent of Anglo-Iranian stocks," he said.

"And what did Anglo-Iranian profits show last year?" Henry George asked.

"I am not sure," MacGregor said, "but I think it was four million sterling, although I believe they expect nine million pounds profit this year."

"And that has nothing to do with the situation?" George said.

"No," Essex said.

"The British Government isn't even considering its oil possession? It isn't at all afraid that a political upheaval might take it all away?"

"Our oil is perfectly safe, Mr. George," Essex said calmly. "I am sure Russia has no designs upon our oil fields."

"I didn't say Russia."

"Oh, get off it, Henry!" Steele said.

"Ah! He is perfectly right in bringing this up," Essex said quickly an l cursed Steele for a fool. "One can hardly think of Iran without thinking of oil. I agree. But this is something bigger than oil. This is Iran itself, and the other small nations who are afraid of dismemberment. Mr. George is simply looking for Britain's self-interest in this affair. Well our self-interest is in seeing the small nations intact, because the small nations have always been our friends, and possibly our strength in Europe."

Essex did not stop there. He gave them a fuller version of British interest in seeing that Iran was not Bolshevized, raped, aggressed, undermined, and selfishly used by unscrupulous foreign powers. MacGregor squirmed through it, wondering how Essex could avoid turning his own remarks upon his own policies; deciding alternatively that Essex was a hypocrite and a liar and then a crazy fool and an ignorant man, but never really deciding which he was. Essex had a way of making a man undecided. Even listening to him became a compromise with his opinions. It gave MacGregor an uncontrollable feeling of being a hypocrite himself. When Essex had finished he turned to MacGregor and said, "Anything you would like to say, my boy?" MacGregor replied, "No. There is nothing." MacGregor felt that Essex had done this deliberately to attach him publicly and privately to all that had just been said. MacGregor warned himself then that he was in a cage with a tiger.

The formality of the gathering ended as Essex stepped away from the fire because he was beginning to perspire in his collegiate sweater. But it was not quite over. Essex was addressed by Gaspar Ford, the white-haired American salesman, who was now indefinite and soluble about the eyes.

"I didn't ask you any questions in there," he said loosely, "because I could see that you were giving it to them straight. Anyway I am really not one of these guys, and this is their day. I am here with Lisa Cort on a mission to get world freedom of editorial opinion, and these Russians are giving us the run-around. Why! These people don't know what a newspaper is. We saw Stalin alright and he gave plenty of assurances, but he talked a lotta baloney about the press understanding its responsibilities. What a thing to say to a guy like me. I've built up the biggest chain of papers in the Southwest and every one of them is paying its own way. There is nothing irresponsible about my business, and who are these people to talk about understanding their responsibilities anyway? Their responsibilities seem to be a matter of sticking their noses into other people's business. You never get an American doing that."

"Gas," Mrs. Lisa Cort Aintree said to him, "you are tight again."

Essex slipped away and spoke to Jack Tanner.

"I have read all your reports, Mr. Tanner," he said.

Tanner obviously didn't believe him, and his grey eyebrows twitched as he smiled slowly and shook his head to show Essex that he could enjoy the joke.

"It's a fact!" Essex said. "The Foreign Office sent them all back to me as a reflection of Russian policy." He made a joke of it and Tanner laughed, and Essex felt that he had captured Tanner. Essex clapped him on the shoulder and passed among the others. He went around them all, missing none and avoiding none, even Henry George who was talking with the tall Englishwoman.

"Mr. George," Essex said. "You are my idea of a good newspaperman. Always asking difficult and dangerous questions."

"That makes you a good diplomat then," Henry George said as if he hadn't a scrap of humour in him, "because you avoid answering them."

"Come. Come. Don't you think I was clear in my answers, Miss Tudor?"

Miss Tudor's open contempt caught his eye as she spoke. "I am sure I don't know," she said.

Essex noticed that her profile was better than her fore-face. He wondered why this obviously well-born Englishwoman, attractive and undoubtedly intelligent, should be so contemptuous of him. It was one of the few occasions on which Essex recognized and acknowledged contempt, and he was uneasy about it. He was pleasant with her and talkative even, but she remained neutral.

"You don't look at all like a newspaperwoman," Essex said to her finally.

She did not answer it and Essex left her gladly.

He was physically and mentally tired by the time they started to leave, and he was glad when the last of them (Gaspar Ford and Mrs. Lisa Cort Aintree) had closed the door in his polite face. He looked around for MacGregor, but only Melby was there. He thanked Melby for the help, and went upstairs to his room to take off the confounded jumper and pants and change into a good grey suit. Then he phoned Katherine Clive to tell her that it had gone well.

MacGregor was talking with Hamber and Steele. He had brought them to his office and he was showing them a duplicate copy of Essex's cable. They leaned against Essex's big desk and read it with interest because it quoted their stories. MacGregor had already torn off the Foreign Office comment.

"I thought you might like to see it," MacGregor said when they had finished.

"Thanks," Hamber said. "I'm glad it got through."

"I wanted to ask you about it," MacGregor went on. "We were having a private conversation the other night and I thought you would know that. Even so, it isn't at all what I said to you."

Hamber looked surprised. "That is a fair report, MacGregor, not only of what you said, but of what you meant. As for its privacy: I am a newspaperman, and it is my job to tell the readers of my newspapers what is going on. I gave you a good break, MacGregor, and everything that I wrote is correct."

MacGregor felt a nice cool anger take hold of him but he restrained himself. "There is nothing very correct about it. I did not at any time say to you that Essex's first task here was to get the Russians out of Iran."

"You implied it," Steele said.

"No, I didn't; and if I did you had no right to use it anyway."

"Look, MacGregor," Hamber said. "It's a newspaperman's job to reveal all the facts of events, whether they are obtained by statement or implication. I have simply revealed the facts of the situation. Anyway, it was a favourable story so what are you griping about?"

"It's not a favourable story at all," MacGregor said less calmly. "I don't believe that we are here simply to get the Russians out of Iran. If I did believe it I wouldn't be here at all."

"Let me tell you this, MacGregor." Hamber had been holding his coat and he put it on now with Steele's help. "You are complaining out of turn. Nobody objects to the British getting the Russians out of Iran. In fact if you British don't get rid of them, then we Americans will have to do it for you. You shouldn't complain about that story and you shouldn't deny your attitude."

"It is not my attitude."

Hamber ignored it. "Furthermore," he said, "it's the best line to take in America and I know it. Anyway, how do you think our stories got to America?"

"I don't know and it's not important."

"Yes it is important. Those stories were sent to London in your own British diplomatic bag, MacGregor. That is one of Melby's Samaritan services to the correspondents. He gets it to London and it is cabled from there. So I don't see that any part of your complaint is valid. If you British want your case put properly in America then you will have to let Americans do it, because we know how it can be done. If it seems imprudent to you, wait until the showdown with Russia really comes and then you will see that it wasn't so crazy. We will have won over American opinion for you, and the U. S. State Department will be able to back you up completely."

"On principle," Jackson Steele said then, "nothing can stand in our way, MacGregor. Don't you see that it is the people who will finally settle these issues and that the people must be informed? America is a democracy, and the first strength of a democracy is a free Press, and a free Press means an informed Press; and we can't hold back information which is necessary to the better understanding of a situation. You are making this a question of ethics; we are making this a question of principle. At least I do. It would be wrong of us to hold back information which the American people should have, no matter how we got it."

Since there was no use discussing something so confused, MacGregor waited with disinterested silence while Steele delivered a further argument. Then, considering MacGregor's adamant silence as impossible stubbornness, they left him with a few pointed remarks about his peculiar attitude to this situation; an attitude which did not seem to tally at all with Essex's; an attitude which they considered contradictory and confused and therefore responsible for any misstatements they may have made.

MacGregor admitted that they might be right and he was still looking out the window and watching them disappear from the Embassy lights when Katherine came. She stood by him until he noticed her and replied to her amused greeting.

"Did you accuse them of misrepresentation?" she said lightly.

He nodded.

"What did they say?"

"That it was my own fault."

She laughed at him. "Well, wasn't it?"

MacGregor did not feel like laughing. "No. I don't think so."

"Perhaps it was my fault for not warning you," she said.

MacGregor could have agreed with her but he didn't.

"How was the conference?" She was quiet and enticing.

"Alright."

"Did they ask you expert questions?"

"There were a couple of questions about the reforms and about oil."

"What reforms?"

"The Azerbaijanian reforms," he said.

"Ah! We object to them I suppose?"

"That was the question."

"What did you say?"

"Nothing. Essex told them we objected to the methods used in effecting the reforms."

"Wasn't there a revolt or a revolution?"

"Yes, but the Russians probably had a hand in it; and the reforms may be their idea entirely. I don't know."

"So you don't agree with the reforms?"

"I wouldn't say that," he told her cautiously. "I'm just not sure about them."

"What did they want to know about oil?" she went on with persuasive confidence.

"One of them suggested that our only interest in the welfare of Iran was in our oil concessions."

"There must be some truth in that," she said. "Isn't there?"

"Yes. But it needn't be our only interest in Iran."

"It needn't be, but *is* oil our only interest in Iran?"

"I would like to know that myself," he said.

"You have certainly been looking puzzled about something," she said. "I am puzzled myself. What is Essex really trying to do: just get rid of the Russians, or get a better hold on Iran, or simply hold on to what we have already?"

"Something of each," he said.

"Is that British policy in Iran now?"

"It looks like it," he said.

"And you don't like the idea of Essex perpetuating it?"

That was where MacGregor stopped. She had found his irritation. He wanted to talk with someone just to clear it all up in his own mind, but he mistrusted his own motives in talking with Katherine Clive. He always found himself with a loose tongue when he was with her because she made any conversation seem reasonable and natural, and half cynical, and alright. But he suspected her. Since her friendship with Essex he had been thinking that she was on the other side. He did not even know what the other side meant, except that it was Essex in some way; either Essex personally, or Essex on Iran, or Essex on this mission. He was on edge after listening to Essex this afternoon and he felt taken in by her sly pleasantry.

"Were you looking for Essex?" he asked her.

"No," she said and left it provokingly unfinished.

He watched the red stars on the Kremlin light up, a sight he had come to anticipate. He supposed that she had already been to Essex. He watched her put her arms behind her back. She was apparently in no hurry, and his silence didn't worry her. "Have you finished for the day?" he asked her.

"Not yet," she said and sighed. "I think I have been in Moscow too long. I spend half my time wandering aimlessly about the Embassy from one room to another with little excuse, and I don't seem to do much work. I can't sit in that room of mine all day: it's beginning to bore me." She was not worked up about it, in fact she was expressionless as if the whole thing weren't important.

"I thought that you had finished work this morning," he said.

"I had," she said, "but Clark-Kerr sent Michael Curtis back from the Balkans and everything he wants is suddenly urgent. He might as well have gone straight on to London and got it all there."

"What does he want?"

"Information on a few Bulgars, and some of our complicated intelligence reports on Hungary. They are really wasting their time."

"Are they?" he said politely, not wishing to probe.

"Of course they are," she said. "They are supposed to be broadening the Balkan Governments to include some of the politicians that we like, but

I can't see the Russians or the people who have taken over those countries suddenly deciding to give it all back to the wretches who were in power before. They would be fools if they did."

"It seems to be the same in every country," he said.

"You should work in this Embassy a little while to find out how true that is. Although the new lot seem to be as bad as the old in some cases," she said sourly, "so it's a devil's choice. It's like your Iran. The reformists have the Balkans too, but who are they? One never really knows whether the reforms come from the population or the Russians. I don't suppose it matters really, just so long as something is changed. Do you care if your Azerbaijan reforms come from the Russians?"

He had asked himself the same question and never found an answer. He had half an answer in that he didn't want anyone in Iran, and he had another piece of it in believing that the Azerbaijanians could probably make their own reforms, but in real substance he had no answer. "It would be better," he said to her, "if nothing in Iran came from any foreign influence."

"So long as there is oil in Iran," she said, "there will always be foreign influence, so you might as well pick the best of it."

He thought she might be right, but he did not like it and he did not comment.

"I came to see you to ask about Professor Onegin," she said then.

"Did you find him?"

"Are you sure he is a professor?" she said.

"Yes. I am fairly sure."

"I was talking with the Moscow University and the only Professor Onegin they know is a pathologist from Kiev. He has nothing to do with geology. Do you know his university?"

MacGregor shook his head.

"Pity," she said. "I don't think you will find him. Couldn't you write a further argument and send it to one of the Russian geological journals?"

"I could," he said, "but I haven't assembled enough new evidence to make anything of it."

"Then what could you do if you saw him?"

"I don't know, but I could argue with him to begin with. He had only seen the brief version of my paper when he wrote his. I sent him a fuller version but he didn't acknowledge it. If I could see him I think I could convince him that he was wrong."

"Are you sure you aren't wrong?" She was trying to provoke him again.

"I could be wrong," he said, "but I don't think I am."

"Then I'll find him for you," she said as she left, "just to find out if you are really so good. I suppose you are," she said and left him wondering why she hadn't laughed aloud at him.

Chapter 8

Some fool in London is holding us up," Essex told Mac-
Gregor, "and if we don't get an all-clear to-day to present that Note then
we might as well pack up and go home. It is Friday," Essex said, "and the
week-end is always difficult for getting anything out of London. Monday
will be too late. I suppose they are having a Cabinet Meeting about
it."

MacGregor was catching some of Essex's impatience by simply watching
him walk up and down the room.

Essex said, "I think it's this damned Embassy, MacGregor. Too isolated,
too introverted. Come on, and we will go out and get at Moscow. I feel
like submitting myself to some of this peasant culture. We shall go out
and travel on their underground or their Metro or whatever they call it.
It may revive us both."

They walked to the Metro at Ploshod Revolutzi and they went down
the crowded escalators and were crushed by the people plunging through
the narrow bomb doors on the station level. They missed the first train
and Essex walked up and down the station inspecting the bronze statues
set in the red marble columns, telling MacGregor that it was nice marble
but poor statuary. They were obvious foreigners and they attracted the attention of the crowds boarding and leaving the trains, but Essex went carelessly among them, swinging the black ebony stick he had taken from the
Embassy hall. When they did mount a train they were caught with fifty
others at one door, and it was a mad scramble in the swaying block of
people to get through the train doors before they closed. They were
stared at, and they were crushed each time the train stopped at a station,
but they rode the full length of the line to Arbat, and then they came
back and walked through long marble tunnels to the Khimki line. When
one of the marble stations particularly attracted Essex they sprang out
of the train at the last minute and inspected it and caught the next train.
They were busy at this for almost two hours and then Essex decided he
had seen enough.

"I feel better," he said when they were back on the street. "Odd to see
an underground of marble. It is baroque and a little naïve, but it is a
magnificent effort, don't you think, MacGregor?"

"They should put the effort into building more houses," MacGregor
said, "or to improve some of the buildings that are falling to pieces."

"Buildings are just buildings," Essex said, "and I don't suppose they can
build palaces for everybody. Let them have their palaces underground —
even if it is for a few minutes every day. It must be stimulating for them
to come out of their drab homes and spend a few minutes every now and

then in that marbled wonder. It seems very clever and not at all a waste of effort."

MacGregor did not argue.

"Let's get back and see if anything has come in," Essex said. He had wanted to feel that at least MacGregor understood his annoying situation in having no word from London, but MacGregor remained uninfluenced and as cautious as ever, even a little more silent. It was a disappointment to Essex, who settled it by outwalking the Scot as they went back to the Embassy. Drake met them with the information that London had replied.

In Drake's room Essex read the cable and slapped his leg. It was almost a *carte blanche*. In fact it was better than he had hoped for. It gave him a clear hand to do anything: write the Note and follow it up and take any other steps he thought necessary. There was one proviso. Drake should present the Note.

"Well Francis," Essex told him. "The Note is ready and the sooner we get it to them the better. When will they see us?"

"It depends on too many factors. You can never tell with these people."

"I know one thing," Essex said. "This Note will stir them up. We shall have a chance to get at them now." Essex took MacGregor with him and they went to their own room and put all the papers they needed into Essex's embossed portfolio. The portfolio was a delicate thing with a golden crest on it, and Essex watched MacGregor as he handled it carefully. "That's my lucky pouch, MacGregor. It's a fifteenth-century courier pouch worked by Ghiberti for Cosimo de Medici." Essex touched the design in its corner. "Ghiberti usually worked in bronze but this is one of the first examples of tooled leather. Beautiful isn't it? It was given to me by the King of Italy for refusing to treat with Mussolini until he had recognized the monarchy. You will be coming to Molotov with us," Essex added.

MacGregor was curious. "Why is Sir Francis presenting the Note?" he asked.

"Putting it on an ambassadorial level is a subtle hint to the Russians that this involves our whole relationship. He is the man to do it, don't worry."

MacGregor was not worried.

"In this situation it is better that he do it," Essex went on.

MacGregor didn't need convincing, but apparently Essex wanted to convince himself that Drake was the proper man.

"Don't be so hard on Drake with that silent opinion of yours, MacGregor," Essex said. "He is an interesting fellow when you get to know him. Did you know that it was Francis Drake more than anybody who made Foreign Office policy on Spain during the Civil War?"

"No, I didn't know."

"Yes," Essex said reminiscently. "It was he who influenced the Foreign Office to an understanding of Spain and Franco. Of course it wasn't that he liked Franco so much. No. It's more than that. He knows that Franco must bring back the Bourbons. Francis believes that England must have a strong single force controlling south and southwestern Europe and he therefore leans towards kings and the Church. He is Catholic himself, you know, and that is why he is a little frustrated here. He can't do much with his Catholicism. He needs to be in Catholic Europe to make the best of his diplomatic hopes for a great Catholic bloc friendly to Britain." Essex suddenly turned to MacGregor and said: "You know—you are not interested enough in people, MacGregor. You should have asked me about Francis Drake. I'll never object to telling you about other men if it will help you to understand them. Now with Francis it is just a matter of understanding his Catholicism. It's not only a religious and a diplomatic attitude with him, he is æsthetically Catholic in all things. I think Francis just missed going into the Church, and he has never forgiven himself for it. He was one of Balliol's best papal scholars in his day, and he made several very important discoveries in pre-Norman church documents or something like that. Oddly enough, though, Francis didn't marry a Catholic. Married a County girl—Claude Pintot's daughter—a frail and silent woman. They have a daughter named Antonia, about your age MacGregor. A devil. Everything the gods forgot in her parents they gave to Antonia. She is a ruffian and a heathen and a wonderful wild girl who probably lives immorally and sinfully, but who enjoys life none the less. If Francis had brought her to Moscow this whole city would have been a different place for him, full of fires and hells and scandals. As it is, he finds it nicely safe and quiet, but he doesn't like it anyway." Essex thought for a moment. "He will like presenting this Note. It is one of the few acts of diplomacy which is complete and satisfying in itself. At least it will give us something tangible to use on the Russians. Come on, and we will go up to Francis and run through the documents with him. Do you think you have a little more confidence and consideration for him now, MacGregor?" Essex asked with mild irony.

MacGregor smiled, not quite knowing what to say.

"Anyway," Essex sighed, "it will be interesting to see how Molotov takes this one. I don't think he will like it."

But it was not Molotov who eventually received them. That evening it was Vishinsky who took the Note.

Vishinsky met them at the Foreign Office and greeted them as if this would be a bout to enjoy. He looked to Essex like a hungry lion good-naturedly welcoming his victims. He was a solid man with a grey face and a continuous icy twinkle in his eye. His tongue was sharp and always a mixture of rapier-like humour and relentless irony. Essex decided to leave everything to Drake until he discovered whether Vishinsky was as clever as he looked.

When Drake presented the Note, Vishinsky said "Ah, a Note" as if he were pleased with the beginning of the contest. "What does it concern?" he said conversationally as he read it and handed it to Troika, who was there behind him. They were in Vishinsky's book-lined office, seated on the usual matching couch and chairs. Vishinsky had put on horn-rimmed glasses.

"It concerns the political situation in Iran," Drake said precisely. He spoke slowly so that Joyce — the Embassy translator — could catch every word. "We deplore the disorderly situation in Azerbaijan, Mr. Vishinsky, and remind the Soviet Government that its interference in Iranian affairs is a violation of the 1942 Treaty. We insist that an immediate commission of enquiry be set up by the Treaty signatories to investigate the situation in Azerbaijan and take practical measures to restore government authority in that province."

Vishinsky's expression did not change, he looked neither surprised nor annoyed. "The British Government seems to be very worried about a little democratic activity in Iran," he said to Drake and smiled with thin lips.

"Very worried," Drake said solemnly.

"Your accusations are serious," Vishinsky went on.

"We are not accusing," Drake replied calmly. "We are simply stating the situation in its real form. We have tried to get satisfaction from the Soviet Government before, but we have been continuously rebuffed. The situation in Azerbaijan is worsening every day and we feel that the Soviet Government is ignoring our interest in this matter."

"We have had little chance to ignore British interest in Azerbaijan," Vishinsky said, still smiling as Troika spoke the effluent Russian. Like Molotov, Vishinsky was a rapid talker, and Essex had already decided that they both belonged to the same hard-headed diplomatic school. "Still, if there is anything that the British representative wishes to discuss I am ready to talk about it."

Essex had MacGregor beside him on the couch. "Tell Mr. Vishinsky, MacGregor, that we want to discuss the whole problem of Azerbaijan. We are not merely complaining. We want to institute practical measures for Azerbaijan's return to government authority. Tell him this would require a proper conference and ask him when it would be convenient to begin."

MacGregor didn't want the responsibility Essex was giving him, but he told Vishinsky in reasonably good Russian what Essex had said, making it as impersonal as he could. Vishinsky listened and nodded his head so that his grey hair shone in the white light. It was then that MacGregor felt his real responsibility and his real interest in this mission. He realized that he was talking to Vishinsky and transmitting this important message. He lost any conception of its having anything to do with Iran. He was interested in the contest between the men in this room, and he waited for Vishinsky to accept or counter Essex's proposal.

"We cannot see that Soviet policy in Iran requires a conference," Vishinsky said. "If Lord Essex is suggesting a conference concerning Iran, then he is in the wrong country. As Mr. Molotov has told him, Iran would be the place for such a conference."

Essex listened to MacGregor's translation and felt that this was a lawyer's answer. In fact this was a lawyer's room and a lawyer's atmosphere: the books in their bookcases looked like law books with their pale binding and red stripes on the backs. If it hadn't been for the long portraits of Lenin and Stalin, Essex would have thought himself in the chambers of a sharp-tongued Continental barrister, a prosperous and clever fellow who seemed to know far too much for comfort.

"Tell him it isn't the conference I want so much as the real settlement of the disturbed situation in Iran," Essex told MacGregor. "It is a danger to Middle Eastern peace, and you might add that we are anxious to settle it before the next meeting of the Security Council in London at the end of the month."

"Ah!" said Vishinsky happily. "I can see that Lord Essex must be anxious indeed, when he mentions the Security Council. We are anxious too. There are situations in Greece and Indonesia and other parts of the world which we are anxious about. As for Iran: she is one of our neighbours. We are therefore more concerned with a peaceful situation there than anyone else."

"Then let us get down to a practical discussion," Essex said.

"What does Lord Essex call practical?"

"Anything that will arrange the restoration of authority in Iran."

"That could be called interference," Vishinsky said.

"We are not suggesting interference," Essex said and MacGregor could not help translating his slight annoyance. "We have a traditional interest in the welfare of Iran and that decides our attitude in this matter."

MacGregor did not do well with this translation. Vishinsky waited while he sought the proper phrases, and then turned to Troika. "Tell Lord Essex that in admiring tradition he is underestimating the laws of history. The first law of history is change, and the Soviet Government recognizes all social change which improves the lot of the mass population of a country."

"We are highly suspicious of the changes taking place in Azerbaijan," Essex said with a calculated impatience.

"We see no reason for such suspicion," Vishinsky said.

"There is every reason for suspicion when the province of a sovereign

141

nation is split away and declared a separate state by a group of adventurers."

"You are misinformed," Vishinsky said. "Azerbaijan remains part of Iran. No split-away has occurred. The present Democratic Administration has no separatist intentions. Azerbaijan is merely expressing its right to self-determination, a right which the Allies themselves recognized and encouraged after the first war, only then it included Soviet Azerbaijan and the intentions were different."

"That was the past," Essex said.

"We have the past continuously in mind," Vishinsky interrupted. "Iranian provinces on our borders have always been rich prizes for foreign intervention and political interference. Until now Azerbaijan has been a tool in the hands of adventurist Khans, unmercifully exploited for its riches and loaned unscrupulously as a springboard for attack on Russia by larger powers. A dejected and downtrodden population have had little chance of determining their own affairs. That situation is changing now. A new democratic force has arisen in Azerbaijan, and its aim is the vast improvement and education of the people. In this we have a friendly interest. We are interested in seeing all Iran a progressive and democratic country, a strong, independent, and friendly country unthreatened by its backwardness and poverty, and uninfluenced by any political clique which will safeguard the interests of foreign capital and domestic landlordism."

"Mr. Vishinsky talks of Soviet interest in this situation."

"A very justifiable interest."

"I would remind him that Britain also has an interest in Iran."

"True," Vishinsky said slyly, "but there is a difference. Our interest in Iran is that of a neighbour, British interest is that of capital investment."

"Perhaps," Essex said tolerantly, "but we will not have our interests threatened by the interference of another nation in the internal affairs of Iran. For Iran's sake as well as our own we intend to preserve our rights, Mr. Vishinsky, whatever the cost." Essex spoke mildly, almost quietly, but the threat was clear.

"We are glad to hear Lord Essex state his country's policy so frankly."

"I think frank discussion is needed," Essex said. "That is why I suggest a conference to settle the situation in Azerbaijan."

"Perhaps our first consideration must be this Note," Vishinsky said.

"It is merely a statement of our views on the subject," Essex said, not wanting to have the Note interfere with the possibility of a conference.

"True," Vishinsky said, "but it must be considered nevertheless. I shall have to hand it to Mr. Molotov, and no doubt he will find it something of a surprise. I am surprised myself to receive such a hostile document."

"It is not a hostile document." Drake leaned forward. "It is a fair complaint." The Russian's last remark had been too much for Drake, and he felt it his duty to defend the Note, since he was technically responsible for it.

"The complaint is invalid," Vishinsky said to Drake. "Iran was discussed by Mr. Molotov and yourself several weeks ago, it was discussed in detail at the Moscow Conference, and now Lord Essex is in Moscow discussing Iran."

"And in all discussions the Soviet Government have refused to take any action," Drake argued.

"Naturally," Vishinsky said, "because British proposals for action have suggested interference in Iranian affairs and that we refuse to do."

"We are not suggesting interference," Drake went on. "The British and Russian past in Iran has always been conflict, sometimes direct conflict. The best way to end this trouble is to sit down and settle it once and for all."

Vishinsky, no longer smiling, said, "The rôle of Czarist Russia in Persia is not the rôle of the Soviet Government in Iran. We are not concerned with rivalries or foreign interests in Iran; we are concerned with Iran itself. Whatever the problems — they exist in Iran. No conference between us can settle Iran's difficulties."

"But it could settle British-Soviet differences," Essex said.

"In that regard there is the Note to consider first," Vishinsky said.

In saying it Vishinsky seemed to be cracking a joke with them, making his point as if they too could share the joke. It was lost in the translation and only MacGregor sensed the delicate twist by which Vishinsky had turned the Note against Essex.

Essex guessed its intention, however. "The Note is intended to clarify the situation," he said. "Nothing more."

"It has," Vishinsky told him.

"Then we may expect further development," Essex said, knowing it was over.

"I will deliver the Note to Mr. Molotov," Vishinsky said, implying that this was all he could do, but implying it with a smile on his lips and a look in his eye which said to Essex: I have enjoyed this, but it is really a waste of your time trying to put such a thing over me.

MacGregor saw that too, and thought Essex was going to be indignant again. Essex yawned a little and stood up and gave his pouch to MacGregor and said: "In that case I will expect to hear from Mr. Molotov." He shook hands with Vishinsky and for a moment they seemed to be good friends.

As they walked to the door Vishinsky said to MacGregor, "And what do you think of the situation in Iran, Mr. MacGregor, after living there for so long?"

"I don't know," MacGregor said, embarrassed by want of an answer.

"I should like to go and see what is happening there. It is five or six years since I was in Iran, Mr. Vishinsky."

"You don't have to visit Iran to understand what is happening there," Vishinsky said, chiding MacGregor for his caution; but he shook Mac-Gregor's hand warmly and told him that he must see and enjoy Moscow while he was here. Vishinsky said good-bye again and left them at his office door. Troika left them only when they were on the street.

It was late afternoon and the Rolls-Royce was waiting at the curb for them. Essex waited until Drake got in and then he put his pouch on the seat and said, "I think MacGregor and I will walk back, Francis." He put on his astrakhan cap and buttoned his lined coat. "That hot-house atmosphere in there dulls the senses." He took the cap off again and threw it in the car. "I'll come up and see you when I get back. Can you find our way back, MacGregor?"

"I think so."

"Then let us walk briskly."

"Was that the end of the mission?" MacGregor asked Essex as they stepped it out.

"What gives you that idea?"

"I thought Vishinsky had brought it to a dead-end."

"On the contrary." Essex laughed grimly. "Vishinsky was in a corner. The Note shook him, my boy."

"Wasn't he more or less refusing to talk about Iran any further?"

"Naturally," Essex said; "but that isn't the end of it."

"No?"

"It's the next step that will be decisive," Essex said, and added less certainly: "It has to be decisive. On that Note they must decide whether they will talk with us about Iran. And they will talk. They must talk. They know the consequences if they don't."

MacGregor, too, had been containing himself. During the interview his one moment of insight into the contest between Essex and Vishinsky seemed to have made all diplomacy suddenly clear to him. "When you render down all that talk between you and Vishinsky," he said, "it amounts to something a little terrifying."

Essex was forced off the iced curb by a party of Uzbeks in long padded cloaks. "Terrifying?" he said as MacGregor folllowed him on the road. "Are you going to start worrying every time we argue with the Russians?"

"No," MacGregor said, "because you were hardly arguing about Iran. The real issue seemed to be the threatened consequences if the Russians didn't talk about Iran."

Essex grunted. "You are right there. They realize now just how far we are pushing them, and how much farther we are willing to go."

Essex was deliberately calming himself down, taking everything Mac-Gregor said as an emetic for himself. "You try to define things too much, MacGregor," he said with tense patience. "In this sort of thing the obscurity of the ultimate limit is a comfort. Definition is the business of the politicians and the generals, not the diplomat. A bold threat is useless and unnecessary. A subtle implication is a better implement. It enables you to attack and manœuvre, and if necessary retreat. It enables you to imply far more than you are willing to take responsibility for, and that gives you strength in the council chambers. Cold definition could ruin this case. In fact international intercourse would be destroyed in a bog of facts and violent irritations if we all defined our attitudes and our ultimate intentions too clearly. Vishinsky will know what he is faced with. He will define for himself the strength of our little ultimatum."

MacGregor was trying to think of Essex as a sinister man, but Essex was an open-faced Englishman with a pipe in his teeth. Yet the British intention seemed to be that of grim counterbalance of Russia, whatever the cost, and MacGregor wondered why it hadn't occurred to him so simply and alarmingly before.

"Is it necessary to strike out at the Russians all the time?" MacGregor asked. "Hasn't the war done away with some of our antagonism?"

"Don't mix foreign policy with popular sentiment," Essex said in reply. "The problem for us is one of politics and geography, not sympathy. We must contain Russia politically and geographically, that is our foreign policy and on it depends the existence of a sensible Europe and a manageable world." Essex had talked himself back into a feeling for his rôle. He had almost ridded himself of the dejection of the Vishinsky talk, and was convinced again that he had put Vishinsky in a corner.

"The trouble is," he said finally to MacGregor, "these Russians are too elusive and enigmatic. Still, we are fairly safe in assuming their . . . er . . . discomfort. It is now a matter of waiting for Molotov's reaction."

"How long will you wait?" MacGregor asked.

They were crossing the road near the Bolshoi Theatre. "A day or two. My dignity will not allow us much longer than that," Essex said in a moment of humour and honesty.

MacGregor smiled, but he was hoping that Essex would not precipitate their departure now. He had acquired an intense desire to stay with Essex and see his mission out.

The realization that this mission went far beyond a dispute about Iran was still new for MacGregor. It was like that moment in physical research when you found you were on a new, unthought-of direction — a direction which opened up a complete new picture of the work in hand. His task in Moscow was exciting and repulsive at the same time, but he wanted to see it out.

Chapter 9

Miss Williams took off her glasses and waited while Essex finished his conversation with MacGregor. These two men began their day so differently that she could not help making a mental note of it. Lord Essex was always voluble and full of discussion and energy; Mac-Gregor always seemed quiet and restless, as if each day signified something lost for him. Essex she liked to hear and MacGregor she liked to observe, and she sat now and listened and watched as they finished discussing yesterday's meeting with Vishinsky. After dictating his briefs on the conversation to Miss Williams, Essex seemed more irritated than when he had begun, and there was complaint in his voice. He was saying that he did not feel like waiting here even two more days.

"By their evasive behaviour they are asking for the worst," Essex said.

"I suppose they are."

"I doubt if it's possible to get any clear answer out of them."

MacGregor agreed; and yet he did not want to agree. He did not want Essex to juggle with Iran any more; yet he did not want Essex's mission to break disruptively with the Russians — that was too big a failure to enjoy contemplating.

"I am inclined to return to London and let these people face the consequences," Essex said, his impatience rising.

"Wouldn't it be complete failure if we left now?" MacGregor asked.

The failure MacGregor meant was total undesirable failure; but the failure Essex understood by that was his personal failure. It was a cold reminder for him.

"Don't worry," Essex said with a mixture of annoyance and confidence in MacGregor. "I shan't leave here before we get something out of the Russians. Just read that last paragraph back, will you, Miss Williams?"

Miss Williams adjusted her glasses again. " 'It seems to me,' " she read, " 'that Vishinsky was far more willing to talk about Iran than was Molotov. This may be a mere comment on the man himself; but in fact there was a little more give-and-take between us yesterday than was the case in talking with Molotov. It will be clear from the briefs above that the Russians are determined to have their own say in Azerbaijan, no matter how far we push them. However, I think I left Vishinsky with a clear impression of just how serious we think this business is, and just how far we are willing to go. I am sure he will transmit this to Molotov or Stalin and warn them that we are willing to go the limit. I intended it that way, and in conjunction with the Note I feel sure that our hopes of achieving something are considerably better than they were when I left London.' "

"Yes, that will do," Essex said. "Let Sir Francis have a copy too."

Miss Williams waited again because Essex had not told her to go, and because she wanted to talk with him. "Is there anything else?" she asked him.

"No, I don't think so."

"I was wanting to ask you, Lord Essex, if you knew how long you would be here?"

Essex looked surprised.

Miss Williams explained quickly. "I received word from London last night that I am being transferred. I am supposed to leave Friday."

"That's rather soon, isn't it?" Essex said.

"Yes sir, but if you need me I could stay for as long as you were here. I will have to let them know how long I will be delayed."

"Do you want to stay and see this through, Miss Williams?"

"Oh yes sir, I suggested it to Mr. Melby."

"Well, we would be sorry to lose you. Tell them another ten days or two weeks. We shan't be here that long, but that will give you some time to play around with. Is that alright?"

"Yes, and thank you very much."

"Where are you going next?" Essex asked her.

"Stockholm; but I am trying to change with one of the other girls who is going to Paris. Katherine Clive has also been transferred to Paris."

"Miss Clive?" Essex said. "Is that a fact?"

"Yes."

"When is Miss Clive supposed to be leaving? On Friday also?"

"Yes. That is the day the plane goes." Miss Williams went to do her typing.

Essex looked over at MacGregor. "This will be a dull place without Katherine Clive," he said ruefully. "She could have waited until we had gone before running off."

Essex was making a joke and MacGregor was smiling with him, but both of them were quickly realizing the gap which her departure would make for them. To Essex she was becoming something different, even distinctive, and he did not want her to leave. He would not accept it as fact. On the other hand MacGregor accepted it as if it had been ordained. He knew that if Katherine Clive left Moscow it would be the last he would see of her. He could not believe that he had expected anything but quick termination of his acquaintance with Katherine. But he knew now that he had hoped in some obscure way to go on knowing her.

Essex was already on the phone to Katherine. "If you can spare a couple of hours this afternoon," he was saying to her, "I should like to take you up on that offer to see the Orthodox churches."

MacGregor listened intently.

"I shall pick you up at two o'clock," Essex said as she apparently agreed. "Right downstairs. Yes. I shall have a car."

There was a distinct silence when Essex had hung up.

"I don't suppose you are interested in churches, MacGregor," Essex suggested.

"No. I'm afraid not," MacGregor said, knowing that he had been politely turned aside, knowing also that he was aggravated by this suggestion of competition.

"I thought not." Essex sealed an envelope he had been addressing. "Have you familiarized yourself with the problem of the two Turkish provinces yet: Kars, and what is that other one I can never remember?"

"Ardahan."

"Yes. Have you read up on it at all?"

"No. I have a few documents about it but I haven't read them."

"The Foreign Office is expecting the Russians to present a Note to the Turks about them. They might use it as a sort of retaliation for our Note, so you had better assemble what you can about it. The Embassy is sure to have plenty of material. Have you ever been to Turkey, MacGregor?"

"No."

"It's one of the few countries in the world I don't like," Essex said. "I was there just before I went to Washington, trying to keep the Turks out of the war. I had no hope of persuading them to become an Ally, because France had just fallen. They were ready to go in with the Germans. It was all I could do to keep them neutral for a few important months by simply persuading them that they were not sure that Germany would eventually win. They were up to every shameful trick to extract promises of post-war support in exchange for their neutrality, but I never did play their game. I left that to Dr. Schmidt. I think the only promise we ever made them was to guarantee continuation of their control in the Dardanelles. Now they are getting at us to block Russian demands for a say in the Straits."

"Are we supporting them against the Russians?" MacGregor said.

"Certainly. We can't have the Russians in the Dardanelles." Essex was going out. "I am paying a visit to the Americans this morning," he said. "If anything comes up just give me a ring. I shall be back for lunch."

MacGregor watched him go, knowing that Essex was avoiding the routine of the morning. He did it every morning, breaking each tendency to habit as quickly as he could. MacGregor did not like habit himself, but he liked a proper order and sequence to work, a system and a classification of each task as if it were a whole continuation and process of work which would eventually arrive at a given point. Long hours of identifying and classifying microscopic fauna had given him an automatic desire for routine and order in his work, and Essex's continuous upsets were discouraging to real effort. Besides that, MacGregor had no more desire than Essex to read the summaries and the London reports this morning. He kept at it for a while, but then he went up to see Katherine Clive.

It was the first time he had been in her office and he was embarrassed somewhat by its importance. She sat sideways at a business-like desk, her feet crossed on a low table as she thumbed through a large indexed book on her knees. He looked around the efficient room, observing the tables of papers and files and the bookcases of thick official volumes. Her head had been bent down and her hair had covered her face. As she looked up she tossed her hair back and folded it carelessly over her oval ears.

"You are the last person in the world I expected to see come in here," she said without putting down her feet. "You are not the visiting sort, Mr. MacGregor."

"I am here on business," he said.

"Of course."

A red-headed girl sat in a corner desk typing, and Katherine said to her "Helen. This is Mr. MacGregor who is here with Lord Essex. Miss Helen Boyle," she said to MacGregor who had seen the girl occasionally in the passages. She was thin-faced and she was tucked away inside herself and she went quickly back to work.

"What could that be?" MacGregor said and pointed at the volume on Katherine's knee.

"It's not as important as it looks," she said. "I am just looking up the Provisions of the Hague Conference of 1907."

It meant nothing to MacGregor.

She drew a breath: "It's a dull business. I'm checking a complaint we are making about some British property in the Baltic countries."

"Diplomacy seems to be more than half complaint. What is the trouble about now?"

"One of our most respected chemical corporations, who supplied Germany with phosphorus and sulphates before the war, is trying to get two million pounds compensation out of the Russians for destruction and seizure of property in Latvia."

"They have a slim hope," MacGregor said. "Having seen a little of the Russians."

"They have no hope," Katherine said, "but we don't like to lose these opportunities of complaining to the Russians about something. I suppose the Russians do the same thing in London. It's a rotten waste of time."

"I gather that you won't be wasting your time here much longer," he said.

"Oh?"

"Haven't you been transferred to Paris?"

"Who told you that?"

149

"Everybody knows everything about everybody else here," MacGregor said, repeating one of her own indifferent explanations.

She laughed. "I haven't been transferred to Paris," she said, "but I can go if I want to. They are so short of people these days that the choice is always there."

"Will you go?"

"I haven't made up my mind," she said. She was honestly intrigued by MacGregor's quick knowledge of her situation, even though she guessed that it came from Ella Williams.

"I would have thought you would be glad to get out of here," he said.

"I will be glad!" she said.

MacGregor had no more to say on the subject. Katherine Clive behind the desk was the same woman, but with additional barriers of position and professional self-possession. She might have detected his own reservation because she laughed at him and put her feet down from the small table and jumped up and came around to him to sit on the edge of her desk.

"What I came to see you about," he said, "was some material on the Turkish provinces which the Russians are claiming as Armenian. Where would I find all the Embassy documents and information on it?"

"We can get it for you," Katherine said. "Would you mind, Helen?"

Miss Boyle was already attending to it.

"Where do you live when you are in London?" Katherine asked him.

"In South Kensington," he said.

"With your family?"

He shook his head. "I have a room just off Brompton Road."

"Is that where you lived when you went to the Imperial College?"

"That's right," he said.

Katherine looked carefully at his smooth face until she detected freckles under his eyes, small and very faint freckles. They made his eyes seem too quiet, almost too gentle. "How much of your work have you lost after five or six years away from it?" she said.

"More than I like to think of," he told her.

"Do you try to keep up with your micropaleontology?"

"There is no way of keeping up," he said. "You are either in it or out of it, and at the moment I am very much out of it."

"But surely you would have some means of knowing what was going on."

"I can read the few monographs that come out on the study of specific fossils, but the real work of micropaleontology has to be done in the laboratory. There aren't any all-embracing books on the subject, so the only micropaleontologist is the practising micropaleontologist."

"What on earth made you take up such an obscure subject?"

"I wouldn't call it obscure," he said to avoid the question. "It's simply a new field of study in geology. It is still highly specialized, that's all."

Miss Boyle came back and gave MacGregor a large Manila envelope tied with red tape. Also a brown-covered dusty book which she said was Curzon's *Armenia.*

"How was Vishinsky?" Katherine asked him as he started to leave.

"Alright," he said from the door.

"The way you are going now," she said, "you will be here long after me, although your boss doesn't seem to mind being here. We are going out to see the churches this afternoon."

"Yes I know," he said and left her.

While Essex was out looking at his churches, MacGregor spent the afternoon before the fire reading the documents on the Turkish or Armenian provinces of Kars, Ardahan, Van, Bitlis and Erzerum. He then turned to Curzon's *Armenia,* a volume dated 1854. It was an account by the Honourable Robert Curzon of his experiences with the Anglo-Russian-Persia-Turkish Frontier Commission for settling border disputes in Armenia. He had almost finished it when Jane Asquith telephoned and asked him if he would like to come over for coffee, after dinner. He said he would be delighted, and he had settled back again to finish the book when there was another interruption. This time it was Miss Williams.

"You will ruin your eyes," she said, and turned on the light.

"I am forgetful when I am reading," he said and stood up.

"I always seem to be turning lights on for you." She was more confident than MacGregor had seen her before.

"You seem to be pleased about leaving," he said.

"I only hope that I can get to Paris."

"I have never been there," he said conversationally.

"I was a schoolteacher before I went to the Foreign Office," she said, "and I went to Paris on one of the summer excursions. I have always wanted to go back. Do you have any hope of getting there, Mr. Mac-Gregor?"

"None," he said.

"I hope to have three weeks' leave in London first."

"Then you will probably come back with us."

"I should like that," she said, and left MacGregor in the quiet room with Curzon and Armenia.

Melby had gone to Leningrad and MacGregor went on reading over dinner, finishing the book by the time he went to the Asquiths. He did not bother to put on his overcoat to walk across the courtyard, but he arrived at their door with his hands in his pockets and his shoulders hunched.

"You are like John," Jane Asquith said as she brought him in. "I have to force an overcoat on him — like a schoolboy."

"It's only a few steps," MacGregor said apologetically as they went inside.

Asquith and Katherine Clive were playing chess at an inlaid table before a large English radiator. Katherine looked up, but Asquith simply took his pipe out of his mouth and waved it vaguely at MacGregor, spattering ash over the worn carpet. He then moved a chess man with such violence that Katherine returned her attention to the game.

"When will you two finish?" Jane asked.

"It's finished now," Asquith replied. "In another move she will be checkmate. How are you MacGregor? You stand behind Kathy and watch her play this game without imagination. Do you play?"

"Yes."

"Then we must meet. Anybody would be better than Kathy. She plays the game without attempting to understand the importance of what she is doing. Look at the position of those two men of hers." He had his fingers on them.

Katherine pushed his hand away. "Mr. MacGregor can see for himself," she said.

"You can only play your bishop," Asquith told her impatiently.

"John, she defeated you in the last game," his wife said.

"By luck only. She reduces the whole game to a tactical play. I admit I can't cope with such a circumscribed mind."

"You are all pretence!" Katherine said and moved her knight. "Now you are in check, and I doubt if you can get out of it." She was still concentrating on the board, fingering a thin gold chain she wore around her exposed throat. The long lines of her neck gave her features additional length, breaking up the threat of her straight eyebrows and straight lips. In the moment of concentration MacGregor saw her very briefly without adult behaviourism, but it was gone in an instant. "Why don't you sit down?" she said to MacGregor, moving up on the long piano stool to make room for him.

"Take your eyes off MacGregor," Asquith growled at her, leaning forward and puffing at his pipe and pulling and twining his plentiful hair and long moustache.

"It's your move!" Katherine said.

"I have moved," Asquith bellowed, "and you are checkmated."

Katherine tapped her teeth with orange fingernails. She was in no hurry to see that she was defeated. "Is there any way out of it?" she said to MacGregor.

"Don't try to involve MacGregor," Asquith said. "Leave your passion out of it."

"Is there?" Katherine said to MacGregor.

MacGregor shook his head. "He enticed you into that trap."

152

"Of course I did," Asquith shouted. "Jane. Your champion is defeated."

"Then it must be the result of your rudeness and shouting," Jane Asquith said from the kitchen.

"Why don't you play him?" Katherine said suddenly to MacGregor.

"Not on your life," Asquith said. "Not when you suggest it. If MacGregor is a man of purpose then he would defeat me. That would only embarrass the both of us to mollify your own sense of defeat. We will not be used by you, Katherine. Go into the kitchen where you belong."

Katherine stood up. "You know quite well he could beat you," she said and helped Jane Asquith with the coffee.

It was served in small cups and poured straight from a small brass pot. It was thick powerful Turkish coffee which you sipped slowly and washed down with iced water. It was the only coffee that MacGregor liked.

"This was made for you particularly," Katherine told him.

"I thought that living in Persia would have given you a taste for it," Jane Asquith said. "You see I have the proper utensil." She held up the brass pot.

"Where did you manage to get it?" MacGregor asked.

"One of those American correspondents gave it to me."

"Which one?" Katherine said.

"I don't remember his name. He has very dark hair and looks like Stalin."

"Jeb Wills?"

"Yes," Jane said. "He brought it from Teheran. He is a very nice boy."

"A nice boy!" Asquith complained. "Foreign correspondents. Men with dead hands."

MacGregor sat near Jane Asquith (who was knitting) and watched Katherine and Asquith keep up an apparently violent discussion of each other, all of it highly personal and insulting. Asquith's eyes were alight, and he tugged at his drooping moustache with vigorous enjoyment. Katherine was being stirred into sharper and sharper comment, and MacGregor was expecting her to lose her temper at any moment. The break never came, however, and Katherine simply became calmer and more cynical and more critical, the phase of Katherine which MacGregor disliked and mistrusted.

She had turned to MacGregor now to say: "I have just been reading about oil in Iran." She was asking for his comment so that she could argue with him.

"Geological or political?" he asked.

"Political," she announced. "It's all about the last Shah sending for the manager of the English-Persian fields and tearing up the British concession in his face. If it's true it must have been a delightful moment."

"It's true," MacGregor said, "but it didn't get the Shah very far."

"It got him better terms and more money."

"It didn't get rid of the English-Persian Oil Company," MacGregor said.

"He didn't want to get rid of it," Asquith interrupted. "He simply wanted more money without additional responsibility. A sound investment. That is the sort of fellow that makes other people's Empire possible. Sells his birthright to a foreigner."

"If he didn't sell it we would take it anyway," Katherine argued.

"I doubt that," Asquith grumbled. "It's easy these days to buy a nation, but it's quite difficult to take it by force."

"Who would stop us in Iran?" Katherine said to MacGregor.

"It's hard to say . . ." MacGregor began.

"Don't be cautious," she said. "Would the population resist us?"

"They might."

"They couldn't," she insisted impatiently. "They are incapable of ordering their own affairs and incapable of expelling foreigners."

MacGregor did not want to be further embroiled with this contrary-minded Katherine but he was angry enough to argue with her. "We seem to be doing it for them," he said with mild sarcasm.

She took him up. "Haven't we a right to protect our oil?"

"Perhaps — but not in the name of Iranian integrity."

"We are just taking our cue from the Russians," she said. "Can we afford to be honest with ourselves when the Russians are not? Haven't they set up a puppet government in Azerbaijan for the sole purpose of interference?"

"I don't think it is entirely a puppet government," he said.

"How do you know?"

"I don't know," he said irritably.

Asquith had been watching with pleasure the dispute he had so subtly transferred to MacGregor and Katherine Clive, but it was too good to miss. "In this situation," he said to Katherine, "MacGregor's judgment is better than yours because he knows more about Iran."

"His judgment has gone astray," she said.

"And so has yours," Asquith replied. "You have been out with Harold Essex."

"At least I am not moralizing," she exclaimed.

"Neither is MacGregor."

"Of course he is. He has become quite a moralist."

Asquith got up off the floor. "You confuse morals with virtue."

"I am not confusing anything," she said.

"Yes you are!" Asquith said accusingly. "A moralist is a man who is concerned with good by deliberation and sacrifice; a man of virtue is a man to whom goodness comes naturally. You are a fool to accuse Mac-Gregor of morality, because a little observation should have shown you otherwise." Asquith took this golden opportunity of expounding his idea further and he paced up and down. "Of all men the moralist is the most dangerous and the most worthless because he is a martyr to his goodness. Goodness is unnatural to him. He acquires it as a priest acquires it — by unnatural practices. In politics it leads him to assassination, and in religion it leads him to hypocrisy. The moralist is a Brutus and a Pope. Now whatever MacGregor's attitude, Kathy, it is achieved by honest investigation. It comes naturally to him from his human experience and not from any metaphysical contemplation, and not from any moral grovelling in search of the ideal human character. MacGregor is not a moralist. He is simply suffering for his education in political morals, and if I am not mistaken he is actually beginning to see shadows behind our subtle ultimatums to the Russians. He is probably not at all sure why he is here and what he is doing. What unhappy devil of chance dropped you into this business, MacGregor? Are you going to go on stumbling around with a conscience like a bush fire about Iran, or are you going home?"

"I am not going home," MacGregor said quickly to stop any additional accusation.

"Well that is some advance," Asquith said. "Do you still look upon your work here with Harold as one world, and your science as another? Is that still one of your escapes?"

"It's no escape," MacGregor said. "It's a fact."

"How is it a fact?" Asquith demanded. "What you do here is just as much your responsibility as what you do in your geology. Don't you see that they are finally inseparable in deciding your ultimate activity?"

"No, I don't see that at all," MacGregor said. "What I do here is completely separate from what I do in my own work. One has nothing to do with the other."

"One may decide the other," Asquith insisted. "All your science is decided by the shape of the world you live in; and it is the political world which will decide your scientific activity."

MacGregor shook his head. "A scientist is a scientist, a politician is a politician, and a diplomat is a diplomat."

"I can't understand how you scientific fellows can be so ignorant," Asquith said in dismay. "Only a moment ago you were showing a glimmering of understanding, MacGregor. Some day the total picture of your responsibility will no doubt stare you in the face, and I should like to be there to see what happens when a man like you makes the real decision of his life." But Asquith was forgiving MacGregor, and he looked at the

Scot as if he were trying to decide MacGregor's unknown decisions for him. It seemed too much for Asquith, for the life went out of him for a moment. "Kathy was saying that you were reading up on Armenia," he said peacefully.

MacGregor nodded.

"Why bother?" Asquith said. "Harold should know all about the Armenian dispute. He took it up once before, in Paris just after the First War. Then it was a dispute with the Turks."

"All our disputes these days seem to be with the Russians," MacGregor said.

"Who else is there to dispute with?" Katherine said.

"Anybody else would do," MacGregor suggested.

"Everybody else co-operates," she said.

"You might be right." He could see that she was determined to argue with him.

"Why the devil don't you go on arguing instead of allowing her to brow-beat you into agreement?" Asquith complained to MacGregor. "Why don't you go on and finish a thought instead of stopping half-way? She knows exactly how to get you in a corner, MacGregor, and you are fool enough to be pacifistic about it."

"Does he embarrass you, Mr. MacGregor?" Jane Asquith said.

MacGregor denied embarrassment.

"John usually sees in other men what he should seek in himself," Jane Asquith went on. "He claims so much insight into others that I think he must be afraid of himself."

"Don't make a bogy out of me," Asquith said to her.

"Then don't be so rude," she said calmly.

"And stop being maternal with MacGregor," Asquith said. "He is intelligent enough to look after himself."

"If he was intelligent he would ignore you," Katherine said.

"It's Katherine you must ignore, MacGregor." Asquith stood over her for a moment as if he were looking at a painting to understand it. "Katherine is like Saint Veronica," he said. "She might wipe the sweat from your brow and treasure the imprint of your face upon her handkerchief; but give her a chance to take hold of you and she will eliminate your face from living memory to make it a copy of her own. That is her conceit," he emphasized brutally.

"Who on earth was Saint Veronica?" Katherine asked to irritate him.

Asquith shook his head as if Katherine's ignorance were an unforgivable sin. "It was Veronica who soothed Christ's face on His way to Calvary," he said.

"I have never heard of her."

"If you go to the Vatican," Asquith instructed her impatiently, "you can see the veil still there with the imprint of His face upon it. I once made the mistake myself of visiting the Vatican with a famous Italian biologist, and I asked him in bad Italian to show me the *Veronicella*. It was some time before I realized why my biologist friend left me without a word. *Veronicella* is apparently a genus of sluglike pulmonate gastropods and nothing in name to that sacred veil."

"That sounds like one of those obscure situations you spend months in planning," Katherine accused, "just so that you can carry your no-Popery into enemy territory."

His wife said he shouldn't blaspheme like that.

"Blaspheme!" Asquith protested. "I am idol breaking."

"Must you be so vehement and murderous about it?" Katherine said.

"Am I as murderous as the Crusader with his sword?"

Jane Asquith brought him brandy and glasses. "Perhaps this will stop you," she said. "Let Mr. MacGregor taste it first."

Asquith poured it and said, "You don't drink this stuff, do you Mac-Gregor?"

"I don't mind brandy," MacGregor said. "I dislike whisky."

"I am surprised that you touch any of it. You look pious."

"Pious and moderate," MacGregor said, knowing enough to keep the joke upon himself so that Asquith could not take it further.

"I suppose your father was a drunkard," Asquith went on casually.

"Not that I know of."

"One excess is usually the result of another," Asquith sighed. "Take my brother, Lord Cachelot. A sportsman and a drinker, a born inebriate. His children are growing up stupid with excessive moderation because of his continuous tippling. I warned him to take it easy so that his children will have their own chance to tipple sensibly, but he calls them sober fools and does his best to set them a bad example."

"Phillip's only trouble is his gout," Jane Asquith said. "He is not an inebriate or a tippler."

"You defend him because he is stout and sporty."

"At least Phillip can ride a horse," Katherine Clive taunted.

"Horse riding is a clever occupation for egotists only."

"And Phillip is witty."

"He is a wretched idiot, a buffoon."

MacGregor sat outside the talk that went on between Katherine Clive and John Asquith and Jane Asquith about the habits and cruelties and loves and family and money and sport of relatives and friends whom he didn't know and who were beyond him. It wasn't rude of them to talk this way. On the contrary. They were half implying that MacGregor was part of it, and were therefore being kind with him. MacGregor understood that, and nodded and smiled when he had the chance, realizing that

157

this was Katherine's world but it was not his and never could be. She would not let him out of it, however.

"Aren't you bored by all this gossip, Mr. MacGregor?" she asked.

She was making a fool of him now. "Should I be?" he said.

"Yes. Unless you know the people."

"No. I don't know them." He restrained himself because any reply more damaging would have included the Asquiths.

"What sort of people do you know in London?" she said.

"Ordinary people."

"But who are they? Are they all like you? So careful with themselves?"

"Perhaps they are not quite as wild as your friends seem to be," he said.

"They must be awfully dull."

Katherine went on being mocking and harsh and occasionally tender, but more often than not vicious. MacGregor did not know why she was so contrary-minded and so anxious to disturb him. He could not help looking back into his brief association with other women to explain Katherine's caprices. Of two women he could judge her by, both had been quiet and agreeable beside Katherine Clive, and not at all comparable with her in any of their habits and contradictions. Yet they too had given him little peace, he had to admit, though for a different reason. One of them had been a pallid calm Swedish girl named Malin Alving who had deliberately made his acquaintance in his first year at the Royal College. She had been a second year geology student and she had always puzzled him because she had expected far more of him than he was willing to offer. He had been glad when she had gone back to Sweden; yet he would not be glad when Katherine left Moscow. The other of his brief acquaintants had been an Englishwoman as quiet and gentle and understanding as Jane Asquith, the complete reverse of Katherine. Yet she was a woman he preferred to forget. She had been the wife of one of the geologists at Fields, and between herself and MacGregor there had developed a rather silent friendship that came out of her immediate understanding of his dislike for Fields. Though there had never been a moment of close personal relationship of any kind between them, he had come to depend more and more upon her presence and her friendship at Fields as the place became increasingly unlikable. It was the peculiar life in that hot compound which had given the relationship more significance than reality, and MacGregor wanted to forget about it. With Katherine Clive in her present mood, however, he found the comparisons he was making inevitable. It gave him no clue to Katherine's behaviour. It simply added to his irritation, because in the comparison with Malin Alving and the Englishwoman, Katherine was a woman full of fire and intelligent disagreement. She stood apart from them and from all others.

She was by him now, cupping her elbows with her hands, hunching

158

her shoulders so that he had a fleeting glimpse of some voluptuousness.

"I must go," she said. "I haven't been in bed before midnight for weeks."

"Yes, you look tired," Jane Asquith said.

"I heard you coming in at two o'clock this morning," Asquith told her.

"No you didn't," she said. "I was with Jeb Wills at the Bolshoi, and he brought me back before twelve."

"Then it must have been Wills leaving."

"That doesn't embarrass me," she said.

"Must you do this early morning work so often?" Jane Asquith said. "Surely someone else could do it."

"I like finishing early, Jane. I am getting too restless to sit all day in the Embassy being a dutiful civil servant. I am sorry I have to leave you alone with John."

"MacGregor will manage him."

"I must go also," MacGregor said.

"Oh?"

"Let MacGregor go, Jane. No doubt he has something to say to Katherine."

"You are always very welcome," Jane Asquith told him. "Whenever you feel like it, please drop in." She picked up a book from the hall stand. "Don't leave your Persian book, Kathy," she said and picked up Vodka who had suddenly appeared.

MacGregor bade them good night as Asquith opened the door.

"I should like to stand here and listen to your conversation," Asquith said to them. His wife pulled him gently inside and closed the door.

MacGregor held Katherine's arm as they walked on ice.

She gripped his hand because of the dark uneven walking. "I suppose you think I am a bit of a dog," she said finally, as if this had been on her mind.

"Why?"

"Don't behave so blamelessly about it," she said.

"Are you going to fight with me?"

"If necessary. You are annoyed because I argue with you."

"I haven't said a word." He was not taking her too seriously.

"I know you haven't, but you have such an air of being thoughtful and intentional and honest that I could kick you. Your arguments are all wrong anyway."

"You were warning me a couple of days ago not to be taken in by all the accusations I will hear about the Russians. You change your mind quickly."

"Certainly I change my mind. I change it all the time."

"So I see."

"Don't be virtuous."

"It's impossible to talk with you," he said angrily.

She laughed quietly. "Don't take any notice of me," she told him and put her hand lightly on his fingers.

"I seldom do," he said.

"At times I am a thoroughly bad egg. I don't like to be this way with you. Perhaps I like you too much to put up with your objective attitudes. You are so annoying at times and so confused that I want to irritate you."

"You might be more confused than I am," he said.

"Don't say that," she said to him. "Let me do the accusing."

They were standing near her door.

"Have you decided whether you are leaving on Friday?" he asked.

She shook her head. "I don't know that Paris would be any different from Moscow for me," she said. "I would like to leave here with a little more purpose. Your friend Essex was persuading me to-day not to go."

"I see," he said thoughtfully.

"I really like you when you are so wary of me."

He brought up his hands to hold her as he stepped up into the doorway, but the book she was carrying dropped on the ice and he blushed and stooped to pick it up and heard her laugh, but not unkindly. When he straightened up she put one hand on his face and kissed him casually but warmly upon the lips and let him go.

"Good night," she said cheerfully.

MacGregor was too surprised to reply.

Chapter 10

Essex began the day wearing a very old pair of trousers and a tweed jacket, with a woollen scarf around his neck. He sat at his desk looking mountainous and cold. He glanced at the papers and reports from London and pushed them aside impatiently.

"Did you ask if there was anything from the Russians this morning, MacGregor?" he said. "This is just about the deadline."

"I haven't asked," MacGregor said, "but I can do it now."

"Ring up Francis Drake and ask him."

MacGregor rang Drake, who answered his question with an impatient No and hung up.

"Well," said Essex. "We shan't get far unless we can get talking with these people. Everything depends on that, MacGregor. But I shan't be too patient. To-day is the second day we have been waiting for their reply on the Note, and two days is long enough." Essex went back to his cables, until one item of news was too much for him. "Here is that Senator Pepper taking the side of the Russians again," he said. "Did you read it, MacGregor?"

"Not yet."

"It says that he brought a message to Americans from Stalin: *Do not praise us; do not scold us. Base your judgment on facts, not rumours.* Now what would you think of a statement like that?"

"It sounds fair enough," MacGregor said mildly.

"Fair enough! The Russians are always asking for some special consideration from the world, MacGregor. Some day we will get tired of listening to them." Essex unlocked his middle drawer and took out a quarto loose-leaf book and started to write in it as if an important thought had just occurred to him. He used his quill, but he had difficulty with it and he chose another and wrote with it until that too spattered ink on the pages. He swore and shouted to MacGregor for a knife.

"I don't have one," MacGregor said.

"Then take these quills and sharpen them." Essex threw the quills across his desk and MacGregor leaned back to get them. "Get a razor blade or something and get a point on them, will you?"

"How do you do it?" MacGregor asked.

"Just pare them to a curve." Essex didn't look up from his writing which he had continued with a fountain pen. "And make sure that the tips are not too soft or too hard. They have to be flexible and fine."

MacGregor went to Miss Williams and asked her for a razor blade. She gave him a broken penknife and leaned forward and said to him very quietly. "What is the matter with Lord Essex this morning? Has he got a cold?"

"I don't think so," MacGregor said and shaped the quills. It was difficult because the quills were not consistently hard or soft, and the surface was oily. MacGregor had precise and capable fingers and he worked lightly and efficiently with them. Miss Williams watched him as he bent over the small task, admiring his ability to concentrate on any task. He returned the knife and took the quills back to Essex, wiping the residue of ink from his hands with his handkerchief. He dropped them on the table near Essex without saying anything and went back to his desk.

"Damned good, MacGregor," Essex said as he tried them. "Not one man in a hundred can sharpen a quill properly. You must have done it before."

"No."

Essex inspected the others. "Then you must have good hands. I usually make a mess of them myself. I suppose you develop good fingers from

161

working with your hands in laboratories. Your work has been in laboratories, hasn't it?"

"Most of the time."

"As you get used to this work," Essex said to him, "don't you feel that it is a better choice than science? Don't you feel that it is more active and more direct and more satisfying?"

"More direct perhaps," MacGregor said, "but not more satisfying."

Essex guessed that MacGregor was not quite as positive as he appeared about his work. It made Essex feel a little better about his own, and gave him the patience to go through all his morning's documents. But Essex had no intention of grinding out his shift monotonously. There was a Greek reception in the early afternoon, so he left his routine and took MacGregor with him.

"This will show you another side of the life," Essex told him, as if it had become a duty to convince MacGregor that diplomacy was the life for any man who had the chance to follow it.

It was a mistake, however, and Essex knew it the moment he arrived at the reception. He took one look at the collection of minor diplomats and ministers and secretaries and wives, and despised the whole lot of them. They were as miserable a collection of second-raters as he had ever seen. It was his first look at some of the Moscow diplomatic corps and he went quickly through them with one of the Counsellors — the little bouncing Mr. Maximos. MacGregor was forced out of it slightly, but Essex kept bringing him to the fore as they were introduced to these polite people. Essex became shorter in temper but Mr. Maximos became more enthusiastic than ever, which meant that he held Essex by the elbow or touched his back or patted his arm. Maximos was formally attired and wore a white flower in his black coat, and he kept up a running commentary on the terror of the EAM in Greece until Essex told him that he was sure he had other duties to perform and thanked him for his generous welcome. Essex then retired to the staircase and sat down with MacGregor, out of reach of the other guests because none would dare come and sit next to Lord Essex on the staircase.

Only John Asquith joined him after going around the entire gathering and insulting every diplomat personally. He had been received marvellously and joyously as a result, but he tired of it and took a bottle of champagne to the staircase and finished it with Essex and MacGregor, looking down upon the gathering and discussing the people with sadistic delight. His wife was down there being genuinely nice to everybody and trying to cope with the admixture of awkward young men who couldn't speak English and awkward wives who felt their own inadequacy when they stood beside this thin and saintly Englishwoman. When the time minimum was up Essex descended the staircase, flanked by Asquith and MacGregor, to make an unobtrusive exit. He was seen to the door and to the car and even a few steps along the road by Mr. Maximos, who did not see Essex's slight shudder as they left him standing in the gutter with Asquith, who was waiting for his own car.

"Well, that was a mistake," Essex admitted to MacGregor.

MacGregor knew how to take advantage of it. "Are most receptions like that?" he said with a smile.

"No, but you will probably have to wait until we return to London to see the thing properly done, and as it is now we might be back in London in no time at all."

"Perhaps to-morrow?" MacGregor said, not quite believing it possible.

"It's possible," Essex said.

They were still in Moscow the next day, which was a Thursday, and Essex said to MacGregor: "If these Russians think we are going to go off home and leave this dispute unsettled, they are very much mistaken. I have no intention of leaving here without something settled, and if they think they can freeze me out they are more stupid than I thought. I can wait here until Doomsday, and I intend waiting until I get some tangible answer out of them on our Note."

MacGregor discovered that he was pleased Essex wasn't giving up.

"Perhaps we will leave on Saturday," Essex said, "and take Kathy Clive with us." He was intrigued with that idea, and it cheered him up considerably.

He went alone in the afternoon to another reception.

This time it was a celebration at one of the South American Embassies. The Ambassador, José Salado, was a man of hot tongue, rasping voice, and vigorous sensual energy. He took to Essex immediately. They both had a passion for miniatures and all other forms of the portrait art. Salado's Embassy was full of miniatures, and he took Essex up to his marble-walled bedroom and showed him a remarkable collection of finely painted French portraits on white mother of pearl, a combination which gave scintillating perception to the bored French faces. Essex was surprised when Salado told him they were purchased in Moscow, and he listened with interest as little José Salado told him their reasonable price in English pounds. Salado suggested that they go shopping for miniatures some time, and Essex agreed readily enough. As the party thinned out, Salado was undiplomatic enough to leave it. He persuaded Essex to hurry around to one or two of the Commission shops before they closed. Since he was leaving with Essex, his guests would just have to persuade themselves that he was leaving them for some sort of diplomatic business, important business. It was nothing new for him to walk out on his own guests.

José was like that, and everybody knew it and forgave him. They forgave José everything but his love and trust in the Russians. He was alone among the established diplomatic corps of Moscow in showing any sympathy for the Soviet regime. When the conversation at diplomatic parties came around to the boorishness and stupidity of the Russians (as it always did), José Salado would conduct a one-man defence of Russian socialism, foreign policy, domestic policy, economics, morals, and art. He could conduct his defence in six languages with perfect fluency and taste, and since his education and reading and culture were a mixture of French, Spanish, Italian and English, he had the advantage over all his fellows in any argument. He used the advantage of this diverse culture and knowledge ruthlessly and unashamedly. When his opponents wished to disparage him they attacked from another direction. They drew attention to his passion for young women, his overflowing enthusiasm for the ballet, his hoarse voice, and his sparrowlike habits. Even these weaknesses were difficult accusations with José, because he acknowledged such habits as gifts rather than curses. In fact the man was irrepressible and his small fiery eyes dared any man to challenge him. He even made friends with the new Embassies who were considered outside the pale: the Poles, the Jugoslavs, the Bulgars, and the slightly more acceptable Czechs. Because his country had little serious business to do with the Russians, he seldom saw Stalin or even Molotov. When he did, it was an event for the entire diplomatic corps to talk about. He was eccentric enough to get on well with them, and he made jokes with Molotov which no one else would think of. In that he was an important Moscow diplomat.

Essex knew enough of Salado to place the man. He came from a very old Spanish family, well known and quite historical. His wife was the direct descendant of Maria, second daughter of Louis Philippe of France. Her family was associated with that of the Conte di Savoia, whom Essex had known quite well in Florence. In that sense, José Salado was the only man worth a diplomatic damn in Moscow. All the others were part of the new school which Essex rejected: stupid sons of merchants and political fathers; tobacco millionaires; upstart landowners from miserably poor countries; and political appointees from the Americas. Salado was almost alone with Essex and Drake in being a carry-over from the great tradition. Yet Essex despised the man after he had been with him for an hour. He considered Salado too bold for a foreigner — too clever and too witty and too full of energy and too eccentric.

As they rattled over the Moscow streets in Salado's old Russian Zees car, he explained these Commission shops to Essex, using his hands and his elbows to express himself. "These shops are where you find great treasures," he said. "Here they sell you the intimate objects of no historical value which the degraded Czars left behind them. Miniatures, china, porcelain, silver, and wonderful Faubourg jewelry." Salado was almost on fire as he spat the words out. "The State allows citizens to sell goods through these shops for a fixed price. The State takes 10 per cent and gives them the rest. Have you money?"

"No."

"I will lend you some."

"Perhaps I will not buy anything to-day."

"You will take one look and beg me to lend you money."

The woman driver stopped the Zees in a narrow street and turned around and said something cheerful to Salado, who laughed and replied in sharp Russian. He led Essex into a dull-windowed shop which displayed a few large vases. It was piled to the doorway with desks, pianos, pictures, candlesticks, bureaus, and large ivory ornaments, all of it worthless and barely visible in the darkness. But the glass counters which lined the walls of the shop were well-lit and filled with delicate artistic jewellery. There were pearls and jewel boxes and stick-pins and ear-rings, and even a pair of sapphire cuff-links. They looked at them all as Salado pushed his way around the counters through the crowd, pulling Essex after him.

To a plump motherly woman in a shawl, Salado said "Madame, this is an Englishman. He has seen the miniatures you have sold me and he also would like the best of what you have. Show us something tremendous."

The woman pointed non-committally at the glass counter where there were half a dozen miniatures of all sizes up to the shape of a book page. There was also a long jade cigarette-holder and a patent-looking enamel box, small painted fans and blue porcelain figures. Essex looked at the selection and realized quickly that the miniatures among them were really excellent. He peered through the glass, which he rubbed clean with his glove. He pointed at one, a tiny round locket-shaped portrait of a man done in sharp yellows and reds and greens. The woman gave it to Essex and they looked at it. The portrait was obviously that of an early nineteenth-century Italian, and his eyes twinkled and his stiff moustache made his stout face look wild and devilish. Essex knew immediately that he wanted it, and he tried to read the name which was written under it in minute gold letters, but his eyes were not that good, and he would not ask Salado. He told Salado he was interested in it. Then Essex had to listen to Salado being gay, cunning, witty, and friendly to the woman in a language which was impossible to understand.

"Do they bargain?" Essex asked.

"No," Salado said in horror. "These are State shops. Don't suggest such a thing. I was asking her for some cameos for you, but she swears she will not get any more for some time."

"How much is this miniature?"

"Two thousand roubles."

"What does that mean in pounds?"

"Forty English pounds. Marvellous, isn't it? Exquisite. Look at the evil goodness in the man. Eh? You want it?"

"Have you got any money, M'sieur Salado?"

"Hah!" Salado clapped him delightedly on the arm and roared: "What did I tell you! Here. Take it all." Salado gave him a bundle of money. "Buy some more."

"I'll arrange for you to have it back to-morrow. Just the two thousand."

Salado took the money back and counted out the two thousand and Essex put the miniature in his overcoat pocket. Then they went back to José Salado's Embassy so that Essex could get his own car.

"You must come in and have a drink of Vodka with marmalade in it," Salado said.

"I'm afraid I must go out this evening, and I have an early appointment for dinner," Essex said, not wishing to be too ungracious.

"Then we must do this again." Salado pumped his hand.

"Yes." Essex was non-committal. "I will have the money sent around to-morrow. It was very kind of you to let me have it."

"Please!" Salado cried. "Don't say such things. I shall be insulted if you send it around at all. Good-bye, Lord Essex. Are you happy in Moscow?"

"Confident would be a better word," Essex said.

"Here you can be happy if you wish. A marvellous country. Good night."

Essex leaned back and let out his breath as the car rolled out the gate.

Back in his room, Essex unwrapped the miniature and looked at it again. The colouring was so fine that the impression of light and shadow, cheek and chin, was almost third-dimensional. The eyes were like two tiny blue crystals of light, and the black moustache bristled from the man's heavy red lips. Essex turned on the bed lamp and tried again to read the small gold name. After straining his eyes and detecting three or four letters, he realized that the name was *Geronimo*. Essex put the miniature down on the table and let his curiosity work on the name. The only *Geronimo* he had ever heard of was a Western Indian who had fought his own war of independence against the Americans and unfortunately lost. This man was no Indian. He was a fat, happy, Hogarthian Italian, and his face looked up at Essex as though he were about to laugh uproariously. In fact it was a challenge to Essex to find the answer to his name.

Essex had enjoyed a satisfying day and one last pleasure remained. He telephoned Katherine Clive to remind her that this evening they would attend the Bolshoi Theatre's performance of the ballet "Giselle." Katherine said she had not forgotten about it.

Chapter 11

B<small>EFORE</small> Katherine left her office for the ballet she looked again at Drake's weekly confidential summary to Sir Bertram Cooke, which had been read by no one but Drake and herself. The major part of the report was Drake's weekly estimation of the political attitudes of the Russians, but in this particular summary he included a comment on Essex's mission. He outlined Essex's activity so far, and concluded that in his (Drake's) opinion the discussions on Azerbaijan would not succeed. The Russian attitude was one of delay and humiliating contempt for Britain's interest in the matter, and this attitude would not change, whatever special emissary was sent. Nothing could come out of the mission, and its continuation could only mean further irritating rebuffs from the Russians. Such missions, Drake reminded Sir Bertram, were of no real value because they cut right across the work which was properly done by the Embassy. The sooner this particular mission was terminated, failure or not, the better it would be for British policy in Russia.

Drake had not made a point of her reading about Essex. Ostensibly Katherine had been given the summary to check some details on the British properties seized in the Baltic states. She guessed it was Drake's intention that she read about Essex's mission, and she did not know whether to be angry or amused. She was not sure why he had done it. His last remarks in the summary concerned MacGregor, a peculiarly indifferent fellow according to Drake, and a man who was hardly fitted for the difficult task given him. This amused Katherine, and she thought it a pity that she could never tell MacGregor of it. Essex too. Both would have something appropriate to say about Drake. But they would never know of it. Even so, Katherine did not like knowing Drake's confidential opinion of them. It was awkward to know, and she thought Drake had shown bad taste, particularly in his pointed comments on MacGregor.

"What do you think of MacGregor, Helen?" Katherine asked her secretary who was putting a cover on a typewriter and blowing rubbing dust from her desk.

"I barely noticed him," she said.

"Then what was your impression of him?"

"He's got marvellous skin," Miss Boyle said. "It's like china."

"Is that all?"

"His pants are baggy."

"Hm!"

"As a matter of fact he looks a little like a professor."

"That's very near the mark," Katherine told her.

"Is he a professor?"

"No, but he might as well be."

"He looks out of place here," Miss Boyle said, "and I don't think John Melby likes him. I don't suppose he cares much about that."

"I doubt if he knows," Katherine said. "He is the sort that never knows what other people think of him. And as you say — he probably doesn't care anyway."

"Good for him," Miss Boyle said. "Shall I look back to-night to see if anything has come in for Michael Curtis?"

"No, I'll do it when I come home."

"Are you going to the Red Army Theatre?"

"I put that off," Katherine said. "I'm going to the Bolshoi to see 'Giselle.'"

"You had better hurry."

"I shan't be late," Katherine said. "I am never late."

They were not late for the ballet, but they were still in the marble foyer when the bell rang. Katherine led Essex through hurrying Russians who wore strange silk dresses and pressed blue suits with large orders in their buttonholes. A uniformed attendant shuffled the two of them into a box and locked it behind them.

"It's a pity to waste such a beautiful theatre on ballet," Essex murmured as the overture started. He had been surprised at the Bolshoi from the moment he had entered it. He had thought that the Bolsheviks would spoil it, but he recognized here the serious atmosphere of a well-run theatre. They had not taken away its rich red furnishing; and all the gilt facings were freshly painted right to the high ceiling. The theatre was packed to its six tiers, and below in the parterre there was not an empty seat.

Essex forgot his prejudice about ballet in the first act of "Giselle" and at the entr'acte he said to her: "This is the best of their culture, no doubt."

"By no means," she cried as they joined a large circle of people who were walking around in the large upstairs foyer. "Their music and drama are quite as good. Their opera is better than you will see in London — and far more frequent. In fact, there is no place quite like it for theatre and music, so don't be grudging about it."

He was not grudging about it. When they had seen the ballet through she said: "Have you ever seen anything like it?"

"I don't believe I have," Essex said. "Not in ballet anyway."

The Embassy Humber took them silently home.

"Are you coming up to have some coffee out of my thermos bottle?" Essex asked at the Embassy door.

"No. I have a little work to do," she said.

"At this hour?"

"It's simply a detail."

"Then I shall wait for you," he told her.

"No please don't. I shall get it done and go straight to bed. I have to be up very early in the morning."

"Are you leaving to-morrow?"

"I am not sure yet," she said. "I am ready to leave, but I am still un-decided."

"When will you know?"

"I shall think about it to-night."

"If you like to wait you can come back with MacGregor and me."

"When do you expect to go?" she asked him.

"Within a week I should think."

"I suppose you are about ready to give up and go home."

"Not at all," Essex said. "I shall leave here when my work is done and not before. But that shouldn't take me very long, providing I have a clear run."

"London might tell you to give it up," she said.

"I hardly think so," he said in surprise at such a suggestion.

"Do you have anything to do with Sir Bertram Cooke?" she asked him.

"Not a thing. He is Drake's man."

They stood silently at the staircase for a moment.

"Perhaps you should wait in Moscow and educate me further," he sug-gested.

"If I go," she said, "I shall go to-morrow."

"Are you sure you wouldn't like some coffee?"

Katherine gave it some thought and then refused again. They parted at the staircase.

Chapter 12

DURING the evening Vishinsky had sent word that he would see Essex on the following day.

"I believe we have turned the corner," Essex told MacGregor with fresh morning energy. "Once we get them discussing Azerbaijan, we can force them to make concessions. It won't require much. Just one compromise out of them and we will pry loose their grip on Azerbaijan."

"What do you imagine changed their mind?" MacGregor asked with genuine curiosity.

"The Note of course. What else?"

"They might be worried about your mission failing," MacGregor said.

"How the devil would my failure upset them?"

"Perhaps they don't want trouble with us. It looks as though there will be real trouble if we don't settle this dispute."

"You can be sure there will be trouble," Essex said ruefully. "And incidentally MacGregor," Essex said, "I had a cable from London this morning and they are quite satisfied with your explanation of those American newspaper stories. You must be doing rather well in this work. Any other young man would never know if London had been placated or not."

MacGregor was not interested in Foreign Office goodwill at the moment. He had placed before Essex a half-dozen typescript pages.

"What is this?" Essex asked him.

MacGregor was as casual as he could be. "I noticed in the brief from the India Office yesterday that they suggested seven or eight men who could help to widen the Azerbaijan Government. This is a short dossier I compiled on five of them. I thought you might be interested, particularly if you are seeing Vishinsky to-day."

"I am most interested," Essex said. "How did you compile this? From your own information?"

"No, from our files."

"What sort of men are they?" Essex asked.

"Not so good," MacGregor said.

"I suppose you want me to reject them?"

"I think you will when you have read about them. I didn't choose the worst. I simply took those whose names I knew. Of the five men, all but one opposed the Allies during the war, and two of them were under our surveillance for a long time."

"Which two were under surveillance?"

"Aga Tabrizi and Jafar-I-Sadik."

"Ah yes," Essex said. "I recall their names."

"They are the two men the India Office want particularly in Azerbaijan, because they are Moslem fanatics. As far as they are concerned the Azerbaijanian Democrats are atheists and unbelievers and should be hanged. They want a holy war upon the Kurds and Armenians in Azerbaijan, and the restoration of religious authority."

"Religious fanaticism is simply good politics in the Middle Eastern countries," Essex said. "Those fellows aren't quite as vicious as they appear."

"They are not the worst," MacGregor admitted. "The really bad specimen is Kazim, who was once a governor of Azerbaijan. He has put down several other Azerbaijan revolts, mainly by wholesale executions. The last time three thousand people were shot, and he has a nice habit of having his victims executed in their own homes."

"You can throw him out then," Essex said. "Are the others so bad?"

"Yes, but not so obvious."

"Have you offered me alternative men?" Essex asked.

"No, I didn't have time to get that far."

Essex dropped the typed pages to one side. "Find me six better men and you have made a point," he said. "We are not deliberately favouring these doubtful specimens, MacGregor. They are simply the best of a bad lot, and they are men who recognize government authority. And after all we are still here to restore Iranian Government authority over Azerbaijan."

"With men like these?"

"They are no worse than any of the others," Essex said.

MacGregor bent over for his documents but Essex stopped him. "MacGregor," Essex said and leaned back in his chair. They were silent for a moment. "There is a book I want you to read. If you go into the library you will find it on the small shelf near the door. It's called *An Ambassador of Peace.*"

MacGregor got the volume, and Essex thumbed through its pages. "There is a passage here which is particularly apt to our mission, and I think it might show you the historical necessity for what we are doing. This book was written by Lord d'Abernon. He was British Ambassador to Berlin before the First World War, but this is a defence of the Locarno Treaties of 1925. I had never bothered to read it before, because I disagreed with Edgar d'Abernon's opinions, but I picked it up the other day and I find it very true to the present situation. Locarno, of course, was the first attempt to create some kind of Western Bloc to stop the Russians. Ah yes, here it is. Are you listening?"

MacGregor was listening.

Essex read: " 'Resistance to communistic propaganda, the maintenance of peace in Europe, the avoidance of another Great War, the establishment of security for respective frontiers, the preservation of society on existing lines, were capital objects of British policy [at Locarno]. But there was more than this. England's stupendous and vital interests in Asia were menaced by a danger graver than any which existed in the time of the old imperialistic régime in Russia. Hostility to England or jealousy of the intrusion of British civilization into Asia were indeed of old standing. For the last seventy years of the nineteenth century, rivalry between England and Russia had been a dominant fact in history. But the Bolsheviks disposed of two weapons which Imperial Russia lacked — class-revolt propaganda, appealing to the proletariat of the world, and the quasi-religious fanaticism of Lenin, which infused a vigour and zeal unknown to the officials and emissaries of the Czar.'. . .[1]

[1] From *An Ambassador of Peace,* Vol. I, Introduction, "The Russian Danger." By Edgar d'Abernon (Hodder & Stoughton, London, 1930, 3 vols.)

"Do you know anything about Locarno?" Essex asked him.

MacGregor said he knew very little about it. "I only remember reading somewhere," he said, "that it was our policy at Locarno and the agreements reached there which made Hitler's rise to power possible."

"There has always been a great deal of criticism of the Locarno agreements," Essex agreed, "but it's worth looking into the proceedings again to understand the reason and the sense of our policies. Read d'Abernon and you will see how our policy wasn't so mistaken then; any more than it is mistaken now. If you are ready," Essex stood up, "we had better be going."

Vishinsky met them with his usual thin-lipped smile, but it broke into lively good-humour as he greeted them in Russian. For a few moments Essex felt that Vishinsky really meant his good-fellowship. MacGregor also held a cheerful conversation with Vishinsky in Russian. Though Essex couldn't understand a word of it, he could tell by Vishinsky's sharp eyes that he was making wiry jokes with MacGregor. Essex decided then that Vishinsky had something to offer them.

"MacGregor," Essex said. "Tell Mr. Vishinsky that I am surprised that he is not in Rumania broadening the Government, and add that we are very pleased to see him." It was lightly ironical.

Vishinsky offered them *papirossa* (cigarettes). "We are glad to see you still here," he replied instantly. "We had thought that the British Note was the termination of your mission." He had not taken his eyes off Essex.

"Only the beginning of my mission," Essex told him good-naturedly, and decided to be a little more careful. Vishinsky was so intent upon every word said that he seemed able to detect any hidden implication in Essex's polite English. Again Essex felt that he was being received in the chambers of a clever lawyer rather than paying state visit to a deputy Foreign Minister. As they sat down, Suchkov and Troika came in.

"How are you?" Suchkov articulated in English. His big square face opened into a smile as he gripped Essex's hand in his fist and squeezed. They sat down again and Essex waited silently.

Vishinsky began by nodding his grey head at Suchkov. "While I am in Moscow," he said to Essex through Troika, "I thought I would introduce you to Comrade Suchkov."

"We have met before," Essex told him.

"Mr. Suchkov is an Azerbaijanian himself," Vishinsky said, "from Soviet Azerbaijan. We thought that if you wanted so anxiously to talk about Azerbaijan, you might as well talk with a man who knows the subject."

"That is the very reason I brought Mr. MacGregor with me," Essex said.

"Then no doubt these young men will appreciate each other," Vishinsky said. "But before anything is said, it must be made clear that we cannot talk about Azerbaijan as a pawn in a game. We can only talk about Azerbaijan in its own right. It is not the business of any government to interfere or juggle with the historical course of events in that country."

"That is the last thing we wish to do," Essex said quickly. "We share joint responsibilities in Iran, Mr. Vishinsky. That is the level on which talks should take place."

"We have no objection to the British representative talking about our joint responsibilities," Vishinsky replied implacably. "If Lord Essex has suggestions for improvements in our joint rôle, then we will listen to him as we have always listened to representatives of Great Britain. But we will not parley on Azerbaijan's balancing rôle between Soviet and British interests. While we are always concerned about our relations with Britain, we will not bargain those relations over the body of Iran. For that reason we have also rejected the British Note as invalid and hurried, and not indicative of the British Government's sincere regard for good relations with the Soviet Union."

"I protest!" Essex said with real indignation at the sudden, casual method Vishinsky had chosen for rejecting the Note. "The Note has the full voice of the British Government and the British people behind it. It shows our deep concern with events which are taking place in Iran. It seeks to solve this problem amicably."

It was Vishinsky's turn to become indignant. "There is *no* other way of solving it than amicably," he said, "and veiled threats are not amicable thoughts. The British Note is not the expression of one friendly power to another. It shows distinct hostility as well as suspicion and threat. That is why we reject it as not a true statement of British policy. We regret your suspicion. That is why we are arranging for you to present your attitude and information to Comrade Suchkov. We welcome this opportunity to hear the *British point of view*." He said *British point of view* in English.

"Has Mr. Suchkov the full authority of the Soviet Government to conduct these negotiations?" Essex remembered past instances of delay. Colleagues had told him that Soviet negotiators were powerless. He couldn't imagine this young peasant having full powers from anybody.

Vishinsky feigned surprise, and smiled. "Has Lord Essex the full authority of his Government?" he asked.

"Naturally!" Essex said.

"Then I must reply with the same expression. Naturally Mr. Suchkov has the full authority of his Government. But I must correct you on one point. You talk about negotiations. We are negotiating nothing. Mr. Suchkov will exchange information and discuss our mutual rôle in Iran. There is really nothing to negotiate."

"We appreciate these warm considerations by the Soviet Government," Essex said in a flat voice.

Vishinsky and Suchkov talked for a moment. "Is four o'clock in the afternoon suitable for our meeting?" Suchkov asked Essex.

"Certainly. Where?"

"Here at the Foreign Office," Suchkov said. "Somebody will show you to another room."

"Alright?" Vishinsky added. (That one Russian word — *Khoroshaw?*)

"Yes."

Vishinsky relaxed as they left. He was alive with encouragement for Essex's enjoyment of Moscow: theatres, ballet, music. Soon also there would be Soviet elections, and Lord Essex might like to see how Russia went to the polls. One suggestion followed another, and Essex listened politely but remained properly English and reserved.

On the other hand, MacGregor and Suchkov spoke as if the few minutes left for their private conversation was not enough for all they had to say. Essex heard snatches of their conversation about Iran, and finally about Professor Onegin, the Russian petrologist.

"He is busy working for so many of our geological organizations," Suchkov said, "that it is hard to say where he is. He is not in Moscow, and I think he is in the Urals. But if he does come to Moscow I will let you know. If you want to send a letter to him I could do that for you."

"It doesn't matter," MacGregor said. "I wanted to see him in person."

"I will keep trying," Suchkov said with serious consideration.

For a moment they spoke together in Russian, and whatever they said was between the two of them alone. Essex had the impression that these two had forgotten their mutual rôles in a diplomatic argument about Iran. He did not like it, and he cut it short with his farewell to Vishinsky. Saying good-bye, Essex and Vishinsky exchanged delicate smiles which were carefully poised and opposed, like good foils with the *boutons* taken off.

Chapter 13

INSTEAD of feeling successful, Essex felt that he had achieved nothing. Suchkov was not the man he had come to talk with. It was useless negotiating with a man who could not make decisions, and Essex knew that Suchkov was powerless. Moreover it was an indignity to conduct negotiations on such a low diplomatic level. Essex almost decided to give up the whole mission and go home.

Nor did John Asquith improve matters. "You might think your Note achieved its purpose and forced their hand," he said cheerfully, "but

Notes mean nothing to the Russians. We have handed them too many Notes for the method to be effective any more. I remember the Americans delivering a Note to the Russians in 1933 complaining of some Russian threat to the China border. I remember the reply. It was a great loud laugh at the Yankees for having the temerity to deliver a Note to a government they did not even recognize. The Russians are so used to being accused and threatened in diplomatic complaints that you were a fool to deliver a Note to them at all. You haven't influenced them, Harold, and you are a greater fool if you think you have scared them. If they have decided to talk with you, they are just being generous. It will amount to nothing. You might as well give up now and go home."

Drake was equally discouraging. Giving them to Suchkov (said Drake) was a deliberate slight by Vishinsky. Essex replied warmly that he could get what he wanted out of any of them, whether it was Stalin or Suchkov. Anyway he might let MacGregor handle Suchkov. In reply to that suggestion Drake told him he was making a mistake, and added by the way of information that MacGregor was a bad influence and happened to be infatuated with his assistant, Katherine Clive. Essex made that a great joke by saying calmly: "We're all infatuated with her."

Nevertheless Essex was suddenly fed up with the mission and all its ramifications, including MacGregor. He was not admitting failure. He could not think in such terms. He decided that he had merely lost interest. There was little for him here, except perhaps Katherine. He was waiting for her now, filling in time writing a note to the Foreign Minister suggesting that it was a waste of time for him to remain here any longer. He might as well return to London early next week.

For that matter it would be quite interesting to return to London next week — taking Katherine Clive with him. He needed Katherine now. He had rejected many women, but here was one who stood so much higher in his estimation that he thought of his mother and waived some fears of dangerously committing himself. When Katherine came she confirmed his need. She made a challenge of her presence. She looked at the quill in his hand and said "What on earth are you using that for?"

He twiddled it in his fingers. "I prefer it to those fountain pens. When you write with a quill you really write, you don't scratch your way along the paper."

"Isn't that some kind of pretence?" she said.

"Perhaps it is," he admitted gracefully.

"Where are we going?" he asked as he turned out the lights and closed the door behind them.

"I am taking you to a Russian home," she told him.

"Oh?" He took her arm. "I have ordered a car."

"No car," she said. "We can walk."

Essex didn't mind, in fact he was pleased. He wanted to talk to Katherine. He wanted to find out something about himself. He wanted to know where Katherine Clive would fit in if he did take her back to London. He had a feeling that he was about to decide if Katherine could come completely into his life or not. It was further consideration than he had given any woman since his mother had died; but it was natural enough in view of the impression Katherine had made on him from the outset. Yet a lifetime of prejudice had to be overcome, and that would not be easy at all. He needed to talk with her to convince himself that he was plunging in the right direction.

As he took his coat from the hall he saw MacGregor outside.

"Is MacGregor coming?" he asked Katherine.

"Yes. I thought it was time you both had a little education."

MacGregor seemed just as surprised and displeased to see Essex.

A persuasive and felicitous Katherine had insisted to MacGregor that he make this visit. MacGregor had thought it decent of her, and he had been ready to forget the occasion when she had put him off to have lunch with Essex (something that still rankled). But seeing Essex now, he felt that he had been cheated again. She had made no mention of Essex's attendance, and apart from being irritated with Katherine, MacGregor was sadly disappointed. He could not continue a discussion begun with Katherine before dinner when she had called on him to suggest this outing. The discussion had developed from her questions about to-day's conversation with Vishinsky.

She had sat before MacGregor's fire being very pleasant, and MacGregor had told her that the mission was taking its first real step. He had found his tongue unusually free, as it always was when Katherine was co-operative.

"What do you call a real step?" she had asked him without cynicism.

"Talking with Suchkov," he had said without hesitation. "It will be easy talking to him because he understands Iran. It gives Essex a chance of settling the dispute now — if he can just once see Iran as a problem in itself and not as a part of our own affairs."

She had smiled to hear it, and she had been a little cynical. "Can Essex see it that way?"

"Why not?" he had said. "Essex may not like the Russians, but surely he can see that giving Iran a chance is the best possible thing for us."

"What about the Russians? Will they see it in the same light?"

"Suchkov will. He knows that Iran must be given an opportunity of settling its own problems — not told what to do nor handed over to the corrupt old ministers. I'm sorry now that I know so little about this business of negotiation." The admission had seemed a little foolish, and he had confused it further by explanation. "I never realized before that one man could have such a golden opportunity of doing so much. If I knew enough, and had the authority to talk with Suchkov, I think we could both see what had to be done. If I knew more about this diplomacy," he had said, "I might have a chance; but I am just realizing how ignorant and disinterested I have been."

There the discussion had ended because Vodka had walked in and sniffed sadly around Katherine's ankles. He had been wet and bedraggled, and Katherine had taken him home, leaving MacGregor with an unsatisfied desire to explain himself further. MacGregor had then looked forward to this evening's meeting to continue the discussion. Katherine had a way of asking the most pertinent and vital questions, and in answering them MacGregor found that he answered his own problems and cleared out some of the confusion. Now there was no hope of talking with her. Why did she have to bring Essex!

The two men greeted each other politely and the three of them marched silently out the Embassy gate, Katherine between them and holding them both with her warm fingers.

"Well, you two!" Katherine said after a long silence. "Talk."

"We talk all day," Essex said grumpily. "How far is this place?"

"Not far," she said and they walked on silently.

"How did you meet this Russian family?" Essex asked eventually.

"Through Jack Tanner," she said.

"The Communist?"

"Yes."

Moscow was unusually dark and the air was very clear. It was not a smoky city, and MacGregor felt his hands and sensitive skin free of grime for the first time in a year or more. Through the clear night, Katherine led them across a square towards a Neon light advertising a cinema and then along a small street and through an opening formed by two dark buildings. MacGregor instinctively made a mental chart of their route, and he wondered how far they were from the river. The dark snow-piled courtyard shut him off from all landmarks, and he was in the sort of place he had often wondered about in Moscow, a four- or five-storied building on the street, worn and old but well-kept and clean, and inhabited by unknown people.

"Do any of these Russians speak English?" Essex asked Katherine.

"Caradoc speaks perfect English; his wife just enough."

"Caradoc?" Essex said. "That is a Welsh name."

"He is Welsh. I suppose I should tell you that he is the clown at the Moscow Circus. His wife is Russian; she is an acrobat."

"Are you taking us slumming?" Essex asked.

"Don't be rude," Katherine replied without being annoyed.

The clown was an old man, and he lived at the top of the dark building.

His one room was so small that the quilted brass bed almost filled it, but Caradoc himself was small enough for it, and so was his wife. He was a little red-headed old man, old enough to consider age the only real human division. He lumped Essex and MacGregor together as impersonal young men among a million other young men. He immediately took for granted that they had come here to attend everything he said. Katherine was something different, however. The grizzled little Welshman showed a natural affection for her and he leaned upon her shoulder as he sat down in the horsehair rocking-chair near the small oil stove. He had a stiff right leg, and as he sat down it straightened out with a snap and his young Russian wife pushed a footstool under it. He thanked his wife politely, and she smiled back at him as a man who had all her consideration, companionship, and deep respect.

Katherine watched Essex and MacGregor closely because she wanted to see how they would get on with the clown. She herself knew what to expect of Caradoc because she understood him instinctively, had done so since the first time she had seen him in the centre of the Moscow Circus ring. He had not bounced around the ring in ragged trousers, tumbling and fooling like a normal clown. He had simply appeared alone on a dais under a spotlight. On that particular occasion Caradoc had displayed himself as the miserable conscience of Pierre Laval. By the writhing of his compact, expressive, creaking body; by the movements of his small head and his grizzled face; by the intonation of his words; and above all by the terrible satire of their content, he had created a picture of the degradation of Laval. He had spoken in Russian, but Katherine had understood most of it because of its English accent and its simplicity, although Jeb Wills had needed to translate some of it. From Laval he had turned to satirizing the generals of the invading German, Italian, and Rumanian armies. Then he had turned more lightly upon Russian officials, policemen, women, tram-conductors, Metro crowds, foreign visitors, street-boy scallywags (with whom he seemed to sympathize most), and all the characters of life that surrounded anyone in Moscow. He was always political, and he never moved from his small dais, nor did he make any costume change except to pull and swish the long frock coat he wore. The Russians had long thought him as great as Chaplin; and after seeing him Katherine had agreed. She had also been impatient to know the little Welshman — of whom the rest of the world knew nothing. At their first meeting, Caradoc had been indifferent to her presence. She had expected nothing else. But by arguing with him in his own biting terms she had provoked his attention. Now she was respected and liked by both Caradoc and his young wife, Maria. From taking little notice of Maria, Katherine had gradually realized that the young Russian acrobat was a woman without a trace of any human vulgarity and deception, in fact Katherine thought at times that she had never seen a woman with more natural dignity. She was the only human being whom Caradoc treated gently, as if he had found in her an ultimate creation, unqualified for derision.

Katherine had brought Essex and MacGregor here not only for their education, but to make her own observations on their behavior with the clown. It was an examination in their taste for human relationship. To pass it they would have to measure Caradoc as she measured him; fall in with his ways as she had done; grasp his significance with something of her own instinct; and then cope with him as a sacrilegious old man whose satiric barbs found every target. She was therefore more intent upon the men she had brought here than upon the usual fascination of Caradoc himself, and she was getting ready to pass judgment on them. She would watch one against the other and see who survived the measure of the clown. It was an important test for each of them.

In the first surprise of their surroundings both Essex and MacGregor were silent and stiff-necked. They both sat uncomfortably on the hard small chairs in the warm corner of the room, while Caradoc asked them with deceptive politeness how long they would be in Moscow and what they were here for. MacGregor bent down to stroke a cat and left Essex to answer it. Essex ignored the question and demanded in return how Caradoc had come to leave his native England to become a clown in Russia. Caradoc's mildness faded and he said that he had left his native Wales to become a clown in first one foreign country, England, and then in every other country in Europe until he had arrived at the least foreign of them all: Russia.

It had begun well, but Essex was taken off guard by Caradoc's reply. Essex retired a little and Katherine explained to her colleagues just what sort of clown Caradoc was. She said he was not really a clown, but a satirist.

"I am nothing of the sort," Caradoc snapped. "I am a clown. I have always been a clown, and I will always be a clown. Until I was sixty I was tumbling in the sawdust like all the others. I gave it up only because I became too brittle to fall without cracking my senile limbs. I was forced to take up a stationary position, and it has made a stationary clown of me. For fifteen years I have been a clown who hasn't found it necessary to fall in the dirt. There is nothing more to my work than that. I am a clown who stands still," he concluded irritably and rocked on his rocking chair and lifted his other leg stiffly and placed it on the stool before the small cylindrical oil stove. The naked yellow light caught the wrinkles in his sandy face and lit the few red and white hairs which made a halo round his shining crown.

Katherine pursued this subject deliberately, knowing that Caradoc enjoyed arguing about it. She told them that Caradoc had been compared with George Bernard Shaw and with Charlie Chaplin, and that he corresponded regularly with both men, both being among the few outsiders who knew and admired him.

"You are like our Russian critics," Caradoc complained. "They deny that I am a clown so that they can give me half a chair in heaven with Shaw. Well I am a clown, and I don't want to share anything with Shaw."

"Ah, but Shaw is also a clown," Essex said by way of a good-natured compliment. "A rather impressive clown."

"Shaw is too stupid to be a clown," Caradoc said calmly. "He knows nothing about men. He might be a fool, but he's not a clown. Now Chaplin is different. He suffers like any other man, whereas Shaw is too clever to suffer anything but prolific old age." In the change of his voice and the squinting of his face he had been a sad Chaplin one moment and a senile Shaw the next.

Essex smiled despite himself, and MacGregor sat silently near Caradoc and rubbed the cat's chin. Caradoc went on attacking all clever men, and his list of stupid-clever men encompassed so many great figures that he eventually bundled them all together and said disgustedly that they were necessary in life only because they gave the simple man a chance to be different. Furthermore, these clever men were so bad, that it was only in view of their evil that a simple man could show a little good without being persecuted as a dangerous criminal.

Essex disagreed because he believed in great men. He had realized now that the only way of meeting Caradoc was to behave without any inhibition at all. Otherwise Caradoc would soon make a fool of him, not a vicious fool, but an ordinary human fool. This Essex refused to be.

Strangely enough Caradoc left the polite MacGregor alone, perhaps because MacGregor was talking with his wife in Russian. Katherine was with Essex. She saw MacGregor momentarily as something pallid beside the vigour of these two older men. She was annoyed with him and annoyed with Maria for not letting him face Caradoc on his own, as Essex was doing.

By now Essex and Caradoc had reached the generalities of history, and it was almost a straightforward argument between them, an argument in which Caradoc was accusing Essex of being stupid enough to see war as inevitable.

"There will always be wars," Essex admitted and added that England would always win them, "just as we have eventually won this war."

"England is always winning wars," Caradoc said in his high-pitched lilting Welsh-English, "but she is now beginning to lose the war between wars. However — now that you have won this war what do you expect the world to do? Fight another?"

"No, it should settle down and behave itself."

"How?" Caradoc was deceptively solemn.

"If nobody tries to change things too much, then nobody else will get discontented or afraid or angry, and we will all settle down peacefully."

"No revolutions?" Caradoc said, his voice an exact copy of Essex's.

"No revolutions!" Essex said. "When people have a little more food, and when their houses are rebuilt and their shops are full, they will stop being so radical and go back to normal living. Radicalism is always fresh when destruction is fresh. It wears off, and Europe will wear it off very quickly."

"So radicalism isn't a force to be taken seriously at all." It might have been Essex asking himself a credulous question, it came so exactly from Caradoc's lips as Essex's voice and Essex's question.

Essex would not fall into the trap of ridicule. He remained straightforward. It was his only protection. "If you are asking me to make allowances for the necessity of radicalism, I cannot. If I did I would have to allow internal considerations to decide international situations, and that would be ridiculous. It would be stupid of me if I worried about the conflicting forces in every country near and far before I made a decision which concerns, say — the Russians and ourselves. I cannot worry about who is right and wrong among the minute political forces that always rumble underground in every nation. I have one concern, and that is our part and our own right in this world."

"In view of what you say," Caradoc said primly, "there is one thing I would like to know."

"Yes?" Essex was suspicious.

"It is simply that I often wonder whether the English diplomat acts upon his own convictions, or whether he submits entirely to the convictions of his changing governments." This, Caradoc said in a mimicry of diplomatic verbiage.

"A little of both," Essex said, not at all upset, but surprised all of a sudden that he should find himself sitting in this small circle in a dim corner of a bare room talking to a clown, whose comments he treated warily. "Actually governments change but policies remain," Essex went on. "Within the policy you obey your own convictions until they conflict with the particular government's attitude."

"And then?"

Essex smiled. "You compromise or you resign," he said.

"Then tell me what British diplomacy is supposed to do. Eh?"

"It is supposed to preserve the British Empire," Essex said good-naturedly, realizing that he was the only Englishman alive who could be Lord Essex and at the same time tell a clown in Moscow what to expect of British diplomacy. "We make treaties," he said, "pacts, alignments, blocs, and alliances which will guarantee our national safety. We prevent other alignments which are hostile to our security and to our historical rights in other lands. Whatever happens, we guard our life-lines. Since they encompass so much of the world, we are always vitally aware of our responsibility in other lands."

"I suppose you in particular are vitally aware of your responsibility in Iran," Caradoc said. Again the perfect words of diplomacy.

"Naturally," Essex said. "Iran is vital to us."

This reply concerned MacGregor. It was a direct answer to MacGregor's own question: Could Essex just once forget British self-interest in Iran? Listening to Essex MacGregor decided over again that Essex would never make any consideration outside his loyalty to British interests. It was all hopeless, Suchkov notwithstanding. Essex would go on negotiating for a piece of cheese or a barrel of oil, but the sight of Iran would never reach him.

Essex did not stop there. Having accepted Caradoc as a sly but worthy listener, he went on to explain in a comfortable way that British diplomacy was flexible without being changeable. The British diplomat achieved his purpose where achievement seemed impossible. This required patience, largesse, and a determination never to be insulted nor to go away empty-handed.

Essex was feeling a new confidence in his mission. He had talked himself into it. His hopelessness about Suchkov was dispersing, and he was suddenly anxious to begin his talks with the square little Russian. Suchkov would be a mere beginning. His confidence rose higher and he stood politely to help Mrs. Caradoc carry a small table across the room. It contained a carafe of vodka, black bread, cheese, a square of bully beef, radishes, and four white sandwiches of powdered egg.

They drank the vodka, toasted each other, toasted the English, the Russians, the Welsh, and the Scotch. All the time Katherine tried to bring Caradoc and MacGregor together in dispute, but Caradoc would not fight with him and MacGregor remained quiet and annoyingly unprovocable. Katherine felt let down. Caradoc should have rough-handled MacGregor as he rough-handled everybody else, herself included. Perhaps he saw some of the same qualities in MacGregor that he saw in his wife. Katherine did not want to accept such a thought, but looking at the Scot she knew he could be nothing else by his appearance but a man of no presumption, and a man of slow conviction. Caradoc must like him, although they had said very little to each other. Perhaps it was because of Maria's easy way with him.

Whatever the reason, Katherine begrudged it because she preferred a man to come out and meet his fellows as Essex had done. Essex had enjoyed this meeting; MacGregor had simply accepted it. It was a choice between Essex's worldliness and MacGregor's simplicity. In irritation with MacGregor she chose Essex and gave him her attention. Essex, however, was busy charming Mrs. Caradoc with compliments on her English. He was so pleased with his conversation that he felt his evening to be complete. It was therefore timely when Caradoc snored angrily from his chair and thereby announced that their call had ended.

They went out quietly to avoid awakening him. Mrs. Caradoc lit a candle and led them downstairs, saying good night to each of them in careful English, finally kissing Katherine.

As they came into the dark streets, MacGregor was still thinking of the clown. Caradoc reminded him of the oldest and most respected paleontologist in England, Professor Edwin Hills. Because he was undoubtedly the greatest English paleontologist and because he was eighty years of age, Professor Hills had established his right to say what he pleased, in his field and out of it. Professor Hills commanded you to attend and be still, and MacGregor had never felt any discomfort in accepting it as requirement for listening to him. It was something of the same thing with Caradoc. And just as Hills had always produced something instructive, Caradoc had revealed for MacGregor (accidentally perhaps) the hopelessness of Essex. Now there was no more thought of discussing diplomatic prospects with Katherine. In fact, MacGregor was thinking how satisfying it would be to hear the old Professor again. He must get into one of his lectures when they returned to London. Hills still managed his three or four lectures a year and no doubt he would go on with them until he dropped dead among his fossils.

While MacGregor was thoughtful, Essex was being cheerful. He had one thought in mind: getting at Suchkov to-morrow. He decided that the best way of tackling Suchkov would be to present him with a written outline of demands for improving the situation in Iran; then back it up with plenty of examples of Russian interference. MacGregor would supply the evidence, and he must instruct MacGregor about it when they returned to the Embassy so that they could be ready for Suchkov to-morrow. It would be something to satisfy MacGregor's organizational mind. It was a good scheme, and Essex had an idea that it would work. Already his renewed confidence began to show. He walked vigorously and took deep breaths of cold air. Katherine thought he was overdoing it and decided that Essex had been just a little too clever and too well-met, and now he was being smug about it.

Without thinking, Essex took her arm. "So you take me to a Welsh-man," he said, "and tell me he's Russian. We are the only people who can produce weird beggars like that. Shaw is an Irishman and Chaplin a Whitechapel Jew, and here is this fellow a Welshman from Aberystwyth."

Katherine walked silently between her companions wondering how two men could be so stupid, so disappointing, so full of themselves.

Chapter 14

T HE Rolls-Royce held the slippery streets of Moscow very well, but Essex was nervous and he felt like telling the driver to slow down. He sat back and put up with it, drumming his fingers against the frosted window, and disliking MacGregor's patient silence. The whole interview they had just had with Suchkov had obviously made no impression on MacGregor, whereas Essex felt himself still tense with the control he had summoned to end the interview politely. As for Mac-Gregor: there were times when the silence of an assistant could be an advantage; but there were other moments when it became too much. Why the devil didn't MacGregor make some comment or pass some word on that wretched fellow Suchkov?

"The trouble is we didn't hit the man hard enough," Essex said irritably. "As I told you last night we had a chance of presenting an overwhelming case to Suchkov, showing him just how much we knew of Russian interference in Azerbaijan. I rather expected you to put in a word to-day and support me with more examples than you had listed," Essex said.

"Sorry," MacGregor said. "I didn't know."

"It's no use being sorry now, and you should have known. Actually nothing would get through that thick Russian skull anyway. I suppose Molotov picked his stupidest man just to annoy me. The Embassy should have known about Suchkov. They should have been able to warn me that he was a useless dolt, and that I would simply be wasting my time with him. I don't think I can tolerate these heavy-handed Russians any longer. In fact I'm sure I can't."

MacGregor was not taking much notice, knowing that Essex was always in a state of temper after one of these unsuccessful interviews. It would wear off.

The Rolls turned into the Embassy gate and MacGregor leaned across to open the door for Essex.

"Bring my pouch," he told MacGregor, "and we'll go straight to work."

"You have the pouch," MacGregor said and pointed to it.

Essex had it gripped like a vice in his hand and under his arm.

"Then come along!" he said.

Their office room was cold because the fire had died down. MacGregor was sent to find one of the servants with more coal. The man came and Essex paced impatiently while the fire was raked and re-stacked. Miss Williams also returned, and Essex told her to be available. Essex had transmitted his nervousness to all of them except MacGregor. The man who had stoked the fire dropped a small shovel on the way out and Essex jumped. Drake arrived, and he too seemed nervous. MacGregor sat still and turned over page after page of the files he had brought back. He knew that Essex had lost the day and he thought it Essex's own fault. MacGregor knew that Essex had planned to overwhelm Suchkov, but in this case Essex had been asking for retaliation. Essex had received the reply from Suchkov which had upset him so much, a reply which Mac-Gregor would often remember since it expressed so much of his own feeling on the subject. It was a lesson which MacGregor had often wanted to deliver himself to Essex.

"I have been reluctant to reduce this discussion to your provocative level," Suchkov had said to Essex, "but I have no choice. The trouble is that your whole premise is wrong. You are claiming that the Soviet authorities began and influenced the existence of the Democratic Party. That is the basis of all your statements. The simplest way to discredit your absurd claim is to tell you about Iran, of which you are apparently ignorant. The people of Iran are oppressed, poverty-stricken, and miserable with hunger and disease. Their death rate is among the highest in the world, and their infant mortality rate threatens Iran with complete extinction. They are ruled without choice by feudalistic landowners, ruthless Khans, and venal industrialists. The peasants are slaves and the workers are paid a few pennies for a twelve-hour day — not enough to keep their families in food. I can quote you all the figures you like to support these statements, quote them if necessary from British sources. I can also quote you the figures of the wealth which is taken out of Iran yearly by the Anglo-Iranian Oil Company, of which the British Government is the largest shareholder. Two hundred and forty million pounds a year is taken out of Iran by your oil company: a hundred times the total amount of Iran's national income and ten thousand times the total national income of the working people of Iran. By such natural resources as oil, Iran is by nature one of the wealthiest countries on earth. That wealth goes to Britain, while Iran remains poverty ridden and without economic stability at all. It has no wage policies, no real trade unions, few hospitals, no sanitation and drainage, no irrigation, no proper housing, and no adequate road system. Its people have no rights before the law; their franchise is nonexistent; and their parliamentary rights are destroyed by the corrupt method of election and political choice. The Iranian people suffer the terrors of a police regime, and they are prey to the manipulations of the grain speculators and the money operators. The racial minorities suffer discrimination and intolerance, and religious minorities are persecuted for political ends. Banditry threatens the mountain districts, and British arms have been used to support one tribe against another. I could go on indefinitely, painting you a picture of misery and starvation and imprisonment and subjection which must shame any human being capable of hearing it. Yet you say that the existence of a Democratic Party in Iran has been created by the Soviet authorities. You underestimate the Iranian people, Lord Essex! The Democratic Party has arisen out of all this misery and subjection as a force against corruption and oppression. Until now the Iranian people have been unable to create a political party because the police system prevented it by terror and assassination. Any attempt to organize the workers and peasants was quickly halted by the execution of party leaders and the vast imprisonment of its followers. The Iranian people, however, have a long record of struggle and persistence, and they do not have to be told by the Soviet Union where their interests lie. They are not stupid and they are not utterly destroyed. They still possess the will to organize a democratic body and follow it into paths of government. The Soviet Union has simply made sure that the police assassins did not interfere, particularly in the case of Azerbaijan. To talk of our part in 'creating' the Democratic movement is an insult to the people and a sign of ignorance. We do not underestimate the Iranian people, and as far as we are concerned the Democratic Party of Azerbaijan belongs to the people. It is their creation and their right, and it cannot be broken by wild charges which accuse the Soviet Union of its birth. We did not create it, and we have not interfered in the affairs of Iran. On the contrary, it is the British Government which has interfered continuously and viciously in Iran's affairs."

Essex had his own picture of what had followed, and he was telling Drake about it. "Suchkov," he was saying to Drake, "made a long speech about the misery of Iran, and then proceeded to accuse us of interference. The trouble is he didn't even make a good job of it. He is so slow-witted that he could only repeat the stock accusations. I could have made a better case against us myself, but we won't go into that. He really thought he had finished me."

"Well how did you end it?" Drake was sitting on his window-sill waiting for Essex to finish so that he could go. He had something else on his mind.

"I simply tossed the documents across the table at him," Essex said. "They contained our demands and our listed cases of Russian interference. I told him 'Alright! You want our case without accusation. There it is. There is our specific proposition. Widen the Azerbaijanian Government with representatives of other parties, instruct the Azerbaijan rebels to allow Iranian Government troops to enter Azerbaijan, cancel all these new economic and political measures, guarantee anew Iran's right to rule Azerbaijan, and allow British representatives free access to all parts of Azerbaijan.'"

"I doubt if it had any effect on him," Drake murmured.

"It had its effect. Those big peasant hands picked up the papers and I could see them shaking. He then looked at me as if I were a brick wall, and he said rather stupidly that he had no power to speak for the Azerbaijanian Government. It's an autonomous authority within Iran, he said. The Soviet Union cannot speak for it nor interfere in its body. He said it was an internal affair, and that any idea of broadening the Azerbaijanian Government should be put to Azerbaijan, not to the Russians. The Soviet Government was very willing to transmit the idea to Tabriz for consideration, but he would have to study the documents before he could discuss it further. That was that. He didn't know where he was. When I asked him if he would like to discuss this matter again he mumbled the usual nonsense about getting in touch with us. I didn't waste any more time. I shook his clumsy fist and left him."

Other than the straightforward argument about Iran, there was something else that bothered Essex. He could not understand the Russian political line. They talked in political terms which he had failed to recognize, and worst of all — to anticipate. What Essex wanted now, more than anything else, was a man who could give him the key to Russian scheming. There was no one in the Embassy who could do it, he knew that much. For that matter it was really MacGregor's job. MacGregor should have laid bare Russian policy for him long ago.

When Drake left, Essex stood up and looked out the window at the Kremlin. "I often wonder, MacGregor, why you don't give me a little more lead on the Russians. It is really your job; and an explanation of a man like Suchkov would have saved me that stupid conversation to-day."

MacGregor knew he was being given a share of the blame. He didn't like it but he kept safely quiet, knowing he was too ready to argue with Essex.

"Couldn't you have given me more support to-day?" Essex did not turn around.

"I don't quite know what you mean by support," MacGregor said.

"What I wanted was an overwhelming case against Suchkov, not only in document but in quoted example. You should have replied to Suchkov's Iranian nonsense with your own evidence of the situation."

"Our evidence was in the document you gave him."

"Surely you had more."

"Quite a lot more, but none of it was any good."

"What was the matter with it?"

MacGregor did not hold back any longer. "Like all the rest of our information from Iran, it was wild and unreliable. I have been trying to let you see that since we came here. We have plenty of examples of Russian interference, but too many come from worried carpet dealers or scared bank officials or unreliable gendarmerie. Even the best of what I listed in the document was bad, and what remained was worse. There is little in the lot of it that the Russians need take seriously. We don't know what is really going on in Azerbaijan, and I don't think we can pretend to know."

"You are allowing the Russians to influence you, MacGregor!" Essex accused.

MacGregor in defence was equal to anything that Essex said. "No sir," he said. "I am simply beginning to understand something about this argument between ourselves and the Russians which I never understood before. We are arguing with the Russians about Iran, but because of our ignorance they are in a better factual position than we are. That's all."

"It's by no means all," Essex said, a little calmer for MacGregor's anger. "This is not simply an argument about information. This concerns the creation by the Russians of a puppet government in Azerbaijan, and that stands above whatever we lack in information. In presenting our case, however, we needed a whole indictment. You should have supplied sufficient facts for it. Why couldn't you get them!"

"To get that sort of information you would have to go to Azerbaijan yourself," MacGregor said, "because we will never know what is going on there by the evidence supplied from London. I would have thought that if we wanted to accuse the Russians of establishing a puppet government in Azerbaijan we would first find out what was really happening there. As it is we don't know. The only real example we have of Russian interferences, for instance, is the case of the Russian who stopped Iranian officers from proceeding to Tabriz. Every other example outside that is open to doubt. That may not matter, because the real argument seems to be about the Azerbaijanian Democrats. We are rejecting them completely, although we know nothing about them. We simply consider them dangerous rebels, and that is where our argument begins and ends. I have only read their statements of policy, which I summarized and put on your desk the other day, but from these I don't see anything dangerous about them at all. We claim they are out to confiscate and nationalize everyone's private property and use revolutionary methods to establish their power. Well they certainly intend confiscating some of the large estates to parcel up among the peasants, but they say nothing about nationalizing the few industries or seizing the banks. In general the programme suggests land reforms which will give some of the land to the peasants, bank reforms which will do away with money speculations, and market reforms which will prevent the landowner holding back needed supplies of grain for high prices. If we are really worried about the dangerous situation in Azerbaijan and Iran, our only hope is to go there ourselves and find out what is happening. Then we might be able to argue with the Russians."

"All that is the wonderful sort of stuff the Russians would understand,"

Essex said. "Perhaps you are the man who should argue them out of Azerbaijan."

It was pronounced with an edge, but Essex quickly realized that there was more in the cynical suggestion than he had really intended. MacGregor might still be a means of getting at the Russians. They had a ready-made respect for him, and his peculiar ideas probably appealed to them. Used subtly, but properly, MacGregor could be a valuable lever. He must give it some thought.

Chapter 15

DRAKE read the London cable instructing Essex to abandon his mission, and he asked himself if this was the result of his own note to Sir Bertram Cooke. Whatever the inspiration, the Foreign Office was being rather casual about it. This was not a special cable to Essex. It was part of the diplomatic instruction which the Ambassador received daily from London. There in this morning's list was a short note telling Essex to come home. Drake thought of taking it down to Essex himself to see the effect, but he rang Katherine Clive and asked her to come and see him.

"Where are we on that last Russian memorandum?" he asked her, as a vague preliminary.

"On reparations?"

"Yes. I didn't get a chance to read it all. What are their complaints now?"

"They list factories and industries in our occupied zone which they think should be dismantled," she said. "There is also that old demand for one of the Krupp plants at Essen, which they refer back to the Potsdam agreement. There is also a claim by Zhukov that we have a large German Army still intact, and that we are actually arming some of them. He says that we have a German Army of 100,000 at Stockhausen and reminds us that all German military formations should be disbanded. Actually it's the Control Council's business. I don't know why we get it at all."

"No doubt London sent it on for our edification," Drake said.

"Do we still need edifying?"

Drake sighed. "One always needs edifying here."

Katherine waited, knowing there was more than this.

"One other thing." Drake put a hand to his grey hair. "What days do the Russian planes go to Berlin now? Is it every day?"

"I don't know. Three times a week I think, but I am not sure."

"Ask someone to find out will you. Lord Essex and MacGregor will probably be leaving us to-morrow." He watched her closely.

Surprise was not beyond her. "Really?" she said flatly.

"Yes. It's in this morning's list." Drake put his white fingers on the foolscap pages, finding it hard to conceal delight in London's method of recalling Essex.

"I suppose Harold had finished with the Russians anyway," Katherine said, disliking Drake's sweet pleasure.

"It seems that the Russians have finished with them," Drake smiled. "Poor Harold had a bad day with Suchkov yesterday. He'll be glad to get these Russians out of his hair. They seem bent on irritating him and insulting him."

"No doubt Harold can hold his own," she commented.

"Perhaps. But they are certainly making it difficult for him." Drake liked his rôle of defence and sympathy for Essex. "Here is the final touch." Drake handed her a large white card which was neatly engraved in Russian italics. It was an invitation to a reception being given this evening by the Russian Foreign Office. "You know who that reception is for?" Drake said.

Katherine put the card down.

"It's for half a dozen Azerbaijanian rebels who are up here on some kind of mission," Drake said. "It's one of those deliberate Russian insults, aimed directly at Essex. To make it worse they invite us."

Katherine laughed. "Well at least they are giving you a chance to throw it back in their teeth. All you have to do is go along and look pleased about it."

Drake did not smile. "No one from this Embassy will go," he said. "Our attendance would imply a form of recognition for these Azerbaijanians, and we have no intention of falling into that trap. It's one of those cunning affronts which make the Russians so difficult to get on with."

"Aren't they too stupid to be that cunning?"

Drake put on his glasses and said quite stiffly that the Russians were stupid and cunning at the same time. "Would you like to take this cable down to Harold?" he said to her. He had intended to be a little more subtle about it, subtle enough to underline Katherine's relationship in that quarter, but his primness had come to the surface too quickly. "He hasn't seen it yet, so he doesn't know that he has been recalled."

She took the foolscap sheets and strolled out without saying anything.

Essex had spent the morning drinking Russian champagne. Two bottles had been brought to the office for him, and he had sat by the fire to consume it. He had insisted on MacGregor sharing it with him, and Kathy found them seated on the couch with their legs stretched out before them, talking and drinking and being friendly after yesterday's contest. Essex had refused to put pen to paper this morning because the less written and remembered about the Suchkov interview the better.

"Champagne at eleven o'clock in the morning?" she said as she sat down.

"Get a glass MacGregor," Essex said and waved his hand across the room. "Get the water glass from the small table there. Do you mind drinking from a tumbler, Kathy? If I had known you were coming to visit us I would have ordered another bottle, in fact I think I shall send Miss Williams for another."

"I haven't time to sit here and drink," she said, and looked from one to the other. They were both in very good spirits and pleased to see her, yet she felt like an interloper at this advanced stage. Essex was pushing a chair near the fire for her, and MacGregor was pouring champagne into the tumbler, a most unnatural-looking act for MacGregor to perform. His studious face was flushed, either with the blazing fire or the champagne, and he seemed to be unusually cheerful about something. Essex on the other hand was being happy by purpose and application, and he was obviously glad of her presence for the distraction she brought. Essex flourished himself about her. MacGregor sat down and smiled at her; not as if she were in the room at all, but as if he were thinking pleasantly of her in absence. This MacGregor was the same MacGregor who had been so self-contained with the Caradocs. She still wanted to upset him, insult him if possible; in fact the impulse to hurt him and damage him before Essex was so strong in her that she was surprised at her own vehemence, and therefore suppressed it. She behaved very coolly.

"I have never seen either of you looking so detached from Moscow," she said. "What are you celebrating?"

"There is never anything to celebrate here," Essex said. "We are just breaking the monotony. We must gird ourselves for another attack."

"That may not be necessary," she said and gave him the cable.

Essex read it and said "Well I'll be damned." He was not annoyed yet. He was incredulous and amused, and he read it again. "Here MacGregor," he said. "Some stupid fool in London is trying to be clever. What on earth makes them think I would leave here now? How long have we been here?"

"Ten days!" MacGregor read the cable and also felt indignant.

"Ten days and they want a miracle," Essex said to his friends.

He could not say much more about it, although he felt like telling them exactly what this meant. If he had been a lesser man he would have been insulted by this telegram. Being Essex, he could only assume it to be the illicit interference of someone like Bertram Cooke or Alastair Cutler. They had not wanted him on this mission in the first place, and no doubt they were doing their best to make it impossible for him. He wanted to explain this to Katherine, but not a word of it could reach her. One thing, he thought as he looked at Katherine and realized how remarkably young and sure she was, if I do go back to London I will certainly take Kathy with me. There will be something absolutely satisfying in that, whatever happens on this mission. "I wonder what the devil prompted this decision," he said, and it was as far as he could go.

"I suppose the Foreign Office has decided it's hopeless," MacGregor said. He did not quite know what to say, but he attempted to console Essex.

"No they haven't!" Essex said irritably. "Where would they get such an idea? Certainly not from my reports." The only occasion on which he had declared the mission hopeless was in the letter he had written to the Minister last night, but he had torn it up.

"London might have heard about the Azerbaijanians arriving in Moscow," Katherine said casually. "Did you know about the reception this evening?"

"I know about it," Essex said irritably, "but London doesn't."

"Then no doubt some intrigue has been going on." Katherine went off without finishing her champagne. They both asked her to stay, but she said she had work to do. She had been distant like this with both of them since their evening with Caradoc, and neither understood it.

"She may be right," Essex said. "Someone may have meddled."

"In the Foreign Office?" MacGregor did not like this development.

"God only knows where," Essex said. "It could come from any quarter. Too many people did not want this mission to take place at all. I have a reputation in some official quarters, MacGregor, of being too willing to talk with the Russians. That is the trouble with the Foreign Office. There are so many people with fingers in the pie that you can never be sure what influences are at work against you. Of course the influence could have come from somewhere else, from outside the Foreign Office. I am hanged if I know. But I am certainly not going to be sacrificed on any political altar. I have no intention of being a Gordon abandoned at Khartoum."

MacGregor felt an alarming sense of guilt. In his last report to Sir Rowland Smith, his superior at the India Office, he had suggested that negotiation in Moscow was a waste of time, and that the best place to talk about Iran was in Iran. MacGregor had made quite a case of it by showing how the actual situation in Iran was so much different from the situation being negotiated in Moscow. He had written it in one of his moments of distrust and impatience with Essex. Moreover, all his reports to the India Office had followed similar but milder lines. He could not believe, however, that they were responsible for Essex's recall. He would not believe it, and yet the dangerous thought was there. He hoped that Essex would never see his reports, and he asked himself how he could have been so stupid. Why couldn't he see then, as he could now, that this mission of Essex's had to succeed? It was still hopeless to expect consideration for Iran out of Essex, but it was better that he talk about it in Moscow than break off completely with the Russians. That was too dangerous because of the larger international issues involved.

"MacGregor," Essex said thoughtfully. "I have to see Molotov."

"Perhaps I could ring him," MacGregor suggested.

"You wouldn't get him."

"Shall I try it?"

"No. It's a waste of time, and he would be evasive anyway. I have to get him in person; and there is one way to do it. I think we will go to that reception this evening." Essex rocked on his heels and suddenly became pleased and even warm with the thought. "Yes," he said enthusiastically in discovery. "I think I'll surprise them. They don't expect me there, that's certain. Well by God we'll make the grand gesture and turn up. It will be that co-operative spirit the Russians are always asking for. Moreover, if the British Embassy attends, then every other Embassy will be there, I can see to that. Molotov will know it also, and he dare not be unfriendly after such an act of good grace. I'll go up and tell Francis."

MacGregor felt better, and he was anxious to help.

"You had better get Katherine back here," Essex told him from the door. "Tell her to let every Embassy in Moscow know that we are going to this reception, particularly the Americans and that chap Salado and also the newspapermen. But it must be done carefully and not at all deliberately, in fact she might be able to arrange it so that they find out for themselves. In the meantime draft a cable to London telling them that we will not be coming back, and then sign it with your own name and send it off." That was his answer to the slight he had received this morning.

Drake listened to Essex's scheme and stood up to face Essex more adequately. "It's unheard-of, Harold," he said incredulously. "If you attend that reception you will be giving *de facto* recognition to these rebels."

"Nonsense," Essex said.

"It is not nonsense. The Russians will take recognition for granted."

"Let them," Essex said. "They will find out how wrong they are when we resume our talks. In the meantime it is imperative that I see Molotov quickly."

"I tell you it's a dangerous precedent," Drake insisted.

"Dangerous my eye. We are not putting anything in writing. What are the Russians going to do? Claim that we have officially recognized these rebels because we attend a reception in their honour? They are not that stupid. All we have to do is go along and show our faces, and the Russians will never recover from their astonishment. It's a nice little jolt at them. You should enjoy it."

"I will not go, Harold." Drake sat officially down. "It's folly, and I will not be part of it. Nobody in this Embassy will go either. I will forbid it. My responsibilities continue beyond yours, and I know the danger in what you are doing. You are making a bad mistake."

The mixture of anger and humour which Essex experienced was partly due to the champagne. The trouble was he couldn't separate the emotions properly. "You have no vision, Francis," he said calmly. "Never have had it and never will have it. The only way to handle the Russians is to be daring and surprising with them. I am not going to let an opportunity like this go by because of your official scruples. Don't be a fool, Francis."

Drake was white. "This is my Embassy, Harold, and nobody from here will go to that reception. I suggest strongly for your own sake that you do not go either."

Essex sighed. "Of course I will go."

"Then I will make it clear to London that I opposed it."

"Make it clear to anybody you like, including old Bertram Cooke." He left Drake and went back to his office to find Katherine in conference with MacGregor.

"Can you get word to the Embassies?" Essex asked her.

"It's simply a matter of telling one or two people," she said. She was enjoying this, and her wide straight mouth was not quite so taut. "The rest will know about it in no time at all," she said. "They will all be there. What are you doing? Being cunning again?"

"All in the spirit of friendship," Essex said.

"Yes, I know," she said.

"Now don't be suspicious, Kathy. I just had a suspicious Drake on my hands."

"What did he say?"

"He will forbid anyone in the Embassy to go."

Katherine rubbed her straight nose. "You don't say?"

"Yes. Will you come?" Essex asked her.

"How can I if I am forbidden?" she said, laughing at him.

"Well, if you change your mind we will be downstairs at seven o'clock," Essex said.

"If I went," she said languidly, "it would be the end of me."

"At seven o'clock," Essex called after her.

Miss Williams came in, and Kathy (in passing) said "Hullo Ella." Miss Williams had MacGregor's cable typed out and she put it on his desk.

"Would you give it to Lord Essex," he told her.

"Is that your cable to London?" Essex asked.

"That's right."

"Then I don't want to see it. Just send it off, Miss Williams." Essex was only now beginning to feel annoyed with London's cable this morning. He hoped that MacGregor's reply would be insulting enough, and ceased to think any more about it. "What about these Azerbaijanians, MacGregor. Who are they?"

"Melby sent the names down, but I have only heard of one of them."

"Which one is that?"

"His name is Mirza Jehansuz."

"Is he a Communist?"

"No." MacGregor could not help smiling and he wiped his lips with his tongue. "He is actually some kind of enlightened landowner. Mirza before his name is a title, and he has always been very well known in Azerbaijan. He has been trying to establish schools there. He must be an old man by now. He was one of the Constitutionalists."

"I want to know what they are up here for," he said. "I suppose they are here to get their orders from the Kremlin or to get some military equipment. Find out what you can about them at this reception, MacGregor."

"I intended to," MacGregor said.

"Find out what they are up to, and particularly if any of them are military men."

"I'll find out what sort of people they are," MacGregor said. "I am curious about that myself. But I am not going to pry secrets out of them."

"Well find out what you can. It's part of your job."

MacGregor almost shrugged.

"And don't be Quixotic!" Essex said. He was off again. This time to see John Asquith. He needed someone from the Embassy with him.

Asquith was sitting on his chair with his long legs stretched flat across his desk over papers and books. He cocked his right eye as Essex came in, but he did not put his feet down. A large fire was literally roaring in the giant marble fireplace and it threw out long golden reflections on the red linen walls. Essex stood with his back to the fire looking at the faded wealth of the room.

"John," he said tentatively. "How do you feel?"

"Lazy," Asquith said slowly. "I am not up to one of your schemes."

"What are you working on these days?"

"What do you want to know for?"

"Are you still chasing yourself around the Balkans?"

"Poland," Asquith corrected. "I am trying to do the Russians out of a trade pact they have made with the Poles, but I am failing gloriously."

"You should be in Warsaw." Essex lit his pipe.

"Oh no. We believe it's all a matter of estimating what the Russians are doing, and then putting a stop to it. So here I am guessing what the Russians are doing. The Russians are minding their own business and getting on with their work. That is what we should be doing. The trouble with England these days is that there are not enough heads resting on the row of spikes along the Tower. That is where we should have our brains. Better there than fooling with this nonsense." Asquith scattered files and papers off his desk with a kick of his foot.

"Now you have to pick it up," Essex said like a calm father.

"That is another mistake. There is always someone to clean up the mess we make. Miss Curtis," he shouted. "Miss Curtis." A round and vigorous young woman came in and Asquith said: "Just pick up that mess will you and throw it all in the incinerator."

Miss Curtis was already picking up the papers. "These are the Warsaw summaries," she said disapprovingly.

"I don't care. Burn them."

Miss Curtis stacked them neatly on Asquith's desk. "I had to type those out this morning." She spoke precisely, indignantly, and left the room with a long reproachful stare at Asquith's two large feet.

Essex laughed and came to the desk. "How the devil do you ever get any work done at all?"

"That rebellious woman does it all," Asquith said contemptuously. "She is the daughter of a coal-miner. More brains than I've got, but nothing else. No sense at all."

Essex put the warm bowl of his pipe to his cheek. "Are you busy to-night?"

"I know what is coming," Asquith said. "I heard all about it. What are you trying to do? Singe Drake's beard?"

"You know what I am trying to do," Essex said with a reminder of their long intimacy. "I have to get at Molotov again. Did you hear about the damned telegram?"

"What about it?"

"Somebody has been meddling," Essex said bitterly.

"You ought to be glad. Go home and leave this nonsense to other fools."

"Now be sensible for a few moments."

"That is what I am saying to you. Be sensible and go home."

"Are you coming with me to-night?" Essex said impatiently.

"Of course not." Asquith twisted his long hair and frowned at Essex. "I never go to these things. And if I did I wouldn't go to-night to be part of this pretty little war you are having. You should leave Kathy out of it too. If you want her, why don't you just take her and get it over and done with."

196

"You're hopeless."

"The trouble with you is that you are licked and you don't know it. Poor Harry. Have a good time old man," Asquith shouted after him. "Come and tell me about it in the morning when the battle is over." Essex had gone. Asquith looked at his feet and then at the neat pile of the Warsaw summaries. With a vicious kick he scattered them on the floor again. He had finished for the day and he went home to find comfort in the existence of one adequate person, his wife.

Essex wasted the rest of the day impatiently. He spent most of it in his own room, reading a little, memorizing odd verses of Pushkin, and drinking another bottle of champagne. He enjoyed the luxury of preparing himself slowly for the evening. He had a bath, shaved, wore silk socks and kid pumps, attached the rows of miniature medals to his jacket, admired his diamond shirt studs, and looked at the result in the mirror. With his fresh face and his straight back he looked no more than thirty. His hair was the only mistake. It was getting too thin, and too much grey appeared in it. He put plenty of oil on it to give it a shine, and he was looking for his brushes to give it the final touch when he saw the miniature of the laughing Italian. Essex looked at it closely as he had done a hundred times since buying this colourful fellow. Who the dickens was Geronimo? Most miniatures of that period were portraits of respectable merchants or polite noblemen. Geronimo was neither merchant nor nobleman. Essex was still thinking about it when he put on his braided coat and went downstairs to wait for MacGregor, and possibly for Katherine.

MacGregor came — in a tweed suit. He took his trench-coat from the peg in the hall and put it on as he joined Essex. His face shone with its close shave, and his schoolboy's hair was brushed neatly back. By heavens he is a queer fellow, Essex thought. He looks like a good Scot but he is too intent for a Scotsman.

"I should have warned you to bring a formal jacket," Essex said to him, thus taking upon himself the responsibility for MacGregor's tweed.

"I don't possess a formal jacket," MacGregor said.

Essex laughed. When MacGregor was good-humoured and friendly he was a man to have with you. "Now we just need Kathy," Essex told him. "Did she say whether she was coming or not?"

"No." MacGregor was preparing to go out the door. He obviously did not expect Katherine to come. Essex stood and watched the staircase.

Katherine did not come down the staircase. She came through the front doors of the Embassy. She came with the brisk cold air — as part of it. Though she wore her fur coat, she was not bundled up in it, and her head was uncovered. Beneath the coat she wore a light blue gown that touched the floor over her golden slippers. She rubbed her hands and put on her gloves. "Well?" she said as they stood for a moment. "Are you coming?"

"Kathy," Essex said and drew a breath. "You've got the beauty of the Russian snows in you. Come along. We shall go to the Imperial Ball."

The car was waiting for them. It was not the ambassadorial Rolls-Royce but Asquith's Humber. For that pettiness Essex could have kicked Drake solidly in the trousers. He settled back next to Katherine and forgot about Drake.

MacGregor sat in the small tip seat and felt a complete stranger to the two people behind him. In one instant of seeing Katherine sweep through that door, he had lost sight of her as any Katherine he knew. This was simply a Katherine that Essex knew. Perhaps it was her sudden elegance in a drab Moscow, or perhaps it was his own unexpected sense of smallness, but the two people behind him were not part of his world. This court beauty had destroyed the other Katherine, and both were lost to him. He sat still and felt as lonely as he had ever felt in his life.

"What did Drake say, my dear?" Essex was asking her.

"Nothing. He doesn't know yet."

"I am sorry to put you in this fix," Essex chuckled.

"Nobody ever puts me in any fix," Katherine reminded him.

It wasn't far and the Humber swung into the short drive of a large mansion which was spilling light from its high Georgian windows.

"This is another one of those sugar-beet millionaire houses," Katherine told them. "Fortunate gifts to the Revolution."

"Does Molotov live here?" Essex said. The car rolled up an incline to the porticoed door of the house.

"No. No one knows where Molotov or any of the others live. They don't believe in exposing private life to public view in Russia. This is just a house for receptions and foreign visitors."

Inside, they looked straight up a marble staircase and Essex was delighted with such a magnificent aid to a proper entry. They left their coats with hurrying old men at the foot of the stairs where racks were overflowing with heavy winter coats, fur cloaks, great-coats, gold-braided caps, and astrakhan hats, and a mixture of ordinary caps usually associated with the worker. Exposed now, they began the climb under the casual inspecting eyes of four men with typewritten lists at hand.

The click of Katherine's golden heels on the marble stairs cleared a path for them among the others coming and going. Essex and Katherine walked together and MacGregor was behind. MacGregor tried to catch a whole picture of Katherine who seemed to be gold and blue all over, but he saw each part of her separately. The top of her sky-blue dress was sewed thick with gold, and her ears were hung with two thin pendulum ear-rings which tinkled with light. She had nothing at her throat, and though her collar-bones looked a little too bony they were part of her beauty, part of her wide face and long neck and graceful hair. Essex, by his slow gracious step on those stairs, was showing her off and Mac-Gregor knew it.

At the top Katherine said "Where is MacGregor?" and turned around. He was right on her then, and saw all her face quite close to his.

"There you are! What are you doing back there?"

"I'm just taking my time," he said politely.

She looked puzzled for a moment, but Essex took her arm. She was not really perplexed about MacGregor. She knew that he did not like her glittering sophistication. Knowing it, she was worldly enough to be cynically amused by his silent antagonism. She put him out of mind and turned her attention to being the English Katherine that Essex wanted her to be. MacGregor stood behind and did not follow them: he walked to a table of sweetmeats on the landing and ate a few pieces of licorice and then made his own way among the people.

Essex looked casually about him as he entered the first white reception room. It was obviously a ballroom. It had a parquet floor, a gallery for the musicians (who were seated there and waiting), and a giant crystal chandelier. Ahead of them was a long reception line leading to Molotov who was shaking hands and bowing a little greeting to each group who filed by him quickly and formally. So they really mean it! Essex thought about the reception. He stood among bejewelled women and bemedalled men, Russians, foreigners, diplomats, and newspapermen. He did not move with the queue. He waited and relaxed and thanked his lucky stars that he had decided to come to this reception. He was going to be very satisfied with it, he could tell that instantly. He eased Katherine out of the line, and stood talking with her, knowing that next to Molotov he was the central figure in the room. He felt that God had personally given him Katherine for this occasion. MacGregor too was very much what he wanted: MacGregor in his tweeds, Mac-Gregor with his scientific appearance; no one but the English could produce a man like the unpretentious MacGregor, and no one but Essex could have such a modest fellow and such a beautiful woman in the same entourage. He could not have planned it more to his taste.

Essex knew what he was doing, and he glanced occasionally at Molotov until he was sighted. Molotov left his position and came forward, his round face beaming and his black gold-braided uniform giving him the erect poise of a small man. He bowed to Katherine and greeted her in Russian, and then shook hands vigorously with Essex. He was still speaking in Russian, and Essex turned around to have MacGregor translate it. Only then did he see that MacGregor was not with him. For a moment he was isolated and unprepared. He recovered quickly and replied to Molotov in wholehearted English, saying he was delighted to be here and pleased to see Mr. Molotov again.

Katherine finally rescued him. "Mr. Molotov says that you arrived just in time. He was beginning to give up hope of seeing you again."

"Can you tell him, Kathy, that I am surprised to find him still in Moscow. I thought he had gone away somewhere." The subtle reprimand was enough. The requirements he had of Molotov could wait. As Katherine struggled with her Russian, Molotov led them over to his own group: Vishinsky, Maisky, Mikoyan, Litvinov, and the sick-looking Korin from the Foreign Office. Essex was left with them as Molotov returned to his guests, and for a moment Essex felt himself among friends. Only the day before leaving London he had read a most authoritative, positive, and confidential report which said that Maisky and Litvinov were both in disgrace and disfavour, primarily because of their sympathetic outlook to the west. It was very possible, the report said, that Litvinov had actually been sent away, and that Maisky had been confined to his quarters. Essex knew by looking at these men that there were no restrictions upon them, and he wondered what fool had sent that report. Melby probably. He spoke with them all, except Litvinov who was called away, and then passed on. The formalities over, he turned upon the reception to enjoy himself.

The reception room was now crowded, and Essex knew better than to stand still in it. He began to move around and see these people, feeling that this was his most Russian experience. Katherine held his arm and people made way for them. Without moving his eyes from the casual level, he asked Katherine who this person and that person was. She knew them all: the diplomats in their white shirt fronts, and the Russian generals with medals on both chests. "It's Russian Kathy," he said generously as he looked at the generals and thought of Chekhov. "It may be Bolshevik, but it's Russian." She smiled and pointed out Budyenny, a small thick-set fellow with large long moustaches which stood out from his face as he laughed about something. "He is a cavalry-man," Essex told her. "I have read that he could split a man from top to bottom with a cavalry sword, and I can believe it now that I see him." Katherine went around the others. "Dekanozov," she said and nodded at a small dark man. Ehrenbourg —the grey-haired writer with a curmudgeon brow and angry lips and a bitter slump to his shoulders—was talking gaily with Lepeshinskaya, the Communist ballerina. There were other writers, actors, actresses, ballerinas, generals, commissars, musicians, composers, opera singers. Simonov and his thin blond wife walked by them and Essex followed them with his eyes and thought they looked more Rumanian than Russian. Zoya Fedorova, the Girl from Leningrad, plump and smiling, greeted

Katherine in English. Then Katherine drew his attention to a delicate and pale women who stood quietly with a grey-haired man. "Oulanova," Katherine said. "That is our Giselle." Essex glanced at her and said: "She looks consumptive."

"Are the Embassies here?" Essex asked.

"The Czechs and the Poles and the French, and one or two Americans. Most of them have turned up, if not all of them." She looked around her again. "I wonder what MacGregor is doing," she said.

"We can forget about MacGregor," Essex told her.

The room was full by now and they were finding it difficult to move. Essex stood by one of the alcoves for a minute, getting his bearings. A dark grey-haired little man made a formal bow to him and approached.

"Good evening Lord Essex," he said in excellent Cambridge English.

"Good evening," Essex said.

"Good evening Miss Clive."

"How do you do," Katherine said. "This is Sobhi Ala from the Iranian Embassy," she told Essex.

"My Ambassador asked me to attend," Sobhi Ala said to Essex from his grey face. "We were not going to attend, but when we understood that you would be here, we reconsidered our decision." He folded his dark hands over his red-sashed stomach.

"Do you know your fellow countrymen from Azerbaijan?" Essex asked him.

The Iranian rubbed his bristled moustache. "By name only," he said.

"This is your chance to find out what they are up to." Essex could not help having his fun and he was feeling excellent.

"I have strict instructions not to contact them."

"You shouldn't be like that," Essex smiled. "They will not contaminate you."

"I'm sure you underestimate them, Lord Essex." Sobhi allowed his slow English to drip from his delicate lips. He did not look very much like an Iranian, and his voice did not sound Persian. His face was small, but it was well chiselled. His grey hair and bearing and dress and attitude were European, in fact they were English, as English as his accent.

"My Ambassador is most anxious to see you," Sobhi said quietly as Essex looked down upon him. "We are most anxious to understand what has occurred between yourself and the Russians."

"Hasn't our Embassy sent you full reports?" Essex said.

"Of course. Of course. But we would like to know your impressions."

"If you read those reports, you are as well informed as my own Government," Essex said cheerfully. "There is nothing more that I can tell your Ambassador."

"I see. I shall tell him so, Lord Essex. Thank you."

Sobhi Ala bowed nervously and left them.

Molotov was finishing with his guests and everybody else was standing around looking tired. Essex walked slowly to the front of the room with Katherine upon his arm, and they arrived at just the right instant. Chairs were being set up, and Molotov was already seated, surrounded by what Essex supposed were Azerbaijanians. He saw young Suchkov talking to an old white-haired man who sat next to Molotov. A moment of anger came back at the sight of Suchkov. Essex knew again that he must succeed with Molotov this evening: it was Molotov with whom he must continue the discussions. Suchkov nodded, unsmiling. Essex sat down three or four rows behind him. As they settled themselves on chairs of gilt and red velvet, Litvinov and an American Embassy secretary sat down in front of them. Katherine leaned forward and said, "How are you Mr. Litvinov?"

"Miss Clive." The pudgy Russian stood up and bent over Katherine's hand. "I saw you talking with Maisky but I was called away before I could greet you. How are you? You know Mr. Richmond Eddy of the American Embassy?"

"Yes. And you know Lord Essex?"

"Of course."

"How do you do Mr. Litvinov." Essex shook hands with both the American and the Russian. "It is a pleasant surprise to find you here."

"Well, our paths are always crossing," Litvinov said. His English was thick, but Essex had always found it understandable.

"How is Mrs. Litvinov?" Katherine said of his English wife.

"She is well." Litvinov looked around. "She is here somewhere."

"You seem to be a man of leisure these days," Essex said carefully.

"No. I am so busy," Litvinov corrected, "that I haven't even time to travel."

"We at the Foreign Office miss you Mr. Litvinov."

"Do you?" Litvinov was pleased. "I shall be back in London some day."

"I hope so," Essex said.

Richmond Eddy, the American Secretary, leaned forward to interrupt them. He was a tall and wavy-haired young man and Essex disliked him at first sight. "The Azerbaijanians are sitting with Mr. Molotov," he said and grinned.

"Really," Essex said disinterestedly.

The orchestra in the gallery began to play and Essex settled back to make a pretence of enjoying the entertainment. He had never liked diplomatic entertainment, not even in Washington where Mrs. Roosevelt had presented some of the world's best singers and comedians. This was something similar. There was Russian salon music to begin with. Katherine pointed out its composer, Shostokovitch, and Essex was more interested in

202

the man than in his music. There were opera singers and recitationists, and finally a ventriloquist with two tennis balls which he held on the edge of a screen. The balls were painted with faces, one of General Franco, and the other of the Angel Mussolini in heaven. Essex enjoyed this, although he didn't understand the dialogue, and it was apparently too funny for Litvinov to do more than laugh. Yet it was all dull entertainment, and only saved for Essex by its Russian savour. It was over when Molotov stood up, took the arm of the old Azerbaijanian beside him, and led the way out of the room.

Essex knew better than to be left behind. With Litvinov as an escort, he took Katherine in the line behind Molotov and the commissars and the marshals, and followed them through one room after another. Each room contained a large table packed with food of all descriptions and colour and taste and purpose, including numberless bottles of wines and spirits. There were also delicate wine glasses and stacks of beautiful crockery and decorative old silver. Waiters were lined up in each room waiting for the guests. It was a buffet supper but there were plenty of tables for those who wished to sit down.

Molotov took his party right through to a small room with a little more seating accommodation. The surge of people behind the leaders stopped before reaching the small door, knowing that this was reserved for the honoured guests. A few inquisitives swept through the censorship of the white-gloved guards who acted as major-domos.

Molotov invited his own guests to a large round table set in an alcove. Essex and Katherine were brought to it. Katherine was being so Anglo-Saxon, and so conscious of her good and ancient breeding, that Essex forgot about Molotov in a moment of new admiration for her. This was what he expected of a woman, and should all else fail he would have the satisfaction of taking Katherine home. He was determined about that. Molotov welcomed them in expressive Russian again, and Essex felt lost without MacGregor. Troika was here to translate, but Essex needed his own voice. He was then introduced to the Azerbaijanians, of whom he had taken little notice. Molotov did this himself as if he were enjoying a special delight, in fact this whole reception might have been arranged deliberately for this meeting.

The white old man among them was Jehansuz, and he shook hands with Essex and said in English that it was many years since he had spoken with an Englishman. Essex wondered just how old this ancient was, and where he had learned his English. Essex had no time to inquire because Molotov had brought the others. Jehansuz was introducing them to him. There were three of them.

"This is Abbas Akka," Jehansuz said shakily of a medium-sized young man with dark hair and dark eyes and unsmiling countenance. He compressed his lips and looked at Essex without knowing who he was. He was dressed in a new blue suit, and Essex considered it foolish of an Oriental to wear such dull European clothes. It destroyed natural poise. "Abbas is a teacher," Jehansuz said, and his failing eyes almost cracked with a faint smile. "A religious teacher, a good Moslem, but a teacher none the less."

The second of them was a middle-aged man who wore a long black frock coat and had a hooked nose, much white in his eyes, and steel in his mouth. "Mirza Hassan," Jehansuz said and held the Mirza's shoulder. "He and I have been friends all our lives. He was once a student of mine, but I could never teach him English. He is the author of many text-books on our language."

Only the third man impressed Essex. He was tall, thin, and obviously a man of action. He had tight piercing eyes, and his hands were hard and bony as he gripped Essex. He wore European clothes, but Essex hardly noticed them because the man possessed enough mountain grace to overcome any such encumbrance. He was the youngest of them, and Jehansuz treated him as if he were his own son. "This is one of the great young men of Azerbaijan," he said to Essex. "Sheikh Hasad. Hasad is Kurdish, although his mother was a Babi poet of wide reputation. She was carried off in a Kurdish raid by Hasad's father, and here you have the combination of Kurd and poet." Jehansuz looked at Essex and calmly asked him if he was impressed.

"He is a hard and fierce-looking specimen for a poet," Essex said.

"Perhaps our poets are different from yours," Jehansuz said and Essex laughed.

The others were already seated. Vishinsky had arrived, and he shook Essex's hand and sat down at the round table beside the Moslem, Abbas. Molotov had already taken Katherine to the table of food, and she returned and sat between Maisky and Budyenny. Essex broke away from the old man and attended to his appetite.

He did not make a pretence about this meal. He chose food from the table with care: chicken, Russian salad, green salad, two roast potatoes, and one small green onion. He ate deliberately and slowly, talking only when necessary to Jehansuz on one side of him and Maisky on the other.

"Are you going to be in Moscow long?" Jehansuz asked him.

"No. Not long," Essex said and wondered if Jehansuz was taunting him.

"I'm afraid we will also be here a short time," Jehansuz said. He wandered off into his own thoughts. "I have never been to Moscow before, and I need more time to see it." He was irritable about it. "As it is we are too busy."

"You are here on some kind of economic mission aren't you?" Essex said casually. "Wheat, or timber, or something like that?"

204

"No. No. We are here to talk about education."

"Education?"

Jehansuz was painfully slow. "Are you surprised?" he said and raised his white eyebrows and then looked as if he had forgotten Essex.

"I don't quite understand why you would come here to talk education."

"This is the only place we can come to," Jehansuz said.

"Oh?" Essex waited with interest.

"Yes. Our Russian friends are the only people who have experimented so extensively in simplifying the teaching of the Azerbaijan language. They have an Azerbaijan of their own, you know. They tried unsuccessfully to Latinize the alphabet, in fact they gave the idea to the Turks. It failed with the Azerbaijani, however. What they have really done is to limit and condense the alphabet into a comprehensible thing. This is very important for us too, because our country is in bad need of education. I have devoted my life to it," he said as if he had said this many times in his life. "I sold my family properties many years ago and attempted to establish schools, but our Iranian administrations have prevented any advance because of their corruption. The Government money for schools has gone into the pockets of the officials, and we have been taxed for nothing. There are so few schools in our province that not one thousandth of the children can attend them. We also suffer the forced use of Persian, which is not our language: it is entirely foreign, and it is too much to expect the people to study in one language and speak in another. That is why we must teach our own Azerbaijanian language."

"Are you planning on educating all your peasants?" Essex asked drily.

"Yes." Jehansuz nodded.

"Don't you think that might be difficult?"

"No more difficult than educating anyone else, once we begin."

"I was going to ask you where you learned English?" Essex raised his glass in reply to Molotov who had been toasting the teachers of the world.

"First an English governess," he said, "and then Oxford."

"Oxford?" Essex was not really surprised since it seemed natural enough. "We are always glad to see you fellows there," Essex said as if Jehansuz were a twenty-one-year-old Indian student. "And how will you achieve this dream of educating your peasants?" Essex asked. "By revolution?"

"Revolution?" It was simply a word to the old man. "We need something more than revolution," he said. "First we must do away with the corruption, and then with the foreign influence which destroys us. Then we can think of revolution."

"Foreign influence?" Essex murmured. "Russian influence?"

Jehansuz lost his old age for a moment and looked at Essex and put his two scrawny hands together and bowed his head and raised it again. He was smiling. "Perhaps there are worse influences than the Russian," he said. "But we are not discriminatory about it. All foreign influence must go." He put his fingers on the table. "We have a poet," he said. "The great Mirza Hassan . . . "

"The Kurdish boy?"

"No. No. A man who is now dead, a man who was a hero in all Iran. He has written so: 'Hearts palpitate and breasts rattle. See! The wealth of the world is a carcass. Every wazir of the country receives bribes from the foreigner. Do not wear these clothes of glory for a few days.'" Jehansuz had forgotten for a moment the point he was making, and he waited to think of it. "Perhaps only by education will we ever throw off the foreign clothes, or perhaps by revolution. What does it matter so long as we achieve our purpose?" He had forgotten Essex again, and he sat still as if he were too old to really care any longer for this struggle for education and sovereignty.

Molotov was between them now, raising his glass and addressing the whole table. "Here you have two men who obviously understand each other, talking without any thought for their surroundings," he said. "May the understanding continue." The vodka was consumed and a chair was brought for Molotov, and Troika stood over them ready for this meeting. Jehansuz was nodding his head and patting Molotov on the shoulder like a schoolboy. Essex knew that this was his moment.

"Understanding is usually a matter of quiet conversation," Essex said to Molotov. "It would be simple to settle our problems if we could bring all diplomacy to the dinner table."

"If we did that," Molotov said with a great deal of feeling, "we would simply ruin our digestion." He put his hand on his stocky diaphragm.

Essex felt for his pipe. "Perhaps it would be worth our digestions for the results it would achieve," he said wisely. He unwrapped his leather tobacco pouch and looked thoughtfully at Molotov. "Too much negotiation fails for lack of understanding," he said, "and there is no place like a dinner table for comprehending your fellow man."

"I think you are making a point," Molotov said, warm with vodka but still impatient with English circumlocution. He clinked (almost smashed) glasses with Essex in the meantime and they drank again.

Essex was not abashed, in fact he was pleased that Molotov had made it easier for him. "The truth is," he said. "I think you and I understand each other, Mr. Molotov; over the dinner table or over the conference table or over a glass of vodka." They drank again. "You are the man here that I can talk with, and the man I came to Moscow to meet. I think between us we could settle much of the little problem we have been discussing. I had been hoping that you would arrange a further meeting

206

so that we could finally do away with a completely unnecessary issue between Russia and Britain."

Molotov looked across the room at Suchkov. The young Russian was talking with MacGregor. "I think there are two other men who understand each other," Molotov said, and Essex followed his glance and saw MacGregor. Molotov was smiling at Essex as if he had said something to please him.

"Understanding is not enough," Essex said quickly. "With it there must be decision, and I suppose we must depend upon ourselves for that."

Molotov stood up. "Anything we decide will probably rest with those young men anyway. Wouldn't you and I be wasting our time?"

"Perhaps those young men could answer that better than I," Essex said. "Why don't you ask them if further talks between their chiefs would be worth while?" Essex made it into a challenge, because this was the exact moment to use MacGregor. Essex knew that MacGregor did not want the talks to break off. If MacGregor said so to Molotov, it might very well be effective.

Molotov smiled noncommittally and passed on to the young Kurd.

By now the rest of the room was filled with minor diplomats who hovered around the principal table and drank the toasts and laughed at the jokes and offered to be part of this gathering. Being so much on the edge of it, they felt uncomfortable fools. Yet they were impelled by the pretence they must make of their own importance to remain and go on being fools. It made Essex uncomfortable to watch them and he was glad when Molotov finished the session by making his way out of the room, followed by his entourage, beginning now to toast various diplomats and Russians whom he met. He stopped at the very edge of the room to talk with MacGregor and Suchkov.

"Mr. MacGregor," Molotov said. "I hope you have met our Azerbaijanian guests."

MacGregor recovered from his surprise. "Two of them," he said apologetically.

"You must talk with Doctor Jehansuz. You know him?"

"Yes." MacGregor looked at the old man, who was almost asleep in a corner.

"Are you surprised to see him here?"

"I am surprised to see anyone in Moscow," MacGregor said. "That is, I am surprised to be here myself. Everything is a surprise." It was not a very coherent statement and Suchkov laughed.

"It's a pity that you must leave so soon," Molotov said.

"We wanted to stay a little longer," MacGregor replied and found himself going further: "Lord Essex had hoped that we could all meet again." He did not like to make the point, but he still felt his responsibilities.

"Do you think it would serve any purpose?" Molotov took off his glasses and squeezed the nose hinge and put them back on again.

"I think Lord Essex is intent on seeing you," MacGregor said with undiplomatic honesty.

"You imagine our meeting would be worth while?" Molotov asked again.

"Perhaps it is the only chance left," MacGregor said.

"Then we might arrange it," he said and raised his glass to MacGregor. MacGregor had empty hands, and he turned quickly around to find a glass. "You shouldn't allow an Englishman to stand empty-handed in Russia," Molotov told Suchkov. "Get him a glass and drink a toast for me. Both of you." He had no time to wait for the drink to arrive, and he went on out of the room, the important Russians with him.

Essex waited awhile and then excused himself and joined Katherine and moved out. He looked over at MacGregor talking with the Azerbaijanians, and tried to catch his eye, but MacGregor was not taking any notice of Essex. He had walked away.

"He's been rather odd all evening," Katherine said to Essex. She had by now become angry with MacGregor for not seeking her out. Any guilt she felt about it had gone, all blame was upon MacGregor. She decided that MacGregor had cheated her of some curious expectancy she had of him.

"He has been very odd," Essex said. "Where the devil has he been? I needed him."

Katherine took his arm. "You shouldn't have given him champagne so early in the morning," she said. "In fact you should never give him champagne at all. It doesn't fit him and it makes him boorish." The blame was now upon Essex and MacGregor.

"I think I have had enough of this," Essex said. "Would you like to go?"

"Yes," she said. "I am getting irritable and sleepy with that heavy Caucasian wine."

When necessary, Essex could be unobtrusive in his exits, and they moved quietly to the staircase.

"What about MacGregor?" Katherine said. She was unwilling to leave without MacGregor. She wanted to satisfy her anger with him and insult him if possible.

Essex wanted to talk with MacGregor, but MacGregor was still set on avoiding them. "MacGregor seems to have done very well on his own," Essex remarked sourly. "Let him continue to do so. He can find his way home."

She did not insist. "He was being very stiff-lipped about something," she said. "I don't know how you put up with him at times."

They went down the stairs and waited while their coats were discovered among the mountains of clothing. Essex had nothing with which to tip the old men, but he did not feel badly about it here. The Humber was called for, and as they waited and went out they heard the noise of the reception above them solidifying into a dull hum of chatter and laughter and music and singing.

"How was Molotov?" Katherine asked as they sped home.

Essex knew the import of that question. "Alright," he said noncommittally. He did not want to think about Molotov now. He still did not know whether Molotov had agreed to talk or not. MacGregor might have a clue, but Essex could only wait now, although waiting was as annoying to him as growing old. He put the whole issue out of his mind and turned to Katherine. "You know you really are a beautiful woman, Kathy," he said and held her arm. "Thank God you are English." Katherine did not move from his grip.

At the Embassy Essex said: "I have a bottle of champagne upstairs. Would you like to come and share a glass with me?"

"Do you have anything to eat?" Katherine asked.

"The housekeeper usually leaves me biscuits and cheese."

"Then I'll come for the cheese," she said.

The snow was still falling. The courtyard and the iron fence and the road and the river were thick and soft with it. The cold air was bracing, but they hastened to the fire in Essex's room. The biscuits and cheese and a "Thermos" jug of cocoa were on a small table.

"Can I begin?" Katherine said. She heard her own voice and it sounded brittle.

"Certainly." Essex took her coat. "But haven't you eaten enough food?"

"I don't like reception food," she said. "I never eat it."

They did not talk as they ate and drank, and the warm fire and the champagne eased them into a comfortable quietude. Neither wanted to disturb it, and yet Essex had to disturb it because he needed more of Katherine than this. It would be difficult, however. Katherine sat beside him, accepting his proximity, enticing him with her scented warmth, and yet offering no real encouragement. Essex needed her co-operation, and he waited for it, but he waited too long and Katherine suddenly stood up.

"I am falling asleep," she said. "I must go."

"Would you like to stay?" Essex said softly.

She picked up her coat. "No. It wouldn't do any good," she said and Essex did not know what she meant by it. He could see that she was tense. He stood before her and gently put his hands on her arms, hardly touching her. She did not release herself immediately but she shook her head and said "Sorry Harold," and turned away. She stopped at the door and became the normal Katherine so that nothing awkward should remain. "Do you think you will be here long?" she asked. It was another way of asking about Molotov.

"No. Not long," Essex said. "You really must come back to London with me."

"When Drake finds out about to-night I shall have to go back. Good night, Harold, and stop drinking champagne. Go to bed." She closed the door and Essex was left with any thought he had about Katherine.

Katherine walked slowly down the main stairs. A sensation of shivering warmth had taken hold of her. She wondered if the wine had caused it or if it was still her curious irritation with MacGregor. She hurried outside into the cold air. The snow quietened her considerably, but she did not want to go in until she felt absolutely calm. She walked out of the Embassy and across the road to the river parapet. She leaned on the fresh snow and looked at the reflection of the Kremlin lights on the white river. She was still shaking from the odd sensation, and she began to rub snow on her face. She started in quick fright as someone said "What are you doing here, Kathy?"

It was MacGregor.

"My dear MacGregor," she said and dropped the snow. She held his trench coat and almost clung to him. MacGregor was surprised, and as instantly tense as Katherine herself.

"There is snow all over you," he said and pulled off his gloves and began to wipe the snow away from her hair and from her eyebrows and chin. She held tightly to his coat, tighter, until he could not help gripping her shoulders. He could hear her breath shaking as she drew it deep inside her. "My dear MacGregor. My very dear MacGregor." It was so soft that he could just hear her. He did not know what to do, and yet he set his teeth as if to shake her. He was defeated by the damp fur coat, and for a moment he was about to release her, but she took his wrists and put his hands softly under her coat on her warm shoulders. She held him tight again and offered an open face and open warm eyes, and she was saying again "My dear MacGregor." He bent his head down, seeking the shape of her face. He was not very considerate of her, but she held him tenderly and gently in encouragement. She almost drew his breath for him and MacGregor lost the last moment of restraint.

Chapter 16

THE NEXT morning Essex felt convinced that he had made a full impression on Katherine the night before. He was even glad now that he had let her go — and had not pressed his advantage too far. There was a streak of cantankerous resistance in Katherine, not resistance to himself personally, but simply a crude antagonism to British diplomacy in his person, and this he could overcome at leisure. If Katherine were to be taken into his life he did not want to spoil their relationship by impatience. Katherine had to be handled carefully. Yet of one thing he was certain: Katherine could at this moment be his. If he had to go back to London without seeing Molotov then there was no doubt that she would come with him. He was sure of that.

He breakfasted with Drake, not because he wanted to, but because Drake (as well as some other fools in London) had to be placated. Under the circumstances all officialdom had to be placated — in case his talk with Molotov did not come off. To this end Essex had already sent off an early morning cable to London, explaining his actions and suggesting — not stating — that he should remain a few more days to finalize matters. He had also taken a look at MacGregor's cable replying to his recall. Fortunately MacGregor had been careful in his reply, and Essex felt grateful for the Scot's natural restraint.

Placating Drake was a more difficult proposition. Essex achieved it by painting such a picture of Russian chagrin at his arrival last night that Drake grudgingly admitted that it might not have been such a bad thing after all. It was all that Essex could hope for, knowing that Drake would complain to London anyway.

"What do you really hope to achieve with Molotov, Harold?" Drake asked him over coffee. "Isn't it clear that he intends ignoring all our efforts at compromise? Why else would he have invited those Azerbaijanians here?"

"They are nothing but a handful of schoolteachers," Essex said. He believed it because none of them had known of him. They must be obscure schoolteachers. "Certainly Molotov intends ignoring us if he can, but I'm hanged if I intend to let him get away with it."

"I don't see how you can effect any change in his attitude at all."

"Molotov is no fool," Essex said. "He knows that if I go away from here with nothing settled, then we really make this an open fight. And if they like the UN organization so much they will not like being the first nation accused by it. They will avoid us if they can; but there is a point reached where it is too dangerous to avoid us; and Molotov knows it."

Drake was not deceived. "You are being more desperate about it than Molotov," he said. It was one of those rare occasions when he could speak his mind. He had Essex on the defensive this morning and he was taking advantage of it. "You can't embroil him, Harold, and I think he is sitting back feeling confident."

Essex knew that he had reached rock-bottom on this mission when he had to put up with this from Drake, but he did put up with it. "You underestimate me, my dear Francis," he said. "Molotov is not such a hard nut to crack. He is difficult simply because he keeps out of the way. Get at him, and the rest is comparatively easy. If he comes out of hiding once more then I will have him."

"Perhaps!" Drake was not unkind enough to persist. There was something else, though, which he had to bring up at this opportune moment. "I really think that you have been at a disadvantage here," he said to Essex.

"Oh?" Essex was surprised.

"Yes. You would have been better off if you had brought a really good assistant with you, Harold. It was bad luck getting a peculiar fellow like MacGregor. I am sure that he has been more hindrance than help. Much of your difficulty in coming to grips with the Russians has been a sheer lack of good material and expert co-operation."

"You may be right," Essex sighed wearily and accepted the commiseration.

"What do you plan to do with MacGregor?"

"I don't plan to do anything with him," Essex said. "When we return to London he goes right back to the India Office where he came from."

"Well the man might be of some use," Drake said. "The Intelligence people have suddenly realized that we have a geologist in Moscow."

Essex raised a blond eyebrow. "What do they want of him?"

"Frankly I haven't looked into it, but it's something to do with geological data. There is some Polish fellow he has to talk with. It's one of those obscure technical affairs. I'll have a talk with MacGregor about it."

"If I know MacGregor," Essex said, "you will have trouble on your hands. He will most likely object to doing it . . . on principle."

"I shan't be as patient with him as you are," Drake said.

"He can be stubborn!" Essex enjoyed the thought.

"I can also be stubborn," Drake said. "MacGregor can stay here until he does the job, that's all there is to it."

That's what you think, Essex said to himself. He made no comment, however, and the indirect ultimatum to MacGregor remained.

MacGregor himself was already at his desk, waiting for Essex and reading the mail. There were a few papers from the *Quarterly Journal* of the Geological Society, and two letters from his mother. She wrote very quiet letters and MacGregor felt a gentle relaxation settle upon him when he read them. She asked him about the food situation in Russia, and wondered if he had met the Russian petrologist who had disputed him over the rock facies of the Khush plateau. MacGregor smiled when he read this. His mother had never spoken of her disappointment, but MacGregor knew that she was sorry for his last five years of wasted effort. The war had not passed her by, but she considered it a waste for her son to be anything but a paleontologist—in the war or out of it.

MacGregor glanced through both her letters again. There was no interest there in the diplomatic mission which brought him to Moscow. Instead there was a faint inquiry about when he would be back, and about when he would be returning to his proper work. There was also a reminder that his father's books were still his and ready for him anytime he wanted them.

He folded the letters and put them in his drawer out of sight. He was sorry that they had come this morning. Among the confusion of thoughts in his head there was a real doubt about the effect that Katherine would have on his mother, and vice versa. There was too much division between them, the main difference being that his mother kept herself to herself, whereas Katherine was an extraneous human being who deliberately brushed against others. Perhaps they might get on very well together, both having a calm respect for each other. He hoped so, because these were the only two people in his life now.

Actually Katherine had suddenly occupied all his life, including any thought he might have about returning to his proper work. He was still bewildered by Katherine, still amazed by her complete relationship with him. She had made no doubt about making it complete, and MacGregor was lost again in the thought of her overwhelming tenderness, of the gentle care with which she had taken away his doubt and his hesitancy. The thoughts of it filled his mind so completely that he shook his head as if to create it over again. He was lost in the unreality of their association, and yet there was one clear thought that dispelled any fantasy. Katherine had given to him something that seemed equivalent to her whole existence. What he must now face was the equal decision of his own life.

He knew that he had already made it. A man's life changes so suddenly that decision is really unnecessary. His mother was anxious for him to get back to his own work. He knew now that he would never go back to it. Circumstances had placed him in this new life and had taken him along so rapidly in it that there was really no choice required. Even if the choice were necessary then it would not be difficult. On the one hand he had lost all touch with his science and had already forsaken it. On the other hand he had started well with Essex and he had tasted the possibilities of what he was doing. He wanted to fulfill the chance he had of implementing changes in Iran, and above all he wanted to be equal to this world of Katherine's. She had given him everything of herself, nothing held back and nothing half-given. Could he ask her to go back with him to his own work and abandon her own life? Was that possible? The answer was a straightforward No. He had to put himself on her side, and the work he was doing now was Katherine's side of life. It went with Katherine, therefore the choice was already made. For a moment he felt utterly destroyed and dejected, and nothing seemed worth the decision he had made. It was not a real decision at all, but there seemed to be nothing he could do to change it.

"Good morning, Mr. MacGregor." It was Miss Williams. "You are early this morning. Didn't you go to the reception last night?"

"Yes," MacGregor said, "I was there."

"Did Katherine go?"

"Yes." MacGregor knew that Miss Williams wanted to be told of the reception; that was the right of her position; but he could not put his mind to it, and he offered her nothing further. She felt unwanted, and blushed and left him, but he hardly noticed it.

Essex brought a more welcome brusqueness. "Where did you get to last night?" he said to MacGregor. "I needed you."

"I thought you would be better off without me," MacGregor said calmly.

"Better off? How did you think I was going to make myself understood? You knew I wanted to talk with Molotov."

"Wasn't Troika there?"

"Of course he was there, but I needed you, not Troika."

MacGregor was not upset. "Sorry," he said. "I really thought that you and Kathy were doing the job properly." He could afford to be generous with Essex about Katherine now, in fact he felt decidedly satisfied in being generous. Yet it did not occur to him that in succeeding with Katherine he had won a contest over Essex. He simply felt himself on a better footing with Essex. "Did you settle anything with Molotov?" he asked.

"No."

Essex wanted to ask MacGregor what he had said to Molotov last night, but he couldn't get it out. It had a suggestion of dependence on Mac-Gregor, even though Essex told himself that he had cleverly planned it that way. "Molotov will see me," he told MacGregor. "So we need to be ready. The Russians want a way out of this gracefully. I think I will give it to them."

MacGregor asked the question expected of him. "How?"

"I shall offer Molotov a Commission of Enquiry into the situation in Azerbaijan," Essex explained. "We have all the details somewhere. They were worked out in London for the Minister's conference, but they weren't used. We will use them now. I'll be satisfied if we leave here with an agreement to establish an Anglo-American-Russian Commission on Azerbaijan."

"To operate in Moscow?"

"No. In Azerbaijan. These people can't be shaken on their home ground."

"Surely they won't agree to it," MacGregor said.

"Yes they will," Essex argued. Was everyone going to overrule him this morning? "They will consider an Enquiry a means of delay. Most Enquiries usually are. However, it can always be made a real thing, and you can crack open a situation any way you like — providing you have the majority of the Commission on your side — which we will have in this case."

"I suppose that means the Americans," MacGregor said and repeated his argument that the Russians would not agree; they would see through it.

"Not the way I present it," Essex said.

"Can it be set up from here?" MacGregor asked.

"I don't propose to set it up. All I want is the decision on it. Then we can go home satisfied, and London can do the rest. No doubt Molotov will want to bring the Azerbaijanians into the Commission, but then we can throw in Teheran, and with the Americans as well, we will have a majority. Did you talk with those Azerbaijanians and find out what they were doing here?"

"Yes, I spoke with all of them."

"Are they up here to talk about schools?"

"I think so."

"Are any of them Communists?"

MacGregor shook his head. "I don't know, but I doubt it."

"Any of them soldiers?"

"No. Definitely not."

"Well we don't have to worry about that lot," Essex said and forgot them.

"Where do you imagine you will go from here?" MacGregor asked him suddenly.

It brought Essex's head around quickly. "I didn't know you were so interested in my future, MacGregor."

"I was thinking it has been pleasant working with you," MacGregor said.

"I am glad to hear it." This was interesting.

"There is something I wanted to ask you, as a matter of fact."

"Oh?"

"Would you mind?"

"Go ahead."

"Were you ever anything but a diplomat?" MacGregor asked slowly.

"A soldier," Essex said, still surprised.

"Did you have to make a choice between them?"

"Not really. I always considered the Army a collection of heroic play-actors who refused to grow up. The real choice was limited anyway.

215

Church, Army, Foreign Office. As far as I am concerned the Foreign Office was the only life. Why? Are you contemplating the profession after all?"

"I was just thinking about it," MacGregor said.

It was careful, but Essex guessed there was something drastic behind it, and he became curious. If MacGregor was thinking about a diplomatic future, then he was surrendering his one shred of advantage over Essex. In a peculiar way MacGregor had been unbreakable because he had never cared one way or the other about the job he was doing. If now he intended making this his profession, then he had instantly lost his annoying independence. Moreover (and MacGregor must know it) the one hope he had of achieving anything would depend on Essex's own goodwill. Essex was already enjoying the possibilities of the situation.

"You're in luck," Essex said to him. "Drake has just the assignment to start you off. It can be a side-line to your work with me. You had better go and talk with him about it."

"What sort of assignment?"

"Oh something about geology. I don't know. Drake will tell you all about it." Essex was deliberately perfunctory: MacGregor probably expected him to be encouraging about his future in diplomacy, offering him advice and assistance and guidance. If MacGregor wanted it he would have to pay for it by a more sensible outlook and a more loyal co-operation.

"Is he expecting me upstairs now?" MacGregor asked.

"No." Essex looked at the back of MacGregor's sandy brown head and wondered what gave him such an air of willing participation this morning. He decided to make the most of it. "We'll get done with this Commission problem first," he told MacGregor. "Just get Miss Williams will you, and the files. You can see Drake later."

When MacGregor eventually went to see Drake, he was still smarting under the demands which Essex had made on his restraint. For some reason Essex had been bent on humiliating him this morning. Essex had made him feel a fool more than once in discussing the detailed form which this Commission should take in its presentation to Molotov. Despite MacGregor's natural capacity for attention, Essex had turned him into a hopeless idiot; had finally tangled him up so completely that he felt depressed with the hopelessness of ever understanding the simplest requirements of diplomatic work. Now there was Drake.

"I don't understand the details of this job," Drake was saying to him, "but in general the requirement seems to be technical information. It's simply a matter of utilizing your geological knowledge."

MacGregor had looked through the typewritten instructions which Drake had given him. At a glance he could see that they were specific

216

demands for information on Russian geological exploration. The first question wanted all the available details on Russian geologic investigation of areas where uranium could possibly exist. MacGregor did not have to read much further. "Who wants the information?" he asked Drake.

"Need I tell you who wants it?" Drake said.

Again MacGregor felt a fool. "No," he said. "I suppose it is quite clear that Military Intelligence wants it." It was a cold admission but he did not want to avoid it. This was something he must understand without deception.

"You are not shirking it are you?" Drake said ominously.

"It isn't exactly my job," MacGregor replied.

"I understood that Intelligence was your job during the war. Weren't you some kind of a geological informant to the Long Range Desert Group?"

"Not quite," MacGregor said, "but near enough."

"Then consider this a continuation of your war effort," Drake ordered.

MacGregor kept hold on himself. "Isn't that assuming we are at war with the Russians?" he said.

"It's assuming nothing." Drake put a pen down angrily and looked up. He had kept MacGregor standing, and he had been making a pretence of busyness. "Are you going to start arguing about this also?" he said.

MacGregor shook his head. "I am not arguing," he replied calmly but grimly.

"Then you can get on with it."

"There is one thing," MacGregor said (and he asked himself bitterly if this was the compromise he must make, if this was a task he must accept without question as being a duty and a routine of the diplomatic profession). "Where is this information to come from? I can see that some of it is just a matter of assimilating survey reports, if I can find them. What is the other source?"

Drake relished MacGregor's obvious repugnance. "When you have read the instructions and understood them, then you can come back to me. I will arrange to have you contact a certain gentleman who will give you most of the information. Nothing must be written down, mind you, and you must return those instructions to me the moment you have memorized them. The details which this particular fellow will give you must also be memorized and retained until you return to London. It's very simple," Drake said.

How the necessity for quietly accepting this task had become mixed up with the compromise he owed Katherine Clive, he didn't know. Yet it was there. He did not fling the papers in Drake's face and walk out, he did not tell Drake that the whole idea was a rotten piece of hypocrisy whatever title of duty it was given. He said nothing. He did not tell Drake that he would accept the commission, but he took the document and went away with it. Fortunately Essex had gone to lunch and he did not have to face him again. The one person he must see now was Katherine. He must convince himself that what he was doing with himself was right, and for that he must talk with Katherine. He locked the brown Manila envelope in his desk drawer, along with his mother's letters, and phoned Katherine.

"Good morning," he said uncertainly.

"Oh hello there," Katherine replied lightly.

"Are you alright?" He heard the hesitant echo of his own voice.

"Certainly!" she said.

"I wanted to see you for a moment, Kathy."

"Oh? What about?"

"Nothing in particular," he said.

"Have you had your lunch?"

"No."

"Do you want to come skating to-day?" she asked.

He hesitated but he said that was alright.

"What size is your foot?" Katherine asked.

"What size?" He had to think of it. "Oh 8 or 9."

"I'll have to find you some skates," she said with practical thoughtfulness. "I think Melby might have some, but I am not sure. Why don't you meet me on the tennis court in five or ten minutes?" she said. "I'll see what I can do."

He thanked her and heard her talking to Miss Boyle before she had put down the phone. For five minutes he tried to see why the morning had suddenly turned against him, why in the moment of one great decision of his life there was such a contradiction and a doubt. A great deal depended on Katherine.

She was late, and MacGregor had been sitting on the bench of the tennis court for fifteen minutes before she arrived. By then he was cold, even though he had been stamping his feet. Katherine looked as though the cold had become part of her life, and she stood before him dressed in a red jumper and a woollen cap and carrying a leather jacket and two pairs of skating boots. MacGregor stood up quickly and nearly slipped on the ice. He looked at her and smiled a little, not knowing what to expect of her.

"You look so serious," she said. She did not pay deliberate attention to him. She put the leather jacket on the bench and sat on it. "There are your skates," she said. "Helen Boyle found them for you."

"Thank you." He sat down beside her.

She was already taking off her shoes and pulling on her skating boots.

MacGregor waited for her to say something more important to him, but she lifted a boot and said, "Push it on, will you?"

He pushed it on.

"Get your skates on," she said and looked up at him. She was the same Katherine with the same persuasive hands, but she did not accept the embarrassed confidence in his eyes.

"Do you really want to skate?" He glanced at the boots in his hand. She didn't look up. "What else?" she said.

"I wanted to talk with you," he said.

"Oh? What about?" she repeated.

He was puzzled. "Isn't there anything to talk about?"

She sat up and looked the same and behaved the same; she was the Katherine Clive he had first seen on this rink; even her lips were impersonal. "You are certainly very serious this morning," she said.

"Yes. I'm afraid so." He was worried about her now.

She knew it and said quickly, "Aren't you afraid to spoil it?"

He was relieved. "Is that what is worrying you?"

"I'm not sure," she said almost huffily.

MacGregor tried again. "It is difficult to explain all of this, Katherine."

"What do you want to explain?" She stood up on her skates.

"Myself, principally," he said. He took off one of his boots. His sock had a hole in it. He did not hurry. He pulled on one of the skating boots as if it required deep thought. "Whatever I do, I want to do it properly. It's very important for both of us," he said. "You see, I have been thinking of staying at the India Office. . . ."

"Come on," she interrupted. "Get your skates on."

MacGregor could resist his thoughts no longer. Now he was hurt.

"I wanted to see how we could work this out," he said deliberately.

"Work what out?" Katherine shook her head impatiently. She was trying to be something else but she was coming out the way she always came out: cursory and somewhat disinterested. She watched his bent head jerking as he pulled on the second skate, and she wanted to apologize. She pulled on her gloves and kept quiet.

"Isn't there anything to work out between us?" he went on grimly.

"Darling. You're so serious." Was there mockery in that?

"I don't feel like skating," he said with as much control as possible.

"Aren't you going to try?"

MacGregor knew that his pride was so damaged, already, that anything more would be too much. Why was Katherine acting this way? Surely she understood that something had happened. He didn't quite believe her attitude; its death-dealing blow hadn't struck him yet. But he looked at her, standing upon her skates and swishing her hair around and waiting for him, and knew that possibly he had made a tremendous mistake. He was afraid to think of himself, of what he had decided in relation to Katherine. Was she completely casual about it? He didn't believe the quick realizations he was reaching in his staggering mind.

"I suppose I can give it a try," he said about the skating.

A single look at MacGregor's confused and tightened face was enough to show Katherine that it was foolish for him to suffer the silly indignities of trying to skate. Yet she did not stop him, even though she wanted to.

"Don't let your ankles bend," she said to him.

He was standing up, but he was not smiling. He did not have the light-heartedness or the complete abandon to be able to laugh at himself and forget his physical pride. On the contrary, he was intensely concerned with himself at this moment because he knew that Katherine had torn down the very essence of reality and sincerity and warmth which he had made of their relationship. Instead of being ready to abandon himself, to laugh at himself, he was more in need of his self-possession and physical calmness and pride than at any time in his whole life. To be a fool at this moment would be disastrous and would be a dangerous addition to the confusion and to the attitude now forming itself in his mind.

"Come on," she said.

He moved forward and his legs gave way and he fell awkwardly and completely on his side, his arms and head flinging themselves loosely at will.

Katherine laughed.

MacGregor was red, and he tried to smile. He was thinking again of Katherine and her ability to laugh and see him like this and reject any other attitude which might sanctify their relationship.

"You're too stiff," she said. "Relax."

MacGregor tightened his lips and tried to calm the shivering anger which was rising in his stomach and making him weak and more confused. Was this woman playing with him, even torturing him? If so, he would not break for her.

"Don't swing your arms, darling."

MacGregor knew how stupid he looked as he half walked and half stumbled across the ice, swinging his arms wildly to keep balance, and feeling the blood flooding his whole face and neck and ears. He was afraid to look at Katherine because she was doing this to him.

"You're too serious about it," she said again. "Relax."

He fell sideways, mostly on his face. Katherine bent over him to pull him up and she could not hide the pity in her face. Why was he doing this? Why did he want to destroy himself? Why did he say so casually that he would compromise himself so foolishly for her? Stay in the India Office! Did he want to destroy himself utterly? Did he want to succumb to these silly snobberies, to these narrow and petty stupidities and restric-

220

tions? . . . MacGregor, she wanted to say, what are you doing down there on the ice? Get up. Get up and we will go away.

"I don't think I'm much good at this," he said as he brushed his face and threw back his disordered hair. He spoke with a voice which was tighter than a high-pitched drum. "I actually wanted to talk with you, Katherine."

"There's plenty of time for talking," she said. She had not wanted to encourage him up on his feet, yet he accepted it that way, and he got to his knees and then prepared to rise. He looked at her carefully before he stood up, and Katherine knew that MacGregor was gone forever. If he had bled openly he could not have shown more how much he had been wounded. He got up and started carefully. He almost succeeded in making a few moves on the skates, but he came to a soft patch and he dived forward and really fell flat on his face.

Katherine did not laugh. She stood near him while he lay there a moment. She felt all of the breath go out of her as she thought he might be hurt. But he bent up slowly and turned around. It was either the fact that he had hit his nose, or it was the ice; but there seemed to be cold tears in his eyes. She could see his hand shaking as he sat up and started to undo his boots.

"I didn't come out here to make a fool of myself," he said slowly, with terrible calm. "I didn't come out here to do this. It must be my own fault. But I thought that you were honest in . . . " MacGregor could not express himself. He pulled off one of the boots and unlaced the other one wildly.

"In what?" she said, and she sounded ruthless instead of panicked.

"In yourself!" He stood up without looking at her and walked across the ice on his stockinged feet.

"Are you blaming me for something?" She half followed him.

"No." He shook his head and looked up at her as he sat down. He did not disguise his contempt and dislike, and his overwhelming pain. "I might have known it. You can't help it. Have you ever been sincere in your whole life?"

"You are so virtuous," she said. "But I still don't know what I have done."

"If you don't know, it's no use trying to tell you."

"Don't be stupid, and don't be childish." Katherine was angry with him because he was behaving like a prig, like a simple-minded peasant, and like an egotistical fool. She wanted to hurt him for his self-centred and unsophisticated emotions.

"It really made no impression on you, did it?" He was bitter now.

"What?" she said and felt so sorry for him.

"Must I give it words?"

221

"You make too much of an issue of everything."

He pulled on his shoes and bent his face to hide himself. The mixture of anger and destruction was too much for him. It came out of him with no restraint. "I would have committed any foolishness, and any compromise," he muttered, "because I had never been so sure of myself and of you. You will never know what I was about to do to myself. You will never know anything because you are true to your own deceit and your own morals. I was never so sure of anything, yet you were never so casual as you are now. I suppose I am a joke; but by God I would sooner be something to laugh at than be what you are, Kathy."

She curled her lips. "Oh my. What a fool you are."

"Yes. Oh yes. I admit it."

"No you don't. You don't know why you're a fool."

He stood up. His coat was wet and his tweed trousers had a large round patch of dampness down one side. His hair was loose over his head and his tie was over his shoulder. His cheeks were wet and his hands were rigid with cold. His thin nose was white in anger and he kept his lips closed tight. He put the skates neatly together on the bench as he rearranged himself. His anger came back. "I believed that you felt as I felt," he said. "You are incapable of any feeling. You are a cheat. Why did you choose me to satisfy yourself? Why didn't you choose one of your own people? Why not Essex? Why me? Am I so easy to pass by?" He was walking across the ice to the door in the wire fence.

"You're such a fool. Such a fool," she cried from thin angry lips.

MacGregor did not turn around to see Katherine close her eyes against the cry which she kept inside her. She was crying because she did not know if he was right or wrong. She was saying to herself that he must be right. Why had she done this to him? Why hadn't she been born as straightforward and simple as this one man? What was it that made her destroy something which had for a moment seemed priceless? Was it so difficult to be simple? *Why can't you see that I don't mean what I have done! You are too stupid to see it. Oh, MacGregor, I am no good for you anyway.* She must cry out.

Katherine stood up and skated quickly to break the stricture of this emotion. She had to free her blood and calm her mind and take away the complication and questioning of herself and her emotions. If she did not calm herself she would wail like a child.

Her skating was the last act of her deception to MacGregor. He saw her as he turned back along the outside of the fence to trudge through the snow. She might as well have laughed outright at him: to be able to dismiss him so casually. It was conclusive, and he needed to know nothing more about Katherine Clive. He had saved himself, and almost destroyed himself. He wondered if he could ever feel calm or normal again, for no matter how far down into his emotions he reached for sanity, he found a scar already there. He knew he could forget his anger, but for his shame he could never forgive Katherine.

Chapter 17

Dɪᴅ Kathy entice you out there to watch you fall on your face?" Essex was sympathetic but he could not hide his whole-hearted amusement.

MacGregor sat down at his desk and took no notice.

"Drake and I watched the performance from upstairs. What was she being so vicious about, MacGregor?" But Essex was really saying to him: I know that a row like that could only come out of some intimacy between you two; what was it and how far has it gone and what has happened now — has Kathy turned you out and made a fool of you? Aren't you a little stupid to think that you could cope with a woman like that? Why don't you leave it to other and better men?

MacGregor sat stiff and quiet, despising Essex.

"Well, you can forget all about it for the time being," Essex said. "We have an American coming to see us. If the Commission idea is to succeed we will have to have their help. Did you meet that wavy-haired fellow at the reception?"

MacGregor shook his head.

Essex looked at MacGregor's frigid back and felt sorry for his previous remarks. But what was up between him and Kathy? What was Kathy wasting time on MacGregor for? He must have been hit hard. He might as well have time to recover, Essex thought generously, and addressed MacGregor in such a way that his attention was not required. "I don't fancy bringing the Americans into this at all," Essex said almost to himself. "They are inclined to take things over these days, and I have an idea that the price for their co-operation might be a big slice of influence in that part of the world — at our expense of course. They are developing a large interest in the Middle East, and the danger of ignoring them is worse than that of co-operating with them. We are trying to hang onto what we've got down there, while the Yankees are coming in and taking everything they can put their hands on. We are on the defensive and they are on the offensive. They have the dollars, unfortunately. All we have is our political experience and skill. Where we do have a good sound economic footing, such as in Iran, what do they do but come and try to interfere with that too? That is our wealth down there in Iran, but who is handling it? Millspaugh and all sorts of strange financial geniuses from Milwaukee. Other geniuses from Chicago are running the police and the Gendarmerie and even the army now. You import a gangster specialist from Chicago to handle a miserable collection of peasants! Aren't the local brutes efficient enough? Now they are starting to run the hospitals and the street-cleaning departments, and even the palace. How can a good American stomach a king? Yet you observe our friends swallowing feudal courts and kings and then spitting up Democracy and the American Way of Life. I know that we are fairly hypocritical at times, but compared to the piousness of the Americans we are a nation of honest men. Unfortunately they are about to skin us too, MacGregor; but I suppose it's either that or losing everything. At a pinch I would sooner kiss the dollar than embrace the fanatics who are trying to change everything all over the world."

Essex had not finished, but Miss Williams had entered.

"Yes? Yes?" Essex had lost patience with the nervous Miss Williams.

"Mr. Eddy has arrived," she said. "He is with Sir Francis."

"Then he can wait with Sir Francis," Essex said.

"Yessir." Miss Williams had a moment of defiance with Essex, but no more.

"I didn't take to this Eddy chap at all," Essex said to MacGregor. "But I suppose we had better tackle him now."

MacGregor was handed some folders, and he followed Essex to Drake's room. MacGregor was introduced to Richmond Eddy and they sat down around Drake's desk.

"Well, Mr. Eddy," Essex said, "are you any relation to that popular singer?"

The tall American shook his head and showed white teeth and said No.

"Always like to ask Americans if they are related to somebody," Essex said. "They like to be related to the Mayor or the Chief of Police or the President or the film actors. Of course I should have guessed that you were no relation. You're dark and thin and you have an Italian nose."

Richmond Eddy's poise had gone already and Essex was now in a position to begin. "I suppose you have been informed about our talks with the Russians?" Essex said.

"We have the Washington reports," Eddy told him.

"You know our relative attitudes, Mr. Eddy?"

"Yes. You don't seem to be getting anywhere," Eddy said.

"I wouldn't exactly say that." Essex laughed outright. "We are about to do something about a Commission of Enquiry into Azerbaijan. Don't you think that is a step forward, Mr. Eddy?"

"Yes. Oh yes." Eddy smoothed his hair.

"We're interested in your attitude to a Commission."

"I should think we would support it," Eddy said.

"Good. So you understand what's going on in Iran."

"Certainly. But we look at Azerbaijan as part of the whole picture."

"Ah. The whole picture." Essex nodded.

"Yes. It's quite obvious that the Left Wing and Communist elements, who have seized Azerbaijan, are Russian-inspired. The Iranian Ambassador to the United States, Mr. Husein Ala, has already said that the revolt was engineered by the Soviet Union. This agrees with our own Teheran reports. We think that it would be better for Iran if the Russians were to leave as quickly as possible. We already suggested — in a Note to the Russians — that all our troops be withdrawn by January 1. They replied that they had no reason to advance the evacuation date."

"We went over that with your Embassy in London," Essex said. "Mr. Bevin had suggested the same idea to the Russians previously. The whole idea of early evacuation failed. That's why I am here, Mr. Eddy. That is why we need this Commission. If we cannot hasten the departure of Russian troops, then we can try to save Azerbaijan. If we can count on your full support in the Commission . . ."

"Naturally our attitude is one of personal disinterest," Eddy said.

"Naturally."

"We are not partisan in any way."

"Oh, definitely not. Definitely not."

"Good. Then let's get down to business."

The details were simple. There was no nonsense between them. They were serious men talking on equal terms. Richmond Eddy's wavy hair did not matter any more. Richmond Eddy knew what he was talking about, and this was not going to be a one-sided affair. Mr. Eddy pointed out the importance of the American position in Iran in view of the large number of American experts in that country. Of course they were not official United States Government experts. Nevertheless! . . . and the American attitude began with that *Nevertheless*. When Eddy had finished, Essex had become the partner of Richmond Eddy in an undertaking. It only remained to put it over the Russians. It was Drake who was sceptical about that part of it.

"I doubt if the Russians will swallow this so easily," he said.

"I tell you, Francis," Essex said, "that they want a way out of this which will prevent our bringing the issue to a head in UNO. This Commission is perfect for them, and it also gives us a chance to get them out of Iran."

"It will require more than a Commission of Enquiry to shift them," Drake said.

"The Commission will only be the beginning," Essex insisted.

The discussion went on. Meanwhile MacGregor's quiet presence was forgotten, and he was solemnly contemplating his predicament.

He had no idea why he should be here in Moscow listening to these men. He certainly did not belong here. This Embassy had become a dangerous little corner of the world, planning the exact shape which the world must take. It was not his world. It belonged to these three men. They were so sure of themselves; so compact; so positive that they were right. In facing them MacGregor knew that they were wrong. These men really are plotting, MacGregor said in surprise to himself; and here I am in the middle of it. If I don't get out soon it will be too late.

As if there was no time like the present for beginning to get out, Mac-Gregor excused himself and left them. Essex watched him go and was not surprised, but Drake did not like it at all. Nothing was said, but it was not long before the conference ended. "Well my dear chap . . ." Essex stood up with Eddy . . . "it has been most satisfactory. We really see eye-to-eye on this thing, and that is important. We can settle the whole affair."

Eddy shook their hands.

"Good-bye," Essex said. "It was nice of you to come."

"I'll expect to hear from you," Eddy said.

"When I have heard from the Russians," Essex told him.

Essex anticipated a further little scene with MacGregor, but MacGregor had disappeared. He had gone to the Moscow University to see if he could find Onegin. He failed again, but this time he found a Professor of Paleobotany who knew Onegin, but didn't know where he was. He had not heard of MacGregor's dispute with Onegin, but in an hour MacGregor had explained it, and they had discussed all aspects of the dispute. The botanist was an Armenian from Erivan, on loan to the Moscow University from the University of Armenia. He was very dark and very Armenian, but he spoke Russian so softly that MacGregor found it hard to understand him, particularly with his heavy Armenian accent. They had finally talked about Azerbaijan because the professor had only recently heard that his brother had come back to Soviet Armenia, after fleeing to Iran twenty-five years ago to avoid Turkish persecution in Kars. In a moment the professor had revived the curse which all Armenians put upon the Turks, and with the mention of Kars, Adahan, and Bitlis, he practically rose and cried with anger that they were Armenian provinces and that no Armenian could be at peace until they were returned to Armenia. It was a man and not a mere scientist who was talking, but MacGregor could not separate one from the other. Even here, even in the midst of science, they were talking of Armenia and Azerbaijan. It was inescapably connected. Actually the professor knew nothing of Azerbaijanian politics, and MacGregor left him, promising to send him a copy of his paper on the rock-facies of the Khush Plateau.

So far MacGregor's mental control had been adequate for suppressing the flood of thoughts about Katherine, but after a lonely dinner in his room he knew he could not escape going over his shame again. Not yet, however. He sat down to write a letter to Professor White, asking him if he could go back to English-Persian when he was out of the India Office. He did not want to go back to English-Persian: it was part of this same great dispute. But better English-Persian, and his own work, than the danger of absorption in this diplomatic trickery. Even with this thought, he realized that he could not entirely cut himself off from responsibility to his job here. He could leave the work in London, but Essex was still here deciding Iranian affairs. MacGregor knew he could not abandon his own responsibility to Iran.

Nevertheless he wrote the letter to Professor White.

Jane Asquith knocked and came in and was surprised to find him sitting at his desk. "I thought you had gone to bed with a cold," she said. "I rang to ask you over for coffee. John Melby said you were not well." She had in one hand a small bottle and a teaspoon, and she was ready to bully him gently.

"I'm alright," he said, still surprised.

"Are you sure?"

MacGregor put on his coat. "I am alright," he repeated.

"I thought you had fallen on the ice and hurt yourself."

"Did you see that performance also?" he said to her.

"I didn't see anything." She was looking closely at him, her perfectly elliptical eyes conducting a gentle scrutiny of his features as if she were worried about his state of mind. "If you are feeling unwell you ought to take some of this quinine. It's bitter, but it stops a cold. Have you had malaria at all? Perhaps it's just a fever?"

"I haven't had malaria," he said.

"We have it from time to time." She was looking about her. "You're a very neat and tidy person, Mr. MacGregor," she said, and he remembered Katherine saying the same thing. "When I married my husband I often wondered how I could turn him into a model of neatness, but I have given up now. He enjoys being out of place. He is like Katherine."

"Please sit down," MacGregor said.

"I am not disturbing you?"

"Good heavens no. I was just writing a letter."

She sat down in the winged chair. "I don't suppose you will be here long." She was so impersonal with her presence that MacGregor relaxed.

"A few days more," he said and sat down.

"Will you be glad to leave?"

"Yes." He ran his hand through his hair to straighten it and flatten it. "It's been interesting here, but I want to return to London."

"I would have thought that you would not like London," she said.

227

"I don't particularly," he said. "I am just anxious to see what the world looks like from there again."

"Is it so confusing here?"

"A little too confusing," he said.

"I believe you are doing very well here. Will you stay in the Service after you return to London?"

MacGregor shook his head. "It's not for me."

"I had thought you might."

"I considered it," MacGregor said and looked away into another desert for a moment. "I thought I was so far behind in my own field that I would be better off in diplomatic work, but I changed my mind again."

"Were you good at your scientific work?" she asked.

"I might have been," he said, "but I am far behind now."

"Could you catch up?"

"Yes, but it would never be quite the same again. I was just writing a letter to the man I used to work with at English-Persian, asking if he would take me back. I am not sure if it's worth finishing."

"I am sure it is," she said.

"It's not quite that simple," MacGregor told her. "I don't like English-Persian."

"I had thought they were an excellent organization."

"They are," MacGregor said. "They make it easy for us. They allow any of their scientists plenty of scope. It isn't so much the organization as the fact that it exists in Iran."

"So you don't want to go back to them?"

"No. But it is the only place that I can do my work properly. I will go back there if I can, but I doubt if they will have me now."

"I think you are underestimating yourself, Mr. MacGregor."

"Thank you," he said.

"I mean it."

"Are you urging me out of diplomatic work, Mrs. Asquith?"

She did not treat it so lightly. "No. Oh no," she said. "There is a great deal that can be done in diplomatic work, Mr. MacGregor." She interrupted herself: "I can't go on calling you Mr. MacGregor. What does Kathy call you?"

"It depends on how insulting she wants to be. My name is Ivre," he said.

"I suppose that is a family name. But you sound angry with Katherine." He shrugged.

"She is very fond of you, so I hope you don't quarrel with her." MacGregor said nothing.

"I have known Kathy a long long time and I know her very well." Jane Asquith was arguing delicately with his silence. "She is not as hard as she seems, you know. I think she hurts people despite herself, never deliberately."

"I don't think I can agree with you."

"But you must. She does terrible things, but she is very sorry for them afterwards. She is always hurting herself by hurting other people."

"Nothing would upset Kathy," he said.

Jane Asquith appealed to him again. "She is not an ordinary girl, Ivre, and she is changing a great deal. Please don't get angry with her. She is fond of you because you are sane and very honest. She believes everybody here to be a cheat, and she gets very angry with them and it makes her cynical at times. You should understand that."

"My understanding of Katherine is quite different," he argued.

She smiled. "I know that she is unpardonably cruel at times, but it is really not her fault. She was brought up in a rather odd family, a very good family, but erratic and unhappy. She has always been running away from them, as far back as I can remember her, even as a school girl. Katherine could easily have fallen in with their ways and their surroundings, she could have been a wild young thing around Mayfair and the hunt clubs, but she has always run away from it. The result is she is often confused, and she doesn't always understand herself."

"Am I wronging her so much?" MacGregor was surprised that he could feel so peaceful, even about Katherine.

"Of course she is very willful and destructive, but not with you. Not with you, I assure you." She shook her head convincingly.

"You are putting up quite a fight for her," MacGregor said.

"Actually it's for both of you."

"Did Katherine tell you anything?"

Jane Asquith hesitated. "Katherine is rather reluctant about such things."

He was none the wiser for that answer, but he did not try to analyze it.

"She is very reluctant about many things," he said without much anger. "She might think me sane and honest, but she calls me a fool for it and even makes me feel a fool."

"Now you are angry."

"No," he said slowly and hopelessly. "It's just that we are not at all pleasant with each other at the moment. I might have made a fool of myself, or she might have made a deliberate joke of me. I have lost any feeling of blame for it." His eyes were full with the cold.

"Take the quinine," Jane Asquith said and stood up. "Do not feel so angry with Katherine, and forget whatever she has done. I think you are rather shy, and I am sure she has been very rude, but you are both too sensible to be childish and fight with each other." Jane Asquith found a glass and put a teaspoonful of the quinine in it and poured water from a jug to fill it. "Here," she said. "Drink it and go to bed. Remember too that Kathy thinks badly of herself."

"I can't believe it," he said and drank.

Jane Asquith held a wry face for him, and when he had put down the glass and tied his thin face in hard little muscles of distaste, she produced a chocolate. "I can never get used to the taste of it," she said. "Yet it always makes me feel homesick for India, even the smell of it."

MacGregor chewed the sweet and appreciated Jane Asquith. English-women were admirable when they were like Jane Asquith. They did not wail at funerals, and they did not break up with a single blow of misfortune or climate. Yet they were sympathetic enough to be Oriental, warm enough to be Armenian, and intelligent — like Katherine Clive. Intelligent and vicious — the Katherine Clives.

"You must go to bed," Jane Asquith said to him. "Good night."

A few minutes later Drake sent word that he wanted to see Mac-Gregor immediately. MacGregor put on his jacket and went over to the Embassy and found Drake in a very cordial mood.

"I have just been talking with the Russians," Drake said. "It seems that Harold's persuasiveness with Molotov last night has brought you some success. They have suggested a meeting with Molotov at midnight, and I took the liberty of accepting. Is that alright?" Drake neatened his cuffs and looked at MacGregor with a cynical pretence of deference.

MacGregor knew enough to look back and say nothing.

"There is also a telegram from London," Drake said, and by his air of satiric confidence in MacGregor he was indirectly repaying Essex for defending MacGregor. "I gather that they want you both back there."

"When?" MacGregor was neither rude nor polite.

"Immediately."

MacGregor made no comment and they remained at uneasy peace.

"I want you to go and get Lord Essex," Drake said abruptly.

"Where is he?"

Drake smiled sleepily. "He is at a restaurant with Miss Clive."

MacGregor gave nothing away under Drake's glance. "Why not telephone?"

"Not to a restaurant, not in this country. I'll order a car for you, Mac-Gregor, and you can go and collect him. There is another thing. Did you go through those lists of questions on geological data yet? If you're leaving so soon you had better do something about it quickly; otherwise you might have to remain and finish the job."

MacGregor said briefly that he hadn't forgotten about it, and left the matter there.

Drake's Rolls-Royce took MacGregor in smooth privacy to the Aragvi Restaurant, but he was glad to get out of the car. Its comfort gave him a feeling of insidious deceit. He slammed its door and walked down the dim flight of steps into the restaurant. Shashleek, yogurt, garlic, pickled meats, pork, and all variety of spices had impregnated the dusty walls with Oriental sweetness. It was Georgian but it could have been Persian, and he felt homesickness in the pit of his stomach. He heard a thin orchestra playing apologetic Caucasian dances, and when he turned into the arched room with its long tables, he was almost back in Teheran, until he saw Essex and Katherine dancing on the small floor near the orchestra.

He had waited for this moment to see if there would be another surge of anger with Katherine, but he felt nothing more than casual bitterness. He stood and watched them. They were neatly matched and evenly proportioned to each other and absolutely balanced in their movements. MacGregor had never danced in his life, but all the sensuousness of these movements in their forbidden yet restrained intimacy developed a violent and unreasonable jealousy in him, and again he felt a dislike for Essex which was quickly transferred to Katherine.

When they stopped he followed them to their table. They were surprised to see him, Katherine more than Essex. She seemed to forget herself for a fraction of a second and she was smiling at him until she curled her lips. MacGregor looked away.

"MacGregor," Essex said. "What's up?"

"Nothing." MacGregor liked his own coldness. "Drake arranged a meeting with Molotov for midnight. I thought I had better come and tell you."

"Well? What time is it?"

"About ten-thirty."

"In a hurry aren't you?"

"I'm in no hurry," MacGregor said, "but I thought you might be."

"Thank you very much."

"Sit down," Katherine said to MacGregor.

MacGregor took off his coat and sat down. He wanted to be quite settled in their presence. He told Essex about the cable from London ordering their return. "I thought you might be interested in that also," he said.

"I'll be interested in that when I have finished with the Russians," Essex replied; but it did not sound convincing. It was clear that this time London meant what it said, Essex or no Essex.

"You must have some of our champagne," Katherine said sweetly to MacGregor.

Essex called a waiter and said in brief Russian, "A glass," and pointed to the champagne. The black-coated old man went away and came back with a champagne glass and poured some champagne for MacGregor.

MacGregor did not hurry. He looked around at the half-deserted room where rather sad Russian civilians and warmer-blooded Red Army men were drinking vodka and enjoying too much rare food. Dishes were still being served, and each one that passed MacGregor brought another good smell of home with it.

"So now you are homesick," Katherine said to him very politely — too politely and too loosely.

MacGregor did not like her insight and he said nothing.

"Why the devil should he be homesick?" Essex said.

Katherine spread her romantic hands. "You really don't know how much of a Persian your MacGregor is," she said to Essex.

"Oh?" Essex's voice rose.

"You would never think to look at him that he was also deeply emotional. Look at those thin features and those lovely straight eyes and that lick of hair. How delightfully calm you look, Mr. MacGregor."

"I feel calm," he said and wondered how much she had been drinking.

"I thought you might be troubled," she murmured.

He shook his head.

"I thought you two had finished your arguing at lunch time to-day," Essex said. "I don't want to hear any more of it. Don't talk to each other at all if you are going to bicker so politely." Essex called for a bill. "As for you, Kathy," he said, "you had better start making up your mind whether you want to come to London with me or not. Do you have a house in London?"

"Only Uncle Paul's, and I hate the place."

"Then I shall have to put you up," Essex said. "I have plenty of room."

"Is your house empty?"

"More or less."

"They should take it away from you," she said. "Take them all away and make them good habitations for the wretches who live in the gutters. What a wonderful sight it will be to see you all thrown out in the street."

"Shall we go?" Essex said benignly, and offered Katherine his arm.

"Come along Mr. MacGregor," she said very nicely.

In the car Katherine fell into silence, and MacGregor could not tell whether she was soft and warm beside him or merely crushed with him in the narrow space.

"This is damned annoying in a way," Essex said about Molotov.

"Never mind," Katherine said affectionately.

At the Embassy they both helped her out, and for a moment she held an arm through each of theirs and laughed as if it were a great joke. Still laughing she turned to MacGregor. Her face drained of its humour, and for a moment she looked ill as she compressed her lips and said

232

again as she had said before: "You are such a fool. Such a fool." She walked away and both men knew better than to go with her. They stood and watched.

"That certainly finishes you, MacGregor," Essex said cheerfully.

"I suppose it does," MacGregor said cynically — but now he was not at all sure.

Chapter 18

THE DISCUSSION with Molotov was brief and decisive. Essex put all the frills on his plan for a Commission. There were plenty of ways of putting over a plan like this, all within the scope of the present situation. The skill in presenting it lay in the refinements, and Essex knew them all. He presented it briefly, sharply, importantly and factually. He created an atmosphere about this Commission which made it the quintessence of common sense and goodwill. He made it so logical that any man arguing about it would be a fool.

Nevertheless, Molotov argued.

"As I understand it," Molotov said. "You suggest that a complicated committee be set up to test the validity of the democratic movement in Azerbaijan, and that we should all agree to act upon the decisions or findings of this committee."

"That is putting it crudely," Essex said.

"It is a plan which neither Britain nor the Soviet Union has the right to implement, or even consider," Molotov said and shook his head.

Essex retained his air of absolute common sense. "I don't follow your reasoning," he said to Molotov.

"It's very simple." Molotov raised his two hands to Essex, his most common gesture. "We have no right to interfere in the internal affairs of Iran. Occupation does not give the Soviet Union or Britain the right to impose their will on the Iranian people."

"I see that it is hopeless arguing about it," Essex said. "To us, however, the Commission of Enquiry is a fair means of testing the Soviet Union's faith in this matter."

"Is this discussion to test our faith, Lord Essex?"

It waited there for a moment, but Essex already felt the collapse of his whole scheme. It had collapsed, in Essex's estimation, because it was hopeless trying to talk the Russians into a British point of view. Essex had put up his brief fight, but he had lost the spirit of the discussion. He could rouse no argument and no new thought.

233

"What is it that Britain really wants?" Molotov said suddenly.

"A Commission of Enquiry!" Essex repeated, as if Molotov were a fool.

Molotov shook his head. "We can't see that it would serve any purpose."

"Then I see no reason for continuing these talks," Essex said in quick and angry decision. "We wanted to settle this calmly and sensibly by direct negotiation with the Soviet Union," he said. "It is quite obvious now that we must apply other methods of settling it, because we cannot allow such an uneven situation to exist in Iran. I regret the Soviet Union's attitude in this matter. I believe that you will soon have cause to regret it yourselves."

Molotov did not appear worried about that.

Essex stood up. "Then we might as well terminate this discussion now."

Molotov shrugged a little. "As you wish," he said. He did not argue, but he did say that he regretted their failure to reach agreement. "No proposals have been put forward by the British representative which were anything but interference in Iran's affairs," he said. "Discussion on that basis is hopeless. I believed before that it was hopeless, but you persuaded me that another meeting might be of some use."

They shook hands and Molotov turned to MacGregor. "I can do nothing more," he said as if he were apologizing to MacGregor. "The real trouble seems to be British lack of understanding of the situation in Azerbaijan."

"Then it's a pity we haven't had a chance to go there," MacGregor said. Molotov said nothing in reply.

While he waited for MacGregor to say good-bye to Suchkov, Essex took out a snuffbox which he had found in his coat pocket this morning. He took a pinch and held it to each nostril, inhaling it twice with violent sniffs. "If that is all," he said to the astounded Molotov, "then I bid you good day!"

Chapter 19

THEY spent just another day in Moscow. In its own way it was one of the most eventful days in Essex's life, for it saved him from suffering complete defeat.

In the morning he went with Katherine to visit the Tretiakoff Art Gallery, and it seemed typical of Essex that, at the moment when he should be defeated and making serious farewells to Moscow, he could go to an art gallery.

"Katherine," Essex said to her when they had left the Embassy behind. "I wanted to ask you about London. I am expecting you to come, you know."

"Are you really?" she said seriously.

"Yes. I had counted on it."

She waited, and the Kremlin clock chimed in the distance.

"I'm sorry to rush you," he said, "but I expect to leave to-day or to-morrow."

She was a very sane Katherine this morning. "What would be the point in my going with you?" she said. "What exactly do you intend me to do?"

Essex was near to saying that she should marry him, but he was not that defeated. That might come; it might be necessary; but not yet. "You could work with me; I could arrange that."

"And MacGregor?"

"He can go back to his morphology or paleontology or whatever it is."

She laughed. "You would be making a poor exchange."

"Don't be coy," he said. "What about it?"

"I wonder if I would be any good to you, Harold. You and I could never really agree. I seem to be going the other way from you."

"What other way?"

"I don't know. It's just the other way."

"I don't understand you."

"Never mind," she said. "It's not worth going into."

"I think it would be a good thing for both of us if you came to London," he said honestly.

"Would it?" She did not give him any more definite answer. She was still thinking about it, and Essex decided to let the matter drop for a little while.

The Tretiakoff Gallery was a dull building from the outside, and Essex quickly decided that it was equally dull inside. He was not really interested in anything here. All he wanted was Katherine's word that she would come back with him. Katherine seemed bent on avoiding the decision by giving him an education in Russian art and provoking unnecessary argument about it.

For Katherine's sake he showed some interest in the Ikons on the second floor, and in one painting of Repin's. It was the study of the Cossacks replying derisively to Sultan Mahmoud's demand for their surrender. The picture of these amused and mocking men telling the Sultan to go to the devil appealed to Essex's own sense of defiance, and then to his sense of humour. None other of Repin's painting interested him. Katherine told him instructively that the Russians considered Repin their

235

greatest painter, but Essex passed by most of his work with quick contempt. After Repin there was contemporary Soviet art, and he was genuinely curious about it. It was all heroic and revolutionary, whether portraiture or landscape. Too many of the portraits were of leading Soviet political and military men, from Stalin down.

"Ah Kathy, you can see that this is junk! Do we have to see the remainder of it?"

"You wanted to come here," she said.

"Yes, and I have seen enough. I wanted primarily to talk to you about London. Can't you make up your mind and get it over and done with?" As if to speed her decision, he bundled her out of the Tretiakoff.

Essex asked her once more about London, arguing that her job had finished here anyway; that Drake was no use to her any more; that she had been long enough away from home. He was not asking her to come back, he was provoking her into it.

Even in this last moment she would still not give a definite answer. "I don't know that I want to go back to London yet," she said. "I wouldn't mind a holiday somewhere else first, in the mountains, or in the sun. I don't like London in midwinter."

"The winter doesn't worry you," he told her.

"Perhaps it doesn't," she admitted, "but I'm not sure about going back. I'll let you know when I make up my mind."

That was all the answer he could get, and there the matter remained.

Essex had a feeling that MacGregor was responsible in some way for Katherine's hesitation, but he could not logically see how. Katherine had deliberately made a fool of MacGregor, and there was no way in which MacGregor could influence her. Yet the balance between himself and MacGregor and Katherine was not settled yet, and Essex had discovered that he could not settle it by himself.

He had an afternoon siesta in his warm room and then called Miss Williams and asked if there was any news about a plane. She said there was a Russian plane going to Berlin early to-morrow morning. She had booked three seats on it, the third being for herself. Essex told her to make it four seats and didn't offer any explanations. He kept Katherine in mind because he did not want to think now about his return to London without her. It would be difficult enough with Katherine. Without her it would be his most miserable homecoming in a lifetime of diplomacy. He had been so sure of succeeding where the Ambassadors and the Foreign Ministers had failed. He had to succeed where others failed: that made him Essex. Not that he had failed. London had asked him to come back. Very well. If they wanted him back before he had finished his job here, then the responsibility was on London. Moreover, he had been the terminator of these discussions, not Molotov. It was he who had arisen and called a halt. There was no failure. There was a deadlock, but no failure.

At six o'clock in the evening, Stalin sent a messenger to the Embassy and wondered if Essex would like to come and see him. Essex was shaving.

"The old man has never done this before." Melby was excited in bringing this news to Essex. He made little sense of his announcement that the envoy was waiting downstairs with a large black Packard.

"Did you leave him sitting outside in his car? Essex asked farcically.

"No. No. He is in the library."

Essex went on shaving. "Give him a drink of whisky and tell him I'll be down when I have finished dressing. Get MacGregor and tell him to wait for me in the library."

Melby made the mistake of inquiring how long Essex would be.

Essex gave him time to realize his error. "Do you want me to hurry, Melby?" he asked with lazy sarcasm.

"No. Oh no."

"Then don't fluster. I shall be down when I am ready." He went on shaving with deliberate strokes, although his own elation could not prevent a smile cracking the dry lather on his cheeks. When Melby had gone he said aloud, "By God I must have shaken Molotov!" and he hurried despite himself.

Drake came. It was the first time Drake had visited him in his room. He wanted to hurry Essex, but knew better. "If you don't mind," he said to Essex, "I'll come with you."

"What for?" Essex said, tying a bright bow tie.

"I know it's your night," Drake said, "but I should like to put one or two matters to Stalin that we have been trying to settle for some time."

"That might not be a good idea, Francis. This Iranian issue is too important. I don't want it confused with other problems. Do you mind?"

"Whatever you say. But I should like to go along anyway."

"Please," Essex said.

"And if you don't mind I'll bring John Melby with me."

"If you don't mind," Essex said, "I'd rather not."

Drake left him without arguing that point.

Stalin might as well have come in person, the way the Embassy had stirred into life even at this late afternoon hour. Miss Williams knocked quietly on Essex's door and then stood no more than a foot inside his room and asked if he would want any of the documents unpacked. "No, my dear lady," Essex said. "To-night we will be talking something bigger than documents." Having satiated Miss Williams with charm, he put a silk handkerchief in his top pocket and strolled along to the library where Melby and MacGregor were attending Stalin's emissary. The whisky had been provided as ordered, but it remained untouched by the visitor, whom Melby introduced as Professor Stein. He was an unimportant and disappointing figure. He looked to Essex like a German Jew, a clever man who was quietly amused with himself. He had white hair and was pale and academic. He asked Essex in lilting English to forgive the informality, but Comrade Stalin had just heard that Lord Essex was preparing to leave Moscow. Stalin was anxious to talk with him before he left.

Essex waited for a leisurely moment and then clapped his hands like a circus master. "Shall we go," he said. Professor Stein found himself urged out by a firm, confident, and self-possessed Essex. Drake and MacGregor followed as an entourage.

En route to the Kremlin in Stalin's black Packard, Essex asked the Professor about Stalin's health, and the Professor amused himself by referring to stories in American newspapers which always pronounced Stalin a sick man, but always found him strong and well when they least expected and wanted it. It was a short drive, and they turned into the Kremlin through the main tower gate from the Red Square. As the car approached the gate a blue light shone and a bell rang. The car slowed up as it went under the bricked arch of the guard post, and a blue uniformed guard glanced inside briefly and saluted. Essex was ready for scrutiny and formality, but the Packard went on into the Kremlin grounds and stopped at a drive-in between two buildings. They were at the large yellow palace — the building with a round dome at one corner. MacGregor identified it as the dome over which flew the spreading red flag he had seen from the Embassy, across the river.

Professor Stein preceded the three Englishmen into an entrance hall and then to a modern grey lift which was attended by a blue uniformed guard who saluted and took them to another level. They followed Stein along a carpeted corridor which was bare-walled and precise, and though this was a palace, the only indication of it was the tapestry curtains at one end of the corridor. MacGregor looked around him and guessed that this had been turned into an administrative building, but there was no hurrying of people, and the only noise of activity came from a typewriter in one of the rooms behind high white walls.

The Professor opened one of the doors and they were shown into a small room which was half panelled in oak. The walls were new white, relieved only by a decorative ceiling with egg-and-dart moulding. A picture of Kalinin hung at one end of the wall near a porcelain stove. The oak furniture consisted of four or five leather-covered armchairs and a round polished table with a set of straight-backed chairs around it. The room could have been a small conference room combined with a reception room, and it rather surprised Essex who had expected to see proletarian bareness or Oriental luxury. The Professor asked them to be seated, and Essex and Drake chose the armchairs. MacGregor sat in a plain chair near the stove. The Professor was walking to another door when it opened and Stalin came in. They all stood up.

Whatever these three men expected, they had a common moment of excitement here. Drake had met Stalin before, but he had never ceased to be curious about this man, a curiosity which he could not define and which he did not like. MacGregor was surprised to find himself standing here about to meet such a distant and mysterious figure. For Essex it was something entirely different. He was first of all concerned with the possibilities which Stalin brought for success or failure of the mission. Then he considered Stalin as a man, perhaps as a great man. If he really was great, then Essex would very soon know it. If he wasn't, then Essex would place him in his proper place in no time at all. Yet Essex knew that the first impression was in Stalin's favour. He came forward to Drake, who happened to be the nearest, and shook hands with him and said a few words in Russian. It gave Essex a chance to adjust his picture of this strange Russian.

Stalin was dressed in a dark green Army uniform with large gold embroidered stars on the epaulettes. Essex observed that he wore no decorations. That too was in Stalin's favour because illustrious figures needed no such distinction. Essex was surprised to see that Stalin was a little shorter than himself, but he had a straight back although he was quite relaxed. Essex liked a man to stand up straight. Stalin was broad and solid with very little shape of age around him. He was unhurried, and Essex could see in this a natural dignity and an instinctive calm. Such natural poise Essex considered rare in anyone but an Englishman, and he scrutinized Stalin's face for lines of deeper concern and conflict. There were none, and Stalin looked younger than his sixty-odd years. His hair was greying and so was his thick moustache, but his brown eyes had never worn glasses, and they were set in a calm estimate of the universe round about him. Essex felt that there was no division of any kind in Stalin, no uncertainty, nothing small and nothing remote, nothing indirect and nothing confused. Essex decided that Stalin must be a well-bred man.

The Professor translated as Stalin spoke his quiet Russian. "Comrade Stalin says he is very pleased to see you, Lord Essex, and he hopes that your stay in Moscow has been satisfactory." It was not intimate nor was it formal, and Stalin waited for an answer.

"Tell Marshal Stalin," Essex said to Professor Stein, "that we were about to leave your country in high disappointment, but now we feel hopeful again."

Stalin nodded and said *Khoroshaw*.

239

MacGregor, still trying to estimate the reality of his situation, found that he was shaking hands with Stalin and exchanging a formal greeting in Russian. Stalin carried it further and said that he was always pleased to see young people, particularly when they came to Moscow and could speak Russian. He said to Essex that he hoped the young men which the Soviet Union was sending to England were as capable as Mr. MacGregor. MacGregor nodded solemnly. The Professor translated it for Essex, who put back his head and laughed and looked at Drake until he too smiled a little. Stalin motioned to the chairs and they sat down. Stalin eased himself into one of the armchairs. He rested his elbows on the arms, entwined his fingers, and waited while Professor Stein offered cigarettes.

As Stalin produced a pipe Essex saw his opportunity for informality, and he reached in his top pocket for his own pipe. It wasn't there. For a moment Essex thought that he had left his pipe behind, and this seemed a terrible blunder under the circumstances. He found it in his inside pocket and he relaxed again. "Let us hope that we see eye-to-eye in everything else," Essex said as he brandished his pipe at Stalin.

Professor Stein was amused. "Comrade Stalin offers you some of our Caucasian tobacco. He is particularly proud of this supply because it is a gift from his native Georgia. It is strong."

"The stronger the better," Essex said with nice bravado. "You might tell the Marshal that this is real luxury for me. Tobacco is hard to get in England these days, particularly good tobacco."

Stalin nodded and pushed his thumb in his pipe bowl and told Essex to take the box with him. Essex had planned for that reply. He thanked Stalin, already fancying the subtle and nonchalant use he could make of the tobacco in England, Stalin's Georgian tobacco. Stalin smoked for a moment as if waiting to see if the Englishman wanted to say something, but Essex knew that it was better to wait for Stalin, who obviously did not mind taking his time. Stalin addressed Essex directly but it was Professor Stein who carried the meaning. "Comrade Stalin would like to know why you are leaving Moscow, Lord Essex."

Essex did not want to be ordinary, but he had to equal Stalin's authority. "Tell Marshal Stalin that I would be wasting time if I stayed here any longer. Our negotiations, as he must know, have broken down."

The Professor continued: "He knows of the negotiations and he would like to know your frank and honest opinion as to why they broke down."

Essex's immediate emotion was not directly concerned with the success of his mission. He wanted nothing more than to impress Stalin. "I will speak very frankly," he said. "Our negotiations with the Soviet representative about the difficult situation in Iran failed because of a lack of understanding of each other's terms. Unfortunately we did not attend

240

Voltaire's dictum to define our terms before we began. The result was disagreement on all issues. We did not understand our opposite ideas of sovereignty, pacts, occupation, legal rights, legitimate national interests, and self-determination. These confusions, plus a certain amount of in-born suspicion, made agreement impossible. We regret it considerably, because the situation in Iran is a deterrent to the friendly relations be-tween the Soviet Union and Great Britain." Essex stopped for transla-tion, puffing thoughtfully at his pipe while the Professor caught up with him.

In his statement Essex had sacrificed a good opportunity of appealing to Stalin for immediate conciliation and compromise. He did this de-liberately to impress Stalin with a show of unbiased and intelligent under-standing of the real difficulties.

Stalin merely nodded his head and drew his lips over his pipe and said nothing. If he had been impressed by Essex's honesty and intelligence he did not show it, and he waited for Essex to go on.

Essex hunted for the instincts which had carried him this far, because he understood above everything else that Stalin could actually be convinced. Essex had no idea of what would convince Stalin, but he knew he had to be honest.

"I should like to point out," he said earnestly, "that Britain's interest in Iran is not one of interference. We have long had an intimate associa-tion with Iran. Iran's modern history and advancement owes much to British friendship and assistance. We also have large economic interests in southern Iran which are vital to our existence as an Empire. Most of our oil comes from the oil refineries in Abadan, and this is a consideration we can't ignore when watching the developments of power within Iran itself. So that when we show concern with the development in Azerbaijan, it is not in any way directed against the Soviet Union. It is real concern with the freedom and integrity of Iran, which we wish to preserve at all costs."

Essex gave Stalin a chance to reply but the Russian's capacity for silence seemed infinite. Essex now became fluent with so attentive a listener.

"We look at the revolt in the northern province of Azerbaijan," he said, "as a direct political influence on the whole country. An influence which is not natural nor spontaneous, but one which is perhaps inspired with the lessons of Soviet history. We are not a Fascist state seeing danger in his-torical change. We are simply an Empire. Yet we have no imperial con-trol over Iran. Our economic interests are no more than the Soviet Union herself is seeking in the north. But the regime which has seized power in Azerbaijan is a regime of revolution and confiscation. The situation in Azerbaijan could become an example for all terroristic organizations, if it were allowed to succeed. Not only that, its success would really destroy Iran's sovereignty, and that is the clear aim of the separatist policies of the Tabriz regime. They have used murder and plunder as a means of getting what they want; they have instituted reforms which we believe to be ahead of any real change demanded by the people; and they have threatened war with the real Government of Iran if it interferes in their partisan activities."

Essex felt that surely this must stir the Russian, but Stalin said nothing.

"In coming to the Soviet Union," Essex went on, "I had hoped to show the Soviet representatives that there was another side to the developments in Iran, the side which we see from the comparative position of disinterest."

Here Stalin questioned Professor Stein on the word *disinterest*. Professor Stein assured him that disinterest was the word Essex had used.

As Essex went on, the reason of his own arguments seemed clearer to him than ever before, and he was more convinced than ever that by reason alone could Stalin be persuaded to change the Russian attitude. He was not sure why he felt as he did: perhaps it came from watching Stalin seated so calmly in his leather chair: silent but nodding occasionally as the professor mumbled his running translation. Yet the combined effort to impress and convince Stalin had taken Essex as far as he could go. When he had finished he began to worry about the show he had put on. He waited for Stalin to comment and decide.

Stalin looked at his dead pipe and then spoke to the Professor, who turned to Essex. "Comrade Stalin," he said, "thinks that Lord Essex has apparently been misinformed about the true situation in Azerbaijan."

Essex waited, but there was nothing more. Was that to be the summation of everything he had said! Essex recovered. "If we are misinformed," he said, "it is because we cannot move freely in Azerbaijan. The Soviet authorities have prevented British representatives from making a study of the situation."

The Professor told this to Stalin and replied again: "Comrade Stalin asks if British representatives are still anxious to make a study of the situation in Azerbaijan."

"Certainly."

"Comrade Stalin would like to know if you are personally anxious to do so."

Essex hesitated only a moment. "Indeed I am," he said.

"Then Comrade Stalin personally guarantees that the Red Army in Azerbaijan will not hinder you in any way. He suggests that if a personal study will assist in settling this misunderstanding between us, then we are most anxious to co-operate with you in any way. He invites you to study the situation at first hand, Lord Essex. Would that be satisfactory?"

Essex had not expected it, and he did not know whether it was a trap or a deception or a delay. Yet it was too spontaneous to be anything very cunning. For his own sake Essex accepted it, because he needed its salvation. Already he could see his hopelessness turning into successful accomplishment. This would be the biggest step anyone had made in this quarrel with the Russians. It would strengthen his position so much that London would consider it a remarkable achievement. No doubt they would also see in it an importance beyond the Azerbaijan issue. It was a new chance. "I would be very happy to accept that invitation," he said, "and I believe it would be instrumental in establishing a real compromise. Since time is short, however, we would only be interested if it could be done immediately."

"Naturally," said the Professor.

"What does Marshal Stalin think?"

"He says he would be delighted to arrange for a plane to take you and your staff to Tabriz to-morrow, if that is not too soon."

"Not at all." Essex was calculating quickly and sharply. "But I believe it would be better if I went to Teheran first, because I would have to consult our Ambassador there. With Marshal Stalin's permission I would like to approach Azerbaijan from that direction."

"Everything will be arranged," the Professor said. "Our authorities will be fully instructed and the plane will be at your service to-morrow. Comrade Stalin wishes you *bon voyage,* and he looks forward to the pleasure of seeing you again." Professor Stein was smiling at Essex with his self-contained eyes.

"It is understood that we will be perfectly free to move unhindered and undirected in any way?" Essex put away his pipe and stood up.

"Certainly. Although your personal safety . . ."

"That is our responsibility," Essex said definitely to the Professor. "Then the plane will be ready to take Mr. MacGregor and myself to-morrow?"

"Yes," said the Professor.

Essex nodded with satisfaction. This was ultimate victory after all.

Drake interrupted his satisfaction by addressing the professor. "I was wondering," Drake said, "if we might discuss a few more problems of policy with Marshal Stalin. Many issues are outstanding, and we would like to have certain things clarified."

The Professor told it to Stalin and replied: "Comrade Stalin would like to know what needs clarifying?"

Drake spoke abruptly. "Several points of Soviet policy in Germany and Poland and the Balkans are confusing, and we would welcome some method of understanding the Soviet attitude. Perhaps I could see Marshal Stalin again at an early date?"

"Comrade Stalin says that it is better for issues like that to be settled by the authorities established by both countries to deal with them."

"These mainly concern broader elements of Soviet policy which we don't understand," Drake said desperately.

The Professor talked with Stalin again. Essex wanted to kick Drake in the ribs, but Stalin accepted Drake as he accepted the others. MacGregor in particular observed this. He had been much impressed with the man, but seeing him so tolerant of Drake was disappointing.

The Professor was explaining to Drake that Stalin did not understand how any broad issue of Soviet policy could be unclear. "However," said the Professor, "to avoid misunderstanding in the future, he would like to furnish Sir Francis with a guide which will explain Soviet foreign policy. First, he says, the Soviet aim is a stable and lasting peace for all nations. Secondly, security for Soviet frontiers. Thirdly, peaceful and friendly governments in adjacent countries with which Russia may maintain good-neighbourly relations. Fourthly, strengthening of international co-operation on the basis of the principles of equality of states and with no nation dominating others. He says that this will explain the broad Soviet policies now and in the future, and if this outline is applied to anything which is unclear, it will act as a solvent to the problem."

"Unfortunately the problems are more specific," Drake began, but Essex was already taking his leave. Stalin handed the box of Georgian tobacco to Essex as they were shaking hands. Stalin was also saying goodbye to Drake, who abandoned any hope of pursuing this to the end. With MacGregor, Stalin was more direct since there was no language difficulty, and he asked if MacGregor had seen something of Russia.

"Very little, unfortunately," MacGregor said.

"Come back and see all that you can," Stalin said as he shook hands. His eyes held MacGregor's for a moment as if he shared a sly secret with the Scot. "Since it was your suggestion to Mr. Molotov that a visit to Azerbaijan might be of some use," Stalin said to MacGregor, "I will be most interested to hear your personal views on the situation there. Perhaps you could let me know?"

"Yes, I will," said the surprised MacGregor.

Fortunately Professor Stein had not translated Stalin's remarks, and MacGregor hoped fervently that Essex would never hear them. He did not want Essex to know of any part he had played in sending them to Iran. If Essex ever found out that his assistant had been somewhat responsible for this new turn in events, then his punishment upon the meddler would be instantaneous, and they might never get to Iran at all. To be of any use, this achievement had to be Essex's. MacGregor knew it, and apparently an amused Stalin knew it. MacGregor let out his breath, and was glad that the talking was over.

Stalin walked to the door with them, and finally said that he hoped Essex would be satisfied with what he saw in Azerbaijan, and that he would understand what was happening there.

"I will be convinced by anything that is fair, reasonable, and honest," Essex said in his final attempt to impress Stalin, "and I give you my word that I will not be prejudiced by past considerations."

With adieu, they left.

Chapter 20

I WAS wondering when you would turn up," Katherine said to Essex as he walked into her office. She was sealing letters and she held a taper near her soft face for a moment and then crushed it out with her fingers. "How was Stalin?"

"Amazing fellow." Essex ruffled the loose hair on her forehead.

"So are you," she said carelessly. "You have given me the devil of a time getting you out of here. These are all yours." She gave him the official envelopes. "For London."

"Kathy," he said. "Rather unexpected things have changed my plans a little," he said.

"I can see that," she commented. "You are smug and happy."

"Do you blame me?" He sat on the desk close to her. "I seemed to have done rather well to-day. I think I pulled something off with Stalin."

"*Mm!*"

"Don't be so wise and cynical." She was making it hard for him to discuss the idea of Katherine leaving Moscow with him. It was an awkward idea now. It was alright taking her to London, but it would be difficult taking Kathy to Iran, and rather unnecessary. The circumstances had changed so radically that his immediate need for Katherine had changed at the same time. He did not want to lose her; he wanted this relationship when he returned to London; but it simply wasn't as necessary now as it had been. "About London," he said. "You know we are heading for Iran now?"

"I know." She waited.

"I expect to be back in London in a couple of weeks," he said.

"Oh?"

"Yes," he said. "You can get home alright can't you?"

"I should think so." Katherine leaned her knee against the desk to push back her chair and look at him out of the glare of the desk lamp. Essex looked at her set English face and at her wide head and self-possessed

245

mouth, and he hated any idea of ultimately losing Katherine. It was unfortunate that something more important had interrupted him here.

"I'll give you a note to my man in London," he said, "and I'll cable him. I can still put you up."

"Don't bother," she said, and he did not know how she was taking it.

"I'm sorry we couldn't go back together," he said gracefully.

"My dear Harold," she said, "I hadn't decided to go back. Don't place too much importance upon it." She yawned with her arms above her head.

"I actually came to invite you to dine with Drake and me," he said.

She stood up. "I am having dinner with the Asquiths."

"You can have dinner with Jane any time," he said and put his arm loosely through hers and tried bullying her a little.

"No," she said. "I want to be there this evening." She was laughing at him and he knew it. "Turn out that desk lamp will you?" She stood at the door, keeping it open for the light it gave from the hall.

"Are you sure you won't come?"

"Not this evening," she said.

Essex was courtesy-bound to have dinner with Drake, otherwise he would have gone over to the Asquiths with her, since she seemed so set on going there. He was bored with the thought of eating a silly dinner with Drake. "I shall drop over later on," he told her as they parted at the stairs. "I'm sorry about London."

She was still laughing silently at him, and Essex felt that he had lost his advantage with Katherine. She waved a casual hand of dismissal and walked very successfully down the stairs.

Now Drake, Essex thought, as he began his last rites in Moscow.

Drake was having a dispute with MacGregor.

"I am glad you have come," Drake said to Essex. "You might remember, Harold, that we asked MacGregor to use his technical background to acquire some geological data."

"Yes. I remember," Essex said, "but I doubt if he has had the time to do much about it." He sat down to enjoy the scene.

"That may be so," Drake went on, "but I went to considerable trouble to arrange an urgent meeting with this Polish fellow who has so much material that we want. MacGregor, with fine scruples about not spying on the Russians, has refused to go and see him. The Pole is waiting at the National Hotel for him now. Perhaps you can persuade MacGregor where his duty lies."

Essex raised a hand. "Leave me out of it," he said jovially. "This is between you two." He began to fill his pipe.

Drake found a successful Essex as unbearable as an argumentative MacGregor. "I'm afraid you must intervene, Harold," Drake insisted.

"MacGregor is the only man here who can understand the technical material which the Pole has available. This is the only chance we have of getting it. MacGregor must go."

"Well MacGregor?" Essex said.

"Sorry," MacGregor said and shook his head disinterestedly.

Essex watched MacGregor and knew that behind his detachment there was an absolute determination not to go: the set of his thin features and the tight grip of his Scottish jaw were all the indication Essex needed. He knew MacGregor. He smiled and leaned back. "Must you be so adamant?" he asked MacGregor.

"Yes, I think so." For a moment they understood each other, and MacGregor was calmly challenging Essex to argue with him, to take sides with Drake. It was almost a taunt, an inexplicable revolt in MacGregor against Essex as well as Drake. Essex smoked patiently for a moment. He had to have MacGregor in Iran with him; he needed MacGregor. To-morrow he would be leaving Drake. There was no need to decide his attitude: Essex shrugged and said no more. Let them fight it out.

"This cannot be treated so lightly," Drake said.

"No," MacGregor admitted agreeably. "It can't."

"It would not take long to see this man." Drake was as near appealing to MacGregor as he could ever be.

MacGregor said nothing.

"I don't believe you intended doing it in the first place," Drake said.

"Perhaps not," MacGregor said. "Perhaps not."

"Well, I shan't argue further." Drake's anger was now making his calm voice shake. "Your attitude will be adequately reported to London."

MacGregor did not want to walk out on Drake, but he looked at Essex as if to warn him of the possibility. By a slight movement of his head Essex told MacGregor to leave. That gesture was saying: Go on, I will look after Drake, there is no point in fighting with him.

MacGregor agreed. He became polite. "You will excuse me," he said to Drake, and added as a necessary afterthought, "I would like to thank you, Sir Francis, for every kindness I have received at the Embassy."

"Good night young man, and I shan't forget your behaviour."

MacGregor inclined his head in careless acknowledgment. He was leaving when John Asquith stood at the door. "Ah, MacGregor," he said. "I was sent to get you for dinner. Have you finished with him, Francis?"

"Indeed I have," Drake said.

They all expected Asquith to make some comment on the obvious hostility of the scene, but Asquith apparently didn't care what had been going on here.

"When did you get back?" Essex asked him.

"About an hour ago," Asquith said, and he didn't care either about their meeting with Stalin or their intended departure to Iran. He said nothing. He took MacGregor and left.

Mad as a hatter! Essex said to himself. He thought about MacGregor going over there to dinner. He decided to get away from Drake early. Already Drake was telling him that London must be given the facts of MacGregor's refusal.

Essex sighed. "Give them the facts," he said. "I couldn't help you with him, Francis. MacGregor is a stubborn fellow, and there are times when it's useless arguing with him."

This provoked Drake further, but by mutual control and consent they allowed the matter to drop. They went to dinner and Drake suggested that Essex telephone London and tell them he was going on to Iran.

"I don't think so," Essex said and laughed to himself. He was not going to give any decision like that to London. He would get to Iran and then let them know. It was Drake's final attempt — and failure — to put Essex on the road to doing the formal thing by his profession. Thereafter they talked sensibly about their mutual acquaintances in the diplomatic service, and they finished the dinner at peace. After a suitable delay over brandy and coffee Essex rose to end it.

"Well, Francis," he said. "I think I shall call it a day. I don't suppose I shall see you before I leave, so let me say now that it's been damn nice of you to put up with us. We have been extremely comfortable." Not too much said and not too little.

"It has been nice having you, Harold," Drake shook hands with Essex briefly and smiled. "Unusual things always happen when you attend a situation; but we seemed to have enjoyed the excitement. I hope we meet in London."

"I will look forward to that. Good night old man."

"Good night. I hope there are no mishaps this time."

Essex hoped so too. He didn't need mishaps on this expedition to Iran. To have first-hand experience of the situation in Azerbaijan was all he required. Nothing would be more valuable in any showdown on the issue. He just wanted to get there and see what could be done. The Kremlin had already phoned him earlier, to suggest that they be at the Moscow airport at 7:30 to-morrow morning to catch the good weather. Essex didn't want any mishap, but he had no doubt that the unexpected would happen to him. It always did.

At the Asquiths he was greeted by John, who had opened the door for him. "Here is Harold looking like a forgotten schoolboy. Come in," he said. "Come in. Jane, get him a drink. He obviously needs it."

Essex entered the living room with Vodka at his heels. He bent to pat the spaniel, who scrambled around the chairs and the carpets. "Hullo boy. Hullo boy," Essex said and watched Vodka leap onto the couch

248

between Katherine and MacGregor. There he sat, his tongue out, his bright eyes upon Essex, barking attention to the two people who sat on either side of him. Essex did not need Vodka to show him that a truce was in force on the couch. There might not be deep friendship between Katherine and MacGregor, but there was at least toleration. That was the Asquiths' doing. Essex knew that they liked MacGregor, and he knew that they found him a very suitable companion for Katherine.

"I suppose you are tired after such a day," Jane Asquith said to Essex.

"Yes. You look tired," Katherine added, and still she laughed at him. "Sit down, Harold, and tell us about Stalin."

"Hasn't MacGregor given you the details?" Essex said as if he couldn't be bothered with it. He sat on the hassock near the fire and stretched his legs and invited Vodka to join him.

Vodka stayed where he was.

"MacGregor's powers of description are limited," Katherine said. "He merely says that Stalin is absolutely self-possessed. Did you find him so impressive?"

"Of course he did!" Asquith came from the kitchen with a bowl of ice. He put it on the floor, pulled up a chair, and sat over the bowl brewing drinks. His method of mixing a cocktail was to pour a large portion of this and a large portion of that into the bowl of ice, stir it with a ladling spoon, and then pour it into the glasses. He gave Essex a long drink and said: "Any man with more self-possession than himself impresses Harold. He envies it in any man, particularly when he finds it in a foreigner."

Essex ignored this as the remark of a man under the stimulation of this throat-raking concoction. Between the mockery of Katherine, and Asquith's derision, he felt that he had his hands full. Nevertheless, he could not keep quiet on the subject of Stalin. "Yes," he said. "There's no doubt that Stalin is self-possessed. Yet I had the feeling that he was a man who could be absolutely ruthless when necessary. Wouldn't you imagine so, MacGregor?"

MacGregor said No — he didn't think so.

"Ah nonsense," Asquith said to MacGregor. "Certainly he is ruthless. He has to be ruthless. There would not be any Russia at this moment if he hadn't been as bitter with his enemies as they were with him. Purges, for instance, are essential. We will never be anything ourselves until we have a few in England. As for the war: Stalin was no doubt very harsh with the Germans. He did not look upon the war as a sport between gentlemen. He is too civilized for such a conception, and as a civilized man he was naturally a ruthless warrior."

There was further argument about Stalin, each of them having his exact but different opinion. It was a genuine dispute in which all four of them took an equal share. Their voices rose as more of Asquith's

249

concoction was downed, and soon Vodka left the couch and crept away from the noise to settle under Jane Asquith's chair behind her sheltering legs, his head on the floor. Jane Asquith listened and said nothing until it became too personal and too angry. She then quietly blamed her husband for the whole argument, and asked MacGregor if he had many friends in Teheran.

It was such a violent change in the temper of discussion that at least it calmed MacGregor. "Well no," he said. "Not many."

"I suppose most of your friends were Persian?"

MacGregor was still rather fluent with the previous argument. "Most of my school friends were Persian," he said.

"Did you go to a Persian school?"

He nodded. "My father would not send me to the English or French schools."

"So you knew none of the foreigners in Teheran?"

"We lived with a Russian family for a long time," he told her. "But I think they have come back to Russia now."

The others had also paused for breath during this conversation because they would not interrupt Jane Asquith. John Asquith whistled impatiently under his breath and snapped his fingers for Vodka and cried *Hoish*, but the dog would not move from his wife's chair.

"You have never been there have you, Harold?" Jane Asquith was saying.

Essex shook his head. "It's new territory for me," he said.

"Poor Harold," Asquith interrupted violently. "Now you are in for it."

"In for what?"

"You are about to be frightened out of your wits," Asquith said and ladled out another glass for himself. "When you get to Iran you won't be talking over conference tables. You will be there in the thick of it where you can't escape the responsibility for what you are doing. You think it will be simple down there. But the sight of the place will frighten you. Every shout in the street will sound like a revolution. Ask MacGregor. You are about to see the raw material of your polite negotiations and it will scare you out of your wits."

"As usual," Essex said, "I'm hanged if I know what you're talking about."

There was little use in Jane Asquith's trying to stop her husband now and she didn't try. Asquith pulled at his long moustache. "You simply refuse to think about it," he said.

"About what?" Essex demanded, humouring him.

"About the mess you are stepping into. You'll never understand it."

"What is there to understand?" Essex said, exasperated now.

"If I thought it would do any good I would tell you," Asquith said contemptuously. "But you will never understand the world you are trying to make. *I* understand it, but it doesn't do me any good. In fact it's worse to understand what you are doing, because you become a hypocritical coward without the belly and the courage to revolt against the plotting and the scheming. I can't complain about you, Harold. You are stupid but honest. Look at me. I know everything, absolutely everything, always have and always will. But I am a bigger fool than you are, because I obey all the rules I despise. For that matter I now have a worse job than yours."

"Oh?" Essex said. "What now?"

"The Czechs!" Asquith announced.

"What the dickens are they involving you with the Czechs for?"

"That revolting mass of hypocrisy, the Labour Government, are about to blackmail their Czechoslovak brothers. Bah! I prefer the Tories."

"You are just getting sour, John," Essex said.

"I am always sour," Asquith said bitterly. "Last time it was a soap factory in Riga. This time it's a chemical trust in Prague. It is supposed to be ours. Ours! A British-owned appendage to a German cartel. The Czechs nationalize it and I am supposed to go there and de-nationalize it — hand it back to our Trusts."

"What's the matter with that?" Essex smiled.

Asquith shook his long unhappy head. "I wouldn't mind doing it for the Tories, but to hear our Socialists being so protective of the cartel is more than even I can stomach. The Labour Government nauseates me. They are a cheap blackmailing lot; filthy, immoral; playing with the balance of power like all the others. They will ruin us. If we are left with a friend in Europe when they have finished, it will be a miracle. *I* am to begin on the Czechs."

"What did you expect?" Katherine Clive said. "You are always laughing at other people for expecting so much of any British Government. Now you are expecting it to hand over several million pounds to the Czechs without a word. Are the Czechs any different from anyone else?"

"Do you think I care a hang about the Czechs?" Asquith shouted.

"Then what are you complaining about?"

"You're as stupid as the others. If you can't see what a miserable business it is performing these little tricks for a Labour Government then there is no hope for you either."

"Why don't you tell London to go to the devil?" Essex said.

"Yes. Why don't I?" Asquith said.

The others had nothing to say.

Asquith turned upon MacGregor. "Let this be a lesson to you," he said with sudden fury. "This is what happens to a man when he hasn't the stomach to make up his mind when he is your age. It's too late when

251

you are my age. You too Kathy! Don't be so stupidly sure of yourself."

"What's he talking about?" Essex said to Katherine.

"You wouldn't know," Asquith said. "MacGregor: At the first opportunity you leave this man. Do you hear me?"

This embarrassed MacGregor but he said "I hear you."

"When you get to Iran go off and leave him."

"What do I do then?" MacGregor said.

"How do I know. Go and live in the hills or dig your oil wells; but leave him. You too Kathy. You get away from here. Go down to Iran with MacGregor and make sure he leaves Essex. Get him out of the way. And listen to me Kathy:"

"I'm listening."

"You are ignorant and you are vain, and you are too stupid to understand what is happening to you. You think you know where this world is leading you. Bah! You don't know at all. You are smart because you can say to me *What did you expect?* That is just too smart. I know what to expect of governments, but I am still shattered by it when it comes. Do you think I can laugh at political cynicism? Can I laugh simply because I expect every move I make to be a trick? Can I laugh because I know it? You vain stupid woman: I know everything but you don't know anything. Should I start telling you what we are trying to do in Poland? Rumania, Hungary, even Germany? Or do you know all that too? Will you say *What did I expect?* Don't be any more foolish than you can help! I know what to expect, and these days it is always rotten with plots. We are all rotten. We will go on being rotten while irritating women like you are being smart, and clever men like Mac-Gregor are sitting in the middle of your little lives waiting for what you expect. You are hopeless. And so long as you are hopeless we're all hopeless. Can't you see anything happening which is bigger than your conceit? Don't you see what is before you? Don't you? I know you can't answer me because you allow your petty little surroundings to decide your habits and your morals and your entire existence. Oh you revolt alright! But all your pallid little revolts are a waste of time. Why don't you go home and see where your anger really lies? Why don't you look around the world and see what is happening and allow that to decide your life? While you two are sitting here quibbling, we are becoming a nation of unholy partners and purveyors. The old hypocrisy was bad, but it was almost honest when compared with our present standard of deceit. We are now led by worthy men with their feet among the people — whom they betray so easily and immodestly. It is your fault, but neither of you is intelligent enough to see that nothing else matters. You get tangled up in this little incident of Harold's, and you think you are persons of human intellect with a sense of passion and virtue and responsibility. You are miserable little wretches, wasting your time. Go away from here. Leave me alone. Go out and fold your useless hands like Melby's pasty fingers. Go and smash your brains and your bodies under a tramcar. They are no use as they are. A man with a limb to use and a particle to think has got to use them, but not among the tiny people who swagger and skite and sit in this building warming their hands and quaking at their shadows. Get out of here. Go home, both of you. Go away and see if there is anything left of you before it is too late." Asquith towered over them for a moment, his face drained white and his angry eyes unseeing.

Jane Asquith took the glass from his hand and said softly: "I knew this would happen. You are getting terribly maudlin, John. I think you must be asleep on your feet. You might as well go to bed."

Asquith allowed his wife to lead him away, and though he made a long sound of disgust, possibly with himself and possibly for his friends, he went out without saying another word, without looking back, and without saying good-bye. It was clear that they meant nothing to him any more. He went right away from them, and Vodka rose from the floor and went with him.

"Poor old John," Essex said. "Knocked himself out with his own brew."

The other two said nothing.

Jane Asquith came back immediately. "He's alright," she said calmly. "He was travelling all day and he is not used to so many cocktails. It must be affecting him a little. I think I had better stay with him for a while."

Katherine stood up. "He'll be alright," she said.

"I'm so sorry," Jane Asquith told them.

"Can't say I blame him!" Essex said cheerfully, deliberately.

MacGregor wanted to say something in the same voice, but he kept quiet.

"Good night Jane," Katherine said quickly.

"Yes." Essex leaned forward and kissed Jane Asquith on both cheeks. "Good-bye Jane. I'll see what I can do about all this. Say good-bye to old John for me will you? We'll see you again somewhere and I hope it's at home. Time he came home. Good-bye my dear. It's been nice seeing you again."

"Good-bye Harold," she said. "I shall tell John. It's really terrible of him to go off like that." Jane Asquith put her hand forward for Mac-Gregor but she then leaned forward and kissed him lightly as if Mac-Gregor needed it for his unhappy face. He did not like to see Asquith like that. "He did not mean to be quite so harsh," she said to Mac-Gregor and smiled. "He is very fond of you. He is very fond of all of you, and he will be very sorry when he realizes what he said."

"No," MacGregor said with a faint smile. "I think he'll be pleased." It was the least he could do.

He stepped out with the others, and for a moment the three of them stood in the snow without wanting to understand anything about themselves or about Asquith or about their departure. From this sort of situation there was nothing definite at all in their parting. Nothing had concluded their relationship and they were all left in doubt. In a few words, however, Katherine made it definite and clear.

"Good-bye you two," she said briefly. "How nice it has been to know you both." She was lumping them together and doing away with them very casually.

It was so unimportant of her that MacGregor was angered again. He was surprised to find that he had expected Katherine to be less careless, to be less explicitly final. He had wanted Katherine to correct everything, as if she could do it by one word or one gesture. At least she might have offered some hope of it in the future, in London, anywhere. Not this Katherine, however. She was finished with him. The truce forced upon them by the Asquiths had been mere forbearance on her part. To Mac-Gregor their brief mutual toleration had given him another hope for Katherine, almost against his will, but there anyway. At the Asquiths he had watched her closely, had reminded himself that this could be the last time he would see Katherine. That alone had dispelled a great deal of his former bitterness. But now she had pushed him away again. By her casual farewell she made this leave-taking as final as it could ever be.

"Perhaps we should go and drink my coffee," Essex suggested.

"No," she said. "Take MacGregor with you this time."

To Essex that remark was directed not at himself but at MacGregor. He saw in it a clear indication that Katherine was by no means finished with MacGregor. The way she stood there, facing MacGregor, not turning a hair in Essex's own direction, told Essex enough. Katherine expected MacGregor to make some move, some offer to her. Essex didn't like it, and he saw again what a very serious threat MacGregor was to his own relationship with Katherine. She was by no means finished with MacGregor. Essex was left suspended with this thought as Katherine left them.

"Queer," Essex said. "Everybody's queer," he said irritably. "Be on time to-morrow, MacGregor. Good night."

"Good night," MacGregor said.

At least the morning was clear when they stood upon the airfield, watching their bags being thrown into the Russian Douglas. They were drinking hot coffee, served by one of the Embassy drivers from the

Humber. They were now full of coffee; early-morning coffee, breakfast coffee, and this consignment. It gave warmth and diversion from the lonely sound of sleepy aeroplane engines being warmed up across the dim field. Their Douglas was starting up, and the Russian crew had taken the wooden locks from the tail and the rudder. A small grey-haired Russian told MacGregor that they were ready. He was the pilot and his khaki jacket was thick with ribbons. Korin from the Foreign Office was standing with Essex, sharing the coffee as they made their official farewells. MacGregor stamped his cold feet, impatient to go.

"I forgot to return that book of Nicolson's I borrowed," Essex said to Korin. "I think I packed it away in my bag."

"It doesn't matter," Korin said as they shook hands. "We will soon have it in Russian. Perhaps you could send me his next book."

"Yes. I'll do that," Essex said.

A distinctive station-wagon suddenly cut in from the perimeter runway and came across to the plane. Katherine got out of it, well wrapped in her furs and wearing high boots. She ran across to them, followed by two men and Miss Williams.

"Hullo you two," she shouted. "Wait for us."

"Kathy," Essex said. "What the devil are you doing?"

"Here are Hamber and Steele. They want to come with you."

The two correspondents had their luggage, and Hamber explained that they had their exit visas and Iranian visas, everything they needed, if Essex would take them.

"If you're all clear," Essex said. "Get in."

"That's swell," Hamber said and they ran to the plane.

"You had better get in too, MacGregor," Essex said.

MacGregor was being asked by Miss Williams where he would be in London. He gave her the address. "If I don't get to Paris I hope to be in London," she said. "I do hope I see you. Good-bye. I am so sorry you are going."

He stood near Katherine.

"Why don't you come along?" MacGregor asked Katherine suddenly.

Katherine stopped warming her hands. "Would you really like that?" she said.

"Yes, I think I would."

She hesitated and then shook her head. "It's too late," she said.

"Is it?"

"You know it is," she said.

He nodded and turned away and climbed into the soft-walled plane. He took the first seat and looked out the window to watch Essex and Katherine talking and he knew that Essex was also suggesting to Katherine that she come. She shook her head and playfully eased him towards the

255

plane, and then stood back near Korin and Miss Williams as Essex left her. The moment Essex was inside, the mechanics pulled up the steps and closed the door with a metallic bang. Essex sat heavily in front of Mac-Gregor and cleaned the window with his glove, waving to Katherine.

Katherine had already gone back to the station-wagon. Only Korin and Miss Williams stood there as the plane bounced along the runway and turned into one of the lanes and took off and away from Moscow.

BOOK II
MacGregor

Chapter 21

O APPLES *of the earth. Little suns to warm your winter*
stomach. Summer days to roast your frozen belly. Little domes to keep
away the wind. O apples of the earth...

MacGregor listened to the old man selling his sweet potatoes which
he roasted slowly over a small charcoal fire on a barrow. *Yer-elmasi:*
apples of the earth. His barrow was still a landmark on the Maidan-i-
Shah, but his black old face was no more grizzled than it ever had
been. His fingers were long and very dirty, and they sorted the hot crack-
ling potatoes without feeling the roasting heat. He looked up for a moment, and MacGregor waited to see if he would recognize the young
Ferangi who had bought his potatoes thirteen or fourteen years ago. The
old man's red eyes indicated nothing, a little puzzlement perhaps and a
little resentment at the foreigner's stare, but no more. MacGregor laughed
at himself and at the old man and walked away.

He made his way slowly up the wide street which led to the British
Embassy. The street faced north and disappeared into the first slopes of
the Elburz Mountains which made a shadow of Teheran. MacGregor
could see the high granite peaks cutting deep into the blue sky ahead.
They were covered with fine snow and they rose up with fluted sides
from the edges of Teheran, standing there like barren whitewashed
rocks. Drifts had filled the steep valleys and crevices, and the whole lot
was frozen with stillness.

It was a good home-coming to see the sharp ridges and the high peaks
of the Elburz, but, whatever MacGregor saw of these mountains, he told
himself that his home-coming could not be complete until he had seen
the shallow plateau which was hidden to the west towards Kazvin.
Nothing was so much Persian to him as that hard, baked, rich, pebbly,
tableland, which flattened out the Elburz into a rich plain. There the
yellow dust was buried in the muddy villages, and when he could see
the green vineyards and the tall poplars and the rolling limestone hills,
he would satisfy his long nostalgia.

Until then he was finding that the reality of Teheran did not coincide
entirely with his sentimental memory of it. He did not like the shapeless
wooden shops which were now glass-windowed and filled with Western
alarm clocks, pocket knives, combs, pins, artificial jewelry, and badly-
made clothing. The city had become a Western abortion. The broken-
down busses scraped crazily along the roads, and the skeleton droshky
horses almost fell with every step. Water-carts and mules and strings
of camels held grimly to their ancient paths in the wide streets, but they
made a mockery of this new Western façade. Teheran had always been

the same in MacGregor's lifetime, but this fresh view revealed its ramshackle ugliness for the first time. The Western façade did not deceive him. He knew that the wide streets and the marble Banks and the American cars were a mere frontage, because he knew that this particular wide street turned off behind the Telegraph Office and narrowed down into the old bazaar where buildings tumbled upon each other and the entire life became a compact tangle of buying, selling, eating, drinking, and the washing of filthy bodies in open drains. Taken in relation to the older city, these spacious thoroughfares were an achievement in town planning.

MacGregor walked around an emaciated beggarwoman who lay half-naked across the footpath. She ordered God to destroy her, or alternatively send a miserable coin from the pocket of a charitable passer-by. Her small child with swollen belly followed MacGregor and called him Father, Lord, Khan, Sweetness-and-Light. MacGregor had no money and he crossed the road. Escape was not so simple. There was a leper who dragged himself along in the dust near the half-finished Opera House, and he told MacGregor to pause for a moment and consider the degradation of a man whose life depended on the bounty of strangers.

These were the details his memory had conveniently hidden. He had expected to see beggars, but the actual sight of them revolted him. The poverty revolted him. The whole picture about him was one of wretched degradation, and in two days the picture had not changed in his mind. He had not fallen easily into the normal blindness of anyone inhabiting a city; he had not been here long enough for that. To MacGregor the people still appeared strange, and in their threadbare European clothes he knew them as he had never known them before. The women, for instance, in their twisted black stockings and awkward broken shoes, had not been as easily reformed as the streets. They still wore a pretence of the veil, usually a tablecloth which they held at their chin with a tightened fist. MacGregor could just remember when the last Shah had wiped out the veil and the national costume. He had wiped it out alright, but he had replaced it with his ugly combination of East and West.

As an army officer rode down the middle of the street on a white horse, MacGregor admitted cynically that the Shah had done better with the army. The officer was a major, and he wore a heavy buff coat trimmed with gold and padded heavily at the shoulders. He saw nothing with his half-lidded eyes, and behind him a soldier rode a large bony animal and bore the officer's silver-hilted sword. The women, the officer, the teeming streets running with dirt and poverty, the small boys, the glazy-eyed opium addicts, the lepers and the beggars — they were all inseparable from the mountains. Yet as long as he saw the mountains they did not matter. He was home as long as he heard the tongue and understood the humour and saw the dusty peaks.

At the Embassy gate he waited for a moment to hear the curses of a small man who was carrying a large wooden bed on his back. The bed had slipped against the Embassy wall, and the tall Indian who guarded the porticoed Embassy gate would not go to the man's assistance. The little man cursed the Indian's family and religion and spat two or three times on the wall. MacGregor got behind him and hoisted the bed back into position.

Ya 'umm," MacGregor said in warm Persian. "Save your curses, save your breath."

"A curse is all I can afford to spend," the bed-carrier said, "and I don't mind spending it upon the little-English who would steal it out of my belly if they could get down there. Little-big-Englishmen and their *soofee* slaves!" This was directed at the Indian guard, whom the Persian considered a servile imitation of his English masters. He adjusted his head-piece and bent double under the weight of the bed. He could not see who had helped him, but he shouted his thanks as he staggered away. "You are certainly the Light-of-my-Eyes," he said to MacGregor, "but about the English: no doubt Allah will do something about barren-izing the English who sit like little puddles of water in their great prison. God be with you!"

"God grant you your wish," MacGregor replied politely.

MacGregor watched him go and then passed on through the Embassy gates.

The Embassy was a large compound entirely surrounded by a high mud wall; it occupied most of a whole city block in the heart of Teheran. Its position was a reminder of other and better days when the nation had been administered from within this compound. At the same time the wall was a reminder that the Englishman himself insisted on being left alone. Once inside, the noise of the street was lost, and it became a quiet retreat in a small forest of eucalyptus. MacGregor walked down the gravel road to the Chancery and felt like a traitor to the world outside.

The Chancery was a low building with black doors, and MacGregor used the public entrance and pushed the bell. He was greeted deferentially by another Indian, who took him along the fortress-like passage to Colonel Pickering's office. There Essex was stretched out on a heavy old horsehair couch set near a large fire. Colonel Pickering sat at a roll-top desk, his back to the door. Pickering was as much a part of this room as the furniture and the walls. He was a quiet, grey, handsome and elderly military man in a tweed suit. Near him there was a high stool and a tall accounting desk which held a large bottle of ink. It was all ready for a clerk to come and perch there, and yet it had long been un-used. So had the files in the wall niche, for they were mellow with the settled dust of years. Old photographs hung on the walls and at a glance they looked like a record of long-forgotten army commands and long-dead soccer teams. It was all Victorian, and it still bore the imprint of the India Office engineers who had designed it. There was a fire for the winter, and on the low cobwebbed ceiling a single-bladed fan was ready for the unbearable heat of the summer. This office was still an outpost of British Colonial administration, and yet the cracked and yellow wallpaper could not hide the certainty that the walls were made of mud.

"Sit down, MacGregor," Essex said with a short twist of his head and a squint of his blue eyes. "Pickering is just going to outline a few details about this country for me. You have met Pickering haven't you?" Essex raised a lazy hand in Pickering's direction.

"Yes. We met last night," Pickering said and turned around. His kind eyes smiled at Essex in his relaxation, and then turned to look at MacGregor.

"Actually we met about fifteen years ago," MacGregor took his trenchcoat off and put it over a leather arm chair and sat on it.

"Lord Essex was telling me that you were an old Persian," Pickering said, "but I did not know we had ever met."

"It was down on the Abi River, near the Kuh Brab."

"Fifteen years ago near the Kuh Brab?" Pickering said and smiled. "What were you doing down there, or what was I doing down there for that matter?"

"I don't know what you were doing," MacGregor told him, "but we were looking for Jurassic fossils. I think you were on your way to Dizful; there had been a lot of shooting down there; down farther actually. I can remember my father calling you a fool for going down that way alone."

"Was your father old Fyffe MacGregor?" Pickering was really surprised. "Yes."

"How stupid of me. I didn't connect the two. Of course, you are young MacGregor. Always losing yourself around the countryside. We all thought the Hamadans had you on one occasion. Well I'll be damned."

"Old times, eh?" Essex said.

"I thought you had followed in your father's footsteps," Pickering said and lit his pipe from a box of English matches. "Geologist wasn't he? Weren't you down at Fields with English-Persian?"

"Before the war," MacGregor said.

"MacGregor got himself a Military Cross at Tobruk," Essex told Pickering.

"Well — the Foreign Office should be glad to have you."

"India Office," MacGregor corrected.

"I say. That is a piece of jolly good luck for you," said Pickering, showing gentle enthusiasm for his own department. "So now you are back here. Your father would be proud of you, MacGregor."

"I doubt it," MacGregor said. "He once forbade me ever to enter this compound. I don't think he would like it at all."

Pickering thought this a great joke and held his matchbox over the top of his pipe as if there were a high wind blowing through the musty room. He was an outdoor man, and all his gestures were physically outdoors.

"How are you finding Teheran?" he asked MacGregor.

"I had forgotten how miserable everything was," MacGregor said.

"In what way?" Pickering murmured.

"Well: the Persian must be the most long-suffering individual on earth. I wonder how long he will put up with his misery."

"From what I have seen of the Persians," Essex said, "they'll put up with it for a long time yet. They are too simple to do much about their poverty. They might be a little more civilized than the Arab, but they seem to be just as lazy, and as madly argumentative. Hopeless people."

"Not as hopeless as you might think," MacGregor said.

"That's true," Pickering added, reluctant as he was to support a subordinate against a superior. "They have an amazing capacity for discipline once you break down their reserve."

"MacGregor doesn't believe in discipline," Essex said.

Pickering had not yet fathomed Essex and his highly personal remarks, so he changed the subject as best he could. "Are you being properly looked after?" he asked MacGregor. "Where did we put you up?"

"I'm living with some old friends. Persians."

The emphasis MacGregor placed on the word made Essex chuckle. Pickering said "Oh?"

"At Professor Aqa's," MacGregor told him.

"Ah yes. Old Aqa the biologist. Cambridge man," Pickering told Essex.

"There were a couple of Oxford men in Moscow," Essex said.

"Aqa must be over eighty," Pickering said thoughtfully. "He was a pretty old man when I came here twenty-five years ago."

"He's eighty-three," MacGregor said.

"Is he a full-blooded biologist?" Essex asked.

"Certainly," MacGregor said.

"Amazing."

"What's amazing about it?"

"Can't imagine such a thing as a Persian biologist," Essex replied. "Ah well, I seem to be thoroughly ignorant of this country. But between you two gentlemen I ought to acquire a little more accurate knowledge."

263

Essex glanced slyly at both of them. "Yet I'll bet that you two will not see eye-to-eye on the political situation at all. Not at all."

"I'm sure we both understand the situation fairly well," Pickering said.

"Perhaps," said Essex, "but the Russians made MacGregor into something of a Bolshevik. You will have to watch him, Pickering."

"Really?"

"Yes. He doesn't like the way I go about my business. Eh MacGregor?"

"I don't mind how you go about it," MacGregor said. "It's really the business itself I object to." He could say this to Essex because he was no longer dismayed by Essex's extrovert humour: Essex's status had undergone a change. They were now among the ultimate benefactors or victims of their mission, and instead of it being a day-to-day struggle for one conference or another, they were faced with the raw material of their plans, plus the picture of degradation and ignorance and corruption and poverty, all of which became their responsibility. In this situation Essex's habits lost their importance. In this situation, too, MacGregor's responsibility doubled and trebled, became infinitely more deliberate, and at the same time more confused. Also: his old contempt was returning, a contempt for anything within this Embassy wall. He resisted it as being unreasonable. Yet he found himself thinking, for instance, that the bed-carrier was worth two of any man he would ever see here. There would never be an Englishman who could curse to such purpose and intent. The thought was so extreme that MacGregor warned himself not to go too far with it. Now that they were in Iran, too much depended on him in this mission, and he did not want his contempt seeping into it. But of two things he was sure: Essex would not get a grip on him again; and he intended having as much say as he could in their activities here. In the meantime there was another influence upon Essex.

"It's very simple to understand this country," Pickering was telling Essex. "You just have to understand what the last Shah did for it. He set this country on its feet. He was really just an army major who led a revolt against the Kajars, but one can forgive him for making himself Shah. It's incredible the way he did it."

"I suppose he had the army behind him," Essex said. "You can do anything with the army behind you. Wasn't he in one of the Russian Cossack brigades?"

"In Liakoff's Persian Brigade. They were Russian-trained," Pickering said, "but they were the best force in the country at the time. Even so it was not terribly easy for Reza. The whole country was rotten with corruption and full of revolt. It was a dangerous situation because the Russians had just had a revolution. Iran was ruled by a Kajar named Achmed who was selling the country piece by piece to any foreigner who would buy it; concessions for building roads, for cultivating tobacco, drilling oil, anything at all he could sell. Unfortunately it was the Treaty that Achmed made with us which brought the whole structure toppling down. The Treaty was misunderstood by the priests and the merchants, and they started the revolt. Reza picked it up, and it wasn't long before he had the whole country behind him. Reza started off by making himself War Minister, then Prime Minister. Shah Achmed saw what was coming and got out of the country, so Reza made himself Shah. That was in 1925. Until he came to power the whole country was a disunited conglomeration of robber landowners, rival merchants, and tricky priests. It was not a nation at all. Too much graft and too many rival tribes. Kurds, Lurs, Bakhtiaris, Kashgais, Turkomen; they all raided and robbed as they pleased. They took no notice of any central Government. The first thing Reza did was to go out with his army and clean up the lot of them. He wiped out the old warrior chiefs, smashed up the fiercest of the clans, and even shifted a lot of them around as sort of hostages against raids. He broke up their independent authorities and forced them to obey his rescripts. It was the first time in centuries that this country had been something like a single state, probably the first time since the Sassanid Kings or at least Abbas. Then he started on the mullahs, the priests. These people are Shiahs by religion and their priests were particularly vicious."

"I always thought them Moslems," Essex said from the couch.

"Shiah is a sect of Islam," Pickering said. "There are two sects in the Moslem religion, rather like our own Catholics and Protestants. The Arabs are Sunnis and the Persians are Shiahs. There is more ritual in the Shiah — more like the papists."

"John Asquith would be pleased to hear that," Essex said to MacGregor. "John has the idea that the Moslems are too intelligent to put up with popery."

"It's really not a very good comparison," Pickering admitted. "It is simply a matter of ritual and descendancy. Shiahs claim they have the real authority of Mohammed by direct descendancy from Ali, who was Mohammed's cousin and son-in-law. The Sunnis say the authority of Islam is not hereditary, but elective. It simply makes the Persian Shiah more bigoted."

"You would never think it," Essex said. "I haven't seen a mosque in the place."

"The Persians have never been very religious," MacGregor put in briefly.

"That is true," Pickering said, displeased by the interruption, "but the mullahs, the priests, have always had a pretty tight grip on the law and the merchants and the schools. But Reza broke it," he said to Essex. "He wiped out the religious authority without wiping out the religion. He destroyed the mullahs' influence on the State, the schools, and the general customs of the country. He even forced the women to abandon the veil and ordered the men to wear European clothing. It was all part of his great job of modernizing this country."

"Is it modernized?" Essex said.

"This city used to be a mud village with an old Kajar wall around it. Reza tore it down and built these wide streets and new buildings, built a university, factories, a new railway station, an aerodrome, banks, a new palace, and even that pathetic Opera House down the street."

"Amazing!" Essex said, but only MacGregor appreciated its intonation.

"Why, I remember the day when Reza decided that one-storey shops were inadequate for the nation's capital," Pickering said, "so he ordered every shop on the main streets to be two storeys high. Take a look at them when you go outside. They are all two storeys. He could get the thing done. In that you had to admire him."

"The only thing MacGregor admired in him," Essex said, "was his dislike of the English. MacGregor believes that all good Persians hate the English."

"Good Persians and good Scots," MacGregor said.

Pickering detected the first real hostility here and he avoided it. "Actually we got on quite well with Reza," he said. "He was always afraid of the Russians. We understood him on that issue and helped him where we could. Of course this country means oil to us, and we were very grateful to Reza for stamping out the spread of Bolshevism. Unfortunately he began to hate the Russians so much that he started to act like a German. He admired Hitler and allowed large numbers of German agents to operate all over the country. They became a dangerous influence when things weren't going so well for us during the war. That is why we occupied the place in '42. We had to put the old man away, unfortunately, but we did it the best way. We gave him a fairly comfortable life down in South Africa, but he died soon afterwards. At least he had the satisfaction of knowing that his son was on the throne. The Russians didn't want him but we insisted."

"And the son?" Essex said. "Any good?"

"We miss the strong hand of the old man," Pickering said without descending to the vulgarity of comment upon a reigning king. "That is why we are having this nonsense now with the Tudeh Party and those separatists in Azerbaijan. It's beginning to get serious."

Essex had not stirred from the couch but he agreed with Pickering that it was becoming serious, in fact that was an understatement. "What are we doing about it?" he asked Pickering. "Anything at all?" He was suggesting as usual that the formal policies would be achieving nothing, and that he had come here to get some action.

266

"Well, we are trying to encourage the right men in the Government and around the Shah," Pickering said, "but it needs something rather drastic. Some kind of strong leadership which can pull the country together. We have good influence among the southern tribes, but that is simply self-protection for our fields down there. Iran needs something quite new, something strong enough to bind it together again. Curiously enough it might turn up where it is least expected."

"Ah?" Essex was interested now. Interested enough to sit up.

MacGregor was also interested. His academic respect for another man's proposition had prevented him disputing Pickering in his discourse, and he had sat through it impatiently. Now he attended Pickering more closely.

"What is this new force?" Essex asked.

"The Mohammedan religion," Pickering told them.

"What the devil can we expect from the Mohammedan religion?" Essex lay back on the couch.

"It's hard to say at the moment," Pickering announced carefully, "but it is quite clear that the councils of the Shiah hierarchy are violently opposed to the Tudeh Party, and of course the Tudeh are at the root of the trouble all over Iran."

"In Azerbaijan?" Essex asked.

"The Democratic Party in Azerbaijan is really the Tudeh Party. They are one and the same thing, and the Tudeh forms the backbone of the Azerbaijan separatist movement. Fortunately the more religious Mohammedans are absolutely opposed to the Tudeh Party. Though the Shiah hierarchy isn't as strong as it used to be, I believe they are the only people strong enough to organize a full-blooded opposition to our Tudeh friends. Of course it's impossible to calculate the existing religious influence in Azerbaijan, but we are counting on its being strong."

"What do these Shiahs think of the Christian English?" Essex said cleverly.

Pickering enjoyed the question, and he answered it with a twinkle in his eye. "Any religion is better than none," he said. "All non-believers are the same to the Mohammedan, but they respect Christ and despise an atheist, particularly a Bolshevik atheist."

"It sounds a bit hopeless to me," Essex said. "There is nothing tangible in waiting for a religious revival."

"It isn't a revival that is necessary," Pickering said. "All we want is a closely knit organization with ready-made associations all over Iran. The revival can come later. In the meantime I think that some sort of Shiah council is being convened, either here or in Meshed. It may be the beginning of the rejuvenation of a Moslem political body. Unfortunately the Persians are not Arabs, so we can't interest or enthuse them with the idea of Pan Islam and the Arab League. But some other form of co-operation might be worked out for them, so that we knit these people in with Iraq and the Arab nations. That would change the whole aspect of Middle Eastern politics. It would also strengthen the Iranian attitude to the Russians, and favour us considerably. That is why we are counting on this religious factor coming off. It's most important, don't you think?"

"More important than you will ever know," Essex said. "We need something to shake at the Russians. Any influence which is extra-political may be just what we want, and it may solve our problem in Azerbaijan. That province has to be brought back into the national authority, by the scruff of the neck if necessary. If we can't get at the Azerbaijanians on a political level, then we may be able to capture them on the religious level. If we bring them into central authority again by a universal religious appeal then that is all we need."

"There is only one difficulty to that," MacGregor said, satisfied now that this was a diabolical scheme, but cunning enough to make a more subtle argument against it.

"Yes?" Essex said.

"If you start a religious crusade here it will eventually turn against all foreigners, including ourselves," MacGregor told him.

"Well — that should satisfy you at least," Essex said sarcastically, but he looked over at Pickering to have confirmation or denial of this theory.

"There is some truth in that," Pickering said. "It's not going to be easy to appeal to the Persians' religious sensibility and keep it within its proper bounds."

"Keep it from becoming anti-British," MacGregor said.

"They could be shown that the alternative was atheistic Bolshevism," Essex said. "We ought to really decide something about this." He was up again.

"Why don't you wait until you have seen what is going on in Azerbaijan?" MacGregor said with dignified insistence. He was not fighting Essex now, he was making a genuine suggestion.

"That is leaving it too late," Essex said briefly. "We must have some basis to work on when we go to Azerbaijan."

"Actually it's being straightened out now," Pickering told Essex. "Fox is preparing a sort of brief for our conference to-morrow. I don't know how important he considers this religious issue at the moment, but he will have *something* for you."

"Good," Essex said. "I want it all clear-cut," he said. "I came down here to settle this thing, and I intend to do it as soon as possible. And don't worry, MacGregor. You will get to Azerbaijan in due time. Just don't be too simple-minded at this stage of the game. We are here to

268

restore Azerbaijan to Teheran authority. I can't put it any simpler than that for you. We may be a little ahead of ourselves on this religious business, but it is a good thing to prepare. I agree with you, MacGregor, that it depends on what is happening in Azerbaijan, and I intend to find that out. But it will also depend on understanding what the Russians can do, and what I can do to forestall them."

"I don't see how the situation can be judged from down here," MacGregor argued again. "Why don't we wait until we get up there?"

"There is no time to wait, and no reason to wait. The issue is still the same, whether we are here or in Azerbaijan. I am not going up to Azerbaijan simply to be convinced one way or the other about some show the Russians will put on for us. This is already a clear-cut issue."

"It may be clear-cut for us," MacGregor said, "but it may not be so clear-cut for the Azerbaijanians. You have to spread things out a bit here," he said in earnest appeal to Essex. "You can't have everything cut and dried. They are peculiar people that way."

"I don't care how peculiar they are," Essex said vigorously, "I am not going to be led by the nose. This Azerbaijanian business is going to be settled once and for all. When I go to Azerbaijan it will be for a purpose. I will not go on some wild-goose chase up in those mountains to satisfy anybody's whim about the rights and wrongs of some harebrained political idiocy. What I see will be made use of. What I do will have its effect."

"I have an idea you might be in for a surprise," MacGregor said stubbornly, taking maximum advantage now of his right to full participation in this conversation.

Essex ignored him. "What about that car?" he asked Pickering. "Any news of it yet?" Essex was now standing up near the fire.

"They put it on the train at Ahwaz yesterday," Pickering said. "Those oil people are not too keen on parting with their Fords, but it will be worth your while waiting for it. It's the only car that can take the country. They have had them fitted out for it: extra water and petrol tanks and a condensor. If you are going off the main roads you are going to need a vehicle that can get you there and back, otherwise it's too risky. Apart from other dangers there aren't any spare parts in those regions. There might have been a few once, but the Russians stripped the territory very thoroughly."

"When will it get here?"

"To-night perhaps, or to-morrow. We'll get you off the day after to-morrow at the latest. We'll have everything fitted out for you, so don't concern yourself about it."

"I'll leave it to you." Essex was ready to leave.

"I'm not too keen on that route you're taking," Pickering said. "That country is getting wild again, and the Kurds are out of hand at the moment."

"I'm not doing it for fun, Pickering. It's the way it has to be done, isn't it?"

"I'm afraid so."

"Right. Then I leave the details to you. Come on, MacGregor."

MacGregor picked up his coat and shook Pickering's hand at the door and then followed Essex up a few steps and along a carpeted hall into an oak-panelled room. Essex had expected someone to be here, but he shrugged and closed the door behind him.

"I expected that newspaper johnny, what's-his-name."

"Hamber," MacGregor said.

"Yes. He rang me up and said he wanted to see me about something. I told him to be here at four, but he hasn't turned up. That's bad manners, isn't it?"

"You're late," MacGregor said. "It's twenty to five."

By mutual consent they had forgotten any difference which passed between them in Pickering's office; Essex because he wouldn't make it important, and MacGregor because he was hopeful of persuading Essex to picture Iran with more scientific detachment.

"Perhaps he is waiting in the room down the hall," Essex said. "Go out and take a look will you Mac. It's down on the right."

It was unnecessary because Hamber knocked on the door and walked in with Steele behind him. Hamber's eyes seemed swollen and they were open with provocation, like his lips and short cut hair.

"You said four o'clock, Harry," he complained. "I've been waiting about an hour."

"If it's too late for you old boy, we can make it another day."

"Oh no. You can't pull that on me, Harry." Hamber opened his large American leather coat and sat down. "We know you're going up north to-morrow or the next day so it's no use trying to avoid us in the meantime."

"Have you been talking to MacGregor?" Essex feigned surprise.

"MacGregor would never talk to me," Hamber said. "He has never forgiven me for that crazy business about your arrival in Moscow. You ought to teach him how to get over these things," Hamber told Essex.

"Apart from that," Essex said. "What seems to be worrying you two?"

"That trip into Azerbaijan," Hamber announced. "Steele and I want to go along, if it's alright with you."

"Hm." Essex walked about the small room touching porcelain ornaments and opening and closing the glass doors of the standing bookcases and looking at two small oil paintings of Queen Victoria in youth and age. "Of course you know we are guests of the Russians."

270

"That's perfect." Hamber stood up happily. "You can invite us too."

"But it's rather more complicated." Essex had come around to face Hamber. "I don't know much about this country old chap, and that is why I am leaving it to MacGregor. If MacGregor says you can come, then there you are."

Hamber's open eyes were worried for a moment. Essex enjoyed Hamber's quick apprehension. "Just ask MacGregor," he said, and he was glad to see MacGregor stretch his legs and go on playing with an old pistol he had taken from the wall.

"What can MacGregor decide that you can't?" Hamber asked.

"He knows the country."

"What about it, Mac?" Hamber stood near MacGregor with his hands in his pockets and a cigarette on his soft lips.

"I think you're being ribbed, Hamber." MacGregor looked up, almost grinning. "This is not my expedition."

"Then what about it, Harry?"

"I still refer it to MacGregor."

Hamber was lost between them, but he looked at MacGregor.

"I still say Lord Essex is ribbing you." MacGregor balanced the pistol in his hand.

"Well one of you ought to be serious," Hamber said.

"I can't do anything more than that, old chap," Essex told Steele. "Get it out of MacGregor. Of course he might feel a little more serious tomorrow."

"I don't trust that," Hamber growled.

"Then sit down old boy, and keep trying. Would you both like whisky?"

"Yes," Steele said. "And one for MacGregor."

"Of course you realize how important it is for us to go along," Hamber said as Essex pushed a bell button.

"No. How important is it?"

"This whole fight is going to fall into Washington's lap before long; and then you'll need all the help you can get." Hamber was certain of that. "Nothing much can be done in the U.S. unless public opinion is ready for it; and Steele and I are set on doing something about it."

"Is that why you want to go to Azerbaijan?" MacGregor said.

"Absolutely," Steele replied. "And it's your duty to see that we get there."

"Duty? Duty to whom?"

"Humanity, civilization, culture, democracy," Steele said.

"MacGregor is a practical man," Essex put in. "You can't convince him along those lines. Duty is intangible to a man of science."

"Duty to humanity should be the first consideration of a scientist," Steele said.

"And a journalist?" asked MacGregor.

"Also!" said Steele.

"Bloodthirsty sort of duty," MacGregor grumbled. "Never saw anybody so keen on starting another war as you are."

"We don't want war," Steele argued. "That is up to Russia. If she behaves, then there will be no reason for war. I might remind you that there are worse things for humanity than war; and one is the barbarism of Red Naziism. That is becoming the issue with Russia, and that is what you fellers have to realize. Russia is a Nazi state."

"I don't know much about that," MacGregor said. "But I think you might be a little confused. Perhaps you resent the Russians being so sure of themselves; or are you indignant about them ignoring your atom bomb?"

"Leave the atom bomb out of it," Steele cried, as if an improper reference had been made to his sister or his wife or his mother.

"That's hardly possible," MacGregor pursued him cruelly.

"It's got nothing to do with this issue."

"It seems to have everything to do with every issue, particularly when you are so anxious to fight the Russians. That doesn't seem like dutiful behaviour to humanity."

"Just a minute," Hamber interrupted Steele's possible anger. "Let's forget about humanity for a while. Put it on the diplomatic level, MacGregor. Diplomatically, you can see that it's important for us to go along with you."

"You can't have it both ways," Essex said. "Either you appeal to him as a scientist with a duty to mankind, or you treat him as a diplomat; but not both."

"Well, which is he?" Hamber did not mind falling into Essex's humour.

"MacGregor?" Essex walked to the door as he spoke. An Indian orderly appeared and Essex told him to get the drinks.

"Neither," MacGregor said. "So it's not much use appealing to me on either level."

"Then it's all a matter of MacGregor's humour," Essex said. "I'd concentrate on that if I were you. He still thinks you are being fooled about his permission, but I assure you it is up to him."

The whisky arrived and they were silent while the Indian boy poured it out. He gave them each a glass with a green bottle of soda.

Hamber tried one last tactic. "I have an idea that MacGregor is afraid we will see just how spontaneous his Azerbaijanian friends are," he said.

"They might be more spontaneous than you think."

"Nonsense," said Hamber. "Political revolution is not in their line."

"You must read Iranian history," MacGregor said. "One revolution after another. One revolt against one Shah after another. I think there have been three revolutions since 1900, and I might add that conditions for revolution here are more difficult than they were in America in 1776. It seems to me that the Americans have lost their spontaneity. No revolution in almost two hundred years. Those spontaneous Americans!"

"It's not much use telling MacGregor about Iran," Essex said. "I've already tried that, and he doesn't like it at all."

"Alright. Alright." Hamber held up his hand. "I don't want to get into a fight with you, MacGregor. It's impolite. I just want to make that trip to Azerbaijan."

"What for?" MacGregor said. "You know all about Azerbaijan."

"But a little physical proof goes a long way when you have a fight like this on your hands."

"I'm afraid your little crusade will get you into trouble, Al," Essex said. "I don't think the Russians will like it."

"I deliberately plan to annoy them," Hamber announced.

"That will keep you out of Moscow."

"My only regret in leaving Moscow was in leaving Kathy Clive, whom I love passionately. Otherwise I don't care if I ever see the place again." Hamber finished his drink and put the glass on a brass tray.

"I'm surprised that Kathy couldn't keep you there," Essex said.

"Kathy and I understand each other so I don't waste my time wanting her. I leave that to Jeb Wills. Jeb won't leave Moscow while she is there. He wouldn't even come down here with us. That's alright for Jeb, but Steele and I have a job to do on the Russians."

"Who is Jeb Wills?" Essex asked.

"Dark, wide face, intelligent, cynic, expatriate. Nice guy for Kathy. You must have seen him at one of the conferences. He is the man. Every guy in Moscow wants Kathy Clive, and Jeb is the only one to make the grade."

"I didn't know Kathy had any attachments," Essex murmured bluffly. He looked at MacGregor, but the Scot was deliberately avoiding the conversation.

"I didn't either," Hamber said. "But if she has any attachment it's Jeb. He has outlasted all the others and he is the right type. No fuss, and no bother." Hamber shook his head. "You two didn't have time to appreciate Kathy. It takes a couple of months at least to appreciate what she does to Moscow life."

"I'm afraid your Wills chappie is in for a bit of a jolt," Essex said. "Kathy is due to leave for London almost any day."

"Jeb is due to get out too."

273

"Funny I don't remember him at all."

"You'd pass him by." Hamber had finished with the diversion and he came back to his real concern. "What about it, Harry? Do we go?"

"Come back and ask MacGregor to-morrow."

"Well, stir him up in the meantime."

"I'll see what I can do," Essex told them. They were leaving, with their American leather coats and their new lambskin caps. "But don't count on anything, because I may not be able to convince MacGregor that it's his expedition."

"Good-bye MacGregor," they said, "and watch that sense of humour."

"Don't worry about it," MacGregor replied. "It's absolutely spontaneous."

Essex was pleased, and he closed the door and slapped MacGregor on the back and walked him over to the fire-place. "Good chaps," he said, "but they need deflating every now and then. You are just the man to do it. You are certainly learning how to deal with them, my boy." Essex finished his drink and stood near MacGregor. "Who is this Wills that Hamber talks about?"

MacGregor had been avoiding this since he had left Moscow. He had censored himself rigorously from inside, but now Katherine had been forced on him from the outside. This was his third day away, and in these three days Katherine had been constantly rising to the top of his thoughts. For no reason, and at all times of the day, he would find a memory of Katherine ready to take hold of his mind and occupy it indefinitely. He had allowed an occasional thought to succeed, but whenever possible he subjugated her for later consideration. He could not avoid the reckoning any longer. Katherine was always walking with him and laughing at him, provoking him into argument, disputing and then agreeing with him, despising him then slyly liking him. And more than anything else there remained those few hours of complete understanding and gentleness. It was always there in his mind. But in every other memory, Katherine was tantalizing him with her mocking eyes and straight lips and loose shoulders. No picture of any human being was so complete for him, yet none was so easily destroyed by the recollection of one incident. His humiliation made him blush, even at this instant, and his anger forced him to shake himself free of Katherine completely. That one memory was too much for him and he could not face it again.

"What about that feller, MacGregor?" Essex was asking.

"He's rather quiet," MacGregor replied. "He seems to be a nice chap. I met him one or twice."

'Can't believe Kathy would attach herself to an American. Can you?"

"Why not?" MacGregor would not let Essex off lightly, nor himself. "No. I can't quite grasp it. Still — all women are basically the same, and

Kathy is apparently no exception if she is fooling around with this Wills fellow."

Essex answered a phone which had started to ring, and he told somebody he would be there — somewhere. "I've got to change for dinner Mac," he said in returning to MacGregor. "I wanted to tell you about the short conference we are having to-morrow regarding our trip. We'll have the experts there, and everything will be mapped out: route policy, and an interesting job for you. Ten o'clock here to-morrow morning. Alright?"

"Alright." MacGregor did not go as quickly as Essex wanted him to go. "I wanted to take you home for lunch to-morrow," MacGregor said, "to meet Dr. Aqa. I have known him a long time, and I think he could explain a great deal about this country. You ought to see a few people who have nothing to do with the Embassy." This was MacGregor in the real capacity of expert and adviser.

"Good lord, MacGregor, what do you think I've been doing in the last two days. I have seen practically every Minister in the Persian Cabinet, and almost everybody except the Shah himself."

"Ministers are hopeless," MacGregor said. "I'd like you to see something more before we go up north. This country is more complicated than it appears, and I thought we might get around down here first."

"Plenty of looking around to do when we go north," Essex argued.

"We ought to see what's going on here first. Then it would be a fair comparison with anything we see in Azerbaijan."

"I hardly think the comparison is necessary."

"Perhaps not. I just want you to see this country as it really is, and not as a couple of Ministers think it is. I could show you quite a lot. If you could really spare the time it would be worth while. Very much worth while."

"We haven't got the time, MacGregor." Essex had lost his familiarity and he was brief and final. "I might try and make your luncheon to-morrow, but don't count on it. I expect to get word from London in the morning, so it's going to be a busy day and we'll need every second of it."

"We could put off our departure by one day to see a little more around here."

"Not on your life. We want to finish with this place and go home."

"I hardly think you are giving it a chance."

"Don't be sentimental MacGregor, and be a good chap and come at ten to-morrow. It's quite important. If you have nothing better to do to-night you might talk to Jack Adams. He's been trying to get hold of you."

"That's one man I don't want to talk to," MacGregor said. "I'll see you to-morrow. Good night."

"Good night Mac."

275

Chapter 22

T<small>HE</small> conference was held at 10:15 A.M. around a mahogany table in a silent Embassy reception room. There were four men present besides Essex and MacGregor: Colonel Pickering, Jack Adams, L. B. Shaw, and Sir Samuel Fox. MacGregor had never seen the last two before, although he knew of them. Adams was a young enthusiastic Englishman with an open face which was not regulated properly by an American bow-tie beneath it. L. B. Shaw had been introduced to Mac-Gregor as a "fellow geologist," but this nondescript man had modestly corrected that to "engineer." Finally there was Sir Samuel Fox, special adviser to the Embassy, who sat at the head of the table. If Sir Samuel had been a woman he would have delighted in arranging formal little teas; but being a man and a diplomat he delighted in arranging formal little conferences which he brought to order with a serious clearing of the throat.

"Gentlemen," he began. "I have called this conference in order to coordinate our plans for Lord Essex's mission to Azerbaijan. As you know, we consider this mission most important, perhaps decisive; so I thought I might say a few words about the British position in Iran to-day, if Lord Essex has no objections."

"Not at all," Essex leaned on his hand. "Be interested."

Sir Samuel put on horn-rimmed spectacles and looked at his notes. "Gentlemen," he said. "The British position in Iran to-day is decided by oil. The Empire's largest supply of oil comes from our fields in southern Iran. The wells and refineries in southern Iran are owned by a limited company, of which the British Government possesses 52 per cent of the stock, and therefore the controlling interest. Our agreement with the Iranian Government," he continued, "allows for the payment to them of two cents on every barrel refined. In return we are guaranteed the defence and protection of our equipment by the Iranian Government. We employ over one hundred thousand Persian workmen, some of them from the tribes of the districts, and others from the surrounding villages and towns. Any questions, Mr. Adams?"

"No sir." Adams held his bow-tie.

"Then please sit still."

"Yes sir."

"I hadn't expected anything so interesting," Essex whispered to Mac-Gregor. "This looks like a meeting of the Pickwick Club; Snodgrass, Winkle and all."

Sir Samuel cast a sidelong glance at Essex, not a reproachful glance but rather the look of a patient clergyman waiting for the attention of his lordship. "We cannot place too much importance on the rôle of local politics in affecting the British position in Iran. Sometimes our wells and pipe-lines have been seriously damaged by raiding tribesmen, but we have had no difficulty so far in maintaining law and order in the area. No. Our trouble is not with the tribes. Our real problem is to keep 100,-000 Iranian workmen productive. You should appreciate that problem Mr. MacGregor, since I understand you have worked for some time in the area as a geologist."

MacGregor nodded and felt like Sam Weller.

"Excellent. Now: under the last Shah, political parties and unions were illegal. To-day, under the terms of the Allied agreement on Iran, political parties and unions are technically legal again. However, there seems to be an extreme to everything, and we find in Iran an extremely dangerous political organization called the Tudeh Party, or People's Party. Strangely enough, Britain helped to found this party early in the war to combat the growing German influence. Unfortunately its leaders have grown ambitious and rebellious. Now they may be considered the most radical force in Iran, and directly influenced by a neighbour to the north. Perhaps Lord Essex would like to make a comment at this stage since he recently has arrived from that country."

"No. No." Essex blinked his eyes. "Go ahead."

"And Mr. MacGregor?"

MacGregor shook his head. He was suffering from uneasy anticipation. He was waiting now for the point to all this.

"To-day, the Tudeh Party aims at direct political action in all Iran," Sir Samuel said. "It has organized itself on the basis of a need for a revolutionary change in Iranian affairs. It is organizing unions among the workmen and peasants. Its final aim is the political control of all Iran and it is very anxious to seize our wells and refineries.

"Therefore," said Sir Samuel, "our first duty must be to halt the activity of the Tudeh Party; not only in Azerbaijan, but in all Iran."

Sir Samuel had made his point, amid the *Hear, hear's* of his small audience, including the amused Essex. MacGregor was silent, and Essex thought it dull of MacGregor to be anything but amused. MacGregor must see in Fox an interfering old devil, a cunning plotter. Essex was more amused than ever.

"Finally," said Sir Samuel, "there is another danger, the real danger in fact. It is the threat of this Red influence spreading not only over Iran, but over Iraq, Syria, Palestine, even Egypt and Turkey and Greece. Need I say more, Lord Essex, and need I wish you God speed and Good luck in this vital mission you are undertaking? Thank you, gentlemen."

The long figure sat down, calling on Pickering to outline Essex's route to Azerbaijan.

"We've given you easy stages," Pickering told them cheerfully. "We don't want to wear you out. However, it will be tough going, and plenty of unforeseen difficulties can upset you. Since the Red Army is in occupation, it's hard to say what will happen. Anyway we have done our best. Alright sir?" he said to Essex.

"Go ahead," Essex said, serious himself now.

"The route covers a lot of territory; most of it is extremely difficult, mountainous, and wild. We have our own men all over the place, but the tremendous prestige of Lord Essex travelling freely, and with rank and authority from the British Government, is the key to the mission. Your public appearance and contact with our friends up there will be of more use than anything we have been able to achieve since the Russians took over. Much will depend on you, MacGregor, because you will have to do most of the talking for Lord Essex."

Not me! MacGregor told himself.

Pickering went on to outline the roundabout route they would take from Teheran to Tabriz. "This way," Pickering said, "you will take in Khamseh as well as the Ardelan plateau."

"But Ardelan is Kurdistan," MacGregor said in surprise.

"That's right," Pickering said. "You are going right through Kurd country. Perhaps you are now beginning to appreciate your task."

MacGregor's pleasure at the proposal to go through Kurdistan almost outweighed his intense dislike for the entire operation. Yet he was more suspicious than ever when he realized that it had been planned without him.

Essex tried to anticipate MacGregor's suspicion by saying privately to him that they would talk over the scheme between themselves afterwards, but MacGregor was not placated, and to cap it off Sir Samuel called upon L. B. Shaw to explain MacGregor's own particular job.

"We have everything documented for MacGregor, and he can study it," Shaw said in the voice of a reluctant man. "We want Mr. MacGregor to investigate Russian activity in oil and mining. That route through Urmia is to take Mr. MacGregor through an area which we understand to be the site of new Russian drilling and prospecting for oil. Apart from that we want to know if the Russians have done anything about copper, iron, and other minerals of the Zagros. It's all documented, Mr. MacGregor." Shaw sat down as unimportantly as he could.

"I should like to mention here," said Sir Samuel, "that information is not as important on this mission as your presence. This technical job of yours is secondary to the main act, Mr. MacGregor, and the main thing is always to show yourselves everywhere; show yourselves as representatives of the British Government. Naturally, however, we must not interfere in any way in local affairs, nor must we abuse the privileges the Russians have given us. I think that's all, gentlemen. Any questions?"

There were no questions. Essex looked expectantly and apprehensively at MacGregor, but MacGregor sat still. Sir Samuel thanked them for their attention and said good day and walked in tall dignity from the room.

Jack Adams came down upon MacGregor immediately, asking about John Melby and others in Moscow, and quickly complimenting MacGregor on his jolly good luck in making this trip. MacGregor had no time nor tolerance to cope with Adams at the moment. He excused himself when he saw that L. B. Shaw was waiting for him. Adams turned upon Essex with intent eyes and MacGregor spoke with Shaw, taking from him the written outline of his technical job in Azerbaijan. Shaw flicked over the pages without attempting to explain the contents — as if he might have been ashamed of his own handiwork. He did not attempt any polite conversation, but he made a brief mention of the fact that he had known MacGregor's father, and added uncertainly that he was rather surprised to see his son in this room. He then excused himself and left MacGregor feeling unpleasant and unhappy about L. B. Shaw.

Essex walked MacGregor into the passage and along to his room. "Come on and we'll talk this over," he said. "I know how you feel my boy. I knew you wouldn't like this sort of planning, so I kept you right out of it."

"I am very pleased that you did," MacGregor said.

"I didn't think you'd like it." Essex was sincere, affectionate, and concerned.

MacGregor appreciated Essex's gesture and he was careful. "We were supposed to go to Azerbaijan to satisfy ourselves honestly about what was happening there. Now, we're going into it with a definite idea of interfering as much as possible."

Essex was equally careful. "Cheer up," he said. "It's not as bad as you imagine it to be." Essex glanced at MacGregor to display his confidential eyes. "Don't place too much importance on the attitude of our friend Sir Samuel. He is inclined to see this as a rather local issue about oil, and he overemphasizes the details. These experts never can conceive the whole picture at all. It's more important than oil, and even more important than the Middle Eastern issue. It's ourselves and Russia. So don't get worked up about the idea of interference. We are really not interfering at all. We are simply manœuvring and balancing our forces. You've got to see sometime, MacGregor, that you dare not sentimentalize about the remote ideals of this or that group. The issue is our very existence as a nation, which is more important than a local squabble between rival politicians. Anyway, we would be doing this country a great service if we untied it from Russia's apron-strings. Look at it that way if you like."

"I don't think you mean that seriously," MacGregor said.

"Well, not too seriously," Essex said, "but you're prejudiced."

"I may be prejudiced." MacGregor laughed suddenly — even good-humouredly — "but I should know something about this country."

"You're the expert," Essex conceded.

"That is why I should like to inform you a little more correctly."

Essex smiled. "You've never tried to inform me, MacGregor."

"You can't inform anybody about Iran by just telling them about it You have to see it to understand it."

"Fine. And we are going to see it."

"With conclusions already drawn, and for the specific purpose of interference." MacGregor spoke quite calmly. There was no bitterness between them, only an interesting sort of respect and good-nature. "I'd like you to see that we are interfering too drastically. We can't just assume so completely that Azerbaijan is in the hands of dangerous men and vicious Bolsheviks. I suppose it's all in the way you see Iran. I'd like you to see that Iranians are just as serious about their politics as we are; perhaps more so. The Iranian is a vigorous individual with definite ideas about the right and wrong done to him. It's easy for these journalists to laugh at the idea of political spontaneity among the Iranians because they look on these people as dirty, stupid, childlike natives who stare open-mouthed while the wonders of the West are offered to them."

"Surely it's true," Essex said.

"No, it isn't true. They are not like that at all. They want proper government, the same as anybody else. They have certainly tried hard enough to get it, but they haven't had a chance. We have done a great deal to prevent them getting real government. It may shock you, but we have always wanted corrupt administrations. Since the Reuter concessions sixty years ago we have behaved like American gangsters, using threats, money, and even war to extort privileges and concessions which amounted to owning the country. At one time we had complete control over the administration, over the entire wealth of the land, the banks, and the army. It's rather silly to say the Iranians are unpolitical when you realize how quickly we had to hand back those concessions. This country rose to a man against us. We gave in hastily, but we managed to cling desperately to our oil concessions."

"And if it hadn't been for prompt physical action," Essex reminded him, "we would also have lost our oil concessions. Where would we be without that oil, MacGregor?"

"I don't know. I can see that we have to have the oil, but we should not interfere in Iranian affairs to get it."

"I think you are worrying yourself unduly," Essex told him. "We can't be too bad an influence. We may not be reformers ourselves, MacGregor, but at least we do not fight people who are really trying to improve the country. You must admit that we did not resist the last Shah, and he certainly reformed the place as best it could be reformed."

"It has become a habit to pass all compliments to Reza Shah," MacGregor said, "even though we dethroned him. All reforms and modernizations are supposed to be his idea. Yet he simply took over the power of a popular revolution which we resisted at the time. He took power as a despot and he was little better than his predecessors. These people are getting fed up with despots. They obviously want some kind of better government, particularly in Azerbaijan. I think if you could see that, you could understand what I'm getting at. That revolt in Azerbaijan doesn't have to be a Russian idea. It is really the continuation of five or six revolutions, all of them trying to get rid of corrupt governments. This time they seem to be succeeding. Our idea is to stop it. If you could realize how corrupt this country is, you would understand the advantages of such drastic reforms in Azerbaijan. Every level of Government in Iran is corrupt from top to bottom, including the Court, the police, and the parliament. Government is organized corruption. The Ministers prey on the population like buzzards; they arrange taxes, laws, finances, famines; everything to the purpose of making money. The last Shah might have wiped out some of it; but that meant he became the biggest grafter of them all. He controlled the little fellows, and took the best of everything for himself. By the end of his rule he owned about a fifth of this entire country. He is not the hero we think he is, and his police regime was as brutal as anything the Germans had. Though we co-operated with him, he was a little tougher than the others and he always held out for more. Once, he threatened to wipe out our oil concession, but we bought him off. He could always be bought off, like all the other grafters."

Essex waited to make sure that MacGregor had finished, but MacGregor had been thinking about how far he should go. Both men looked at each other, balancing their development at this point.

"The truth is — we can't buy off the Tudeh people," MacGregor said. "Nor the Azerbaijanians. So we come here to do something about it."

"That's right," Essex said firmly.

"I can't agree with it, in any way."

"Don't be a fool. We must halt this revolt. We can't afford to fail, MacGregor."

"We can't do anything else but fail," MacGregor said. "Whether we

281

want to or not — unless we come in here with troops, and I don't think we want that."

"There are all sorts of methods short of war." Essex was Essex again. "What we do here will be one step. It not only concerns Britain and Russia, it concerns America and other Allied countries. Actually this dispute may be forced into the higher councils for settlement. Would that satisfy you?" he asked.

"It would simply be a device for getting our own way," MacGregor said. "It would be no improvement at all."

"You're putting yourself in a difficult position, MacGregor."

"Yes?"

"You seem opposed to our mission to Azerbaijan. It looks as if you don't want to come at all."

"Perhaps you're right," MacGregor said as casually as he could.

Essex was not angry. "I should warn you against your own self-righteousness, but I can't worry myself with your conscience. I simply suggest that you make up your mind quickly whether you want to come or not."

"That is very simple . . ." MacGregor began.

Essex stopped it there. MacGregor was about to announce his refusal to go to Azerbaijan. That was clear. Essex would not have it. He needed MacGregor now more than ever, and he would not give him an excuse to walk out. Essex wondered how in God's name he had picked such a complicated and demanding assistant. "I don't want to hear anything you have to say now," he said to MacGregor. "I am too tired to argue with you. Go and forget all about that nonsense you heard here this morning, and remember that this is no time for high-minded moralizing. You are in a serious situation."

"I am quite serious . . ."

"Perhaps," Essex interrupted again, "but at times you can be more self-righteous than a cartload of parsons." He led MacGregor to the door by the elbow. "Go and walk around the town and buy something. Where do I have to be for your luncheon to-day, and at what time?"

MacGregor wrote the address on a strip of Persian newspaper and tore it off.

"You read the local papers?" Essex said.

"Yes."

"In the vernacular? In Persian?" Essex looked at the script for a moment. "*Hm.* That must be amusing. What's it called?"

"Tudeh."

"Ah! Well, I shall see you at lunch."

Chapter 23

MacGregor certainly had no intention of going to Azerbaijan.

He walked home and confirmed that again and again to himself. It was no use trying to be an Englishman planning an Englishman's Iran. Their Iran was not his, in fact Essex and Pickering and Adams and L. B. Shaw had spoiled his home-coming. He did not want to have anything to do with their schemes, and so Essex and his expedition could go to the devil.

Now he missed Katherine. If Katherine were walking here with him she would be weeding out his doubts with her cynical probing. Why not go with Essex, why blame Essex for an Embassy attitude, why be so moral at this stage of the game? There was little use in irritating himself with these questions. They had to come from Katherine. Only her cynical accusations could provoke his arguments and thus clarify his thinking. He wondered if Katherine herself was ever confused. No! But another picture of Katherine suddenly came home to him. Those cynical comments of hers were really based on a clever understanding of political issues, more understanding than he had himself. This was a surprising realization and it gave Katherine new and undiscovered possibilities; but it didn't help him. Now that he wanted Katherine's arguments he could not have them. He concluded unhappily that there was little likelihood of his ever hearing her arguments again.

His single comfort was in being home. He walked to Dr. Aqa's with a genuine sense of returning to his own home. His mother lived in the small village of Shipbourne in Kent, and during the war MacGregor had considered his home to be in Kent because he needed some identification with England itself. Now, in the streets of Teheran, he knew he had no home but somewhere here. He covered a complicated pattern of streets so that he could pass the familiar wealthy houses with their high-walled gardens. Aesthetically every Persian loved a garden, however miserable or poor he was. To understand this was to understand something essential in the Persian character; but it could never be explained — not to Essex anyway. He could picture Essex's face if he tried to talk significantly about gardens.

MacGregor entered the high wooden gates of the old grounds to Dr. Aqa's house. He walked between the stripped fruit trees which flanked the gravel path. He knew all these trees, particularly the apricot tree which had supplied his mother every year with large yellow fruit for jam. The peaches, plums, and almond trees had filled this garden with colour in the spring. Separate from the others was Dr. Aqa's rare nectarine tree which had been a gift from some distant professor of the University of California.

All this fruit seemed to be fruit of high mountain air and good dry soil. It was a little too dry now, and it was unnourished and unturned. The glass-house was also neglected, but the abundant hedges of rhododendrons and laurel and privet and green floss and roses were well-trimmed and not too woody. The hedges flanked a tiled rectangular pool, deep and clear with mountain water. It was free of dirt, but leaves were frothing up at one end of it. MacGregor stooped and scooped out the leaves and threw them under the shrubs. He held up his wet hand, and the dry air and sharp sun had dried it by the time he reached the house.

The house was hemmed in by tall eucalypts, and it was built low, square, and surrounded by verandahs. It was built of old mud brick, red, and its flat roof was bordered by a low railing. In sharing this house with their good friend Dr. Aqa, the MacGregors had lived here in five years of summer and winter, and MacGregor himself had spent his summer nights sleeping on that roof under a mosquito net. He remembered the crisp sound of the summer wind that came down the Elburz and cut through the eucalypts and scattered insecure leaves down upon the roof in wavy gusts. It was a sound and sense as exciting to him now as it had been in those warm nights. It was a memory which MacGregor needed for his youth; a less complicated MacGregor than the MacGregor who entered this house now.

He went straight upstairs to his own room. He opened the shutters and lay on the low posterless bed and stared at the cabinet which shelved some of the first rock samples he had collected fifteen or sixteen years ago: granites, gneiss, and crystalline schists, limestone, sandstone, and a few pieces of bituminous coal. They were still there, more forgotten than deliberately remembered. In the fire-place there were two large green crystals, like solid pieces of glass speckled with white flaws. He had once tried to dissolve them but his small furnace had exploded and smashed a dozen panes in the summer-house where he had established his own laboratory.

It seemed to him now that he had been quietly wild and experimental as a boy, and exceptionally untroubled. In those days there had never been any doubt in his mind about his future because there was only one world for him: that of scientific investigation. Now there were a dozen worlds — and only a few days ago he had nearly abandoned the work of a lifetime! That would not occur again. Rather than tolerate this life of officialdom he would better go back to English-Persian. At least he would be back here in Iran and doing his work. In the meantime he was trapped with Essex, and if he conceded an inch on Essex's plans for Azerbaijan, he would be hopelessly entangled again.

He did not want to think himself into further dejection, so he got up and went down to the library. It was dark, although a low fire burned in the grate. He liked this small Oriental room with its low divans, cushions, carpets, carved tables, silver trays. Persian miniatures hung at eye-level on the panels between the bookcases, and MacGregor looked at them carefully. He had never bothered to find out about these delicate scenes because he had taken them for granted as a boy. He could see now just how ignorant he was of all culture outside his science. Apart from a good sense of design, resulting from the intricate study of fossil patterns, he had no knowledge or appreciation of any art. All the objects in this room meant little to him: the Sassanid bronzes, the early prayer carpets on the walls, the short lumps of sculpture from Persepolis. He turned to the Persian miniatures again and touched them with respectfully ignorant fingers as if they could estimate the quality which made these hunting scenes such important works of art. He was so affected by his ignorance that he was seeking a book on Persian art when Dr. Aqa arrived.

"Here you are," said the Doctor and turned out the lights and marched to the shuttered windows. "I don't know how often I tell Hassan to open these shutters. He has some idea that daylight will kill me. Wasting daylight." Every word was emphasized by a vigorous movement of unlatching and throwing open the three sets of shutters. "He goes around shutting up the place, expecting me to die peacefully in darkness at any minute. Do I look like a dying man?" Dr. Aqa stood erect before MacGregor, a little brown nut of a man with Mongoloid eyes which danced in the new sunlight. He had a small spade-shaped patch of white beard, and he held it aggressively upwards.

"No." MacGregor had smiled, it was impossible to avoid the spark of this man. "I have never seen you looking fitter. You have pink cheeks."

"Pink cheeks and good eyesight." Dr. Aqa put his arm through Mac-Gregor's and measured himself beside the younger man. "I can remember you measuring your height beside mine as a boy. As it is you are only equal to me because I am shrivelling with age."

"That's not so," MacGregor told him. "You keep your back straighter than any young man."

"I dare not do otherwise." Dr. Aqa bent stiffly. "Every time I bend I expect my entire bone structure to shatter into brittle little fragments. That is undoubtedly how I shall die. I will shatter to death."

It reminded MacGregor of Caradoc, and he told Dr. Aqa about the clown.

"He would have done better to keep on with his acrobatics," Dr. Aqa said. "As for me: I will not sink peacefully into oblivion like your respected father. Death is an explosion. Now how are you feeling, eh? Do you sleep well?"

MacGregor was conscious of the Doctor's close inspection. "I don't seem to do much else but sleep," MacGregor told him. "It's the mountain air I suppose."

"I wondered why I hadn't seen very much of you."

"I have been wandering around the city. It's a little strange to come home under these circumstances, and so unexpectedly."

"So! Is it still home?" Dr. Aqa rubbed his hands and stirred the fire.

"Yes. That is the first thing I discovered."

"That's good. That is very good. I realize that I had forgotten you were English at all. You have always been something of myself, and I am Iranian. I am glad you are at home." He bent down and dropped coal on the fire. "Damn this Russian coal," he said. "Look at it crumbling. Ten good lumps from Newcastle are worth a hundredweight of this terrible stuff." He stacked and prodded the fire like a swordsman at work. "I had wondered," he went on, "if the war had re-located you. Loyalties became so important during the war. I could well imagine you forgetting your Iranian loyalties."

"Perhaps I was an Englishman for a little while," MacGregor said wryly. "But not for long. I can't escape having been born and bred here, so now I am a good mixture, with just a little more English in me than before. The war must have done that for me."

"No doubt the war has affected us all," the Doctor said briefly. "Nobody has escaped, least of all the man of science. I have also wondered how you felt in the war: a young man of science. How much more intensely you must have realized your responsibilities. How much more you feel them now."

"What is left of a man of science after six years away from it?" MacGregor said — not without a trace of bitterness and self-pity.

"I don't know." Dr. Aqa looked surprised. "How much of you is left?"

"Not much," said MacGregor.

Dr. Aqa was as impersonal as any professor with any student. "It should be simple for you to fit back into your work," he said.

"I can go back to English-Persian, but I don't feel enthusiastic about it."

"English-Persian is a different issue altogether," Dr. Aqa swept it away: "Of course you don't want to go back to English-Persian. No scientist owes responsibility to the oil companies of the world."

"Then what is the alternative?" MacGregor asked, now thoroughly depressed.

"Son," said Dr. Aqa, "I can't tell you what else you can do because I don't know. I can only say this: if you have lost six years of your life then no one else will pay it back but yourself. I would like to have the wisdom to tell you the alternatives, but an old man's wisdom is really fear. Young men have no fear. To pay yourself your own price you must act fearlessly, you must follow your convictions and your understanding with absolute purpose. The world is no longer an oil-company world, that surely must be your starting point because more than ever we scientists must discriminate with our labour. We should no longer serve these large bodies which assist the domination of one country over another. We have begun a new age, Ivre. That terrible weapon touched the real power of science, and it has made this world an entirely new place. The mismanagement of human affairs can now endanger our entire existence. There is our first consideration. Of course you understand this better than I do because you are young, with an entire lifetime ahead of you. What can I tell you? Here I am in this remote land, isolated and unimportant. How much more clearly your great scientists of the West must see this issue, particularly those men who have brought about this change! How much clearer their understanding must be! How much more they can tell you of the alternatives before you!"

"They can't do anything of the sort," MacGregor said sorrowfully. "Some may know what comes next, but most of them are just as confused as I am."

"They have no right to be confused," Dr. Aqa said and raised a small bony fist. "A man of science has more responsibility than other men because his work gives him a clearer understanding of the objective world. If he cannot see that human affairs have become the deciding factor in science, then he has no right to be a scientist."

MacGregor felt that his own problem was somewhere lost in the maze of Dr. Aqa's excited fears for all science and all humanity. The Doctor had not given him a chance to explain his situation more specifically because this matter of scientific responsibility was a favourite with the old man: touch a point of it and an exposition would follow. Nevertheless it did not cover MacGregor's problem in general terms. "It is one thing to realize the importance of human affairs in science," MacGregor said, "but what does a man do about it?"

"Any honest man will soon find out that the understanding decides his action. I am assuming of course that a scientist is an honest man."

"Honesty isn't enough," MacGregor argued. "You need some kind of basic approach which can explain all human affairs and make a man's actions clear."

"Now you are touching the realm of political theory." Dr. Aqa considered this a limit beyond which he would not go. "Honesty is good enough as a beginning," he said. "Honesty plus scientific objectivity and the natural enjoyment of living among your fellow men. Nothing can be done alone. We can't live outside our own society — I say that as a biologist. Our individual problems are part of the total problems of all society, and that is where real understanding can begin."

MacGregor had not intended taking this discussion any further, but he needed someone to argue with, and he told Dr. Aqa that he was not going to Azerbaijan with Essex.

"Why not? Why not?" The Doctor raised his hands in surprise.

MacGregor explained his distaste for the Embassy plans.

"Why worry?" the Doctor said. "Is it so important what this man Essex does?"

"It can be decisive," MacGregor said.

"Can he be influenced; or is he hopeless?"

"Not entirely."

"Then why don't you go with him? Once you get him away from Teheran you might teach him sense. What do you want of him?"

"Nothing more than a little honest appreciation of the difficulties here."

"Go with him," Dr. Aqa said. "Use your influence."

"My influence would mean nothing. His mind has been made up for him. He isn't interested in Iran. He is only interested in British position in the Middle East, or in getting rid of the Russians. This whole country will pass right over his head."

"Then he is hopeless. Let him go and you stay here with me."

That was not the answer for MacGregor. He did not want to be told to stay.

"Don't worry too much about him." Dr. Aqa held MacGregor's shoulder for a moment. "He can't do much in Azerbaijan."

"I am not so sure of that," MacGregor said. "The Embassy is busy deciding what sort of a country this will be, and Essex's trip is very much part of it." He was surprised and disappointed that the old man couldn't see its importance.

"Didn't you say he was coming to lunch to-day?" the Doctor asked.

"Yes. I asked him because I thought you might be able to teach him something. He thinks he is among savages who cannot rule themselves."

"So I am to be civilized, eh?"

Dr. Aqa paced up and down for a moment as if civilization needed energy.

"He is really a decent fellow," MacGregor said.

Dr. Aqa's eyes danced again. He was going to enjoy this. He stood by the window looking out at the garden. No doubt he was contemplating his part. He was still there when Hassan, the black Arab from Kuwait, announced the arrival of Essex: "His Excellency the Englishman," Hassan said, and Essex appeared.

"Dr. Aqa," Essex said as the old man turned around. "I must say that it is rude of me to come so late but I was most unfortunately delayed." Already Essex was not sure if that was sufficient. "Actually my driver had some difficulty finding your place. I hope I haven't inconvenienced you." They were shaking hands. "Ah, MacGregor," he said and half expected MacGregor to translate for him.

"My dear Lord Essex," said the Doctor — and there was never an English voice more English. "Time is the first thing you must understand in our country. To us time means eternity, nothing less. You have made an excellent beginning."

There was more of this bemused conversation about time, and then the Doctor invited Essex to sit down near the fire.

"I was just looking around at your library," Essex said. The walls were stacked with books and they were even piled on the floor in places. "The complete biologist," Essex said.

"Less than half of them concern biology," Dr. Aga told him.

Essex had caught sight of the miniatures on the walls and he crossed to look at them. "By heavens," he said. "Are these originals?"

"Yes." Dr. Aqa gave MacGregor one of the table lights to hold for more light. "That one you are looking at is a Behzâd."

"Ah," Essex said as if a treasure-house had been revealed. "What a lucky man you are to have him! What a lucky man."

"They belong in a public place where everyone can see them," Dr. Aqa said. "I have a few years left to enjoy them so I keep them here."

"What is this other one?" Essex had passed to the next of them.

"It's from the *Shahnama*," said the Doctor.

Essex was busy inspecting the small patches of ivory and paint. "How did they achieve such delicate blues?" he said. "I have never seen an original Behzâd before."

"The finest collection of Persian miniatures used to be in the Museum of Fine Arts in Berlin," Dr. Aqa instructed him. "I hope they have not been destroyed." He seemed to consider their safety Essex's responsibility. "We are anxious to have them returned. It's the least we can expect, don't you think?"

"I am sure you are absolutely right," Essex said, passing from one to the other of these half-dozen miniatures, MacGregor following him with the lamp. MacGregor wondered where this little play finished and their common interest began. He felt stupid to be so completely ignorant of what they were talking about. Essex had the advantage of him here. There was no pretence about Essex's appreciation of these miniatures.

"And this?" Essex asked of the last miniature.

"It's an unknown — earlier than the Herat school. There you have the first real impressionism. El Greco was influenced by this particular period of our miniaturists, and so was Van Gogh, in fact much more so than is generally acknowledged."

Essex straightened. "I am often sorry that our early English miniaturists concentrated on portraiture," Essex said. "Think of the influence this free panorama might have had on our latter-day painters."

"No. No," said the Doctor briefly. "The English portrait forms were excellent and they did influence portraiture tremendously, particularly the early Hilliards and the half-dozen Plowmans and the occasional Holbein."

"I had a small Plowman," Essex said, "but I gave it to the Victoria and Albert Museum. I still have two Cosways, both signed on the back."

"Ah. Cosway. Now Cosway learned the use of flat colour by studying our miniaturist." The Doctor and Essex were still standing near the wall and MacGregor still held the light for them. "Cosway was the one man of your painters who had imagination. His stained drawings are unequalled, and yet Smart was a greater man. Smart always finished his work beautifully, even though it was fairly straightforward. They were both excellent men. Only the French have equalled them. The French give the form more life and verve, don't you think? I suppose the Gallic War manuscript is as good as some of our own descriptive scenes."

"I have never seen it, to tell you the truth," Essex said.

"Are you an Oxford man, Lord Essex?"

"Yes."

"Then you are familiar with the enamel collection in the university gallery."

"I was."

"Is it still there?"

"I should think so."

On it went, and MacGregor was lost. To the Sassanid bronzes and the bas relief from Persepolis and the carpets on the walls. MacGregor heard for the first time that a piece of brocade on the wall had been worked by Romans who had been captured in Persia by Shakur the First and taken to the south to build the Shakur barrage, but started a weaving industry there: the rugs of Mecca originated there. It was MacGregor who had come to learn, not Essex. He hardly said a word as these two men went on with their discussion. By the time lunch was served they had passed on to literature. Over lunch they argued about Coleridge. Dr. Aqa found him a hopeless mystic but Essex insisted that it didn't matter whether he was a mystic or not, he was a good poet.

They did not move for coffee but sat in comfort at the table as Hassan cleared it, drinking the small cups of black syrup as Dr. Aqa led them over the field of literature like a huntsman leading the pack over the fences. His last word was upon Omar Khayyam, whom he considered a better astronomer than a poet. The Persians thought him a mediocre poet compared with Saádi and Firdousi and Hâfiz, who were the great poets of Persia. Omar Khayyam was a rather beautiful English creation by Fitzgerald. There it ended as the second hour passed.

"Well," Essex said as he rose to go, "I'm afraid we forgot the purpose of my visit. MacGregor wanted me to learn something about Iran from you," he said to the Doctor.

"Nothing that I can tell you will make any difference," the Doctor said and crinkled up his high cheeks. In such moments he looked and spoke like an old man — short and sharp. "You are an intelligent man, and if experience does not teach you then nothing will."

"I hope you will dine with me when I return from Azerbaijan," Essex said. "We can continue this discussion."

"It's difficult to count on anything at my age," Dr. Aqa told him.

"Well, I have something that would interest you." Essex told him about Geronimo, admitting ignorance of painter and subject.

"Do you read Stendhal?" Dr. Aqa asked him.

"On occasions."

"In *The Red and the Black* you will find fleeting glimpses of a Spanish or Italian singer whose name was Geronimo. That must be your man."

"That is the only clue I have had," Essex said appreciatively and shook the Doctor's hand. The Doctor looked cunningly at MacGregor as if to ask him if enough civilization had been covered. Yet not all of it had been a game, and it was clear that Essex and Dr. Aqa had satisfied each other.

"Are you coming with me, MacGregor?" Essex asked at the door.

"Do you want me for anything in particular?"

"No, nothing in particular."

"Then I'll come along later, if you don't mind," MacGregor said.

They walked down the gravel path. "Just so long as you appear before five," Essex said. "There is one thing that you can do for me. I want you to give Jack Adams an outline of our activity in Moscow. He is keen to come along on this expedition."

MacGregor took that as a warning from Essex that other men were available besides himself. Essex was waiting to hear MacGregor agree to make the trip to Azerbaijan. MacGregor said nothing. He was still determined not to go; but there was still time for other influences to work on him. He could procrastinate until he was affected one way or the other.

"Don't forget Adams," Essex said as he got in the car.

"No, I shan't forget," MacGregor stood back. He was not jealous by nature, but the suggestion of Adams making the trip irritated him. "I'll be along later on," he said, and watched Essex drive off.

Chapter 24

At four o'clock MacGregor was waiting in Essex's room at the Chancery when he heard a woman's laugh which flushed the blood to his sandy face. There was only one woman who laughed like that.

He waited to hear it again, standing near the thick wooden door of the room and making up his mind to go out and see who it was. He was standing there when Katherine opened the door and stopped short in surprise at his poised figure before her.

"MacGregor!" she said. "You scared the daylights out of me."

MacGregor was equally startled by their sudden encounter at the door.

"Why were you standing there like that?" She closed the door behind her.

"I thought I heard you, but I wasn't sure," he said in recovery. "What on earth are you doing down here?"

"I am on my way home," she said.

"To England?"

"Yes. The American Ambassador's plane was coming down, so Jeb Wills and I hopped on it. I want to get some clothes in Cairo anyway. Twenty-four coupons won't go far in London. Also I want some sunshine after that miserable winter. Have I given you sufficient reason?" She raised her straight eyebrows to look at him with amused but intent inspection.

He had taken her outstretched hand. "When did you get in?" he asked her, realizing that his pleasure must be showing itself.

"About an hour ago."

"Have you seen Essex?"

"No, I was looking for him here. Are you waiting for him?"

"Yes. But it's better to see you again," he said.

"Be careful," she warned him. "Do not be too pleased." She touched his arm lightly, and her black cloth glove gave the gesture deliberate and subtle intimacy.

"I think I am too careful," he said, still feeling the pleasure.

She looked for a moment as if she were going to deflate him with one of her sly remarks, but the intention changed with the look on her face. "Would you take me somewhere for a cup of tea? We left at some ungodly hour and I am dirty and empty. I must look rather scraggy."

"You know quite well that you look clean, well fed, and absolutely well slept."

Katherine laughed and took his arm and enjoyed his pleasure.

"I seem to be homeless," she told him as they walked out. "Jack Adams is trying to find me a place to live for a few days. All the Embassy houses are full because all sorts of people have arrived here from the south. What is going on here?"

"You might call it something of a campaign."

"So your troubles have begun again," she said. "Poor MacGregor."

"They haven't begun yet," he said but did not go further.

They were out the gate and she stopped him to look north to the mountains. "I'm sure I'm going to like this country," she said. "Look at those magnificent peaks. Is it easy to get to them?"

"To the foothills," he said. "You can do it there and back in a day."

"I must go up there before I leave."

MacGregor moved her on and asked her what Drake had said when she left.

"What could he say?"

"I had an idea that he didn't want you to go," MacGregor said.

"He was so glad to get rid of you that one more blow made little difference."

"I feel sorry for him."

"Don't be malicious," she told him. "What are those people selling over there?" She pointed to a barrow across the road where two men shouted their products at the top of their sing-song voices.

"Chestnuts," MacGregor told her.

"Ah. I love them," she said. "Could we get some later?"

"Embassy people don't walk the streets here eating chestnuts," he said.

"Don't they?" She was ready to cut him to pieces for that remark but again she relented and laughed at him.

He did not appreciate his escape, but he decided to be careful of his remarks. He didn't want to fight with Katherine. He was still enjoying his surprise at seeing her again, and yet he wanted to suppress it as much as possible. He helped her over a flowing sewer and they walked through the dark hurrying people. He took her to a Russian tea shop with large windows, through which they could see stacks of Russian sweetmeats and all kinds of cakes and cream puffs and chocolate biscuits. Katherine stopped before the window to look at them. She told him what a wonderful sight it was and what a wonderful place to take her. MacGregor told her it was owned by White Russians and principally patronized by Red Russians from the Soviet Embassy opposite, also enclosed in a brick wall. He took her inside and they sat down at a marble-topped table in a corner in semi-darkness and away from the few Armenians who sat talking loudly near an orchestra stand. Katherine asked for a full lunch and MacGregor ordered it from the Russian menu. They sat looking across at each other for a moment.

"I thought you would both be in Azerbaijan by now," she said. "The trip is still on isn't it?"

"There is some confusion about it at the moment." He leaned his head down on the palm of his hand and rubbed the back of his neck. "I more or less told Essex that I wouldn't go." He had been waiting to tell her this; and he waited now for her reply.

She took it calmly. "You leave an expedition which you created yourself?" she chided him.

"I created it?" He stopped rubbing his neck. "Perhaps I did." He was amused with the irony of it. "I apparently created a monster."

"Well what's the matter now?" she said as if he must tell her eventually. "What's been going on here?"

"An interesting scheme," MacGregor said, "for creating our own opposition to the local political bodies who are threatening us on all sides. Essex and I are supposed to be some kind of scouting party for the plan in Azerbaijan."

"Is that why you won't go?" She implied pettiness, and there was an edge of Moscow disparagement showing through now.

He wanted to explain himself better. "I haven't actually pulled out of it definitely," he said.

"Why not?" she asked sarcastically.

"I can hardly leave Essex flat," he said and added that he wanted to see Azerbaijan anyway. "It's a long time since I was up north, and Essex plans to take in the mountain districts."

Instantly she forgot his problem. "How mountainous is it?" she asked.

"The way we're supposed to go cuts right along the Zagros. That is all mountain, or most of it anyway."

"High mountains, with good slopes like those beautiful peaks at the end of the street?" She was so engrossed in the subject that MacGregor let his own affairs pass and shared her appreciation.

"Yes. High ridges with deep valleys," he said.

"Ah, you are lucky to be going into that country, Ivre. I have dragged myself all over the slopes of Austria and Switzerland but they never really scared me enough. They were always too neat and compact and sensible. This looks like ferocious country. Will you go into that range I flew over this morning?"

"No. We'll go to the west of it. It's more interesting country."

"How are you going to travel?"

"In a Ford station-wagon."

"Are there roads?"

"Dirt roads, mountain roads."

"Just you and Harold?"

"And a driver I suppose."

"How long will it take?"

"Two or three weeks."

"Do you think I might go with you?"

He had been looking round to hurry the waiter, and he brought his eyes back. She was prepared for that because she was looking at him so impersonally that he could have kicked her shins under the table, and he nearly did so.

"What for?" he said, flat and disinterested, yet suspicious.

"It's just what I have been wanting to do."

"It will not be a picnic . . ." he began.

"Don't get angry again. Could I go?"

"Kathy," he said. "Why ask me? Why not ask Essex?"

"Now MacGregor! It's your expedition."

For the first time he believed that it was his expedition; but he thought there was something behind all this. "Have you been talking to Hamber?" He was puzzled now.

"No. What's he got to do with it?"

"Nothing." MacGregor thought again. "You ought to ask Essex." He was willing to pass it off as cynically as that.

"Perhaps I will," she said and MacGregor was convinced that she was up to something. It was not at all the attitude he had expected of her.

The waiter brought Katherine her plate of borsch and she began eating it without any preliminaries and without the slightest discomfort at being watched by MacGregor. She had apparently forgotten the whole conversation, and was concerned only with the borsch. It was MacGregor who returned to it.

"I should think Essex wouldn't want you around." He was trying to provoke her. "You would cramp his style a bit, and he is inclined to be serious about this trip."

"Do you really think I might cramp his style?" She swallowed the floating egg-yolk and pulled a face as it went down.

"I'm simply suggesting what he will think."

"Apart from the mountains," she said with her eyes on her eating, "what are you expecting to do with yourself, MacGregor?"

"I may not go." He still hoped to provoke her.

295

"You must go," she said calmly.

"Why?"

"Harold will go anyway and do whatever he wants to do. Sitting on your backside in Teheran won't change the situation for you." She still did not look up and she was still impersonal, but this was what he wanted to hear.

"Would you have ideas about influencing him?" he said. "Is that why you want to go?"

"I will simply go along to see the mountains." She looked up and watched him lick his dry lips. "It's rather amusing when you lick your lips like that," she said. "You always look as if you are in the middle of a hot desert. Were you fond of the desert?"

"Yes. No. Not always. Only when I was in it." He still did not know, now, how to switch his mind about as Katherine did.

The waiter brought a thick plate of *bœuf Stroganoff*. "I don't think I would like the Libyan desert," she said. "When were you supposed to leave for Azerbaijan?"

"To-morrow. If you want to work on Essex you haven't much time."

"There's plenty of time," she said. "I'm beginning to get quite excited. It's such a wonderful idea."

"I wouldn't be too hopeful if I were you." MacGregor sipped some of the Russian tea. "Essex will say it is complicated and probably too dangerous."

"Is it dangerous?"

"I don't think so."

"Is it complicated?"

"I don't know." He realized that he was almost discussing this as a serious proposition. "I'll tell you one thing. Essex was almost willing to have Hamber and Steele come along." He felt cunning and full of plots.

"Are they going?"

"No. It's nothing to do with them. If I do nothing else I'll make sure that they don't go."

"You're not being prejudiced are you?"

"Of course I'm prejudiced." That was another unexpected trick he had performed, to his own surprise. Katherine was expecting a heated denial, and strangely enough he felt better for the feeling of honesty which his admission gave him. "Those two prejudice any sane man."

"Bravo!" she said. "This is a lovely *bœuf Stroganoff*. I don't know when I enjoyed a meal so much. I love you for bringing me here."

"It was your own idea," he said.

"Don't be so frightened by honest sentiment." She finished with the *bœuf Stroganoff* and ate flat bread soaked in honey and cream until she was exhausted by it. She relaxed a little in her chair.

"Can Adams find you a place to stay?" he asked her.

"I don't know. Of course I could stay at that odd-looking hotel where Jeb is, but that should be unnecessary. I hate hotels."

"If you are really hard up we could do something about it at home. The whole house is empty. Very empty."

"Your house?"

"No. But Dr. Aqa would be delighted to see an Englishwoman enter his house."

"Is he Persian?"

He nodded.

"I wouldn't be in your way would I?"

"I don't think so."

"Perhaps I'll take you up on that. Do I have coffee?"

MacGregor called the waiter and the coffee was brought. She sipped it appreciatively. She had enjoyed the meal, and MacGregor told himself that she was considerably more robust than her careless manner indicated.

"Incidentally," she said. "Drake put in a rather warm complaint to Bertram Cooke about that job you wouldn't do for him. He also wrote a complaint to someone named Rowland Smith in the India Office — an old crony of his."

"He's the chief of my section," MacGregor told her.

"I don't think you have to worry," she said. "Harold will look after you when you get back. He is really rather fond of you. Did you know that?"

"I'm fond of him," MacGregor said.

"Are you?"

"Certainly."

"You're not afraid of him are you?"

He looked disgusted.

"I don't mean afraid," she said impatiently. "Perhaps I mean awed."

"Why should I be awed?"

"I think that's what I should ask you," she said. "Always remember that a man like Harold hangs on by the edge of his teeth."

"Hangs onto what?"

"Whatever he's hanging onto," she said. "Of course he'll never let go, but he's not as solid as you imagine him to be. Don't let him fool you."

"I don't understand."

"Certainly not. That's why you should go along to Azerbaijan with him. You would be victor in that interesting contest, and I shall love watching you both. If you didn't come out on top there would be something wrong with some of my conclusions about the universe, and that may be possible. Very possible. Shall we go now?"

As he asked for the bill he remembered with a start that he had no Iranian money.

"What's the matter?" She was leaning on her chin.

"I haven't any Iranian money," he said. "I forgot to pick it up this morning."

She did not laugh outright. She watched him with amused eyes, and waited while he explained the situation to the Russian waiter, but when an argument began she touched his arm lightly and handed him a large purple note.

"Is this enough?" she said.

It was an Iranian five-hundred-rial note; it was more than enough. He gave it to the waiter, who had remained unstirred by the entire charade.

"I just remembered I had it," she said while they waited for the change.

"Where did you get it?" He suspected her of deliberately holding out to see how he would get out of the mess.

"I swapped my roubles with Holmes. I was going to buy some stockings with it, but I couldn't bear to see you in trouble."

"I'll pay you when we get back to the Embassy," he muttered.

"No hurry," she said. She took the change direct from the waiter and smiled as she left a small note for him. "Let's go, and I'll see what Adams has done about my room. Do you think Harold will be at the Embassy now?"

"He may be. I was supposed to see him at four o'clock and I'm an hour late already. You'd better come in with me. I want to see how you do it!"

At the Chancery Essex bellowed for them to come in. He clapped his hands together as he saw MacGregor. Then he saw Katherine and shouted his surprise. She kissed him lightly on the cheek and sat on the edge of the desk and pulled off her gloves and told him about MacGregor having no money to pay the luncheon bill. MacGregor sat down to watch her persuade Essex to take her to Azerbaijan. She mentioned nothing about the trip. Essex was too busy getting her straightened out. He wanted to know why she hadn't gone direct to London. She told him about the clothes she wanted, the weather she wanted, the Ambassador's plane leaving, Jeb Wills suggesting they go.

"You could have bought clothes in Sweden," he said. "Why didn't you go that way?"

"I don't like Sweden," she said. "Too many women there."

"This is a rather long way about," he argued. "Still, it's nice to see you. Have they settled you somewhere?"

"No," she said. "It looks like I'll have to stay at the hotel with Jeb."

MacGregor felt nothing about Wills because he knew that Katherine was beginning to work on Essex. He was surprised at his own appreciation of her skill with Essex. He was actually enjoying it.

"I think we could get you better accommodation than a hotel," Essex told her.

"Don't bother. We won't be here long." She looked at MacGregor. She was still the fulcrum between these two men, except that MacGregor had gained an advantage in standing away to judge her better. "Actually," she said to Essex, "I thought you were going to Azerbaijan."

"So I am. To-morrow."

"What a pity. Couldn't you delay it for a few days?"

Essex looked hard at MacGregor and shook his head. He could do no more.

"Never mind," she told him. "Are you going to Azerbaijan, Mac-Gregor?"

MacGregor knew his part. He shrugged.

"That reminds me," Essex said after a perceptible thought. "I expected you earlier, MacGregor. Since you are so late we can go over and look at that Ford car and the equipment which Pickering is fixing up. Come on Kathy, you might be interested in this. The car arrived this morning. They will have fitted it out by now."

They went across the compound to a small gravelled turn-around near a white villa. A yellow desert-painted Ford station-wagon (almost new) was parked near the verandah. Colonel Pickering and a dark angry-looking native were standing over a large assortment of equipment which had been spread out on the verandah. Essex introduced Pickering to Katherine, and the other man stood respectfully aside while the English-man talked, and MacGregor glanced at the equipment.

"This is your driver," Pickering said to Essex and pointed to the native. "His name is Aladin, an old Afghan name which originally came from Ala-ud-din, Chief of Ghor. We find Aladin much simpler. He speaks all the dialects of Persia, having lived here most of his life. He did a spell in the Indian Army and he's one of our most trusted men. Knows the Kurd country thoroughly and speaks most of those dialects there. He even speaks English. Aladin, speak English!"

"What shall I say, Sahib?" Aladin bowed, and showed his white teeth.

"That's enough," Pickering said.

"Yes sir." He bowed again, and turned to include MacGregor who was standing apart. MacGregor's estimation of Aladin was simply that no man could have a more villainous-looking face than that berry-stained Afghan, whose features were lined from his wide harsh brow to his solid grizzled chin with the tightened-up ugliness of a tribal assassin. He was neatly dressed in a khaki coat which fastened right up to the neck with the gold buttons of the General List and Embassy service. He was clean and erect, and MacGregor looked at him again and liked him and then passed over him to Pickering, who was explaining the equipment to Essex and Katherine.

Pickering went over the equipment on the Ford piece by piece, the high running board, the cut-off mud-guards, the condenser on the radiator, the sand-tracks rolled up and jammed against the bonnet, the shovels, the water bags, the large box of spare parts in the back. Then the equipment on the verandah: all of it emergency, since they would really find all their needs catered for at caravanserais and private houses en route; but it was as well to have it. There was a small tent, three sleeping bags, blankets, petrol stove, extra cans of petrol which fitted into brackets at the side of the car (German clamp-top petrol cans, MacGregor appreciated the choice because the English variety leaked badly), a few plates, knives, spoons, mugs, a large supply of maps, an oil compass, a small axe, a set of chains for the tyres, two spare tubes, a small tarpaulin, a first-aid kit (army medical type) and two large boxes of canned foods unopened and well marked with the listed contents. Everything was there, and Mac-Gregor knew that Pickering understood his business. Each group of items folded up into some kind of canvas wrapper or container, dust-proof and water-proof. MacGregor could see nothing lacking, except perhaps a coil of rope, but he said nothing. Nevertheless, the equipment had begun to stir his feeling for the expedition. Now he really had to make up his mind.

Essex was also delighted, and he went over every item with Katherine and Colonel Pickering, complimenting Pickering on the good job done. Katherine prompted his enjoyment more when she kneeled down and felt the sleeping-bags and looked into the first-aid kit and read the contents of the food-boxes.

"It's wonderful," she said and gave Essex her hand to be lifted.

"Well MacGregor?" Essex finally came to him.

"It's all you need," MacGregor pronounced.

"Pickering," Essex said. "You've done the perfect job. The head of the expedition is satisfied." It was pleasantly sarcastic and assumptive.

"What time do you want to get off to-morrow?" Pickering asked.

"How about eight o'clock?" Essex said to MacGregor.

"Fine." MacGregor was noncommittal and disinterested. It had nothing to do with him.

"Did you hear that, Aladin?" Pickering told the Afghan. "Everything ready, including yourself, at 7:30, in front of the Chancery. I'll check you up and then you can go around for Mr. MacGregor and be back here by eight o'clock. Is that clear?"

Aladin bowed, showed his large teeth, and said nothing.

MacGregor refused to admit to himself that he would go with Essex. On the other hand he still did not come right out and refuse to go. He looked at the tyres on the Ford, inspecting them for cracks. They were new and in excellent condition, and he was finally satisfied that this car would be well prepared for the jolting it would suffer on those unpaved roads.

"There is one more thing, Lord Essex," Pickering said. "We haven't all the personal documents required for yourself and MacGregor from the Soviet Embassy. They should have been here by now."

"Get hold of the Ambassador and shake him up," Essex said. "Remind him that Stalin will not like it if we're held up."

"I'm sure he knows that already," Pickering said.

"Well, tell him again," Essex said. "I'm a little tired of these petty officials being mixed up in my affairs."

Essex was out of sorts over it, but Katherine buoyed him up with her enthusiasm for the preparations. MacGregor listened for a while and then told Essex that if he had nothing more for him he would go.

"Did you see Jack Adams?" Essex asked him.

"No. I waited for him. Are you going to take him?"

"I'm not sure," Essex said. "It depends on whether I need him or not. I'll see you at eight in the morning," Essex ordered.

MacGregor had no time to say anything to that. Katherine interrupted. "Just a moment, Ivre. I think I will accept your offer of a room. Shall I come now?"

"By all means," he said.

"What's all this about?" Essex said.

"MacGregor's offered to put me up," Katherine told him.

"I'm sure that you don't have to bother the old gentleman," Essex said of Aqa. "Leave it. I'll fix it up. That's all, MacGregor."

Katherine was obviously going to remain with Essex to further her own cause, so MacGregor left them and went home.

Dr. Aqa was having his afternoon sleep, and the house was dark and dismal. Hassan had closed the shutters again. MacGregor sat in the library trying to read Sir Denison Ross's compilation on Persian art. His father had given him this book, and finding it here had been a surprise. He had never read it and now he wondered why. But his mind was not on his reading. He was making a mental check on his requirements, in case he should go with Essex. He had everything: boots, jumpers, trenchcoat, half-a-dozen clean handkerchiefs, and enough razor blades to see him through. He could save his suit by wearing his army barathea trousers and one of his tweed jackets. He remembered that there were no flashlights in the Ford's equipment; it might be a necessary item. He went over it all again until Hassan announced dinner.

Dr. Aqa was late and they ate silently as Hassan brought small dishes of spiced vegetables, Indian curry, and stewed fruit.

"You had better eat well," Dr. Aqa said to MacGregor. "You're leaving to-morrow, aren't you?"

"I'm not sure." MacGregor did not want to go into it.

Dr. Aqa folded his hands and observed MacGregor with patient, honest,

Persian scrutiny. It was not impolite, it was deliberately fatherly, and MacGregor sat still under it.

"You're a good boy," Dr. Aqa said to him. "You are just feeling the sadness."

"What sadness?" MacGregor said.

Dr. Aqa lifted his hands, palm upwards. "Any sadness," he said. "This is a whole nation of sadness, of primitive sadness. Have you seen all your old friends?"

"Some of them," MacGregor said, "but most of them have gone away."

"Whom did you see?"

"I saw Rhé and our old friend Chabar at the Ecole Normale."

"Ah yes. Then you really are at home!" Dr. Aqa said it as something new. He must have forgotten their conversation of lunch time.

"More so every day," MacGregor told him.

"Good. I'll abide with that. I hope you have a good trip. We will have plenty to talk about when you come back." Dr. Aqa put out his thin skeleton hand. MacGregor enjoyed Dr. Aqa's careful planting of such important ideas. "I'm off to bed," the old man said. "I now sleep fifteen hours every day. Death itself can't mean much more than that. Good-night my boy. Have a good trip."

MacGregor watched him move carefully up the stairs. Hassan walked behind him mumbling in Arabic that an old man like the Doctor — the Pride of Biologists — should not have a room upstairs. He should be modest and self-effacing and admit his age and his creaking limbs and move downstairs. The Doctor grunted argument with every step, and MacGregor turned away because he did not like to see the Doctor so near to absolute muscular disintegration. MacGregor returned to Denison Ross's book, but he got up from time to time to look at the Behzâds and the other miniatures, trying to find in himself the answer to this necessary sense of art and beauty. He had forgotten Katherine Clive completely when Hassan opened the library door and Katherine stood there, her fur coat open and her black and gold scarf hanging from her brushed hair and cold pink cheeks.

"Am I still valid for your room?" she said.

"I thought Essex was looking after you," he said. "Come in. Come in."

"I have four large suitcases out here," she nodded backwards as he reached her.

Hassan was still there and MacGregor told him in Arabic that this was *el Sitt* Clive who would stay here the night. Was there a spare room?

"It sounds so odd," she said as she dropped her coat with a shrug of the shoulders into Hassan's waiting hands. "Is that Persian?"

"No," he said. "It's bad Arabic."

"Is he an Arab?"

302

"From Kuwait. A Bedouin really." MacGregor found explanation of Hassan an excellent antidote to his surprise and to his view of Katherine's black dress and gold sequins. "He was bought as a slave by the Doctor's father, but by now he is a member of the family." He took her into the library. "He almost married one of the Doctor's cousins about thirty years ago. She died of typhus."

"How old is he now?"

"About sixty. He was bought when he was five or six."

"And he still speaks Arabic?"

"The Doctor has never allowed him to speak anything else. The Doctor has tried to send him back home, but Hassan calls on his family and makes himself unhappy. He considers them all crude and uncivilized. He used to give me hidings for eating green peaches."

"Young MacGregor getting a hiding," she said.

"Excuse me and I'll see about the room." MacGregor went out. Hassan whispered to him that *el Sitt* could sleep in the small room near his own, since it was all prepared. While MacGregor took up some of the luggage, Hassan served Katherine with coffee. The Arab smiled good-naturedly as Katherine carried on a warm conversation with him in English, a language he did not understand, having forgotten the few words he once knew.

"This is a lovely house," Katherine said when MacGregor returned. "I never expected anything like this." She looked around her.

"What did you expect?"

"Oh. I don't know."

He sat down opposite her, removing his book from the chair. She looked at the title and put down her coffee and glanced through the book.

"This surprises me," she said. "I didn't know you knew anything about art."

"I know absolutely nothing," he said. "Particularly about Persian art."

"Well that's comforting," she said. "Neither do I." Katherine was on her best behaviour. She was sitting neatly forward on the edge of her chair with legs modestly together.

"I'm a little late in catching up with myself," MacGregor said. "Artistic ignorance is something that never worried me before."

"You have to start somewhere," she said. "I'll borrow that book myself if I may. I can't bear not to know something I must know." She then deliberately shamed him by asking why he hadn't looked at the galleries of Moscow or London, or even of Cairo where the relics of the ancient Egyptians should at least have interested him. She was not very serious, but her attack went home. He knew how ignorant he was, and how inexcusable it was. When he made no defence to her teasing, she dropped the subject.

303

"Where is your Doctor Aqa?" she asked him.

"Gone to bed."

"I think I should go to bed too," she said. "I have to get up early in the morning, and I'm sure I won't get any sleep to-morrow."

"Oh?" He knew what was coming.

"You sound like Essex," she said.

"What are you getting up early about?" he asked.

"I shall have to re-pack my things in the morning. I am far too tired to do it to-night. Tell me, should I wear ski trousers and boots, or will that be bad for the general atmosphere of the expedition?"

"Did Essex say you could go?"

"Certainly."

"When did he agree?"

"Oh I don't know. I had dinner with him. Do you mind?"

"What did you tell him?"

"I simply complicated his life so much that he was glad to take me."

"I can't quite believe it," he said. "Are you sure he wasn't pulling your leg?"

"I hardly think so. Incidentally, Al Hamber and Steele were around at the Embassy trying to find you."

"Are they going too?"

"I don't think so. I rang Jeb Wills. He said they were pretty mad about not going. Wait until they find out I'm going."

"And Adams?"

"I can't imagine Harold taking that bubble of a man. He only wants one man with him and that is you, so don't be jealous of Jack Adams."

He took her out of the library and upstairs. What had she done with Essex? He knew she must have pushed and pulled Essex one way and then another with hints, suggestions, jealousies, and every other wile which she could use with subtle skill. Which Katherine was this? She was like a neutral shade of Katherine. He did not resent her skill with Essex. He was pleased that someone could make such easy use of him. Mac-Gregor felt that he had an ally here, an ally who could show him Essex from the inside. But for how long would this neatly balanced Katherine last?

He turned on the light of her room and explained the bathroom facilities in the hall and said that Hassan would wake her at 6:30. She asked him where he slept.

"Next room," he said.

"Are you coming to-morrow?"

"I might."

"It would be rather awkward if I had to go with Essex alone."

304

He laughed.

"You don't think I would go with him?" she said.

"I am sure you would."

"I am glad you realize it," she said. "He once offered me your job, and that's about all it would mean really. I am sure that doesn't worry you, but it might be something to consider. What about my ski pants and boots? Will they be alright?"

"Women have always worn trousers in Iran," he said. "You'll be alright."

"Do you have any soap?"

"Take as much as you like from the bathroom."

She leaned on the door. "It's a pity we fight," she said calmly and suddenly.

MacGregor nearly lost himself as he stared at her, but the shadow of other times and the sense of foolishness came on him again. He suffered the memory and bade her good night. He was ready for bed when he heard her calling him from her window. He leaned out to see a white shadow shivering and holding her arms about herself.

"I simply wanted you to make this trip," she said. "I couldn't really go without you."

"I wouldn't let you go without me," he said.

"I might even help you influence Essex," she said cheerfully.

It was enough for both of them and they parted at the window.

Chapter 25

Jack Adams was ready to go with them. He was standing in the drive with his kit when Aladin arrived at the Chancery with Katherine and MacGregor.

"Are you coming?" Katherine asked with cruel astonishment.

"I think so," Adams said happily. "Pickering told me to be ready." He was dressed in jodhpurs and a sheepskin jacket. "I haven't seen Lord Essex yet. What a day!" It was a clear bright morning and the first red haze of the early sun was spreading over the quiet city. "Glad you could come, MacGregor," Adams said.

"So am I," MacGregor said.

Essex and Pickering arrived, and the sight of MacGregor brought a broad smile to Essex's face. "You see," he said to Pickering. "He couldn't resist it."

Pickering nodded and asked Adams if he was all ready.

305

"Absolutely," Adams said and kicked his bags and waited for someone to say that he was going. He was like an eager schoolboy.

"Well," Essex said quickly. "We will just have to work this out."

Pickering did not disguise his look of disagreement with Essex.

"Just come inside a moment," Essex told Pickering.

They went back into the Chancery, while Katherine and MacGregor and Adams waited, knowing that a discussion was taking place about all three of them. Katherine walked to the gate to look at the Elburz and the early morning sun. MacGregor sat on the car and wondered whether the argument between Essex and Pickering was the choice of himself against Adams, or Adams against Katherine. Adams sat on the running-board beside him, subdued by apprehension and suspense.

By the look on Pickering's quiet face, Jack Adams knew that he had lost. Pickering forced a dry smile. "Sorry Jack," he said. "Looks as if I'll have to keep you here."

"That's alright, sir," Adams told him.

Now MacGregor felt sorry for Adams. He also felt that he was responsible for the man's disappointment; but in this situation four Englishmen were better saying nothing. Pickering, being the gentleman, had taken it all upon himself. Essex said "Sorry Jack" and wasted no more time. He sat with Katherine in the back seat of the station-wagon and MacGregor sat in the front with Aladin. It was 7:45 by MacGregor's watch when they started off, leaving the disappointed Adams and the reluctant Pickering waving a casual farewell.

They were silent as they lost sight of the Elburz and negotiated the streets of Teheran. When they reached the outskirts and began to leave Teheran, it was Katherine who broke the silence as if she were responsible for it. The movement, the expanse of wide open plateau to the left and the mountains to the right, were more effective conciliators. They enjoyed the Ford singing on the brief good road, and they felt the freshness of the day filling them with expectancy. By the time they had passed the twenty-odd miles to Karaj, they were associated with warmth and pleasure, satisfied with their good fortune in making this trip.

An Iranian Gendarmerie post halted them near Karaj. A long pole blocked the road, and Aladin blew the Ford's klaxon. A soldier ran from a small barrack building (with loop-holes) which nestled at the foot of a bare hill. A crushed and dusty officer of the Gendarmerie followed him leisurely. Aladin shouted at them fiercely to hurry up because an English Ambassador sat in the car. The soldier lifted the pole, but the officer told them to wait. He walked to the Ford and looked in.

He had probably never seen anybody more English in his life, MacGregor thought. The officer's unshaven lips fell loosely apart when he saw Katherine. Her hair was brushed tight back so that her proportionate

English face looked unmistakably feminine. Essex wore a corduroy-leather jacket and a soft shirt; a short camel's-hair coat lay across his knees. The officer pulled his head out quickly and saluted and looked at MacGregor apologetically.

"Where is the Russian post?" MacGregor asked him in Persian.

"Two kilometres along," the officer said. "Are you going to Tabriz?"

"Yes."

"Be careful Excellencies." The officer leaned forward again and looked serious. "They have shot Englishmen going this way. They steal and rob every automobile which goes up the Khorrem Darreh. Do you have weapons?"

"No," MacGregor said, "and who shoots Englishmen?"

"The *Moscovs* — the Russians. Also those bandits who have seized Azerbaijan, raping every woman in the countryside. Be careful of your own sweetness-and-light in the back seat. I really advise you to turn back now. We hear all things here. Ten or fifteen people are killed every day between here and Kazvin. All foreigners except the Moscovs are shot and quartered and robbed. There are none of our Gendarmes up there because they have all been killed, so you will find it murderous country. Not only that, all women have been distributed between the rebels. They are being publicly ravaged in the streets of the villages and towns. You should insist on an escort of the Shah's bodyguard, or you should stay in Teheran which is safe. In God's name!"

"Thank you," MacGregor said politely. "We will be returning in some weeks and we will tell you what it is like."

Aladin drove under the barrier and they were not stopped again until they reached the bridge over the Karaj River. There was a similar pole across the road. A Russian stood guard, a submachine-gun across his chest. He wore a green winter smock and a side cap, and he had three medals on his tunic. MacGregor gave him the passports with the small slips in them from the Embassy, and also the large official document from the Soviet Ambassador which said they were free to travel without hindrance from Soviet forces wherever they wished in Azerbaijan, by the direct orders of Marshal Stalin himself. As the soldier looked carefully and meticulously at all the documents, Katherine pushed open her window and pointed up at a ridge which cut into the mountains.

"Look at the beautiful gorge," she said. "What is it, MacGregor?"

"The river divides the Shemran Mountains from Khalagan range," he said. "It goes right through to that mountain you can see in the distance. That's the Kachang Peak."

"What wonderful country." Katherine swept her arm towards the stony river bed which was flat and open on either side, but tapered up into comfortable banks as it went deeper into the mountains. The banks near the bridge were wide and silted. The white water occupied a narrow pebbled lane in the wide river bed. It was fresh and clear, and MacGregor told them that this water had once been carried into Teheran every morning in skins for Fath Ali Shah. He liked Katherine for enjoying it so obviously, and he told her that the place was really called Suleimaneh because of a hunting lodge which one of the Shahs had built on the slopes. The hunting lodge had been paid for by the raids on the distant Kurdish territory of Suleimaneh.

"What sort of game do you get here, MacGregor?" Essex said.

"Mostly ibex and antelope and a lot of pheasant and grouse and bustards." MacGregor waved a hand at the mountains. "On the other side of the Elburz there are leopards I believe, but I've never seen one. There are some bears, but not down this far any more."

"It looks like wild boar country," Essex said. "Is there underbrush up there?"

"In the valleys." MacGregor had put his hand out for the documents which the Red Army soldier was folding neatly. The soldier had read the large document, but he did not appear as impressed as MacGregor had expected. He came forward and looked in the car and said one word in Persian: Weapons?

"We haven't got any," MacGregor told him in Russian.

The shaven head of the boy stretched in a grin as he heard his own tongue.

"Where are you going?" he said.

"Tabriz," MacGregor said, not wishing to complicate his life by describing the route.

"Tell your driver to go slowly through the town," the Russian said. "An old woman was killed this morning by a truck carrying wheat. Persians are very reckless drivers, and the people will throw stones at you if you kill anyone!" He saluted and allowed the pole to rise. They passed over the bridge and through the low mud township of Karaj, yellow with dry dust and not yet caught by the dampening rains which came down from the Caspian and over the Elburz later in the month.

"What was that Persian fellow saying to you back there, MacGregor?" Essex asked.

"He was telling me we would be raped, robbed, and quartered." MacGregor put all the documents in an envelope and handed back Essex's and Katherine's passports.

"He seemed to have said more than that."

"He warned us not to go into Azerbaijan at all. Apparently every Englishman who goes this way gets killed."

"What Englishmen have been this way?" Katherine said.

"None that I know of."

308

"Villainous-looking specimen," Essex said. "Dirty people."

The good road had ended and though the surface was still paved, the shoulders of the road were crumbling. The Ford bumped and shook and crashed through dust as they avoided large trucks, busses, mules and camels, all occupying the centre of the road. The mountains on the right were still close, but the rolling hills were coming closer on the left. The road went through orchards and vineyards, perimetered by low yellow mud walls and inhabited near the road with mud huts and small adobe houses. The few groves hardly made any impression on the bare plateau, and in the absolutely still air the surface of the earth seemed baked by summer sun and warm air. MacGregor relaxed on the warm leather of the front seat, his elbow leaning on the wooden door. It was luxury; a home-coming that began to satisfy him again. The comforts of privilege and importance were apparently worth while. Katherine also made it worth while. Any issue to be settled with Essex was far away and unimportant.

They were at peace.

The bad roads shook them until Essex protested. Aladin slowed down and they travelled slowly enough to pass the morning in pleasant geographical discussion. They stopped at the hotel in Kazvin for lunch, and MacGregor told them that this town had once been the capital of Iran. So had Tabriz, Isfahan, and ancient Rai.

MacGregor thought he might as well start properly by impressing Essex with a little history, but he was not a good storyteller and he doubted if Essex was impressed. "This was once the stronghold of the Assassins," he told them. "I think it was captured in the eleventh century by one of their chiefs, Hassan Sabbah. He built a castle on the top of a high rock about forty miles from here and called it the Eagle's Nest. The Mongols destroyed it but the Sefavi Shahs rebuilt it and used it for unwanted diplomats and court nuisances, whom they threw out of the windows into the gorge below. Haroun el Rashid was also here: he built the mosque and the city walls."

Essex grunted and Katherine ate hungrily.

As they left Kazvin MacGregor remembered one thing more. "Somewhere in the town there are the graves of two English Ambassadors who died there of fever in the seventeenth century."

"You don't say?" Essex liked that. "Perhaps we could locate them when we come back this way . . ."

That was better, and as MacGregor saw it now, this would be a comfortable and uneventful tour. A pleasant atmosphere had settled upon them. Nothing could quite disturb it. MacGregor had almost fallen asleep in the summery air, when they were stopped at the beginning of a long shadowed valley.

"What now?" Essex leaned forward impatiently.

"Another road block," MacGregor said.

"They've painted the pole red and white," Katherine said.

Standing before the pole at rigid attention, waiting for the Ford to stop, was a small dark soldier. MacGregor thought he was another Russian. Then he identified the soldier's cap as Iranian, although the blouse and boots were Russian. The soldier wore a submachine-gun swung on his chest, and he held his hand at its stock like a man to whom this interesting little weapon was still a novelty and an importance.

"Papers." The little man shouted in Turki as Aladin stopped the Ford a few feet from his upraised hand.

"What for now?" Aladin shouted back.

The soldier came forward and put his foot on the running board.

"This is Azerbaijan," he said.

MacGregor handed him the papers. "They're all in Russian," he explained.

"Of course." The soldier was scornful. He looked at the passports and the documents and touched the large seal on the special document from the Soviet Embassy. He spent some time on them, and he inspected the passports thoroughly and looked at the pictures. He looked inside the car, and he too was surprised to see Katherine, who smiled at him. He almost relaxed his intense self-discipline. MacGregor knew him then as a man who was not long a soldier; he took himself too seriously. Nor was he a soldier by livelihood. He was an enthusiast who enjoyed the importance of what he was doing. He looked at the Ford critically and carefully. He walked around the front and looked at the condenser pipe on the radiator and at the sand-tracks. He walked around the back and inspected the four-gallon cans in the brackets, the strapped-on shovels, and the equipment in the back. He came back to Aladin who was stonily silent in deference to MacGregor, who was handling this. Aladin's normal habit would have been to hurry up this ignorant fool who was holding up the Ambassador, and the entire inspection would have been argued at every point by Aladin's effective tongue. Now he sat staring back at the upstart.

The soldier walked around to MacGregor and spoke in heavy tongue. "You are not *Moscovs*?"

"We are English," said MacGregor.

The soldier looked at the handful of papers again, obviously understanding none of the written Russian. "English?" he said doubtfully. He stood back and looked at the whole picture of these people again, at the Ford and its occupants. He made his guess, which was more important to him than the papers. "Where are you going?" he said and relaxed a little.

"Tabriz."

The soldier thought for a moment and then pushed the papers into

MacGregor's hands. "They are all in order." It was something of a disappointment.

"Thank you." MacGregor inclined his head.

"Englishman," the soldier said formally, "I must go several kilometres up this road, on my duties. Will you let me ride with you? I will stand on the side, thus." He stood on the running board.

MacGregor eased him off. "That's alright." MacGregor opened the door. "Get in."

He was awkward with his submachine-gun as he squeezed in and closed the door. He signalled to another silent guard who held the rope which controlled the pole. It swung up and Aladin drove under its red and white belly into Azerbaijan.

The guard was silent and watchful as Aladin manipulated the gear lever on the steering wheel. He looked carefully at the Ford's elaborate dashboard, at the square clock and the decorative speedometer and at the heater near his knees. He said nothing.

"How is the situation in Azerbaijan?" MacGregor began.

"We have our own government," the soldier said cautiously, "also our own army and officialdom. I am part of the Azerbaijanian Army."

"I understand there is a new Parliament also," MacGregor said.

"I am not sure." The soldier shook his head. "That would be in Tabriz. Quite a lot must be happening in Tabriz."

"Do you know of developments there?"

"It is too far away," the Azerbaijani said.

"Would you know anything about the Kurds? Are they raiding again?"

"I would not know." He disliked being so ignorant, so he reversed the procedure and asked MacGregor the questions. "Have you come from Teheran?"

"We left there this morning," MacGregor told him.

"Do they know there, what has happened here?"

"Not very clearly."

"I wonder that the Gendarmerie allowed you to come. They are preparing a battle with us. Did you know that?"

"No," said MacGregor. "I didn't."

"They have tried several times to bribe me."

"What for?"

"To go with them to Kazvin or Karaj where they would torture me for information about our army. They have kidnapped five of our men in two days and hanged three of them in the fields near by to worry us. They have already sent soldiers from Teheran with artillery. They lie carefully in a dry river, a *fasakh* to the south of here, waiting. Did you know all that in Teheran?"

"No. We heard nothing of it."

"It is mostly the Gendarmerie who are interfering with us. They are even hanging and shooting people at night as far north as Saidabad near Tabriz. Only last night two of our own men were hanged from the telegraph poles you are passing. They had come to Ka'hak to estimate the land. They were shot and killed and hanged by the Gendarmerie. Did you know this when you passed through Ka'hak?"

"It seemed very quiet in Ka'hak." MacGregor shook his head.

"I have heard that a *Yengi Duna* — an Americani — is now in command of the Gendarmerie. Is that true?"

"Yes." MacGregor remembered the Turki derivative, turning Yankee Doodle into *Yengi Duna.*

"Will he bring *Yengi Duna* soldiers to fight us in Azerbaijan with the Gendarmerie?"

"I don't think so," MacGregor said as definitely as he could.

"You have come from Teheran, perhaps you would explain why a foreigner is the principal general of the Gendarmerie."

"He is only an expert who advises them," MacGregor offered.

"Must a *Yengi Duna* advise them to kill us? We are very bitter about it, and about the *Yengi Duna*. Should we find the *Yengi Duna* who gives such good advice we will hang him on that telegraph pole. If you will stop here," he said to Aladin, "I will get out."

As he alighted his weapon bumped the door; he blushed and apologized. He asked MacGregor how long they would be in Tabriz.

"About a week," MacGregor said.

"I heard that we have captured the Mayor and the Governor. I don't know if it is true. I will be here when you come back, and you can tell me what is happening. I can then tell our Captain, who needs information. I am Safar, which is also the name of a calendar month. I hope you are not molested by the Teheran Gendarmes who are roaming secretly all over the place, and who become bandits at night. May your entire journey be smooth and satisfactory, and a thousand thanks for allowing me to travel with you. *Salaam.*" He stood back and saluted self-consciously, hitching up his submachine-gun, MacGregor returned his Salaam and his salute as they drove off. Behind them Safar could be seen avoiding the grey dust thrown up by the Ford, and already walking steadily and directly back to the post.

"What did he want?" Essex said.

"He liked the Ford, and simply wanted to ride in such an elaborate car."

"Cheek!" said Essex, but he didn't resent it.

"No. No," MacGregor said. "He was very proud and reserved, and I think he must be a craftsman from the North. A short journey like that with you is a sign of respect." MacGregor told them what the soldier had said, excluding nothing about the Gendarmerie.

312

"I thought he was going to kill us with that gun," Katherine said. "He seemed unnecessarily affectionate with it."

"It looked like a Russian gun," Essex commented. "I suppose the Russians are arming these people rather well. Rather well."

"I thought it was one of those German pistols that open up," Katherine said.

"What was it, MacGregor?" Essex asked.

"A British Sten gun," MacGregor lied confidently.

"It is the same as Colonel Pickering's weapon," Aladin said quietly to MacGregor in Persian.

"Is it?"

"Yes. He put it under the front seat. It is there now."

MacGregor looked at Aladin's large face for a moment. He shouted at Aladin to stop. As the Ford swung to the side of the road in its own dust, MacGregor leapt out of the car and pulled at the front seat, ignoring the questions from Essex and Katherine. He found the gun, a Thompson, wrapped neatly in a soft leather case. He grovelled for the drums, and he swept them out as he pulled the gun from its case. He did not look at it. He gripped the short tough barrel and went to the front of the car and swung the gun onto the solid bumper bar. He swung it twice like a heavy axe until the wooden stock was splintered and smashed, and the springs and blocks were scattered on the road. He flung the barrel over his shoulder into a muddy ditch, and he swept up the drums from the running-board and pitched them deliberately one by one as hard as he could into the fields. He kicked the leather cover off the floor as he got in, and he slammed the door with shaking hands and told Aladin to drive on.

It had all happened so quickly that there was quiet until Essex said in a tight voice, "Was that necessary, MacGregor?" He was controlling himself in deference to MacGregor's being a fellow Englishman who could not be shouted at before Aladin, who was an Afghan.

"Yessir!" MacGregor heard the shaking edge on his own voice, and felt his quick breath swamping his dry mouth.

Essex closed his teeth. "Pickering simply put that in for an emergency."

"It is not necessary in this country," MacGregor said.

They were silent because they did not dare push their angers any further before Aladin. The Khorrem Darreh was forgotten; the green valleys were ignored; the pleasant river near the road and the tall poplars and fresh orchards were passed uncritically; and they rode silently over the bumps towards Zenjan, the capital of the administrative district of Khamseh, where they would spend the night and make their first official calls in Azerbaijan.

Only Katherine hummed softly, perhaps in anticipation of the interesting times ahead.

Chapter 26

It was almost dark in the valley when they drove along the muddy road into Zenjan. They came into the town between thick stone walls, tall plane trees, and along the soft flat curves of the Abhar River. Instead of lying in secure darkness the whole town of Zenjan was brilliantly lit by powerful carbide floodlights from the low buildings and the mosques. MacGregor thought at first that it must be a religious festival, but as they drove through the narrow single street the town appeared deserted. Shadows clung to the dilapidated mud houses, and MacGregor felt for a moment that they were being trapped into its desertion. Though the streets were absolutely empty some of the houses showed dim light and signs of occupation. MacGregor did not like it at all, and Aladin slowed down.

"What's the matter here?" Essex said.

"Something is happening." MacGregor put his head out to look about.

"Is this where we see this Governor fellow?"

"Yes," MacGregor said slowly, still looking about, "but his estate is off the main road to the left, across the river. Stop at the end of this street Aladin and I'll look around."

When Aladin stopped they heard rifle-shots.

"Shooting?" Essex said.

"Sounded like it." MacGregor got out. He stepped into a pot-hole because he had raised his head to listen. The sky above the white lights had clouded over, and rain had already swept down the hills across Zenjan to make the town black and wet. "It's behind us," he said about the shooting and got back in. "I wonder what those floodlights are for."

"Probably to make good targets of us," Essex suggested, and decided that they ought to get out of here; but MacGregor was taking his time.

"Take the next big turn left, Aladin," MacGregor said. "If anything happens, keep going but be careful."

Aladin bumped the car around the next corner, and the Ford skidded in the mud and nearly hit a thin stunted tree as Aladin straightened it in time to avoid half a dozen shouting figures with rifles who came from the narrow streets and leapt in front of the car. Aladin began to whip the car through them, and the back wheels dug into the gravel. They were stopped dead by a road block of oil barrels on which was mounted a glaring petrol floodlight.

"This has all the aspects of an ambush," Essex said.

"Don't say anything in English," MacGregor said quickly. "Wait."

The men came in from both sides and in front and were on the car, shouting in Turki. They jumped onto the running boards, creating confusion among themselves. MacGregor pushed on the door and threw some of them off. He got out and shouted at them in Persian and Turki to clear the road and stop swarming over the car. What did they want? It was an unidentifiable figure on a small horse who stopped the noise and argument. He rode up to MacGregor and asked him who he was and what he was doing on this road. MacGregor took a chance and explained who they were, having the time and sight now to identify the Azerbaijanian soldiers in their Russian boots and Iranian caps.

"This road is blocked," the figure on horseback said. "There is trouble further up. Why do you want to use this road?"

"We want to get to the estate of the Governor," MacGregor said.

"What for?"

MacGregor explained themselves again and asked what was the trouble.

"Never mind that," the horse-rider said. "You will not be able to call on the Governor. Follow me and I will take you to a captain. Do not attempt to ride me down because there are more road blocks ahead."

Essex cursed himself for not understanding the language. Every bump on the car had pleased him, every motion of threat and experience had delighted him, yet he forced himself to order MacGregor out of this. "We can forget the Governor," he said. "Remember we have Kathy aboard."

"Kathy is alright," MacGregor said impatiently and turned around.

Katherine also raised a loud complaint. If they were going to restrict themselves on her behalf she might as well get out and go back to Teheran now.

"She'll be alright," MacGregor repeated.

"Perhaps," Essex said. "But she is a woman and I haven't as much faith in these Persians as you have, MacGregor. Turn back," Essex said, but without conviction.

"If Kathy is willing to take the chance we should go on," MacGregor insisted. "We might as well find out what is going on here."

"I don't like it," Essex said, but his attitude belied his words.

"There is no use going back now," MacGregor said again and told Aladin to drive on behind the rider who was waiting for them.

There was no arguing with MacGregor now, so Essex accepted it, as he had wanted to accept it all the time. Katherine remained cleverly silent, allowing MacGregor to argue for her. Ahead, the rider shouted for the men to remove the road block.

"Oh no," they said and insisted on searching the car for weapons and Gendarmes. The rider was overruled on this and MacGregor saw that they could not escape inspection so he leapt out of the car and told the soldiers to look. "Only two men," he said. He stopped the others who were still excited, and he took the flashlight and shone it in the back of the car while the soldiers pushed and prodded the tarpaulin wrappings and felt for arms. The boxes worried them, but MacGregor said they were food boxes and slammed the back shut.

The road was then cleared and they drove through. Aladin switched on the lights and they watched the swinging rump of the horse until they reached two large trees. The rider dismounted at a small mud house, and nobody rushed them. They waited.

"What did that howling mob want?" Essex said. "And who are they anyway? Gendarmerie?"

"No. They are the new Azerbaijan Army," MacGregor said. "They were looking in the car for Gendarmerie. There is some kind of a pitched battle going on here, just down the road."

"What about the Governor?"

"This is his road, but I should think the Governor is blockaded."

"These rebels have probably strung him up," Essex said. "MacGregor," he ordered. "Don't take any nonsense from these people, you understand that."

"I thought he did rather well back there," Katherine said.

MacGregor had almost forgotten Katherine because she had been so quiet. He turned around and said, "You always surprise them, Kathy."

"They surprise me," she said.

The rider returned with a short man wearing a black cap.

"Are you English?" the short man asked in Persian.

"Yes," replied MacGregor.

"Then speak some of the language."

"What would you like me to say?" MacGregor said in English.

"That's alright," the short man said — still in Persian. "What are you doing here?"

MacGregor explained again that in the back of the Ford there was an English Ambassador who had been asked by Marshal Stalin in person to inspect Azerbaijan to see if the Russians were interfering in local affairs.

"There are no Russians here," the rider put in.

"You had better come into the house," the short man said.

"What about the Governor?" MacGregor remained where he was.

"You can't reach the Governor," the short man replied. "He has shut himself up in his estate. I will explain it if you would come in. It is dangerous to make too much noise on the roadway. They have a few field guns."

He led them across the muddy road to a small, bare, low, cracked adobe house. It was lit with a kerosene lamp, and a shed door set on boxes served as a table. As they entered it the short Azerbaijian saw Katherine for the first time. He hastily looked around for the one chair in the room, and wiping it with his black cap he asked her to be seated.

"Are you the Captain here?" MacGregor asked him.

"No. I am an engineer from Tabriz. My name is Javat Gochali."

MacGregor told him their names, titles, and functions.

"What's the town lit-up for?" MacGregor asked him.

Javat had a very serious face, a naturally serious face which met every situation with deliberate thought. "The Gendarmerie and the Governor's men have been raiding the town at night," he told MacGregor. "Now we must keep it well lit so that they can't hide themselves in the buildings to kidnap and rob."

"But where is the Governor?"

Javat began solemnly. "He has surrounded his entire estate with an army of vagabonds, Gendarmes, and private cavalry. He was appointed by Teheran as Governor of Zenjan District, so he refuses to acknowledge any rescripts from the new Azerbaijanian Government in Tabriz. He will not meet us on any terms. Instead he threatens to invade Zenjan. We have enough troops to protect the town, but the farms and the peasants in the surrounding districts are being raided. He is kidnapping women and murdering anyone who resists him. We are trying to keep him in check, that is why this road is blocked. His troops are about a kilometre from here. We face him, and hold the town."

"Are you going to attack him?" MacGregor asked.

"We do not want any battles," Javat said, and his voice opened up a serious world which was centred right here in this dim black hut in the heart of Zenjan. "We have only asked him to co-operate. I have been sent from Tabriz to organize the district according to the new laws, and to re-arrange the land and the administration for our new autonomous Government. All this the Governor refuses to acknowledge. We don't like to force a battle, but it might be necessary if he continues to resist."

"Just a moment," MacGregor said. He translated and explained all this to Essex who had been waiting impatiently. Like all translators, MacGregor shortened his version so much that Essex decided he was not being told all. MacGregor assured him that Persian was a lengthy language, that he had told him everything.

"Go ahead," Essex said. "Ask him about this Governor."

"Actually," Javat told MacGregor again, "the Governor is hoping for reinforcements and field guns to reach him from Teheran or Hamadan. He tried to prepare a field for aeroplanes to land, but we flooded it with a canal we control. He has the Chief of Police of the district with him. They threaten to destroy every person and every house in his area if we attempt to dislodge them. The Governor has even threatened the destruction of Zenjan if we do not clear out and leave it to him to administer as before."

MacGregor had forgotten the subtle difference of the Turanian from the Iranian, and Javat was the total remainder of Turanian distinction: of ruggedness, short strength, and rather heavy stringiness which made Azerbaijanians the best soldiers in Iran. His face was so solid that it could have been assembled by a thumb rubbing flat pieces of clay on a modelling block. His shaven head was probably a Russian influence, but in everything else he was patriotic. The black eyes and dark eyelashes, the thick stubble on his controlled face, all of it made a picture of a man who had little sense of himself, a man with a quiet fanaticism for what he was doing.

It made MacGregor curious to know what Javat had in store for himself. "Will you be the new Governor of the district?" he asked Javat.

Javat did not smile. "No," he said. "I am simply the representative of the Democratic Administration, our new Government. I have no title. I am here to re-arrange the district."

"Aren't you a little late? Didn't your revolt take place some time ago?" MacGregor forgot his responsibilities to Essex in favour of his own interest in the situation. To see a man sitting here in this broken-down hut waiting to depose a Governor was something new to MacGregor in Iran. He hadn't expected this change to be so simple.

"We can't do everything at once," Javat told him, "and we have been waiting two weeks now for this Governor to talk with us. We can't be patient much longer because the crops for next year must be planted."

"What's he saying?" Essex said, finding it impossible to wait any longer.

"Just a moment . . ." MacGregor said.

"Well get on with it," Essex said. "I don't want to wait around here."

"He is explaining what is happening," MacGregor said impatiently.

"Why must you see the Governor?" Javat asked MacGregor.

"We are officials," MacGregor explained. "Our contact has been with officials in Teheran. It may be unfortunate but it is necessary because our official contact is with the *Dawlat* — the State."

"That may be alright in Teheran," Javat said, "but it does not apply here."

"It applies for our Ambassador. He is really a Special Envoy. He is important because he will report his attitude to the English Government when he returns."

"Does he understand what we are trying to do in Azerbaijan?"

"He knows something of it."

"Does he know anything of this Governor he is so anxious to meet?"

"Very little."

"Did you know that he and his cohort, Fajami, had hanged every man who attempted to form a Democratic Party here, and that others were tortured by having their lips cut off, their eyes gouged, and their genitals

318

removed? Did you know that the Governor refused to acknowledge our democratically elected district Endjumens, and used the Gendarmerie to disperse them?"

"As I said," MacGregor told him, "we have been limited to official contact in Teheran and we know nothing of the situation here."

"Is the Governor expecting you?" Javat understood MacGregor's caution.

"Perhaps. Does he have contact with Teheran?"

"He may have radio. We don't know. You must explain to your Ambassador that it is impossible to see the Governor. It is unnecessary and it is dangerous."

"I can't agree that it is unnecessary," MacGregor said.

"I can show you all the evidence you may need to know this man."

"It would be better if we saw him personally," MacGregor insisted.

"It is dangerous."

"Why?"

"He is treacherous; and it will be difficult for you to enter there."

"MacGregor," Essex said. "How long is this going on?"

"He's telling me about the Governor," MacGregor said. "I was telling him that we want to get in there. He holds the keys, and we can't get far unless we talk him into it. Do you want me to go on?"

"What does he say about the Governor?"

MacGregor told Essex all that Javat had said. MacGregor further explained the siege and the possibility that this would become quite a battle because of the crops.

"Ask him one thing, MacGregor. Ask him by what right he is deposing this Governor."

MacGregor knew what the answer would be, but he asked Javat and translated the reply. "He says that he is not deposing the Governor. He is trying to initiate changes in the administration, which the Governor opposes by force."

"By what *legal* right does he do this?" Essex persisted.

MacGregor went on transmitting the questions and delivering Javat's answers. "By the legal right of a properly elected Constituent Assembly of Azerbaijan, which passed laws reforming the land and the administration. He says the Governor refuses to recognize the authority of the Constituent Assembly."

"What does he want to do with this Governor?" Essex asked. "Does he want to talk with him or does he want to fight it out with him?"

"He says he wants to negotiate with him."

"On what terms?"

"He says that terms would be part of the discussion. There can be no

319

terms until the Governor is willing to talk, and he has refused to talk with them."

"Does he intend taking away the Governor's property?" Essex said.

"He says not necessarily."

"And the Governor's police force and army?" Essex asked.

"He says that would be something else."

"He does not intend to execute the Governor?"

"He says he should be hanged because of the murders he has committed; but he'll save himself if he talks with them now and compromises."

"Tell him," Essex said, "that I will talk to this Governor and arrange for some kind of discussion."

MacGregor was suspicious. "What do you have in mind?" he asked him.

"Never mind that. Tell this fellow that I'll talk to the Governor."

MacGregor told Javat and transferred the reply. "He says we will not be able to get in there. The Governor's men will shoot us up before they know who we are."

"Ask him if he can get a document to the Governor."

"He can get it there, but doubts if they could collect a reply. He doesn't think much of the idea."

Essex took several envelopes from the inside of his short camel's-hair coat. He leaned forward to MacGregor and gave him the letters. "This is an introduction to the Governor from Teheran, explaining who we are. It is in English and Persian. You had better write another note to the Governor in Persian saying that we will come in by car about an hour after this note is delivered, adding that unless he wants more trouble he had better let us through."

"I don't think it will be very effective," MacGregor began.

"Just write it and give it to this chap to deliver. Ask him if he's got a fire around here somewhere. It's getting damned cold. Are you cold Kathy?"

"Only my feet." She stamped them slowly.

"This must be rather boring for you," Essex told her, as MacGregor explained to Javat about the document and asked for paper. MacGregor wrote laboriously, listening with half his mind to Essex and Katherine.

"It's not boring," Katherine told Essex. "Your friend the Governor must be an interesting fellow: cutting off people's lips."

"You have to allow for a certain amount of exaggeration," Essex said.

"Do you have ideas about saving his neck, Harold?" Katherine stood up and balanced on her toes and heels as she moved her feet inside the boots.

"His neck is safe enough," Essex said, "and I don't care about his neck anyway."

320

MacGregor gave Javat the note, and he agreed to deliver it somehow. He then took them into another small room in the hut, where there was an oil stove. A dozen soldiers were sleeping on the floor and Javat told them to make room. They all went away and Javat spread two blankets on the floor near the stove. He apologized for the wretched circumstances and went off with the letters to the Governor.

"I hope you are inoculated against typhus," Essex said to Katherine. She threw off her coat. "I don't believe in inoculations," she told him, and sat on the blanket. "If you are not going to use your coat, Mac-Gregor, would you lend it to me?"

MacGregor gave her the trench-coat and she sat on it instead of her own sealskin coat. That was the sort of conceit which made MacGregor dislike Katherine all over again. It seemed to be the conceit and the assumption of her upbringing. To so misuse his coat could be flattering, but it was more like an insult. It was a manner and an attitude which would never change in Katherine. It was always there on the surface like an extra skin.

"Are you sorry you came with us?" MacGregor said, looking down at her.

"Not as long as I am warm." Outright denial of anything was beyond her. "When I am cold I tell myself I am a fool to be here. But it is beginning to look interesting. What did that little man say his name was?"

"Must everybody be a little man to you, Kathy?" MacGregor demanded.

"Sorry." She was surprised. "I really didn't know his name."

"Javat. Javat Gochali."

"I don't think the Governor has much chance," she announced. "There is something about these men who start changing Governments, particularly Governments such as this one must have been. They are always men who look immovable. I bet you Javat has been in jail," she said to MacGregor.

"Oh?"

"There is something that gives such men their certainty," she said.

"You think jail does it?" Essex said, scraping out his pipe.

"Not necessarily." Katherine folded her trousered legs like a leopard subsiding. "It's usually what they go to jail for. I often wonder if there are Englishmen with that look. I can't imagine it, but there must be plenty. It's a very political-looking face, don't you think Harold?"

"He looks like a grim Puritan," Essex said. "No wonder the Governor is holding out."

"Would he tell you if he had been a political prisoner, Ivre?"

"I should think so."

321

"Could you ask him?"

"Why not?" MacGregor said.

"You might also ask if he has been trained in Russia," Essex said, but he hardly meant it. "He dresses and behaves like a Russian."

"I think it's his boots," MacGregor said. "They are certainly Russian."

"So are his politics," Essex added.

"Why don't you give him the benefit of the doubt, Harold?" Katherine said. "Wait until you have seen the Governor and then you can compare them both. Be scientific about it."

"I'll leave the scientific thinking to MacGregor," Essex said.

MacGregor saw that they were tossing the subject back and forth like a tennis ball, so he went out to get something to eat, and to see if Aladin was still guarding the Ford.

It was dark, and though the moon was up, there was heavy rain in the sky. After getting his bearings MacGregor could just see the Ford. It was off the road near a broken-down wall and a tent. He could hear men talking as he approached.

He called to Aladin.

"Sahib," came the reply from one of the goatskin tents.

"That's alright," MacGregor said in English as he saw Aladin run forward. "I wondered if you were being looked after. Are you alright?"

"Yes Sahib. I am sharing a fire."

"With the soldiers?"

"These men are not real soldiers but labourers from Tabriz and peasants from the fields," Aladin told him. "Did they tell you about the Governor? They say that there will be a battle soon."

"Yes. What else do they say?"

"They want to go back home. They have been waiting here a long time."

"Do they say why they are setting upon the Governor?"

"They explain a great deal about his cruelties. What do they expect? Cruelties are normal to the Persians, and there is nothing unusual about this one. We are all cruel when we have the chance, isn't that so Sahib?"

"Perhaps."

"They also say that they will be given land. There is so much land belonging to the Shah up here that they expect it to be divided among the peasants. They say they will receive seed and implements from the Government. I don't see why they are down here if they are going to get land where they live."

Three or four soldiers had come out of the tent and they stood close to Aladin and MacGregor, listening curiously to the English. MacGregor spoke in Turki and greeted them and they greeted him in return. He asked them what was going on. They told him briefly that the Gover-

322

nor's men had been seen over the other side of the town, raiding. Then they drifted carefully away. Aladin got a carton of chocolate from the Ford, and as MacGregor returned to the house he heard more rifle-shots, closer and thicker. He gave the chocolates to Katherine. Essex was now seated beside her, his pink face a rosy flush with the heat.

"Car alright, MacGregor?"

"Yes."

"Is that more shooting?"

"It's up the road," MacGregor said.

"That's your letter being received," Katherine said.

"These people seem to take everything a little too seriously," Essex complained. But every rifle shot delighted him. A little touch of war made a man feel young again, and it was an experience he had hardly expected to have again in his lifetime.

"How long do we wait?" Katherine deferred to MacGregor.

"Not long." MacGregor took the bar of chocolate she handed up to him.

"I'm actually tired," she said. "Move over Harold so that I can lie down, and you sit down somewhere, Ivre. Towering over us like that is most impolite."

"I think Javat is back," MacGregor said and went into the other room.

Javat was sitting at the rough table pushing maps out of the way. "Your letter should have been delivered by now," he said. "I heard some activity."

A soldier came in the door with a samovar and a tray of glasses. He set them down and greeted MacGregor and Javat, and poured out the tea. Javat told him to take two glasses into the next room. As MacGregor sipped the hot sweet liquid, Javat asked him if they would influence the English Government in any way when they returned. Influence them about Azerbaijan.

"Yes," MacGregor said. "This Ambassador has great influence."

"Why does he want to see the Governor?" It was a private question now.

MacGregor avoided it. "It may be educational for us to see the Governor," he said.

Javat dismissed the idea with a slight lift of the mouth. "This Governor is a cowardly man. You can learn nothing from him. He will surrender and weep the tears of Allah when he knows that we have enough strength to take him. Your Ambassador does not intend to encourage him?"

"My Ambassador does not speak Persian," MacGregor said.

"Your assistance in settling this dispute may save time and human life." Javat held his chin. "We wish to finish with this nonsense and get on with other affairs in the district. We have a great deal to do."

323

MacGregor wanted to know exactly what Javat had to do; but it seemed a ridiculous question because no answer could tell MacGregor the task which faced this man. MacGregor asked instead how long it would take to institute the reforms. He had no sooner mentioned the question of time than he realized that this was equally stupendous.

"It will take some years." Javat was not overwhelmed by it. "It is not simply a matter of distributing land and correcting the administration. We must educate our entire population, from the oldest to the youngest. They will never understand what is being done if they are not educated to it. We are a backward people, backward and illiterate and unhealthy and unsanitary and ignorant. All of this has been the strength of the shahs and the khans and the mullahs for a thousand years. Ignorance, filth, and opium; excellent weapons to maintain order and corrupt administration. Now we must change our entire mentality. We have grown to consider corruption and misrule an inevitable part of our lives. Now we must do away with a thousand years of indoctrination to evil and poverty and inequality and robbery and murder — all of which we have considered normal in our political affairs. Not only that, we must train officials and police who are not corrupt and brutal, something we have never known in Iran. There is also the fight we must begin for sanitary conditions. You must know our country, because you speak its language; therefore you will know of the disease, the poverty, and the wretchedness of the people. We must institute first the economic reform which will change these terrible conditions. Then we must attack it for what it is, with new ideas, and with education for sanitation and health and preventative arrangements. We must also wipe out the large opium habits of the population. More than 50 per cent of our population here are opium addicts, even the children. Our children are our first consideration: seven in ten die before they reach the age of ten years. We must reduce that to a normal level, and we must provide families with good clothing and good housing and good economic conditions. It will not be easy because we have not forced ourselves forward by revolution. We have not passed any laws which will do away with landlordism altogether. Nor have we socialized our industries and our national wealth. We are doing this according to the rescripts of our democratically elected Assembly. That means we must proceed without sharp delineations. A great deal of what we must achieve is new to us, and in that we must seek help from the technicians of more advanced countries: like your own. You can see that it will take some years."

"Do you have any experienced men at all?" MacGregor was trying to understand the matter-of-fact approach of Javat, who presented the world-shaking problem of changing and reforming Azerbaijan as simply a task of application.

"None," said Javat.

"And yourself?"

"I am an engineer."

"Are you a Communist?"

Javat moistened his lips. "I am a member of the Democratic Party," he said.

"These are peculiar questions because they are details which must be known. You will understand that my inquisitiveness is official, and that I do not intend impoliteness."

"Politeness is a drop of honey in a pool of bitter words." Javat shook his head. "A man can value understanding more. Can you understand us, Englishman?"

"I believe so."

"You have lived in Iran long?"

"For most of my life." MacGregor saved him the questions. "I am not a state official by profession," he said. "I am a geologist."

Javat interrupted. "A technician!" he said.

"Something like that."

"You estimate the earth, not so?"

"Yes."

"You have worked in Azerbaijan, or simply for the English oil company?"

"My father has worked here a great deal, and I did so when I was younger. Your maps probably have much that he surveyed and investigated."

"We have heard that there is wealth in our mountains: iron, steel, and coal, all of which remains undiscovered and unworked. Is that true?"

"There are some mineral resources in the Zagros and the Elburz."

"Enough for great industries to rise here?"

"I'm not sure." MacGregor wanted to smile, but Javat's intensity prevented him. "There is probably some coal and iron and copper and I believe tin. I don't know what you could do with them, but they are there alright."

"Do you know if we have men in Tabriz who can estimate the earth so casually and so well as you do?"

"Certainly."

"Would you have time to look about the district and tell me more? Is it difficult and complicated?"

"There should be maps which could tell you."

"We are not properly organized, and I doubt if maps can tell me all that I would need to know. Would you have time?"

MacGregor shook his head slowly. "I don't think so."

Javat subsided a little. "I expect too much."

"No," said MacGregor, "but is it so pressing?"

"We have much to do."

"But you couldn't do much," MacGregor said incredulously. "It's an enormous job."

"We could begin," Javat said.

"It's more complicated than that. You're an engineer. You know you can't start mining and industry without machinery and technicians. You can't do it with the peasants from the fields."

"We have no choice," Javat said.

MacGregor shook his head. He did not know whether Javat really understood the size of the undertaking he was so intent on beginning. If he did understand it, then MacGregor had never met a man like him before. Was this the way that reforms were introduced? By men who ignored the height of the wall they must climb? MacGregor did not know whether to laugh or admire. This was something new and something worth pursuing.

MacGregor had so much to find out from Javat that half an hour of further questioning covered little ground. They were interrupted by the arrival of a captain. "Most Favoured Captain" Javat titled him in his polite introduction.

He seemed to justify his title. He was a mild man, small, cheerful, with blue eyes and a halo of thin grey hair. He used such polite Persian forms in his conversation that MacGregor had to interrupt him with the necessary corrections of verbs and pronouns to contradict formally the Captain's self-effacing modesty. MacGregor guessed him to be of the official class whose habits were more elaborate than the simple needs of Javat. He was probably a civil servant from Tabriz.

The Captain told them that the letter had been delivered, but nobody had attempted to acknowledge it except by an exchange of shots. If the Ambassador wanted to go up the road he had better go now because they had heard the Governor's men removing some of the barrels from the road, in expectancy of a car.

"Is it safe?" Javat asked him.

"Nothing is safe," the Captain replied with a shrug. "But if the Pillar of Light wishes to reach the Governor, he had better do so now."

MacGregor got Essex and Katherine who were awake and talking. Javat told MacGregor he would go with them as far as their own road block. He put on his cap and followed them into the wet darkness to the Ford, where Aladin was now dozing on the front seat. Essex awakened him and got in the back seat after Katherine. MacGregor sat with them. The Captain (saluting Katherine) and Javat sat in front. They told Aladin in Persian to proceed up the road, but carefully and without lights. They would tell him when to stop.

326

"Is this Javat coming all the way?" Essex asked MacGregor.

"I don't think so. We ought to see the Governor first." But MacGregor asked Javat anyway.

Javat thought for a moment, but it was the Captain who vetoed the suggestion. He said that the Governor would hold Javat as hostage, so MacGregor told Essex that they didn't like the idea.

"Alright," said Essex, "but how is he going to talk to this Governor if he doesn't come in there? Ask him if he will come should I send for him."

"He says he will come if you send the car back and indicate that the Governor is willing to talk with him."

They were stopped before the road block by firing. The Captain and Javat got out of the car and ran forward to a barbed-wire trestle which MacGregor could see on the road ahead. The shooting was very close, and MacGregor got out and followed Javat to the barricade where two soldiers watched opposite sides of the road.

"It is dangerous," Javat said again. "They are shooting all along the road."

"What in Heaven's name are they shooting at?" MacGregor looked ahead at the muddy road.

"Shadows," said the Captain.

"We'll take a chance," MacGregor told them. "How far up is their barricade?"

"About five hundred paces."

"Can you move this wire now?"

"Whenever you wish," the Captain told him.

"You might as well do it now," MacGregor said. "We'll turn the lights on and drive fast. How is the road?"

"The same as the one you have travelled." Javat stood up from his crouching position. "I will stay here. We will do our best to reach you if something goes wrong." They exchanged formal expressions of departure, and MacGregor went back to the car thinking of Katherine.

"You will have to stay here Kathy," he said to her. "They will probably take pot-shots at us. Don't you think it would be better?" he said to Essex.

"No," Katherine said. "That's ridiculous." She was immediately angry.

"How safe will she be here?" Essex asked.

"Absolutely safe. Are you afraid to stay with Javat, Katherine?"

"Certainly not, but I prefer to go with you."

"It's probably better if you keep out of this," Essex told her. "Are you sure she is absolutely safe back here?"

"It's as safe as the British Embassy itself," MacGregor said.

"I think it's better, Kathy. I'm sorry." Essex put his arm around her shoulder and gave her a friendly hug.

MacGregor opened the door for her and Katherine got out silently. She still objected to being left behind, but she was obviously determined to make no embarrassing fuss about it. MacGregor took her to Javat and explained that she was remaining here until they came back for her. Javat nodded and said he would take her back to the house.

"For Heaven's sake don't leave me here all night," she said. She bent forward and put the side of her face against MacGregor's ear.

MacGregor sat in the front seat with Aladin and told him to turn on his lights and go like the devil and watch the pot-holes in the road. They did not want to crack up in the middle of this amateurish no-man's-land. As they started, MacGregor turned around to look at Essex. Essex was sitting erect, and MacGregor knew that Essex had calculated this as clearly as he calculated everything. He would not be shot at, because he was an Englishman, and if they did shoot they would miss him anyway. It was only the bumping of the Ford which broke Essex's posture, he had to grip the front seat to hold himself in position as Aladin drove the car in quick curves around the hazards of the road.

As the road curved and the trees cleared and the lights lit their path ahead, they saw another road block, of barrels. MacGregor listened for any firing, but the Ford's engine made too much noise. He sat with his head bent a little, ready to drop down if something happened. He could not see if there was a passage through the barrels and it was not until they were almost on them that the narrow passage became visible. Aladin did not slow down but scraped the car through the passage.

Then the movement began.

Mounted men came in on them from both sides. Aladin slowed down to avoid hitting them, and running men jumped on the car and told Aladin to keep going until he reached a large gate. The mounted riders galloped beside them, still shouting. A soldier on the running-board put his head in and looked carefully at MacGregor and showed the nose of his rifle over the door. They were stopped at a large brick gate, and were told to get out by a tall man in polished boots. They were immediately crowded by soldiers and by mounted men. The man in polished boots told Aladin that he would remain here, and ordered MacGregor and Essex to walk to the house. He was brusque and authoritative, and MacGregor knew him to be a regular army officer by his bearing and his manner and his boots.

MacGregor was separated from Essex by several soldiers, and they were both swept quickly along the gravelled path through a row of cypresses, black in the moonlight, fringing a wide and beautiful garden. MacGregor could see the house ahead of them, a traditionally low, square, large Persian villa with two marble stairways leading up to its verandah. They were halted at the steps as the officer felt MacGregor's coat for weapons and then gripped his arm while he turned to shout at the mounted men to get back to the road. He called them clumsy uncircumsized dogs for riding on the garden.

With some of this bucolic anger the officer gave MacGregor a light push up the steps so that MacGregor fell lightly on his hands. He straightened up and said in Persian direct from the English. "I'll break your neck if you man-handle me like that again." He used the familiar form as an insult.

The officer obviously contemplated kicking MacGregor in the groin. Even in the moonlit darkness MacGregor could see him poised for the action, but he stopped and shouted and cursed again and called on Allah to send a thunderbolt to strike this unbeliever down.

"For such foulness and profanity," MacGregor said, feeling the sickness of anger, "I can only hope that you are buried unwashed and that you are blinded so that you can never behold your Shiah paradise."

"In the name of God! I should kill you for such insults."

"What are you shouting about?" Essex said.

"This fool is man-handling me and I am objecting to it."

"Good," said Essex. "I had to crack one of these fellows. Tell him if he doesn't stop this insulting behaviour I'll go right back and leave this Governor to his fate. Tell him."

"I will not flatter him that much," MacGregor said. "Now you might understand why there is trouble up here."

"Never mind the moralizing. I've put up with enough for one day."

"You're putting up with a lot for this Governor."

"I have something to do," Essex spoke calmly, "and I'm not going to argue with you here and now. Come along." He walked up the steps behind the officer, who was furiously whacking his long sword against his boots. "We'll settle this with the Governor. And lower your voice MacGregor. Remember you are an Englishman."

"English be damned," MacGregor said. "I'm not going to sacrifice good Persian insults for the sake of being English."

"Alright, alright." Essex preceded him inside the ornamental front door and then passed through dark carpet-hung partitions to a small reception room. It was lit by a petrol lamp and it was furnished with worn Louis furniture. Trays, divans, cushions, photographs, praying mats, coloured glass ornaments, and gew-gaws overcrowded the room. The officer said Wait. He left two soldiers at the door as he went out.

"There's something brutal about that man," Essex said of the officer.

"What do you expect?" MacGregor was still angry.

"Calm down young man," Essex said. "We have a lot to do."

A servant in a frock coat and a felt skull cap — a *kulah* — opened a door behind them. He bowed very low and said *Excellencies please enter this way*. Essex marched ahead of MacGregor, his dignity established by the correct amount of prepared indignation. MacGregor felt his own inadequacy, being unable to pose, and unable to calm his anger. It was only when they were in the large well-lit room that MacGregor appreciated the humour of their situation. The room was empty, and their entrance had been wasted.

"I must say I'm putting up with a great deal," Essex slapped his hips with his pigskin gloves. "Where the devil is this fellow?"

A thick curtain of beads parted, and a plump headbowing man with a broad smile came in. He was wearing a white waistcoat and his boots were topped with grey spats. Holding his golden fingers together, he pressed them to his spacious diaphragm as he murmured the formal welcome and stated the necessary humilities. MacGregor guessed he was not the Governor, but Essex addressed him as the Governor because if he wasn't the Governor, he damned well ought to be the Governor.

"What sort of behaviour is this!" Essex spoke in English with insistence that the man understand it or go to Hades. "It might be appropriate for you to rough-handle your servants, sir, but when you are foolish enough to insult our person and our official position by sending thugs to escort us here, I must say that you are asking for trouble, and you probably deserve the miserable end you are about to suffer. Do you understand that?"

MacGregor did not wait to see if the round smiling man would understand. He took delight in translating Essex's anger into Persian. He added strength to it by utilizing the refinements of the language. He was satisfied when the happy man's face tightened into proper seriousness.

"I am not the Governor," the man said in Persian. "I am Ghazan-i-Manjil, the Chief of Police of this district, and I am thoroughly confused by what you say. I don't know where to hide my face." The Chief of Police was catching his breath to show his astonishment. "What beasts could have shown you such impoliteness! We gave instructions that you must be received with the utmost official politeness. We were deeply grieved that we could not arrange for an *Istikbal,* an official entry. I can only beg your pardon and assure you that the wretches who were responsible will be horsewhipped and thoroughly beaten. Your Excellency must consider himself too lofty to be troubled by such ignorant and stupid louts who are not human at all but simply brainless idiots whose mothers could be dogs and apes. They will be punished severely. In the meantime we offer you our entire household, which we consider unworthy of your honoured presence and inadequate for the regal importance of

330

your person. I will take you immediately to the Governor." Breathlessly the Chief of Police waved a half-dozen armed men aside and plunged through the bead curtains ahead of Essex and MacGregor. MacGregor was translating literally everything the Chief of Police had said, and Essex felt a little better until MacGregor told him it was the polite language of a hypocrite.

They were taken into an official reception chamber, a long and narrow room. Running down the middle of it were two long inlaid tables, white and black in the shadow of the high petrol lamp above. The tables were packed with glass dishes and round globes and draped wine-bottles and mosaics of coloured China. At the end of the room under a latticed window sat the Governor.

He was dressed in a black coat which reached his knees and he sat erect, with a silver-topped walking stick held in his right hand. He was black-haired and black-bearded, although he looked too old for such colour to be real. Behind him were more than a dozen men. They sat and stood silently as MacGregor walked up the long carpet to the Governor.

MacGregor and Essex had to mount two steps to reach him and he stood as they reached the last step. He did not bow nor incline his head but immediately addressed Essex in meticulous Persian which MacGregor found carefully assembled and well delivered. It was the same address of formal welcome and obeisance to a guest: the house was humble and inadequate and it was already lit up by their presence. There were apologies for the surroundings and the times, and curses for the worthless creatures who had besieged him in his house and robbed him of his jurisdiction and property and appointed rights. As he finished, and before MacGregor had time to translate, the Chief of Police interrupted and unfolded the statement of Essex about their reception, stating to the Governor that he had already ordered those responsible to be whipped and beaten. The Governor repeated the curses on such beasts and re-stated the apologies. He sat down and looked at the two Englishmen and said in slow English, "Do you understand what I have said?"

"Yes," Essex replied. "I can guess what you have said."

"I am apologizing," the Governor said and looked at Essex with authority. He was a man of natural dignity and forceful bearing, and his voice was commanding as he asked them to be seated. They sat on gilded chairs facing him. MacGregor noticed that Essex was pacified by the Governor's civilized appearance.

"You know who I am?" Essex began.

"We are honoured to know you by the letter," the Governor said in English.

"You know of my mission to Azerbaijan?" Essex had built up his voice into equal authority. MacGregor admired his ability to see the needs of the moment.

"As it is written here, I know of it. We praise God that you have arrived safely. You have seen how we are beseiged by a great force of Russians and other enemies of religion."

"We know your situation," Essex said, "but we have come a long way to-day. We have come from Teheran, and we did not come prepared for these circumstances. However, I think that our comforts can wait until we have discussed this situation further with you."

MacGregor did not know whether Essex knew the strength of the reprimand he was delivering the Governor in referring to their comforts. The Governor took it at its face value and banged his walking stick on the floor and called one of his retainers forward and told him in Persian to see that the chambers prepared for the guests were heated, aired, and well supplied with necessities and servants. He then insisted to Essex that they rest immediately and wash the dust of travel off their tired skins, and also eat before deigning to assist this miserable self.

"It will be much simpler," Essex said without moving, "if we settle a few details first. Perhaps you would like to tell me something of the situation here."

"Then we must make you more comfortable." The Governor rose. The retainers and the scribes dispersed as the Governor waved his hand. One whispered to the Governor, but MacGregor could not hear what he was saying. The Governor caught MacGregor's intent eyes. "You speak the dialect?" he said in Turki. MacGregor looked stupid and the Governor rubbed his nose and stepped off the dais and preceded Essex and MacGregor through his entourage to an anteroom, where he seated them in large leather chairs and called for coffee and wine and sat down in a high-armed throne-like wooden chair, while two servants stood behind him against the wall.

"It is a long time since I have spoken English," the Governor began. "I spoke it a great deal at the Court of the late Shah, who admired the English language and insisted that we speak it. But in five years of my life here I have had little occasion to use it, except to read the English weekly newspaper called the *Sphere*. You will therefore forgive my clumsiness."

"Your English is excellent," Essex said. "My assistant, Mr. MacGregor, will be saved a great deal of translating." MacGregor smiled because he could see that Essex was not going to be talked down to. There was something of a contest between Essex and the Governor on this issue, which Essex would win. MacGregor knew that much already.

"You speak Persian?" the Governor said to MacGregor.

"A little," MacGregor said.

"He speaks fluent Persian," Essex said. "His modesty is misplaced."

The Governor ignored Essex's boast. "We are most interested in how you came through Zenjan to here." The Governor concentrated on Essex. "Did you have some kind of authority with the Russians or the rebels who surround us?"

"We had no trouble," Essex said. "I am in Azerbaijan at the suggestion of Marshal Stalin, therefore I have no difficulty." Essex took coffee from a servant who held a tray.

"Did you see anything of the disposition of their forces?" the Governor asked.

"We are not particularly interested in such information. I am more interested in what you have to say about this situation here."

"The situation is our tragedy," the Governor said. "We are surrounded by Russians on one side, and by rebels on the other. I have at my disposal some two thousand loyal troops and police, and a hundred of my peasants who are ready to resist all attacks. Our forces are inferior to our enemy's because the Russians have brought up tanks, guns, and even aeroplanes. We are only holding out by the superiority of our magnificent courage."

"Where are the Russian troops?" Essex asked him.

"They face us to the south." The Governor waved an arm to indicate their large numbers and their direction.

"How do you know they're Russians?" MacGregor said.

"We have captured several of their men."

"We may see them?" MacGregor began.

"Never mind," Essex interrupted. "What do you hope to achieve by this magnificent resistance?"

"We hope to maintain resistance long enough for the rest of the world to understand what is happening in Azerbaijan and come to our assistance, as indeed you have at this moment. We are a handful of men here, holding out against all the forces which the Bolsheviki hurl upon us. We are men who feel our responsibilities enough to resist as martyrs all Russian interference in our affairs. A lesson for the rest of the world, Your Excellency. We are fighting the world's battle and it is in the interests of our British friends to appreciate the Russian danger as we do. That is why we have hoped for help before it is too late."

"What about your peasants and your population?"

"They are loyal to me and to the Shah," the Governor said. "The forces attacking us are Russian, led by a Russian general of great experience. If there are Azerbaijanians among the rebels, then they are thuggees, murderers, and political criminals whom the Russians released from the jails. A few of my people might have been led astray by promises of loot, but my peasants here are loyal and will resist to the last man. We are willing to martyr ourselves now to show the world its responsibilities and its real enemy."

"Are you sure you are martyrs?" Essex said.

The Governor almost stood up, but he needed no dramatic effect. His bearded face and black countenance and the way his hands were folded on the top of the walking stick were evidence enough of his determination and his courage. "I am a Shiah," he said, "and I am a Persian. What is a life compared to belief in the blood which creates it!"

Essex had lit his pipe, and he folded his fingers over the stem and stretched his legs. "Martyrdom is a worthy method of defending a principle," he said, "and if you feel that this is the only way to defend your principles then I will do nothing to dissuade you."

"I am only interested in my people and my country," the Governor said with dignity. "If another course of action will achieve more, then I would willingly sacrifice my principles for the higher good."

"Ah." Essex had taken it all with flat acceptance, and MacGregor was waiting to see what would come next. MacGregor had watched Essex working up to something, and he knew it was due now. "Of course your martyrdom is your own affair," Essex went on, "but I would like to point out that you are not alone in this struggle for the preservation of your independence. Great Britain is aware of your plight, and we have taken it upon ourselves to preserve Iranian independence, whatever the cost. For that reason I have just been to Moscow for my Government. My specific task was to halt the Russian interference in Iran, and to restore the authority of the Central Government in the province of Azerbaijan. That is still my mission. I am not on a wild-goose chase nor on a polite tour of inspection. I am here to preserve whatever it is possible to preserve of Iranian independence."

"Excellent," said the Governor in delight.

"With this clearly in mind, I feel that any martyrdom of your forces at this moment is a trifle unnecessary and wasteful. You would do better to preserve what you can of your authority, your establishment, your influence, and your strength. Though the situation may look hopeless at the moment, there will be a time in the near future when your existence will be of greater value than your martyrdom. Need I say more?" Essex did not seem to be as interested in the Governor as he was in MacGregor who was watching him carefully, his thin face expressionless but his eyes suspicious and his ears pink. It was the Governor who looked at both of them and smiled a little.

"I place myself in your hands," he said to Essex, bowing his head.

"I don't want you in my hands," Essex replied with annoyance, looking away from MacGregor. "This is your affair."

"What do you suggest?" the Governor raised his hands in appeal.

"Get that fellow here whom you haven't mentioned yet. Talk to him."

"What fellow?" the Governor frowned.

"What's his name, MacGregor?"

"Javat Gochali."

The Governor pushed the air forward with his throat. "That man is a Russian agent and a traitor, an enemy of religion and a union agitator. He is an animal, a mongrel to say the least. He has seized the lands and the town. He seeks only to loot my home, steal my property, and hang me from my own verandah post. *Ghasam*! I will not cross my breath with his."

Essex rose. "You are obviously intent upon self-sacrifice," he said. "In that case I can do nothing more for you, and I am wasting my valuable time."

The Governor was agitated, but he persuaded Essex to sit down again. He raised his hands. "What else can I say of this man, Your Excellency? He is everything I say he is."

"That may be so, but he's got you in a corner."

"But you cannot trust him."

"What harm can he do by coming here?" Essex said disgustedly.

"I am not afraid for my person," the Governor protested forcefully, "but if I am to talk to him it means some form of compromise, and I cannot take his word on anything."

"Then take mine," Essex said. "I will see that he talks fairly. I can give you my word on that. If that doesn't satisfy you then I can do nothing more."

"What can I hope to achieve by talking to him?"

"You can hold onto some of your property and no doubt some of your establishment. I suppose you will be deposed as Governor, but that is not important. Your only hope is to save what you can, and the only way to do it is to talk with this man. He is obviously powerful, and everything seems to depend on him."

"He impresses you with such importance?" the Governor asked incredulously.

"He doesn't impress me at all," Essex said, "but it is obvious that he is one of the ringleaders of this dispute. If you don't talk to him he is going to come in here and throw you out. You have little choice."

"You are right." The Governor clapped his hands. "I will send for him."

Essex interrupted him. "They don't trust you any more than you trust them," he said. "I will send for him. I have already arranged it. He will come here on my word as an Englishman for his personal safety. Is that understood?"

"Of course," said the Governor.

"Do I have your word on that?"

"Naturally!" The Governor touched his forehead.

"Then I will send for him. If you have my driver brought in I will instruct him. I would also like to send for my other assistant."

"Please!"

"My assistant is a young lady," Essex said carefully, in warning. "I cannot risk her being treated as we were treated in coming here. Will that happen again?"

"I have already had those men who mishandled you punished and beaten," the Governor said. "There will be no repetition of that, I promise you."

"Alright," Essex said. "Get my driver."

"First I will have you escorted to your chambers and you may speak with him there in privacy. I will personally arrange the safe-conduct of your car." The Governor rose and indicated two men who had been waiting at the door. The Governor bowed and told Essex and MacGregor to follow them.

They were taken outside and along a tiled path, white with wet moonlight. It cut through a garden of hedges and flowers and small trees. The garden was walled in on both sides; but through the onion arches in the walls MacGregor could make out the shape of horses tethered on one side. They also passed a pool, and beyond it they entered a small house. A long covered corridor connected it with the large house, a corridor they were obviously not supposed to use.

The house was prepared for them. It was small and warm. A servant indicated their luggage on the floor of the sitting room and bowed out. Essex dropped his gloves and coat on a deal table. MacGregor knelt to see if his suitcase was intact. It was still locked and untouched.

"You had better go back with Aladin," Essex said, breaking MacGregor's deliberate silence. "That fellow will not take Aladin's word for anything, and I want you to see that Kathy is unharmed."

MacGregor shook his head. "It's no use bringing Javat Gochali here," he began.

"Why not?"

"These people want to get hold of him. That's obvious."

"They can't do much if we're here with him," Essex argued. "What good will it do them if they harm him?"

"Persian Governors are great believers in hostages," MacGregor said. "This one is no exception."

"I have given my word on Gochali's safety. Just get him here, I'll be responsible for the rest of it."

MacGregor said No. "I can't tell him to come. I would sooner tell him to keep well away from here. Kathy also."

"Do you think they dare harm anyone while we're here? What's the matter with you?"

"I don't feel your impulse to preserve the existence of this sort of man," MacGregor said. "You don't seem to understand what is happening here at all."

"I know enough of what is happening," Essex said. "I'm not as stupid as you seem to think. Your ideas are not always very sensible, my dear MacGregor. There is not much use letting your superficial views of this little incident decide your actions. Our decisions are governed by the larger issue, and that is my understanding of what is happening. Always remember that. This petty nonsense going on here is unimportant in itself; its real importance is its shape in what we are here for."

"I leave that to you," MacGregor said, "but I'm not going to tell Javat Gochali to walk into this trap." MacGregor took off his coat. "Katherine is also better where she is," he repeated.

"I'm amazed at my patience," Essex raised his hands. "It's just as well I respect your motives, MacGregor. I shall go back myself."

"Then I'll go along with you," MacGregor said and they turned silently to inspecting their luggage while they waited for Aladin.

When Aladin came he was no longer fierce in countenance. He was scared and worried and surprised by all that was happening to him. When he saw Essex and MacGregor his large eyes filled with tears. "I thought they had murdered you," he said. "I have been locked up and guarded by soldiers. I don't know what has happened to the car. I'm sorry for that, but they took me away with guns at my back."

"That's alright," Essex said soothingly.

"I have been locked up," Aladin said, "and I think they were preparing to whip me. They were asking me about the rebels."

"Nonsense," said Essex. "They would not dare harm you." He gave Aladin his coat to hold while he got into it. "We are going back for Miss Clive and Gochali," Essex told him. MacGregor picked up his own coat and followed them into the garden.

They were escorted again by two soldiers to the Ford. It stood where they had left it, and five men were sitting in it. They were ordered out by the officer, who came up behind MacGregor.

"There's the man the Governor pronounced punished and beaten," MacGregor told Essex. "Let's see how he behaves this time."

The officer kept away from them and turned his back as they stepped into the car. He shouted something at the mounted horsemen, and he stepped on the running-board near MacGregor. They drove slowly to the barrels of the road block. There he jumped off. The barrels were parted and they went through the gap. MacGregor leaned out, half-expecting the officer to spring a trap on them, but as Aladin switched on the lights and picked up speed, there was no ambush and no firing. They came safely to Javat's road block and Aladin drove as fast as he could down the lurching road to the house.

Katherine was waiting for them. She shouted to ask them if they were alright.

"We're alright," MacGregor said.

"We heard them shooting when you went in," she said. "We thought you might have been hurt. They sent somebody to find out, but they didn't come back. Did they actually shoot at you?" She stood between them and held them both.

"No. No," Essex said, as they entered the sorrowful house. "They're a little too free with their ammunition, nothing more. I came back to bring you along with us so that you can have a decent meal and a decent bed to sleep in. MacGregor came to tell you to stay here."

"Oh nonsense Ivre," Katherine said.

"Here's the gentleman I want to see." Essex and Javat met in the room of yellow light.

"Mr. Gochali speaks some German," Katherine said. "We've been having quite a long talk. Isn't that so?" she said to him in English.

Javat smiled seriously, a little embarrassed.

"Do you really speak German?" Essex said in that tongue.

"*Ein bisschen,*" Javat said. "*Nicht genug zu verstehen alles.*"

"*Das ist genug,*" Essex said and watched MacGregor as he told Javat about the Governor. Essex explained how he had arranged some kind of compromise, giving his own word for Javat's safety. Javat did not understand because Essex made no attempt to simplify the rhetoric or the grammar. Javat turned to MacGregor. It would be better if MacGregor explained it in Persian.

"He wants you to go with him to the Governor," MacGregor told Javat. "He talked the Governor into agreeing to speak to you, by pointing out that he should try and save some of his establishment instead of losing it all."

"What did the Governor say?"

"He swore he would never speak with you; but he changed his mind. He will speak with you, but only with the purpose of saving what he can of his own belongings and authority."

"That is natural," Javat said, "but it will not be my consideration. I am only interested in establishing the new administration and preventing a battle."

"You warned us that this Governor is treacherous," MacGregor reminded him.

"Yes he is."

"He was interested in your importance. I think he may want to make a hostage of you. A hostage against his own safety."

338

Javat shrugged. "It's worth the risk."

"I advise you not to go," MacGregor said.

"What are you saying to him MacGregor?" Essex said.

"I'm telling him that you want him to go, and I'm advising him not to go."

Essex interrupted in German, this time simplifying it enough. "It is on my word for your safety that you come with me," Essex said. "If you wish to settle this without a struggle, then this is your opportunity."

Javat nodded. "I will come," he said and began rolling up maps.

"Do you want to come, MacGregor, or do you want to stay here?" Essex said.

MacGregor was stung. "I'm coming," he said. "I want to see how you manipulate this."

"Kathy?" Essex said.

"Of course! Aren't you being a little high-strung about it?" she said to MacGregor. "It's not like you at all."

"He's disturbed because they were rather tough with us for a while," Essex taunted MacGregor. "I hope you are sorry you smashed that weapon this morning."

MacGregor had learned enough disrespect to ignore Essex. He ignored both of them and helped Javat with his maps and his documents.

Chapter 27

Having taken away MacGregor's temporary ascendancy, Essex hustled his entourage into position. The Governor met them in the reception room, surrounded by his Chief of Police, his Mayors, his Lords of the Villages, his personal bodyguard — and his Colonel of Troops, who had welcomed them roughly once but not again. The Governor sat at a small table and faced Javat. With Javat sat his Most Favoured Captain, the little Tabrizi, who had insisted on coming as some kind of support and protection for Javat. Behind them and away from the table, Essex and MacGregor and Katherine sat and listened to the Governor, who stared angrily at the two men who faced him.

The Governor began the negotiations by addressing Javat in Persian. "You are a traitor, a usurper, an enemy of religion, and a desperado. You are paid by the Russians, and you have sacrificed your birthright for their gold and their patronage. I am accursed to have you seated in my house, and the chair on which you sit will be burnt when you leave. How dare you sit there in pretence of equal place and with lifted eyes. Down to the floor, and I will kick you. Prostrate yourself before me now and I will save your head and forgive your impertinence in coming here. Dog."

In the stillness that followed Javat said: "If you have finished we might begin."

This brought another outburst from the Governor.

Javat ignored it and spread his maps on the table. "I have maps of the district here," he told the Governor, "and I will begin by pointing out our intentions and how they will affect your own lands."

The Governor's fist smashed down on the table. "You sit there like a lord and think that I will speak with you as an equal," the Governor roared. "I will order you beaten. I will cut out your tongue for such insults."

Javat waited.

"Must I suffer this in my own house?" the Governor went on. "Must I have this man spoiling the air I breathe? Must I sit patiently while he produces maps to tell me what I must do with my land?"

Javat looked at MacGregor and raised his hands in hopeless gesture.

MacGregor wondered how he had put up with the insults this long. "We did not bring this man here to be insulted," MacGregor said to the Governor. "We brought him here to arrange some kind of compromise. If you insult him again you will insult the Ambassador. If it goes on we will leave immediately."

"Am I to bear this wretch's impertinence; the way he sits there?"

"Is he to bear your insults?" MacGregor replied.

"I should strike him down."

"Do you want to wait any longer?" MacGregor asked Gochali.

"No," said the Most Favoured Captain with the blue eyes. He stood up. "If this is why we came, Englishmen, then your good intentions have been wasted. We will not submit to such indignities. We can settle this by other means."

Essex by now was impatient. "What's all this about?" He had to pull MacGregor by the sleeve to have himself heard.

"The Governor is trying to scare them into submission by insults. Javet hasn't had a chance to say anything yet because the Governor's abuse is a little more than a man can stand. Do you want to do something about it?"

"Tell them to get on with it and stop shouting."

"Speak to the Governor," MacGregor said. "He's the man."

Essex leaned back to put some nonchalance into the atmosphere. "I don't know who is insulting who," he said to the Governor, "but if either side resorts to insults then I will call the whole thing off. You might translate that for Gochali, MacGregor."

"The insults came from the other side," MacGregor said.

"Tell him anyway, as fair warning."

340

MacGregor told Javat who unrolled his maps and began again. The Governor kept quiet. "Before anything else is discussed," Javat said. "It must be understood that the organized force which is resisting the authority of the Azerbaijan Administration must be surrendered. That is the first step to any arrangement between us."

The Governor called upon God to give him patience.

"As a force, it will be disbanded," Javat went on, "and its regular officers sent back to Teheran, with other officials who were sent here by the Teheran Government."

"Excellency," the Governor said in English. "Must this be forced upon me? This man is offering terms like a conqueror."

"What did Gochali ask, MacGregor?"

"He said they would first have to discuss the disbanding of the Governor's army before anything else could be arranged."

"Tell Gochali that he must present all his terms before that can be agreed to. That is fair bargaining."

"I doubt if Javat is in a bargaining mood," MacGregor said.

"At least he has to present all his terms before the Governor can agree to surrender," Essex insisted.

MacGregor explained it to Javat who talked with his Captain.

"I will present the terms," Javat said. "But there can be no terms unless this army and this force is disbanded, and our authority implemented. You will be able to keep your house," he said to the Governor, "and your gardens and a limited amount of land, enough to maintain yourself but no more. We have decided that the rest of the land will be given to the peasants and the small holders whom you have ruled so brutally with your police and your army."

"I could cut off my ears for hearing such insults. What impertinence. What misery!"

"What now?" Essex watched the Governor's face swell and explode.

"It's hopeless," MacGregor said. "Gochali states his terms but the Governor considers every word an insult. Perhaps you could calm him down again?"

"I'm getting tired of this," Essex said. "What's the matter with them. Don't they know how to conduct a discussion of this sort?"

"They are not diplomats," MacGregor said, "and nothing will be achieved as long as the Governor finds it impossible to address Gochali as anything but a slave and a dog."

"Well, let Gochali address you, and you can address the Governor," Essex said to MacGregor.

"No sir," MacGregor said with surprising heat.

"Don't you two start arguing," Katherine whispered. "You are being watched rather carefully by that collection of ruffians over there."

"This whole affair is ridiculous." Essex looked sternly at the Governor. "Let Gochali state what he wants, and you state your answer. That is all that is required," Essex said impatiently.

"He wants my ruination," the Governor cried.

"Do you want to refuse his terms?" Essex asked.

"I ask you, Your Excellency! Must I submit myself to the orders of a beggar and a traitor?"

"Do you have any alternative in mind?" Essex said.

"We will resist."

"And that is your answer?"

The Governor raised his head and breathed heavily. "I cannot embarrass you by such an answer, since you were gracious enough to arrange this discussion in some attempt to preserve our integrity. I will try again, Excellency. I will try again."

"Give it another go, MacGregor," Essex said. "Start them up again."

"It would be simpler and more appropriate if I spoke with the Russian general who is really in command," the Governor said to MacGregor in Persian. It was a more subtle blow at Javat. "Perhaps you could persuade him to come here."

Javat was finally stung. "There are no Russians with our forces," he shouted at the Governor. "We are all of Azerbaijan, unlike thee, who comes from the south, born a Luri khan and a youngest son and parcelled up here to make your own fortune by your own corruption."

"You yourself are from the clownland to the north!" the Governor roared.

"I am of Zenjan and all my fathers before me," Javat cried.

"You are a traitor. You are threatening me with Tartars from Siberia and Mongols from China; with Russian artillery and tanks and machines. Traitor."

"*Agha* MacGregor," Javat turned around. "I invite you and your Ambassador to come with me now, to travel wherever you wish about the district. Should you find a Russian among us, other than those upon the main highway with the road blocks, then I will submit myself to your jurisdiction."

"Betrayer!" The Governor's hand shot forward to Javat who stood back away from it. The men behind the Governor shouted at Javat. The Most Favoured Captain stood and shouted back at them.

"Stop them," Katherine said to MacGregor. "Something will happen."

Essex clapped his hands and stood forward and hit the table with his open palm and said in English: "Gentlemen!" They ignored him, and they all went on shouting, including MacGregor, who eventually shouted them all down.

342

Essex was now ready to abandon the whole affair. "I have had enough of this," he told them sharply. "If you want to talk you will have to learn to talk properly. What is the use of shouting at each other? I'll give you until to-morrow to cool off, and then I'll try once more. But no more shouting."

"It's hopeless unless you can persuade the Governor to change his attitude," MacGregor said. "To-morrow will be the same as to-day."

"To-morrow we will begin differently," Essex said. "I will see to that myself. But it is no use continuing now. Gochali can come back to-morrow if he wishes. What does he say?"

"He says he will take no more insults from the Governor," MacGregor told Essex. "He will return only if you guarantee a basis of equality in discussion."

"Alright. Alright." Essex stood up. "Send him back in the car. Tell Aladin to pick him up to-morrow morning some time. Now," Essex said to the Governor, "I would like to retire to my rooms."

They dispersed in grim silence, Essex following the Governor, Katherine waiting a moment with MacGregor. She did not like to see MacGregor so careless with himself; and to see him shouting and fighting had been most disappointing, most irritating as well. She had seen something in him which had taken MacGregor out of her world for a moment. A sane MacGregor could be handled, but not this one.

"Are you coming?" Katherine said to him.

"I'll just go back with Javat to see he gets there alright."

"Shall I come with you?" she said.

MacGregor shook his head. "I won't be long."

There were no farewells between the Governor and Javat. They faced each other for a moment of silence, then the Governor muttered that death was too good for the dog.

MacGregor took Javat and the Captain back in the Ford. They left him at their own road barrier and waited while Aladin turned the car around. They thanked MacGregor for escorting them and told him to be careful.

"I'll be back for you to-morrow morning," MacGregor said.

"No. Don't bother yourself," Javat said. "Just send your car."

"It's no bother," MacGregor told them. "I shall come myself."

They insisted that they could get there alright.

"As you say," MacGregor said and bade them good night.

When he was back at the Governor's estate, MacGregor made sure that Aladin had a place to sleep and then walked around the garden to the small house, escorted by two of the Governor's men. To annoy them he stopped near the tiled pool and found a couple of winter flowers to pluck and smell. Their flavour was outdone by the heavy aroma of spices and meat which met him in the small house. Katherine and Essex were already seated at a table laden with food.

"At last," Katherine said to him. "Harold insisted that we wait for you."

MacGregor gave her the flowers. "Go ahead and eat," he said.

"Have you ever seen so much food? You can tell us what all these dishes are. Come on, Ivre, I am starved."

He watched Katherine break the long stems of the flowers and put them in her tireless hair. She was dressed in a pink quilted dressing-gown which reached to her slippered feet. Her face was smooth and her pink lips were clean of lipstick. He noticed everything as he always did with Katherine, and he tried to estimate how this situation was affecting her. She had sat through the angry negotiations very quietly, as if it could never touch her personally. Yet she had her sympathies, and they were clearly with Javat. What she could not see was the wonder of the change they were watching. To see a man like Javat defying a governor and his army and demanding their surrender was almost too much even for MacGregor. Knowing Iran he had always expected revolt, and he had always believed the Iranians capable of revolt; but to see it in practice was so surprising that its significance was too great to understand immediately. He was a little unnerved by it, and yet caught up in it immediately. He did not draw back from taking part in these events. He was very much part of this situation.

"Did your friends get back alright?" Essex asked him.

"I left them at their road block."

"Good. Your things are in that room over there. We are doubling up if it's alright with you."

It was alright with MacGregor. He was in opposition to Essex, but he was not upset about it. Essex kept his political emotions out of their private affairs for the most part and MacGregor was learning to do the same. Essex would have to be watched, that was all.

"What are all these dishes?" Katherine asked him again.

He looked under the covers and found rice *pilau* and rice *chilau, kabab,* Persian omelettes, mutton with currants, *yoghurt* with honey, sweet-meats, iced sherbet, small chocolates, and in addition some thick red wine. He gave her the Persian names, but she was not really interested.

"After all that arguing we have earned the meal and the bed," Essex said as they ate. "These people are worse than children. They must be exactly the same to-day as they were a thousand years ago. Odd to think that they were the people who contested the Greeks. I always think of the Archaemenids and the Sassanids when I think of Persia, but I suppose I shall think otherwise now. I just can't connect these people with Cyrus and Darius. No. I am disillusioned, MacGregor." He poured wine from a red decanter. "Why, the very road we came up to-day was once the

344

Golden Road to Samarkand. Marco Polo must have travelled on it. Did you realize that, Kathy?"

Katherine shook her head. Her mouth was full.

"I suppose these unfortunate people never recovered from the ravages of Jenghiz Khan, who destroyed their irrigation system, something it had taken them 500 years to build. I think it was underground, wasn't it, MacGregor — some sort of artesian arrangement with complicated channels and wells? I know Jenghiz wrecked it and ruined the country. They have never recovered. And the Lord only knows who followed the Mongols. Russians, Tartars, Kurds, Arabs, Afghans, Turks. Were the Turks down this far, MacGregor? Would you know?"

"They were," MacGregor said. "But you left out the British. We were here when we were fighting the Bolsheviks after the last war."

"Of course," Essex said, "but that's not history yet. We built the railways didn't we? Only signs of improvement in the place."

Since Essex had mentioned railways MacGregor reminded him that the British had promised four years ago to complete a section of the Teheran–Tabriz line, to assist war supplies going to Russia, but had never done so. Essex said, Naturally: that would have connected Baku to the Persian Gulf by rail. The India Office had made sure that such a dangerous thing never happened. The line would remain unfinished unless these Azerbaijanian rebels completed it for the Russians.

"Give MacGregor some wine Kathy," Essex said to end it. "This is excellent. Is it a local product, MacGregor? Is this what they're fighting about?"

"I doubt it." MacGregor sipped the red wine. "It's probably Kuchan wine, or perhaps *Khullar* from Shiraz."

"Ah," said Essex. "I remember Gibbon writing that in every age the wines of Shiraz have triumphed over the laws of Mohammed. I'd like to see Shiraz. Do we go anywhere near it?"

"Not this way."

"I've heard of Shiraz. It's something to do with one of their poets," Katherine said.

"Sa'di," MacGregor told her. "He is buried there."

They talked about Iran all through the meal, as if its atmosphere added taste to the food. Essex said that somewhere in Persia there was a tablet on which Darius had listed the extent of his empire. MacGregor told him it was at Bisitun, and if he wanted to come back that way it was still there to see. He enjoyed their questions about Iran because he knew the countryside well. It also gave him a chance to encourage Essex away from his set itinerary, telling him that there was plenty to be seen away from their political route. Essex was not diverted.

"I told the Governor to send for Javat and his Captain at ten in the morning," Essex said. "We can take our time about getting up. If they settle their argument to-morrow we will leave immediately. We shan't waste time here. How long will it take us to reach our next stop, Mac-Gregor?"

"What exactly is the next stop?"

Essex got his papers and told MacGregor it was Bijar.

"It's three or four hours to Bijar," MacGregor said. "Who do we see there?"

"We are supposed to stop first at a place called Yangikand," Essex said. "I forgot about Yangikand, such a marvellous name too. Some fellow there named Babr Haslan." Essex read it from an envelope.

"Is that a letter to him?"

"Yes. It's from one of the Persian General Staff. Do you want to see it?"

"No thank you." MacGregor did not want to be contaminated with Essex's documents. "I'll leave that side of it to you."

"What side of it?" Essex said.

"Your side of it," Katherine interrupted and stood up. "I'm about to go to bed," she said. "Don't you two sit up here arguing all night. That's all you seem to do these days, argue with your looks and your grunts and your preferences and your silences. Give it up and go to bed, both of you."

Essex also stood up. "I admit I've had enough for one day," he said. "I'll see you people in the morning." He yawned and went to his room.

"You look awfully mean about something," Katherine said as she walked around MacGregor, running her finger down the deep ridge at the back of his neck.

"Does it show?" he said.

"Not really. You get an oppressive look at times. When last did you have a haircut?"

He put his hand to the back of his neck. "I don't know. Just before I left England, I think."

"Did you know we had a call from the Governor while you were away?"

"No. What did he want?"

"He came with the food and a couple of dozen servants."

"Huh. What happened to the servants?"

"Harold sent them away."

"That's not very polite."

"We were talking about your friends — Mr. Gochali and the other one."

"Oh?"

"The Governor seemed to think that a little intimidation would go a long way. He has a theory that they would understand a good honest-to-God thrashing."

346

"What did Essex say?" MacGregor asked quietly.

Katherine laughed. "Harold ignored it. What could he say?"

"I don't know," MacGregor said unhappily.

"Well don't worry about it. Go and sleep it off," she told him. "Good night."

Chapter 28

MacGregor was awakened by a fresh morning breeze. It came through the narrow window, which Essex had opened to its limit. The wind was dry, coming from the south-east. The rain had been blown away. MacGregor looked at Essex's broken features facing him across the room. He was still asleep, his mouth a little open, and his neat hair ragged on the pillow. Even so, the man looked self-possessed and not at all inelegant. MacGregor got out of bed irritated by Essex's poise — awake or asleep.

MacGregor went to the primitive bathroom and shaved painfully in cold spring water from the tap. He washed his feet and his torso and swung his arms about to circulate the blood. It was almost ten o'clock by the time he had dressed quietly and left the room. Essex was still asleep. As he went out MacGregor noticed that the dishes and the food had been cleared from the sitting room. He almost tripped over an old man who was seated outside the door on the short verandah.

"*Agha*," the old man said. "I was sitting here waiting for you. Do you want anything?"

"No, Uncle," MacGregor said.

"There is hot water in a kettle under my feet if you need it."

"Put it in the bathroom for the *Khanum*," MacGregor said.

"The *Khanum* is awake and inspecting the garden."

MacGregor looked around. "Where?"

"She walks everywhere." The old man smiled. "When the soldiers see her they will think she is a black-eyed houri from paradise. Is she Turkish, Excellency?" The old man stood up, emboldened by MacGregor's politeness.

"She is English." MacGregor walked down the steps.

"The Turkish women are supposed to be the most beautiful in the world." The old man followed him a few steps. "I think that is a legend perpetuated by Turkish women to counteract the true stories of their ugliness. Even the *bul-bul*" — the Kurd — "will not look at a Turkish woman. Turks are Sunni dogs, and their women are Sunni monsters.

347

Ha! I am a man who can always put a Turk in his place. The other way, Excellency! She was looking at the horses," he shouted weakly.

MacGregor walked through the arches in the mud walls and found himself on the edge of wide fields and orchards which stretched level and cultivated to the foot of the low hills. The garden boundary outside the houses was now an encampment. Tents, carts, mules and fodder were sheltering along a broken mud wall, and a corral had been made of broken mud bricks under a giant sycamore tree. MacGregor walked through the damp sunny grass to see if Katherine was looking at the collection of rangy horses. She was not there. He stood up on the broken wall and saw a huddle of low buildings which looked like stables. They were situated at the end of a poplar avenue. He found his way to the avenue by cutting through an orchard of ripe oranges — late Valencias. He picked an orange and felt its warm skin as something of the day itself. The sky was clear, and the yellow air was warm enough to dry the earth but sharp enough to be brisk. As he walked along the gravelled avenue between the straight poplars, he threw the orange in the air and caught it.

Katherine called him from behind. She came running along the road telling him to wait. He turned and stood, smiling and squinting into the morning sun and wondering what she was so energetic about.

"Where are you going?" she said when she reached him.

"I was looking for you. How long have you been up?"

"About an hour. This is a lovely place. Look at those poplars and this road and that vineyard, and the sun. It's like the Avenue Middelharnis."

"Is it?" he said in ignorance.

"The 'Avenue — Middelharnis' is in the National Gallery," she said. "Right inside the first door."

"Oh — a painting!"

"It is like this — the poplars, the vineyard, the fields, everything except the man tying up the vines."

"Is it English?"

"No. It was painted by a Dutchman named Hobbema. When Crome died he whispered *Hobbema, how I have loved thee.*"

"I don't think I have ever been inside the National Gallery," he said.

"Then you shouldn't admit it."

"I suppose not."

"It isn't really important here," she said in concession. "This is much more interesting. If you have been all over this countryside it doesn't matter a damn whether you have ever been inside the National Gallery or not. This is much better. It is nice being here with you on such a morning."

He also found it pleasant. Katherine was tolerant this morning, probably because the weather was good. He smiled at his own cynicism, but admitted that this could hardly be the natural Katherine: a normal uncomplicated woman who would not turn on him. He did not want her normal and uncomplicated. She would not be Katherine at all. Nevertheless, he enjoyed the respite of peace with her. "I gather that you like Iran," he said.

"Odd isn't it," she replied. "It must be you. I like watching you behave as you do with such seriousness. I don't know anything about the place, but I only have to look at you to see that it is full of all sorts of things I would never notice alone. I simply watch you and see what you're seeing."

He nodded and wondered how long her pleasure would last.

"Are you afraid of your sentiments," she said, "or are you being inarticulate to embarrass me?"

"Nothing that I could do would ever embarrass you," he said.

"That's not quite true. You really humble me at times."

This was certainly a different Katherine. She was deliberately showing him a more delicate side of her many crystal surfaces, and she appeared to be a little self-conscious about it. MacGregor was too warmed by the sun not to take advantage of a rare opportunity.

"Perhaps I should humble you more often," he said.

"Perhaps you should," she agreed mildly. "But it wouldn't do me much good. The real trouble here is my stupidity and my ignorance."

"Don't be so subtle . . ." he began.

"It's not subtlety at all. You are so damnably simple and at home in this country; but I am different. I don't understand what is going on here yet, so don't you be smug about it. My problem is much greater than yours." She walked stiff-legged to look at her dusty boots. "Do you have any polish?" she said. "I dislike wearing dirty boots."

"Give them to the old man back at the door. What is this problem you are talking about?"

"Good heavens," she said. "Did I talk about problems?"

"You did."

"What do you think will settle this dispute with the Governor?" she said. "That is quite a problem, isn't it?"

"It's not what you were talking about."

"Oh yes it is. I was watching you getting worked up about it yesterday."

"If you had understood what was being said, you would have been worked up yourself."

"I doubt it," she said. "I am not involved personally in this, as you are. I can see what it all means but that isn't enough. It's enough for you because you are fortunate in being something of a Persian yourself. Unfortunately I feel personally outside this dispute between Javat and the

Governor. Look at that one-legged sparrow washing himself in the pool of water." She stopped. MacGregor waited for her to continue what she was saying, but she watched the sparrow.

"He's not one-legged," MacGregor said. "The water is cold and he keeps one leg warm while the other is in the water. Actually it's a little late for him to be around: he should have moved south by now."

"How far south do they go? To Africa?"

"No. No," he said. "Just below the snow belt. It's good luck in Persia to see a sparrow so late in the year. For women, it usually means the birth of a son."

He looked down at her as she sat on her heels to watch the sparrow. He expected her to go on talking about herself, but she had put the whole conversation aside.

"Do you think there might be horses in those stables?" she asked as she stood up. She pointed to the low building off the road ahead. "They look like stables. I was looking at some of the cavalry horses near the house. They were miserable beasts."

"Most horses in Iran are," he told her. "They have good mountain horses, scraggy-looking, daring sort of animals, particularly the Gulf horses. But most of these around here are *yabus,* just any horse."

"Do you know anything about horses?" She was surprised.

He shook his head.

"Do you ride?"

"My father and I had to use horses on occasions," he said.

"Then let's take a look at the stables. I have heard of a big horse they have in Persia like an English hunter. What would that be?"

"I suppose it's the Karabagh. Thick in the withers. Where did you hear about it?"

"I have a mother who is a hunting maniac," she said. "So was I until I was old enough to know better. I can faintly remember a lot of excitement at Sunninghill when a Colonel brought home a Persian hunter. He was too big for a woman, but my conceited mother wasn't happy until she had mounted him. He was a beautiful beast. He took my mother into a ploughed field and for no reason at all he lay down and rolled her in the mud. Since then I have had a soft spot for Persian horses, but I have never seen any."

MacGregor was less interested in her explanation than in her undisguised and bitter dislike for her mother. He did not like to see such a thing, and yet his sympathies were with Katherine. He knew nothing about her mother, but he knew instinctively that Katherine was justified in denouncing her: he was already a silent partisan with Katherine in her disloyalty.

They turned off the avenue along a muddy track. The stable atmosphere clamped down on them like an odorous blanket as they approached a brown mud building. It formed a U and was lined by a low verandah supported by rough wooden posts. There were soldiers on the verandah preparing harness and saddles and bags, ready to leave. They stopped to look as Katherine and MacGregor entered the stable courtyard.

They were watched by soldiers standing near the buildings and the dung fires. A larger group of men in the centre of the compound took no notice of them. They were more interested in something in the dust. MacGregor heard some of them shout casually (as if in warning) that a *Ferangi* had arrived with his lady. There was silence. MacGregor felt Katherine grip his arm.

"What's wrong?" she said. "Are we making that much impression?"

"They don't expect to see women down here," he said. "It's alright."

"What's going on in there?" She nodded at the group before them.

"I don't know, but we might as well find out."

They pushed their way through until they were standing at a perimeter of soldiers who formed a barrier around two figures lying in the dust on their backs. The bare legs of the two men on the ground were tied to a trestle and their bloody feet were held in the air by its cross-piece. Mac-Gregor could not see the faces of the men because of the awkward and unconscious twist of their necks, but he pushed forward until he could see who lay on the ground. It was Javat Gochali and his Most Favoured Captain.

Katherine cried, "What have they done to them?"

MacGregor was trying to break through the soldiers. They shouted at him and held him back. "They've been bastinadoed," he told her incredulously.

"What is it? What has happened to them?" she said.

"They've been beaten on the feet with birch rods."

"Can't you get through?"

He could not get through. He shouted to Javat and the Captain, but they lay still in the orange cream of the earth. Their necks were twisted awkwardly from their raised bodies, little pools of blood lay beneath their feet. Javat's black cap lay away from him among a dozen broken birches. The Captain's Russian boots were stuck gaudily upon the cross-pieces of the trestle which held his feet.

"Have they killed them?" Katherine said. "What a terrible thing!"

MacGregor stopped fighting with the soldiers. "They're unconscious," he said. "How the devil were they caught? Kathy. Go back and get Essex. Tell him to find the Governor and come down and cut them loose. I'll keep trying here."

"Can't you break through?" Katherine was pushing at the soldiers.

"When you're out of the way," he said. "Go on."

"Kick them," she said.

"Go and tell Essex, and get the Governor," he said. "Go on."

"Will you be alright?"

"Yes. Go on."

Katherine pushed and beat her way through the soldiers. She ran across the courtyard through the collection of carts and harness and disappeared behind the buildings.

MacGregor was held back by two soldiers who had linked their arms. When he tried to move around them the next two linked arms and faced him. He told them again to let him through and they said it was impossible. He threatened them and cursed, but the press of soldiers accumulated around him now and hemmed him in. They told him that it was not their doing, that they were carrying out orders. MacGregor ignored them and struck the arms of the soldiers, but they did not break their grip. One of them shouted at him that next time he did that he would be dealt with. MacGregor knew it was hopeless. He pushed his way out of the crowd and shouted for their officer, whoever he was, to come out. He shouted for the officer again and asked the men for him, but they shrugged and told him that there was nothing to worry about because the Governor himself had been down here and had ordered the beating. What was he shouting about? Everybody was bastinadoed at some time or other, it was no shame, and these two were simply sleeping it off.

MacGregor was ready to make a frustrated plunge into the mass of soldiers again when he saw Aladin coming out a wire door in one of the buildings. With him was the booted officer who had manhandled MacGregor last night.

"Cut them loose," MacGregor shouted to the officer without preliminaries.

"You sing like a sparrow," the officer said. "Cut them loose yourself."

"Tell your men to clear the way."

"Lord of the Universe," the officer said to MacGregor, "clear the way yourself."

The soldiers were laughing. MacGregor's anger dropped to the level of bitter control. He saw Aladin watching him carefully. He was trying to warn MacGregor with his white unhappy eyes.

"What are you doing here?" MacGregor said to him in English. "And how did Javat and the Captain get here?"

"I brought them, Sahib."

"Here?"

"Yes, Sahib."

"When?"

"Early. The Governor and the officer sent me to get them. I thought it had been arranged because you wanted to leave early. His Excellency told me last night that I was to go for them. It is not my fault, Sahib. Do not curse me."

"Never mind that. How long have they been tied there?"

"Two hours, Sahib." Aladin looked nervously at the officer who was suspicious of their English. "The Governor was here to begin it. He began the beating himself, and it was kept up until a little while ago, even when the men were unconscious. It was not my fault, not my fault."

"Why didn't you come and get me?"

"I have been locked in a room under threat of my life."

MacGregor knew it was still impossible to get through. He did not try. The orange he had picked was still in his hand and he flung it over the heads of the soldiers. He waited silently, ignoring the insults of the officer and the nervousness of Aladin and the laughter of the men, until he heard Essex shout for him. He came with Katherine, striding across the compound in riding breeches, his corduroy jacket over his shoulders.

"What is this?" Essex was saying. "MacGregor, are you alright?"

"Yes. Did you bring the Governor?"

"I couldn't find him." Essex held Katherine tight to safeguard her. He looked at Javat and the Captain on the ground. "What a barbaric thing to do. That stupid Governor has broken my word," he said fiercely. "Clear the way there."

Essex pushed one of the soldiers who did not move but who did not resist very vigorously. MacGregor saw the doubt on their faces now. They realized the importance of Essex. He could see that the officer himself was unsure. MacGregor pushed again as Essex stood off and broke the joined hands with his angry fists.

"Get out of the way you beggars." Essex was red with anger. "MacGregor, get one of those bayonets and cut them loose."

They broke through the soldiers. Essex ignored the half-hearted threats of one of them, snatched a bayonet from the same man's scabbard and followed MacGregor. MacGregor bent over the Captain's feet and tried unsuccessfully to undo the twine. He found his pocket knife and cut the strands loose. The Captain's soft slashed legs fell awkwardly into the little pool of his own blood, and MacGregor helped Essex cut Javat loose. Javat was now looking at them with dull eyes. Essex stood away and allowed MacGregor to handle the man's feet and legs which were swollen, cut, and stripped, so that the soft flesh hung from the toes and the arches. MacGregor put Javat's legs down carefully and Katherine applied towels, a practical requirement she had brought with her. Mac-Gregor took two of the towels and applied them to the Captain's legs and feet. They were worse than Javat's, and they seemed lifeless. Mac-Gregor avoided the thought in his mind as he attended the limp Captain.

Essex kept the men away and cursed the Governor for breaking his word. The Governor arrived in time to receive Essex's denunciation.

"This is a beggarly thing to do," Essex said angrily, "breaking my word like this. Do you realize that they had my word for their personal safety? Not your word. My word."

The Governor raised his hands in protest. "I knew nothing about this. It was done without my orders." He was angrier than Essex.

"Aladin will tell you that the Governor began the beatings himself," MacGregor said to Essex. He was still binding the Captain's feet with towels, knowing there was something hopeless about what he was doing.

"Are you a brute as well as a fool!" Essex said to the Governor. "Get some stretchers for these men. Get some attention."

"But Your Excellency," the Governor said. "It is not a bad custom in my country. Even a royal prince is bastinadoed without shame."

"It is illegal," MacGregor said.

"I don't care what you have to say about it." Essex raised his voice. "You are dishonoured. You have dishonoured me. You stupid man."

"Excellency!" The Governor turned and bellowed at the soldiers to go away, so that they would not see him suffering such indignities. "Excellency," the Governor said with more firmness. "It was the right thing to do. These two rebels will understand my position now. They will not argue with me any more. They will realize that I intend to implement my authority. They will not bargain and behave as lords of my own fields. They will see their folly now and behave sensibly. That was your purpose in assisting me. You simply do not understand our methods. After all, I did not hang them, so do not be angry."

"I'm not angry, and I understand your methods. You are a fool, and I gave my word for these men's safety. There is no explanation for what you have done to me. Get assistance for these men."

The Governor cursed the officer and told him to have these two men carried to the buildings, and to send someone for the doctor. The Governor's imposing figure, his beard, his commanding gestures, his rolling voice, sent the soldiers tumbling away. They returned with stretchers and carried Javat and the Captain into one of the harness rooms.

"MacGregor," Essex said. "Watch these men and see that they get attention. Where is the car, Aladin?"

"Behind this building, Sahib."

"MacGregor. When these men have been attended to, put them in the Ford and come and get us. We will pack your things."

"He may not be safe here, Harold," Katherine said. Her hair was falling over her face and she could not push it back because of her bloody hands.

"If anything happens to him," Essex said to the Governor, "there will

354

be a squadron of RAF planes over here in no time at all, believe me!"

"You are safe. You are safe. But you are not leaving?"

"Of course we are leaving."

"But Excellency. You will leave us with nothing and in more dangerous circumstances than before. I swear these men will see reason now."

"Don't be silly. These men are half dead, and you broke my word."

"I told you not to overdo it." The Governor turned upon his officer and repeated the curses, applying them to the officer's mother and religion. The officer said nothing but stood aside uncomfortably.

"Come on Kathy," Essex opened the wire door.

Katherine had washed her hands under a pump in the room. "I don't like leaving, Ivre," she said. "You had better come too."

"I'll be alright," MacGregor said.

"No you won't be. We can carry the men with us to the house."

"No," he said. "Go on. I'll be there."

"Please," she began.

"I'm alright," he said impatiently.

"Yes. Yes," Essex told her. "Come along Kathy. The sooner we leave this place the better."

They had gone, and MacGregor looked down at Javat, whose white face was coming to life.

"We are getting you out of here," MacGregor told him. "Is there a doctor at Zenjan?"

Javat nodded and turned towards his Captain.

MacGregor stepped over Javat and looked at the Captain, who was heavily limp and not white but almost pink and relaxed, his grey hair softened by the dust and shaped away from his dusty face. Javat watched MacGregor, and his eyes asked the question. MacGregor said that the Captain was alright. He walked up and down until a tall thin man in a dirty black overcoat arrived.

He did not greet MacGregor. He looked at Javat and then at the Captain. He touched the Captain's forehead and looked at his hands and feet and eyes, and sighed. Then he took the towels off Javat's feet.

"I haven't any equipment with me," the man said in Persian.

"You're the doctor?" MacGregor said.

"Yes. I did not know you spoke Persian. That one is dead." He nodded at the Captain. "He must have died from shock, unless he has been beaten elsewhere and has internal injuries which would kill him. Probably shock. No doubt he is not used to this sort of thing. This one is alright, but I have nothing to fix him with."

"We are taking both of them to Zenjan," MacGregor said.

The doctor nodded. "That will be the best. Get them away from here. It is no place for a civilized man. I would go myself, but my family is

355

here." He was an elderly man with nervous hands and threadbare trousers. He stood up and said there was nothing much he could do. "Take them out of here," he said.

MacGregor called Aladin and told him to get some of the soldiers.

"Just keep his feet up," the doctor said as he looked down at Javat.

"Are you sure it is alright to move him?"

"Yes. He will feel nothing."

The soldiers came in with the officer. They took Javat and the Captain to the Ford which was waiting on the dusty road.

At the house Katherine and Essex were ready with their suitcases. Katherine looked at the awkward situation of Javat and the Captain in the back and went back into the house for pillows. MacGregor didn't tell her that the Captain was dead, but she quickly guessed it.

The Governor appeared and began his protests again. Essex took no notice of him so he turned to MacGregor.

"You must tell the Ambassador to take me with you," he said agitatedly. "Do you hear me?"

"Tell him yourself," MacGregor replied.

"He is far too angry," the Governor said, "and you must see the situation I am in now. You must see the wisdom in taking me out under your protection."

"I don't see the wisdom of it at all." MacGregor closed the door.

The Governor put his head in the car. "Excellency, Excellency . . ."

"Go on," MacGregor said to Aladin.

The Ford jumped forward and the Governor almost lost his head, saying *Excellency, Excellency*.

The booted officer leapt on the running board and held on as Aladin drove through the garden to the Governor's road block. Fortunately it was clear. Aladin slowed down to go through it and the officer jumped off.

The officer did not attempt to save himself as the Governor had done. Instead, he cursed MacGregor with anger and vehemence. It was so foul and provocative that MacGregor opened the door of the Ford to get out. The officer waited for him and laughed at MacGregor's flushed face and spat twice in the dust at his feet and then called on his soldiers and on Allah to witness the Englishman who was too cowardly to reply. MacGregor caught the officer by the front of his green uniform and pulled him awkwardly around and pushed him half into the front seat of the Ford on his back, and then fell on him and told Aladin to go, go on, move, for God's sake to move.

Aladin took the Ford roaring through the open barrier as the soldiers came running at them. The door was open and MacGregor's and the officer's feet were hanging out as they struggled in the bumping car.

The door lurched with the car to crack MacGregor's calves as he pushed the officer down off the seat onto the floor, avoiding his groping hands and pushing a knee into the officer's stomach. Shots followed them, and Aladin was shouting in his own tongue and pushing the officer's hands away from his legs. MacGregor got the back of his arm on the officer's head and he shouted at Aladin to hold the officer's flaying arm from scratching his face. Aladin was occupied with the twisting bumping Ford which suddenly skidded and crashed into a ditch with its back wheels. He lost control. The Ford almost stopped and they piled upon each other. The back wheels spun and the bump seemed to have cracked the whole car. Aladin regained control. MacGregor pushed the officer flat on the floor and kept him there.

MacGregor turned his scratched and breathless face on Essex, who was calling him a crazy fool, and on Katherine who was trying to straighten the unconscious Javat. He looked through the back to see if they were being followed, but they had reached the barbed wire of Javat's barrier which took them into safety. MacGregor called the soldiers at the barrier and asked them if there was a hospital at Zenjan. They ran up and looked in and saw Javat and the Captain, and shouted among themselves until one of them came running, bread in his hand and in his mouth. He stuffed his handful of flat bread into his pocket and stumbled over his gun as MacGregor opened the door and made room for him. This time, the officer's legs would not fit and he began to kick so that the soldier had to hold the door open a little. MacGregor pushed him down again.

"Look at your face," Katherine said then.

"What did you take him for?" Essex demanded.

"I don't know." MacGregor was breathing so deeply that his chest ached. He felt for his handkerchief to wipe his face, catching his breath through his mouth. "But this is the specimen who worked on Javat and the Captain."

"Well throw him out," Essex said.

"Oh no!" MacGregor wiped the scratches which came around his right ear and his neck. He loosened his collar to avoid its friction, and he felt another strip of raw flesh on his forehead.

"Turn him loose," Essex said. "We can't do things like that."

MacGregor sniffed and blew his nose and ignored Essex.

The soldier directed them along a village road to a small blue and white house, a house built for an official, a tax-gatherer, or a police-officer. It was now a primitive army hospital, guarded by two peasants who sat on the steps talking. A young man in a Russian smock came out when they called him, and between them they got Javat and the Captain into one of the small rooms where an agitated old woman was al-

357

ready pumping a primus stove to boil water. MacGregor gave a brief explanation of events to the young doctor, who was already looking at Javat. MacGregor left him and went outside.

He said nothing to Katherine and Essex and stood quietly in the sun. "I suppose the Captain is dead, isn't he?" Katherine said.

MacGregor confirmed it.

"This is terrible," she said.

"And Gochali?" Essex asked.

MacGregor sat down on the running board. "I don't know," he said. "They are working on him now." He watched the booted officer, who had been turned over to the two peasants. They did not know what to do with him and were obviously afraid of his contempt. He was brushing the dust from his boots and looking triumphantly from time to time at the mess he had made of MacGregor's face. MacGregor dabbed at himself and waited for the doctor.

It was a long time before he appeared. MacGregor asked about Javat.

"He is alright," the young man said in Persian. "His right foot is broken below the ankle, and he is severely cut and bruised. He is suffering from shock, but otherwise he seems to be alright. Naturally he was in great pain and it will be some time before he regains consciousness again."

"And the Captain?"

The doctor shrugged and raised his clean hands. "It was a great shock to his system. Too much for him. Perhaps he was beaten on the stomach or the head, although I see no evidence of it. He was not a strong man and not a young man. He must be a town man of regular habits. The shock probably killed him. You had better let me attend your face."

MacGregor went inside with the doctor and held a basin of water while his wounds were bathed in a boracic solution. He asked the doctor if he was serving with the Democrats' Azerbaijanian Army — with Javat and the Captain.

"Not exactly," the doctor said. "I was serving my compulsory year in the Iranian Army stationed at Zenjan. When the revolt started I set up hospital here for anyone. I am not an Azerbaijani myself. I come from Khorrom-Shah but I suppose I am now considered a rebel for helping these people, and therefore an exile. I cannot go back now."

"I would like to explain to someone just what happened," MacGregor told him. "Is there an official with whom I can talk?"

"I have sent for them," he said. "I am sorry we have no anti-tetanus injection for you. We have little of anything." He was painting iodine across MacGregor's face. "Scratches are always worse than clean wounds, particularly when they might have stable dirt in them. You must be careful."

With his leg bandaged and his face painted MacGregor went outside again.

"How are you feeling Mac?" Essex asked him.

"Alright."

Katherine gave him a glass of tea which the old woman had brought out.

"Are you well enough to move on?" Essex asked him.

"Yes, but we can't move on yet. We have to explain all this to someone."

"Didn't you explain to the doctor?"

"Yes I did, but we will have to wait for some of Javat's people to come. They will not be long."

"I'll wait for a little while," Essex said patiently, "but not long."

MacGregor was too irritated to argue with Essex. He sat down and ignored them all. He was getting impatient by the time one of the Azerbaijanians arrived. He was a major, still wearing the uniform of a regular army officer but supplemented by an odd sidecap. After he had seen Javat he came out to MacGregor, who began to explain the incident again; but the Major pointed to the booted officer.

"Is this the one responsible for it?" he asked.

"The Governor was responsible," MacGregor replied. "This one simply carried it out. He did a great part of the beating."

"Would you be willing to tell more of the details to our Colonel?"

"Certainly."

"Perhaps you would come with me to our headquarters?" the Major asked.

MacGregor said "Please!"

Essex felt that he had been patient enough listening to so much talk in another language and he told MacGregor that they should now move on, explanations being over.

"We should wait and see what we can do," MacGregor told him. "We can't make this mess and then simply clear out."

"We did not make this mess," Essex replied.

"I think we did," MacGregor said stubbornly.

"Well, when you have calmed down a little we will go on our way."

"Harold," Katherine said casually. "We are impolite if we leave so abruptly."

"What the devil is the point in getting more involved?" Essex argued.

"Because we are partly responsible for what happened," Katherine said.

"We are entirely responsible," MacGregor insisted.

Katherine agreed.

Essex denied it, but Katherine's partisanship was too much for him. "I shan't argue about it here," he told them. "I don't mind waiting

359

for both of you to calm down and see reason, but I am not going to involve myself further in this dispute, and I forbid MacGregor to take any further part in it."

"I am about to go to their headquarters to explain it," MacGregor said.

"Then you go alone, and don't expect us to be here when you come back."

Katherine clicked her tongue. "Don't be childish," she said.

"I am perfectly serious," Essex said. He was unconvincing.

"In that case," MacGregor said, "just leave my belongings on the verandah."

"I forbid you MacGregor . . ." Essex began, but he was too weary to continue arguing.

"Shall we go now?" MacGregor said to the Major in Persian.

"If it will not inconvenience you," the Major answered, sensing dispute.

MacGregor got in the jeep and Essex watched silently as he drove off. "Where did you get this vehicle?" MacGregor asked the Major to take his mind off Essex. "From the Russians?"

The Major made an elaborate defence, explaining that the Americans had supplied jeeps to the Iranian Army and when the revolt had occurred in Azerbaijan, the Army had fled and left them obligingly for the Democratic forces. MacGregor did not think it quite that simple, but he did believe that it had been captured from the Government forces.

They arrived in the streets of Zenjan. The rackish town was functioning normally in daylight but it was patrolled by groups of Azerbaijanian soldiers in their Russian boots. Much of the starch and stiffness went out of MacGregor as he passed the coffee shops, the shouting barrow merchants, the urchins in the streets. They turned into a small Gendarmerie post next to a brassworker's shop, and they could hardly hear themselves above the hollow sound of the furnace and the anvil. Inside it was quieter.

A very neat but stocky colonel welcomed him and they sat on hard chairs on a bare floor before a coal fire. The Colonel articulated every word for the Englishman until MacGregor replied in rapid Persian and settled the whole matter of how this conversation should be conducted. The Colonel was relieved, and MacGregor wasted no time telling him about Javat and the Captain. The Colonel listened quietly, but when MacGregor had finished he did not ask about Javat and the Captain. He knew that the Captain was dead and that Javat was alright, but he seemed to take their plight as something to be expected. What more could be said about it? In this attitude he seemed to be less of a revolutionist and more of a regular soldier, and MacGregor guessed him to be such. MacGregor was further convinced that the Colonel was a regular soldier when he began to show most concern with the disposition and extent of the Governor's forces. The Colonel brought out rough maps to show MacGregor where they thought the Governor had placed his men.

MacGregor hesitated for a moment to think about what he was doing — taking part in this military discussion; but he knew he was already committed against the Governor. He told the Colonel that he knew little, but he estimated the Governor's strength near the entrance gate, and the reserve of men camped near the house and at the stables. From his casual and undeliberate observations he corrected some of the details on the Colonel's map, and when he had finished the Colonel asked him if he was militarily trained.

"Only during the war," MacGregor said.

"I thought you were experienced," the Colonel told him warmly. "Yours is the only expert information we have had about the Governor's forces. Most of it so far has come from our untrained peasants who notice little or exaggerate too much. Now we are clearer about our position."

MacGregor was not pleased. He did not want the bad taste of war entering his life again. He had finished with that. But he could not help asking the Colonel what he planned doing.

"We must be careful," the Colonel said. "We are outnumbered and outarmed, but we have been smuggling arms into the peasants on his estate. In a day or two we will arrange matters for some co-ordinated action."

"Can't you do anything before then?"

"I don't think so," the Colonel said. "We must arm as many of the peasants in there as we can. The situation will depend on the strength of the Governor's resistance. You have seen the man; do you think that he will resist well?"

"I doubt it," MacGregor shook his head. "He tried to come out with us. I think he has had enough, but I don't know about his army."

The Colonel said that the Governor's army was inferior in morale and purpose to his own, which he claimed modestly as the best army in Iran because it was an army of very determined and very angry Azerbaijani. He turned to his maps again to show MacGregor how he proposed to come in on the Governor from two sides, complaining about the lack of cover in the open fields. MacGregor took one more step.

"You could get two small detachments up this watercourse," MacGregor told him and pointed to it on the map. "I could just see it from the house and it has a lot of cover when you get near the road. You could get men up it at night and if they were careful they could not be detected, even in daylight."

The Colonel was surprised and delighted and agreed to do it and asked

MacGregor to remain and see the operation, but MacGregor said he must leave.

"Is your Ambassador in such a hurry?" the Colonel said.

"He doesn't want to become involved any deeper," MacGregor said.

"And you?"

MacGregor shrugged. "There is nothing much more I can do," he said.

"You have been most helpful," the Colonel told him happily. "But tell me one more thing. Is it true that the Americans are already leaving Iran?"

"I believe so."

"When will the British Army leave?"

"In March when the occupation is up," MacGregor told him.

"It will be a good thing when everybody has gone," the Colonel sighed.

"The Russians also?" MacGregor said sourly.

"The Russians also!" the Colonel replied. "We have always been afraid of the Russians in Azerbaijan. This time we have been glad of them because they have left us alone; but we don't need them here."

"Have you been to Russia, Colonel?" MacGregor had earned the right to ask such a question. He suspected that the Colonel was more experienced militarily than most Iranian Army men.

The Colonel smiled. "Are you thinking that I am a Russian Azerbaijani, or perhaps an Iranian Communist who was trained in Moscow?"

"No," MacGregor said and there was no smile in him. He was going through all this with a grim acceptance of his own sudden participation. "I am simply curious. Forgive me."

"It is a natural thing to be curious about." The Colonel was still amused. "Particularly for an Englishman. Englishmen in Iran are always worried about the Russians, as worried as we are."

"That is not quite my problem," MacGregor said. "These are questions I myself will be asked officially, and I like to know the answers."

"Ah! I like that," said the Colonel. "If you must answer for me you will find it simple. A few months ago I was a staff officer of the Imperial Army at Mianeh, and here I am to-day a staff officer of the Azerbaijanian Army at Zenjan. If you are asked about my military training, then you must explain that I was a cadet of the Imperial Staff College at Teheran and was sent to Turkey by the last Shah to train with Kemal Attaturk. But if you are asked about my political training and my free will, just say that I am of Ardebil, a good Azerbaijani who does not need to be taught the political sense of self-determination."

MacGregor said he had been well answered. The Colonel replied that he had been well accepted and remembered to thank MacGregor for bringing in the booted officer.

"What happened to him?" MacGregor said.

"First he will be questioned," the Major put in.

362

"And then?"

The Major shrugged and the Colonel laughed.

MacGregor said it was time he went. The interview ended.

The Colonel went back to the hospital with him to see if Javat had regained consciousness. As the jeep came through the village and approached the blue house, MacGregor saw that the Ford had gone. It was nowhere in sight.

He didn't believe it. Essex's threat to leave him behind had been the same as MacGregor's own threat not to come on this mission at all. Both men had understood each other enough to realize that their conflict might be real, but complete division was unthought of. MacGregor could no more walk out on Essex than Essex could walk out on him. Whatever their conflict — there was something between them which made that impossible. Essex must know that their personal dispute could not be decided like this. He should not have gone. MacGregor felt cheated by Essex and deserted by Katherine.

The jeep stopped at the steps and MacGregor jumped out, forgetting the Colonel. He hurried inside to see if they were there. Katherine was standing near an old black oil-stove, looking unusually pale.

"Did Essex go?" MacGregor said, still incredulous.

"He went with Aladin to get some petrol. Somebody stole ours from the tank."

MacGregor felt his whole face relax. Behind him he heard the Colonel click his heels to Katherine.

"Oh no," Katherine said as she guessed his thought. "He wouldn't leave you here. For one thing I wouldn't let him. For another he seems to be afraid of parting with you. He ought to be back now. Javat is conscious, by the way."

They went into the engineer, but he was barely awake and he still could not speak. The young doctor told them not to remain long because Javat had been drugged and would sleep. Javat looked at MacGregor's scratched face with his solemn eyes.

"The officer with the boots," MacGregor explained his face and smiled a little. "I brought him back for you." He said nothing about the Most Favoured Captain; there was nothing to say. "I am leaving," he said then, "but I will look for you when we come back."

Javat nodded.

"The Colonel knows everything," MacGregor said.

There was no way of expressing themselves further except to feel that each understood the other. Nothing more than that was required, so MacGregor left him. Outside, Essex was just arriving in the Ford.

"So you are back in time," Essex said to him. "We were about to leave. It's after one o'clock already. We'll have to get a move on. Are you ready?"

"If you are," MacGregor said.

"Is Gochali conscious?"

"Yes."

"I'll just have a few words with him."

MacGregor waited in the sun, having time now to think about their part in this incident. He blamed Essex for its tragic outcome. Essex should never have trusted the Governor in the first place; should never have persuaded Javat and the Captain to enter that estate; should never have offered the Governor so much encouragement. This was the result of Sir Samuel Fox's plan for Azerbaijan, and MacGregor was more violently opposed to it than ever. Already his personal sympathies were with Javat, and he thought that his political sympathies were somewhere in the same direction. More so since Essex was forcing him to take sides. Essex had made a mess with his interference. He had to be blamed. Even the Most Favoured Captain's death was his direct responsibility.

"Come on then," Essex said as he came out with Katherine. "Let's go."

Aladin started the Ford and they got in. The Colonel stood at the door of the car as they were about to move. He gripped MacGregor's hand and then impulsively wrenched a pistol from the holster on his belt. He put it through the window for MacGregor. MacGregor tried to refuse it but the Colonel dropped it on his lap.

"Take it," he said as they moved off. "You may need it on the road. Let it be my gift of appreciation for you. Take it, and adieu," he shouted.

MacGregor had no choice. To be adequately polite he should have offered in return a more elaborate gift, but the Colonel had arranged it so that this was impossible, and Aladin was well on the road to Zenjan by the time MacGregor could think about it.

"Are you going to throw that one away too?" Essex said to him.

MacGregor ignored Essex. He pulled back the barrel of the pistol to make sure there was nothing in the chamber, then he pulled the spring clip out of the butt and emptied the bullets into his hand. He was not surprised then to see that this was a Nagant, a Russian weapon. Essex should know that, he thought cynically.

"I am glad that's over," Essex was saying. "How is your face, MacGregor?"

MacGregor told him it was alright.

Essex did not attempt further conversation and he watched the road until they were out of Zenjan. Just along the main road beyond the Colonel's headquarters they passed the green figure of the booted officer. He was hanging from a telegraph pole.

"Good Lord!" Essex cried. "Is that the same fellow?"

Aladin slowed down.

"It's the same fellow," MacGregor muttered unbelievingly.

"Well you certainly brought about his downfall," Essex said drily, and in that statement he was retaliating for what he felt of MacGregor's blame. They were equal now. MacGregor could not avoid his own guilt in this. He was already beginning a moral argument with himself for bringing about the man's destruction, an argument which would never finish for him.

Katherine was the most shocked. "Go on. Go on," she said to Aladin. Aladin speeded up, and the swinging figure passed from sight.

"What a nice diplomatic mess this could make, MacGregor," Essex growled.

"Don't be so immoral with your diplomatic concern," Katherine said.

"It's unfortunately a fact. This could be dangerous," Essex said.

MacGregor had to agree with Essex. The full significance of their interference had now reached both men. Their double interference had caused so much damage that it could stir up a diplomatic explosion if it ever became generally known. MacGregor could not avoid his share of the blame, but the diplomatic guilt worried him less than his personal guilt. He felt already that Katherine was blaming him for the death of the officer.

Essex saved them from unhappy silence. "These people are simply barbarians," he said to them. "They beat, hang, and murder people like a lot of primitive savages. They have no feelings, no sensibilities, and apparently no honour."

Katherine stopped him. "Let's hear no more about honour," she said.

Essex was startled. "You're in a moral state of mind to-day," he said. She let it pass.

Essex went on, settling back into his seat. "I was wondering," he said, "if that crude form of beating on the feet was the same punishment which Alexander inflicted on Bessus for the murder of Darius. I suppose it was. These people certainly haven't changed in a thousand years," he said disgustedly.

Thereafter they left the whole matter alone, but it remained a bitter issue between them, even though they could not talk about it again.

Chapter 29

As THEY turned off the main road MacGregor was too occupied with his own thoughts to take notice of their direction. The figure of the officer still swung like a pendulum before him. Yet as he calmed down he almost lost some of the guilt because he was not entirely Christian in his attitude to death. He had not escaped the influences of fatalism in a youth spent in this Moslem country. Mass death he deplored in Christian terms; but in the matter of individual death he was more philosophically an Oriental. The death of a close friend in the war was an overwhelming tragedy that could still cause him fits of inexpressible sorrow. Conversely, the death of an enemy like the officer must be accepted as natural and desirable. It was simply a matter of deciding that the officer was a sufficient enemy. He might have been in political terms, but MacGregor could not quite convince himself that this was an adequate justification.

Depressed, he sought distraction in his surroundings. The Ford was travelling on a narrow road which had degenerated into a mere pasty indentation along the rocky bottom of a dried-up river-bed. It was so bad that Aladin had slowed down to a few miles an hour. MacGregor expected the better road to begin again, but when the track became worse he knew that something was wrong. He asked Essex for the maps and told Aladin to stop. He got out and compared the bare red countryside with the War Office map, doing his best with the meagre topography.

"We have missed Yangikand anyway," he said. "We are way to the west of it, in fact we must be half-way to Nasirabad up the old river-bed."

"What town were we looking for?" Essex asked him from the car.

"Bijar."

"Can we get there this way?"

"We'd never get there on a road like this," MacGregor said.

"Then turn back," Essex told Aladin. "It's late and we don't want to wander around these roads at night. Go back to that town we missed: Yangikand is it?"

Katherine got out of the Ford. "If you don't mind," she said to Essex, "I'll stretch my legs while he is turning. Women weren't built for this sort of thing."

Essex joined her as Aladin drove on to find a spot wide enough to turn around.

While Katherine and Essex made quite a business of the arm and leg stretching, MacGregor strolled to a sandstone ledge across the river-bed. He was at his lowest ebb, depressed, isolated, and as unhappy about himself as he had ever been. He climbed up on the sandstone ledge and casually inspected it. He had made this trip with every intention of collecting rock samples from the mountain areas; and knowing the route, he had anticipated samples of these particular sandstones. He dug his fingers into the rock without enthusiasm or intent; but once into its surface he could not avoid interest in it. He moved along, looking for a good lump which could be broken off so that its inside could reveal more than its eroded surface. He found a short protrusion but he could not dislodge it with his hands. He felt in his pockets, found the pistol there, and was hammering at the rock with it when Katherine stood below and asked what he was doing.

"Collecting a few samples," he said grumpily. "Where is Essex?"

"He went off into the wilderness somewhere." She climbed up on the ledge near him. "What sort of rock is it?" she asked.

"Sandstone," he said. "Marl-sandstone."

"Are there fossils in it?" She was looking at MacGregor, not at the rocks.

"Some of it is plant-bearing," he said.

"I suppose all this country is sandstone." She looked around her, enjoying the expanse.

He crumbled the edge of the rock in his fingers. What was Katherine up to now? She was being deliberately conciliatory. "Most of the mountains here are granite overlaid with chalk-limestone," he said evenly. "The valleys are usually sandstone like this one. It's true of all the north."

"Did your fossil hunting ever include those large beasts which roamed around in the prehistoric world? Have you ever found remains of them here?"

"I haven't," he said, "but a man named Erni found deposits of the jaw-bone of a large mammal."

"What sort of large mammal?"

"Probably one of the Rhinoceridae," he said, "although there was some disagreement about it because no one could decide the history of the sand layers in which it was found. The argument about the sand layers was really more important than the discovery of the jaw-bone; but what is left of it is in the Natural History Museum, if you want to see it. You might have seen it already."

"I've never been into the Natural History Museum," she told him.

"Then you shouldn't admit it," he said, repeating her own reprimand for his ignorance of the National Gallery. It was a fortunate reply because his humour had suddenly come back, and he thought that Katherine might have deliberately led him along to break his unhappiness.

"You really know all these things?" she said and peered at him curiously as if she had never recognized his talents before.

"It's very elementary geology," he said. "You should know some of it yourself."

"Is this what you did with your father? Go around poking up the history of the earth and discovering fossils and prehistoric remains?"

"Among other things."

"What other things?"

"Too technical to go into," he said and put the rock in his pocket.

"I rather thought you had always been deep in a laboratory," she said.

"Only when I went to London and English-Persian," he said. He had already been thinking that he had suppressed too much of his natural inclination to field geology; but it was difficult to combine general field work with micropaleontology; and given the choice he was first and foremost a paleontologist. His absolute preference was still in the large undeveloped field of micropaleontology and he knew that he would never prefer it otherwise — the pleasure of field-work notwithstanding. "In a way," he said to Katherine, "all geologists are frustrated field men, whatever they do. We all want to be explorers, I suppose."

"I can't think of you being exploratory," she said.

"Good heavens," he protested. "Geology is all exploration, particularly now. We are only beginning to explore the earth's surface. We have barely started."

"I thought geologists knew all about it."

MacGregor knew that she was leading him still farther with a deliberate desire to make him talk, but he did not resist it. He decided that she had sufficient interest, either in himself or in the subject, to attend what he was saying even standing against this rock looking out across the sandstone hills that dropped far away into the Talar valley. "We really know very little about the earth and we know nothing about its origins, although we are on the way to knowing something, largely because we are co-operating with the other sciences, particularly physics and astronomy."

"I heard that those subjects were largely a matter of mathematics these days," she said.

"So they are," he agreed, "but they are all interrelated with geology. Everything in science is interrelated. With fossils for instance the geologist meets the biologist, the zoologist, the physiologist. In history we meet the archaeologist and the anthropologist. My father was a good archaeologist. We often worked with some of the Americans who were investigating the river civilizations in the south."

"If geological work is so fascinating I don't see how you can keep away from it."

"In Moscow," he reminded her, "you were supporting diplomacy against geology."

"Of course I was," she said. "You were using geology as an escape from the issues of diplomacy, and being infuriatingly smug about it. These days you don't seem to be avoiding issues so I can afford to be generous."

He thought of himself as a hangman, as a participant in a political decision, and as a geologist whose responsibilities had been stirred by Javat's ambitious questions about the resources of Zenjan and by the warmth of the sandstone in his pocket. "The more involved in issues I become," he said, "the less I know what I am doing in the middle of this affair. What are we doing here anyway?"

"I ask myself the same question." She sighed elaborately. "I am fascinated by our peculiar behaviour, particularly yours."

"Are you objecting?" He was ready to argue with her.

"No. I was quite impressed."

Essex appeared and climbed up to them. "What are you gossiping about?" he said and looked from one to the other.

"We're enjoying the view," Katherine told him.

Essex looked around at the countryside. "Not much view from here," he said. "How is the face, MacGregor?"

MacGregor's scratches felt like a mass of raw ant-bites and he had to screw up his face to deaden the pain a little. "It's a little sore," he told Essex. He thought it strange that Essex should be so worried about his face. It was not really his face which Essex worried about. Essex seemed to be making a gesture of concern for MacGregor, a concern which had originated in their dispute at the Governor's estate. MacGregor sensed the subtle change and sensed his own strength in the situation. There was mental satisfaction in his action against the Governor, but it was satisfaction which he did not allow to develop. He was too confused about his motives to enjoy the taste of decisive participation.

"Where is that wretch Aladin?" Essex said then.

"Perhaps he has gone off and left us," Katherine suggested.

"He's too cowardly to do that," Essex muttered.

"That man looks so fierce," she said of Aladin.

"He's as timid as a camel," Essex said as Aladin came back with the Ford.

They went down the slope in something of a scramble and climbed into the Ford. Aladin told them that there was something wrong with the car, it was barely pulling.

"It's just this damned road," Essex said. "Go on."

Aladin put the car in gear. It strained forward as the engine raced.

MacGregor could feel the heat of the engine. "Something is definitely wrong with it," he said.

"Keep going until we get off this bad patch," Essex instructed.

The darkness was catching up with them. The sun had disappeared behind the hills to the southwest. They sat uncomfortably while the Ford struggled along. They were out of the little ravine and on that flat bed of the river, with bare rolling country either side of them, when the Ford seemed to strangle itself. It whined and the engine died. Aladin revved the engine and it moved a few feet, but the effort was too much. It stopped with obstinate finality.

"Now we're for it," MacGregor said. "It sounds like transmission trouble."

Aladin tried the gears. Though the engine was running well enough, the car was dead and it would not move.

369

"Let me have a go at it." MacGregor moved over as Aladin got out.

"Can you drive a car?" Essex said. "Why don't you let Aladin handle it?"

"I'm not trying to drive it." MacGregor engaged the clutch on all gears. "I'm trying to see what is wrong with it."

"Won't it move at all?" Essex was leaning forward.

"No."

"Then what's the matter with it?" Essex asked Aladin.

"I don't know Sahib. It may be gears."

"It's not the gears." MacGregor switched off the engine and stepped out. "It's probably the half-shaft. They always seemed to break in the Fords we had in the desert, but only after quite a hammering. Get out the torch Aladin and we'll have a look underneath it."

"Can you do something about it?" Essex's voice was rising.

"I don't know. I know very little about cars." MacGregor took off his coat and went around to the back of the Ford and lay down on the rocks and wormed his way on his back under the car.

"Put something under you," Katherine told him.

"I'm only going to take a look," he said. Aladin handed him down the electric torch and then straightened up.

"Go on," Essex said to Aladin. "Don't stand there looking happy. Get under there and see if you can help Mr. MacGregor."

"He can't do anything," MacGregor said. He was looking at the indentation on the axle casing. He could see that they had hit something very hard, and he remembered the bump which had cracked the car as they fled from the Governor's house. He crawled out and asked Aladin to jack up the car.

"Well?" Essex said.

"I don't know," MacGregor replied. "We'll have to take the wheel off."

"They told me this car was almost new," Essex said.

"It must be that hard knock we took this morning."

Aladin was under the car jacking it up. MacGregor found the tools and unrolled them and pried off the hub cap. He began to unscrew the holding nuts of the wheel, but it became awkward as the raised wheel turned. He asked Essex to put his foot against it. Essex folded his arms and balanced himself and put his riding boot on the tire. MacGregor jerked at the brace and the wheel turned and Essex nearly fell over.

"Let Aladin do it." Essex stood away.

"Don't give up so easily," Katherine told him. "It's a change to see you two working together. Go on."

MacGregor had taken off the nuts and he stepped back to allow Aladin to handle the wheel. It came off easily and MacGregor wondered what he was supposed to look at next. He told Aladin to take off the hub casing, and they watched silently as the Afghan worked on it. When the casing was off, Aladin stood up with a small piece of metal in his hand.

"Yes," MacGregor said. "The half-shaft is broken."

"Can you fix it?" Essex pulled on his coat.

"I don't think so. What do you say, Aladin?"

"No Sahib. We must have a new part. They are very difficult to get, even in Teheran."

"I suppose that means it's impossible out here," MacGregor added. "You might as well wipe off this vehicle," he told Essex.

"Let's have a look at where we are again," Essex said.

"We're absolutely nowhere," MacGregor unfolded the map from his pocket.

"What's this place?" Essex kneeled down with him and looked at MacGregor's finger identifying their position by the light of the torch. "Hajiabad. That can't be far away."

"You won't find a half-shaft there," MacGregor said.

"I'm not looking for a half-shaft. I'm looking for a place where we can get in touch with someone."

"Do you want to go back to the main Tabriz road?"

"I don't intend going back anywhere," Essex said. "Isn't there some other way out of this without going back?"

"Not unless we abandon the Ford," MacGregor told him.

Essex stood up and looked at Katherine. "This would happen," he said. "Damned bad luck from the beginning, or damned bad driving. What would happen to the car if we left it here?" he asked Mac-Gregor.

"It would be stripped to the last bolt."

"Do you think we might find a team of horses in this place Hajiabad?"

"Probably," MacGregor said.

"That is obviously what we must do," Essex said. "Aladin can stay here and watch the Ford. We will go and arrange for horses to pull him in. Then we can see how to proceed."

"We can't get far in this country without a vehicle," MacGregor warned him.

"Then we'll have to get one at Hajiabad."

"Most unlikely," MacGregor said. "It would be simpler if we bedded down here and tried to get back to Zenjan in the morning."

"We're not going back there," Essex said, having no intention of limping back after such a dramatic exit. "There must be some Russians around here somewhere. We can get the broken part out of them, or at least some transport of some description. We had better get to this

371

place Hajiabad as soon as we can. Could you get us there, MacGregor?"

"It shouldn't be difficult."

"Then we might as well go. How long will it take?"

"A couple of hours."

"Alright. Do you hear that Aladin? You stay here with the car, and we will go to Hajiabad and send back some horses or mules or something to pull you out. And don't go to sleep and have the car stripped."

"Sahib," said Aladin. "There are Kurds here — now that the snow is on the mountains. They will probably find me and overpower me and steal your belongings."

"Then hide our bags in the rocks somewhere."

"They would torture me to discover them, Sahib. It would be safer if we remained here until morning. Then it would be simple for me to guard the car during the day."

"Nonsense." Essex had put on his coat, and was filling his pockets with chocolate and oranges and thinking of his other needs. "We can't wait around here because you happen to be scared. Colonel Pickering told me you were the best man he had, but you don't seem to be living up to your reputation. I wouldn't like you to disappoint Colonel Pickering."

"Yes Sahib."

"MacGregor. Give him that pistol."

"No Sahib," Aladin said nervously. "No pistol."

"Why not?"

"They will certainly kill me if they discover I have a pistol."

"Alright. But don't go to sleep. You can do your sleeping to-morrow. Get out the food box and take what you want."

"It wouldn't be a bad idea if we ate something before we left," MacGregor said.

Essex was reluctant now to admit any wisdom or authority in Mac-Gregor for suggestion or directive. "The sooner we get to this village the better," Essex said. "We can eat there."

"It won't be much of a village," MacGregor argued. "I think you're expecting too much of it. It's probably a few mud hovels and a dozen people."

"That's all I'm expecting," Essex said. "Are you ready?"

MacGregor had been cutting a circle of compass degrees from the bottom of the War Office map. "I haven't a protractor," he said. "Do you have a pin, anybody?"

Katherine gave him a pin and he stuck it through the rough protractor onto the small point he had marked on the map as their position. He got the position of Nasirabad roughly and then walked away from the car to place the small compass on a rock. He found his position and then said, "Alright. This will be rough, but let's go."

"Do we really have to walk?" Katherine said. "It's getting so cold."

MacGregor pulled on his greatcoat. "We're lucky it isn't raining," he told her. "This place is always wet at this time of the year."

"Is that a desert we have to cross?"

"Not quite," he said.

They said good-bye to Aladin, who bowed from the waist in token of his obedience in remaining; thus placing upon them the responsibility for his mutilation or his death. He asked Allah in his own tongue to forgive and preserve them, whatever happened to him.

"You'll be alright," MacGregor told him. "Just don't show any light."

They left the dried river-bed, and began without ceremony to walk across the hard tableland which had turned purple in the evening haze. They walked in silence until Essex damned his riding boots and the cold wind. MacGregor and Essex allowed Katherine to set the pace, and she did so at a speed which was obviously intended to embarrass them, but they kept up and said nothing about it. If there was any further humour in the spectacle of three English travellers racing across an unknown part of the Median plains, then none of them had the mind to see it at this moment. Their peculiar grimness was only softened by the appearance of a Kurd with five mules.

They saw him pass over a rise before complete darkness blocked all their vision of distance. He was not far away, and he was taking their own approximate direction. They caught him as he climbed another rise, and he cried his religion and his honesty as the three strangers descended upon him from the early night.

"Are you devils?" he said in Persian.

"Don't be afraid," MacGregor told him. "We are travellers. Our car has broken down and we are making our way to Hajiabad."

"I am not afraid," the Kurd said in rough and unhappy Persian, "but there is a limit to a man's understanding. Mine is ignorance rather than fear. Who but three devils would appear like that, from nowhere. Now I see a beautiful houri with you. Two divs and a houri."

"We are travellers," MacGregor repeated seriously as they stood with the Kurd at the head of his first mule, "and we will not harm you."

"What kind of people are you who dress like that?"

"We are not devils," MacGregor assured him. "We are English."

"Englishmen? Divs? What do you want of me? I am a Kurd from Suleimeneh taking my skins and hides to Hajiabad where an armed caravan awaits me. What do you want of me?" He was dressed in Kurdish robes with swirling baggy trousers, tight at the ankles. He held a short-barrelled rifle before him in some defence and in some offence. He was grey-bearded, but he was not an old man, and he wore a Kurdish head-piece of handkerchiefs wound about a felt cap. He stood away from them with his five mules behind him. The mules were laden with large bundles of skins. As the animals moved nervously, the bundles on each side of them swayed and creaked like a rolling ship. The smell was enough to indicate the quality and tension of the hides, and Essex took out his handkerchief and coughed and blew his nose.

"What's he saying, MacGregor?"

"He thought we were devils."

"Did you tell him we were Englishmen?"

"That's the same thing as far as he's concerned," MacGregor said.

"What language is that you speak?" the Kurd asked quickly.

"The English tongue."

"You are Christians?"

"Yes."

"Then you are Armenians!"

"No. English."

"*Armeni* are Christians," the Kurd said decisively.

"So are the English," MacGregor said carefully, "just as Kurds and Arabs are Moslems. I assure you that we are English. Our machine has broken down and we would like your help in pulling it to Hajiabad. Your mules could do that easily."

"My five mules are loaded with skins, *Armeni*," the Kurd said.

"It would be simple for your mules to pull the car," MacGregor insisted. "It is a short distance back in a dried river-bed. We could pay you well for your trouble."

"No, *Armeni*," said the Kurd. "I do not wish to be rude, but my skins are worth more than you could pay me. Furthermore I fear for my property in this quick darkness, unescorted. You may be well-dressed bandits. I must go on to Hajiabad."

The arguments were formal and polite, that is the Kurd's rifle pointed at them as MacGregor tried to persuade him to go back with them for the car. Essex produced money. The Kurd showed interest; but he shook his head and prepared to leave them.

"What's the matter with him?" Essex said.

"He doesn't trust us," MacGregor said. "He's afraid we'll rob him."

"That is absurd," Essex protested. "Tell him he has a gun, and we haven't."

"I've gone into all that. He will only come back for the car when he has delivered his hides to Hajiabad. Nothing will make him go back to-night with those hides on his mules."

"Then he can give us a lift," Katherine said.

"I can't see you riding on those filthy hides," Essex told her. "I'm sure they're verminous."

"The hides are covered with felt matting," MacGregor said. "Two of the mules have no hides. One has boxes of dried figs, and the other is his

374

own riding mule." MacGregor did not wait to discuss it any more with Essex. His own aching leg and head decided him, and he bargained with the Kurd to allow them to ride. At fifty rials MacGregor became tired of bargaining and he handed the Kurd the money and told Katherine to ride on the bare mule.

"Do I sit side-saddle?" she said as he helped her on.

"Sit any way you like," MacGregor told her. "Side-saddle is probably more endurable."

"The second one has the boxes," MacGregor told Essex who was lighting his pipe to condense the atmosphere a little.

"I think I shall walk," Essex said.

MacGregor ignored Essex and scrambled up on the hides of the third mule. He told the Kurd to go ahead as he settled himself against the felt matting to counteract the rolling motion of the bundles and to prepare himself for the gait of the animal. The Kurd kicked his mule in the stomach and began the real movement of the caravan.

"Kathy," he heard Essex say. "You're the only woman in the world who can ride a mule and look absolutely comfortable." He was walking beside her.

"I can assure you that I am not comfortable."

"Then get off and walk."

"I never walk if I can ride," she said. "I might as well be sore in one place as another."

"Kathy," Essex said again. "What do you think of this country?"

"If you mean this desert, I don't like it at the moment."

"Don't deliberately misunderstand me," Essex said. "Do you find anything about this place at all which could appeal to you, with the exception of its ancient history?"

"With the possible exception of Turkey," she said, "I've never yet been in a country that I did not like. What's the matter with this? Have you ever seen such glorious country?"

"It's a wilderness," he said. "Where? Oh where are the plains of Nishapur, and where are the Ivory Gates to Paradise? In this bitter emptiness! Here!"

"Why not?" she said. "Do you expect your ordered woods and gardens, and your green and shaded lanes?"

"Not at all, but I expected some vision of ancient splendour. You can't tell me for instance that you are impressed with the nobility of this population."

"No," she said. "I find them dirty and poor."

"Do you like that?"

"Not particularly. Dirt is a sin, and poverty an evil; but I prefer them to some of our own submissive orderliness. Where? Oh where are the

Yeomen of England?" Katherine shifted her position with suitable groaning and complaint.

"*Armeni.*" The Kurd had dropped back to walk beside MacGregor's mule. "What do they talk about?"

"Religion," MacGregor said as a near translation.

The Kurd was delighted. "That is something to discuss with a Sunni like myself. Would the Khan be willing to discuss religion with me?"

MacGregor addressed this to Essex. "The muleteer would like to discuss religion with you," he said.

"Oh?"

"He wants to know why a Christian is not a Mohammedan. If there was one prophet, Jesus, why couldn't there be a second prophet, Mohammed? He would like to know your answer as a Christian to that."

"Tell him to watch his mules. We seem to be going round in circles."

MacGregor was in a mood to put Essex into a predicament, and he told the Kurd exactly what Essex had said, and waited for the answer.

"Is he angry with me for something?" the muleteer asked unhappily.

"No. He is angry with himself and many other things." MacGregor was sorry for the rudeness and he retracted quickly. "He is an important man who has much on his mind, and he does not intend any rudeness or anger."

"It doesn't matter," the Kurd said philosophically. "The anger of great men has its blessing: when the desert dust rises to the sky it is a sure sign of rain."

MacGregor translated the reply to Essex as a form of forgiveness.

"Is he being impertinent?" Essex said.

"No. He did not want to embarrass us by showing that he was hurt, so he made a compliment of your anger. Kurds are very proud; also very polite."

It was dark now but MacGregor knew that Essex looked back.

"I suppose I deserved that," Essex said.

"You certainly did," Katherine told him.

"Perhaps you had better apologize for me, MacGregor."

MacGregor apologized to the Kurdish muleteer for Lord Essex. The Kurd turned it again by blaming God for not creating all men with a common language and a common religion so that they might understand each other better. He offered to continue the discussion of religion.

"No thank you," Essex said to MacGregor. "Tell him I respect his Belief, and I'm sure he respects mine, whatever it is. That will be satisfactory for both of us."

MacGregor sighed in the night. "He says you are absolutely right," he told Essex. "He adds that there is really no difference between you and him as men, except that he wears the baggy and uncouth trousers of the Kurd, and you wear the subtle trousers of the Armenian."

376

"I hope you're learning something from this man," Katherine said to Essex. "He is obviously a born teacher."

"What is it I am supposed to learn?" Essex asked cheerfully but wearily.

"Everything you don't know," Katherine said. "Particularly about those trousers you are wearing."

"What's the matter with them?"

"Nothing. It really isn't anything to do with your trousers."

"Isn't it?"

"No."

Essex was lost. So was Katherine. There was nothing more to be said.

Essex put his two hands on the boxes of the second mule and pulled himself up as the Kurd came around to help him. The moon was out and MacGregor saw Essex before him, seated comfortably and naturally upon the mule, smoking his pipe. He moved easily with the awkward gait of the beast, and MacGregor admired again the natural dignity and poise which held this man together, even on a mule. For a moment Essex was untouched and uncomplicated, and MacGregor understood something about Essex for the first time: he understood this simple dignity and it made him regret that Essex would never learn the lessons of other men. Apparently Katherine also regretted it.

Katherine was now announcing that she could see the tiny lights of Hajiabad.

The soft hills ended as suddenly as they had begun. After a short flat approach, Hajiabad appeared on a slight rise. In the frosted light of the sharp moon, it was a huddled-up cluster of red, pink, brown, and yellow faces of flat walls which barely rose above the earth. It was quiet and caught by the empty blue space about it. In its centre there was a slender pillar of silver light. It was a slim minaret, cast tenderly on one side by a lunar shaft, and on the other by a purple shadow.

"Thank God," said Essex, "for the Mohammedan religion. If it produced nothing else but its minarets it produced enough. Nothing embraces space so naturally, so perfectly, as the symmetry of these wonderful towers."

"Those wonderful towers are unusual here," MacGregor said. "This one must have been built as a watchtower for Kurdish raids."

"MacGregor!" Essex complained. "Don't say things like that. For God's sake don't explain it. If you want me to understand this country then let its æsthetic beauties do their own explaining!"

Katherine denounced MacGregor in the same terms.

MacGregor was silenced and he did not try to explain the shouting which the Kurd launched before them as they approached the narrow mud street of Hajiabad. The Kurd shouted *"Chabadar,"* as he clapped his hands and helped Essex and Katherine off the mules.

377

"What's he shouting about?" Essex had to ask.

MacGregor was no longer a man who could resist explanation. "He is shouting the word they use to announce the arrival of important visitors. It is supposed to clear the way, but it will actually bring everybody out to see us."

"What time is it?"

"Nine o'clock," MacGregor said.

"See if you can hurry this fellow to get back," Essex said.

They had to fall into single file as they entered a narrow lane of mud hovels. The village was little larger than the dozen huts expected, but it did boast a caravanserai with a roof. The lane stopped dead at a mud wall. Through a hole in the wall they entered the courtyard of the caravanserai. Its occupants had collected to see the officials who warranted the shout of *Chabadar,* and the children and the dogs made a high-pitched din as the Kurd shouted the explanation of the strangers: *Armeni* whose machine had broken down and who had appeared on him out of the night. This explanation went on to considerable length.

"Well MacGregor," Essex said. "What's going on?"

"The Kurd is explaining that we are Armenians. As far as I can make out he is telling them that we crashed in an aeroplane."

"What's he saying that for?"

"To give us more importance," MacGregor said.

"Is this a Kurdish village?"

"No. But I should think Kurds come here during the winter when they migrate from the mountain slopes. I can see a few here now."

"What's all the noise about?" Katherine asked as the shouting continued.

"They're having a little fun and a little excitement at our expense," MacGregor said. "They are calling for a light to take a good look at us."

"Ask them where we can find the Russians."

"We had better wait until they satisfy themselves about us. We can look around and see if we can find a place to sleep."

"Can you see any Russians?" Essex asked.

"None."

The courtyard was small, and it was already filled with large bundles of skins which were guarded by Kurds whose authority and ownership were marked by their silent rise from crouched positions before a charcoal fire. MacGregor greeted them elaborately in Turki. Katherine stood near him, impressed, as those tall cloaked men leaned on their guns and returned a solemn greeting, then plunged into animated discussion in Kurdish with the muleteer, belabouring him with blows and kicks until he leapt behind MacGregor for protection. They let him alone when MacGregor explained that they had delayed him. The Kurds apologized

378

for not being able to provide them with more suitable transport and better company than the muleteer.

The caravanserai was a square mud building with a broken door which hung on its top hinge. There was a short verandah, and a few tables and chairs made it a coffee shop. MacGregor called into one of the rooms for the proprietor. He came out of the crowd who watched them. He was a small, grey, sick-looking Persian with a hooked nose and a sorrowful face. He explained to MacGregor that the only room he could offer them was one which was too humble for their occupancy. Nevertheless he asked one hundred rials for a night's lodging. MacGregor insisted on seeing the room, after declaring that he would not pay that price for a palace. They went through the broken door into a dark passage which led to a mud stairway. They stumbled up it as Essex lit his cigarette lighter and held it over his head. On top there was a low-ceilinged room without a door and with a small hole in the roof. The floor was mud, and the permanent smell of onions and cooking rose from the cracks in the floor.

"It is above the kitchen," the Persian said. "It is warm, and very good for sleeping. I will have my son block the hole in the roof with straw to keep out the wind."

MacGregor began the necessary violent arguments of rejection, continuing it until they were taken downstairs again and through the kitchen (where two women sat on the floor) and into a small room which possessed a few pieces of broken furniture, two worn rugs, and a window of coloured paper. The inn-keeper lit an oil lamp and Katherine and Essex sat down on a low and dusty couch as MacGregor continued the interminable argument for food, water, light, covering, and mattresses to sleep on. He ended it with a shout which brought the blood to his face, and the proprietor of the caravanserai went out, mumbling and turning to argue with MacGregor's back.

"Must we have these long discussions every time we want something?" Essex asked.

"No," MacGregor said. "We could sleep outside and go hungry."

"Sorry," Essex said good-naturedly. "So this is the caravanserai? Can't we do better than this?"

"He'll bring mattresses and covering, and water for washing. We'll eat later."

"Did you ask him if there are any Russians around?"

"Yes."

"What did he say?"

"He said he had never seen a Russian in his life."

"Those confounded Russians are never where you want them. Where is their nearest military post?"

"He doesn't know. It won't be nearer than Zenjan or Bijar."

"That far?"

"There is some kind of Iranian army post on the other side of the town," MacGregor said. "I'll go over there and see what they can do, but I don't think we will achieve anything here."

"How is your leg?" Katherine asked him, watching his awkward movement.

"The bandage is slipping."

"Why don't you sit down for a moment?" she said.

"We'll be here for days if we don't get onto this right now." MacGregor was feeling kind to no one. "It would have been better to spend the night at the Ford, and then go back to Zenjan. We will not find any spare parts nearer than that, and we're likely to get stuck here."

"Then we'll go on without the Ford," Essex said. "All we have to do is show our credentials to the Russians and we'll get transport."

"When you find the Russians!" MacGregor said and left. He was out in the courtyard when Katherine caught up with him and walked with a spring in her step to indicate her lightness and her friendliness.

"Are you angry at me also?" she said, as they walked through the hole.

"I'm not angry," he said. "I'm annoyed."

"What for?"

"It was a waste of time coming here."

"Don't be so sure," she said. "It will do Harold good to suffer a few discomforts."

"It's a little late for that," he said.

"You do not adapt yourself to a situation very well, do you?"

"When necessary . . ." he began.

"In fact for a man of your profession you cling to one line of thought with amazing stubbornness. You ought to take advantage of Harold's predicament instead of objecting to your own."

"Ah, it's impossible for him to understand what is happening here."

"If it's impossible for him," she said, "it's impossible for me."

"Why do you say things like that?" he said.

She didn't have a chance to reply. MacGregor had stopped to ask the youngsters — who had been following them in the darkness — where the soldiers were. They pointed up a small road and ran ahead as MacGregor gave information about himself and Katherine in answer to their daring curiosity.

"What were you saying to them?" Katherine asked.

"They were asking me where we came from, and whether you were really a woman, and if it was true that we had come in a flying machine. I told them it was all true."

"That I am a woman?"

"Very much a woman," he said. "Sometimes it overwhelms me."

380

"I can't believe it," she said.

"You're a woman alright," he said, and mumbled something in Persian.

"What was that?"

"It wasn't exactly meant for you," he said.

"I'm sure it was. What did you say?"

"I said that the ocean had taken the pearl of your womanhood to see how such pearls could be made."

She was quiet. "You are always surprising me," she said slowly. "Did you really say something so delicate?"

"It's simply the way things have to be said in Persian," he told her. "If you and Essex want to be æsthetic you should learn this language. It has more to offer than the sight of a mosque."

"Do you think I could learn the language?"

"Are you serious?"

"Of course I'm serious."

"You would find it very easy." His voice boomed from the hollow street of mud and straw. "You would probably be good at it."

"Perhaps you had better start teaching me."

"Please!" he said. "You can never really understand what is happening here unless you speak the language, although I have the feeling that you understand some things here better than I do."

"Hardly," she said, "but I can see how important it is to know what is going on in this peculiar country."

"Yes?"

"And how important it is for Harold to know what is going on."

"I'm sorry about Essex," MacGregor said. "He will never really know."

"Harold may be impossible," she said patiently, "but you must keep at him. He is very important, and he is going to be more important when we return to London. So will you be. Something big is going on, and Harold is going to decide some very serious issues; so it is worth a little patience to keep at him."

"I know how serious it is," he said.

"I don't think you do," she said. "You are going to be surprised at some of the peculiar situations in London. I'm sure of it. This trip is not simply important because of what is happening here. It is part of much bigger things."

"I know that too," he said.

"Then you mustn't get impatient with Harold. It's awfully difficult for him to understand. Believe me, I know. He has a tremendous amount of influence, and if you can convince him of anything here, it may change a great deal of policy that is being made in London."

"It's not much use trying to think in such diplomatic terms when we are way out here," he said and she did not argue further.

The military post was a former prison with a long courtyard before it. It housed ten to twenty soldiers. They were Gendarmes — Teheran Gendarmerie — and they sent for their officer who was sitting in a neighbouring coffee shop. When he came MacGregor saw instantly that he was a *hashash*: an opium addict. He was a young man with an old face, half-bearded and patched with dark shadows. His eyes were swollen and red and brimming with the unhappy tears of unattainable forgetfulness. He did not greet them, but stood on his heels with his eyes trying to grasp the significance of Katherine, who held a red-gloved hand to her slender throat. He could not see MacGregor at all. When MacGregor asked him where the Russians were, he closed his eyes so that he could force his words through a converging tangle of mental chaos.

"He's sick," Katherine said.

"He's drugged," MacGregor told her.

The officer laughed, swayed his head, and looked at Katherine's red gloves. "You are *Moscovs* who come to bribe me with a handful of red rubies. I am incorruptible. Go away and tell them that. I am incorruptible. Go away . . . go away . . ."

He had caught his tongue among his teeth, and he closed his eyes again to fight for some glimmer of coherency and clarity. He held one of the soldiers as he lost his balance because of his closed eyes, and he closed them tighter as if to limit the confusion. He cried and shook his head from side to side, and the tears ran slowly off his cheeks, disintegrating when they met his hard black beard. His face had tightened all over, and he lifted his head so that he could strain his neck muscles to breaking point. He clenched his whole face into a struggle for a single bead of sanity. He was clearly fighting a lost battle and fighting something which he had fought before. In terrible desperation he cried again and again: *Creator God. Creator God.* In this effort to call upon his Maker he achieved the moment of bitter sanity he needed. It destroyed him immediately. His whole face broke and he moaned and swayed and fell on the floor. The soldiers half-lifted and half-dragged him into another room, and they returned to answer MacGregor's questions about the Russians.

"The Russians," said one, "are at Zenjan. That is the nearest."

"No," said another. "Bijar and Nasirabad, and down by the bridge that covers the road to Maragha."

They argued, and MacGregor did not attempt to pursue it. He thanked them, and as he left one of them said: "*Agha.* The Russians are everywhere and they are nowhere. They are the little ghosts that haunt us." They laughed and MacGregor laughed, and he took Katherine away from their friendly shouts and their continuing argument about the exact location of the nearest Russians.

"Well?" Katherine began.

"They don't know where the Russians are. There are none around here."

"And that miserable fellow?" She held his arm tight with the memory.

MacGregor shrugged. "More than half the population are opium addicts," he said.

"Don't dismiss it like that," she told him impatiently.

"I'm not dismissing it," he said softly. "I'm trying to show you what it really means."

"But are they all like that?"

"Not that bad."

"But why . . ."

He lifted his hands. "To forget the difficulty of keeping alive. To keep out the cold, to forget their hunger and their misery."

"They ought to prevent it," she said.

"Who ought to prevent it?" he asked slowly.

"I don't know. Who allows it? Who is responsible?"

"The gentlemen in Teheran to whom we give our unqualified support. Opium helps to keep the population too stupefied and too broken to do anything about their miserable conditions. We support men here, knowing that opium is part of their means of maintaining position and authority. If you really want to know who is responsible, I suppose we are. Some of our most influential friends in the Government are landlords of large opium-growing areas."

"Wasn't there some kind of international control of narcotics set up?"

"They arrested a few Kurds smuggling opium in the belly of their camels into Iraq and Turkey."

"Surely we could really stop it."

"Certainly."

"How little we know of these things," she said.

"All the world could know and it wouldn't mean a damn," he said bitterly.

"You're wrong," she argued. "That is the trouble. Nobody knows these things. Even I didn't know and here I am right in the middle of it. I don't think anyone in England would like it if they knew."

"They will never know," he said.

The children had followed them again, and Katherine gave one of them a bar of chocolate, and told him in kind English to share it with the others. He ran off followed by the others, who caught him and began a vigorous battle for its possession.

Katherine watched them unhappily. "I didn't mean to cause that," she said.

She was more concerned than any Katherine he had heard before, and she was completely undisguised. He had a brief glimpse of her natural honesty, and he was surprised at its intensity. Yet, with such a thought came the memory of the trust which he had once offered her, and which she had turned back on him with such hard-bitten cynicism. He wondered if he would ever be able to find her honesty without stirring the memory of her dishonesty.

At the caravanserai Essex was lying on the couch which had been covered with a grey blanket. A small oil stove burned in the corner of the room, and sitting on a mattress near it was a Persian in a long bottle-green robe which reached to his ankles and which covered a light yellow garment of the same length. It was an unusual costume for modern Iran, and MacGregor was not surprised when he saw it all topped by a beard and a peaked green turban.

"May God be with you," the stranger said to MacGregor.

"Peace be with you," MacGregor replied. He bristled a little because the man had addressed him as an infidel. By simply allowing God to be with you and not peace, the Persian had announced his religious fanaticism. There could be no peace for an infidel.

"This fellow has been gabbling away since he came here," Essex said. "He had that stove and a few other things brought in. He has also been trying to show me some kind of letter. Find out who he is and what he wants."

"He's a Sayyid," MacGregor said.

"Oh?"

"He's a descendant of the Prophet," MacGregor said. "They wear green like that, but I haven't seen one of them so elaborately dressed for many years."

"Is he a priest?"

"More or less," MacGregor replied. "By his greeting he is obviously a fanatic."

"Well get him out of here."

The Sayyid held out the letter again. He was asking MacGregor if he spoke Persian, and if he could read this letter which he offered as his credentials, having heard that they were Englishmen who were travelling officially in the district. MacGregor took the letter to the oil lamp to read. Essex said never mind that, and had he found the Russians?

"There aren't any Russians here," MacGregor said, "and no one knows where we can find any. Our best hope is to go back to Zenjan."

"We're not going back," Essex said, "and we had better do something about getting that Ford here."

"Do you want to know what's in this letter?"

"Is it important?"

MacGregor licked his lips. "It's a letter from the Chief of sub-Provincial Intelligence of the Iranian Imperial General Staff."

"What about?"

"It says that the bearer has the full confidence of the General Staff and calls upon all agents of the Iranian Government to give him full assistance in his work."

"What work?"

MacGregor began one of the long discussions in Persian which annoyed Essex so much. In deference to Essex he foreshortened it by stopping the Sayyid half-way. "It's rather complicated," MacGregor told Essex. "He says that he is here to restore the teachings of the true religion to the God-forsaken people of Azerbaijan. He says the Russians have corrupted the true believers, made them worthless atheists, and created a political party of nonbelievers who have seized power in Azerbaijan. He says he is here on a holy crusade to effect resistance to these unbelievers, and to create a political religious party which will fight the Democrats and create a corner of the true faith in the heart of Azerbaijan."

"Why here, in this God-forsaken village?" Essex said.

"He says there is hope of real success here."

"Is there?"

"He says that he is known here, and that the Democratic Administration has not touched this area yet because they are afraid of the Kurds. Several Democratic organizers who did arrive from Teheran were hanged as traitors and unbelievers. His own party, which is the Religious Will Party, is strong here because he has organized it well. He is expecting great assistance soon from Teheran. In fact this is the work of our religious revival," MacGregor added.

"What is he wanting of me?" Essex asked.

"I haven't got that far," MacGregor said, and recommenced the discussion in Persian with the Sayyid, asking him what he wanted of Essex.

"I seek assistance," the Sayyid said.

"We are Christians," MacGregor told him. "Would you seek assistance from infidels and unbelievers against your fellow Mohammedans?"

"There is no God but God, and Mohammed is his prophet. I ask this in God's name, and not in the name of the prophet."

"What do you ask?"

"Your assistance. We are very poor, and influence is an expense."

"We have no money," MacGregor said.

The Sayyid was insulted at the mention of money, but he recovered and went on. "If you would speak in great public to the people of the district and explain that soon the English and the Americans are coming to fight the Russians, and that it would be well for them (if they wish to live) to do nothing now that will compromise them. Order the people not to assist the Democratic infidels, who are Russian agents."

"Even out here in the middle of nowhere!" MacGregor said in English.

"What now?" Essex demanded.

385

"He wants you to make a speech telling the people that we are about to fight the Russians, and that it wouldn't be healthy for them to assist the Democratic Administration."

"He wants me to give a speech?"

"That specific speech," MacGregor said.

"Tell him I couldn't do that," Essex said lightly. "Tell him I haven't my Government's authority to make such a statement at this time."

"Tell him it's all nonsense," Katherine interrupted. "You shouldn't be so tolerant of such talk, Harold. You only encourage it further."

"Don't worry," Essex told her. "I'm sure MacGregor fills in where I leave off."

"I certainly do," MacGregor said. "I told him you would report him to the Allied authorities if he said things like that."

Essex was not serious. "Tell him to come back to-morrow. I'm too tired to struggle through this now."

"He says that to-morrow is a religious holiday."

"That's too bad. Is it Friday to-morrow?"

"No." MacGregor was not interested enough in the Sayyid to pursue it any farther with him, even in requiring an explanation of the religious holiday. He was surprised when the Sayyid did explain that to-morrow there would be a *ta'ziya* — a passion-play — to commemorate the murder of the Shiah saints by their rival Mohammedan sect: the Sunnis. Mac-Gregor knew that this was Muharram, the month of mourning in the Arabic-Persian calendar, and the correct month for the *ta'ziya*. But the real *ta'ziyas* had been forbidden by the last Shah, who had limited any display of religious fanaticism to the flying of the black flag over a house or mosque. The Sayyid was obviously being clever and very free with his religious interpretations, and for obvious political reasons. MacGregor said (exactly as Essex had said) that it was too bad the Sayyid could not re-turn to-morrow, and bade him farewell. The Sayyid left with some mur-mur of complaint which MacGregor could not hear.

"Now we have to get the Ford," MacGregor said.

"Do you think our friend with the mules can find it alone?" Essex sat down heavily.

"That is risky in too many ways," MacGregor said. "I'll have to go with him."

"Oh no, MacGregor," Katherine said.

"You've had enough for a while," Essex told MacGregor. "I had bet-ter go."

"I don't think you could find the way," MacGregor began.

"I'll manage," Essex grunted moderately. It suggested that MacGregor was underestimating Essex's technical ability to navigate himself back to the Ford. It was something of a challenge to MacGregor.

"You have to be careful here," MacGregor argued mildly. "Anything at all can happen."

"True." Essex pulled on his jacket.

"Also, you won't be able to get along, not knowing the language."

"I'll get along," Essex replied. "You just find the fellow with the mules and set us going. That's all that will be needed. Come on."

MacGregor knew that Essex had decided very definitely that he would go for the Ford himself. There seemed to be some kind of an appeal to MacGregor and to Katherine in what Essex was doing. Katherine did not leave the room with them, and Essex paused to say rather quizzically: "I hope I can trust you two to behave yourselves."

"I should resent that," Katherine said, but she did not turn it on Essex as sharply as she could have.

MacGregor recognized Essex's appeal to Katherine but MacGregor was too tired to acknowledge its rivalry. He wanted to lie down somewhere to deaden the throbbing pain in his legs and the ache of his burning face. First, however, he must get Essex on the way. He thanked Heaven that Essex was a good sport and didn't mind riding five or six miles on a mule to haul in a car. While Essex made a meal of the last chocolate and fruit they had brought with them, MacGregor went to find the muleteer and argue the price for his services.

Chapter 30

WHEN ESSEX had gone MacGregor ate well of the sticky rice which the inn-keeper supplied, and then allowed Katherine to re-bandage his leg and clean the scratches on his face. He accepted the best mattress without much argument and he lay down on it to sleep fitfully — worrying about Essex. Katherine apparently had more confidence in Essex's ability to look after himself, for she slept very successfully without turning or sighing, and MacGregor restrained himself from awakening her as he waited for Essex to return.

She was awake when Essex did return. She sat up as he came in.

"Are you alright Harold?" she said quietly.

"Yes. Go back to sleep."

MacGregor turned his head. "Did you have any trouble?"

"A little," Essex said. "We had a bit of bother getting the car out of that river-bed. That's all."

"Did you eat?" Katherine was very solicitous.

"Yes. Go back to sleep."

Essex was already taking off his riding boots, having called Aladin in to help him. He then bade Aladin good night, undressed, wore his silk pyjamas, and bedded down on the couch which they had left for him. MacGregor heard him sigh with pleasure and he was asleep before Katherine or MacGregor. Both lay and listened to his steady breathing, and when Katherine fell asleep MacGregor lay awake thinking of both these people who were so difficult to know but so very worth while knowing.

He went to sleep with this good feeling, and he was the last to awaken in the bright morning which illuminated the room through the paper window.

He was so stiff that he grunted involuntarily when he sat up. Katherine and Essex were not in the room, but Essex's riding boots faced him across the floor. It was cold, and he tasted the warm odour of cooking. By his hunger he guessed that he was quite fit and fresh, despite his soreness. His headache had gone, and he touched his facial wounds with his fingers. They had hardened, and they were already part of his face, and he forgot them and felt his fresh beard. He took off his pyjama trousers and pulled on his baratheas, and then pulled on his socks and boots. His suitcase had been brought in, so he found his towel and went into the courtyard.

Like most caravanserais in the north, this one had all rooms opening onto the small courtyard. Stalls for the merchants and travellers were alternated with stables to utilize the warmth which the animals created. The Kurds had gone, and Aladin was now importantly placed in the centre of the courtyard before a fire, cooking in his pots from the tins of food. The Ford was behind him and he shouted angrily at the small boys who tried to get into it. He was pleased to see MacGregor, and they exchanged a little of the banter which comes so naturally in conversational Persian. It was natural for them to talk in Persian because it was more expressive than English.

Aladin had a tin of water ready, and MacGregor stripped to the waist and began washing as Aladin poured the water for him. He asked Aladin about the journey from the river-bed. Aladin said that Essex had arrived just in time, because he had heard Kurds around. Aladin had expected the worst as they made the slow journey here behind the mules, but Lord Essex had slept most of the way in the back seat of the Ford. Moreover, Essex had already taken Aladin with him this morning to enquire about other transport, about Russians, about horses. He had been sent back to cook the breakfast. Essex and the *Khanum* had gone to see the mosque.

Aladin was pouring water over MacGregor's head, keeping one eye on the breakfast and the other on the car, and apparently none on the direction of the water. Katherine and Essex arrived, and it was enough distraction to send a stream of water too far down MacGregor's back and he bellowed at Aladin for a towel.

Katherine laughed with delight. "Aren't you cold?" she said as he groped for the towel.

"Damned cold," he said. He rubbed his neck and shoulders, and straightened up and kept the towel around his shoulders as he turned around to face them. Katherine was without lipstick and her cheeks were pink in the sharp air of the morning. Essex was unshaven but he also looked polished. He did not wear his riding breeches; he wore corduroy pants and brown shoes.

"Look," Katherine said. "I had my boots cleaned."

MacGregor flayed his arms to get warm, and she noticed the scar across his stomach, a tan scar which was wide and smooth and dangerous.

"Where did you get that?" she said.

He folded his arms over it. "That's a burn."

"What happened?"

"Truck caught fire," he said and went inside.

He dressed, combed his hair, and felt the beard under his neck. He decided that he would rather let it grow than struggle through shaving. He went out again and they all sat on the running-board of the car to eat breakfast, coated and padded against the sharp air, but preferring it to the rank smell of the caravanserai.

Aladin had prepared them link sausages, and as the other travellers came out of the stalls and stood near Aladin's fire, the Englishmen were made conscious of their elaborate meal. The onlookers ate flat thin loaves and dried dates and prunes which they produced from baskets. They freely discussed the strangers' elaborate tins of food, and one of them asked Aladin if he might have the empty tins. Aladin behaved with the coolness expected of him, saying it was nothing to him who took the tins.

"If I had a thousand tins of your food," one merchant said to Aladin, "I could be a millionaire. Do you have any to trade?"

"No," Aladin told him briefly.

"Ask your masters," the merchant said. "It is up to them."

"Ask them yourself," Aladin replied.

"Do they speak our tongue?"

"Better than you do."

"Then forgive me," the merchant said to Essex, MacGregor, and Katherine. "I did not know that you understood me. I would like to ask if you need any good Shiraz carpets or some Tabriz silver, or perhaps some bolts of silks and Aleppo cottons?"

"We are honoured," MacGregor replied. "But we need nothing."

"I have anything you would like," came the reply. "I want to trade with your servant for his tins of foods and his utensils and equipment."

"We need everything we have," MacGregor told him.

The merchant was a prosperous man and he had the patience of good manners and good eating, and he pursued his request leisurely and carefully and with good humour, until it was clear that it was hopeless. He then gave his attention to a fellow merchant (an older man) who was saying that he had always been impressed with the English trading methods. In his business it had taken the honesty of an Englishman to place Iran in the most important position in the world.

"Oh?" MacGregor said. "May I ask your trade?"

"I trade in the finest quality opium," the old merchant said. "My products are all fresh, pure, unadulterated, stamped, and correctly weighed. We owe this refinement of our commodity to a serious and high-minded Englishman who came to Isfahan many many years ago, and showed us that purity and reliability in our product would guarantee a regular demand for it. We have never adulterated our opium since that day. To-day it is the finest in the world, fit for men, women and children, ideal for regular consumption, and without the excessive reactions which one usually suffers from the heavily oiled opium of the East. For bringing honesty to the opium trade, we owe so much to that remarkable Englishman that I would like to take the liberty of presenting you each with a small silver box of our product — the very finest little black pearls of constant enjoyment."

"I hasten to state my unworthiness," MacGregor said.

"On the contrary," the merchant replied. "My gift is unworthy of your illustrious heritage."

MacGregor rejected the three small silver boxes, and told the curious Katherine and Essex of the illustrious Englishman who had brought all this upon them, having put the opium manufacture of Isfahan on such a sound moral basis.

"That's the funniest thing I've ever heard," Essex said.

The memory of the drugged officer was still fresh in Katherine's mind and she did not think it funny at all.

"If he comes from Isfahan," Essex said to MacGregor, "what is he doing way up here?"

"I've just realized that this is an opium village," MacGregor said. "Can you smell that rotten-apple odour?"

"Yes."

"That is the opium in its liquid form. This merchant is probably here to buy the raw product."

"Give him a couple of tins of food, and we'll take the boxes," Essex said.

"No." Katherine shook her head.

"My dear Kathy, don't be so boorish."

"It's disgusting," she said.

"Good heavens. Are you worried about that Englishman?" Essex was delighted with that Englishman.

"It's a terrible thing," she said. "We can be awful people at times."

"Ridiculous." Essex performed the exchange himself, more in the spirit of a purchase than in an exchange of gifts. Essex was immediately sorry when he realized that Katherine was more disgusted than he thought possible. He changed his mind about offering her one of the silver boxes as a reminder of an amusing incident. He himself would tell of the incident — including the story of the Englishman — when he produced the silver box in more civilized surroundings. He intended to use it as a snuffbox.

To divert attention from his mistake with Katherine, Essex stood up and told MacGregor that he had found a barber. They both needed a shave. Also, he wanted to discuss with him the difficulties of getting to Bijar.

"I investigated the situation rather thoroughly this morning with Aladin," Essex said as they walked to the barber. "There doesn't seem to be any kind of transportation available, or anything at all that goes to Bijar, and I'm hanged if I know where we can find any Russians."

"I don't see why you're anxious to go down to Bijar," MacGregor said. "It's not Azerbaijan at all. Bijar is in Ardelan District, and that is Kurdish. Aren't we supposed to be concerned about Azerbaijan?"

"You keep trying to throw me off my route," Essex said good-naturedly. "There is a very particular reason for me going to Bijar. I know it's Kurdish. I even hope to get farther across Kurdistan to Sinneh."

MacGregor noticed that Essex was already grasping the geography of the country. He had obviously gone into this particular part of the route in great detail. "Is it so important?" MacGregor said again. "Can't we skip all that part of the world and turn north?"

"I'm surprised at you sometimes, MacGregor." Essex helped Katherine over a mud puddle and ignored the curious peasants who watched them. "We have discussed this many times, and you never seem to grasp the significance of this part of the world in relation to the Empire."

"Are you talking about Azerbaijan or Kurdistan?"

"Both. At the moment I'm thinking of Kurdistan. Both Bijar and Sinneh are in Ardelan, which is right on the border of Iraq isn't it?"

"Yes."

"And we have large populations of Kurds in Iraq haven't we?"

MacGregor said that he knew that.

"In fact Kurds inhabit the areas all around Mosul," Essex went on, "where we have some of our largest oil fields in Iraq, and other vital interests and communications."

"I know that," MacGregor said again. "How that oil worries you!"

"Well then. Do you wonder that I'm interested in Ardelan or Kurdistan, or whatever you like to call it. Whatever these Kurds do in this part of the world will have a direct effect upon our Kurdish populations in Iraq. And vice versa, I suppose. We want a friendly border on this side of our Kurdistan, a border of people who are not being scooped up by the Russians. For all we know the Russians may have started an independent Kurdistan movement to include our Kurds in Iraq."

"There have always been moves for an independent Kurdistan."

"Well we can't have that sort of thing on our Iraq borders," Essex announced.

"You are not going all the way down there just to find out if there's a growing Kurdish plot for independence?"

"Not I," said Essex. "We have enough sources of information from that part of the world, and we have sent some rather good chaps in there from Iraq. I have all the information I need. All I want to do is to show the Kurds that the British Government is aware of them enough to send a man like myself down there. Also, we might be able to persuade one or two difficult Sheiks to be friendly. Most of them can be bought I believe, but there are some who need more deft handling as things begin to get serious up this way."

"I'll be interested to see how you make out."

"I presume that you intend to come along."

"Certainly."

"And I hope you will lend me the benefit of your vast experience."

"I won't be of much use to you," MacGregor said dully.

"Don't worry," Essex told him. "I'll see that you are useful. First we have to get down there, and we have to hurry up about it. I can't waste any more time in this place."

MacGregor waited, knowing that Essex had already made his plans.

"Aladin can go back to Zenjan and find some Russians and get the part he needs," Essex began judiciously. "We three can go on to Bijar and either wait for him there, or go on to Sinneh and wait there instead."

"How do we get to Bijar or Sinneh?"

"By horse," Essex said simply.

MacGregor did not laugh. It was so typical of Essex to suggest such a thing that MacGregor was not even surprised.

"I took Aladin and went into it rather thoroughly this morning," Essex said. "Horses seem to be cheap here. It's apparently a rather complicated business to hire them because you have to hire a whole caravan and entourage, and the horses you hire are rather poor. We spoke to one fellow this morning who is willing to sell us four horses and the necessary equipage. All we have to do is to go along and pick out the beasts we want. What do you think, Mac?"

MacGregor looked at Katherine, who was expressionless.

"Can you ride?" Essex asked him.

"In a fashion," MacGregor said.

"Well then, what is the difficulty?"

"Horse travel is too slow."

"It's quicker than waiting here, and we can make Bijar in less than two days."

"It's rough going."

Essex nodded. "I know that," he said, "but I am keen to see a little of this countryside from a horse. It's the natural way to travel here. In fact Kathy and I are rather set on the idea and we anticipate the experience. Eh Kathy?"

Katherine shrugged, but she was obviously in this with Essex.

MacGregor could already detect their anticipation, and he did not quite understand it. It would be quite uncomfortable and very slow, and the chances were that they would have to walk a great deal of the way. They had to face hard country and mountains. Yet these two looked as if they were excited about a fox hunt. If not a fox hunt, then some other rare sport which appealed to their Anglo-Saxon imaginations.

"Where did you find the horses?" MacGregor asked.

"There is a horse dealer near the mosque," Essex explained. "He has a yard full of the beasts. A mean-looking collection, but good enough for our purposes and I'll pick out the youngest. Let's get this shaving over with."

They had been standing outside the barbershop for some time, the centre of a great deal of anticipation by the barber. As they mounted the step MacGregor knew what a disturbance Katherine's presence would make in a village barber's shop, but the occasion was too important for such details. They were bowed inside by the pink-faced barber.

It was not a shop but simply a small mud room with walls which had once been washed a pale blue. Now they were almost black, and the heavy odour of sticky jasmine and other cheap pomades had impregnated the whole room. In shutting the door, MacGregor seemed to have locked out the rest of the world. The only light came from a few small panes in the wall, and there were no chairs and no mirror; only one or two recesses in the walls. In one of these a man lay on a ragged carpet, his beard wrapped in cabbage leaves. He was sleeping with his hands upon his comfortable stomach.

"What on earth is that?" Essex pointed to the figure as he took off his coat.

"He is having his beard dyed," MacGregor explained.

"Yellow!" Katherine said.

"That is henna mud." MacGregor took her coat and gave it to the barber. "When the mud is washed out, his beard becomes a sort of maroon colour. It's an old habit among old men."

The barber was a small round man with well-shaven cheeks for a Persian. He was precise and independent. He disappeared behind a rush curtain and produced three small chairs and seated his visitors near a rickety pedestal which held a thin clay vase containing three red roses. Each rose had a small collar of coloured paper holding the petals tight like an opening bud. The collars were used to create a delicate picture of symmetry, in preference to the individual beauty of each rose. MacGregor understood this without thinking about it. Every Persian had a sensitive regard for nature, and it was perfectly alright to give natural beauty an additional design, particularly in the matter of roses and hyacinths. Katherine was aware of no such tender ambition and she thought it crude and primitive. But the roses were a passing moment which neither thought of mentioning.

For his water supply the barber had a clay font which was shaped out of the mud floor. He placed a fourth chair beside it and asked Essex, in deference to his seniority, to be seated. Essex loosened his collar, sat on the chair, and within a few minutes he was swathed about the face with warm damp towels.

"You are the English travellers?" the barber said when the towels were applied.

"Yes," MacGregor told him.

"Are you here to visit the Khan of Malool?"

"No. Our car broke its back," MacGregor said. "Who is the Khan of Malool?"

"The Khan Malool," said the barber, "is the lord of this little universe of Hajiabad. The lands about and the village are all his. He himself lives in Teheran, but he sends his nephews to administer the district."

"Is this all poppy country?"

"Every *bir-abassi-batman* of it!" said the barber, wrapping another towel around Essex's straight neck. "It makes the Khan as wealthy a man as the Shah. I understand that his house in Teheran is almost equal to the Shah's palace."

"Does the Khan still have his land?"

"At the moment, yes. Perhaps to-morrow or the next day it will be reformed." He placed another towel on top of Essex's head.

"What about the new Azerbaijanian Government, the Democratic Party, have they shown themselves down here yet?" MacGregor asked.

"Twice." The barber raised two pink fingers. "The first one was a small doctor who came one day and sent a letter to the house of Malool stating that he was here to re-arrange the matter of the land and would like to call upon the Khan or his representatives. The Khan's nephew, who calls himself *Ali Beg,* called upon the doctor with twenty men as his bodyguard. The doctor told *Ali Beg* that he must plant corn and barley instead of opium poppies, and also informed *Ali Beg* that he must reduce the rent of the land to the peasants, reduce their taxes, increase their share of the crops, and disband his large bodyguard. This happened right outside my door on the hard ground, on a very nice autumn day!"

"What happened?"

"While his men held the doctor, *Ali Beg* came in here and took my best and broadest razor and personally cut off the doctor's ears, tongue, nose and lips, and then allowed his men to remove the doctor's genitals. He then had the doctor tied behind his horse and he rode away, and we know that the doctor is buried headfirst in cement in a new well which *Ali Beg* is building."

MacGregor was silent as if he were never able to escape the presence of brutality.

"Then the other arrived some two weeks later," the barber went on pleasantly. "What a lion he turned out to be! He wrote no letter to *Ali Beg.* He was a big man with a wide moustache. Not a writing man at all. He did not wait to hear from *Ali Beg.* He went himself, alone, right to the door of *Ali.* We have had no such man since Sattar Khan defended Tabriz. I did not see the death of this second Tabrizi, but I believe he was torn limb from limb by trees or horses or even dogs. I only know that he called upon the peasants in his last words to revolt against *Ali Beg,* and to seize the land if necessary and institute the reforms which they have long needed. I don't think we have had a man like that since Sattar Khan," he said again, and placed the last towel on Essex's soft ears.

"MacGregor!" Essex's muffled voice bellowed from the towels. "How long do I have to put up with this? Tell him to get on with it."

"Is he uncomfortable?" the barber asked.

"He wants you to hurry," MacGregor said.

The barber took a towel from the top of Essex's head and applied fresh linen to his face, and then dampened Essex's impatience by rubbing his scalp gently and expertly so that Essex relaxed to enjoy it.

"I will never be able to understand those men from Tabriz," the barber said. "What sort of men are they who come here without an army at their backs? It is an unreal way of doing things, walking single-handed into the camp of your enemy. What sort of men are these?" The barber shook his head. "They might have been honest men; but is honesty enough for these reformers? Isn't strength important? What is the use of claiming reform if you don't have the strength to achieve it? What do you think, Englishman?"

"I haven't had to face the issue so bluntly," MacGregor said. "It always seems bad to use force, but I suppose it depends on whom the force is directed against."

"Ah ha!" said the barber and whipped the towels off Essex's face. "How true!"

"In this case, perhaps some kind of strength was necessary," MacGregor admitted.

"Strength is always necessary," the barber said.

Essex was puffing and feeling his red face. "Is this Figaro going to be much longer?" he asked MacGregor. "I feel like a beetroot."

"He's been telling me about the village." MacGregor told them what the barber had said while the barber himself chose his razor from a shelf in one of the recesses. He selected it from a group of other implements: scissors, combs, pincers for teeth pulling, cauterizing irons for sores, and the clamp and knife of the circumcisor. He stropped his razor on a broad strap and bent Essex's face over to begin.

"He hasn't put any lather on my face." Essex pushed him away.

"They don't use it here," MacGregor told him. "Go on," he said to the barber.

"He's not going to shave my face unlathered!"

"Try it," MacGregor said.

"He'll tear my face to ribbons."

"Not the way he does it."

Essex was half-convinced, and he allowed the puzzled barber to bend his face again. By tightening the skin in small patches the barber shaved Essex dry, the only water in the process being that on the razor which the barber dipped occasionally in the font behind him.

"The trouble with all these stories," Essex said as MacGregor completed the barber's story, "is their exaggeration. They embellish these things just enough to make you disbelieve the whole story."

"What's exaggerated about it?" MacGregor demanded.

"This talk of lip and nose cutting."

"That's not exaggerated," MacGregor said. "Believe me."

"But how could anybody do anything so horrible?" Katherine said.

"You say that after watching the Governor at work?"

"But there is some difference," Essex began.

"No there isn't," MacGregor replied irreverently. "They are all the same. I can't see why Tabriz didn't send an army down here with those men."

"Are you advocating force, MacGregor?" Essex's voice was hollow.

"If necessary."

"It's always bad when an Englishman thinks force is necessary," Essex said sadly.

"In this country the English know all about force," MacGregor replied. "They have never hesitated to use it."

"Now he is off on one of his moral spells," Essex complained to

Katherine. But Katherine would not join the discussion, in fact she was impatient with them for debating their different points of view. Essex decided that a little too much of the local bitterness had seeped into Katherine. It was unlike her. Since he did not want to cope with a sharp-tongued Katherine, he gave more attention to enjoying the barber. "This fellow is doing quite a good job," he said. "I can't feel a thing. What's he singing to himself?"

"I wasn't listening," MacGregor said.

"Is he satisfied?" the barber asked.

"Yes."

"You were discussing my method?"

"No. We were talking about Hajiabad."

"Have you met the Sayyid who has recently arrived here?"

"Yes. What is this religious festival he is holding?"

"He is being very clever," the barber said. "He pronounces this a time for *ta'ziya,* not because it is the month of mourning, but because it is a time for good Shiahs to remember their religion in the face of so much political activity. As you know, we Persians are deeply political. Here I am talking politics and religion with you in a few moments' acquaintance. We are like that. The Sayyid hopes to make a political impression upon us with his *ta'ziya.* We haven't seen a *ta'ziya* in many years and this way we will be attracted. Since he is organizing a Party here, a religious Party, it is quite clear that he is here for political reasons. He is also here to encourage the Shiah hatred of the Sunni Kurds. Antagonism between our village and the itinerant Kurds would make a great deal of trouble, and would probably stir up all the Kurds along the border."

"Surely the population don't want trouble with the Kurds."

"No. But only a few can see the results of his *ta'ziya.*"

"You expect the Sayyid to succeed?"

The barber shook his head and concentrated on Essex's upper lip. "We are poor, dirty, and ignorant; but we are not fools. Do we enjoy the taxes we pay, and the small returns we get? Do I like to pay the large rents upon this miserable hut? Will we love the Sayyid because he is the man of the Khan Malool? We are afraid to do very much but I say again we are not fools."

He finished with Essex by massaging his face vigorously and then softly, finally rubbing it with a dry towel. "Remarkable," Essex said as he stood up and stretched. "Tell him it was the most unusual shave I ever had, MacGregor."

"I'm sure that will impress him," Katherine said.

MacGregor sat on the chair to enjoy the same treatment, and the barber began by asking how he had been scratched. MacGregor said it had happened in the car accident and told the barber to shave his neck and chin and anywhere else he could. As he sat back and relaxed he listened to Essex and Katherine arguing about the Sayyid and the Khan Malool. Essex thought it all a great joke, and MacGregor felt personally responsible for Essex's lack of understanding. Perhaps he had not explained the barber's statements well enough. Yet Katherine seemed to have understood the division between the Khan Malool and the rest of the world. Was it so difficult to understand? MacGregor was beginning to find himself in this position of mental summing-up whenever he thought of Essex, and he decided that Essex had a hard wall in his mind which could not be broached by thought, reason, or evidence. It could be penetrated by other impressions but MacGregor had no idea what they were. Katherine knew that better than he did. He would leave Essex's education to Katherine, who seemed to be educating herself with remarkable speed. MacGregor almost went to sleep as the barber finished with the towels and shaved what was left of his face.

The barber made a whole refusal of payment, insisting that it would be bad manners for him to accept payment from visitors with whom he had discussed religion and politics. MacGregor forced it upon him, but he protested so loudly that he awakened the sleeping customer whose beard was wrapped in cabbage leaves. MacGregor placed the money on the chair as they left and the barber shouted his appreciation until they were out of sight along the muddy street.

They went immediately to the horse dealer near the mosque. He was a dark man with a shaven head but an unshaven face. He was seated on a bench beside the mud wall of his corral, a charcoal brazier before him. He looked like a Tartar, and MacGregor asked him about it. He smiled toothlessly and told MacGregor that he was not a Tartar. Oh no. He was a Persian from Isfahan, but he had been captured as a boy and taken to Bokhara as a slave. A horse dealer had rescued him and brought him back. Now he was a horse dealer himself. He took them under the wooden plank into a mud corral and shouted at two barefooted assistants to corner four specific horses from a bunch of ten or fifteen. A tall grey horse was isolated and brought to them for inspection. It was thin-legged and spindly with hard visible bones.

"This is not a *Yabu*," the dealer said cunningly. "It is a good Turkoman beast, long-winded and hard-footed. Look at the good condition of his hoofs; and you can see he is a real Turkoman by his long ears and his large head."

MacGregor felt the horse's forelegs, but Essex took over the inspection and rejected the animal. He pointed at two smaller Arab horses with thick shoulders, and nodded when the assistants brought them in. Essex chose four horses of the Arab type, small-looking and broken, but he had inspected them thoroughly and looked carefully at their teeth.

"They look pretty bad," he said, "but they're the youngest horses of the bunch. And they haven't any sores. Some of those other hacks are really in bad shape, and you ought to tell him to do something about those sores, MacGregor."

"They're all so filthy and uncared-for," Katherine added. "Don't they ever comb them down?"

"Not in winter," MacGregor said. "The dirt keeps out the cold."

"The only happy horse," Essex said, "is a clean horse. If we are to ride these beasts then tell him to comb them out. It is cruel to leave an animal so dirty."

"Tell him to clean the mud out of their hoofs," Katherine said. "Look at the filth and the scales. How can they be so cruel?"

"I don't mind the mud," Essex said, "but I do mind those sores."

"They look like tumours," Katherine went on, "and their eyes are swollen with pus."

"That grey fellow over there is blinded in one eye. Look at him turn his head to see what's going on." Essex was revolted. "This dealer ought to be shot for such neglect and you can tell him so from me, MacGregor."

"You might add my damnation also," Katherine said.

"I think the old man is in worse shape than the horses," MacGregor said. He did not mean it as a rebuke. But Katherine blushed and Essex laughed.

"I could kill you when you say such things," she told him.

"I'm sorry," he said with genuine surprise; but Katherine looked at him with quick resentment; and Essex laughed again.

"Are these the four you want?" MacGregor wanted to deflect Katherine's anger as quickly as possible. He pointed to the four Arab horses.

"Yes," Essex said. "I have always wanted to spend a bit of time on an Arab, even if he is rather thick in the neck. With horses as poor as these, youth is the only guarantee of the beast's stamina."

MacGregor had intended to remain quiet about the horses, but he was annoyed by Essex's unintentional snobbery in assuming him to be ignorant of horseflesh. If anything, the lack of intention made the snobbery worse.

"Those four horses have been bishoped," MacGregor said briefly.

"Bishoped?" Essex repeated.

"Old, and made to look like two-year-olds."

"I know what it means," Essex said, "but you're wrong. You can't argue with teeth and I looked at their teeth carefully. They're small and correctly marked."

"It's an old game." MacGregor opened the mouth of the nearest horse by placing his fingers expertly on the nose and the lips. "They cut down the teeth with a dentist's drill and stain the cavity with an acid to give it the markings of a young horse."

"How do you know these have been bishoped like that?" Essex looked at the teeth.

"By the small ridges and lines in the cavities."

"Why didn't you mention it before?" Essex said.

"I was waiting for you to ask me." MacGregor released the horse.

"I assumed you didn't know a damned thing about horses, didn't you Kathy? How do you know, anyway?"

"Shouldn't I know about horses?"

"It's unusual," Essex said forcefully.

"What's unusual about it?" By now MacGregor was annoyed with both of them.

"Did you keep horses?" Essex demanded.

"We had to use them fairly often."

"Ah. Here, in Persia?" Essex said.

"That's right."

Essex understood now. "You had work horses to get you around the country." Experience with horses on that level didn't count.

"Gentlemen!" Katherine interrupted, realizing the division and its reasons. "Shouldn't we get on with our horse dealing? You two can combine your knowledge, although we ought to defer to you, Mac-Gregor, as the local expert. If you know these horses so well, why don't you pick out four, and Harold can make the final decision."

"Go ahead," Essex said. "Pick what you like."

MacGregor plunged among the horses in the mud, and went over them very thoroughly. He kept one of the four Arabs which Essex had chosen, and picked two others which were small Persian cobs rather than Arabs. The fourth was a bigger horse, a Turkoman with no barrel, a singed-off mane, and practically no tail, but with sturdy legs and a solid rump. Mac-Gregor did not ask Essex's opinion, but told the old horse dealer that these would be their choice, depending on price. He had kept the one Arab as consideration to Essex. He was left alone by Essex and Katherine while he haggled over the price for ten minutes. Then he turned to the saddlery. He checked bits and straps and stirrups by pulling and jerking until they broke or resisted. He was finally satisfied with the pile of equipment and told Essex the total price. As a final concession to Katherine and Essex, he told the old man to brush the horses down, clean their tails and manes, and then pare the scales and mud from their hooves. He gave the dealer no money but told him to deliver the horses to the caravanserai within the hour.

They were feeling better as they left the corral and they began to anticipate and discuss the journey to Bijar. They were interrupted by a din which was issuing from the compound around the mosque. A crowd of people had collected around a small dais on which men and children were dancing and chanting. Essex stopped for a moment to watch over the wall and to listen to the high-pitched shouting.

"Is this their *ta'ziya*?" Katherine asked.

"The beginning of it," MacGregor said. "Let's get out of the way."

"What's it all about MacGregor?"

"It's a passion-play," he said.

"Who do they use for a martyr?" Essex said. "Surely not Moham-med."

"No. It's about the martyrdom of Hossain and Ali, the Shiah saints."

"Never heard of them," Essex said.

"Hossain is the Shiah hero," MacGregor told them. "He was murdered by a rival named Shamr."

"Do they go through a long rigmarole of suffering?" Katherine said. "They always drag it out in the Oberammergau."

"They go through everything: the mourning, the families, the whole picture of the killing of Hossain and Ali. It usually goes on for days. It's really a claim that Ali and Hossain are the true descendants of the Prophet, in contradiction to the false religion of the Sunni Moham-medans. In the old days it used to get fierce. The whole population would be worked up into a frenzy, beating themselves practically to death. The actors in the *ta'ziya* were supposed to mutilate themselves and cry for vengeance for Hossain and Ali. It's a bad business," he concluded. "We had better move on. They will turn on anybody if they really get worked up."

They could hear the wailing cries of "*Ya Hossain, ya 'Ali*," as they walked back to the caravanserai. The whole town was excited already by the chanting from the mosque. The caravanserai was deserted. As they sorted their luggage and rolled their needs into bundles to fit the large horse, the chanting and the shouting grew more excited. Essex ignored it for the time being and gave his careful instructions to Aladin as they packed. He wrote several letters for Aladin to take with him. MacGregor also wrote two explanations of their predicament in Russian.

"You go back to Zenjan and get the half-shafts," Essex told Aladin. "If you can't get it there, keep going until you do get it. Put the responsi-bility for it on our Russian friends, and if you have any difficulty phone the Embassy in Teheran. But get it from somewhere, and fix the car and then come on to Bijar or Sinneh."

"But Sahib," Aladin said. "The road to Sinneh is dangerous."

"If it's dangerous for you it's dangerous for us," Essex said. "It's up to you to find us. We'll leave plenty of information behind if we move on. But don't waste time. We don't want to be stuck out in the middle of nowhere waiting for you, and we don't want to stay in Sinneh any longer than we have to. Is that clear?"

"Yes Sahib," Aladin said doubtfully and looked at MacGregor who shrugged a little.

"We're depending on you," Essex told him. "So buck up."

They divided the food, as Aladin explained that he would have to find someone to guard the Ford while he was away. Essex gave him money and said he would have to arrange that himself. Then the horses came, and after another argument about the price, MacGregor paid the money and loaded the Turkoman horse with the large equipment wrapped in the tent. He tied their own bundles behind the saddles, wrapped in blankets. They were ready to go, and they sat down to eat the lunch that Aladin had prepared. By now they were irritated with the continuous shouting of the *ta'ziya*, and it was swelling nearer. Aladin went to the hole in the caravanserai wall and came back and bellowed above the growing noise that the whole procession was coming through the village and heading this way.

"Do you think we might watch it?" Katherine put down her mug of tea.

"Not in the street," MacGregor said. He looked around and up at the flat roof of the caravanserai. Two or three Persian women were up there already, and they were waving their arms and shouting. "We can see it from the roof," he said.

They left Aladin to watch the horses and climbed to the roof by the outside ladder. The Persian women were holding their children up to see. They ignored the foreigners, except to hide their faces with their long black chuddars. From the roof MacGregor noticed the domed mud roofs of all Hajiabad, grey in the greying day, broken only by the few narrow lanes and crooked paths that led from the mosque to the crude square beneath.

Down the lanes and into the square came children, who were running and shouting and clapping their hands and jumping to the beat of small tight drums. Behind them, and at the head of the procession, came a water-carrier who was spreading water out in handfuls upon visionary dust. The real dust rose behind him from the surging people who shouted and jumped and dragged their feet. The water-carrier was surrounded by young men, beating their heads and their breasts and shouting "Ah Hossain. If this water could only have been for our Hossain! *Ya Hossain. Ya 'Ali. Hossain! Hasan!*"

The water-carrier was followed by soldiers on horseback and chanting men, and women and children who wept and screamed. The crowd of onlookers joined in, crying and weeping aloud and beating themselves.

MacGregor tried, but could not explain the chaos of the procession to

Katherine and Essex, who saw it mostly as a mass of howling demented natives, horribly fascinating in their wild frenzy. MacGregor simply pointed out the recognizable characters of the *ta'ziya*: the old bearded man with one arm who was the angel Gabriel; the veiled figures who were assorted prophets, saints, and minor angels; the moaning groups of men, women, and children who represented the brothers and family of the martyrs; and Shamr the murderer, played by a drugged soldier who was beaten and cursed by all.

Then came the central figure of Hossain, the hero. This was the Sayyid himself, wearing the green turban and green cloak and holding a rusty-looking sword high above his head. He was greeted by shouts and praises and mourning wails. As the drums beat harder, the Sayyid brandished his sword and shouted at the top of his voice. With every shout a group of six half-naked men behind him cried "Woe for Hossain! *Hasan!*" and beat their naked backs with thick chains. Behind them came another four men in dirty white shrouds and rags, and covered in blood as they hacked their heads and their shoulders and their ears with bayonets and swords, so that they looked completely mangled and drenched in blood. The crowd called for pity for Hossain and Ali Akbar, and commended these men for shedding their blood in honour of the martyr; but it all came back in glory to the Sayyid representing Hossain. He accepted their shouts of pity as the four men hacked at themselves and fell fainting or exhausted to the ground.

"It's horrible." Katherine had walked away, breaking the fascination. "Why do they do it? Are they killing themselves? Are they drugged? It's horrible."

"It's hardly human," Essex commented unhappily. "What's the point to it all? Why be so frenzied about it?"

"There isn't any point to it," MacGregor shouted above the wailing. "It's your friend the Sayyid whipping up religious feeling for his own cause. This sort of thing is absolutely forbidden. It only causes trouble, particularly here where there are Kurds who are the Sunnis they are denouncing. The Sayyid is trying to use religious fanaticism to stir these people up. It will probably end in someone being killed — a Kurd, no doubt. Then there will be real trouble with the Kurds. The Sayyid is already shouting to the Faithful to reject the atheists who are in Tabriz and who are sent down here to make the people forget their religion and the sufferings of their saints, Hossain and Ali. He is calling on them to support the Religious Will Party of Sayyid-el-Zil. This is what Sir Samuel Fox was talking about when he said that religion was one way of counter-acting the Tudeh Party."

"It's a bad business." Essex could say no more, and they waited on the roof until the *ta'ziya* had moved away along the other streets.

Nothing more was said about it until they were mounted and out of Hajiabad, following the dirt track which would eventually take them to Nasirabad and Bijar. Essex leaned forward on his Arab pony and spoke to MacGregor.

"Who is this fellow, Sayyid-el-Zil, you were talking about?" he said.

"He is the leader of the Religious Will Party — our hope for a religious revival in Iran — our opposition to the Tudeh."

"This is really his doing?" Essex said.

"Absolutely."

"I don't like this sort of thing," Essex said. "I will never encourage such barbaric and superstitious nonsense, and I'll make sure that this Zil fellow is not given our support. It's an insult to the intellect to encourage such black-minded frenzy."

MacGregor was not impressed. He expected more of Essex than disgust. Nevertheless some impression of Fox's political follies had been made on Essex. If Essex could reject the Sayyid so easily then he could also reject the rest of Fox's friends in Azerbaijan. There might be some hope for Essex after all.

MacGregor had an idea that the real test for Essex was yet to come. They were already in Kurdistan, and they were facing the distant Kurdish mountains. With each mile the rise and fall increased, the country lost its smoothness, and the mountains were always ahead: sharp explosive mountains with black shapes against the grey sky, ridged and barren peaks which tangled and multiplied without sense or purpose. In this wild country even Essex could lose his identity.

Chapter 31

KATHERINE rode behind MacGregor and watched him twisting in the high saddle. He changed his position often, eventually raising one leg over the pommel until he was almost sitting side-saddle and squatting back on the cantle. He had his maps on his knees and she could see that this position came from experience. He was bent over his maps as if they held his interest more than the mountains, but he looked up at them from time to time, gazing at the distant peaks rather than at the surrounding hills. Occasionally he made notes on the maps and drew brief diagrams. She supposed that he was making geological observations and she envied him his knowledge of the construction of this country. She would have liked to understand the enormous forces which had carved these mountains out of the earth. It was an expanse of country she felt to be instinctively natural to her. The distant massive ridges, the horizon of unconquerable peaks, the barren valleys and wide plains; they all satisfied Katherine that this was where humanity belonged. She regretted not being born here so that she could see its challenge every moment of her life. This was a country worthy of a man who could conquer it.

As she watched MacGregor she believed that she could see him taking on some of the ungovernable nature of the changing countryside. She knew that to most people MacGregor had a deceptive air of being permanent, but to herself he had always been a changeable man. She saw him at various times as a stern seeker of the truth, as a man easily misled, sensitive, stubborn, patient, calm, bitter, tolerant, and above all completely confused. He was confused politically and personally, and it was somewhere in this characteristic that Katherine's annoyance with him began. To see a man struggling with himself made her uncomfortable, and MacGregor's complications were particularly annoying because she had the feeling that she would suffer the same conflicts if she ever allowed herself to get out of hand. If there was something in existence to decide, then she wanted to decide it. She would not have her mind and her intelligence overcome by any problem. Not like MacGregor. MacGregor had allowed his confusion to get the better of him. If he allowed it to go on much longer, Katherine knew that she would despise him. That was one thing about Essex. He did not fight with himself. Right or wrong, Essex could make up his mind without any difficulty. Essex had a good grip on himself, more so than most men, and Katherine admired him for it and would always choose him in his decisive moments in preference to an indecisive MacGregor. She could get annoyed with MacGregor by just thinking of his slow-witted confusion and his ever-increasing argumentativeness. These days it was enough for someone to say Yea for MacGregor to say Nay. Katherine recognized it as a symptom of a man who was looking for decision in every utterance. He would probably get worse.

Yet she had a vital interest in MacGregor's ultimate decision with himself. What she suppressed inside herself seemed to come out in MacGregor. There was a dangerous similarity between them, one which she would not acknowledge. It added to her impatience with him and with herself, and it continuously threatened their relationship. It was therefore satisfying to see MacGregor at least physically unfettered by the country which seemed to be his own. He had already acquired the slim vigour that went with these wild mountains.

"What luck," Essex said as he came up beside her. "I didn't expect to be so delightfully occupied on this expedition. I actually feel happy about our predicament. You couldn't have arranged it better if you had tried," he shouted ahead to MacGregor. "It will do us all a world of good.

405

Nothing like a seat on a horse to make a man feel human. Eh? Horses are so damnably sane. I must say that Swift knew what he was doing when he chose the horse as the ideal opposite to man."

Katherine told him he was a fool.

"After witnessing such a remarkable display of human frenzy," Essex argued, "and after seeing the level to which the human animal can descend in stupidity and gullibility, how can you deny that the horse is the nobler animal?"

"Is that the only impression that brutal festival made on you?" she said. "Is that the only lesson you learned from it?"

"What other lesson is there to learn, my dear?" he said.

"For you, Harold, it should be a lesson in the evils of human ignorance, and the danger of playing with religious bigotry."

"Now that is a lesson I did not have to learn," he told her. "When I see the human mind being so easily moulded, I have a sense of personal insult. That is exactly what I am trying to tell you Kathy. Try to make a horse do a stupid thing and see how difficult it is. With man it is simple. Man is absolutely incapable of rational behavior. He is born stupid."

"Now you are being ridiculous," Katherine said calmly.

"Oh I admit that the individual is capable of objectivity," Essex went on. "Look at MacGregor, look at myself, even you Kathy." Essex enjoyed his good argument. "But in a mass he is of lower order than the horse. He is not only born stupid, he is inherently cruel and dangerous."

"I am sure you believe that," she said contemptuously.

"Of course I do."

"Then you are quite dangerous yourself for believing such idiocy."

"Then what is the truth, my love?" Essex demanded.

"I am too ignorant to answer that," Katherine replied, "but I know that you are wrong. The only people on the earth born stupid are people like us, born with contempt for everyone else. In that we are not only fools but we are ignorant as well."

"Now you're talking like Asquith," Essex accused.

"Then I have a lot more sense than I thought I had."

"Or perhaps you are talking like MacGregor," Essex went on and looked at the sky. "No. MacGregor is a pragmatist. You are becoming a philosophical nativist." Essex laughed. "I always admire your original attitudes Kathy."

Katherine did not continue it.

Essex compromised gracefully by concluding that a man who could ride a horse was naturally superior to it. He added with new provocation: "For a woman who rides a mule so well, Kathy, you have a rotten seat on a horse. Sit forward woman. Don't sit on his buttocks."

"Are you going to tell me how to ride a horse?" She was more ready to fight him on this score.

"Yes: if you insist on breaking the animal's back. Sit forward. There should be a straight line from your neck to your heels. Your stirrups are too short and your legs are too far forward."

"Listen Harold," Katherine said, "I was taught the forward seat by Melnikoff of the *Haute Ecole*, and I know it cannot be practised on anything but an English saddle. This mediæval war saddle was not built for the long stirrup. Furthermore I haven't been on a horse for three or four years, and there are certain parts of a woman's anatomy which have to be broken into this very gently."

"That is nothing to do with it," Essex said. "You are simply not using balance. You have a good hand position, most women have, but you are sitting too far back. Otherwise you have a good seat," he said generously.

"Thank you," she said.

"You have a rather good seat too, MacGregor."

MacGregor had dropped back to drag in the Turkoman pack-horse. He had its lead around the horn of his saddle. He was paying no attention to Essex.

"There's one thing wrong with your riding, MacGregor," Essex continued cheerfully. "I've been noticing it, and I must say it's typical of you my boy."

"Oh?"

"Yes: you just sit on a horse without understanding what you're doing."

"What is there to understand about sitting on a horse?" MacGregor said.

"Riding is an art," Essex told him. "You make it a task. You just sit down on a horse. You sit rather well but I'm afraid it's all accidental."

"You are probably right," MacGregor said. "I've never made a study of how to sit a horse. I have made a study of these saddles, however, and I agree with Katherine. They are not made for the forward seat. The side bars get in the way of your bones."

"Interesting saddles." Essex did not argue because he was well warned against testing MacGregor's ignorance any farther. "They're a mixture of the American Western saddle and the old McClellan saddle. Double cinches and latigoes and a high cantle and this massive pommel. Damned awkward looking thing and hard as a rock; but I must say they give you excellent support. It's like riding in a chair."

MacGregor was not listening. He was reading his maps again, looking around at the increased density of the small hills and the quick little valleys. They had followed a track since leaving Hajiabad, and it was now taking them along the continuation of the dried-up river bed in which the Ford had broken its half-shaft. The hills were still bare, and yet they were always unexpected in their shape and incline, and they cast long and round shadows on the red earth as the darkness settled above. The light was gradually fading to one end of the sky.

Near the river-bed they passed shepherds with herds of goats, and across one small plateau they could see the black goatskin tents of the nomadic tribes from Ardelan. Twice horse riders in the dying light came near enough to watch them, but remained far enough away to be out of calling distance. It was quite clear that the riders were armed and it was quite clear that they were Kurds. MacGregor wanted to see if Essex was disturbed by these figures on horseback, but Essex looked intrigued without being surprised or worried. Katherine was more interested in the countryside, and so MacGregor did not object when Essex said they had done enough for one day. Essex said he would rather camp out than go into Nasirabad, which was sure to be another village as filthy and as objectionable as Hajiabad.

"How near to Nasirabad are we MacGregor?" Essex asked as they rode up a short hill to look around.

"We're actually south of it since we crossed the river," MacGregor pointed to their right. "It's over there somewhere. We can't be far from the road to Bijar. Do you want to keep going until we hit the road?"

"No," Essex said. "We might as well stop around here. Do we have any water?"

"Not for the horses."

"Are we anywhere near a river?"

"If we move south a mile or so, we come to a river which we can follow to-morrow to the Bijar road. It crosses the road below Nasirabad."

"That's fine," Essex said, and they left the track and moved through the rising hills until they reached the quiet crystal trickle of mountain water which MacGregor said was the *Qizil Uzun*. They stopped on a bare round plateau a little way from the river, sheltered from the mountain breeze by a higher ridge. MacGregor dropped the equipment from the pack horse on a flat corner of the plateau, the edge of which went straight down for fifty feet to the river's edge. He hurried to finish his chores before the last of the daylight.

"Do you want the tent up?" he asked them.

"How much colder does it get here?" Essex was already stamping his cold feet.

"Quite a bit," MacGregor said.

"Oh well, I can stand it if you two can," Essex decided. "It's too late to fool around with it and I'm hungry. But I say! What about the animals? Do you think they're blown?"

"I don't know," MacGregor said. "What do you think?"

"They look alright: they need watering."

408

"I'll do that," MacGregor said.

"What about fodder?"

"There is a little in the pack, but they'll find enough along the river. It's dry brush but they're used to it. I'll have to watch them while you two prepare the cooking. I'm a rotten cook anyway," he said. He was bending his sore legs and feeling his thighs as he took the horses. Katherine was also stretching herself and both men watched her as she pulled the saddle off her cob and dragged the long felt cover from the horse's buttocks. MacGregor told her to leave it on and strap it under his middle. The long blanket was good protection against the cold. He took the four beasts by the reins and led them down to the water. He took off all the bridles and watched them until they stood quietly satisfied. He knew that these horses were camp trained and they would not wander far. He washed himself and drank the cold water as the horses pushed around under the overhanging rocks and among the stones for dried grass and dead bushes. There was a small locked sand bay near by and he drove the horses into it and blocked the entrance to it with rocks, and went back to the camp.

He unrolled his kit and took his small hammer and canvas bag and went off to look for some of the sediments which overlaid the Jurassic limestones of the valley.

Essex did not notice his departure, but when it was almost dark he asked Katherine where MacGregor had gone.

"He's off fossicking somewhere," she said. "He'll be back."

When MacGregor did return the cooking was under way and he was surprised to see that Essex had achieved immediate victory over the petrol stove, something which MacGregor had failed to do in all his days in the Western Desert. Katherine was squatting on her heels before the stove, reading the instructions on a tin of food while Essex puffed on his fresh pipe and dragged the rolled tent and the sleeping bags to the shelter of the rocks which rose above them.

MacGregor stood above Katherine, just able to see her face in the troubled light, and he felt one of the periodical flushes of pleasure which knowing Katherine gave him. It was partly stimulated in his careful mind by the memory of his own intimacy with Katherine. She did not know she was being watched. Her mouth was open slightly as she read, her eyebrows were tight, and her loosened hair was falling down about her ears and cheeks. She was lost until she felt MacGregor's stare, and then she looked up and smiled with surprise, but said nothing.

"You must have been a solemn child," MacGregor remarked as if she had asked him what he was thinking.

"MacGregor!" (She might have been embracing him.) "Pass me the frying-pan."

He bent and gave it to her. "You even squat there like a child," he said. "Shall I get a rock for you?"

"I'm too sore to sit right down," she said.

"That is because you were hanging onto the horse by your hips," Essex told her. "Lengthen your stirrups to-morrow and sit forward on the horse and balance yourself properly."

"Do you like onions, Harold?" Katherine called to him.

"If they drown the taste of that tinned food: yes."

"Do you, MacGregor?"

"If you have any."

"Aladin got them for me in Hajiabad. Would you peel them while I mix this mess in the pan. Is this what you ate in the desert?"

"Some of the time," he said.

"Poor MacGregor. No wonder you look so fragile at times."

Essex laughed. MacGregor peeled the onions, enjoying Essex's laugh because it was quite clear that Essex had mistaken Katherine's affection for cynicism. It pleased MacGregor so much that he was not at all conscious of the time that passed, nor of the unusual mechanical ease with which Katherine had prepared the meal. Nor was he greatly diverted by the pleasure of eating in darkness. He listened to Katherine talking to Essex, and he watched her, and he said very little. He found himself deciding that Essex would never know the delight he expected of Katherine.

When the meal was finished MacGregor went down to the river and washed the dishes and the pan with the fine sand. When he came back Essex had placed the bed rolls under a hanging shelf of rock which almost formed a cave. MacGregor had a sudden inexplicable desire to see what would happen if he left Katherine and Essex to themselves, so he pulled his roll right out to the ledge which overlooked the river. Katherine had gone off somewhere, but Essex watched him carefully.

"What are you doing out there?" Essex said from the rock.

"I prefer to be in the open," MacGregor said cautiously.

"You'll be cold," Essex told him. "That wind is picking up. It's even blowing the clouds away. This shelf is good protection."

"I'll take a chance," MacGregor said about the cold.

"Are you being tough, MacGregor?"

"Perhaps."

When Katherine came back, she knelt on her bed roll and asked Essex where MacGregor had gone.

"I think you hurt him with that remark about being fragile," Essex said. "He has taken his bed into the wide open spaces."

Katherine picked up her bed roll. "I'm sure this rock will fall down on us if we stay here."

410

"Rot!"

"I don't think I like it here either," she said and dragged her roll across the ledge to MacGregor's position.

"You two can freeze if you like," Essex said carelessly, "but I wager you will be in here before morning. I have an idea it is going to rain." Essex had hardly expected Katherine to be so decisive and so sure of what she would do. He was extremely disappointed.

"Do you mind me coming out here?" Katherine said to MacGregor with a sly inference of rebuke for his silence.

"Not at all." He was already in the folds of the sleeping bag, folding his trousers and putting them into the empty canvas holder of the bed roll. "I just want to be on high ground."

"Do you think it would be silly if I put on pyjamas? I hate sleeping in my clothes."

"You'll be alright," he said. "But don't leave anything uncovered. It might rain."

"With that moon?"

Her sleeping bag was a few feet away from his, and she sat down and took off her boots and socks and trousers and jumper and turned her back while she put on a pyjama coat and then awkwardly pulled on the trousers as she got into the sleeping bag. She arranged her clothes neatly in the canvas bag and put them near his and then pulled her short sealskin jacket over the blankets which she had piled upon herself.

"It's so damnably cold," she said as she pushed her feet down and put her head on the small pillow, "but I'm so weary that nothing can keep me awake. Good night Harold," she called.

Essex replied "Good night," his voice sounding far away.

"You too!" she said to MacGregor and moved comfortably under the covering.

MacGregor did not reply. He was wondering how much a man could stand of such proximity, of such grace, care, boldness, modesty, provocation, all in one woman at the one place at the one time. MacGregor was not sure what he had expected of Katherine, but he was disappointed as he listened to her deliberate breathing and her movements of comfort and sleep. Yet anything more would have revived his fear of her eventual dishonesty.

He finally went to sleep, and for a little while he dreamed that he was back in London and that Katherine was taking him for a ride on a London bus. They got off in an endless street and she persuaded him to go into a roofless building, enticing him into it with good-humoured affection. She led him along mysterious dark corridors, holding his arm with a tight grip as security for herself until they entered a large empty room. Here she gently provoked his affection, touching his lips with delicate fingers and ruffling his hair a little. Then the lights of the room flooded on and he was standing in the geological library of the Natural History Museum surrounded by his friends, including Professor Hills and Professor White and Malin Alving and the instructors and lecturers of his university days. They were all laughing at him, and Katherine stood away from him to join them. He was in the middle of this unhappy situation when he awakened. Katherine had been throwing stones at his feet, and he sat up.

"You were certainly struggling with yourself," she told him. "You were so restless that you wakened me."

"Sorry," he said, not yet entirely awake. He lay down again and terminated the subconscious drama by looking at the material sky. It was a blue night, and very white clear clouds scudded in patches across the sky passing right over their horizon in a few minutes.

"My ears are cold," Katherine told him.

"Then put your hat on," he said briefly.

She misunderstood his brusqueness. "I am sorry I woke you," she said, "but you really were in a state."

"That's alright."

"It's very nice out here." She was wide awake herself.

"Yes," he said thoughtfully, "but what are we doing out here?" He put a warm hand over his exposed ear. "There must be a hundred simpler ways of getting to Bijar or Sineh, and I could have thought of fifty of them. I fell too easily into this horse-riding business."

"My dear Ivre," Katherine said quietly. "Harold wouldn't think of travelling into the wilds of Kurdistan except as a mounted man on a horse. Any other way would have been absolutely inadequate for his sense of proportion. I thought you realized that when you kindly left him the small Arab pony."

"He seemed to be set on having it," MacGregor said. "Although I'm pretty sure it will develop stiff legs before we get much farther."

"You were very nice about it," she told him, "and quite angry with him."

"Tell me," he said then. "How did you persuade him to let you come on this trip?"

"Is that worrying you?"

"Shouldn't it worry me?"

"No it shouldn't," she replied. "I did mislead him a little, but not very much. I suppose I can be very persuasive at times but I did nothing more than pull his ear, although he is probably anticipating a little too much on our arrival in London."

"Is that why he has been so sure of you?" MacGregor said.

"Is he sure of me?" Katherine sighed.

"I think so," MacGregor said, and asked her what she meant by Essex's "anticipating" in London.

"Please don't think about London," she said. "We are out here now. I don't care whether I ever see London again." She stretched her arms out and up. "I see why you prefer this to England."

"There is nothing wrong with England . . ." he began.

"I know. I know," she said. "But this country is full of vigour."

"Most Englishmen think it a lazy and indolent place."

"They see nothing," she said. "They can never see beyond their own stupid plotting. In a country like this," she told him, "I would sooner be anything but an Englishman. How can these people bear us? How can they watch us so dispassionately as we move among them? Don't they hate us for our interference? Will they ever take it into their heads to throw us all out?"

She waited for his comment but he said mildly, "Your guess is as good as mine."

"No it isn't," she argued. "You know the language and you know what is happening. Don't they know that we are all here to meddle?"

"How can they know it?" MacGregor said. "Who in Hajiabad, for instance, could know that the Sayyid was part of the long arm of the India Office? Our part in these things is always too indirect and too intangible. Some of it becomes obvious in Teheran, but not enough to have it understood and stopped. Our interference has to be blocked at its source."

"Well you had better start on Harold," Katherine said cruelly. "He is about to become a positive fountainhead."

"I thought he came out of the *ta'ziya* business rather well."

"No he didn't," Katherine said. "You were right in the first place. Harold will never be influenced by the reality of anything he sees here. If he suddenly decides to reject the support of religious fanaticism, it's because he has a purely intellectual dislike for the dark corners of the human mind, including his own. It has nothing to do with the political right or wrong. He really rejects the most general collection of human beings as being fools; and as far as he is concerned nothing can change them. Nothing."

"I still think he learned a political lesson from the *ta'ziya*."

"I don't think so," she said sharply.

MacGregor the pragmatist and Katherine the nativist had changed positions, but of the two of them it was only Katherine who could see why.

"Don't allow these specific incidents to confuse your understanding of what Essex is doing," she said, her breath now puffing white into the cold air. "What you want and what he wants are entirely different."

He said he knew that.

"Then draw a few philosophical conclusions from it," she said.

MacGregor did not concern himself with philosophical or political comparisons between himself and Essex. "All I want of Essex," he said, "is his fair estimate of what he sees. If he can use his own judgment instead of following Fox's policy then this trip will have been worth while."

"He will never use his judgment while he has a policy to follow," she said.

"Policies can fade quickly in these surroundings."

"Not with Harold," she said. "He can hang onto an attitude through anything. No outside influence can touch him once he decides what he is doing. And he has already decided to follow Fox's policy here."

"I don't know about that," MacGregor said.

"I'm afraid I do," she said. "Don't be wishful thinking about Harold, and don't leave it to his fair-mindedness to decide what is happening here. Play your own part and play it for all it's worth."

"I intend to." He lay on his back looking straight up at the night. "Every time he meets one of these Embassy contacts I shall fight it out with him there and then. I don't like arguing with him, but it's the only way, and it may have some effect." He turned around to face her and he silently cursed Essex for riding into Kurdistan; he was so stiff that it was painful even to stretch his legs. "I'll be glad when all this is over and I can get out of it," he said.

"Why?" she said aggressively. "Do you intend to leave the fate of this place in the hands of people like Essex and Pickering and Fox?"

"No. I think this place is better in the hands of its own population."

"That is no excuse for you to ignore it as a political issue."

"I don't ignore it."

"Well, what do you intend doing about it?"

"Surely I am doing something about it."

"Locally perhaps, but you always ignore its wider aspects. This is part of a whole political and diplomatic policy. What are you doing about that?"

"What am I supposed to do?"

"I don't know, but you ought to start making up your mind what attitude you will take after this trip is over. That is when you will really have to act."

"In Iran I know what is right and what is wrong, but I am no good at this game of political intrigue, and the sooner I get out of it the better."

"What do you want to do?" she demanded: "Come back and work for English-Persian?"

414

"It's the only place where I can do my work," he said evasively.

"So you will come back to it!"

"No," he said. He did not want to discuss his future plans with Katherine because he knew how dangerous such a discussion could become, but he had to admit that he would not come back to English-Persian.

"Why not?" She reversed her attitude. "What's the matter with English-Persian?"

"Nothing," he told her. "They are very good people to work for; they have all the facilities I need."

"Well?"

He shook his head. "I couldn't stomach it any more," he said. "The whole organization behaves as if it owns this country. Its existence in Iran is the cause of all our interference. I don't want to go near the place."

"I wouldn't allow you to," she said with sudden casual possession. "Do you intend coming back to Iran at all?"

He felt reasonably safe now. "I don't know" he said. "I don't see how I can come back. There is nothing much I can do here."

"Is English-Persian the only organization that requires a micro-paleontologist?"

"More or less," he told her. "It is such highly specialized work that an oil field is the only place where there is enough information available to do my sort of work."

"Isn't there anything else you could do?"

"I could probably teach at Teheran University, but I'm not a teacher."

"No," she agreed finally. "That isn't for you."

It was unsatisfactory to leave the matter there but MacGregor did not want to pursue it and Katherine sensed it and kept quiet. He liked Katherine for that moment of understanding, and he stretched out his hand as she did likewise, and for a moment they had a grip on each other which neither would loosen, but which neither could exceed. Katherine might be waiting for him, but MacGregor knew that he could go no farther. Yet even with his fear of her he was so overcome by his need for Katherine that he lifted his head to look at her. There was just enough moon to make a perfect silver shadow of her face, a shadow which shone softly through her loose hair. As if the restraint was too much for him he lay back and uttered a sudden exclamation in Persian.

She still had a grip on his arm. "What are you saying?" she said.

He kept his grip of her and said nothing.

She was equally tense. "Is it more about the pearl of my womanhood?"

He still said nothing.

"If it is," she said. "Say it. Say it," she demanded.

He did not hold back any longer and the utterance came out. "I have

415

not ceased, even for an instant, to have you constantly in my mind, so that even forgetfulness has been forgotten by my heart."

She waited, but he did not go on. "There must be more," she said. "Go on."

In a moment he was as quiet as the language he spoke, carrying some of its tenderness into the English. "My beloved has entered the tent, and the bird of my heart has remained bewildered. The candle is put into the lantern and the moth has remained fluttering in dismay."

"Oh. It's such beautiful extravagance," she said.

"It is perfect for you," he said slowly.

"There must be more!" she insisted.

"Yes," he said. "It is endless."

"Then go on."

"Love is mine enemy," MacGregor murmured, "and that is sufficient. You need not, therefore, O sky, take the trouble to oppress me, for where there is an executioner, a butcher is not needed."

"No. No," she said.

MacGregor went on softly. "A city of hearts can be purchased with a single sidelong glance. I beg of you to be slow in taking advantage of my city."

"It is too much," she cried.

"Shall I go on?"

"Yes. Yes."

"I have been asked where is your dwelling place," he said. "And yet everybody knows that your dwelling place is in my heart. But I have lost my heart and I know not where it is."

"Oh!"

"In your face," he said, "which is like the land of Khutan, there is a boudoir of an Abyssinian bride, and in each of your beads of Yemen there is the sanctum of a Hindu idol." He was catching his own breath.

"Please stop," she said. "Please!"

"If you become my garden," he went on, "I will become a rose, and if you become a rose then I will become your lips. If you become a goblet, then I will be your wine, and if you become the wine, then I will be your gurgling sound."

Her fingers bit into his flesh.

"I am a cripple sitting in the wilderness of my want for you."

She suddenly relaxed and released him.

"My tears have made the silver ocean that surrounds me."

She had turned away from him and she was sighing No No No No as she breathed in and out. She lay like that for a long time and they were still. He waited for her to face him and see him again, but with each breath that he heard above the pale wind he knew that she was finally asleep.

Chapter 32

As THEY RODE again in the faint morning MacGregor tried to persuade Essex to go straight through to Sinneh and forget the smaller town of Bijar.

"We have people to see in Bijar," Essex told him. "One of them a very important Kurd."

MacGregor knew about that Kurd. He was Sirda Aziz, a tribal leader who had already made half a promise that should he get control of Ardelan District, he would grant all oil concession in the area to the British, in preference to the Russians. It was quite clear that he didn't like the British any better than the Russians. But he expected surreptitious British military aid from neighbouring Iraq. With this military assistance he hoped to establish a tribal dictatorship over all Ardelan and even north of that into all of Kurdistan. He was one man that MacGregor wanted Essex to avoid.

Essex knew it. "I admire your persistence," he said to MacGregor, "but there is no use trying to divert me."

"I am not trying to divert you," MacGregor argued cheerfully.

"Then what is the point in avoiding Bijar?"

"I am trying to go around those mountains." MacGregor pointed ahead to the concert of ridges which mutilated the sky. "If we go straight to Sinneh we can go through the valleys, but to get at Bijar this way we have to go up into the mountains too far."

"What's the matter with that?"

"This is Kurdish country," MacGregor said, "and we are better out of the mountains. Anyway it is hard going up there."

Essex believed him, and in the general course of events he would have followed MacGregor's advice. But this morning he was suspicious of MacGregor. He was suspicious of both Katherine and MacGregor. They were unnaturally calm and quiet and he did not like that.

"No," he said. "We will go on to Bijar."

"As you say," said MacGregor. He was not in an argumentative mood, although he really did not like going too deeply into the mountains without a better knowledge of the local situation. That was the first law of travel in this part of Iran.

"Do you know the Kurds up here?" Essex asked him.

MacGregor said "No. I know the tribes in southern Ardelan, the Khalhurs of Shahabad and the Gavars, but I know nothing of these northern tribes except that they are supposed to be treacherous."

"What does that mean exactly?" Katherine asked.

"Nothing really," he said. "All Kurds are supposed to be treacherous because so many live by raiding and robbing; yet most Kurds are really cultivators and shepherds. They are all so independent and self-possessed that they are slandered as being treacherous and vicious. Some are probably very vicious, particularly the robber tribes, but most of them are polite even if they are fierce. Who could be anything else but fierce in these mountains?"

"That sounds ominous," Katherine said, and the thought delighted her.

"Up here," MacGregor said, "you are in the lap of the gods. Anything can happen in Kurdistan." He knew this would please them both.

"With Harold along, something is sure to happen," Katherine said to conciliate Essex a little. "He is one of those human beings who always runs into trouble."

"I don't want any trouble," Essex told them modestly. "I just want to do the job and get out of here; but I must say this is magnificent country."

MacGregor allowed his own enjoyment to take hold of him. "If you want to see Kurdistan, the only way to do it is to go into the mountains," he admitted. "We have already climbed a thousand feet since we left Hajiabad."

"Soon we will be at the snow-line," Katherine said. "Look at those great rocks." She pointed to the north where the mountains were getting closer. There was one peak with great folds of rock, and MacGregor told them that this was almost into volcanic country; a lot of the ridges had been thrown up by great earth movements.

"It's getting damned cold," was Essex's comment.

"You wanted to come into the mountains," MacGregor said.

"How far is Bijar?"

"About thirty miles," MacGregor told him. "We won't reach it to-night." He left them then and fell back to make one of his periodical encouragements to the Turkoman pack horse who was a natural scavenger and dragged behind to hunt among the rocks for a few weeds and thin grass.

"What is that dry bush he keeps cropping?" Katherine asked as MacGregor drew abreast again, driving the large animal in front of them with hard kicks in the ribs.

"I don't know what it is in English," MacGregor said, out of breath. "We have always called it by its botanical name, *Rosa berberiffilos*."

"It's a camel's-thorn of some kind," Essex told them.

While the riding was still comparatively easy on open stretches they went on talking, and MacGregor explained the large formations that came in sight each side of them as they went on climbing. They stopped to eat lunch near the first patch of snow. After that the snow increased but never became more than drifts which were caught in the sheltered valleys. A light north-westerly blew, and it caught them when they passed gaps in the converging mountains. They were now away from all roads

418

and villages and well into Kurdistan and climbing higher all the time. It was a day's hard riding, and they weren't sorry when MacGregor said the horses were weakening and stopped them early to camp in a deep ravine. Each of them was so stiff that they took their time in preparing themselves for the night.

Essex unpacked the Turkoman and MacGregor unsaddled the other horses and watered them in the small mountain pools and watched them until they settled down. It gave him a chance to wander up the ravine and collect rock samples from the small outcrops which rose up in the slopes. Of the other chores Katherine would not give up the cooking, saying she didn't mind cooking so long as someone washed the greasy dishes. She was frying bully beef on the petrol stove and asking MacGregor if there were Alpine flowers in these mountains.

"There are all sorts of saxifrage," he told her, "but a lot of the flowers here are the same as English wild flowers." He watched her cutting the beef. "Don't fry mine," he told her. "Just give me the raw slices."

"Don't you like it? It's all the meat we have."

"I don't like it fried," he said.

MacGregor took advantage of the last of daylight to look at his maps again, and Essex came to watch him making notes and to ask him where they were.

"I'm not quite sure." MacGregor did not appear worried.

"Haven't you any idea where we are?"

"We're tangled up in these ravines somewhere." He pointed at the map. "We are alright so long as we keep that mountain on our sharp right."

"What mountain is it?"

"Five Man Mountain. If we go any nearer to it we will be in impossible country. This way we are alright, although we are probably wandering all over the place. I am keeping to the low ground as much as possible."

Katherine called them to come and eat. They seated themselves, wrapped in blankets before a scrub fire which MacGregor had prepared, and ate their bully beef with canned tomatoes. They were waiting for the tea to boil when they were suddenly aware of a tall figure standing near them.

Essex saw him first, as if the man had appeared out of the ground. Essex took his pipe out of his mouth and said in a flat voice, "I say MacGregor. Who is that fellow?"

The tall figure greeted them in Kurdish and he bent down and took a pinch of dust and threw it over himself. He leaned on his stick and touched his lips and his forehead most formally.

"Where did he come from?" MacGregor said.

"He was just standing there," Essex told him.

MacGregor greeted him in Persian.

Thus formally addressed the stranger told them his name. "I am Father Da-ud," he said and touched his forehead again.

"Peace," said MacGregor.

"Peace," said Father Da-ud. "I am the Eighth Angel."

"Welcome," said MacGregor. "You are a Sayyid?"

"No. I am a pilgrim travelling to Mosul to pay homage at the Mountain of the Body where our Saint is buried. I have followed you for several hours and I can see that you are strangers here by the unusual route you take. I come to offer my assistance. If you tell me where you are bound I will direct you through the mountains. I will be glad to show you the best route."

"Please be seated," MacGregor told him.

MacGregor looked closely at the serious man who claimed to be the Eighth Angel. He was undoubtedly a saintly-looking man, a long lean figure with a short white beard, and of very careful physical grace. It was too dark to see more of him, but he did not seem to be a very young or a very old man. He wore a sheepskin *kulah*, which was a Kurdish headdress, and over his shoulder he wore a long felt *aaba* which reached to his ankles. He was very careful in placing his stick upon the ground at a polite distance, and he crossed his ankles and eased himself down and thanked MacGregor for his invitation to join them.

"Well who is he?" Essex demanded.

"His name is Da-ud or David. He is the Eighth Angel."

Katherine had placed some of the food on a plate and she held it out to the stranger. "What makes him claim such a thing?" she said.

"I don't know yet."

Father Da-ud accepted the food after some protest, and he bowed to Katherine when she gave him a mug of tea. He blessed the food by passing his hand over it a few times and began to eat with his fingers. Eating thus was an act of subtle delicacy with him, and when he had finished he wiped his fingers in the dirt and sipped the tea.

"So you are strangers," he said quietly to show that his interest was one of welcome rather than impolite curiosity.

"Yes," MacGregor admitted. He was trying to recall which religious sect made the pilgrimage to Mosul. "We are English officials going to Bijar and Sinneh. We are travelling this route because we know no other." It was a risk to talk of their ignorance but it seemed to be alright with this gentle pilgrim.

"If you are English," Father Da-ud said, "then you are Christians."

"That's so."

"I am a Yezidi," Father Da-ud announced. "I have never spoken with an English Christian before and I am surprised to find you out here in

420

our wilderness." He was smiling at MacGregor and choosing his Persian very delicately, addressing them all.

"My friends speak no language of the country," MacGregor told him, eased into a confidence of the man by the soft articulate tones of his voice.

"I hope my sudden arrival did not offend them," Da-ud said. "Perhaps you should apologize for me. Apologize too for my ignorance of your language."

"Then I must apologize for theirs," said MacGregor.

"No. No." Da-ud removed his hat, and even in the darkness by the small fire they could see his long white hair. "I do not look like an old man but I am quite old," he said, "and I should know all there is to know. At my age ignorance of anything is inexcusable." He was making polite gestures at Essex and Katherine.

Essex nodded back at the Yezidi. "Are you going to hold one of those long and very singular conversations, MacGregor?" he said. "What does this old fellow want? Is he a beggar?"

"He is a Yezidi," MacGregor said.

"Well?"

"A Yezidi worships the Devil."

"This beautiful old man?" Katherine said.

"How does one worship the Devil?" Essex asked.

"The Yezidi claim that it's not much use worshipping God," Mac-Gregor explained, "because it is quite obvious from the amount of evil on earth that God is not all-powerful. They worship the Devil as the more powerful Deity."

"Do they really mean it?" Essex said.

"He's on his way to Mosul where their saint is buried," MacGregor said, pleased with Essex's incredulity. "I'm not quite sure of the details but I am certain that they worship the Devil. There are quite a few Yezidis up north somewhere and there are some in Iraq."

"It sounds very logical," Katherine said. "Ask him about being the Eighth Angel. I'm sure he really is a saint."

"At least he's the cleanest-looking native we've seen hereabouts," Essex commented.

"My friends are interested in your religion," MacGregor told Father Da-ud. "They had never heard of the Yezidi and they would like to know something of your principles."

"You personally have heard of the Yezidi?" Da-ud asked MacGregor.

"Yes, but no doubt improperly."

Da-ud smiled. "Perhaps you have heard that we worship the Devil, and you do not want to believe it."

"On the contrary," MacGregor said. "The *Khanum* was saying how logical it is to worship the Devil."

421

"Very logical," Da-ud nodded gravely. "We call him *Malek Taus* or *Malekul Kut*, 'King Peacock' or 'the Mighty Angel.' To your Christian religion he is Satan and he is Evil. To us he is the Chief of the Angels, fallen temporarily in punishment. We believe that he will be restored to his important position after weeping sufficient tears in seven vessels to quench the seven hells of his seven thousand years' exile."

"Then he really is your God?"

Da-ud held up both his hands. "Please do not talk of our God. We don't like Gods. At the same time we reject none. We even accept Jesus Christ as an angel, but we are like the Mohammedans in believing that he was not crucified. As the Koran says: *They slew him not, and they crucified him not, but they only had his likeness.* Nevertheless we believe that your Jesus Christ will return to earth. We also believe in the prophet Mohammed and in the return of their Imam Mahdi. We embrace all faiths, even the Chaldean and the Zoroastrian and the sun-worship of Babylon. The sun is our Sheikh Shems and the moon is Sheikh Sin, and these we reverence as you would a god. You see we are not bigoted. We merely place King Peacock in a good position, since as head of the Seven Angels he is the most authoritative Deity and the King who casts the largest and most responsible shadow. This is not bigotry, but logic. We venerate the Old and New Testaments, the Koran and the Avesta of Zoroaster; but we do not place any book in a position of authority. Our only authority is the sensibility of men and their absolute goodness. The correctives we seek are to be found in Man himself rather than in Books and Deities."

"And King Peacock?" asked MacGregor.

"If there must be a God, then King Peacock is the logical Deity. That is the importance we give King Peacock. If it is clear some day that there is no need for a God then we will pass King Peacock into the past as a legend, and we will still have the basic faith that Man is his own God and his own corrective."

"Then you are really not a religion at all."

"Please," Da-ud said with his slow smile. "In being religious we reject religion. We feel that this is the honest thing to do. Are you a religious man?"

"No," said MacGregor.

"It is surely unusual for an Englishman to be irreligious."

"It is difficult for any man of science to be religious," MacGregor said.

"You are a man of science? What science? Astronomy perhaps?" Father Da-ud was mildly excited about this possibility of MacGregor being an astronomer.

"No. I am a scientist of the earth itself, of its origin, its structure, and its formational history."

"Wonderful!" Da-ud said happily. "Our respect for men of science is unlimited. We know that they will eventually discover Truth. Scientific irreligion is the hope for mankind; that is why our religion strives to make all men irreligious."

"Surely that is a contradiction," MacGregor said to him. "You make religion and irreligion the same thing."

Da-ud accepted this as a wonderful argument. "In one small effort of your scientific mind," he said, "you have discovered our schism. Mind you, we are not divided. But in being a religion which preaches irreligion we do find that we disagree on the ultimate point of religion. Fortunately the majority of our followers believe that a man must accept irreligion for its practical good and not for its abstract evil. Is that logical?"

"Very."

"We apply this to all human endeavour. Anything for its own sake is bad: whether religion, science, literature, art, or politics."

"You are political also?" MacGregor asked.

"Indeed."

"Active?"

"Indeed."

"In Azerbaijan?"

"Certainly! Unlike the official policy of our Mohammedan and Christian colleagues, we 'Devil-worshippers' actively participate in any movement for the universal good, whether it disagrees with our precepts or not. In this we seriously criticize our Christian and Mohammedan brothers in the terms we were just discussing. Their activity is always religion for its own sake. We Devil-worshippers on the other hand are irreligious for the sake of Man. Having no hierarchy, no priesthood, no bigotry, and no rigid forms, we are free to follow the absolute directions of universal good — whatever these directions mean in the name of politics. We are not bigoted," he repeated.

"If you are not bigoted," MacGregor said, "why do you reject other religions?"

"We do not reject other religions. We accept them all and then reject all religion in totality, including our own. Furthermore we do not claim to be the one true Church, as the Pope in Rome claims for his sect. We simply say that such a claim is impossible, since no one has ever investigated all the religions and sects in the universe sufficiently to say that his is the only true form. Do you see that there is logic in our religion, my friend?"

"Logic," MacGregor admitted in wonderment, "but a little contradiction also."

"No more contradiction than in any other religion."

"True," MacGregor said.

Father Da-ud placed his cap upon his head and stood up. "I will leave you now so that you can sleep without my presence worrying you." He bowed to Essex and to Katherine and leaned on his stick. "Since you are going to Bijar and then to Sinneh and since I must pass through there on my pilgrimage to Mosul, I would be happy to show you the shortest route."

"We have no horse to offer," MacGregor said.

"No matter. Your pack horse will carry me when I am tired."

"Is this route you know through the valleys?" MacGregor asked.

"Some of the way."

"Is it a road?"

"It is neither track nor road," Father Da-ud told him, "yet it is a route. It is known only to the Mukri-Kurds and to some Yezidi travellers like myself. It is not difficult except in climbing one ridge. After that it is very simple, even though it traverses the wildest parts of Ardelan. It is really the ancient Mukri route from Sinneh to the Mountain of the Temple of Solomon, which is their home now."

"Do the Kurds still use the route?"

"Small bands," Da-ud said. "The Mukri do not go down to Sinneh these days. It was more commonly used some two or three hundred years ago, but now there is little use for it. The Mukri or the Sabis may use it if they are raiding again, but I cannot reassure you about such things."

"It's the same risk in all Kurdistan," MacGregor said and the reply pleased Da-ud. "One more thing," MacGregor added tentatively as Da-ud turned to leave them.

"Yes?"

"The *Khanum* would like to know how it is you are the Eighth Angel."

Da-ud kissed Katherine's hand and addressed her as the beautiful Esther. "There are Seven Angels in heaven," he said to her. "Gabriel, Michael, Raphael, Azrael, Azraphael, Dedrael, and Shemkel." He had already stepped back out of sight.

"And the Eighth?" MacGregor called after him.

"The Eighth is Man himself," he said and laughed from the darkness.

Chapter 33

MacGregor accepted Father Da-ud's offer to show them the best route to Bijar and Sinneh. Essex was sceptical of the pilgrim, but he did not object, although he eventually held MacGregor responsible for the events which followed.

424

Da-ud appeared as they were preparing to leave. He squatted on the rock above to watch them and wait to be called down. When Mac-Gregor did shout to him, Da-ud came with the peaceful air of a man about to lead a band of faithful pilgrims out of the wilderness.

"*Marhabba*," he said to MacGregor, using the Kurdish greeting.

"*Marhabba*," MacGregor replied, repeating it thrice as an essential courtesy.

"I shall walk at your stirrup," Father Da-ud told him when they mounted to begin, "and when necessary I shall walk ahead; but the route is very simple."

MacGregor accepted it that way because Da-ud was obviously a practised guide for travellers in Kurdistan. In daylight he looked no less gentle, but it was clear that he was a mountain Kurd. He was not old, he was simply weather-beaten, and his skin was wintry and burnt, but very smooth. His white hair seemed to be the accident of his religion, but it did give him veneration, and as Katherine had said, a devilish-looking saintliness. Essex's only comment on the pilgrim (after hearing MacGregor's translation of their conversation last night) was that the man must be a Communist. Even so, Essex said nothing about his presence this morning and accepted MacGregor's confidence in him as a guide.

To begin with Da-ud could walk faster than the horses because the ground was boulderous and rough. His felt cloak did not hamper him, nor did his long white gown beneath it. He gripped the rocks with his hemp-soled sandals and preceded them agilely through the complexity of sharp hills and twisting valleys. As the country became more chaotic and tangled with ravines and faults, Essex wondered how they could have found a way through here without Da-ud. By midday they were up on a high open ridge which stood well above the sweeping country around them, and Essex was finally convinced of Da-ud's usefulness.

"This is the ancient Mukri route to the north," MacGregor told them. "He says we can follow this ridge right down to Bijar."

"When do we get there?" Essex said, feeling the jolt now to every bone in his body.

"By to-night," MacGregor told him.

But that was not to be so.

A heavy weariness had settled on them as they clung to their beasts and followed Da-ud, who was now mounted casually on the Turkoman pack horse. The ridge had dipped into a basin, and they were almost down at its steep bottom when two horsemen came galloping around the basin's other side, turning through the rocks to come down upon them. They held rifles and they were Kurds. MacGregor turned and Katherine followed his look. The ridge above them was dotted with more Kurds, who waited there for a moment before driving their small horses down the slope in a reckless sliding scramble.

425

"I have an idea they're unfriendly," Essex said.

MacGregor reined up. "Just don't move," he told them.

"I hope you can handle this," Essex began.

"We'll be alright," MacGregor told him hastily. "Don't say anything in English, don't say anything at all." He had barely instructed them when the first two horsemen came up level with them, snaffling their horses into a vicious stop.

"*Marhabba*," MacGregor said quietly and dug his feet into the bar stirrups and gripped the saddle, knowing that it was an old Kurdish habit to knock a man off his horse and then come to terms with him.

There was no polite reply to MacGregor's greeting. The Kurds rode around them and jostled them and shouted to the other Kurds on the slope, and MacGregor backed his horse to squash Katherine between himself and Essex. Father Da-ud had been isolated by the Kurd's whirling encirclement. He gripped the lead of the pack horse and tried to talk with the riders but they would say nothing to him. They were shouting among themselves as more of them crowded around the Englishmen.

"Are these fellows bandits?" Essex growled angrily.

"I don't know what they are," MacGregor said. He was trying to estimate by their dress what they were, but there was little to recognize except that they were all of the same tribe. They were all dressed in swaggering robes, brown over a dirty yellow, with short vests and billowing muddy trousers which were tight at the ankles and tucked in red Turkish boots, curled at the toe. MacGregor's one consolation was their apparent prosperity: they wore silk handkerchiefs in their turbans, and their saddles were studded and tassled in yellow and red, all of it the sign of an organized tribe rather than bandits; but since all tribes could be bandits, MacGregor wasn't sure of them. They were well armed with British service rifles which had been studded with silver tokens, and they propped these weapons on their saddle horns. Each wore a large bandolier of cartridges which rattled with every move of their horses.

"What now?" Katherine said as they were jostled unceremoniously forward up the slope again.

"Just sit tight until we get on some high ground," MacGregor said. He moved close to Katherine and braced himself forward to make the climb. "Watch out that they don't try to knock you off your horse." He could say no more because his horse was prodded with a rifle barrel and they were driven like sheep until they reached the top of the ridge.

They were still together, and MacGregor looked around to decide what to do. They were on the edge of a steep ravine and some of the Kurds were already on their way down. MacGregor knew there was no choice left for them. They were herded down the slope, and MacGregor felt stupid and helpless as he tried to keep behind Katherine to see that

426

she was not pushed about, while Essex did the same thing on her flank. Da-ud had been lost in the scramble and there was no sight of him as they slipped and stumbled in the descent.

"Where do you imagine we're going?" Katherine managed to gasp out as MacGregor came abreast of her. She was hanging desperately to her saddle.

"Their camp." MacGregor held his cob by the mane and neck. "Keep as close to me as you can." He was a little ahead of her now, driven by the surrounding riders who were laughing and joking and shouting as they rode.

She could not keep level with him, and MacGregor heard the awkward clawing of her horse and turned to see the beast go down on his forelegs, throwing Katherine over his neck, her arms spread, her hair flying, and her legs bent up as she turned over and landed on her shoulders on the rocks. She rolled over sideways under the hoofs of Essex's horse. Mac-Gregor was off his horse and almost under Essex at the same time, and he felt the hoofs drag over him as he bent over Katherine. When he was clear he pulled at Katherine's arms to straighten her up and see if she was hurt.

"Let me look," he said and pulled her grazed hands away from her face. Her face was still tight and her eyes were still closed. "Are you alright?" He had taken out his handkerchief to wipe the dirt from her mouth and she opened her eyes and looked up at him.

"Is my face alright?" she said, taking her breath.

"Yes. How are your legs?" He was supporting her as the nearest Kurds held the steep slope near them. She put up both her arms to be helped up as Essex came back. She looked at the mounted Kurds and then released her arms from MacGregor.

"I'm alright," she said sharply. "Let's not make too much fuss in front of these people."

She pushed her hair back and brushed the grit from her knees through her torn trouser-leg. She looked around for her horse. A Kurd held its bridle and she took it from him and pulled some of the stone flakes out of its forelegs. She then mounted with as much vigour as she could muster while a Kurd held the bridle at the horse's mouth. She pulled it free from him and the Kurd laughed with his head back and drove his horse down in the loose stones ahead.

At the bottom of the ravine the Kurds pointed to a great cavern in the side of the mountains. It was really a large verandah of rock, an over-hanging ledge which jutted out from a cliff-face. It sheltered a flat expanse of limestone, wide at the mouth but cavernous in its narrowing depth. At the mouth of it there were horses, bundles of fodder, piles of saddlery, and a small herd of black goats. Since the approach was comparatively level the three travellers collected together again, all of them out of breath. Essex by now was red-faced with effort and indignation.

"Do we have to submit to this man-handling?" he said. "Why don't we turn around and ride off?"

"They would round us up like cattle," MacGregor told him. "We couldn't outride these men."

"Well why don't they loot us and get it over and done with?"

"If they were going to loot us they would have done it on the spot. They obviously want something else of us. It may not be so bad if we are careful."

"Surely they don't know who we are," Katherine said.

"They know we're not Kurds," MacGregor said impatiently.

They were jostled again by two particular Kurds who had made a holiday of this incident. One shouted to MacGregor with insulting vulgarity: "Get on. There is no time for your Osmanli gossiping. Get on. Get on." He prodded MacGregor's horse with his rifle.

MacGregor drew back and called him a Turk and kicked his horse. The Kurd closed in again and cracked MacGregor's horse across the rump with his rifle. The horse shot forward, pig-rooted, and whinnied in pain. The Kurd was about to attack it again but the other Kurds stopped him and Essex rode between him and MacGregor.

"What did the fool do that for?" Essex said to MacGregor.

"I insulted him." MacGregor recovered, wiping horsehair and dirt from his hands. "I don't like him. I don't like him at all."

"Great God," Essex said. "Is this a time for likes and dislikes?"

They had reached the edge of the cavern and the Kurds rode straight into its mouth. The horses' hoofs beat on the hard rock like metal hammers, and as they dismounted they were met by women and dogs and goats and children. Every sound in the cavern acquired a mocking echo; the shouting men sounded like giants, the barking dogs sounded like monsters, and the chattering women sounded like the continuous dash of pebbles in an empty vessel.

Katherine was already off her horse and she was struggling to hold the bridle as a Kurd pulled at it.

"Let him have it," MacGregor told her quickly.

"Where is Harold?" she said.

"I'm back here." Essex was flanked by Kurds who had taken his horse. The three of them were pushed together and they stood like naked women among a crowd of grinning men. The Kurds dismounted and came around to inspect them, and for a moment the situation was funny.

Then Essex said, "That old Devil-worshipper led us into this."

"I don't think so," MacGregor said.

"I'm sure of it," Essex said. "What are they all grinning at?"

428

"They're saying that they have never seen anything like us," MacGregor told him. "They don't seem to be too unfriendly."

"They look unfriendly enough to me." Essex stared back at the Kurds with an equal eye. "Where is that pistol of yours now, MacGregor?"

"It's in my kit on the pack horse," MacGregor said, "and God knows what's happened to the pack horse and Da-ud."

"I suspect that old devil too," Katherine said.

One Kurd scattered the others by shouting at them, and he gestured ahead and took them into a small cave in the cavern's side. It was shaped like a cathedral and it was lit by the yellow lumen of a wick floating in oil. In here the rest of the world was dead, and in an instant the grip of depression took hold on them. Two Kurds sat on their haunches at the entrance to this cathedral and watched them. Left alone, the English travellers stood silently together for a moment. Katherine saw a piece of horsehair matting, and she lay down there on her back. MacGregor gave her his cap for a pillow and Essex looked down at her and worried.

"Are you sure that fall didn't hurt your back?" he said.

"Yes."

"What about your knees?"

"I'm alright," she said.

"Let me take a look," Essex persisted.

"Leave me." Katherine turned on her side. "I don't feel like talking."

Essex looked embarrassed and said to MacGregor: "Well then. What now?"

MacGregor sat down. "We'll find out soon enough," he said. "Why don't you sit down and relax?"

Essex was nervous. "This whole affair is ridiculous," he said.

"Well don't walk up and down," MacGregor remarked with no care and no respect and with no consideration for Essex's position. "We'll just have to wait and see what happens."

"I can't take this sort of thing so casually," Essex said. "You just can't sit there and let these things happen."

"Perhaps you can do something," MacGregor said drily.

"I intend to."

"Please stop arguing you two," Katherine ordered.

"Sorry," Essex said.

"What's the matter with you, Kathy?" MacGregor asked.

"Don't ask me," she said. "I'm alright."

"We won't get anywhere sitting around here." Essex could not be quiet. "Talk to those two beggars over there MacGregor, and ask them what this is all about."

"I've already asked the others," MacGregor said. "They don't know."

"Did you tell them who we were?"

429

MacGregor leaned back. "No," he said. "It might make it worse."

"You've become as mulish as these Persians," Essex said in sudden temper. "One moment you're a wild and argumentative devil; now you lie down there like a dumb mule and do nothing. Remember you are the Englishman — not the submissive Oriental."

"At the moment I feel like an Oriental," MacGregor said. "Whatever is going to happen will happen. You can't do much about it. Sit down."

Essex grunted with disgust and walked to the two Kurds and complained to them in angry English. He then set his jaw and walked right past them. MacGregor sat up to watch. He could see that Essex was angry enough to try anything. The Kurds did not stop Essex. They did not get up. They watched him, and Essex went on walking as if he had a distant gun in his back. The Kurds shouted to someone as Essex disappeared in the darkness of the cavern.

"Where's he gone?" Katherine was also angry.

"He's gone to fight them all single-handed." MacGregor got up.

"Don't you go," Katherine said. "One fool is enough."

"Aren't you worried?" he said to her.

"No. My head is too sore to care a damn what happens."

"Lie down," MacGregor told her without approaching her.

"Go after him," she said with more sanity. "He'll get into a mess. You had better go."

"They'll bring him back," MacGregor replied.

"You are pig-headed," Katherine said and looked beyond the two Kurds for Essex. "Something will happen to him."

"If they were going to do anything to us they would have done it by now," MacGregor said. "It's no use beating your brains out."

"Oh heavens," she said. "Why did I get involved with such a stubborn man. Go and find him."

MacGregor did not move.

"Then I'll go myself." She meant it.

"Lie down," MacGregor told her sharply. "They aren't going to hurt him. If you start wandering about I shall have to go with you and I'm too stiff to walk about, so lie down and let Essex do his own exploring. He won't get far."

Katherine lay down and MacGregor stretched his legs and wondered if he should find out what this predicament really meant. He knew that it would be hopeless to look for the explanation by badgering odd Kurds. He knew it by the senses he had developed in a lifetime among such people. He accepted and faced their detention with stoic deliberation. They would have to wait until the unknown figure of Kurdish decision showed himself. MacGregor guessed that they were physically safe. That was enough for him at the moment. He had no patience with Essex, who had gone out to behave as an outraged and indignant Englishman should behave. Essex would strain their situation and make it even more difficult. MacGregor told himself disgustedly that Essex's right to complicate the world should be limited. He then went out into the wide cavern to find Essex.

He stumbled over rocks because of his stiff legs, and he walked out of the cavern as casually as he could, passing by a group of Kurds squatting around dung fires, and by another fire where women were cooking. He went right to the opening of the cavern and looked at the bright day, but he did not go further. Behind him in the cavern he heard Essex talking. He found Essex near one of the fires addressing three Kurds who sat under a goatskin awning.

"Where is your chief?" Essex was demanding of them in English.

He was answered in Kurdish by one who had a short beard and wore two silver daggers in his girdle. "Does this *Ferangi* expect us to understand him? What is he saying? What an ignorant man he must be to imagine that we speak his foreign language. What is he saying?"

"I don't know what you are muttering about," Essex told them, "but I have an idea that you understand me. Get up and take me to your chieftain."

"There is a man," said the bearded Kurd, "who is losing his dignity. I know that without understanding a word of what he says. *Ferangi*," he said to Essex, "you would do better to show the strength of your silence."

"If you're saying something about your leader," Essex said, "get up and show me where he is."

"Now I am tired of such a voice and of the man behind it." The old Kurd waved his arm at Essex. "Go away. Go on."

Essex was also fed-up. "If you could talk English I would teach you some manners," he said.

"I think I will call the dogs onto him," the Kurd said. "Go away."

MacGregor finally interrupted. "Lord Essex," he called.

"Ah, MacGregor." Essex swung around. "How long have you been there?"

"A few minutes," MacGregor replied.

"Why didn't you help me out?"

"It wouldn't do any good."

"Well, ask them who is responsible for our predicament and find out where the ruffian is."

"That is no good either," MacGregor said. "Come on back and wait at the fire. It's better that way."

"Wait for what?" Essex said in a high voice.

"In a situation like this we should behave morosely and silently," Mac-

431

Gregor said between his teeth. "Any other behaviour, particularly indignation, is a sign of weakness and fear."

"Nonsense," said Essex. "I intend to make enough fuss to find the authority for our detention."

"They won't discuss it with you, and you're making a fool of yourself." MacGregor knew what he was saying, but he had never gone this far before. Patience with Essex had drained right out of him. "You had better come back."

"I don't like that sort of talk, MacGregor."

"This is no time for niceties," MacGregor said sourly. "If you know better than I do you can go ahead; but they are laughing at you. One of them has suggested turning the dogs onto you for your ill manners in disturbing a man at his own fire."

"This is what comes of following that old devil," Essex said. "He led us right into it. You had no business to trust him."

"You wanted to come into the mountains," MacGregor reminded him. "If we had avoided Bijar this would never have happened."

Essex didn't deny it. He could blame, but he could also accept other men's blame, although the responsibility for their predicament would always be argued between them. MacGregor left him and went back to the cathedral rock.

He told Katherine that Essex was alright. She was still lying down, and with her now was a Kurdish girl of ten or twelve. She was babbling at Katherine in full-blooded Kurdish. She was dressed in long yellow and blue silk robes with baggy trousers tight at the ankles. She wore a flat red cap which was fringed with gold disks, and her arms were jingling with thin brass bangles. She was brown and full of Kurdish hilarity, and she begged Katherine in Kurdish to give her some of the red paint on her lips. She greeted MacGregor with a formal and firm *Marhabba*, and she went on talking to Katherine, who was shaking her head in hopeless ignorance.

"Tell her to go away," Katherine said to MacGregor.

"She wants some of your lipstick."

"Some other time."

"She says she knows that you fell off your horse and that you look sick."

"Oh, take her away," Katherine said.

"Her name is Pirusa." MacGregor barely had time to interrupt the little Kurd. "She's offering to look after you."

"Then tell her to stop chattering."

"She likes you and feels sorry for you," MacGregor explained. Pirusa was clicking her tongue and touching Katherine's torn trousers and scraped knees.

432

MacGregor did not attempt to keep up with her chatter, and he noticed suddenly that their kit was in the cathedral. "How did this get here?" he said.

"Our famous guide brought it," Katherine replied.

MacGregor unpacked it and found their small first-aid kit and gave it to Katherine.

"What makes you so disgustingly casual," she said, "and why didn't you bring Essex back?"

"He is out there being indignant."

"Good for him," she said. "Why don't you give him a hand?"

"What does he expect to do?" MacGregor demanded. "Ride out of here with an official apology from some Kurdish Minister of State?"

"Well, we have to get out of this somehow."

"It will be easier if we adjust ourselves a little and talk our way out of it. It's no use trying to get out of it by indignation. We will be alright if we behave properly." MacGregor had unrolled Katherine's sleeping bag beside her.

Katherine was beginning to be amused although she grimaced as she dabbed at her knees with iodine, attended by Pirusa who was still chattering. "Has this sort of thing ever happened to you before?" Katherine asked him.

"Once or twice."

"Is that why you accept it with such annoying indifference?" She edged Pirusa's small face away from its inquisitive position over her knee. "What do you suppose these people intend to do with us anyway?"

"Perhaps nothing."

"Then why did they round us up like cattle?"

"Kurds round up anyone they find in these mountains. We are in their country," he said in ironical explanation. "We might as well remember it instead of claiming some extraordinary right to go where we please. It wouldn't be a bad idea to consider our dignity as well. Essex is overdoing his resentment."

"He's feeling helpless and frustrated," she said, "and I can't blame him."

"He is making a fool of himself."

Katherine finished painting her knees. "Go away while I change," she told him, "and take this chatterbox with you."

MacGregor turned his back while Katherine put on a plaid skirt.

"What is this little gipsy gabbling about," she said. "Please go away." Pirusa looked at Katherine's skirt and laughed with delight. She snatched up Katherine's torn ski-pants and rushed off, her gold disks tingling as she danced over the rocks, laughing with white teeth and wild young eyes.

"She's stolen my pants," Katherine said.

433

"You shouldn't have left them lying there," MacGregor said and laughed. "Anyway, you impressed her. She didn't stop talking about your small nose and your red, red lips, and your delicate skin. She says your face looks as if it had been licked by a kitten."

"Do they speak Persian?"

"No, but it's similar to Persian."

"She makes it all sound like an unintelligible rhyme."

Essex returned, and seeing the kit commented that he never expected to see that stuff again. "Has any of it been stolen?" he asked.

"Some of the food," MacGregor told him.

"I found one of these Kurds who speaks a few words of German," Essex said, "but he just grins and says *Achtung* when you ask him why we are being detained. Surely we can do something MacGregor. Something."

"What?"

"I don't know, but it's not my way to sit down and let things happen to me, and I don't intend to make it my way." Essex was not quite so indignant.

MacGregor's sense of proportion was also returning. "We are hardly in a position to have our own way. Just be patient for a while. They will let us know what it means."

"They can't hold us up like this. Don't they realize who we are?"

"They don't care who we are," Katherine said.

They were still discussing it when one of the Kurds appeared and said that there was food if they wanted it. He commanded them briefly to follow him, and they did so, feeling that a solution to their situation might be forthcoming.

The Kurds were seated around a felt mat, more than a dozen of them, and two women. The food was in rough bowls along the centre of the mat and the men were helping themselves with their fingers. They ate noisily and spoke noisily, and they grinned at the *Ferangi* who were brought among them.

"It's a good sign when we're asked to share their meal," MacGregor murmured to them as a hope for reassurance.

A few of the Kurds moved up after a great deal of shouting, and the three foreigners sat among them, facing the steaming food. There was just sufficient light from an old oil lamp to display the dishes; and at first sight they were all revolted. Even MacGregor was revolted. Every dish looked like the same mess, but some were identifiable as beans and others as cheese and pancake bread soaked in broth. The first move was up to MacGregor, and he dug his fingers into the beans which had already been sampled by his Kurdish neighbour.

"You'll find the bread alright," he whispered to Katherine.

434

"I'm hungry," she said under her breath. "Give me that repulsive bowl you are dipping into. Are they beans?"

"Yes, and they're hot."

Katherine plunged her fingers into the beans and lifted them to her mouth but they fell out of her straight fingers. MacGregor showed her how to bend the ends of her fingers to hold the mixture, and Katherine tried again, knowing that every eye of twenty men and two women were on her as she drew the beans from the tips of her fingers and negotiated her teeth perfectly.

"Bravo!" MacGregor said quietly.

Essex watched but did not attempt the bowls. He took long pieces of meat from a copper pan and put them in the dry pancake bread. He ate calmly, and regarded his Kurdish hosts who appeared in this light to be a God-like collection of men with thin features, fine colourful robes, fierce eyes, straight noses, and bellowing voices. MacGregor watched Essex and felt that there were never two types of men so different as Essex was from these Kurds. Every refined habit which came naturally to Essex was contradicted by a completely opposite refinement in the Kurds, this delicate art of eating with the fingers being an example. It was an interesting thought, but MacGregor didn't have time to pursue it because Pirusa had arrived to pester Katherine again.

"What does she want now?" Katherine asked.

Pirusa had brought back Katherine's ski-trousers. The knees had been stitched with a neat felt patch. Having presented them to Katherine, she began to make quick journeys to the food dishes bringing various bowls for Katherine to try. She was encouraged in the operation by her bellowing tribesmen. She eventually edged her way between MacGregor and Katherine and sat down and began to eat with great appetite.

"They call her Pirusa with the Golden Ears," MacGregor told Katherine.

"Look at the little beggar eat."

"She is the daughter of the Sheikh."

"Which one is the Sheikh?" Essex asked.

"He doesn't seem to be here. One of the women is his wife." MacGregor looked around at the circle of faces, all yellow in the pale oil light. No. The principal Kurd was not among them. Two men were authoritative enough to be Sheikhs but they were not addressed by rank or title as such. These two seemed to be diametrically opposed in every way, and whenever a discussion began they eventually shouted at each other in argument. Both were young, but one was tall and surprisingly blond and blue-eyed, while the other was small and ugly and cynically humorous with tiny eyes which were folded at the corners. All other argument stopped when these two began, but it usually ended in a vic-

435

tory of wit for the small man. The blond Kurd was strong-minded and clever but too blunt for his wily opponent.

Listening to their conversation, to all this conversation around him, MacGregor felt the paleness of their own English appearance and existence. Even Essex's natural dignity was lost in this gathering of proud men. Of the three only Katherine was adequate for this gathering. She had the same command and the same sense of herself as these men, and MacGregor had a new appreciation of the Englishwoman beside him.

"There he is," she was saying to MacGregor. "There is our Eighth Angel."

Father Da-ud had appeared with his usual suddenness and he seated himself beside the small ugly Kurd, but not until he had bowed in their direction and touched his forehead in gentle respect.

"Are you convinced now?" Essex said to MacGregor as he finished his meal with a handful of dates and cheese. "Look at him. Thick as thieves with these Kurds. I tell you he led us into this, MacGregor."

"No," MacGregor said.

"Why must you always disagree?" Katherine said to MacGregor.

They were given small cups of Turkish coffee and as they drank it Katherine tried to cope with Pirusa, feeling cheerful enough to tolerate and even laugh at the youngster. Katherine also watched Essex and MacGregor, and she was pleased by their different methods of coping with the situation. Essex was casual and relaxed. He looked around him from time to time, but he was cleverly ignoring the whole gathering. MacGregor on the other hand remained solemn and rigid, attending quite openly to what was said around him but keeping quiet, almost morose, as occasional gestures were made in his direction and attempts made to bring him into their conversation. She had never seen MacGregor make such a drama of his behaviour, but she couldn't tell how serious he really was. She decided never to let him forget this little act, and she started to chide him for it.

"Is your stern silence necessary?" she said to him. "Aren't they trying to be friendly with you?"

"There is plenty of time," he said.

It was Father Da-ud who eventually brought MacGregor into the conversation by a reference to the comparative sounds of Kurdish and other languages, including Persian and English. MacGregor knew that this was the sort of discussion which a Kurd enjoyed. Anything that touched on the relative merits of different religions, languages, customs, and people, made the Kurd an agitated disputant. Before the discussion had gone far, all the Kurds were involved — the end of the meal had brought more tolerance and a great deal of loud humour.

For his part in it MacGregor did not spare the English language in his comparisons, and when he began to translate common English expressions into the purity of grammatical Mukri Kurdish (as near as he could) the sense of English idiom became so ridiculous that MacGregor laughed with pleasure as if he was hearing its absurdity for the first time.

For that matter — MacGregor thought — how ridiculous everything became by comparison with its equal in another culture. MacGregor took this as a lesson he had never learned before. He had never had reason to compare the refined sanity of different societies. Now that the contradiction of all customs and manners and speech was suddenly revealed, he thought of Essex. All of Essex's superiorities were conditioned, they were not natural at all. MacGregor had always known this without thinking about it, but this new illustration became a revelation to a man who was now looking for an explanation of society. So much was shibboleth! So much of human habit and manner and organization. What made it bad? Not simply comparison with other societies. Nor did natural laws explain human folly. The mistake seemed to be in Man's inability to shape the society in which he lived. The result was a stupid and illogical order of things in which Lord Essex appeared as the ultimate symbol of Man's achievement.

With this thought came a sudden insight into much of John Asquith's behaviour.

"Well thank God you finally broke down," Katherine said. "What was all that fascinating argument about? It must have been hilarious."

"It was all very wild," he said. "I wish John Asquith had been here to take part in it."

"Good old John," Essex said, and he was his normal self again. "Pity he couldn't have come on this trip. Eh MacGregor? Never a dull moment."

Having lost his indignation, Essex was willing to take his surroundings as he found them, and he began to talk to the Kurds through MacGregor. In the conversation the responsive Kurds gave Essex back his lost dignity and even commented in fair apology upon the magnificent vigour of his age. Before they went to their cathedral for the night, they were all talking to their rough hosts. Essex was eventually referred to as *Elchee,* the common term for "ambassador," and Katherine was also given the benefit of their blunt good-nature. Her beauty and poise and horsemanship and courage and pride were admired, first by the men, then by the women, and then by Pirusa with the Golden Ears.

Chapter 34

It was not until the next morning that the Sheikh of the Mukri showed himself to his English guests. It was quite clear from the first moments of daylight that the Kurds were preparing to move. This would decide everything for the Englishmen: whether the Kurds had simply detained them for the night, or whether the Kurds had other plans for their further detention.

The Sheikh entered the rock cathedral when MacGregor was about to load their baggage onto the Turkoman horse. He was a rough man, young and hard and cadaverous. He was dressed in a yellow silk robe, a filigreed Zouave jacket, and wine-coloured baggy trousers. His nose was hooked and his large impersonal eyes were deep in his hollow black cheeks. In his youthfulness there was a hard shadow of old age and authority. This he turned upon Essex so that he appeared to Essex as the expected figure of a tribal lord: native, barbaric, and crude. After inspecting Essex, the Sheikh's impersonal eyes passed to Katherine who was equally impersonal with curiosity. Katherine's curiosity concerned the absolute masculinity of the Kurd; and she decided by his cold stare that he was a dangerously honest man, a man of uncertain youth and age, but of certain and approaching mortality. MacGregor in turn waited for the Kurd to observe and greet him. He saw what Katherine saw, but more by familiarity with Kurdish features than by Katherine's romanticism. He knew that the Kurd was young, probably no older than himself, yet obviously he was aged by some advanced sickness which made him brief, hard, and commanding.

The Kurd touched his large red turban and greeted MacGregor in Kurdish without feeling and without direct concern. He knew that MacGregor was the man he must address, and from the outset there seemed to be a contest between them in morose dignity and poise: the Kurd in his silks, and MacGregor in his worn rain-coat which hung as dramatically as any robe from his sullen shoulders. They had immediately become a measure for each other, and Katherine was the pleased observer who quickly realized it. For Essex the meeting became another long wait while something was settled for him in another language, and he listened to the grunts and brief phrases with annoyance and distaste.

The Kurd had announced himself to MacGregor as Salim of the Mukri, and had asked MacGregor the direction and intention of their journey in Kurdistan. MacGregor knew the danger of dishonesty with this man and did not attempt to conceal any information at all. Nevertheless, in telling Salim who they were he spoke as stubbornly and morosely as

438

any Kurd, showing resentment but not submission. There was little between them until MacGregor asked if their way was now clear and the detention over.

"You intend going to Sinneh?" Salim asked.

"We must go to Sinneh. We have a machine waiting there, and we must travel from Sinneh to Tabriz to see the officials of the new government."

"There is nothing you can do in Sinneh!" Salim announced with a wave of his hand.

"That is for us to decide," MacGregor said.

"I have just come from Sinneh," Salim said flatly. "And there is nothing you can do there." He waited for a moment. "If, as you say, you wish to understand our Kurdish situation, then it would be better if you came with me."

"We must go to Sinneh," MacGregor insisted. "Our machine is there."

"I can tell you all about Sinneh," Salim said with an impatient movement of his head. "We have had a great conference there of Kurdish leaders and I can tell you all that you need to know. The great men have left Sinneh, and it is simply an empty walnut for an ambassador now. You would do better to come with me."

"Where?"

"To Takht-i-Suliman, which is on your way to Tabriz. I will send someone to Sinneh for your machine and your servant."

"The Ambassador must see important people at Sinneh," MacGregor argued.

Salim now lifted his two arms and shook back his loose sleeves. He turned his head a little and spat largely and necessarily on the ground, and then plucked longer sleeves of an undergarment to wipe his mouth which loosened enough to show his divided teeth. "Sinneh is unnecessary," he said. "You can have your horses and you will benefit by our escort to Takht-i-Suliman."

MacGregor knew that Salim was telling him that they would come to the Throne of Solomon whether they liked it or not, but he made one show of resistance. "We have no intention of going with you," he said to Salim, knowing he sounded unconvincing; but faced with the inevitable, MacGregor found that he didn't mind if they went along with the Mukri.

"You will come," Salim said and bowed a little. "We will arrange for your servant and your machine. Your *Khanum* can travel with you or with our women: whichever you wish. Your pack animal will travel with ours."

"You realize that we are officials of the British Government," MacGregor said finally, "and that the Ambassador will consider this as hostile and dangerous. He will report it to the Iranian Government, and our own."

"Governments are far away from here," Salim said. "No government has ever delivered a protest to Takht-i-Suliman. You will be secure and well cared for. We will tell you all that you need to know of Kurdistan, and you will be able to tell the Iranian Government and your own Government of the real situation in Kurdistan." Salim wiped his mouth again and looked at Essex who was now asking MacGregor what was happening. Salim was more curious about Essex than the others, and he waited until Essex had finished speaking before he addressed MacGregor again. "If the Ambassador doesn't wish to come with us you must tell him that he is in Kurdistan, and that this is a fierce and lonely country where bandits make travel dangerous. For the *Khanum's* sake he would do better to come with us."

It was not a reason which Salim was offering to MacGregor but a suggestion to assist MacGregor in arguing with Essex. It brought an unconscious smile to MacGregor's tempered lips, even as he explained the situation to Essex.

"It's quite obvious that we are being subjected to some kind of kidnapping," Essex announced. "It's not much use trying to give it any other name or purpose. What does he want of us?"

"I don't know yet," MacGregor said.

"Tell him we won't budge from here."

"We have made fools enough of ourselves already," MacGregor said. "It would be a great joke to the Mukri to see us walking behind their horses over the mountains. We have no choice. You might as well realize it. He is actually treating us rather well by allowing us to ride."

"Perhaps he wants money," Katherine suggested.

"Then offer it to him," Essex said. "I don't mind wasting money, but I don't want to waste time. Ask him how much he wants."

"He may want money," MacGregor said, "but it would be dangerous to even suggest that we have it to offer. Do you have a lot of money?" he asked Essex.

"Enough," Essex said.

"Then keep it well hidden and don't talk about it."

"I'll do something about this business when we get home," Essex said.

"What about you, MacGregor?" Katherine said. "Will you do something about all this when you get home?"

MacGregor ignored this theme of Katherine's. He was looking at the two Kurds who were standing at a distance behind Salim. They had come with Salim and had remained standing quietly behind him. MacGregor recognized both of them. One was the small ugly Kurd, and the other was the large blond with Teutonic features. He had laughed at

Essex and MacGregor, as if he understood what they were saying.

"Do you speak English?" MacGregor asked him suddenly.

The blond Kurd bowed with undisguised mockery. "I am Amir Zada-i-Karadag," he said in bold English.

Essex looked surprised but he said nothing.

"Does he also speak English?" MacGregor nodded to the smaller older Kurd.

"He speaks no language but his own," the blond Kurd said with distaste.

He was interrupted by the small Kurd announcing his own name in Kurdish to MacGregor. It was Salim who explained that both men were his cousins and that both had been delegates with him at the gathering in Sinneh. In Kurdish, both their names were normal titles for ruling families. MacGregor knew that he had to translate them into English to please Katherine and Essex. "These two gentlemen are the cousins of Salim," he said formally to Essex. "This (he pointed to the blond) is the Fair Lord Zada of Karadag, and the other small gentleman is Lord Gordyenne the Invincible."

Despite himself, Essex inclined his head in their direction, and MacGregor enjoyed it, although this was neither the time nor place to be humorous. He was becoming like Katherine — planning humorous situations at unhumorous moments. He was surprised that Essex's humour did not come to his rescue, but Essex's humour seemed to have lost itself in the Kurdish mountains, so much so that he had nothing to say to these men.

"Do you have weapons?" the Fair Zada asked MacGregor in Kurdish.

"No," MacGregor lied. The small pistol which the Colonel had given him was in his coat pocket at this moment, awkward and heavy and in the way.

"Surely you do not travel without weapons." Zada's thin blue eyes were watching MacGregor so carefully that the Scot kept his hands in his pockets.

"We have lost them," MacGregor said with a take-it-or-leave-it attitude.

The ugly Lord Gordyenne turned his dark eyes on his blond cousin. "Are you afraid these delicate foreigners will kill you?" he said. It was insulting, but MacGregor found it less insulting than the hint of viciousness in the blond Zada. Both these men disliked the foreigners. Since they disliked each other as well, it began a contest between them in insults, directed obliquely at Essex and MacGregor. Out of Kurdish politeness, Katherine was spared by both.

Salim interrupted the hostility between his cousins and said: "We will go now. We do not travel at a great speed, but if you wish to come ahead

441

with me, then come now. Your beasts are ready for you." He looked at Essex. "Is your Ambassador angry?"

"No," MacGregor said. Now he had to behave as if they were going with Salim by choice. It deceived no one, but he was not supposed to deceive anyone. "He is happy to travel with you."

"He is not very happy," Lord Zada said with great enjoyment at their predicament. "He looks like a sick old goat." He laughed and left them.

Salim might not have heard the derision. "Why is it that they send an Ambassador here who does not speak Kurdish or Iranian? How can he know about Kurdistan?"

"I was sent with him," MacGregor said, "because I speak some of the language."

"Then you are the important man," Salim said to MacGregor.

"No. He is the important man with the Government."

"But he will know nothing that you do not tell him." Salim had not shifted his eyes from Essex's face while talking to MacGregor.

"He will make up his own mind and his own opinion," MacGregor said.

"Is he a great lord?" Salim asked.

"Yes."

"By family? Or by force?"

"By family."

"And the *Khanum*?" Salim said.

"She is a great lady by family."

"And you?"

"I am neither lord nor slave," MacGregor said coolly and added no more.

Salim walked away, and in doing so he passed Father Da-ud who was coming into the rock cathedral. Salim stopped to shake his hand, greeting him informally in Kurdish. MacGregor could see that the two men were well acquainted. Lord Gordyenne also shook Da-ud's hand and they exchanged a casual greeting on the state of their health, their regard for each other, and the respect, humbleness, and friendship of their brotherly love.

At the sight of Father Da-ud, Essex was irritated again. "I don't like that fellow, and I don't want him around me. Tell him to keep away, MacGregor."

"Don't be like that, Harold," Katherine said. "He's perfectly harmless."

Essex did not reply. The smiling face of Father Da-ud greeted them but he was worried when Essex waved him off. He asked MacGregor if Essex objected to the Devil being among them.

MacGregor tied the bundles to the Turkoman horse to give it balance. "He believes that you led us into the hands of Mukri," he told Da-ud.

"Does he fear the Mukri?" Da-ud did not deny the accusation.

"By no means. He is simply annoyed," MacGregor said. "Where are our horses?"

"Waiting for you. Everything will be safe. We are now travelling with noble men."

"What do these noble men want of us?" he asked Da-ud.

"I'm not sure," Father Da-ud told him.

"Do they want money?"

"Have they demanded it?"

"No. But what else could they want?"

"Perhaps they want your importance."

"What for?" MacGregor said.

"There's a great deal of political activity going on in Kurdistan these days," Father Da-ud explained, "and Salim of the Mukri has been to this important conference of Kurdish Chiefs at Sinneh. Something has been decided. Perhaps Salim wants your assistance or your sympathy. You are important men, and the world needs to know about Kurdistan."

"How does he know we're important?"

"If no one told him then he guessed it."

"Who would tell him?" MacGregor said.

"Aren't you great men known to all your friends in Iran?"

"Did the Russians tell him?"

"My dear friend." Father Da-ud smiled with kind reprimand. "Don't concern yourself about it at all. Salim of the Mukri is a self-dependent man. You are also a self-dependent man: responsible, and important and necessarily proud. Consider Salim as yourself and yourself as Salim; then you need not ask about him. The men to consider and to ask about are his relatives who will succeed him: the Fair Lord Zada and Lord Gordyenne the Invincible. They are men who disagree between each other, who dislike and contest each other for the political decisions of the Mukri."

"Do you concern yourself with them, *Baba* Da-ud?" MacGregor asked.

"Certainly."

"How is it that you, a Yezidi and a pilgrim, are so intimate with the Mukri, and can discuss them so freely?" MacGregor had finished with the Turkoman horse and he was waiting for Katherine and Essex to come with him.

Da-ud did not mind the serious and personal question. "Salim of the Mukri is a tolerant and enlightened man, and I have travelled with him before; many times before." Father Da-ud led the Turkoman horse before them as they walked out to the cavern.

"Isn't he a Sunni Mohammedan and therefore an enemy of the Yezidi?"

"He is a man above religion," Da-ud said. "No man in Kurdistan can be more tolerant, and yet no man can be more dangerous. You are in noble hands my friend, even though you may lose your wealth and your possessions and your importance."

MacGregor admitted to himself now that Father Da-ud was guilty of some part in their detention. He was no longer a pilgrim going to Mosul, but a fellow Kurd travelling with the Mukri in the opposite direction: to the Temple of Solomon, which was the home of the Mukri. Yet MacGregor could not believe that Da-ud had planned this deliberately, even though he participated in their detention now.

Outside, the morning was cold and quiet and fresh snow was on the ground. The Kurd's horses were now bunched together and breathing and stamping on the padded snow as the cloaked Kurds mounted their restless bodies and rode away. Among the horses there was one Arab which was white except for two black patches on its forehead. Its saddlery was red and its stirrups were of some kind of bronze. A large embroidered cape hung over its hind-quarters while it stood patiently awaiting its rider.

"That is the pony to suit you," Katherine said to Essex.

"It must be Salim's," MacGregor told them.

Essex said nothing and mounted his own miserable Arab. He then rode forward to where Da-ud held the pack horse and he took its lead out of the guide's hand. He pulled it behind him and faced MacGregor and Katherine, who were also mounted.

"Now why don't we just ride off?" he said to them calmly. "There is nothing to stop us."

MacGregor did not move. "We wouldn't get over that ridge," he said.

"You take these men too seriously," Essex told him. "Come on Kathy. Are you game?" He was relying on Katherine. This was the sort of defiance she would appreciate. It was an act to restore Essex's proper authority in this expedition.

"It's worth a try," Katherine said. "Come on MacGregor."

MacGregor had no choice. As they turned about he followed them in the rear.

Essex did not hurry. He asked MacGregor for their direction and proceeded at a walking pace over the rocks and up the most gradual of the slopes.

"Just don't look back," Essex instructed them. "Keep going."

"I think it will work," Katherine said as they drew away from the cavern.

MacGregor, most apprehensive of all, was beginning to think so too.

They were almost to the top of the ridge, out of sight of the cavern, when they heard the sound of horses behind them. They hurried on until they were on top of the ridge, and there the journey ended. Two Kurds had cut around the ravine and were already on the ridge ahead of them. MacGregor turned and saw two more coming. One was Salim himself. He was on them before the others and he shouted to his men to go about their own business.

"You are mistaken," Salim said briefly to MacGregor. "This is not the route."

"We know that," MacGregor said. "We were going on our own way."

Salim looked at Essex. "Tell him that our way is your way," he said to MacGregor. "It is dangerous for you otherwise. Tell him so." Salim had recognized the instigator of this diversion, and by the twitching of his hard lips into a moment of humour, it was quite clear that he appreciated Essex's attempt and respected him for it.

Essex realized Salim's impression. "Tell him he has the advantage of numbers, MacGregor." He was being good-natured about it as a sporting contest which he had lost. "You might add that we have the safety of a lady to consider. We therefore travel with him. Let him proceed."

Salim listened and bowed his head, first at Essex and then at Katherine.

"At least he appreciates the try," she said.

MacGregor had been outdone. He saw that Essex had scored a point with Salim, also with Katherine. They turned around with the Sheikh and followed him along the ridge. A Kurd took the pack horse at Salim's orders and Essex was left free to keep up.

They were joined by Lord Gordyenne, black and ugly upon an angry horse, and reprimanding Salim for bothering with these foreigners, telling Salim to let them go on their own miserable way. The Fair Zada was not far behind. He told Salim that it would be stupid to let them go; an honest Kurd would shoot and strip these foreigners without wasting time. The cousins then turned upon each other and cursed the God that kept the other alive.

Essex wanted to know about these two.

"As far as I can see," MacGregor told him, "they have rival ideas about the Mukri. Zada, the fair cousin, is apparently a brigand who thinks a Kurd is born to kill and raid. Gordyenne seems to have political ideas: I don't know what they are, but he is contemptuous of Zada's brutality."

"They both look vicious wretches," Katherine said.

"Particularly the short ugly specimen: Gordyenne is it?"

"Yes, but it's Zada whom we will have to watch. One thing they both agree on. They want to get rid of us. The Fair Zada suggests shooting us, whereas Gordyenne merely wants us turned loose in the wilderness." MacGregor did not take their threats very seriously: Kurds were like that.

They could talk no more then because Salim had set a pace which required concentration. He kept it up, and soon they were so high in the mountains that the clouds lay in the valleys around them. They never left the high ridges except for brief detours of high rocks. Since the ridges were narrow and bare, there was little for a rider to do but follow the man before him. This was difficult because of the rocky surface. The dusted snow supplied some grip for the flat hoofs, but the strain of coping with such uneven ground was as great on the rider as it was on the horse, particularly at the pace which Salim kept up. Whenever there was a brief stretch of flat ridge he forced a canter, and when the large boulders had to be negotiated he did not allow the pace to slacken for better footing. It seemed impossible that any rider could keep this up at all.

"I didn't bargain for this," Katherine managed to gasp out.

It was the only word out of them for more than an hour. Salim rode ahead without looking back and without any consideration of their presence. Behind them was the long line of Salim's entourage, and MacGregor was glad of Essex's determination to keep up with Salim at any physical cost. MacGregor knew by his own weariness that Essex must be in bad shape. On the uneven stretches he could see Essex hanging grimly to the pommel of his saddle and struggling to keep his back straight. MacGregor had already abandoned his posture and Katherine was almost riding side-saddle. There were times when she had both knees up on the horse's neck, a balancing feat which hardly seemed worth the comfort achieved.

Though they kept the pace they were still a great joke to the Kurds behind them. The comment upon their weakening horses and their persons was tireless, and each time Essex's horse stumbled there was a shout, as every Kurd within sight anticipated the pleasure of seeing the Ambassador fall off his horse. MacGregor was thankful that Essex and Katherine could not understand all the comment and therefore would not take it up. He waited for it to cease, but by midday the Kurds were still derisive, and MacGregor felt like calling Salim to order for it. Salim could hear the comments, and this made MacGregor hesitate. If Salim could consider it unimportant then so could he, although he felt a jolt of irritation each time he heard the remarks behind him. Beneath his annoyance, he knew that this was common and normal Kurdish humour, and that no real insult was intended. Abreast of Essex, as they waited to negotiate a stream, he forgot about it in admiration for the old man who was winning a Pyrrhic victory over his decaying body.

"You must be in good shape," MacGregor said to him to break the long morning's silence. His voice was dry and hollow. "My back gave way some time ago."

"How long is this going to keep up?" Essex said, his voice broken by

446

the shaking of his stomach. "We seem to be clinging to the top of the world."

"They are following the ridges to avoid the hellish business of going down the valleys and over the peaks." MacGregor looked at the clouds beneath. "Apparently the Mukri alone know which ridges to follow, and if we were clever we would do a little mapping of the route."

"Go ahead and map," Essex said wearily. "Your friends in the India Office will forgive you all your past indiscretions if you present them with a nice new piece of local geography."

The India Office was far from MacGregor's thoughts. He said that this route might settle the argument about Saladin's ride from Sinneh to Takht-i-Suliman.

"Is there an argument about it?"

"He was supposed to have covered the whole distance in a little over a day, but the geographers say it is impossible." MacGregor swept his arm at the infinity of mountains and ridges which broke the sky. "This must be his route."

"Which way are we heading now?" Essex asked him.

"I don't know. We are always doubling back on the ridges and changing our direction. I don't even know where we are. We haven't passed a village or any other sign of life."

"This is all so awkward and unnecessary," Essex said suddenly. "What do you imagine this Salim will do about the car?"

"I gave him a note to send back to Aladin. I told Aladin we would be waiting at Takht-i-Suliman."

"I hope Aladin has the sense to get in touch with Teheran and tell them that we've been waylaid by these banditti. I don't mind a little diversion by peradventure, but I don't like to be interfered with in this way, MacGregor. You might tell that chief for me, and repeat that I intend to settle with him somehow."

"It's not much use threatening him."

"Then let him consider it a good warning."

"For what?"

"To stop him carrying this game too far."

"He'll do what he wants to do," MacGregor reminded Essex again. "He is not awed by us — and we were trespassing on his territory."

Katherine caught up with them as they crossed the stream. "Is this what they call a leisurely pace? It's going to do me some biological damage if we keep it up much longer."

"Why don't you tell him to slow down a little, MacGregor?"

"Not on my account," Katherine said.

"This fellow ought to be taught some civilized manners."

MacGregor was too tired to laugh at Essex, but he could see that Katherine was suffering intense discomfort. He kicked his horse and cantered awkwardly ahead and caught Salim in a soft patch of snow. He eased back in the stiff saddle as Salim turned to see who it was. Salim's face was glazed with perspiration. His large turban and cashmere shawl exaggerated his face in its length, its fierceness, and its grip of sickness. Salim's blue lips parted for a moment, but MacGregor heard nothing.

"Peace," MacGregor told him. "I will ride with you."

Salim did not reply.

MacGregor rode with him up a new ridge which took them around a high peak. In riding, Salim did not drive his small white Arab. The pony had its own head and it was sure-footed in its nervous insistence on keeping up the brisk pace. It was hard for MacGregor's weak-footed animal to keep abreast.

"Do they go all the way to Takht-i-Suliman?" MacGregor pointed to the parallel series of bare peaks on either side of them.

"All the way," Salim said heavily.

"Is there no road to Takht-i-Suliman? Is it so isolated that we must travel the mountain tops?" He hoped to provoke Salim to save his own pride.

"The Kurdish road is always the mountain tops," Salim said.

"Is it always so rough, and are you always so much in haste?"

"Are you exhausted, Brother?"

"I am here beside you," MacGregor said bluntly.

"And the Ambassador?"

"The Ambassador is an old man, but his back is stiff enough."

Salim was expressionless. "Is the *Khanum* miserable because of the fall she had yesterday?" he asked.

MacGregor knew that Salim was helping him out, but he decided not to use Katherine. "No. If she suffers she has not shown it."

"Then you have miserable horses," Salim decided. "They are too old and too soft-footed for this travelling. They are exhausted too easily." Salim had already curbed his Arab, and the pace was slower.

MacGregor knew how maganimous Salim had been in providing the solution to this complicated balance of pride. Salim had not forced him into an ignominious position of asking that the pace be slackened. That was a great concession. MacGregor relaxed a little, feeling that some of his burden had been lifted by Salim. It was brief pleasure, for Zada rode up and reprimanded Salim for slowing down, pointing out the indignity of allowing a *Ferangi* to influence a Kurd. He was followed by Lord Gordyenne, looking hard and muscular on a quick-rising horse.

To MacGregor Lord Gordyenne took on more and more the appearance of a grotesque gargoyle with his dark spreading face and his thin neck and small shoulders. He contradicted all of Zada's teutonic blondness and Kurdish slimness. However ugly his features, it was Gordyenne's face that decided his real appearance with its lines of inquiry, its intelligence, and its ugly humor. There was also a great deal of anger and quick Kurdish temper in his thick mouth and his broad sensitive nose. His contempt for his blond cousin was everlasting, and he rode down upon Zada and jostled him out of the way. They were all approximately level, and the riding was awkward, until Salim went ahead and left MacGregor between Zada and Gordyenne. They immediately began an argument about MacGregor.

"Here is your victim," Lord Gordyenne said, taunting Zada with the presence of MacGregor. "Do you wish to rob him now, to dispatch him like a butcher and bury him in the snow? Is this the moment you want for your thieving and robbing, Cousin?"

Zada bellowed a reply. "What sort of a man is it who is afraid of bloodletting? Not a Kurd! You are a puking infant, you are sickened by a little bit of killing," he said to Gordyenne. "You are afraid to kill these Christian monkeys." He then shouted ahead to Salim. "Let us dispatch them now, *Ra-is*."

Salim did not turn or pause.

For the first time MacGregor sensed real danger, and he did not like it. Zada was making bloodthirsty fun, but he was beginning to sound serious. Until now MacGregor had not believed that harm would come to them among the Mukri, but now he wanted a quick assurance from Salim of their safety. Salim said nothing. It was therefore possible, MacGregor decided, that their safety might depend on Lord Gordyenne, who hated them as much as Zada but who did not want to use violence on them. Again Gordyenne taunted Zada with his childish desire to destroy the foreigners.

"Why don't you go ahead," Lord Gordyenne said to Zada. "They are infidels. What more does your superstitious mind need? Kill them now. Kill them and rob them and tell the women to pluck out their hearts to feed the jackals." Gordyenne's ugly face turned upon Zada with sudden disgust. "What would you have us be as Kurds? Animals, thieves, bandits; murdering our neighbours and robbing all men who enter the mountains. You are too stupid to be a Kurd, too barbaric to understand the great rôle of the Mukri. Bandit!"

"Warrior!" cried Zada in defence of himself.

"Ravager!" said Gordyenne.

MacGregor expected Salim to intervene now, but the Mukri chief rode on without ears or voice, and he had little concern for what happened behind him. MacGregor decided to take a hand in it himself, and he thought his best plan was to follow the line of Gordyenne, so that at least he might have an ally.

449

"Is the Kurdish warrior a murderer of old men and a defiler of young women?" he said to Zada with as much contempt as his short breath would allow.

"Are you afraid?" Zada said delightedly.

"Of thee?" MacGregor said calmly.

"Take care," growled Zada. "You are an infidel among enemies."

"Does Salim of the Mukri think that also?" MacGregor addressed Salim's back, knowing that Salim must disavow Zada now or never.

Salim merely turned his head and said "Peace."

Lord Gordyenne laughed and his short arm gripped MacGregor for a moment as they came together. "Beware of my cousin," he said morosely, but he was making fun of MacGregor. "I personally have no wish to kill you," he said, "but this ignorant and dangerous cousin of mine would like nothing better. I suggest that you persuade *Ra-is* Salim to let you go on your own way. We don't want you among us. One can never trust the presence of an Englishman. Nevertheless I do not want to see you slaughtered; so a little persuasion and Salim will send you away, and good riddance. Otherwise the butcher Zada will get you. He sees nothing in a Kurd but a man who kills."

Zada had taken enough and he kicked his horse so hard that it leapt forward in a mad gallop, and Zada disappeared in a flying cloud of snow dust, his striped cloak rising around him like a pair of angry wings. They watched him as he cut across a valley and rode along a neighbouring ridge. Then he disappeared again until he eventually appeared among the distant outriders.

"If it wasn't for *Ra-is* Salim," Lord Gordyenne said to MacGregor with his peculiar humour, "Zada would have dispatched you long ago."

MacGregor believed him. He was realizing that this was more than an argument about Essex and Katherine and himself. This sharp contest had placed them in the middle of some bigger dispute between Zada and Lord Gordyenne, a political dispute concerning the Mukri. In the circumstances, Salim was their only security, but Salim said nothing one way or the other. MacGregor thought of warning Essex about their situation, but he decided that it would be simpler if Kathy and Essex knew nothing.

As MacGregor dropped back to join them, he hoped (*Inshallah!*) that Salim was not as disinterested as he appeared to be.

Chapter 35

By the time they entered the high-towered gate of Takht-i-Suliman they were broken and exhausted, clinging desperately to their lurching saddles so that they would not fall off in the surprising darkness. As far as his weary mind would picture it in the darkness, Takht-i-Suliman looked to MacGregor like a temporary mountain settlement, built at the foot of a large rock which offered shelter from cold winds and driving snow. They rode through black groups of mud houses and goatskin tents, greeted by the shouting of women, the barking of cur dogs, the crying of sheep and goats, and the additional bellowing of Salim's riders trying to clear the way.

MacGregor was too tired to listen to what the villagers were shouting and laughing about, but he heard enough to realize that Zada had arrived ahead of them; had prepared a reception of Kurdish laughter for Salim's English guests. Yet they were Kurdish hands that helped MacGregor off his blown horse, and other Kurdish hands that helped Katherine and the silent Essex. Essex could not move his legs and he had difficulty standing up at all. He seemed to have snapped at the hips, and he had no choice but to suffer assistance to the small mud house where Salim stood and shouted orders to his men. Katherine walked and MacGregor walked, but they were little better off than Essex as they entered the hut.

It was one large mud room, one half of it being laid with Kurdish felt matting. It was lit by an American petrol lamp which gave a sharp but confined white light. In one corner was a small oil-burner expelling hot air from its perforated top. It was a soft and wonderful warmth after the freezing stiffness of the night air. They stood near it without saying a word. It was a test of endurance to see who would wait longest before collapsing on the rough cots against the walls. It was Katherine who went first, dropping with a long sigh of disgust on the nearest cot. Essex and MacGregor stood together, warming their hindquarters, saying nothing, but hanging grimly to their upright position. The younger man had less determination but more stamina, and Essex was forced to go before him.

"By God I am done," he gasped and lay down.

In sheer bravado MacGregor took his endurance one stage further and said he would attend the horses.

"Do you want something to eat?" he asked Katherine.

"No. Go away."

"I'm hungry," MacGregor commented annoyingly.

451

"And I've never been so wrecked in all my life," she groaned. "I'd give anything for a hot bath. I'm filthy with horse sweat."

"I'll get the kit and you can have a wash."

"Just leave me and go away."

MacGregor looked for another means of provoking them but the best he could do was to fulfill his boast and stagger outside to attend the horses, which Kurdish women and children were unsaddling with fierce argument. The riders told MacGregor that the pack horses would not be here until morning, and MacGregor noticed with relief that their own mounts had been taken off with the others, so he returned to the hut.

Pirusa was in the room, spreading a quilt over Katherine.

"Golden Ears," he said to her. "The *Khanum* is hungry."

It was sufficient to send her off to get food.

"She couldn't have been riding all day," Katherine groaned.

"She must have been."

"The little devil must be made of rubber. So must you. Lie down somewhere for God's sake, and turn out that light."

MacGregor turned down the petrol lamp and stumbled to the last cot. He started to take off his boots but he lay back without completing the operation. He was already asleep by the time Pirusa came and left the food under Katherine's bed.

It was daylight when Katherine shook MacGregor. "I say, wake up will you."

"What are you doing?" he complained wearily.

"I'm shaking you," she said. "Someone was bending over you."

MacGregor wasn't interested.

"I think he was the one that hit your horse with a rifle the other day," Katherine went on. "He seemed to be contemplating the idea of wringing your neck."

MacGregor groaned and sat up. "It might not have been a bad idea. I never want another day's ride like that one. How do you feel?"

"I can't move," she said as she stretched her arms.

"You look dirty," he told her.

"I'm hungry," she said.

MacGregor pointed under her cot where he could see the cheese and bread. He bent his legs over and picked up the platter and set it on the bed. He looked at his filthy hands and asked her if she minded. She displayed her own which were dirty with leather-sweat and grime. Mac-Gregor looked around to see whether Essex was awake. The "Ambassador" was sleeping soundly on his side with his face flattened into the cushion and his mouth open.

"I must say Harold did well," she said. "He didn't bend his back all day."

MacGregor nodded and cut a piece of cheese and offered it to Katherine with a round of bread. They ate silently and hungrily, leaving only enough for Essex, and drinking from a water skin which Pirusa had also supplied.

When she was satisfied Katherine began to think of her appearance. She was dishevelled and tangled up in her clothes.

"I must be an awful sight," she announced. "I have to wash myself somehow, MacGregor. It's uncomfortable for a woman to remain unwashed for so long, and I've run out of underclothes." She touched the hard pink material at her low throat and then straightened up. "What sort of place is this?"

"I didn't see much of it last night," MacGregor said, "but it's primitive. It must be the home of the Mukri in summer. I don't know what they're doing up here this late in the year." He walked stiffly to the door noticing that their kit was now stacked among the other bundles. The only light in the room came from a framed window with thick green glass. When he opened the door, he was blinded by the blue sunlight which came with the flat push of cold morning air.

"Kathy!" he said from the door. "Come and look at this."

Katherine asked him what it was.

"Come over here," he said without turning around.

She buttoned her jumper and walked in stockinged feet to the door and looked out to see what MacGregor saw.

It was a mountain peak, high and perfectly shaped in a cone. It was very white with snow, and it stood crisply against the blue sky. It rose from a valley which was deep below them, and in the valley was a small lake whose shores were patched with rolled snow, and whose surface was blue and white in frozen reflection.

"I can never quite believe these breathless mountains," she said. "They're wild and yet they all have such absolutely perfect shape. I think that might be the best peak I've ever seen. Did we pass it last night?"

"No. It must be north."

"Let's get out," she said and pulled on her boots.

MacGregor waited for her and watched her as she put on her coat and pulled back her hair until it was tight above her ears. She gave him a crumpled piece of ribbon.

"Tie it," she said; and he tied it at the nape of her neck. "What about waking Harold?"

"Let him sleep," MacGregor said charitably, and they went outside.

Though the plateau of Takht-i-Suliman was sheltered on all sides by mountains, it was high enough to view the ranges all around as far as the eye could see. The inhabitance of the plateau was its least significant

453

detail. The dozen mud-walled houses and the six or seven goatskin tents were dwarfed by a towering white rock which rose above the table-like surface. From the foot of this rock the mud huts and tents were scattered out towards the centre of the plateau. They were supplemented by the slightly visible outline of some historical-looking ruins enclosed in a broken wall containing a few crumbling towers and a large ruin in its centre. The main gate of the ruins formed one of the limits to the plateau village.

They could see the whole shape of Takht-i-Suliman from where they stood, and when they walked forward they came to the edge of the plateau and looked down at the deep valleys and lake, and across at the white mountain.

"What a skiing slope," Katherine said, "if it were only covered all the way with snow. It must go down five or six thousand feet, right into the lake."

"Must you always look for the sporting possibilities of the country-side?" he said to her, recovering some of his humour.

"Well, what do you see?" she demanded.

"Just the mountains and the valleys," he said.

"Oh nonsense," she replied. "You are probably making a brief estimation of how it all happened: What made the mountains? And what made the lake?"

It was true, but MacGregor considered it part of his personal appreciation, an appreciation which was unexplainable, even to Katherine.

"It must excite you to look at country like this and understand it." She looked around her and then glanced at MacGregor.

Now he was surprised that Katherine had recognized the double advantage the geologist had in viewing the beauty of topography. Few laymen ever understood this additional appreciation which understanding the structure gave the expert. It encouraged MacGregor to try and explain it, as if he were letting her in on a secret. "If you know the history of the earth," he said, "it usually adds a little to the wonder of the scenery." It was the best he could do, so he told her of the area. "In the Pliocene period this country was probably a deep fresh-water lake supplied by large calcareous springs. There are still springs all round here. We must take a look for them later on."

"Have geologists been over this part of the world?"

"A few," he told her. "A German named von Stahl, and some of the École Normale Professors have touched it, but no real survey exists because no one has had the time or the opportunity to study the area." MacGregor shrugged with a touch of bitterness. "I suppose its eventual exploration will be limited to the needs of the oil companies or the copper miners. It's a pity. Sometimes I wish that I had a chance to do

454

more field work myself. Given the chance, a field man could make a life's work of exploring these mountains."

She laughed at him. "I can really see you spending your life chipping away at these peaks. This seems to be your natural habitat, MacGregor. That's really the difference between you and Harold. He outpoints you in the civilized world, but up here you are absolutely supreme, my boy. And—talking of civilization"—she gave the word infinite distance—"Have you decided yet what sort of stand you will take when we get back to London? Have you?"

"That depends on what Essex does," he told her.

"No it doesn't. It depends on you."

He did not want her always reminding him of some ultimate decision he must take. It had become an obsession with her. "Wait until we get back to London," he told her.

She replied that he would be leaving it too late. She said that he would be at a disadvantage if he waited until he was in London to decide how he was going to dispute Essex. "But it will be interesting to see you both in London," she said and did not provoke him further.

He thought it would be equally interesting to see Katherine in London. He wondered if she would be the Moscow Katherine, or this more normal woman who could agree so easily and so simply with him. Perhaps she would be different again.

"Once I get up here in these mountains," she said—as if the same thought were in her mind—"I get the same feeling that you must have for them. Perhaps if I had been born here I might have been a different woman." She said this cleverly and took his arm as they walked across to the village which was coming to life with children and dogs and departing horsemen.

They were met in the snow half-way across the plateau by Father Da-ud. He was pleased to see them and he exchanged five or six small bows with MacGregor and then with Katherine. He hoped they had slept well, and added that there was food for them in Salim's tent. Food had also been prepared for them last night but they had gone to sleep too soon. MacGregor said they would eat later when the Ambassador was ready. In the meantime they were looking at Takht-i-Suliman.

"This is the heart of Kurdistan." Father Da-ud embraced the plateau and the mountains. "It is the throne of Solomon, where he held court with his divs and his djinns." He pointed to the tumbling ruins across the plateau. "That was Shiz, the capital of the Medes and the birthplace of the Kurd. Did you know that, my Brother?"

"I know nothing of its history," MacGregor admitted.

"It was also the Kandsag of the ancient Greeks who once conquered it.

It has always been a city for the conqueror. Even the Romans — Antony and Pompey — were here. The Arabs also. They called it Shir and they looted its palaces."

"There doesn't seem to be much left of any palace," MacGregor said. There were a few domes among the ruins but no shape of a building.

"Ah," said Father Da-ud unhappily. "It has always been a city to destroy because it has always been impossible to conquer the Kurds. Our cities have been destroyed, but we have never been conquered. Look." He pointed to the high sheltering rock. "The great temples of the Avestic religion were built beneath that rock. Zoroaster was born here and began his religion here. There too was the fire temple in which Khosru was enthroned, but it was destroyed by Heraclius. Later the Arabs stole the jewelled throne of Kai Khosru and threw it into the lake." Father Da-ud shook his head sorrowfully as if these events had happened in recent tragic years.

When Katherine had heard this from MacGregor she told him to ask Da-ud about the white mountain. That mountain must be important.

"That is the Takht-i-Balkis." Father Da-ud stopped and turned around so that they could see the white cone. "On its very top stood the palace of the Queen of Sheba." He smiled at Katherine and spoke to her in Persian. "She asked Solomon for a palace that was made of nothing but the bones of birds, and it was built in one night by two hundred of Solomon's djinns. It was then attacked by a dragon which Solomon turned into stone. You can see its shape across the hills. Below the peak is the bottomless pit where Solomon housed his divs. It goes through the hot centre of the earth to the New World."

"Did you know any of this?" Katherine asked MacGregor as he translated it.

"I had heard that it was one of the Ecbatanas of the Medes."

"Wait until Harold hears about this place. It will make up for yesterday's ride. Ask him about the other ruin on the high rock."

"He says it was the palace of Deioces; but I haven't any idea who Deioces was. He also says there are several treasures buried here. Cyrus apparently hid the treasure of Croesus somewhere in the caves; and some of the old Avestic jewels are buried beneath the lime sinters on those little hills."

As MacGregor told this to Katherine, Father Da-ud led them through the tents and the houses to the foot of the high rock. Near the ruined wall were two high arches built into natural caves in the hillside. Some of the arches were covered with glazed tiles, and Father Da-ud said that this was the palace of Abhu Mongol Khan who had built it near the remains of the old fire temple. He pointed to a lip, half-way up the

456

rock. He said it was a large basin lake with warm sulphur springs for bathing.

"Are they still usable?" Katherine asked MacGregor.

"Yes."

"Then let's go back and I'll have a bath and wash my clothes. Will it be alright?"

When MacGregor told this to Father Da-ud, he said he would arrange for one of the women to be with Katherine. There were places up there for bathing and washing. No doubt MacGregor would also like to wash away the dirt of travel. Father Da-ud gripped them both by the arm in a fine gesture of affection.

They were now among the goatskin tents near the crumbling wall, and as they turned to go back to their mud house, the children of the tent inhabitants came out and around them, running ahead so that they could look back upon the *Ferangis*. There were two who were very small and could not keep up, their bulky clothes restricting their small movement to no movement at all. They were crying, and Katherine turned around to see what was the matter with them.

"They are all very impressed," Da-ud told Katherine. "Kurdish women are the most beautiful of all women but you are something quite extraordinary. Even the children can see it."

MacGregor translated it with a little of Da-ud's romantic sentiment, and Katherine replied in English by calling Da-ud a good friend. Da-ud was pleased to be addressed directly by Katherine, even in English, and when MacGregor translated her remarks, he raised his hand and bowed with appreciation. MacGregor decided that Katherine knew what to say to anyone at any time, whatever the language difficulty.

Katherine was waiting for the two children to approach her. They were silent and they stood away from her with nervous faces, still crying. "What's the matter with them?" she said to MacGregor.

"Nothing," he told her. "They're shy."

"No. Look at the sores on their faces."

"All children in Persia have sores," MacGregor said.

Katherine squatted and tried to talk to the two children in English. They looked and listened but they did not move. They were small replicas of the Kurdish women, with long black trousers, felt wrapped feet, long coloured jackets tied at the waist, and large winding head-pieces of coloured scarves. They were warm but dirty and ragged. The older children, who now stood watching Katherine, were dressed in the same manner, but they were healthier-looking. They were not dark children but they were walnut-coloured and burnt by the wind and the snow. They were all black-haired and had strong teeth and sharp perfect eyes. They were tall and they were hard, and there was little difference between the boys and girls except in the softness of the girls' features and their long braided hair with its metal ornamentation.

"Tell them to come here, Ivre," Katherine said of the two smallest.

MacGregor spoke to them in Kurdish but they backed away. It was Father Da-ud who called to them, reprimanding them for their fear, and appealing to their affection for himself. They were careful but they allowed him to approach. He picked them both up in one sweep, and they clung to him as he brought them to Katherine. MacGregor watched Katherine to see if she would withdraw from proximity to their sore faces and filthy clothes. She did nothing but turn one face around with an insistent finger so that she could look at it closely.

"They must be terribly painful," she said as she inspected the infectious mess of sores on the child's face. "What causes them?"

"Just their general exposure to every disease in existence."

"It wouldn't be syphilitic would it?"

"There's not much syphilis among the Kurds," MacGregor said. "It's nothing but filth and bad conditions. They live miserably and poorly. They are all infested with lice. Anything can get hold of them: typhoid, typhus, smallpox, even the black plague. They have no doctors and no hospitals, their food is inadequate and their tents and houses are unhealthy. There's nothing to prevent them getting sores like that, and nothing to cure them. Don't touch their faces," he told her.

Katherine ignored him and looked at the other child. This second baby was a small girl who clung to Da-ud's long neck as Katherine took the turban off her head. There were small pustulous sores around her ears and her hair-line. Her whole head was encrusted with scars and sores. The child had not stopped whimpering. It was clearly the whimper of a child who suffered continuous dismay and pain.

"Why don't they wash this dirt away?" Katherine said impatiently. "No wonder she's moaning like that."

"Let her be," MacGregor said, "and keep your hands away."

Katherine had put back the turban. The child struggled to be put down and Father Da-ud let both the children go. They ran away and stood watching again, still crying with the slow deadliness of their unhappy and painful existence.

"Is the *Khanum* upset?" Father Da-ud asked MacGregor.

"Only by the terrible sickness and sores," MacGregor replied.

Da-ud looked unhappy. "We have beautiful children," he said, "but we are ignorant and wretched people, despite our nobility and our heritage. Only a great upheaval can change us. Perhaps you could explain this to the *Khanum* so that she will understand us better."

"She understands it," MacGregor said.

"If thee and thy people understand this, then we have some hope for

458

the political decisions of our future." Da-ud gripped them both again and they passed a group of silent and curious women. Tall and independent figures, they bore the same mixture of vigour and sickness as their children. The women returned Da-ud's greeting in a chorus which tended to announce their lack of subservience to any man.

Da-ud left them and they returned to the hut to organize their bathing requirements. Here a complication awaited MacGregor, something which was to have a far-reaching effect on their situation with the Mukri. In the hut, talking with Essex, was Zada. He was standing near the door speaking in his bold English to an attentive Essex. As MacGregor came in Zada looked hard at him with his still blue eyes, and then strode out abruptly.

"What was he doing here?" MacGregor asked.

"We were just having a bit of a chat," Essex said. "Speaks peculiar English, but it's understandable."

MacGregor had almost forgotten the threat of Zada but it came back sharply now. To see this show of friendliness with Essex was a warning that Zada was danger, and also a reminder of Essex's weakness for scheming. The combination disturbed MacGregor, but he made a quick decision to wait before saying anything to Essex about Zada.

"How are you feeling, Harold?" Katherine sat on the cot near Essex.

Essex put his arm through hers and sighed. "I'm one of God's patient people," he said. "I'm filthy and I'm hungry but my temper is perfect."

She got up. "Aren't you stiff?"

Essex was unshaven and untidy but he still looked comparatively clean and comfortable. "Of course I'm stiff, but I could get on a horse and do it again." Essex watched Katherine and MacGregor as they unrolled the kit on the floor to get towels. "Why didn't you wake me this morning?" he said to her.

"We thought you needed the sleep."

Essex did not like such consideration from Katherine. Since leaving Teheran she had been treating him more and more like a generous uncle, at the same time giving increasing attention to a pig-headed MacGregor. She sympathized too easily with MacGregor, and she had been too easily impressed with his unfortunate activity at the Governor's estate. Essex found consolation in the belief that it was a temporary attitude with her. Once out of these mountains Katherine would cease to be so impressed with the expanding MacGregor. Once in London, Katherine would be Katherine again. Essex looked at MacGregor and admitted the Scot's change for the better. Up here MacGregor had acquired an easy movement which Essex liked, despite himself.

When Katherine had told him about the springs Essex joined in their search for clean towels and sufficient clean clothing.

459

"I suppose you would both like some clothes washed," Katherine said.

"Are you offering to do it?" MacGregor asked.

"I'm making the gesture."

MacGregor shook his head. "You would make a poor job of it," he said and wrapped his dirty clothes in a shirt.

Father Da-ud came back, and with him was Pirusa. It was she who danced them across the plateau to the rock. She led them up a steep rock staircase to the lip of a crater. Over it they descended a twisting path to a small blue lake which they stopped to admire. The impatient Pirusa took them on to a cavern and directed MacGregor and Essex into it, while she took Katherine further around the lake to another.

In the cavern MacGregor found the expected sulphur springs. They flowed up from an unseen source and formed small lapping pools in the flat rocks, eventually flowing out into the crater. Stalagmites rose from the floor to the walls, which were open above to the sky. There was a natural rock slope into the pools and here MacGregor dropped his bundle of clothes and felt the water with his hand.

"Is it hot enough?" Essex said.

"A little too hot," MacGregor told him.

They did not waste time getting into the water. They stood waist deep and washed their clothes, using the rock ledges as washing boards. Mac-Gregor chose this moment to broach the subject of Zada.

"What was Zada talking to you about?" he began.

"Who?"

"The blond Kurd."

"Ah, The chap that speaks English."

"Yes."

"Oh he was explaining a few things about the Kurds. Fierce sort of fellow, but he seems friendly enough."

"How friendly?" MacGregor said.

"He was telling me about the meeting they had at Sinneh," Essex said. "Apparently all these Kurdish chiefs are trying to establish some kind of independent province and they are looking for co-operation. Quite important, actually." Essex held up a shirt and rubbed soap into the collar.

"What sort of co-operation did Zada want?"

"He didn't exactly get around to that," Essex replied cautiously. "He's fishing for something." Essex rinsed the shirt in the warm water. "But you keep out of this, Mac," he said. "I don't want you moralizing and interfering."

"What is there to interfere in?" MacGregor asked the question with the apprehension of an elder brother.

"Nothing yet. But this Kurd may be just the man we're looking for, and it may turn this silly adventure into a profitable mission, so don't interfere." Essex whistled as he rinsed a pair of socks.

"I can't interfere if I don't know what you're doing."

"Good! Just find out what this Salim wants of us, and how long he plans to detain us in the wilderness."

"You don't seem very worried about it," MacGregor said.

"Neither do you old chap. Neither do you."

MacGregor did not want to make a mistake and drive Essex closer to Zada, but he had to warn Essex. "You may not know it," he said, "but your blond friend was rather keen on getting rid of us yesterday."

"Oh?" Essex was not going to be impressed.

"He believes it a Kurd's duty to rob and kill as he pleases. He wanted to dispatch us there and then."

"He was trying to scare you," Essex said. "He probably wants money."

MacGregor pounded a shirt on the rocks. "He scared me alright. I think you would be safer if you kept away from him. You're dealing with a dangerous and vicious fellow. He would cut your throat for sixpence."

Essex laughed and wiped soap from his blond arms. "No doubt he is a passionate man, but he was educated in an English school at Mosul in Iraq, and I have an idea that he has even been in contact with one of our Intelligence men up here, but I'm not sure yet."

"You shouldn't complain about the Russians," MacGregor commented.

"It's your Russian friends who started all this."

"We haven't seen any sign of a Russian so far."

"No but they're here. They are interfering hand-over-fist. Right in the midst of these Kurds."

"How do you know?"

"Zada has been telling me a thing or two about the Russians."

"Yes?"

"Their agent here is the other cousin, the short ugly fellow, what's his name?"

"Lord Gordyenne the Invincible."

"Ah yes. Lord Gordon. There is your Russian interference."

"It that what Zada told you?"

"More or less."

"If he's a Russian agent then so am I," MacGregor said.

"You might be," Essex replied delightedly.

MacGregor snorted in the water. "If you could understand what these men say to each other," he told Essex, "you wouldn't trust Zada. If you want to make a contact here it would be better to talk with Gordyenne."

"Isn't he just as anxious to get rid of us?" Essex argued.

"Yes, but at least he can see beyond killing. He and Zada are obviously fighting for control of the Mukri. Zada plans to make them a marauding band of thieves and mercenaries, whereas Gordyenne at least wants them to behave with some restraint and co-operation with other Kurds. He is less interested in killing than he is in independence."

"You told me all that before," Essex said and waved a hand in the air. "I am not interested in their rivalry. I only want to do my own job. If I can't get down to Sinneh then I shall do what I can up here. Zada may be just our man."

"Any of them but Zada! If he knows you've got money he will bargain with you for anything you ask; but if he can he will kill you for it. So be careful. It's only Salim who keeps him from butchering us now."

"I've never heard such nonsense," Essex said mildly. "You are becoming too impressionable, my boy. I wish you could remember that you are an Englishman and not a Persian."

MacGregor could not reply to that without being insulting.

"I know you're sincere, MacGregor, but you have lost your perspective."

"I don't need perspective to see that Zada is a thief and a robber." He was out and drying himself and dressing. "You always seem to pick the wrong man. At least Gordyenne is trying to do something for the Kurds, just as Gochali was trying to do something for the Azerbaijanians."

"I think you're becoming too concerned in other people's problems," Essex told him. "You will see it all differently when we get back to England. Believe me. You will see our side of it."

"What exactly is our side of it?"

Essex did not hesitate. "We want a man up here we can deal with. A man who will have a say in Kurdish affairs. Zada seems made to order."

MacGregor was too disgusted to reply. He began to collect rock samples.

"Incidentally," Essex added, "I don't think we need tell Katherine about these two Kurds."

"Why not?"

"We don't want to disturb her."

"She's disturbed already." MacGregor refused to have his ally taken away from him. "She knows what is going on."

"I feel we ought to leave her right out of it."

MacGregor decided to argue no further, either about Katherine or Zada. But he had decided to interfere as much as possible in Essex's scheming with Zada. He would go to Lord Gordyenne or to Salim himself to counteract this dangerous move by Essex. The importance of being a fellow Englishman was again forgotten.

Chapter 36

Their equal English pleasure in cleanliness gave Essex and MacGregor a better understanding of each other. As clean and fresh-faced men they sat pleasantly on the cushions in Salim's tent waiting for Katherine.

Father Da-ud had brought them here and he was sitting on the thick carpet between Lord Gordyenne and Zada, who were smoking through separate tubes from the same water pipe. The Kurds were silent. The two Englishmen exchanged an occasional comment upon the woven rugs, the brass trays, the fine silk hangings of the goatskin tent. There were bowls of figs and prunes on the brass trays, and sweet raisin drinks coloured red and pink; but they were too hungry for these morsels. They could smell the more substantial food being cooked at the back of the tent by two argumentative women. Salim was not in the tent. Without knowing where he was MacGregor guessed that Salim's absence had something to do with his health. MacGregor was deciding to find Salim later, when Katherine made her appearance.

First came Pirusa with a series of hopping steps. Then Katherine entered the tent grinning like a schoolgirl and holding a child in her arms. She looked at MacGregor and Essex with startling desire for interest, and she turned the child so that they could see it. MacGregor recognized it as the little girl with the sores. The child had stopped crying and it was grasping the collar of Katherine's sealskin coat with one hand, and Katherine's soft neck with the other. The child smiled at Father Da-ud, who was as surprised as Essex and MacGregor.

"What's this about?" Essex said.

"Don't you like her?" Katherine smiled at the baby, who turned away.

"What did you do to her?" MacGregor asked.

"See. She doesn't cry any more!"

"That's nice," said Essex without knowing what it was all about.

Katherine had brought the child close to them, but it turned away and clung to Katherine with an iron grip. She seemed to know how to hold the child and she told it in English to take a look at these peculiar Englishmen. In the meantime Pirusa explained to Father Da-ud that the *Khanum* had washed the child in the springs and rubbed its head and face with some kind of sweet oil from a silver bottle. She said it was the first time the child had stopped crying in months.

"What did you rub on its head?" MacGregor asked Katherine.

"Is that what the little witch was talking about?" Katherine looked around at Pirusa who held onto Katherine's coat to be part of her. "It

463

was an olive oil mixture I use for my hands," she said. "It softened the sores and got rid of the scabs. Couldn't you tell them to keep her clean all the time, Ivre?"

"Yes, but they'll think you fixed the child with the oil."

"They can have that," she said. "If they keep her head clean she'll probably be alright, but her whole body is covered with them. Hasn't she got a wonderful face? I've never seen such eyes."

"What are all those blotches?" Essex asked now.

"Just sores," Katherine said.

"Nothing contagious is it?" Essex said.

"I don't think so," Katherine told him.

"Is it a good idea to fool around with things like that Kathy?" Essex said.

"It's alright." Katherine shook the child a little and held it away from her so that the child laughed. They all laughed. Salim came in at that moment, and Pirusa left Katherine to hold her father's silk cloak and chatter an explanation of Katherine. Salim said nothing but he looked closely at Katherine, who seemed to be embarrassed by his sudden arrival. She bent down and gave the child to Pirusa who went out with it.

Essex and MacGregor had half-bowed to Salim, and now they sat down again. Katherine sat on a large cushion which Salim had moved in her direction. His long face was drawn and hard, and his black eyes showed even more untouchability than usual. He wore a coarse white silk scarf loosely around his throat. His turban was white and banded with gold, and his red boots were studded with small brass beads. In the large green band around his waist Salim wore two modern steel daggers.

His arrival began the serving of food. The women brought bowls of *pilau* and meats and cheeses and *kababs* and stew, better fare than they had enjoyed in the cavern. While they helped themselves Da-ud addressed a word or two at Salim. He received no reply, but Da-ud seemed to take it as natural. For the rest, they ate in silence until Pirusa returned. She was now wearing a bright scarf which MacGregor knew to be Katherine's. These two had developed a method of talking to each other in their own language without bothering about the meaning. It worked as a form of contact, but even Pirusa became quiet in this solemn gathering.

The real responsibility for this grim silence rested with Zada and Gordyenne, whose enmity seemed to be increasing with every moment, as if it were coming to a head. No doubt the presence of the foreigners added fuel to the flames, and MacGregor decided to get out of Takht-i-Suliman as soon as he could. In the meantime he didn't like this sudden

464

quiet; it was unusual for any Kurd to eat without the vigour of laughter and conversation. Something had to end it.

He began the conversation without preliminaries by quoting the Mullah Do-Piazah's Definition of a silent meal being the meal of thoughtful men who could not stomach their own thoughts. It was half rebuke and half provocation, and it served its purpose by provoking a general exchange of the Mullah's Definitions. Actually they were not the Mullah Do-Piazeh's Definitions at all but each man's own, since each sought to present a Definition that had never been heard before.

Father Da-ud made the first reply to MacGregor by creating a joke upon himself. He defined an Angel as a tattletale in heaven. Lord Gordyenne (to compliment Da-ud) said that an Angel in heaven simply meant that there was a better man in hell. Da-ud laughed and countered that the flatterer was one who prospered at a thriving trade. In genuine paraphrase of the Mullah, MacGregor said that anyone who was not a flatterer was likely to be a truthful man and therefore one who was regarded as an enemy by all. Zada could not remain outside this small competition and he added that in speaking of enemies — the only friend accepted by all was the Pot of Gold. Gordyenne naturally took the opposite view: Gold, he said, was the sweat of the earth. The earth, he said, was the blood of the sun. The sun, he said, was the smallest tear-drop shed by the heavens. This did not impress Zada. The tongue of the poet, Zada replied, was the beggar of words. Hoping to separate these two, the gentle Da-ud said that argument was the unfortunate consequence of Creation. But Salim intervened, a ghost of a smile upon his thin lips. Creation, he said, was the fault of the Kurds: there had to be Kurds so there had to be Creation.

They all complimented Salim for this, but Zada broke the sequence by complaining bitterly and without Definition that the world existed for the sake of the Kurd, but what of the earth did the Kurd possess? He addressed Salim by appeal and asked if the destiny of the Kurd was to be that of the frightened shepherd, the timid peasant, the puny mechanic — all of whom were slaves to politics.

"Is that the only faith you have in the Kurd?" Lord Gordyenne demanded.

"That is your faith, Cousin," Zada replied bitterly. "You want to make our destiny that of conference and talk and political decision. What sort of heritage is that for a Kurd? We come from one conference at Sinneh and now we prepare for another at Saujbulaq. Is this the way for Mukri to behave?"

Gordyenne's ugly face twisted into a mask of derision. "Are we to be a band of thieves?" he said to Salim, "or shall we act as men?"

465

In arguing, both these men addressed Salim. MacGregor could see that Salim was willing to listen to both, and it was obviously the continuation of a long argument between them to influence Salim. Now it was bitter and critical.

"Robbers we are and robbers we have always been," said Zada passionately. "We should boast that we are shedders of blood, raisers of strife, seekers after turmoil and uproar, terrorists, brigands, evildoers of depraved habits, a people all malignant, devoid of all humanity, and scorning the garment of wisdom and peace. That is the Kurd and that is Mukri. God created us ravagers, and by God's will must we remain so."

"Our Cousin loves the foolish words of the *Bustan us Siaha*," Gordyenne said. "It also says that we are a brave race, fearless, and of hospitality grateful to the soul, in truth and in honour unequalled, of pleasing countenance and fair cheek, boasting all the goods of beauty and grace. I say, Brother, that our ravaging is a mistake and our brutality an error. We would do better to be proud of our heritage of independence, the heritage of all Kurds. No one has conquered the Kurd: neither Persian, Assyrian, Parthian, Greek, Roman, Arab, Mongol, or Turk. We have preserved our language and our brief cultures against all history, and we should seek now to preserve it further by uniting all Kurds . . ."

Gordyenne's Kurdish was so much more effective in argument than Zada's that MacGregor felt a moment of pity for Zada. He was like a big, handsome, blond child, trying to cope with something which was beyond him. He had to adjust his arguments more closely to Gordyenne's.

"If we must persuade the Kurds to unite for any purpose," Zada said to Salim, "let us persuade them to unite in sweeping down upon the Luris to the south and the Azerbaijani to the east."

Gordyenne was as angry as his cousin. "I beg you, Salim, never to consider an attack upon the new forces in Azerbaijan," he said. "Their revolt is the beginning of our own revolt, and we must assist their new autonomy."

"If we co-operate with the Azerbaijani then we might as well co-operate with the Persians, and the English," Zada argued.

"The Azerbaijani are now our brothers," Gordyenne said. "The Persians and the English are still our enemies. Half the Kurds are in subjection to Persia and the other half are in subjection to the English in Iraq. We must decide at Saujbulaq that an independent Kurdistan must include our brothers in Iraq. The English and the Persians are our equal enemies."

By now Zada was feeling the frustration of his own arguments to Gordyenne's cunning phrases. "I despise the English and I despise the Persian, the Moscov, and the Turk," he said, "but the English are looking for one strong tribe among the Kurds who will co-operate with them and

466

keep discipline among the others. They are wealthy and they will give this tribe gold and arms. Let the Mukri take advantage of this to make themselves the strongest and most powerful tribe in Kurdistan. What does it matter if the English are foolish enough to pay us for it? We will serve them only as we see fit. What better opportunity could there be for the rise of the Mukri?"

"That is the evil word in your ear by the English among us," Lord Gordyenne cried. "Like their agents at Sinneh, they come among us to look for betrayal."

Zada was triumphant. "Then why do you strive so hard to save their necks, when a dozen times I would have dispatched them with pleasure?"

"I do not want them among us," Gordyenne argued, "but I have no desire to butcher them. Send them away. Let them take their money and their political scheming with them."

"Why send away their gold?" Zada said impatiently. "Let us kill them for it, or reach an agreement for it."

This debate had sharpened the danger so much that MacGregor again looked to Salim for a word of their safety. He knew that it was Salim who kept Zada in check, but as usual the Mukri chief would say nothing. His black eyes looked at the figures before him with the impersonality of a young man who was aware that he was facing extinction and had little care if others were about to share his fate. He had eaten nothing and he sat so still that he was obviously in the grip of insistent pain. MacGregor knew then that the responsibility for getting them out of here depended on the speed of his own initiative. He would have to force Salim to face their situation and let them go. He would also have to prevent the crazy Essex from making any further contact with Zada.

"Why did you stop translating?" Essex was saying to him now.

"Yes. Yes," Katherine said. "What are they saying?"

He had explained Zada's alternatives, sparing Katherine none of the details. He went on to translate Gordyenne's increasingly bitter reply to any suggestion of co-operating with the British, and his demand for Kurdish independence.

"Do all Gordyenne's grandiose schemes for Kurdish independence directly encompass our oil-field areas in Iraq?" Essex whispered, unbelieving it.

"Certainly," MacGregor whispered back.

"This is getting serious." Essex stopped fingering a bowl of sultanas. "Are there going to be Kurds from our Iraq oil areas at this conference they are talking about?"

"There'll be Kurds from everywhere at Saujbulaq," MacGregor told him.

"When does it take place?"

467

"I don't know."

"Well, find out, man."

"I don't think we can be inquisitive at this stage," MacGregor whispered, adding: "Are you thinking of going to Saujbulaq for the conference?" He was surprised at the fierceness of his own whisper.

"We ought to do something about it. This is getting serious."

"Did you think they were playing? I warned you about Zada."

"He's just blustering," Essex said.

"By God he isn't," MacGregor's voice rose.

They were discussing it so intently that they forgot themselves and there was silence among the Kurds for a moment.

"The English are plotting," Gordyenne said with biting discovery.

Da-ud saved the situation by raising his hand and saying a few words.

"What does the old devil say?" Essex asked.

"He says that perhaps the English want to speak."

Before MacGregor could stop him Essex addressed the Kurds as he would address a hostile conference. He stood up. "Yes," he said. "I would like to speak."

Salim kept the others quiet by a wave of his hand.

"I am the English you talk about," Essex said. "Perhaps I should warn you that any attempt to upset the peace of Iraq will be dealt with strongly by His Majesty's Government, whether the disruption is by raid or by politics." Before MacGregor could pick this up Zada was translating it to Salim. "It is very noble of the Kurds to seek independence, culture, and sovereignty," Essex went on, "and the British Government will do all that it can to assist their advancement. But to talk of interfering in the affairs of Iraq is another thing. The Kurds of Iraq are part of Iraq, and they have a greater measure of independence than the Kurds of Persia or Turkey. No one has the right to interfere in their affairs, and the British Government will see to it that no one does interfere. We guard their interests with all the strength we possess. Not only that, the British Government considers any Kurdish conference that discusses the affairs of Iraq as a hostile conference. The Kurds of Iraq will have nothing to do with your schemes for independence and autonomy. We have no objection to a powerful Mukri in Iran, but we reserve the right to take drastic measures if we feel that this conference you talk about threatens British interests in Iraq. Is that understood?"

Gordyenne turned to Salim and cried, "You see!"

The resulting turmoil between Zada and Gordyenne became so fierce that Salim had to shout at both of them, and Da-ud had to prevent them striking each other. No more coherency could be expected and the gathering broke up when Lord Gordyenne stood up and cursed Zada to begin with, and then turned on Essex and MacGregor and called them curs and mongrels and vile purveyors of betrayal and treachery. With this he left, and it was Zada's turn to follow him and laugh.

"Come on," MacGregor said to them quickly. "Let's get out of here."

"By God Harold," Katherine said to Essex. "You're out of your century."

MacGregor did not understand the inference, but he did understand his passing moment of admiration for Essex. Personal odds meant nothing to a man who could deliver such an ultimatum to these men. It was either enormous courage or even greater ignorance of the danger than Mac-Gregor thought possible. MacGregor hesitated, then decided that Salim must be tackled now.

"You go on out," he said to Katherine as Essex led them out, "and don't leave Essex. Don't let him wander around, and keep Zada away."

Katherine had taken Pirusa by the hand. "What are you doing?"

"I'll talk to Salim." Salim had already gone, but MacGregor took Pirusa. "Golden Ears," he said to her. "Can you take me to your father?"

"Does the *Khanum* come?"

"No, but she will be waiting for you where we sleep."

"Are you going to leave Takht-i-Suliman to-day?" Pirusa said.

"I don't know," MacGregor said in English.

He left Father Da-ud to look after Katherine, and he followed Pirusa out among the tents and through the muddy snow paths to a long low shelter.

Chapter 37

MACGREGOR expected to find Salim lying down and behaving as his sickness demanded, but he was not in the compartments of the low tent. Pirusa took MacGregor outside among the other wide tents until they found Salim in a mud stable among his shouting, arguing men who were saddling horses and assembling rifles and blankets at the entrance. Pirusa pulled her hand away and ran off to find Katherine. MacGregor stepped over the equipage and stood behind Salim, who was giving peremptory orders, arguing with his men about number and direction and arrival and return. The argument was equal-sided, and MacGregor could not discover where these half-dozen men were going in such a hurry, but it was his first question of Salim when the Mukri chief saw him and led him away from the stable.

They walked towards the gate of Takht-i-Suliman, and Salim preceded MacGregor up a path of steps which were cut into the hill of rock.

"They are my fastest riders," Salim explained. "They ride to Tabriz."

"Why the great hurry?" MacGregor said.

"Our political affairs require haste." Salim turned his head. It seemed as if the movement had given him physical relief, and he looked at MacGregor with less deathliness, even friendliness.

"Is the Ambassador's attitude the cause of this haste?" MacGregor asked.

The steps finished and a bare rock slope made it possible for them to mount a short rise together. "The Ambassador is not important to us," Salim told him.

"Oh?"

"You," said Salim, "are the important one."

MacGregor climbed the last few yards of the rise without replying. The elevation had taken them onto a cantilever rock which hung out over Takht-i-Suliman. They looked down on the snow-patched goatskin tents. They were just in time to see the six riders amble their horses out the gateway and plunge down a slope of soft snow so that a cloud of white mist was flung high from their rising legs.

MacGregor felt disappointed with Salim for not explaining why the men were going to Tabriz. He said nothing about it but asked Salim another question.

"Ra-is," MacGregor said as they looked at the white peak opposite, "how do your men get English military rifles?"

"By raid," Salim said calmly. "The English illegally arm the southern tribes to protect their oil-fields against a revolt of the Persian mechanics and *farashes*. We raid the southern tribes and take the rifles for our own use. It is equitable. I think you will understand it, even though you are an *Englis*."

"Yes. I understand it," MacGregor said briefly.

"We need your understanding." Salim looked at the mountain. "In all our affairs," he added.

MacGregor knew then that Salim wanted to talk with him as much as he wanted to talk to Salim. "I would like to know why you brought us here?" MacGregor asked.

"Is it important?"

"Yes," said MacGregor. "Did you know who we were when you found us?"

"I knew nothing, except that you were neither Kurd nor Persian."

"Is that why you swept down on us like demons?"

Salim shrugged. "That is the way of the Kurd in his own mountains. You were unharmed."

"Why did you detain us and bring us here?"

470

"You were important *Englis*, Da-ud told me, bound for Sinneh. All *Englis* in the Kurdish mountains are agents. I kept you to see what value you would be."

"Value for what?"

"There are times when every man has some value," Salim said unimportantly.

MacGregor persisted: "As hostages?"

Salim closed his serious eyes. "No," he said. "I wanted to know what important *Englis* were doing in Kurdistan. It is always essential to know what the *Englis* are doing."

"You think we would tell you what we were doing here?"

"Any man would eventually tell me enough," Salim said with terrible certainty.

"You should realize how dangerous it is to capture an important *Englis* and divert him and detain him."

"I know there is always danger in dealing with an *Englis*. It is therefore best to grip him by the throat and deal with him that way."

"The Ambassador is an important man: a Lord and a Minister," MacGregor said. "Any harm done to him would bring quick retaliation from our *Englis bombandaz*."

"Nothing will happen to your Ambassador," Salim said, "unless Zada thinks better of murdering and robbing him than of accepting his political bribes."

"You must prevent it."

Salim looked quietly at MacGregor. "It is simpler for you to prevent your Ambassador dealing so stupidly with my cousin."

"That would not stop your cousin from being so dangerous."

"True." Salim waved his arm impatiently. "But this Ambassador is not something for serious discussion. You are more important to the Mukri, my Brother, and I must talk with you."

"I am of no importance unless the *Khanum* and the Ambassador are secure."

Salim frowned impatiently. "Yes. Yes. The *Khanum* is a magnificent woman and she is secure. The Ambassador is safe enough unless he gets himself into difficulty with Zada. Let us forget him and I will talk to you of great decisions. I know that you are not a crude *Englis* who comes here to ask each Kurd to betray his birthright. Are you really an *Englis*? What must I call thee?"

MacGregor and Salim were walking up and down on the small ledge. "Yes. I am an *Englis*," MacGregor said. "But I come from the north where the people are like the Kurd. We are called Scot and Highlander but we have become part of the *Englis* by understanding."

"You were conquered by the *Englis*?"

"Never," said MacGregor. "Like the Kurd — we have been defeated but never conquered."

"You have achieved autonomy?"

"We have achieved equality," MacGregor said.

"You are therefore not *Englis.*"

"I am *Englis* by responsibility."

"And the other?"

"Scot."

"And more?"

"Highlander."

"Noble enough," Salim said graciously. "I do not hesitate to call you Brother and to offer you the friendship of the Mukri." It was a formal statement of their equal position. It became a basis for free expression which MacGregor accepted immediately.

"I have wanted to ask you," MacGregor said: "When may we leave Takht-i-Suliman?"

Salim hesitated a moment. "You may leave when you wish, and you may have my best horses and an escort." He shook his long head. "Must you leave?"

"I believe so. It is bad to have the Ambassador and Zada scheming for each other's political interests."

Salim stopped walking and they looked around them at the Kurdish mountains. "Could I know what your Ambassador is plotting about?" Salim said. "I do not ask you to betray him but the *Englis* schemes will affect all our decisions at Saujbulaq."

"We did not really come here to scheme," MacGregor said. "We came here to look for Russian interference."

"Among the Kurds?"

"Among the Persians, the Azerbaijani, and the Kurds."

"There are no Russians among the Mukri!" Salim declared.

"No agents?"

"None. There have been mine and oil hunters, but none that spoke politically and none that offered bribes." Salim had finished with that issue. "What is your *Wazir* really seeking?" Essex was now *Wazir*: Minister.

MacGregor terraced the snow with his heel. "He is looking for support against the Azerbaijani and the Russians."

"Has he spoken with other Kurds?"

"No," MacGregor said. "There are Kurdish chiefs in Sinneh who are waiting for him; but that is your problem."

"Yes," Salim said. "I know them. Why does such an important man bother with them? Your petty agents have done well enough with bribes and promises."

472

"He didn't come to bribe," MacGregor said. "He came as an important *Englis* to flatter them and to influence them directly against the Azerbaijani and the Russians."

"Now he hopes to achieve this with the Mukri?"

"With anyone," MacGregor said.

"But what is the real purpose? Is it directed simply against the new Azerbaijani, or is it concerned with the Russians?"

"Both," MacGregor said. "If the revolt in Azerbaijan succeeds, it will eventually extend over all Iran. That would mean the end of English influence and English possessions. We are anxious to prevent the Azerbaijani from succeeding."

"And the Russians?"

"Perhaps it is the Russians we fear the most," MacGregor told him.

"But do your Ministers plan war with the Russians?"

"I don't think so," MacGregor replied. "No. I don't think so. But a lot of our political activity in Iran is to defeat the influence of the Russians, not only here but in all countries of the East, and in Europe."

"And what of the Kurd in this?"

MacGregor closed his eyes against the climbing sun and looked far enough into the sky to see the beginning of tessellated clouds behind the mountains. "We are opposed to Kurdish independence because we fear for our oil possessions in the Kurdish areas of Iraq, and because it would upset all our influence in the Orient. It's just as Lord Gordyenne says."

"We have always known that," Salim said and nodded slowly. "But it is never clear just what the official *Englis* are actually scheming about."

"I suppose we will scheme for anything that will divide the Kurds among themselves," MacGregor said flatly. "We might support one tribe in opposition to another, or we might antagonize the Kurds against their neighbours. We could encourage the Kurd to attack Azerbaijan now, so that both will be weakened and perhaps destroyed."

"If the cold words torture you," Salim said sympathetically of this statement — "then say no more."

"The truth itself is the torturous thing," MacGregor replied testily. "I shed no blood for what I say."

"Then I will bleed for thee," Salim said softly, and they walked again on the snow ledge to salvage MacGregor's temper. "It is very important to hear these things from an *Englis* himself," Salim went on. "I guessed some of it, but I have never been quite clear about the *Englis* purpose and ambition. I have never quite believed in their complex and subtle scheming. To understand it now is to know clearly what must be decided at Saujbulaq because it explains much of our hidden opposition. It is very clear that the Kurd must avoid all these subtle directions. They would lead Kurdish autonomy into quick destruction."

"One thing, *Ra-is*," MacGregor said quickly. "Do not despise the *Englis* for the political plotting of their Ministers."

"I have never thought of the *Englis* with such warmth and understanding as I do now," Salim said as a direct compliment to MacGregor. "If we must plot against them, it is only because they plot against us. If they choose our friendship then never will they know a nobler ally and a truer brother. Knowing this, and knowing of your understanding, I have waited to ask a great service of you."

MacGregor waited, diverted for a moment by seeing Katherine way below them. She was walking with Pirusa towards Salim's tent, and Essex was not with her.

"Yes?" he said as he watched her disappear into the tent.

"It is not a small thing I want," Salim said, "but it is very important to the Kurds, to all Kurds. Perhaps it would be too easy to ask you to simply be a partisan of the Kurds in the counsels of your country, but it is more than that. We ask you to explain our situation so that all people in your country may understand and appreciate our struggle. It is the Kurd who will decide the direction and activity of his own political future, but a great deal of our hope will depend upon the final attitude of friendship or enmity from the powerful *Englis*. Perhaps all over the world there are primitive peoples like the Kurd, seeking independence, political expression, and material progress. There are certain things that we can do for ourselves, but so much depends upon the large countries. Their governments shape the primitive states by rich and powerful influence. Much of the responsibility for our situation therefore depends upon the people of your own country. If they are apathetic and ignorant of our Kurdish aspirations; if they make no attempt to influence the direction of their own government in dealing with our affairs; then all will depend on ourselves alone. That would mean reluctant but necessary and bloody and terrible struggle because I would warn your Ministers that we cannot give up until we have achieved national sovereignty and our equal right among all people. It is therefore a vital and great service that I ask you, dear Brother, because our immediate hope of urgent success will depend on the strength and deliberation of those who oppose our aims. If the *Englis* continue to turn all their influences and strength against us, and against the Azerbaijani, they will choke the first great breath of our free choice as men. It will never destroy us, but it will be a bitter, hateful, shameful thing, and the *Englis* will live forever in our history as despicable wretches who break the spirit of all advancement. That is why we desperately need support among the people and the counsels of your country. So much may depend on it, and so many decisions at Saujbulaq will be clearer and simpler if we know that in your country there is an active partisan of the Kurd; a partisan who understands and appreciates the Kurdish struggle for political autonomy and material advancement: a friend and a true brother. Dare I ask more of thee, *Englis?*"

"It is nothing to ask at all," MacGregor said morosely, as he waited for Katherine to appear again. "We are wrong, you are right. Is a man's choice of these a service to anyone but himself?"

"Forgive me!" Salim was surprised with MacGregor's unhappy justification of himself. "I had ignored the problem as being part of the *Englis* themselves. Nevertheless, it is your specific assistance that we need because you might be the one *Englis* who understands our situation so intimately."

"I am committed to the Azerbaijani, the Kurd, and the Persian," MacGregor said seriously and a little sadly. "I am already opposing my own Minister by talking with you."

"He is an old man," Salim murmured.

"He is a healthy man," MacGregor said, realizing Salim's meaning.

"The Kurdish mountains are full of accidents."

"No. No. That would settle nothing."

Salim blinked. "As you wish," he said. "No doubt he is scheming with Zada at this very moment against our mutual political interests."

"He could be," MacGregor admitted, wondering if Katherine had found Essex.

"In Zada there is always a race between his regard for killing and his crude political ambitions for the Mukri. One never knows which he will choose."

"Then we should go back right now," MacGregor said. He realized that he was cold as he plunged his hands into his pockets and surprisingly felt the warm barrel of the gun in his pocket.

Salim was cheerful as he held MacGregor's arm. "The *Wazir* is a cunning man," he said. "He can look after himself with Zada."

"He's a foolish man," MacGregor said.

"The words of a nervous father," Salim decided.

As they walked carefully down the slope, MacGregor told Salim that they would like to leave when there was some word of Aladin's whereabouts with the station-wagon.

"I will send a rider to the road at Tabin-Tepe to await him," Salim said.

"When should he be there?"

Salim preceded MacGregor down the cut steps. "If your message reached him at Sinneh he should be at Tabin-Tepe to-morrow. It is not an easy route from here to Tabin-Tepe, but it should not take you more than half a day, and you may use my horses."

"Can you restrain Zada until we leave?"

"To-day I will talk with all the Mukri here to make it clear what we must do at Saujbulaq. Perhaps this will calm Zada with a little caution, but I could not guarantee it."

"Why do you tolerate him at all?" MacGregor said with some impatience.

"He is like your *Wazir*, a foolish man, but he is my blood relative and a Mukri. I do not wish to create any more antagonisms and feuds among us. As it is Gordyenne has aggravated his simple mind into brutal desperation." Salim waited for MacGregor at the end of the steps. "Zada is a wild man but I will talk to him, and if he can understand he will obey."

"He can't understand anything."

"We shall see," Salim said.

They had passed under the gate, and Salim had visibly dropped all of the easy flow of personal expression. He was again a still-faced and reserved man of hard features and dangerous impersonality. Even as they walked, he simply left MacGregor without saying anything. It sped Mac-Gregor in search of Katherine and Essex.

Chapter 38

He found Katherine in the house where they had spent the night. She was lying on her cot with her ski-boots off and her sealskin coat thrown across her legs. Her hair was very loose, and MacGregor could see that she had washed it. He hadn't noticed it earlier because she had tied it behind her ears. Now it was spread softly around her face on the patched and coloured pillow, over her wide forehead and her hard cheeks.

"Where is Essex?" MacGregor asked her.

"Damn Essex!" she said.

He had not expected any temperament.

"Sorry," Katherine added briefly.

"What's the matter with you?"

"Nothing." She was a straight-lipped Katherine. "Please don't talk behind me. Come in front of me so that I can speak without breaking my neck."

He walked around and sat on the cot. "You look yellow."

"I should be out of this damn place." She looked at him without considering him at all. "Women are foolish to go wandering around primitive mountains on stupid horses with stupid men. This is what happens

476

to me. It serves me right for being such a damnable fool. Go and find Harold and tell him it's time we got out of here. I've had enough of his lovely adventures."

"Why didn't you keep your eye on him?" MacGregor said unsympathethically, not quite understanding this.

"I never found him, but what difference does it make anyway. You're too stupid to understand what he is doing. You're all argument, but you're so small-minded that you'll never make any serious attempt to interfere with him. I suppose when we get out of here you'll still be lost in that complicated mind of yours, running around wondering what to do while Harold goes right ahead and takes your stupid Iran away from you — Kurds and all. What will you do about it? Nothing. Essex has left you standing there. Good for him!"

"Where is he?" MacGregor said, unaffected.

"He went off to play with that blond Circassian beast. When you find him tell him it's time we left here."

"We're leaving to-morrow," MacGregor told her.

"Have you decided?" she said sarcastically.

"Yes." He halted the acrimonious discussion by leaving her.

He did not try to form any drastic decisions about Katherine: he was too concerned and angry about Essex. Where was he? MacGregor stepped from the door with his head down and he practically knocked Essex over. They gripped each other to prevent their fall, and in the moment of recognition and realization MacGregor said "Where have you been?" It came right off the top of his mind.

The moment was rich for anything, but Essex paused a moment and said, "You're a heavier man than I thought, and what the dickens have you got in that pocket?"

"Nothing," MacGregor said and followed Essex into the house.

By the time they reached Katherine she was sitting up and around and bending down to put on her ski-boots. She looked straight up at Essex and smiled.

"Were you sleeping?" Essex said to her.

"Dozing!" she said without taking her eyes off Essex.

"I feel like a little more sleep myself." Essex leaned back. "MacGregor just made a desperate attempt to knock me over. Did you send him out of here like that?"

"He was in a hurry to find you." She was sweetness and light, and as MacGregor stood there, he could see that she had a tight grip on herself and that, whatever was the matter with her, she would not exhibit it to Essex.

"Were you with Zada?" he asked Essex briefly.

"Are you trying to be angry with me, MacGregor?" Essex murmured.

"You ought to know better than to fool with Zada," MacGregor said. "It's wrong and it's dangerous."

Essex was silent for a moment. "Aren't you going a little too far, Mac-Gregor?" he said.

"No," MacGregor said and went further. "You're not dealing with tribal chiefs in the backwoods of Africa. These Kurds know exactly what you're doing, and you are making a mistake to think that you can juggle their affairs with Zada."

"Are you serious, MacGregor?" Essex was still trying to avoid this.

"Yessir."

"Then I suppose I must be serious." Essex looked from Katherine back to MacGregor. "Your function here is to assist me. I shouldn't have to remind you that I'm not up here for my health. I still represent the British Government, you know, and I still have a job to do. So have you."

"I have just been warning Salim of our dangerous attitude."

"That is too serious to ignore . . ."

"It's all too serious to ignore, and it's a serious thing when you deal with a man like Zada. He isn't even trustworthy for what you want of him, and he's likely to do away with you at his own convenience."

"That's my worry . . ."

"No," MacGregor said slowly, almost regretfully. "It's mine, and it involves us all. You don't know anything about these people and you haven't the slightest idea of what you're doing."

"You don't know what I've been doing and you certainly don't know what you're saying."

MacGregor interrupted again. "I know that you are playing with Zada. Actually you won't get much out of him, because he will not decide the affairs of the Mukri. Their decisions have already been made."

"I don't know what you've been up to, MacGregor." Essex stood up. "But I'll make a final attempt to warn you of the damage of your self-righteous meddling. Will you listen to me?"

"Go ahead," MacGregor said in resignation.

"You ought to know that there are two areas in the Middle East which we consider absolutely vital to our security and perhaps to our whole existence: the oil-fields of Iran and the oil-fields of Iraq. Surely you understand their strategic importance."

MacGregor said nothing.

"You're not a fool, MacGregor." Essex was approaching exasperation. "You know that our fields in next-door Iraq are entirely in Kurdish areas, so whatever else we lose we cannot lose our influence in Kurdistan. We are having a hard enough time in southern Iran as it is, trying to hang onto our fields. Now these Kurds are starting to talk about a

478

sovereignty which includes our Iraqi oil-fields. Kurdish independence indeed! You might as well talk about pigmy independence in Central Africa. It's a false notion and a dangerous notion, just as this plot for Azerbaijanian independence is false and dangerous; in fact it's the same problem. Kurdish and Azerbaijanian independence are mere political tricks against us, and we will resist them wholeheartedly. On the other hand, if this particular tribe wants to be strong, then that is perfectly alright with us. It's always a good thing to encourage one tribe to be powerful as an example in sensible behaviour for the others. Therefore, if I can find one man here who is willing to co-operate with us, why should you resist the idea? You're not a Kurd. You're an Englishman. Enough of this stupidity. What would the India Office say if they heard you were being so obstructive? I don't think they would like it."

To this threat MacGregor replied, unthinking, with one of his own. "What would happen in the diplomatic world if it was known that you were scheming here with a man like Zada?"

"That is not the business of the diplomatic world!"

"It might be," MacGregor announced.

Essex looked at MacGregor as if he were looking upon the face of a friend for the last time. He turned to Katherine and said: "How am I supposed to take this?"

"Any way you like," she told him. "It's time you two put your two little worlds to test. Go ahead: both of you. You might as well settle it now."

They did not settle it. The threat between them had such import that both men recoiled from its ultimate implication. Yet Essex had to warn MacGregor once more.

"Just don't interfere," he said to MacGregor.

"No more of my interference will be needed," MacGregor said unhappily to dismiss it. "We will be leaving to-morrow morning."

Essex did not know what to say. He always felt it an unforgivable weakness to allow a man like MacGregor to upset him. He would not lose control of himself; but he did lose his mental patience, tolerance, friendship, and fatherliness for MacGregor. Without the support of such good-nature, Essex found MacGregor stubborn and interfering, a man he would get rid of as soon as possible.

"We will not be leaving to-morrow," Essex said with sufficient control.

MacGregor knew otherwise.

Essex ignored him and produced a pack of cards and began to play with Katherine. MacGregor lay down on his cot, and though he was stiffer now than he had been in the morning, he went to sleep without any difficulty. He was awakened by the women bringing in their evening meal. Katherine and Essex were still playing cards, but the lamp was lit. It was now evening.

"He's awake," Katherine said, and MacGregor decided that these two had been joining forces again.

"For a man so sensitive to danger, MacGregor, you were sleeping too soundly. You were making quite a racket." Essex was cheerful.

MacGregor gave the comment more importance than it deserved. He thought Essex might be trying to embarrass him, but he was determined to be equal to Essex's smooth forgetfulness of all awkward incidents, so he took no notice of the remark. He replied instead to the greeting of the women who brought the food. One of them said that Katherine was noble enough to be a Kurd. Was she MacGregor's wife?

MacGregor said No, she wasn't.

"Blood relative?" the woman asked.

"No." MacGregor knew what the Kurdish woman wanted to know. "She is nothing to me but a talisman."

"Nothing more?" the woman said.

"No. She is not the woman to share this rude and uncomfortable life."

"Why not?" the woman said. "She is a stern and clever woman."

"Stern and clever," MacGregor agreed. "But a woman of another land."

The tall woman clicked her tongue in disgust with MacGregor, and Katherine asked him what they had been talking about.

"About you," MacGregor told her. He pulled on his boots and asked Katherine the time.

"It's eight o'clock," she said. "You've been sleeping there for about four hours."

"Have you been playing cards all that time?" he asked.

Essex had his pipe loose in his teeth. "I had a little talk with Zada first," he said joyfully, not bothering to look at MacGregor.

MacGregor would not be baited. "I was wondering how you could spend four hours playing card games."

"Don't you play?" Katherine said.

"I can play Snap," he said.

Katherine said "Really?" and placed all her cards in neat order on the bed. "I'm out," she said.

Essex stood up. "Dammit. One more and I would have been out myself."

"You now owe me at least five theatre nights," she told him. "I shall take them all at the Old Vic if you don't mind. Everything else in London is rotten." She stacked the cards. "Incidentally Harold, when do we get back to London?"

"I'm due back before the Security Council meeting at the end of January," Essex said.

"That's about eight days," she said. "We'll never make it."

480

"I have to make it," Essex told her. "The Azerbaijanian dispute is on the Security Council agenda."

"The Security Council?" MacGregor was surprised. In the last few days he had been forgetting about Azerbaijan in the fascination of their entanglement with the Kurds. This was a sharp reminder that Azerbaijan was still the real dispute, even though the Kurds had become part of it. "When did you find out about that?" he asked Essex.

"The day we left Teheran."

"What had the Security Council got to do with Azerbaijan?" Katherine inquired.

"Something about the situation constituting a threat to world peace," Essex told her. "Or that is what John Asquith said."

"And what's John got to do with it?" Now Katherine was surprised.

"Old John has been told to help me finish off this thing." Essex knocked out his pipe. "I just saved him from that Czech job."

"When did you know all this?" Katherine said.

"The day we left," Essex repeated, enjoying the sensation.

"Did you ask for John Asquith?"

Essex nodded modestly.

"But he'll hate it."

"Hate what?"

"This mess," Katherine said. "You've really done an odd thing, Harold."

"What's odd about it?" Essex said. "It's about time he was given something really important to do. It should make him. He is too easy-going and too careless of himself."

"My God!" Katherine said.

The food was forgotten and they were standing around the bench looking at it. MacGregor was now right outside the discussion, even though he felt as Katherine did about Asquith's entanglement. But he couldn't think about Asquith while he was trying to see what Essex's news meant to him. It wasn't surprising, now that he came to think of it, but it brought him face to face with his own decisions on the matter of Azerbaijan. There was no doubt now that he and Essex would disagree on what they had seen in Azerbaijan. If they ever sat down to compare their impressions they would be entirely opposed, but MacGregor knew they would never sit down to make comparisons now. Their differences were too obvious. MacGregor had to admit that he himself still had no clear-cut idea of what he thought of this Azerbaijanian revolt. Perhaps Essex was just as hazy about the total event. Where they disagreed, and disagreed entirely, was on the details. Details like Javat, and the Governor, and justification for revolt, and latterly the same issues among the Kurds. It amounted to complete disagreement on the whole issue, whether they had come to any total picture of the Azerbaijan revolt or not. A disagreement which was final, but not yet settled. Essex was going to settle his side of it in the Security Council. MacGregor knew he would have to do something to dispute Essex, but he had no idea how he would do it.

"Where is John now?" Katherine was saying.

They were dishing out the rice and leaves and dried fish and bread to each other now as if a world of politeness were needed to keep them together.

"John's in London I suppose. He may be in Washington talking to the Americans about it, but I doubt that at the moment." Essex looked at his tin plate of food. "Weird-looking stuff," he said. "What have we got this time, MacGregor?"

MacGregor described the dishes to Essex, thinking that nothing more in British diplomacy would ever surprise him. It was not an unhappy thought, nor was it cynical. The Foreign Office's use of the Security Council was the logical result of Essex's failure in Moscow. He said so to Essex. "It looks," he said, "as though the Foreign Office has finally decided that we failed in Moscow. They must be getting desperate to give it to the Security Council."

"Failed!" Essex said sharply, wondering when this man would learn to drop an argument at the right moment. "That's a stupid remark, MacGregor. Do you think I failed in Moscow?"

"Did we succeed?"

"Certainly," Essex said. "Passing this on to the Security Council is merely the culmination of what I achieved in Moscow. Make no mistake about that."

MacGregor finally decided to stop. Essex's idea of failure and success was beyond him. Essex knew no failure, and perhaps he was right. Mac-Gregor's terms of failure might be Essex's terms of success. Was there nothing left of Essex that MacGregor could understand in his own terms? And was anything of Essex worth understanding? Eating the revolting mess of excellent Kurdish stew, MacGregor had a lonely feeling of being a solitary man against a whole world of Essexes. He was glad Asquith was in this. It took away some of the unreality and a great deal of the bitterness, particularly now that the Foreign Office was resorting to such exaggerated measures.

They said nothing more about it while they finished the meal, huddled round the stove as a mountain wind began to blow fine snow under the door, sending eddies of cold air across the small room. MacGregor was wondering how they would get away to-morrow if the weather was bad, when the decision of their departure was precipitated into a moment of action by the arrival of Lord Gordyenne the Invincible.

482

Chapter 39

FRIEND," Gordyenne said to MacGregor. "Do you understand danger?"

He stood between MacGregor and Essex, flinging the snow off his loose clothes and looking from one to the other. The question did not startle MacGregor as much as Gordyenne's new grotesqueness. Each particle of snow-dust on his dark, hooded face had become an evil jewel.

"Well?" Gordyenne said impatiently.

"What's the matter?" MacGregor demanded.

"My cousin is ill," Gordyenne said, "and Zada is in revolt. Since you are something of the cause of all this I have come to tell you that you will leave here. Your horses will be ready for you and brought here."

"What's the matter with Salim? If he is ill, perhaps we can do something."

"You can't do anything." Gordyenne waved his hand for them to hurry. "Just get away from here. There is a great deal of trouble, and you *Englis* make it worse. We cannot look after you, and Zada will ravage you as soon as he can."

"Where is Zada?" MacGregor was trying not to be rushed into this, but Gordyenne's nervous impatience and harsh announcements were obviously the beginning of a desperate situation.

"He is with his brothers and his friends beyond the gate."

"And Salim?"

"*Ra-is* Salim is well attended." Gordyenne looked about at their belongings. "How long will it take you?"

MacGregor still did not rush into it. He wanted to know more, but his questions made Lord Gordyenne increasingly brief and impatient, and MacGregor had to be defiant to get any picture at all of the situation.

"We can't just go off into the night," he said. "We are ignorant of the mountains and it is dangerous to travel in this storm at night."

"It's more dangerous for you here." Gordyenne expelled a tight breath. "It was only Salim's continuous authority that protected you from Zada, and now Salim is unconscious and Zada is revolting. Zada will kill us all if he can. Though that is our affair we do not want the political responsibility of your murder upon us. Go, Englishman. For God's sake, go. I don't wish to murder you, but you bring the disaster of interference. You create division and conflict wherever you go. Your Ambassador has stirred Zada's ambitions and bribed him with money. Now that he has the money and is in revolt against Salim he will dispatch you without any hesitation at all. Will you go?"

MacGregor knew there was only one answer to it but he hesitated again. "I don't like to run away from a miserable man like Zada."

"Your Christian love for self-sacrifice is wasted here," Gordyenne said. "Go!"

"Can't you control Zada?"

"Eventually; by force and by bloodshed."

Once more MacGregor asked about Salim.

"He was born fatal," Gordyenne said bitterly. "Now his own breath is strangling him. While he was instructing the Mukri about Saujbulaq he was accused by Zada of suffering your bribes and your influence, and it was out of this dispute that he became ill and fell to the floor, blood spilling from his mouth and his nose. With Salim like that, Zada has decided to influence the Mukri at Saujbulaq. Now that he has money, he will force his ideas of raid and robbery upon all the Mukri, unless he is cut down. He has fled to the foot of the mountains, but he will come back here with his supporters prepared for revolt."

"Are you sure he will be back?"

"He is already on his way. If you are not personally afraid then consider your *Khanum,* and consider your foolish Ambassador. He is the first that Zada will destroy so that no man can accuse him of accepting an English bribe."

"What will he gain by that?" MacGregor demanded.

"Are you looking for logic in this situation?" Gordyenne said impatiently, turning to go. "Zada is an anarchist and a fool. He has survived by Salim's authority. This time he will face my authority and he will not be spared at all."

"Can you give me a man to guide us down the mountains?" MacGregor said in inevitable acceptance as he walked to the door with Gordyenne.

"I can give you no one," he said.

"I am sorry about Salim." MacGregor offered his hand to Gordyenne who accepted it without any meaning. "If he gets well then tell him that I will do all that he asked. As for the Ambassador: he is a man who cannot help himself." He was not going to apologize further for Essex, whatever he was thinking.

"It's only the idiot who can't help himself," Gordyenne said about Essex and was gone.

MacGregor expected difficulty with Essex, but he resisted the easy persuasion of exaggeration. He did not damn Essex for being responsible for this great quarrel. He explained the situation very simply. Essex's first attitude was one of nonsense and Essex-disdain. But when Mac-Gregor began to smoulder a little, Essex knew what to do and he turned about and said that he had finished with the place anyway, and

484

that they might as well leave. This was the truth, but MacGregor could see Essex's romantics in operation. The idea of disappearing into the night was all that Essex needed to complete this adventure, and the Ambassador was immediately at work with excellent humour, rolling and packing his kit and advising Katherine what clothes to wear for such a night.

Katherine was displeased by the haste, but her only complaint about it was that some of her laundry was still up in the cave, in fact her best lingerie and most of her woollen stockings.

"I'll get them for you," Essex said. "You can't do without woollen socks."

"You're going up there now?" Katherine said.

"Of course."

"Don't be long," MacGregor told him.

MacGregor had no real intention of taking the glitter from Essex's gesture, yet he had accidentally done so by such easy acquiescence. He gave Essex the electric torch as a final gesture, and though Katherine argued that it didn't matter a damn about her laundry, Essex had to go out into the dark misery and find his way across the plateau to the lake and the cave, and MacGregor did nothing to stop him.

Katherine accused him. "You could have stopped him," she said to MacGregor.

"He's alright," MacGregor insisted. "He likes to do that sort of thing." He was sorry that he had not stopped Essex, but his strict sense of right and wrong had demanded some quick and satisfying retribution for Essex's disruption of the Mukri. "When did Essex give Zada that money?" he asked Katherine.

"How should I know?" Katherine was hostile and was not going to tell tales.

"How much was there?"

"Quite a lot, I should think."

"He's a cunning devil," MacGregor said with nonchalance that impressed himself.

"Peculiar how you now talk of him with exactly the same tolerance that he uses for you. Are you both doing it deliberately?" Katherine was already collecting the remainder of Essex's scattered belongings.

"I'm just cheerful about leaving here," he told her.

"Why?" Katherine disliked his cheerfulness. "You're so definitely at home here."

"That's right," he said, "but it will soon be too active in Takht-i-Suliman. We're better out of the way. What Essex started, our friend Lord Gordyenne is going to finish. I'm sorry that you're going to be put back on a horse again."

"Do we really have to go?"

"Yes," he said.

"Curse the both of you," she said to him. "Everything you do now seems to have such big trouble and small issue about it. Hold this ground-sheet while I stuff these blankets into it, and when you've finished please go out and find Harold."

"He's alright," MacGregor said in exasperation.

"He's an old man," she said. "Go and help him."

MacGregor put his coat on to go out.

"Never mind," she consoled him drily. "If we ever get to London I shall be most polite to you — polite and nice — providing you cease bickering on petty issues and start fighting that large argument that always seems to be going on in your peculiar mind."

As he left she was whistling to herself. In the darkness outside he thought he could hear her laughing, although the wind was blowing hard enough to deaden the sound of everything but the squeal of his feet in the fresh snow. He could not see far. Until his eyes accustomed themselves to the darkness, he was worried about finding Essex at all. Gradually he could see the outline of the tents and the distinguishing features of the rock across the plateau. It was simple to find the rock, but beyond there, he had to grope his way around the large boulders until he found the path that went to the lake. He was watching for Essex's flashlight, and he began to shout "are you there" until he felt foolish and stopped it. He struggled with the sweeping snow and the uneven ground until he saw Essex's light ahead of him. When they met, Essex flashed the torch in his face and asked him what he was doing up here.

"Kathy was worried about you," MacGregor told him.

Essex flashed the torch around. "Why didn't you send her to the devil?" he growled. "It's just a damn good joke for both of us to be stumbling around out here looking for her underwear."

"Didn't you find it?" MacGregor shouted into the wind.

"I can't find the cave," Essex said. "Do you know where it is?"

"Somewhere around here," MacGregor said. "Give me the torch."

Essex would not relinquish the torch. "I'll find the place." Essex knew that MacGregor was here to take him over. Essex was not going to be taken over. He kept a serious grip on himself until they had found the cave and the clothing, and had started on the way back. Then he relaxed and began to plan the advantage of his humour. He was anticipated by MacGregor who walked behind him singing the Highland air of the bloody murder of Ian MacDougall of Loch Buracreagh who tarried too long in his lovely's arms.

"We're fools to be out here, Mac," Essex said over his shoulder.

"Yes sir," MacGregor said, "but she didn't want to lose you."

"Lose me, be damned. She knows that I couldn't get lost. It's just the devil in her. Afraid of nothing. Loves to pull off these daring little schemes."

"Not this time," MacGregor said.

"Don't let her fool you," Essex argued.

"Not for a minute," MacGregor said. "She was worried about you."

Essex shouted a denial, not knowing whether to accept Katherine's concern as compliment or not, and mistrusting MacGregor's interpretation of it. He did not want to go into it further, and he walked on with no more sound out of him than an occasional whistle which was swept out of his mouth by the passing wind. When there were shots from behind them, well beyond the gate, Essex switched off the torch and stood for a moment to see what MacGregor would do.

"Go on," MacGregor told him.

"Is that at us?" Essex did not move.

"No." MacGregor took Essex by the arm.

Essex went on, but he would not be hurried. He told MacGregor about a woman he knew who had Katherine's habit of being too tolerant and too bigoted at the same time: she had wound up marrying a second-rate politician, devoting her life to getting baths for miners. "The sort of woman," Essex said, "who would send you out like this to get her laundry."

"Is that what you predict for Kathy?" MacGregor said.

"Ah no," Essex said. "Kathy may be a woman, but she will not make any mistakes like that. Too realistic, too selfish, too intelligent."

MacGregor did not have time to identify himself with Essex's parable. They had arrived at the hut. Inside, Father Da-ud was helping Katherine put bread and other foods into a bag made of a pillow cover.

Father Da-ud greeted MacGregor as son and brother. "I will go with you through the mountains to Nazli and Sabul," he said. "You can wait there for your machine."

"Where are the horses?" he asked Father Da-ud.

"Zada has driven them all off or stolen them," he said. "We will have to walk."

"We can't walk," MacGregor told Da-ud.

Da-ud sympathized but shook his head. There is no other way. It is dangerous for you here now that Zada has the horses."

"We have too much to carry." MacGregor indicated their gear. He did not intend to leave it. "Aren't there any horses at all?"

"There are asses in the stables," Da-ud said.

MacGregor went out through the back of the house and there were more shots from the top of the rock as he tried to identify the stable tent.

He did not think that he was being shot at, but he ran to a long wall which joined the big rock, and he kept out of sight. He could see the stable as he stood up. The tent had been pulled down at one end and a snow-drift was building up over it. Though Takht-i-Suliman was deserted, he could distinguish figures pulling at the remainder of the tent and he could hear them shouting. He could also see the asses. They were tethered to a single post. Some of them were already loaded with carpeted baggage and boxes.

"They're not going to give up any of these beasts," MacGregor said into his cold teeth. He walked along the back of the wall and avoided the men and the tent until he was level with the tethered asses. He got over the wall and walked carefully among them until he found one of the stolid animals without luggage. He followed the tether of coarse horse-hair rope and began untying it. This was difficult because he could not distinguish the plait of the rope from the twists of the knot, and he had to take off his gloves to pull at the tangle with his nails. He pushed the ass angrily with his knee to get some play on the rope, and with no ado at all the knots came undone and he had the ass free.

To get it back to the hut he had to kick it across the plateau away from the men at the tent. As it complained loudly he knew that someone was shooting in his direction. In a situation like this he knew that the Kurds were not nervous; they simply had no idea of caution because any suspicious figure was fair target regardless of his possible friendliness. MacGregor kicked the ass harder and finally resorted to the Persian habit of pulling the animal's ear. It squealed at such cruelty, but it broke into a trot and MacGregor had difficulty keeping up with it in the snow.

MacGregor's anger with the rope carried him all the way through the experience. In loading the ass he cared nothing for the beast or for the indignant Kathy, who told him to treat it more carefully. Essex commented that the Persian was now in the ascendancy within MacGregor; he had tightened the diamond hitches so much that the suffering ass had kicked up its heels and nearly thrown off all the gear. Even Father Da-ud opposed him, and in holding the tether he urged the beast to see the humour in the situation and be patient towards these desperate people who needed his back. With the ass finally loaded and ready, MacGregor went back into the hut to turn off the oil stove and the lamp. Essex followed him to ask about Salim.

"Don't you think we can do anything?" Essex said. "Get him to a hospital or something. Don't you think we ought to see him at least? Perhaps there is something we can do. Eh?"

"The best thing we can do is to get out and leave these people alone," MacGregor replied. "Salim is unconscious and none of us is a doctor."

488

"Shouldn't we do something about the little girl?" Katherine suggested.

"What?" MacGregor turned down the lamp and blew it out.

"Will she be alright?"

"She's a Kurd," MacGregor said to Katherine. "This is where she belongs. What do you want to do with her? Take her down to Teheran and turn her into a housemaid?" It was unwarranted but he felt relieved to be attacking both of them. "Come on! Come on," he said, "before Zada comes down out of the mountains."

"What are you in a temper about?" Katherine demanded.

"Come on," he said again and slammed the door behind them. "Let's get back to London." He was now enjoying himself, realizing that his free tongue had taken some of his care away. He let them go ahead with Da-ud who held the tether and pulled the ass. MacGregor walked behind, picking up handfuls of snow and throwing them at the beast to keep it moving. He kept this up, adding long Persian insults, until they were well down the mountains and out of hearing of the shots from the rock above Takht-i-Suliman.

Chapter 40

MacGREGOR was never allowed to forget the picture of himself throwing snow at the ass to hurry it down the mountainside. Essex loved to tell it to lend anti-climatic conviction to the whole story of his adventures in Takht-i-Suliman. Essex had recalled and recreated the scene a dozen times on their eventual way to Tabriz, and another dozen times on their eventual return to Teheran. Each time it was slyer in humour and a little less accurate in its detail, but each time it improved as a wonderful story and only MacGregor got tired of hearing it.

MacGregor knew that Essex was leading up to it now, in telling his story to an audience of sceptical newspapermen who looked upon adventure in others as improbable and faked. MacGregor knew Essex so well by now that it was unhappily amusing to see the man unfold his story so cleverly. He was never ahead of his listeners, always planning his pause and sequence so that someone would ask the right question, thus making it appear as if these clever men were squeezing this story out of modest Essex.

From the silence of a deep armchair MacGregor watched Essex perform. They were in Essex's room at the Embassy in Teheran. Katherine sat next to Essex, as attentive as she had ever been. Essex sat peacefully in a rocking chair, his head a little back from his shoulders, his neat flannel suit a good line for his freshly weathered face, and his freckled hands wandering casually over a whisky glass. MacGregor listened to each subtle word as Essex took his time over Takht-i-Suliman. He was giving the half-dozen English and American correspondents wise little pictures of each incident and person: of Salim, Zada, Da-ud, Gordyenne (still Gordon to Essex), of Pirusa, and of the small child with the sores. MacGregor knew by the tilt of his head and by the glaze in his eyes that Essex had already made Takht-i-Suliman a wonderful memory. How could you deny and contradict such a devilish fellow? Would anything stand up against the charm and skill of this man in establishing his knowledge and his experience? You could not doubt the accuracy of anything that Essex said.

Nevertheless MacGregor was determined that he must finally contradict Essex. Since hearing of this press conference he had decided that it would be the occasion when the open split would occur. MacGregor knew the newspapermen would ask for his own impressions of Azerbaijan and Kurdistan, and he had every intention of giving it to them in contradiction to Essex. Curiously enough he had an idea that Essex knew it. Yet Essex had taken great pains in telling him to attend this conference. MacGregor waited for something to develop.

So far Essex had said nothing political to these correspondents. No doubt it would come. Essex would make the whole story a simple lesson in how the British were right and everybody else wrong. The Azerbaijanian revolt was Russian made. Force had been used. The Kurds were being stirred up by Russian agents and were also a potential threat to the peace of the Middle East and must be kept in check.

MacGregor would disagree with it all when these men asked him. He had already disagreed with it in his report to the India Office. It was only half-finished but he had made his case, and he was preparing an additional report for the Foreign Office with particular reference to Essex's mistaken attitude between the Governor and Javat, and his unhappy attempt to forestall Kurdish independence by encouraging Zada into ambitious leadership of the Mukri. It had to come out. Essex knew it and MacGregor knew it, and they were waiting to get to the point.

Now, a cynical and still-resentful Hamber had asked Essex why they had left Takht-i-Suliman in such a hurry, and Essex was replying with easy understatement to a question he had expected. "I really wanted to stay and see the end of the dispute between Zada and Gordon," he said, "but Kathy was ill and there was a little assassination in the air, so Mr. MacGregor arranged for our hasty departure." From there, Essex passed quickly to Katherine's laundry and then to the ass, and he had not miscalculated his audience a fraction. They were all his from the moment

490

he had recreated the scene of MacGregor pelting the ass with snow. In addition it made MacGregor a man who could hardly be taken seriously.

"Did you find your car?" Steele said when the amusement was under control.

"Eventually," Essex said. "We had a dickens of a time getting down the mountains, but our old Devil-worshipper knew every snow-drift. We found a hut about noon the next day. It was some kind of deserted police post, but there was a Russian geologist chappie in it. He made the most remarkable coffee. Best coffee I ever tasted."

"What was he doing?" Hamber asked. "Looking for oil?"

"I don't know," Essex replied. "What was he looking for, Mac?"

MacGregor's voice broke a little because of a dry mouth. "He was a mineralogist investigating a small nickel discovery near Takht-i-Suliman."

"That's what he said!" Hamber murmured.

"That's what he was doing!" MacGregor replied. It was the least he could do to defend the Russian, because the man had finally solved the mystery of Professor Onegin for MacGregor: solved it in such a way that the Scot still felt excitement in thinking of it. The mineralogist had heard of Onegin. He had said that Onegin wasn't a hundred miles away: he was down at the Khush plateau investigating a drilling which the Iranian Government had sunk for oil but had abandoned when the oil-bearing rock had been passed. Onegin had been down there once before because an English paleontologist had decided that the oil-bearing beds had never been passed at all. On that occasion Onegin had disagreed with the Englishman. Now, however, Onegin was taking another look because he wasn't sure. With that, MacGregor had announced in high spirits that he was the English paleontologist. And so Onegin was down at the Khush plateau, still disproving — or proving — MacGregor's theory. For this information MacGregor felt bound to defend the Russian against Hamber. "He was a mineralogist!" he said decisively to Hamber.

"You'll have to believe MacGregor," Essex said. "They were talking for a couple of hours and I have an idea that MacGregor wanted to go off with him. But we had to get out of there and find the car. Actually it was lucky that we were delayed. We just caught Aladin, our driver, at Sanjud. It was Sanjud, wasn't it, MacGregor?"

"Sanjud."

"He was about to leave for the next town. In a mess too. He'd been beaten up by the Kurds a couple of times and the car had been stripped and knocked to pieces. When he saw us he tried to kiss my feet and he started to weep like a baby and kept it up until we got to Tabriz."

"What about the old Devil-worshipper?"

"Da-ud?" Essex said. "Amazing fellow. Simply disappeared when we arrived at Sanjud. He came out of the ground in the first place, and he seemed to go right back into it."

MacGregor had never told Essex about Da-ud; and listening to Essex's brief *passage* about the old man, he decided it was a fair piece of censorship to keep Da-ud's fate to himself. MacGregor slowly held his glass out to the quiet Indian servant and heard ice tinkle on its sides. It was a long long way from the Eighth Angel, whose arrest at Sanjud had nearly ended his long pilgrimage to the tomb of his Saint. Essex's voice tinkled like the glass, and MacGregor blotted it out in recalling Da-ud locked in a sheep-pen, facing his Azerbaijani accusers with no more hostility than one would expect of the Eighth Angel. As the Azerbaijani soldiers had spat on him and called him Kurdish dog and devil and spy he had replied gently that they must forget their hatred of the Kurd: it was false. He had made a formal bow and greeting to MacGregor. But when MacGregor had insulted the men for imprisoning an old man and an ally, Da-ud had shaken his head to suggest restraint. MacGregor was not sure even now why the Azerbaijani had suspected Da-ud of being a Teheran spy. Announcements of Da-ud's friendship with the new Azerbaijanian regime had not placated the soldiers. They had wanted to shoot him, and MacGregor had been forced to invoke the threat of terrible authority to get him released. A deposit of the ass had settled the question of MacGregor's good intentions and he had been allowed to unlock the sheep-pen and take Da-ud away. The Eighth Angel had been untroubled by the incident but he had known that he must leave the village if he chose to remain alive. MacGregor had walked with him to the wide plateau, and there Da-ud had blessed his irreligion and had taken the route to the mountains, presumably to return to Takht-i-Suliman. And here again, in the tinkling of the glass, was Essex. He was talking of Tabriz, where they had really done nothing to speak of, eh Kathy?

"The usual thing," Essex was saying. "We talked to a few politicians and to some of our own chaps up there. Lots of propaganda but we managed to see enough for ourselves."

"Did you see Pishavari, the head of the so-called Government?"

"Ah yes." Essex whistled for a moment. "Sharp feller. Been educated in Russia I believe. Tried to convince us that everything was in order; wanted to drag me all round the town and out to some local election, but I really didn't have time. MacGregor and Kathy went off with him. They're better tourists than I am."

"Did you see the American Chargé in Tabriz?" Hamber asked.

"I believe we did."

"What did he have to say?"

"Now you're expecting too much, Al," Essex said with a smile. "But I'll tell you who else we talked to. You remember the old gentleman who came up to Moscow: what's his name, MacGregor?"

"Jehansuz."

"Yes. We saw him again. Fanatic about educating the nomadic tribes." Essex thought about that. "Hopeless business really on the basis of our short observation of the nomad. Wonderful people, but they are better off as they are: damn good soldiers and free men. Rather like the old Highlander, eh MacGregor?"

"Yes something similar."

There were more questions about Tabriz and the Azerbaijanians, but it now seemed to MacGregor that Essex was going to say nothing committal about Azerbaijan at all; nothing political and nothing decisive. Even in talking of Zada and Lord Gordyenne he had made the issue a simple struggle for power by two men over the sick body of their chief. The correspondents were still trying to commit him on Azerbaijan. They came back to Javat.

"Did you ever find out what happened to Javat Gochali?" This came from a new correspondent: a polite Englishman with a good memory and gold-rimmed glasses, an assured man who spoke with a slight stutter and represented the London *Times*.

"Yes, we found him," Essex replied. He was on non-committal grounds even here, because he had reported the incident at the Governor's in strictly neutral terms. Essex had simply recounted it as an adventure, no mention being made of their own part in it. He had actually given a sympathetic picture of Javat, although he had given an equally sympathetic picture of the besieged Governor. The man Essex made responsible for all trouble was the booted officer, but he had not mentioned MacGregor's part in the detention and destruction of this officer. "Yes," he said, "MacGregor found Javat in one of the hospitals in Tabriz. He was alright. Russian hospital, wasn't it MacGregor?"

MacGregor nodded.

"And the Governor?" the *Times* man asked. "Did they hang him?"

"No. He took *Bast* in the mosque at Zenjan."

"What exactly is *Bast*, Harry?"

"That is legal sanctuary in this country," Essex explained. "I believe you can take refuge in the mosques and the King's palaces and no one dare touch you. The Governor lost his estates after a small battle, but he got to the Zenjan mosque somehow. We saw him on our way back to Teheran. He wanted us to bring him here, but we didn't like to interfere. He was safe enough, and MacGregor thought we would be involving ourselves if we brought him with us."

493

"Well it's all a nice story," said the impatient Hamber, "but what did you get out of all this? You're being terribly clever, Harry, avoiding any political statement. But what does the whole mission add up to?"

"Well it added up to quite a lot," Essex said.

"Since you went there to find Russian interference, would you like to say officially whether you found any or not? The whole world would like to know the answer to that one."

MacGregor put down his glass. There was only one answer Essex could give.

Essex avoided it. "You'll have to draw your own conclusions about that." He was smiling his most tolerant smile at MacGregor, and MacGregor wanted to kick him in the shins. "Officially, of course, it's another matter. I suppose you knew that Azerbaijan was going to the United Nations."

"That's old stuff."

"I'm afraid that is where the British Government will need my information," Essex said. "Sorry chaps, but I can't go any further on the matter of Russian interference."

MacGregor couldn't believe that he was going to leave the subject there.

"Then what did you get out of all this wandering about?" Hamber asked.

"If you really want to know, Al," he said. "I discovered that Azerbaijan was not the only issue at all." He paused. "By no means the only issue."

"Well for Christ's sake," Hamber said. "Go on."

"Before you go on," Steele said. "Can we quote you?"

"Absolutely," Essex said.

"What's it about?"

"It's really about the Kurds," Essex told them and glanced at MacGregor.

MacGregor was ready and thinking: *Here it comes. He won't say anything on Azerbaijan so he's going to denounce Kurdish independence instead.*

"You see," Essex told them with his fingers together. "The one thing that is absolutely necessary to peace and good relations in the entire Middle East is Kurdish independence."

MacGregor was lost from this moment on.

"Kurdish independence?" said the startled *Times* man. "Why?"

"Because the Kurds are facing extinction," Essex said. "They are in a much worse situation than Azerbaijan. In all the tugging and pulling that is going on up here, the Kurds are in danger of being swept into someone's pocket. We must consider their struggle for recognition,

494

autonomy, and self-determination as real and necessary; and in my opinion their aspirations should be assisted and satisfied."

MacGregor groped for an explanation of Essex's reversal, but he was so overthrown that all clear thought escaped him. Why in God's name was Essex switching himself around so completely? In Takht-i-Suliman he had been violently opposed to Kurdish autonomy: now he was actually demanding it. It was a trick, it must be a trick, but what sort of a trick?

"Does this independence include the Kurds in Iraq under British rule?" the *Times* man asked.

"Certainly."

"In Iran and Turkey?"

"Yes."

"Can it be said that your statement is directed at these Governments?"

"You can say it if you wish," Essex replied, "but I'm not saying it."

"Holy smoke," said Steele, "but you're sticking your neck out."

"Is your statement the official view of the British Government also?"

"No," said Essex with brief authority, "but I intend to advise my Government to consider Kurdish independence as a vital requirement for Middle Eastern stability. Independence is the only hope the Kurds have of avoiding extinction and Bolshevization. It is up to the friendly powers of the West to see that all Kurds achieve their self-government and their sovereignty."

"Have you told this to the British Government yet?"

"I've told no one, and heaven help me for telling you. If you look around at my assistant, Mr. MacGregor, you will see that even he is surprised. And I might add that Mr. MacGregor is also a keen partisan of Kurdish independence."

MacGregor was the buffoon who had snowballed the ass. What could MacGregor say? Where was his exposé? Where was the great issue of Azerbaijan and Kurdish independence? What were his objections now? MacGregor looked at Katherine across the dim room. He could barely see her but she had never appeared so well-tailored, so well-brushed, and so untouchably beautiful. MacGregor was a lonely man. Essex had isolated him again. This particular world was not his. It all belonged to Essex, and it included Katherine and the strange geography of correspondents who were men that MacGregor would never understand. He looked back at their poised faces and asked himself what he could say to them now. There was nothing. He felt no affinity to any of them, either as human beings or fellow countrymen. They belonged to Essex.

"Well?" said the sarcastic Hamber. "Are you surprised, MacGregor?"

"Nothing surprises me any more!" MacGregor said.

It was the ridiculous and exact remark to picture his confusion. The newspapermen laughed and Essex smiled. MacGregor blushed and sat rigid and hostile and silent and unforgiving. Even Katherine smiled.

"Wouldn't you like to say something about the Russians at this stage?" Hamber said to Essex. "You've got to say something about them, Harry, otherwise this doesn't mean a damn thing."

"Perhaps everything I've said concerns the Russians," Essex replied warily. "Anyway Al I can leave that to you chaps. I'm sure you'll do justice to that side of the question."

"Can't you say anything?"

"I'd like to." Essex was smiling ruefully, knowingly. "But it's now out of my hands. It's up to the United Nations to talk about Russian activities. They can decide and settle it — I hope."

"With your help," Hamber added fervently.

"Oh, I'll be advising the F.O. on it, and I might be doing the conference work. I'm not sure yet."

"What about Russian interference in Kurdistan?" Steele said.

"Ah. I have to leave something for my report. You fellows can't have everything, you know. In fact you have done rather well." Essex was standing up to finish it. The newspapermen also stood up and they clapped Essex politely to denote their comprehension and their satisfaction. They gathered around Essex for the usual moment of intimate informality. As MacGregor stirred himself out of their way he could hear them asking Essex when he was going back to London.

"They're sending an aircraft up from Cairo to-day," Essex told them. "With a little luck we should all get away to-morrow. Yes! Kathy is coming with us."

"How about a lift?" Hamber said.

"For how many?"

"Three of us," Hamber said.

"Talk to the Air Attaché, Al. Tell him it's alright as far as I'm concerned; but it's an R.A.F. machine and it's up to him. I think it will be alright."

"Thanks," Hamber said. "I want to be in London when you get there, Harry. This is going to blow the lid off the whole thing."

"I wouldn't say that," Essex murmured.

"You've just begun the real battle for the Middle East. Did you know it?"

"Isn't that going a bit too far, Al?"

"Hell, no. You've just thrown in the Kurds and declared war on the Russians."

Essex folded his arms and held his pipe. "Go gently now, Al."

"Are you sure you won't say anything?"

"About the Russians?"

"Yes."

496

"Oh I don't have to, man."

MacGregor was blocked behind Essex by the newspapermen, and Katherine was suddenly standing there, putting her arm through MacGregor's. "Don't look too frustrated," she said. "It shows."

"What's he up to, Kathy?" MacGregor found the words difficult to control.

"You really shouldn't be surprised by him any more."

"Surprised!" he said bitterly. "He has reversed himself on everything."

"Naturally," she said.

"I want to talk with you," MacGregor told her, "if we can get out of here."

"Why don't you wait and leave gracefully?"

"I don't feel graceful," he said between his teeth.

MacGregor was stopped with a touch of the arm and a slow word from a newspaperman. "I say."

"Yes?" said MacGregor.

"My name is Bickford." It was the London *Times* man. "Kathy here knows me, and she was telling me about you this morning. Have you got a moment?"

"What is it?"

"I know you Civil Servants aren't supposed to say much and all that, but I was wondering if you could fill in a few details for me."

"I'm not a Civil Servant," MacGregor said. "I'm in this by accident."

"Sorry." Bickford stuttered a little.

"It's alright," MacGregor said, "but there is nothing much I can say now."

"I hope to be on your plane to-morrow. Would you mind if we talk then?"

"I really can't say much."

"It's just the colour really. Nothing committal."

MacGregor shook his head.

Bickford tactfully dropped the matter and he smiled at Katherine and told MacGregor that she had been a youngster in plaits when last he saw her. "At the age of twelve, MacGregor, she was a Nihilist. Absolute opportunist like all beautiful children. She was in revolt at the time against going back to some Swiss *Töchterinstitut*. Did you ever go back?"

"Certainly not," Katherine said. "They sent me to a convent instead."

Bickford laughed. "You sound like your mother, Kathy." He took off his gold-rimmed glasses and squinted his eyes as he hesitated for a word. "Not quite so beautiful, perhaps, but a little wider in the face and thin-lipped like your father." Bickford replaced his glasses and walked away quite absent-mindedly. MacGregor did not wait for anyone else to approach him.

497

When they were in the low passage outside Katherine complained of his treatment of Bickford. "I asked him to talk to you," she said. "He's an important man to know and if you are careful you can have him on your side. He is sensible and intelligent."

"Everybody seems to be on the same side at the moment," he said cynically.

"That's nonsense," she said. "You've got to learn how to do these things. Just be careful."

"About what?"

"About Jack Bickford to begin with."

"I'm no good at that sort of thing," he said.

"You'll have to be good at it if you want to argue with Essex," Katherine said, "because he's practically perfect at it."

"Nobody can argue with Essex," MacGregor said as he took her into the small dusty Embassy room which he had been allowed. He sat down behind a long roll-top desk. "Did you know that he was going to make that amazing statement on the Kurds?"

"Certainly I knew it," she said. "He told me a couple of days ago."

"Then why didn't you tell me?"

"Why should I? This is between you two. It's nothing to do with me."

"If it hasn't anything to do with you, Kathy, you've been very free with your advice lately on how I should act."

"Yes I have," she admitted. "I have been trying to get you on the road to some sort of decision, instead of allowing you to drift along in that fuzzy argumentative way which ends nowhere. If you are choosing opposite sides to Essex, then why don't you go ahead and choose? If not, you might as well follow in his footsteps. But make up your mind. Fight him or agree with him."

"I could make up my mind alright if I knew what he was up to," he said grimly.

"What do you think he's up to?" Katherine leaned against the desk and faced him. "He is doing what he is supposed to be doing."

"He was supposed to be making an investigation of Azerbaijan to see if the Russians were interfering, and to decide if the Democratic Administration was valid or not. Now he is hedging about it, refusing to come out one way or the other. He also reverses himself on Kurdistan. After his performance in Takht-i-Suliman how can he talk of Kurdish independence? How can a man lie like that, and why? He no more believes in Kurdish independence than he believes in Azerbaijanian independence."

"You're wrong," she said. "He believes what he is doing."

"Never."

"The trouble with you is that you just don't understand the man, and that is what defeats you in understanding yourself. He knows that you

498

were all primed to break loose and deny everything he said. It's been obvious for a week and Harold is no fool."

"He didn't keep silent on Azerbaijan and throw in Kurdish independence just to keep me quiet," MacGregor argued. "There is more to it than that."

"A great deal more," she said and her hard straight eyes were being ruthless with his puzzled face. "If you had any sense you would see that Harold's attitude is his greatest admission of weakness. It's an admission that this revolt in Azerbaijan is succeeding. It's also an admission that the Kurds are about to take the same course. He certainly believes that the Russians are responsible for both revolts, so his beautiful solution is to take one away from them: the Kurdish revolt. He hopes to break the Azerbaijan revolt in the U.N., and if that fails then no doubt he hopes to break it with the Kurds. I know Harold. He has suddenly had the brilliant idea that the Kurds can become the deciding factor in this Middle Eastern balance between Britain and Russia. It's part of a whole policy, and that is the way you should look at it, instead of seeing it as a twist or a turn by Essex and a personal insult as well. You reduce everything to such petty levels of dispute."

"Blame Essex for that," he said. "He makes everything so intangible."

"Don't start talking like that again," Katherine warned him. "If you are going to look upon everything Essex does as intangible then you are going to annoy me. Essex is only intangible because you still don't understand the extent of the political issue you are facing."

"Now you're confusing it," he said. "This started out as a straightforward issue as to whether the Azerbaijan revolt was justified or not, but Essex has confused it with tricks and now you are confusing it with politics."

"No I am not. Azerbaijan is still the issue you have to face with Essex. But it is more than Azerbaijan and more than Iran. That is something you have never been able to understand. Can't you see that it is a matter of a whole attitude for yourself to all politics, to all arguments of foreign policy or political policy?"

"Now you exaggerate."

"No. No. No. You just haven't the vision to see where this should take you. If you continue to fight this for its local issue alone then you are lost, MacGregor. You will never understand what you are doing, particularly when we get to London where the real political battle will begin, more so now that UNO is being dragged into it. If you're going to be so easily confused and defeated by Essex's tactics then I don't want to talk with you about it. You will annoy me too much."

"Why doesn't Essex annoy you for a change!"

"At least Harold knows what he wants and does it."

"You're absolutely right," he said and ran his fingers through his sandy hair. "I can't keep up with this manœuvring. He has me beaten at every turn."

"Well what do you expect? You think you can decide to dispute him or expose him and he will go ahead and allow you to do it? You've got to be clever if you want to dispute Essex. You've got to know how to do it."

"I don't want to be clever about anything." He stood up. "I simply want to stop Essex from doing something that is dangerous: either breaking the reforms in Azerbaijan or taking over the Kurds. All I want to do is to pin him down and show up the unpleasant rôle we are playing in Iran."

"That's all!" she said.

"That's all!" he repeated.

"How were you proposing to do it after to-day's magnificent failure?"

"Any way at all. These reports . . ."

"Reports! Do you think they will impress the India Office or the Foreign Office enough to change their policy here? Do you? It's got to be more than reports. If you want to fight Essex you've got to come out and do it."

"How can I, if he forestalls me every time I decide to do it? I would have disputed him to-day but what chance did he give me? I suppose it will be the same in London. He will keep it all so confused and so intangible that he won't give me a chance to argue with him."

"Then take the initiative yourself," she said.

"How?" he asked dejectedly.

"That's up to you," she said. "But you've got to do it with a political understanding of all the issues: not just the right or wrong in Iran. It's got to be the whole political turmoil in yourself, MacGregor, otherwise it's no good."

He looked at her blankly as they stood facing each other.

"All I ask is that you do something, MacGregor, anything!"

He picked up his coat. He didn't want to hear anything more.

"Where are you going?"

"Home," he said.

"I'll come with you." Her voice was still spanking. "I have to pack."

They left the Chancery and went out into the street, walking silently and with little feeling for each other. MacGregor made the gesture of buying her a hot beetroot, but even as they walked along Firdousi Street eating the hot vegetable there was no sign of good-humour. Ahead was the Zagros, still white in its summits, still the first outline of the hard blue sky. Katherine looked but said nothing. She asked briefly what an old man over the road was shouting about. MacGregor said disinterestedly that he was selling potatoes: little apples of the earth.

500

Chapter 41

IN LONDON, MacGregor lived on Fulham Road just beyond Brompton Oratory. To reach his office he caught the 14 Bus, which went up Knightsbridge to Hyde Park Corner. From Hyde Park Corner he walked along Constitution Hill to Buckingham Palace, and then down Birdcage Walk to Westminster. His office was in the India Office building just off Whitehall, but MacGregor took the long way round Parliament Square to walk by the Abbey.

On this late January morning there was a light fog. The buses and cars and taxis hooted around the square, still using their yellow lights. Everything was a little touched by the fog except the black Ministerial cars that glided through the gates to the House of Commons, under the arm of the special policeman stationed there. It was really less of a fog than a purplish blue smoke. The sun would clear it away in a matter of hours; and though it was neither warm nor cold it was pleasant enough to be without a coat. In this, MacGregor was an alien among his fellow men who were marching into their offices in black coats, morning trousers, Homburg hats, and slim umbrellas. He wore an unpressed tweed suit and brown boots, and his hair bristled healthily for want of washing. His face was weathered and wind-burnt and many a duteous fellow broke his fortress of impersonality to glance with faint hostility at MacGregor's unseasonal face. MacGregor looked back with the aggressiveness of a foreigner who resented the Englishman's identification of unseasonal strangers. He bore this counterattack all the way around the square until he came up Whitehall to King Charles Street. There he forgot it, in his approach to the large stone entrance of the India Office.

His normal procedure was to pass the black-uniformed Commissioner and show his pass without looking at him; so avoiding the issue of whether he should be greeted or not. This morning, as he approached the gate, he changed his mind. Instead of going through it and up to his office across the courtyard, he turned about and retraced his steps to the square.

He bought all the morning papers from a small newsstand and walked down to Westminster Bridge and sat in one of the Embankment kiosks. He was not vitally interested in the newspapers, but they were part of his gesture in refusing to go to his desk. He picked up the first of them. Its main news was that de Gaulle had resigned as President of France, having decided that his task of directing France to liberation had ended: it was also reported that his decision to retire from politics was "irrevocable." The secondary news concerned Iran. The Government of Ibrahim Hakimi had resigned yesterday, presumably to make way for a Government that would be better able to negotiate with Moscow for a settlement of the

501

Azerbaijanian dispute. Since it was Hakimi's Government that had put Azerbaijan on the agenda of the Security Council, it was thought now that the matter might be withdrawn. Negotiations would probably be opened again with Moscow. MacGregor read it and thought for a moment that all his trouble might be over. It was a thought that did not last long because he looked down the page and there was a picture of Essex.

Essex's picture had been on the front pages of the newspapers every day since their return. This picture showed a smiling Essex with a pipe in his mouth and his lucky Cordovan pouch under his arm. This was reported to be a picture of the Envoy, taken yesterday, after he had visited Downing Street to make a report on his extra-ordinary and successful mission to Moscow and Azerbaijan. A sensation was expected when Lord Essex presented his case on Azerbaijan in the forthcoming Security Council meeting. His facts were authoritatively reported to be damning and conclusive evidence of Russia's guilt in creating revolt in Azerbaijan, thus interfering in the affairs of another nation, thus creating a situation for the U.N. to settle. Lord Essex's appointment as special British delegate to the United Nations would enable him to go through with a mission which the British Government had given him some time ago: the job of settling the situation in Iran. Taking it to the U.N. was the culmination of Essex's effort. His representation of Britain on the Security Council was a guarantee that his opinion on Azerbaijan and Iran, together with his evidence, would decide not only British policy but U.N. policy on the situation.

No mention was made of the Kurds. Essex's statement of support for Kurdish independence had created the expected sensation two days ago and the newspapers had announced then that Essex had embarrassed the British Government — serious repercussions from Turkey, Iran, and Iraq being expected. Though MacGregor had looked carefully every day, there had been no story of repercussions from any of these countries. There was a remarkable silence on Kurdistan.

MacGregor looked briefly at the other papers. They said the same thing as the first paper. In one of them he found a social note about Katherine, another regular feature in the newspapers since their return. He passed it over and looked at the more important news. In all of them MacGregor could see Essex's subtle planting and placing of his ideas for Azerbaijan. The two exceptions were the *Daily Worker* and *The Times*. Of the *Daily Worker* MacGregor knew nothing, and he had never read it in his life before. He had bought it by accident with the others. *The Times* reported soberly that Lord Essex would represent Britain as Extra-ordinary Delegate to the Security Council for the specific discussion on Iran. Lord Essex had met the Cabinet yesterday. *The Times* added nothing more. The *Daily Worker* said that Lord Essex had been sent to interfere in the affairs of Iran, after the ignominious failure to bully and threaten the Russians into allowing the Teheran Government to squash the People's Revolt in Azerbaijan. Essex yesterday had the unpleasant task of reporting his failure to the Cabinet.

None of the papers could quote Essex direct. He had still said no word about Azerbaijan, about Russian interference, about anything that would indicate his important conclusions. MacGregor looked again for some word, but found none. Nevertheless there were long stories in each paper around Lord Essex, expanding on his damning evidence of Russian interference in Azerbaijan and Kurdistan. It had been going on like this for two days and MacGregor felt powerless to make any move. Essex was sweeping to victory without committing himself and without saying a word. It was finally too much for MacGregor. His deliberate fingers rolled all the newspapers into a tight scroll and he tossed them into the brown Thames. They spread out on the river and floated graciously under Westminster Bridge. MacGregor had no intention of watching them distend in the Thames. He was making up his mind to go and see John Asquith, and by the time the newsprint was scattered and sunk, MacGregor was in the Foreign Office looking for Asquith's new room.

MacGregor had been in the Foreign Office only a few times before. On every occasion he had gone with Sir Rowland Smith to conferences on the Middle East. He had been a silent bearer of a brief-case full of documents which had never been used, and after that he had avoided the regular assignment to these regular conferences. This solid permanence in Foreign Office affairs had always antagonized MacGregor: there was something threatening and deadly and over-sure in it. The building itself was far more flexible and animate than its regular and eternal inhabitants who demanded such rigid conformity of anyone entering the kingdom. No one could enter the Foreign Office with a contradiction to it and have his conviction untouched and unshaken. This was an atmosphere of such self-conviction and God-like authority that any rival opinion was shattered in the contact. It was more than a man could stand, and MacGregor was an easy victim. In the corridors his convictions were stripped and destroyed in a moment, unable to survive in this consulate of Gorgon. By the time he found John Asquith, there was nothing left but MacGregor himself. Only Asquith saved him from complete extinction.

"I've been waiting to see you, MacGregor," Asquith said, not bothering with formalities. "Didn't have time to go and find you in that other *poco a poco.* How are you, boy? You look remarkably well. Essex looks well, Kathy looks well. Huh! Even so, you might look a bit broken at the neck about something. Did Harold break you, or are you the man that broke Harold? Never mind, sit down and we'll talk about it. Did you come over to see Harold?"

"No." MacGregor sat down in one of the smooth leather chairs. "I came over to see you."

Asquith put his feet on the desk and said nothing.

"Are you busy?" MacGregor began politely.

Asquith nodded, unsmiling. "Harold is preparing to stun as many people as possible with weight of document. He plans to overwhelm the Security Council with a document for every word. I seem to be his first victim."

"No," said MacGregor. "I preceded you."

"You had the advantage of being stupefied on the spot," Asquith said, "whereas I am the impersonal victim of Harold's perpetual bloody quill."

"I thought you could stand anything."

"So I can. So I can."

"I'm wondering if I can," MacGregor said.

"You're too young and too intelligent to be talking like that," Asquith told him. "You should be up like a demon, eating fire and belching smoke. What's the matter? Has Harold got you by the throat?"

"No. I haven't seen him since the day we got back."

"Aren't you still working with him?"

"I'm supposed to be," MacGregor said.

"Well?"

"It's something of a joke. Essex told me he would let me know when he wanted me, but they all seem to be doing very well without me. Haven't done a thing since I've been back. Haven't seen anyone except old Rowland Smith and that was to put in my report."

"What did he say?"

"He told me to be available for Essex, but he had practically forgotten who I was and where I'd been. Wondered what I was doing when I gave him my report. Have you seen any of it?"

"I saw the copy you sent Harold."

"It's useless now, in view of all other opinion."

Asquith had finally moved to the window sill. He sat on the narrow ledge, leaning on one casement and stretching his feet out to the other. "Is it useless?"

"I don't know." MacGregor relaxed for the first time since his arrival in London.

Asquith's face broke into a drooping smile and he pulled on his moustache. "Ah, MacGregor," he said. "I expected you to overwhelm me with argument for Azerbaijan."

"I might have on the first day back."

"Are you losing your simple passion, boy?" Asquith dropped his feet on the floor. "That's bad. All that wonderful sensitive expression, all

504

that revolt and all that anger. That was a heroic report, MacGregor. No one will take any notice of it, but I did."

"That makes two of us," MacGregor said. "All others are wrong and we are right. How do they know so much? How are they so sure of themselves?"

"Who?"

"Everybody. Essex, the Cabinet Ministers, the U.N., the newspapers, and all the people who believe what they read. But it starts with Essex. He has arranged it perfectly to give his picture of Azerbaijan but he doesn't say a word." MacGregor stopped himself there. "I suppose I shouldn't talk to you about Essex, now that you are working with him." He said it so bitterly that Asquith laughed.

"Are you worried about my rotten conscience?" Asquith said.

"No but . . ."

"Let my own twisted mind settle that problem for myself," Asquith told him. "I don't care what you say to me about Essex or your job or yourself, just so long as you're willing to say the same thing to Essex himself. As for me: I have no conscience and no morals. I had to throw them out with everything else when I took on this profession. Go ahead. You don't have to tell me that you disagree with Essex's conclusions on Azerbaijan. I've told you I have read your report. Are you thoroughly convinced that this revolt in Azerbaijan is worth the support you are giving it? Are you?"

"Well, it's better than what existed there before," MacGregor said.

"That's not enough," Asquith said. "Are you willing to support it against every other opinion? Are you willing to accept it in total?"

"I suppose I am. I disagree with some of it, but in general I think it's right. The same with the Kurds. But I just don't follow Essex's ideas about it. Why is he keeping quiet? What is he plotting?"

"Now don't be too hard on him," Asquith warned. "He isn't plotting anything. He is simply making sure that the case will be heard by the Council."

"I thought all that was fixed."

"By no means."

"Then what has been happening?" exclaimed MacGregor.

"Iran put the case on the agenda for discussion; but so far it has only involved a series of Notes from both sides to the Council. The Russians argue in their Notes that Azerbaijan is not a valid case for the Security Council, since the matter is still under negotiation between Russia and Iran. The Persians say that it is a matter for the Council because the negotiations have broken down. The Russians reply in another Note that they are willing to go on negotiating direct with Iran. No doubt Iran will have another Note to-day in reply to that one. On it goes . . ."

"What exactly is Iran asking the Security Council to do about Azerbaijan?"

"They want the Council to discuss Azerbaijan and recommend the withdrawal of all Russia's moral and material support for the rebels."

"But it looks as though the new Iranian Government want to go on negotiating with Russia," MacGregor said. "Do you think that might take it out of the Security Council's hands?"

"Oh no! Whether any Iranian Government likes it or not, we're going to make sure that it does come up for discussion. That's what Harold is doing with all this juggling. He is making sure that the case is accepted as valid for the Security Council. He is building it up piece by piece — in the newspapers, and in that great world conscience which we develop at opportune moments for the protection of small nations. He will make sure that the Security Council doesn't throw it out. He will then put his own arguments forward and he will have such overwhelming support that he will have his own say on the solution to the Azerbaijan problem. His personal experience in Azerbaijan will be unanswerable. I have been working like a black to make it unanswerable."

"Haven't the Russians got an answer to it?"

"Not to Harold's first-hand experience at Stalin's request. No one has an answer to that one my boy." Asquith might have added: *except you MacGregor:* but he knew that he didn't have to say it.

"The Russians were fools to let him go to Azerbaijan in the first place," MacGregor said. "There is obviously not going to be any Azerbaijan left when Essex is finished."

"Do you want the Russians to stay in Azerbaijan?"

"No. No. But I don't want Teheran to come in and break up the revolt. If they all left Azerbaijan alone . . ."

"Are you so dismayed by the effort our United Nations are making to settle the dispute?"

"No," MacGregor said, "but what is the use of someone trying to solve their own problems if all their efforts are going to be nullified by a lot of ignorant men talking around a table a thousand miles away?"

"How long did it take you to reach that estimation of diplomacy? I suppose you are now so disgusted that you want to clear out: go hopping back to Iran, eh?"

"If Essex is going to make the face of Iran, I doubt if I'll ever want to go back there."

"Is that the way you're taking it?"

"That's the beginning of it," MacGregor said.

"Then let's get out of here."

Asquith stood up and took a long amber-headed cane from his desk, and without top-coat or hat he was at the door in a long bound holding it open for MacGregor and gesturing at him to hurry up. There were now two incongruities in Whitehall: one a young unseasonal man and the other an eccentric figure who wore no hat but who carried a cane and brandished it like a schoolmaster's pointer. They were unseeing and uncaring, and Asquith upset the status-quo further when he rapped his cane on the iron railing of the Banqueting Hall as they passed. "Lovely building," he said to MacGregor loud enough for all near-by to hear. "One of Inigo Jones's. You see that window up there?" Asquith stood back on the pavement and pointed with his cane at the upper windows, while a large number of people took a tight grip on themselves and walked by without looking up. "Fourth from the left," Asquith said.

"Yes."

"That's where they dragged Charles the First out and cut off his head," Asquith bellowed. "They should have left a chopping block standing in the middle of Whitehall as a reminder of what can be done if you only have your heart in it." He dropped his cane and strode on. "MacGregor. We are really the ultimate political victims of the Restoration. Most colossal mistake in British history. Don't you think?"

"I've never thought about it," MacGregor said disinterestedly.

"You should. You should." Asquith raised his cane like an accusing finger. "You will never understand our stupidities if you don't understand the history that makes us that way."

"Our stupidities are obvious," MacGregor said. "Too obvious."

"No they're not," Asquith said. "You're just being educated to them by experience. What an advantage you have over all these poor wretches!" Asquith cut a swath through the pedestrians with a swing of the cane. "But it's not an advantage at all unless you put it to use, MacGregor."

"To what use?" MacGregor said. "Writing reports which no one will read?"

"That's something!"

"Is that enough?"

"No."

"Then what else!" MacGregor said.

"I don't know," Asquith replied dismally. "You will have to decide that yourself."

"There is nothing to decide. Who is really interested in understanding Azerbaijan, for instance? Essex has a clear field."

"Ah it's something more than Azerbaijan," Asquith said.

"I know," MacGregor said. "It might be the Kurds and the Middle East and the Russians and the Americans and everybody else."

"If you understand that, then understand the specific issues too, Mac-Gregor." Asquith waved his hand to someone who passed by in a large black Rolls-Royce. "You are almost entirely concerned with your Azerbaijanian and Kurdish friends. That's fine. That's fine. But though they may be the victims of a dispute they're not its purpose."

"I can see that."

"Then be patient." Asquith gripped his arm. "There is a great deal at stake, and no man is quite so qualified as you are to influence some vital political decisions for your friends. It's very easy with your knowledge to decide that the Azerbaijan revolt is natural and appropriate. You make that point very well in your report. Your fierce belief in Kurdish independence is also a wonderful impression, MacGregor, a wonderful and intelligently expounded impression. But it isn't enough to understand Azerbaijan and Kurdistan, and to bitterly claim their right of self-determination. Their self-determination is not an isolated thing in itself; it concerns the rest of the world. As it happens — it is about to be used in international councils as a political weapon for other policies. If you want to participate in these decisions, MacGregor, you've got to understand the objective, the tactics, and the purpose of every nation and every council. Particularly the tactics! There are a hundred different forces at work on Azerbaijan. At the moment its principal usefulness is in deciding a whole attitude and alignment in regard to the Russians, and also in regard to this United Nations Organization."

"Yes. Yes," MacGregor said.

"You might know that too, but consider it a mere beginning to your understanding. Understand the reasons, MacGregor, and you understand the tactics, and when you can understand the tactics you can participate in these affairs effectively. Take a lesson from Harold, whom you are probably ready to dismiss now as an opportunist and a fool. I leave that to you, but remember he is a clever fellow in establishing and propagating his point of view. It's easily done if you know how, and it's necessary to know how. You don't have to do it as Harold does it, by calling in a Hamber and having the unknown source of his opinions originate from New York newspapers. Harold loves to be Machiavellian and though it is effective in establishing his arguments, it will eventually defeat him and deny him. For you, MacGregor, there are simpler and better ways. You can't ask me what they are because I don't know. I might have known once but I don't know any more. All I know is that it's difficult to revolt against a contrary world, MacGregor, and it gets more difficult as time goes on. If you leave it too long you lose the chance — or you become an eccentric like myself, revolting against the petty habits of society but never really revolting against society itself."

"Oh I'm full of revolt!" MacGregor said. "But I know that one man in revolt becomes a martyr and that solves nothing at all."

"Don't be a fool," Asquith said. "There are plenty of people in revolt. Find them, and there's your future!"

"They're in Iran."

"Then go there!"

"I'll see what happens here first," MacGregor told him.

"Good enough!" Asquith cracked his cane on the footpath and they stalked to Lyons Corner House at Charing Cross. There, Asquith surprised MacGregor by leading him down the steps into the popular tearoom. "This," Asquith said, "is my funk hole."

There can be good friendship in a silent attitude to Lyons tea and cakes. After their consummation MacGregor suggested that Asquith had plenty to do without sitting here on another man's problem.

"Anything I have to do is worth escaping, MacGregor." Asquith's voice had lost its bite. "The petty fingerings of diplomacy are poor complement for an intelligent man. It's nice to talk to you. I can work with Harold, but I can talk with you. Devil of a complication. Still — if I've confused you it's your own fault for looking upon me as a hopeful man. Have I confused your problem, boy?"

"You've probably complicated it."

"Do you understand what you're up against?"

"Yes."

"Then should I tell you it's hopeless for you to do anything!"

MacGregor said nothing.

"Do you know what you intend doing?"

"No," MacGregor said in a drooping voice as low as Asquith's. "It's one thing to understand a situation, but it's another thing to do something about it."

"All I can tell you," Asquith's voice was dragging, "is that it's useless unless you know what you're doing. If you want to defy Essex and strike a blow for Azerbaijan, you've got to do it properly, MacGregor. Properly and cleverly and intelligently, otherwise it's hopeless."

"I'm tired of hearing that. It's Katherine's continuous formula."

"Is it? Is it? But Kathy has come a long way my boy, don't you think?"

"I don't know," MacGregor said. "She's too impulsive."

"Have you seen her since you came back?"

"No."

"Whose fault is that?"

MacGregor shrugged.

"You must get hold of Kathy." Asquith rubbed his long hands together. "You supplement each other too well. Don't wait for Katherine to be nice to you. Do you know where she lives?"

"Yes."

"Why don't you go and see her?"

"I have. She seems to be out with Essex most of the time."

"To blazes with Harold," Asquith cried. "Nothing will be bleak and

509

difficult if you have Kathy goading you and provoking you. I thought you two had both been doing rather well by each other."

"Kathy in Iran is one thing and Kathy in London is another." Mac-Gregor did not want to talk about it.

Asquith had no sense of tact in these matters. "She has to find her feet," he said. "Give her time. She's not sure yet how she has really turned out herself. You should get hold of her. She needs you."

"I doubt it."

"I know that Kathy is up-with-the-wind and down-with-the-devil; in passionate revolt one minute and back to her old habits the next. She'll be like that until she can decide one existence against another. At the moment she is running rather hard at being the woman she was, the Honourable Kathy Clive. Ignore that my boy. She'll get over it."

"Her own name seems to be too much for her," MacGregor said.

"Dammit. Is that what's troubling you? I'm disappointed in you. I am the Honourable John Anthony Ahab Asquith, but you're sitting with a man not a name. What's in a name? There's nothing in mine except the Ahab which I got from a paternal grandfather's respect for Herman Melville."

"I care nothing about her name," MacGregor said, "but it's a good reminder that Katherine in London is not Katherine in Iran."

"Nonsense!" roared Asquith. "It's no use behaving like that. If you think Katherine is being a damn fool then you had better tell her so and fight it out. She expects a great deal of you, and it will do her good."

MacGregor would not argue.

"We'll fix the whole thing," Asquith said. "Will you see her?"

"Why not?"

"You can come with Jane and me to the Savoy to-night," Asquith told him. "Kathy will be there; with Essex no doubt." Asquith enjoyed it. "I want to see you and Harold together too."

"Is it his party?"

"No. It's an informal affair for the delegates and official fellers involved with the U.N. That could include you, so you don't have to prejudice yourself and feel awkward."

MacGregor tightened his eyes and denied any prejudice or discomfort.

"Wonderful," said Asquith. "You can exercise some of your passion for Azerbaijan, my boy. It could be quite important if you influence some of the proper men. And you can tackle Essex."

"I thought there were going to be repercussions about Essex's ideas on Kurdish independence." This was something that MacGregor had been waiting to ask.

"Repercussions from whom?"

"The Turks, the Persians, the Iraqis."

"Hah! Are they going to complain when Essex offers them a solution to their Kurdish problems? Wouldn't it be nice: a British-constructed and well-behaved Kurdistan. There'll be no complaints about it, boy, except from the Kurds and yourself and the Russians and that sick chief."

"Do you know what has happened to him?" MacGregor asked.

"No. Would you like me to make inquiries about him?"

"Could you do it carefully?"

"I have an old friend in Teheran," Asquith said, "and no doubt we have sufficient agents among the Mukri tribesmen." Asquith took his cane off the table and stood up. "I'll pick you up at seven, MacGregor. Where do you live?"

MacGregor gave him the address, and as they went out there was a short argument between them about the bill which ended when Asquith said: "Pay it. If you must settle some tidy little sensibility about it, then pay it." They parted at the corner. Asquith went down Whitehall, and MacGregor crossed Trafalgar Square and entered the National Gallery. It was as good a day as any to tackle another confusing world.

Perhaps MacGregor knew more about art than he imagined, but he was lost among the treasures of the Gallery. He tried to cram the whole achievement of art into one day's vision, and the impossibility of it became another frustration for him. He found no answer at all to this precise desire to grasp the significance of art. It was like any other of his problems. Instead of finding answers MacGregor was now asking himself what came next.

Essex was pushing him against a wall of decision and MacGregor could not go on much longer without doing something about it. He looked for natural answers because he was a natural man, but in simple terms he could only think of resigning from the India Office, or going back to Iran in disgust, or writing more reports. He knew that none of these actions would settle anything. They were inadequate and unsatisfactory.

He stood for a moment before a canvas that looked familiar. He had never seen it before but when he saw its title he recalled that it was Katherine who had told him of it. This was "Avenue — Middelharnis," by Hobbema, whose last words were "Crome: how I have loved thee." It really was like the poplar avenue which had passed the stables where Javat and the Most Favoured Captain had been bastinadoed. It was there more than anywhere that MacGregor had felt a moment of choice in his life, but he had no idea how a similar choice could be made in London.

His great idea in Teheran about arguing with Essex for the enlightenment of those clever correspondents was rather poor in retrospect. Who was MacGregor that he should make such public expression? He was glad that he had said nothing; no one would have taken any notice of him. He could realize it clearly here in London where all things came down to their proper level. He would not know how to use the Press and he was afraid of it. Yet what other way was there of satisfying himself and denying Essex but publicly, either directly or indirectly.

As if the difficulty had provided its own solution, MacGregor was given the opportunity of denying Essex publicly when he had left the Gallery and gone home. Sitting in Mrs. Berry's parlour waiting for him was a big healthy man. He was not a young man and it was evident by his thin hair and burnt crown that he seldom wore a hat. He had a grey moustache, large eyebrows, and he wore a good tweed coat. He rose and greeted MacGregor by name, and said in impatient but polished English that he was from the *Daily Worker*. He was Dr. Ross, and MacGregor had heard of him often enough. He was a surgeon, once the King's surgeon, and MacGregor led him upstairs wondering what this unusual man wanted of him.

"Mr. MacGregor," Dr. Ross said without waiting to sit down. "We are anxious for you to give your version of what is happening in Azerbaijan. Since Lord Essex's return to England, an unfortunate and one-sided picture of affairs is being given, and it's about to culminate in a political move against the Soviet Union in the Security Council. I will be frank with you. We believe that you are the one man who can explain the true situation in Azerbaijan and contradict Lord Essex. We would like to publish whatever you can tell us. If necessary your name will be left out of it, but above all we need to know the exact situation in Iran without frills or deceit. It has to be brought out. You can see the situation which is rapidly developing out of the misinformation and the cheating of the diplomats and the newspapers. They are intent on breaking the new government of Azerbaijan as quickly and as vigorously as possible. Your own information is needed now to prevent this political error. Will you do it?"

"How do you know that I would contradict Essex? Who told you?"

"You are not unknown, Mr. MacGregor. Many people could tell me so."

"Not very many," MacGregor said.

"That's not important." Dr. Ross walked up and down the room, his hands in his overcoat pockets. "The important thing is that you publish your version of what is happening in Azerbaijan."

"In the *Daily Worker*?"

"Yes. We will publish it without garbling it."

"But I'm not a Communist!"

"I know that," Dr. Ross said. "That makes no difference. Whatever your politics we are prepared to accept your explanation of what is happening in Iran. You can express it in any political terms you wish."

"Is this for the Russians?"

"Good heavens no. What makes you say that?"

"They are the most concerned in this."

"Are they?" Dr. Ross said sharply. "Isn't it possible that a thinking man could dislike what is happening over Azerbaijan without having it come from the Russians?"

"Yes," MacGregor admitted. "But you are Communists."

Dr. Ross was impatient. "Is that going to frighten you?"

"Certainly not."

"Good. Then you will give us your co-operation."

MacGregor looked hard at Dr. Ross. "I don't see how I can," he said.

"Because we are Communists?"

"Perhaps."

"I see. Is it that you do not wish to be disloyal?"

"I don't think so."

"Then no doubt you do not like the Communists. If so I am sorry about it, but I know that you are more intelligent than to let that prejudice you. You know what is at stake."

"I know what's at stake," MacGregor agreed, "but I could not do it this way."

"Why not?"

"It would not be right, that's all."

"Mr. MacGregor you should be able to distinguish between the big right and the little right. I had understood that you were anxious to express yourself about Iran."

"Indeed I am," MacGregor said, "but not this way."

"What way!" Dr. Ross said. "It's perfectly honest and straightforward. We are not asking you to do anything that would go beyond your own beliefs, whatever they are. If you are worried about the ethics or the fair play of it, then I'm surprised. I would have thought that your experience had taught you sounder moral principles than that." He stood up. "Can I persuade you to change your mind?"

"I don't think so."

Dr. Ross was already at the door. "Then I shan't waste any more time."

"I'm sorry," MacGregor told him as they walked downstairs, "but I can't quite explain it."

"That's alright." Dr. Ross shook a brown hand in the air. "If you are a man of conviction I think that circumstances will change your mind."

"I doubt it," MacGregor said.

Dr. Ross did not argue. He gave MacGregor a grip of his square hand. "Good day young man," he said. He walked out without paying any more attention to MacGregor. He seemed entirely concerned with what lay ahead.

MacGregor did not have to think twice about his refusal of Dr. Ross's offer. It was complete and finished with. He was back again where he had started, still looking for an answer to Essex and to himself. He had made no advancement with the problem by the time he entered the lobby of the Savoy Hotel at 7:20 with John and Jane Asquith.

John Asquith was immediately taken up by two men, and he bounded ahead through a wide lounge and around corridors until they came to a large room in which the people of the United Nations were gathered. When Asquith disappeared into the gathering, Jane Asquith said to MacGregor: "If you don't mind, Ivre, I'll take your arm. I don't like going into these things without some assistance."

MacGregor had an idea that Jane Asquith did it for his sake. Although he did not need it, he felt pleased and at ease in having those gentle fingers on his arm. She did not let him go. Their unknown host greeted them and they passed on through hard-talking men and women until they were at the large windows overlooking a black night upon the Thames. So many people greeted Jane Asquith that MacGregor was thankful for her quiet and undeviating approach to a window sill, where she sat down. "Just lean against the window frame and stand beside me," she said. "The only way to cope with John at these affairs is to brace yourself against a wall and not budge: then he doesn't call at you from all over the place. He'll have everybody at you, Ivre, and I don't want him to embarrass you."

"He cannot embarrass me any more." MacGregor could not help smiling as he kept an eye on Asquith's large head waving about on the other side of the room. He had never had such affection for any man. "He is always the same, isn't he?" he said to her.

"Don't let him teach you his irascible habits," she said, but her smiling eyes belied the words, sanctifying anything that Asquith did and encouraging MacGregor to do likewise.

They had no time to say anything more. In the one minute of their presence in the room, they had been given cocktails and anchovied biscuits, and already polite men and women were upon Jane Asquith with intimate greeting and sweet charm. MacGregor was introduced to them all but he didn't attempt to keep up with the flow of names and faces; and Jane Asquith kept him out of the brittle conversation. MacGregor didn't mind standing with his back to the wall; he could remain here comfortably and easily, observing the world of officials taking time off from creating such an important organization. He recognized few of them, some being delegates and some being deputies and staffs and officials and advisers. They were all polite men, polite in all languages and all ages. The women were all charming, charming to the exact requirement. The most impolite person in the room was Asquith. From time to time his voice rose above all other noise, and then Jane Asquith would look at MacGregor and raise her calm eyebrows and wait for MacGregor's argumentative eyes to find hers. It was a nice world with Jane Asquith, but her husband shattered it by bombarding MacGregor with men to be told about Azerbaijan; men who should know what MacGregor had to say.

It began with a squat grizzled figure named Murphy, whom Asquith introduced as an Australian Ambassador at large in Europe. Australia, said Asquith with a cocked eye, was now on the Security Council; in fact Australia's representative, Mr. Makin, was Chairman of the Security Council. So Mr. Murphy, though not a delegate, was an important man, and would certainly like to know first hand all about Azerbaijan. Mr. Murphy was a little drunk, and though Asquith remarked that he was well known to be an official of the Hat-makers Union in Australia, Murphy told MacGregor that he was also the owner of a hat-making business, having worked up from the bottom of his union to become owner of a hat factory and the employer of two hundred men and women as well as being an official of the Australian Labour Party. When this was settled and Asquith had gone, Mr. Murphy asked MacGregor what it was all about in Azerbaijan anyway: "It's the bloody Russians," Murphy said before MacGregor could answer. "We've got to fight the beggars, fight them down to the last ditch in the Kremlin palace. I'm a Socialist and I'm telling you that the Reds have got to be licked before we get anywhere. I know it's up to England and America, but we've all got to take a hand. This U.N.O. setup isn't worth two bob unless the small nations have their full say, and we represent the small nations. Iran is a small nation, and we intend to see that she has her say and gives the Russians a black eye in the process. If England is finished then Australia can carry on where she leaves off, and this Azerbaijan business is one thing we intend seeing through to the end. It's all done by the Russians."

"If you knew the history of it . . ." MacGregor began.

"Never read history," Mr. Murphy said. "Never read anything. I know what's what, and I don't have to read anything to know what the Russians are up to."

"You're a stupid man," MacGregor said calmly, having learned his lessons from Asquith. "Ignorant and stupid."

Mr. Murphy's mouth opened for a second and his unread eyes sought quickly for the humour in MacGregor's statement. Finding none he set his straight Australian jaw. "Look here," he said. "I don't have to stand for that. What's your name and who are you?"

"My name is MacGregor."

515

"I'll see that the Foreign Office hears about this. I won't have it . . ."

"Then go away," MacGregor said and saw Katherine and Essex enter the room.

Katherine was wearing a red suit, and her hair was pulled tight on her head by a glistening clip of pearls at the back. She was greeted by a woman who held both her arms, and then by a young man who kissed her while Lord Essex stood by, smiling and erect in his grey flannel suit with a blue shirt and a knitted tie. All of this, plus Asquith arriving with another diplomat to be told about Azerbaijan, were just enough for MacGregor. Asquith saved him from the Australian by unceremoniously pushing Mr. Murphy out of the way and introducing the formally dressed foreigner as the representative of his country at the United Nations. It might as well have been the Patagonian representative because MacGregor was barely listening to Asquith's briefing. Asquith disappeared again as the delegate began talking to MacGregor, not about Azerbaijan but about Katherine and Essex.

"That's your Lord Essex coming in," he said to MacGregor. "There is not another man in diplomacy like him. It's only you English who can produce such a brilliant and accomplished diplomat. The French, of course, produce some excellent men, but I'm afraid there's no room in the new France for good diplomats. Communists don't like diplomats and France is rapidly going Communist. Another nation dying in its own ruins. Not enough strength and discipline in 1939. A little more authority in France then, and the Munich pact would have avoided that terrible war. Who is that beautiful woman with Lord Essex?"

"The Honourable Katherine Clive," MacGregor said.

"Do you know her?"

"Intimately," MacGregor said.

"Would you introduce me?" the delegate said.

"Just go up and introduce yourself. She'd enjoy that."

The delegate laughed easily. "Who is the charming lady with the Arab chap? It must be Lady Sybil or is that Mrs. Homer Dupont?"

"I don't know."

"There's Rowland Smith," said the delegate. "Great old man. I'm just reading his Memoirs on suppressing the Cawnpore riots. What were you saying about Azerbaijan? Have you been there?"

"Yes." MacGregor looked at the butterfly collar and at the smooth face and neat white hands and large gold rings. There was nothing that he could say to this man without having the stomach and dignity taken out of it.

"Of course we'll settle it," the delegate said. "Essex will have the Russians flat on the floor, and we can get a two-thirds majority in the Council as well as in the Assembly, although the Russians might use the veto.

Unhappy thing that veto; may allow the Russians to wriggle right out of it eventually."

There were more, one after the other. Asquith brought them, left them, and brought others, all important men to be told about Azerbaijan. There was an American, a young man with a responsible post. Like most Americans he over-estimated the importance of a serious and intelligent-looking Englishman. He knew of MacGregor and spoke to him with the confidence of their mutual position. "I spent the afternoon reading the outline that Essex sent over," he said. "By God you fellers did quite a job in Iran, and I've got to hand it to you. I don't quite agree with the follow-up on your sacred interests in the Middle East," he laughed, "but I don't think Washington will quibble about that yet. I suppose there's quite a lot of your material among Essex's."

"No," MacGregor said. "None at all."

"What's happened to your effort?"

"I don't know," MacGregor said. Was he going to start now a convincing explanation and argument with this American? The American turned the discussion to the problem which everyone in the room was discussing: who would be elected Secretary-General to U.N.O. It had looked for a time as if Pearson, the Canadian, would be elected, but the Russian minority were being obstructive. Pity, because Pearson, being a Canadian, was the ideal man for Britain and America. The Russians wanted Jan Masaryk, but Washington and the Foreign Office looked upon Masaryk as being a Kremlin agent now, and he could be too dangerous as Secretary-General. The American said that he personally favoured the Peruvian delegate, an excellent man and a choice which would favour no one. No one at all. What did MacGregor think? MacGregor agreed with the American and let the man talk himself out, and Asquith replaced him with a thin quiet Frenchman named Danjou who spoke delicately and patiently.

"I understand that you were with Lord Essex in Iran," he said.

"Yes."

"Of course we are waiting anxiously to hear what Lord Essex has to say. It is a peculiar situation in Iran and he could clarify it a great deal. I do not like the easy condemnation which so many of our colleagues have already decided. It is silly to blame the Russians for all the evil on the earth, and it casts suspicion upon our intentions. Nevertheless, if the Russians are interfering in Iran then we must bring it to light. Do you agree?"

"Yes," MacGregor said, "but whose word are we to accept?"

"Lord Essex is an honourable man. I am willing to accept his finding as accurate and decisive, and of course we will decide our attitude in the United Nations by his evidence. I am most anxious to hear it."

MacGregor respected the Frenchman, but by now he was outrun and he knew that it was no use beginning small arguments with any of these men. It required more than the limited chance he had here. He would not convince any of them, so he was better silent. He made only polite replies and even those who inquired intelligently of Azerbaijan found the conversation turned away by MacGregor and they thought him a dull and inarticulate young Englishman with wandering eyes and intense lips, out of place and unhappy and angered too easily. It was uncomfortable talking to him and they left him at the first opportunity.

If there was one exception, it might have been the Greek whom Asquith presented as Leros, an old friend. Asquith said that Leros wasn't the Greek delegate to the United Nations, but he was at least diplomatically concerned with the representation of Greece, and therefore a man for MacGregor to meet. They should have something in common since their problems followed the same lines. Leaving them thus, Asquith relied on their own ideas to bring the men together, but it did not quite succeed. In reply to Leros's questioning, MacGregor admitted that he knew very little about Greece, about British troops in Greece, or about the mix-up in the United Nations concerning Greece.

"Every Englishman should know about it," Leros said excitedly. "We have English troops in Greece just as there are Russian troops in Iran, but no one here seems worried about it. The Russians ask the Security Council to discuss the presence of British troops in Greece but only in retaliation for the complaint against themselves on Iran. That's no good. Nobody will take any notice of it coming from the Russians. Why don't your Labour M.P.'s make a big complaint about British troops in Greece? They are all so worried about Iran, why can't they worry a little about Greece? Do they want British troops to stay there forever? Do they want us to be a British colony? Your Foreign Office certainly treats us as they dare not treat one of your own Dominions. Why — one of our delegates to the United Nations thought it would be an excellent thing if the Security Council discussed British troops in Greece, but where is he now? Back in Greece. A little pressure from your Foreign Office and he is recalled. If it goes on like this, the whole world will be so busy getting the Russians out of Iran that the British soldiers will stay in Greece forever. Don't you think we have as good a case as Iran?"

"I suppose you have," MacGregor said.

"But we are not being allowed to fight it. Besides the delegate going back, the Foreign Minister himself has returned to Athens and will leave the Cabinet because the Prime Minister will not fight the case. I will also be recalled. Any man who opposes British policy in Greece will be recalled by the men whom your Foreign Office has put in power. Why don't your Labour M.P.'s protest about that? Why are they so single-minded

518

about Iran? Let them get the Russians out of Iran, but let them get their own troops out of Greece. Don't you think it is a disgrace?"

MacGregor supposed again that it was. He knew so little about Greece that he could not quite see what Leros was so furiously excited about, and it was useless trying to talk to him about Azerbaijan because Leros's own problem occupied his mind entirely. Perhaps Greece did have a case, but the real argument was about Iran. MacGregor could not get interested in Mr. Leros's appeal for Greece, and Mr. Leros went away to find someone who could, and MacGregor was left again to see who would come to him next.

Of all the people crowded in the room it seemed that everyone had talked with him except Katherine, and when she did come it was Asquith who brought her. MacGregor had been watching Katherine for an hour, and she had always been occupied by endless young men and appreciative old men. She must have seen MacGregor, but she had not given any indication of it. Even now she came with an eye on Jane Asquith whom she greeted and occupied until Asquith tapped her shoulder. "Never mind about Jane," he said, "here is MacGregor."

"I know!" She looked at MacGregor. "What are you doing here?"

"I brought him to see you," Asquith told her indignantly.

"You brought him to talk to all those U.N. people you were so rudely dragging across the room," Katherine said. "What on earth were you doing?"

"Please," Jane Asquith said. "Let's have no family arguments. Ivre came of his own accord and for his own reasons."

"What were they?" Katherine looked at him.

"You're being damned rude to him," Asquith said.

"Go away," Katherine told Asquith.

"Come Jane," Asquith said, but Jane Asquith was already talking with a Slav delegate who kissed her hand and spoke to her in soft-mouthed French. Asquith left them in disgust and MacGregor watched him stand perplexed for a moment with his hand at his drooping moustache.

"Why don't you grow moustaches like John's?" Katherine said to him. "Then you could pull at them instead of tightening up your face like that."

MacGregor was relaxed and he knew it. He was relaxed in the uselessness of his surroundings. It was Katherine who appeared nervous. Her face was pale and smooth and English, and her eyes were larger than usual. There were two small diamonds in the lobes of her ears, almost invisible except for the flashes of light. They were hard supplements to such deliberate eyes.

"You don't look very well," MacGregor said. It began as a challenge. She took no notice of it. "What were you trying to do," she said, "convince all these United Nations one by one?"

519

"I am being what you call clever and sensible," MacGregor said.

"Isn't it rather hard for you? You have such a hopeless look on your face. Haven't you convinced anyone with your careful attitude?"

"Are you like that again?" he said to her.

"Like what, my dear?"

"You're a pain in the neck sometimes. You are now!"

"Don't be flippant." She was maddeningly flippant herself.

MacGregor kept a grip on himself. "If you could make up your mind to be one person, then I would probably have the patience to keep up with you."

"Oh?" She held his eyes and accused him. "Have you made up your mind which person you are? Have you assassinated somebody for your Azerbaijan? Have you cried out your protest?"

"I'm not being impulsive about it . . ."

"You certainly aren't." The sly smile had gone and her face was sharp. "In Iran you were a man about to strike a blow. Have you struck it?"

"No." He sounded unnecessarily defiant. "No."

"Then you're wasting your time here and you dare not complain of me."

"I'm hardly complaining," he said. "I'm simply trying to understand what sort of a person you are at this moment."

"I am the person you think I am, and be damned to you. As for you. If you can't make up your mind to do something, then go back to Persia where you belong. You'll be swallowed up here like any little man unless you can fill yourself up and complete yourself."

"Don't talk in parables," he said. "You're a bigger sinner than I am."

"Don't recriminate." Her hard eyes were at him. "You've done nothing to decide yourself since we've been back, and you are trying to avoid it. I know it. You are dribbling yourself into a puzzled little world of your own. I hate that!" she said. "I hate that! It's a miserable choice for you to have made."

"So is yours." He indicated the room about them.

"What alternative can you offer?" she said.

"None," he said. "You fit this perfectly."

"You're a fool," she said.

"And you are hopeless."

"Then go away," she said. "Go back to Persia."

"Aye!"

She closed her teeth and shook her head angrily and went away.

MacGregor did not quite know how it had happened, how Katherine's brittleness had become serious and how his own ease had turned into anger. It was so final that MacGregor stood against the window sill with all the damage visible. Asquith immediately brought someone else to him. "This fellow is an orientalist," Asquith said. "A Persian scholar, and therefore a man you can talk to. Now talk to him. He says he knows all about the place."

"Not all," the Persian scholar said carefully.

The two words were enough to release Asquith, and the delegate talked to MacGregor in Persian, quoting the commonly taught enigmas of Akel Khan, calling them divine, spiritual, ecstatic things: expressing this with the tips of his fingers like the lips of his mouth until MacGregor was taken out of his own thought by repulsion for the man. His silence was so hostile that the Persian scholar turned to an Arab neighbor for conversation; and again John Asquith came back through the crush of people. This time with Essex.

"Hulloa Mac!" Essex said cheerfully and offered his hand which MacGregor shook in returning the greeting. "I've been waiting to see you. Where have you been?"

"At the India Office." MacGregor had to speak above the diplomatic noise.

"Have you. Have you. I wanted to talk to you. How about coming up to see me to-morrow morning, say at 11:15."

"What for?" MacGregor said.

"Well this is hardly the place to talk about it." Essex grinned. "But I suppose I can mention it. I've asked to have you transferred to the Political Intelligence Department of the Foreign Office, and I think it's going through: permanent appointment and all the trappings."

"Hah!" Asquith said.

Essex ignored Asquith. "I read your reports, MacGregor. That is what really decided me. Any man that can turn in reports like that is right and proper for the Foreign Office. Of course they are wild and prejudiced and young and impassioned, but they've got spirit, MacGregor. They've got spirit. That's the way I started. It will take you a little while to find out what we want and what we don't want, but you'll be with me and I can teach you that in no time. Come in to-morrow and we'll talk about it and perhaps we'll have lunch with Kathy and John if they're not doing anything. A celebration for you, my boy. And MacGregor: Look after that report of yours. It could be dangerous if it fell into the wrong hands. There are plenty of unscrupulous devils around these days." Essex left MacGregor and bent down to talk with Jane Asquith and to ease out of the crowd and sit by her on the window sill. MacGregor was left with Asquith.

"That's nice," Asquith said to him with one eye half-closed.

"Yes. I must be valuable." MacGregor was in no mood to say anything and Asquith did not mind standing beside him with a ferocious look upon his face, as silent and concerned as MacGregor himself. They both looked a little insulted. Nothing remained for MacGregor now, and only a fresh greeting halted his departure.

"Mr. MigGre*gor*." It was a slow and solid voice. "Perhaps you remember me in Moscow at the negotiations with Lord Essex and Mr. Molotov?"

"Suchkov!" MacGregor said. "What are you doing here?"

They shook hands. "I am with our delegation to the United Nations." Suchkov's large dark face and stocky body were enough to give MacGregor a brief moment of pleasant sanity. "Are you well?"

"Yes," he said. "Very well."

Suchkov greeted Asquith, and in English. It was slow and punctuated with Asquith's grunts in Russian.

"Why didn't Mr. Molotov come to London?" Asquith asked him. "We expected him to lead your delegation. We are disappointed that he didn't come."

"When we had Mr. Gromyko at the beginning," Suchkov said, "your Press said that we were treating the U.N. lightly because we didn't send Mr. Vishinsky. Vishinsky was delayed in Rumania; but now that he is here, your Press is asking why didn't we send Mr. Molotov." Suchkov raised his hands. "Are they never satisfied with us, Mr. Asquith?"

"You're too sensitive about our Press," Asquith told him.

"Then why are they always accusing us of things we do not do? They are talking now about our large army, when we are demobilizing faster than America or Britain. To-day your papers say that we are massing troops in Austria and demanding bases in Iceland. What for? Why do they tell these lies?"

"You'll get used to our newspapers if you stay here long enough," Asquith said. "Don't let them worry you. Is this your first visit to London?"

"Yes."

"Are you here as the Azerbaijanian expert?" MacGregor asked him. "I am an adviser," Suchkov corrected. "And you, Mr. MigGre*gor*?"

"I am nothing to do with it," MacGregor said, avoiding this final shame.

Suchkov was surprised. "But surely after your visit to Azerbaijan you are most important. I want to ask you about Azerbaijan, what you saw there and what you have decided."

MacGregor did not want to talk about Azerbaijan now, not even to Suchkov. "I decided what you knew I would decide."

"And you are not part of your delegation to the United Nations?"

"No. I am better out of it," MacGregor said. "And you will have a fight on your hands. What do you Russians think of the tricks we play?"

Suchkov laughed. "We have a good sense of humour," he said.

"You need it," MacGregor said.

"No more than our English friends," Suchkov said slyly. "It's a changing world."

"You're optimistic," Asquith told him.

"You are always too sad, Mr. Asquith," Suchkov said.

"You are absolutely right," said Asquith.

Suchkov told MacGregor that he would like to talk to him at some indefinite time and he departed with the same care as he had shown in greeting them. He had seen the Soviet Ambassador enter the room, and he was at the Ambassador's side like the left wing of a phalanx, a Soviet phalanx.

"I think I'll go," MacGregor said. He bade good-bye to Jane Asquith and forced his way out.

"Let me know what you intend doing." Asquith was pushing through the people with MacGregor, paying no attention to those who called him.

"About what?" MacGregor said.

"Heaven only knows. But let me know."

"I will." MacGregor passed behind Katherine, unseen and unseeing.

"You're a dear friend my boy. I must know. I'm sorry I can't help you more, but you see me in the lion's mouth."

Asquith seemed to be dramatizing the situation unnecessarily. He shook hands with MacGregor in the comparative quiet of the corridor. MacGregor did not like it, and he was glad when he was out on the Strand with the taxis and the buses and the unspecific people.

He needed all the large and personal possession that London could give him and he walked slowly through the deserted streets of Covent Garden to Leicester Square and Piccadilly. He had never liked Piccadilly and he hurried through it, wondering when the American MP's in their white helmets would finally go home. Once out of Piccadilly the Americans were forgotten and he walked slowly through Mayfair to come out at Hyde Park. Through the fenceless perimeter of Hyde Park he kept his mind off the tangle of circumstance by deliberating on his affection for the park. Even the Albert Memorial became a real thing instead of a jest of memory to the great progenitor.

It was here and about the Albert Memorial that MacGregor knew without conscious decision what he would do. There were few trustworthy avenues of public expression open to him. Of those available MacGregor chose the most logical. At Mrs. Berry's boarding-house he sat down in the parlour and spread a few sheets of foolscap on the green-tasselled cloth and addressed a letter to *The Times*.

DEAR SIR [MacGregor wrote]:

In view of the unusual interest at present in the political affairs of Iran, may I make a few observations which are the result of a recent visit to that country with Lord Essex.

Firstly, the Azerbaijanian struggle for a measure of autonomy and self-government is genuine and is locally inspired. The facts of history and existing conditions show that Azerbaijan has always been struggling to overthrow the feudal conditions imposed upon it (and upon the rest of Iran) by corrupt Iranian Governments.

Secondly, the extent of Russian interference appeared to be negligible. In our travels we saw few Russian troops, and in Kurdistan we saw none at all. The leaders of the Azerbaijanian Government are not Russians but Azerbaijanians, and with few exceptions their sole aim seems to be the recovery and improvement and economic reform of Azerbaijan. There may be some Russian influence by indirect means, but I would suggest that it is less than our own influence in Iran which we exercise by direct control of Ministers, political parties, state finances, and by petty bribery.

As for Kurdish independence. The Kurds ask for an independence of their own making, not an independence sponsored by the British Government. Like the Azerbaijanians, the Kurds are seeking real autonomy; and more than that, self-determination. Our present scheme to take them over and use them as a balancing factor in the political affairs of the Middle East is a reflection upon the honesty of our intentions, and a direct blow at the spirit of all good men.

Yours faithfully,

I. A. MacGregor

Chapter 42

In the one day of grace between this action and its consequences, MacGregor was satisfied that he had done the right thing. The act itself was all that concerned him, so he did not go to see Essex. He realized that this would force him to settle quickly with Essex and the India Office and his future, but he did not anticipate any other direct interest in his opinions, except by Katherine, and there was little or nothing of Katherine left for him. Nevertheless, it was Katherine's indirect compulsion that sent him on this day of grace to the Victoria and Albert Museum. This time he investigated only two of the rooms. One contained the delicate Renaissance imagery, which MacGregor did not like. He was an iconoclast, and art or not and Katherine or not, he was suspicious of this beautiful idolatry. He was better off in the long passageway of early iron tracings, comparatives from Italy, Germany, France, Spain, and the rest of the civilized world. He could understand design, and since technique was a continuation of design, he could appreciate the tracery. This was probably a contradiction to Katherine who would have been bored by it, and impatient with him. He therefore investigated it all the more.

For the rest of the day he did not face the reality of the India Office.

He wrote to his mother in Kent and went to bed early. He was awakened in the middle of the night by a hammering on the door. It was Mrs. Berry, and she whispered angrily through the door that it was after midnight and that three gentlemen were below to see him. By the time he had asked who they were she was away down the stairs. He put on his slippers and dressing-gown and pushed back his hair with his fingers and went downstairs to the green chenille parlour. As he entered the room a flash-bulb burst in his face and he was greeted by the three men, one of them with the camera. MacGregor put up his hand as the camera flashed again.

"Are you the MacGregor that wrote this?" one of them said.

"What is it?"

"It's the first edition of *The Times*." The newspaperman handed him the paper, folded to show his letter and his strange name: I. A. MacGregor.

"Who are you?" he asked them.

They named newspapers and news agencies and said that it had taken them hours to find him. They were indignant about it.

"What do you want?" he asked them.

"We thought you might like to expand on this," they told him.

"In what way?" MacGregor was suddenly awake and amazed.

"Since this amounts to a rather sensational contradiction to Lord Essex's conclusions, could you say anything directly about Essex? Just a quote."

"No."

"Isn't your letter a direct attack upon Lord Essex?"

"No. No."

"That's the way it will be interpreted," the reporter said quickly. "Your letter will make it rough on Lord Essex in the Security Council won't it?"

"I don't know."

"What did Lord Essex say about the letter? Did you show it to him?"

Even as MacGregor replied No, three more men came into the room and stood near him silently and began writing. Another photographer came and more bulbs were flashed at him and the questions multiplied as he was surrounded by quick-talking men.

"Has the Foreign Office said anything to you yet?"

"No."

"Have you resigned?"

"No."

"Have you been fired?"

"No."

"Did you write that letter to embarrass the British Government's policy on Iran, or did you write it to make trouble for Essex?"

"That's a ridiculous thing to say," he said.

525

"Did you know that Civil Servants weren't supposed to express their opinions on matters like this, especially in the Press?"

"I'm not a Civil Servant," MacGregor said.

"Then what are you?"

"I'm not a Civil Servant," he repeated.

"Did anybody tell you to write the letter?"

"No."

MacGregor was retreating now and he muttered that he could say nothing more.

"Will you resign?"

"That's my own affair," he said.

There was now half a roomful of reporters and photographers and MacGregor shouted that they would have to excuse him, it was late.

"Wait a minute," one said, "this is important Mr. MacGregor."

"You're exaggerating its importance," MacGregor said in retreat.

"No. We want to ask you about Russia Mr. MacGregor."

"I don't know anything about Russia," MacGregor said.

"Wouldn't you say Russia was acting aggressively in Iran?"

"No, I wouldn't say it."

"Wouldn't you say that Russia is using Azerbaijan to get oil concessions?"

"No."

"Wouldn't you say that Russia is beginning a campaign against the British Empire?"

"No. I wouldn't."

"Are you a Communist, MacGregor?"

"Good heavens, no."

"Are you opposed to Mr. Bevin's foreign policy?"

"I can't answer things like that."

"Are you pro-Russian?"

"Please," he said. "You are making a devil of a row."

He was at the foot of the stairs and a photographer stood a few steps up to take his picture as he raised his hand to avoid it. Others stood behind him and photographed him fleeing up the stairs, an unshaven and unkempt figure with no grace to his back and less to his feet. MacGregor closed the door on his panic and swore between dry lips. His hands were shaking as he closed the cold window and he started when someone knocked at his door.

"Yes?" he shouted.

"Mr. MacGregor!" Mrs. Berry called. "What about all those men down there? It's after midnight."

"Tell them to go away," he said.

"All of them? One says he knows you well, he's an American."

526

"Send them all away, Mrs. Berry."

"Aye," she said.

MacGregor spent a cold night anticipating the morning and worrying about the newspapers. Knowing nothing about newspapers, he did not know what to expect of them. He was no exception to the general rule of newspaper readers and he took them at their face value. If he had any suspicion of them at all it amounted to a cynical acceptance of any of their evils as being natural to newspapers. He had known of endless inaccuracies in newspaper stories, particularly since his service at the India Office, but after a moment of passing anger he had gone on reading them from day to day without seriously questioning their purpose or their accuracy in presenting the news. He had never questioned their approach to human affairs except by these occasional moments of anger. He might have known that a good newspaper was supposed to present a cold statement of events with a fair balance of opposing opinions, but MacGregor had seen time and time again a serious moment in history treated as an amusing incident or as a bright side-line to one man's embarrassment or another man's stupidity, and he had passed it over without having his clear mind insulted and outraged. If someone had pointed out to him the enormous rôle that newspapers played in shaping the world and instructing the people, he would have been politely disinterested. Newspapers were newspapers. You bought them for a penny and you read what Essex said and what unseen reporters said and you threw them in the Thames when they annoyed you. He did have enough discernment to prefer *The Times* of London to the other dailies, but his understanding stopped right there. He had forgotten, like so many newspaper readers, that the London papers without exception had hailed Munich and Chamberlain as Saviours of England. He had never liked Munich and could never forgive its general sanctification, yet he never thought back critically on the newspapers' part in making Munich possible. At the beginning of the war he had been sickened by the London newspapers' gay hanging of the washing on the Siegfried Line, but that too was forgotten. The misconceptions of France, Norway, and Crete were forgotten and so was the terrifying optimism of the early desert reporting. Now there was an attitude for Essex and Azerbaijan and Russia and the United Nations, all good examples for a reader's experience. Yet after so much experience, there was still an easy acceptance of the newspapers. No suspicion of their intention, their direction, their ownership, and their purpose in society. No questions at all, only a faint cynical acceptance which seemed to survive everything, except perhaps the rare personal experience which MacGregor was now suffering.

He went downstairs in the early morning and took everybody's papers out of the box in the hall, and he felt a degrading sickness when he looked at them. In the principal morning paper there were four pictures of MacGregor on the front page. One picture showed an unshaven MacGregor entering the parlour half-asleep. The other three were a serial of his flight upstairs. The caption beneath said that this was the Mr. MacGregor who had denied Russian interference in Iran. It cleverly described the ridiculous scene in Mrs. Berry's parlour, and under each picture was one of MacGregor's brief denials. Under the last picture, which showed his bare heels out of his worn slippers, the caption read *Good Heavens, No!* This was his answer to whether he was a Communist or not.

Most of the news on the page was taken up by a more important version under a large heading which said that the *British Government Denies Civil Servant's Accusations.* There was no direct denial in the long story, but unofficial-authoritative-quarters-in-London-diplomatic-circles were reported-to-have-denied accusations expressed in a letter in *The Times* to-day by Mr. I. A. MacGregor who was Lord Essex's personal assistant on his recent mission to Moscow and Iran. The same authoritative quarters claimed that MacGregor's opinions were unauthorized and contrary to known facts. About Russian interference in Iran, officials would make no comment, but well-informed-circles said to-day that MacGregor's facts were easily disproved, particularly in view of the expected documentation by Lord Essex which was reported to be sensational proof of Russia's misbehaviour in Iran. MacGregor's letter, however, had jeopardized Lord Essex's clear-cut position in the coming Security Council discussion on Iran, and the Foreign Office took a serious view of MacGregor's action in embarrassing the British delegate and weakening the British case. Lord Essex was not available for comment, but circles close to Lord Essex hinted that MacGregor had written the letter because of bitter disagreement with Lord Essex on another issue. These circles suggested that the letter was not a true expression of MacGregor's real opinions on Iran but was simply an attempt to personally embarrass Lord Essex. MacGregor was expected to face serious charges at the India Office; and the Foreign Office was reported to be looking into MacGregor's record. Further developments were expected this afternoon.

MacGregor replaced the newspapers and walked shakily upstairs. He paced about in his room for a few minutes and then began to shave in a basin of cold water because he would not go downstairs to the bathroom where there was a hot-water tap: he was afraid of finding more newspapermen. His hands were still shaking, and it was a strange face in his reflection, a surprised face to say the least. He looked better when he had shaved, but he had cut himself twice and he did not have a clean shirt and his trousers needed pressing and he was not hungry enough to eat breakfast. His room was a back room and he could not see if the men had returned or not. He dressed and put on his trench-coat and gloves and walked slowly down the stairs. The parlour was empty but when he opened the front door flash-bulbs went off again and half-a-dozen of the men were standing around in the small garden. Others were in cars at the gate and MacGregor would say nothing to them as they attacked him with questions again. They followed him until he dodged across the road in the traffic and lost them.

Then it was Sir Rowland Smith waiting for him at the India Office. The gentle old man was seated at his mahogany desk like a jurisconsult, and MacGregor was face to face with the hero of Jacobabad and the bloody suppressor of the fourteen Sikh riots.

"MacGregor," the old man said gently. "I suppose you know what this is about?"

"I think so," MacGregor said.

"You did write that letter?"

"Yes, sir."

Sir Rowland lifted his eyes a fraction. "Rather peculiar thing to do, MacGregor."

MacGregor crossed his legs and waited.

"I suppose you also know that you're in rather serious trouble?"

MacGregor folded his hands. "I came to resign."

"It's not as simple as that," Sir Rowland said carefully. "And I can assure you that your resignation will not be accepted. Would you like to say something about this letter?"

"There's very little I need say," MacGregor replied.

"You must have some explanation for it."

"The letter is its own explanation."

"That's not enough," the old man said, stroking his shining white moustache. "You don't appear to be the disgruntled type, MacGregor. You're not disgruntled are you?"

"No sir."

"Has it got something to do with your relationship with Lord Essex?"

"Not exactly."

"Did anyone tell you to write it then?"

"No one."

"It's hard to understand." Sir Rowland pushed back his chair and did an unusual thing for such a calm man, he paced a few steps behind his desk. "I'm going over to see the Under-secretary in a few moments, MacGregor, and for your sake I want to have some tangible explanation to give him. It won't save you, but it will help you if you have him on your side. Now what is it, MacGregor?"

"I can only repeat what I said in the letter," he said with less certainty.

"But why did you write to a newspaper about it? Why didn't you write to me?"

"I did," MacGregor said, "in my report."

"Well, wasn't that enough?"

"No sir."

"Why not?"

"It was pigeonholed."

"That's something we all suffer, and it's a poor excuse for doing what you did."

"It's not an excuse and it isn't the reason," MacGregor said.

"Then your motives escape me," Sir Rowland said. "I did want to settle that part of it before going any further, but you've said nothing at all that will satisfy me, MacGregor. Actually it's out of my hands now. That's why I can't dress you down and send you back to your desk. I would point out, young man, that it's serious enough when a public servant takes himself to the Press, but it's quite critical when he publicly contradicts and embarrasses a superior, attacks a British government policy, hazards a whole diplomatic mission, and suggests that his Government is involved in blackguardly dealing within another State. What possessed you to do such a thing? Are you a member of a political party?"

"No sir."

"Did the Russians influence you at all when you were in Moscow?"

"Is that a serious question?" MacGregor said indignantly.

"Well, I'm seeking some reason for this peculiar behaviour."

"The reason is my own conviction," MacGregor said. "Nothing more."

"Are you so sure of your conviction, MacGregor? So terribly sure?"

"I think so."

"Then there's really nothing I can do. If you are so misguided there is little use trying to assist you. You have been an excellent man, MacGregor, careful and diligent and occasionally brilliant. You were sent with Lord Essex because of your intimate knowledge of Iran, and because of your facility with the proper languages. Your future here could have been exceptionally promising if you had kept your head. I believe that Lord Essex had actually arranged for your transfer to his section of the Foreign Office, or to the Political Intelligence Department. This recommendation may balance things a little, but you will probably have to thrash it all out before the Service Board. Naturally you will have to refute the letter."

"That isn't possible," MacGregor said.

"Yes it is. It is absolutely essential," Sir Rowland said firmly. "Lord Essex's whole position in the Security Council is jeopardized. As for your own status, much will depend on the Under-secretary and on further developments. I suggest that you sit down and write an apology and an explanation, and address it to Lord Essex so that he can settle with the Press. You might keep yourself available also. That's all, Mac-Gregor."

MacGregor rose and bowed and left.

He had no intention of keeping himself "available." He knew how the army kept men available until their nerves gave way, enabling them to be properly corrected and broken for their misdemeanours. It was too effective a method for MacGregor not to respect it in his present state of mind. He sat down at his desk and without taking any notice of his curious neighbours, striped-pants young men, he addressed a letter to Sir Rowland Smith and wrote his resignation. He had given it to the old man's secretary when Rowland Smith himself came out and called him in again.

"You had better come with me," Sir Rowland said. "I've just been speaking with Lord Essex and he'd like to see you. I'm going across to see the Under-secretary, so you can walk with me. Heaven knows, Essex may have some kind of solution for you."

It was not difficult to walk in silence with Sir Rowland Smith. They did not go across the courtyard but went the long way through White-hall. MacGregor had nothing to say, and Sir Rowland Smith never said anything unless it was necessary. They stepped lively and the old man raised his hat to the Cenotaph and cleared his throat as they passed it. MacGregor could not help coughing politely although he had no hat to raise. There was nothing hostile between the two of them, but MacGregor understood that there was a mental pair of handcuffs bind-ing him to Sir Rowland and preventing his escape. This particularly applied when they were in the Foreign Office. MacGregor now felt the real weight of his sins, and his proper worry began. In the Foreign Office he could see that his letter to *The Times* had been a terrible mis-take, a tragic mistake.

He parted silently and rather reluctantly in the corridors with Sir Rowland, and went to Essex's high-ceilinged office overlooking St. James's Park. Essex was ready for him, leaning his neck against a mantelpiece and dictating to a short white-faced woman. Essex waved MacGregor to a hard chair and went on dictating a note on Security Council pro-cedure. When he had finished and the woman had gone, Essex walked across to the tall clear window and held his hands behind him.

"MacGregor," Essex said with angry sadness and still looking out the window. "I want you to sit down and address to me an apology for publishing that letter. In it, I want you to explain that your remarks were made entirely as a personal attack upon myself, rather than as an expression of your real and honest opinion of the situation in Iran."

MacGregor drew a defensive breath and said nothing.

531

"There's a pen and paper on my desk and you can take your time." Essex had not turned around at all. "If you feel you can't phrase it properly, there's an outline copy of a letter on my blotter which you can use, or which you can simply sign if you wish. Is that alright?" Essex swung around and MacGregor stood up.

"No," MacGregor said nervously. "It isn't alright."

"Oh? Can you think of something better?"

"No."

"Well then," Essex told him. "Go ahead."

MacGregor shook his head. "I couldn't do it," he said.

"Why not?"

"I didn't write those remarks as a personal attack upon you, and they happen to be my real opinion of the situation in Iran." It came with great difficulty.

"We shan't go into that," Essex said. "For your sake, we shan't go into that. It's letting you off lightly, and saving your neck."

"Isn't it too late for that?"

"Don't be cynical, MacGregor. There is only one way to save this situation and to prevent serious trouble for yourself: state that the remarks were made to embarrass me on a personal issue, for no other reason. That way you will save yourself from attacking and ruining a Government policy. That way, you can withdraw gracefully."

"There's nothing very graceful about denying my opinions and admitting them as a petty attack upon yourself."

"It's graceful enough, and believable," Essex said. "I'm trying to save you from serious trouble, MacGregor, and you're a fool not to see it."

"I can see it." MacGregor knew that he sounded annoyingly stubborn. "But I can't do anything about it."

"Then why did you do such a thing in the first place?" Essex paced about. "Why didn't you come to me first?"

"Would that have done any good?"

"I could have stopped you doing such a foolish thing."

"I don't think so," MacGregor said.

Essex did not like that. "Damn it man," he said with rising anger, "I know you are sentimental about Iran and I know that we disagree, but I hardly think you were justified in taking our difference to the Press, either politically or personally. Your letter was a personal affront to my mission and my person."

"Is it a personal affront to disagree with you?"

"Yes. If you do so publicly and literally."

"It was not personal," MacGregor insisted, "and I'm sorry if you take it that way."

532

"Don't be stubborn, MacGregor." Essex had never been quite so angry. "You will have to withdraw that statement one way or the other, so face it now and save yourself a great deal of trouble. I'm getting you out of this as well as I can."

"I don't think I want to get out of it," MacGregor told him. In dispute with Essex he could regain a little of the confidence which the newspapers had taken away from him.

"Good heavens!" Essex hit the desk as he passed it. "You have no alternative. You may be able to ignore the personal implications of your letter, but you can't ignore its political intentions MacGregor. You are trying to smash our case on Iran. With only a few days before the Security Council meeting you undermine my whole authority, you attempt to destroy all confidence in me. That cannot be ignored. You are a public servant and you are not permitted to express your opinions publicly without authority."

"I am no longer a public servant. I have resigned."

"Then you have resigned too late," Essex said. "No one will take your resignation now. They might, if you publicly withdraw that letter. Otherwise you can bet your bottom dollar that they'll have you before the Board. There I could not help you."

MacGregor had nothing to say. He was shaken.

"Can you see the insanity of your position?" Essex said. "Unless you can ease your way out of this cleverly you'll never get out at all."

MacGregor looked out the window and unconsciously imitated Essex's habit of holding his elbows. "I can't argue with you," MacGregor said, "and there is little use in trying to explain myself. I'm sorry for what has happened. I did not want to make an issue of my opinions, but I can't withdraw the letter without denying something I will not deny. That's all there is to it."

"Oh no!" said Essex. "There's a great deal more to it. Can't you see that you've put a thunderbolt in the red hands of our knavish opponents? Can't you see that your stupid letter can ruin our case in the Security Council? You have committed a dangerous folly. If you didn't do it deliberately then damn you for doing it foolishly."

MacGregor stuffed his hot hands into his trench-coat pockets.

Essex used another direction. "We're fighting for our existence, MacGregor, and we are damned near on our knees. Is this the time to express opinions to be misused against us by unscrupulous enemies who haven't your fine sense of moral honesty and political integrity? Do you want to see us bludgeoned to death in international councils? Do you want to have us harder-pressed in the East? Do you want us laughed at for our petty internal bickerings and irresponsible attitudes? Do you want us to

533

become ridiculous like the French? Everybody is at us, MacGregor, and every little mistake we make is another hand at our throat. We can make some mistakes but we can't afford to leave them uncorrected. We can have our opinions, but we dare not allow them the luxury of expression if they are to be used against us. We are not living in an ideal world, MacGregor, we are living in a world which is getting out of hand. We must discipline ourselves to sacrifice some of our better instincts for the sheer necessity of survival. We are the most civilized nation on earth. That is our natural advantage and purpose, and we've got to hang onto it with a terrible grip. If we don't then we can accept the certainty of Communism. In that you have anarchy and chaos and the destruction of civilization and all decent life. Never forget that, MacGregor. You may think that you have a right to your personal opinion, but always understand that you have an enemy waiting to use it against you. We can't help disagreeing among ourselves; that is our right. But in the face of this singular enemy we cannot allow our disagreements to show. Disagreement is the thin edge of the wedge for Communistic political disruption. To give them an inch is to give them a yard. To fight among ourselves is to strengthen their hand. We must sink all common differences before this menace. We've got to stop the Russians. If we don't we can say good-bye to the four freedoms of our existence, to the simple freedoms of any existence. That is the real issue you are facing, MacGregor, not simply personal disagreements and political honesty." Essex rapped sharply on the window to scare away the pigeons. "If you can only get that into your head you will find it easier to sacrifice your own opinions for the common good. It is so easy to be trapped by a narrow outlook Mac-Gregor, and so difficult to understand the wide and vital issues we face. I know you can understand. That is why you will withdraw that letter before it does more damage. You have started something you had no intention of starting. Now stop it before it gets out of hand."

MacGregor listened to Big Ben terminating the hour with a deliberate stroke. It was nicely clear and deep, and so little of the bell was wasted in complicated noise. It was absolutely straightforward. *Boom! Boom! Boom!* and it was ten o'clock. It was as simple as that.

"Sit down," Essex said.

MacGregor undid his coat and remained near the window.

"I'm having lunch with Kathy at 12:30," Essex said. "You might like to come along, if we clear this up in time."

MacGregor was not expected to reply, but he was saved from the embarrassed silence by Asquith, who strolled through the quiet door.

"Ah John," Essex said. "What did Horace say?"

"What do you think he'd say?" Asquith spread his hands. "He's talking to the Press."

"He's not making an official statement is he?"

"No. He is making one of those fancy denials from authoritative quarters."

"He's a fool," Essex said. "Denials will make trouble, and this whole thing can be settled right here if all those Cabinet people will keep quiet. I believe I've persuaded MacGregor to do what should be done."

"Is that so MacGregor?" Asquith asked.

"Not quite," said MacGregor.

"This will have to be decided quickly, MacGregor," Essex insisted. "Otherwise it is no good."

"Give him time Harold," Asquith said. "Give him time."

"There's damn little time to give him," Essex replied. "Why don't you take him with you, John? There's a Cabinet meeting this morning and I can't waste any more time here. Take the letter, MacGregor, and work on it as you will. John can give you a hand." Essex was showing them to the door. "I'll be back in about an hour."

Asquith and MacGregor were in the passage and on their way.

"That was getting damned uncomfortable," MacGregor said.

"Uncomfortable!" Asquith swept downstairs. "You are going to be taken by the ears and beaten to death if you're not careful, but I would have bashed your head in myself if you had signed that letter."

"Essex will bash in my head if I don't."

"It's a fair choice." Asquith threw a bundle of papers on his secretary's table in passing through to his office. "You deserve a beating from someone. I suppose they have all asked you why you wrote that letter to *The Times*. I am another fool and I would like to know myself."

"If you don't know," MacGregor said, "I can't explain."

"That's not a proper answer," Asquith said. "I deserve better."

"I can't explain it," MacGregor repeated. "I had to do it."

"I know that. I know you had to get it off your chest, but why do it that way? Don't you see that you have committed the big sin and broken the big law? There are a thousand rules and regulations for getting at you now. Didn't I tell you that it wasn't enough to simply cry your opinion? It's not nearly enough. To do that and be broken by it is madness. Hang it MacGregor, I said you'd have to be clever about it."

"There was no other way to do it," MacGregor argued.

"Bah!" Asquith kicked the waste-paper basket. "Do you expect to compete with Essex by writing letters to *The Times*?"

"No, but it's a beginning."

"A wretched beginning."

"How long did you think I could sit and be still?" MacGregor exclaimed with a red face. "There was no time for being clever, and I haven't the mind nor the patience to be devilish."

535

"You could be careful," Asquith said, "and not write letters to *The Times*."

"I thought you would understand that."

"I do," Asquith said with closed teeth. "But if I understand something, MacGregor, you can be sure it's dangerous. I sympathize with you, but I can't let you off. I know your situation exactly and I know deeply how you feel and why you revolt. It's because I know it that I want to see you survive it. It's not as easy as you imagine."

"I know it isn't easy."

"Then don't behave with such abandon," Asquith shouted.

"There's no use arguing about it," MacGregor said. "We are complicating an absolutely simple issue."

"Nonsense. We are trying to save your neck."

"I can't go back on what I wrote."

"You may be forced to." Asquith pushed up the ends of his moustache. "Don't you realize that all Kingdom Come is at your heels? You have upset the Persian applecart, my boy, clumsily perhaps but dangerously. This entire building is trying to estimate just how much damage you have done, how much advantage you have given our diplomatic opponents, how much discredit you have done Essex who had such a clear field before him in the Security Council. You've got Harold blue in the face. You've done enough damage already to risk his appointment to the U.N. You've not only threatened all his work but you've put a firecracker under our nice little plot in the Security Council. Harold is rushing over now to find out how much he has been damaged, and to see if the whole show has been ruined. He's scared stiff that you'll pick it up from here and say a lot more. That would really clinch it. You haven't said anything more have you?"

"No."

"Then don't. You're not going to get off lightly as it is. There's going to be more pressure put on you than any one man can survive. Retraction or else! Now for God's sake keep out of the way of it."

"I can't," MacGregor said bitterly.

"You must. Just get out of here," Asquith said. "Go home, go anywhere, but keep away from here if you don't want to swallow your own soul. Don't let them get at you. Don't talk to anyone and don't go near your office. Go home and I'll get in touch with you to-night or to-morrow and let you know what's happening."

"What about Essex?"

"I'll look after Harold."

"I don't like avoiding him," MacGregor said.

"You're not avoiding anything," Asquith said forcefully. "Don't be heroic when you are dealing with cunning men. That is what they expect

536

of an honest man, and they count on it to wreck him. For God's sake don't be heroic."

"Leave that out of it," MacGregor said. "I don't feel heroic. I'm worried and I'm slightly sick and I'm not sure that I can put up with much more of this."

"Then it might be a good idea to go and hide out with Kathy for a few days. She's living with her Uncle Paul and nobody would find you there."

"No," MacGregor said.

"Oh, forget your little battles," Asquith told him. "She'll be pleased to see you."

"It's too late for that."

"You are worse than she is." Asquith complained. "You both need tempering down. When you both admit it you'll be better off."

"I'll be at home," MacGregor said as Asquith held open the door.

"I'll tell Kathy!"

"Tell her what you like," MacGregor replied. Only his lost humour could have made him so impolite, and he was sorry a moment later, but Asquith had closed the door. There was too much in it for MacGregor now. Even Katherine had been injected into his predicament. He was doubtful, a little scared, and uncertain of his own intelligence. He did not want to go home, and he went into the first cinema and watched Noel Coward sentimentalizing on some supposedly happy breed of Englishman. He left it because it was poor substitute for his own real world.

Chapter 43

WITHOUT any letter of retraction from MacGregor, Essex wasted no time. By evening he had broken his silence and issued a statement to the Press, timed nicely so that most night editors would throw out their front pages and place Essex as the principal and rather sensational news of the morning. It was a short statement, a contemptuous denial of MacGregor, a repeated suggestion that MacGregor's attack was unwarranted and personal and not a reflection of MacGregor's true political opinions; in fact MacGregor was a geologist and was politically inexpert and inaccurate, and therefore any statement he could make was suspect. To have done what MacGregor had done was hardly the act of a loyal and reliable subject, and his opinions were baseless and unworthy of a gentleman and an Englishman. The integrity of Iran and the struggle for Kurdish independence had become a sacred trust for the Western Democracies and only the enemies of Democracy would think of making political capital out of MacGregor's erratic and highly personal opinions.

Though MacGregor's letter still stood factually unanswered, Essex's statement was the word that turned it into a national scandal. Immediately and mysteriously one of Sir Francis Drake's Moscow reports on MacGregor was made public. It spoke of his recalcitrance and his disobedience and his refusal to obey instructions, and it summarized MacGregor as a man who was hardly fitted for the tasks entrusted him. Also, more officials denied his statement. Yet more newspapers demanded better satisfaction than denials. The Government should act quickly. Wasn't a whole British policy at stake in this argument? At least one man said he could answer his charges. An Iranian official accused MacGregor of being a Communist in the pay of the Russians; the Iranian Government had all the facts to prove this. From America there was more objective comment by the State Department stating that MacGregor's opinions would not change the American understanding of the situation in Iran. Their own information was contrary to that of MacGregor's and they suggested that anyone who took a minor and disgruntled official seriously was hardly worthy of serious international consideration. The American delegates to the United Nations would never consent to MacGregor's opinions being given serious consideration in that world organization. Moscow radio had read MacGregor's letter each night since its appearance, and the record of his father and his own existence in Iran were offered as proof of his reliability and his accuracy. The BBC decided to have a disinterested observer discuss the question of MacGregor's letter, and they chose Al Hamber the well-known American correspondent of the well-known New York newspaper. Hamber was American and sure and sensible, and he could personally substantiate Lord Essex's attitude and comment, although it was not really a question of one man against another. Hamber said it was a question of the whole integrity of a case which was about to be settled in the international tribunal of the United Nations, the case of Russian interference in Iran. Nothing should stop this case going through as planned, and nothing should prevent Lord Essex from leading the British delegation to the Security Council. Could one man, unknown, dissatisfied, inexpert, a geologist, a clerk, a man who obviously wanted martyrdom, could this one man throw doubt on the rôle and reliability of the British Government and the United Nations? Could this one man be taken so seriously? It was a farce to make such a fuss of a man's opinions when they were not worth it. A farce which could only happen in a democracy where there was free Press and free channels of expression for every man, honest fools included . . . A contrast to those dictatorships which were threatening their small neighbours but who were about to face trial in the United Nations for it. And they must face trial and condemnation. MacGregor's tiny little opinions must not prevent the British case from going through.

This "free Press and free expression" was a new and American element in the scandal and MacGregor suddenly became the symbol of Democracy in the American newspapers, of a democracy which gave free speech even to its opponents. But it was made quite clear that this symbol of free expression ought to shut his mouth or have it shut for him. In England, however, MacGregor's symbolism of Democracy was a little more restrained, but in view of the coming meeting of the Security Council, in view of the serious doubts thrown upon the British delegate Lord Essex, satisfaction was still sought from the Government on MacGregor's letter. If the Government did not do something to squash finally this MacGregor letter, then Britain's name and Lord Essex's name would be mud in international affairs, unreliable mud.

The scandal quickly reached its little pinnacle of effect, but official satisfaction was a slow business, and MacGregor stayed in his room and waited desperately for official satisfaction, because his own situation would be finally decided by it. He did not know how officialdom would satisfy and end the scandal. He had not been called before a Board, a commission, the Under-secretary, or even further by Sir Rowland Smith. He himself had done all that he could to finalize it. He had cleared his desk at the India Office and he had stayed away and not moved outside his room. Everything seemed to be awaiting a common official solution, and MacGregor had reached breaking point when Asquith came to get him. It was the evening of the second day of it and MacGregor was no longer a robust hatless man. He was like any other pale-faced Englishman.

"Some of those newspaper johnnies were still waiting for you downstairs," Asquith told him. "I told them that you had gone to your home in Kent. It is Kent, isn't it?"

"Yes."

"They'll be back again," Asquith said and turned on the light.

"Haven't they had enough!" MacGregor cried.

"They're enjoying themselves."

"Miserable men," MacGregor said.

"Don't blame those fellers," Asquith told him calmly. "They're doing what they are supposed to be doing."

"I know it," MacGregor said, "and it's pretty low."

"We won't go into that now. Get some of your things together and come along."

"Where to?" MacGregor had put on his tie and his shoes.

"You can spend a few days with us."

539

"There is little use dragging you further into this," MacGregor argued.

"You're not dragging me into anything."

"Of course I am," MacGregor said. "It will make trouble for you."

"Ah. Come along. Come along."

"What about Jane?"

"She sent me to get you."

"What about you?" MacGregor asked.

"I told Jane to send me," Asquith said. "God knows I don't want to be slung right between you and Harold, but I'm damned if I can see you doing what I should be doing and have you torn to pieces in the process. I'm doing this for myself. Look at it that way."

MacGregor grasped at it without any further argument. He knew it was now a risk for Asquith to involve himself, but he needed Asquith. He packed a bag with some difficulty because he had few clean clothes. He had a new shirt that he had been saving, and two pairs of badly holed but clean socks. Asquith did not watch him, he was looking at Professor Browne's book on the Persian Constitutionalists, and when MacGregor was ready Asquith announced that he would borrow it.

"It belonged to my father," MacGregor told him.

"So I see."

Mrs. Berry met them aggressively on the way down. "Why didn't you tell me you were going out?" she said to MacGregor. "I just boiled your egg for supper — this month's ration. Are you going away?"

"For a few days."

"Do you want to take your egg?"

"No thank you," he said.

Despite Asquith's persuasion, one of the newspapermen had remained and he faced MacGregor at the door and asked him if he would expand exclusively for his newspaper on his letter to *The Times*. They would publish anything he would like to write, and it would also be syndicated in America.

"No," MacGregor said.

"Where are you going?" the newspaperman asked him.

"To Kent," MacGregor said.

The man followed MacGregor, but Asquith slammed the door of his Humber and roared the engine and shouted "Sorry old chap" and drove MacGregor home.

Asquith lived on Sloane Street in a red brick house. It was a famous house built by his grandfather, General Lord Cachelot, after his successful Indian campaign with Napier in 1851. It was just as the General had left it, and MacGregor benefited by the Victorian serenity. He was given the room upstairs which Asquith had inhabited as a boy, and Jane Asquith said it was small but warm and told him that dinner was already waiting. She gave him a hot dinner and MacGregor said nothing about his predicament until they had moved into the library. MacGregor then complained sullenly that he didn't understand the attack on him.

"Nobody makes any reasonable reply to the letter," he said. "They accuse or they deny or they attack, but the whole thing is so elusive. What are they so desperate about me for?"

"Time is getting short," Asquith replied, tasting good brandy with his irritable lips. "In a few days the Security Council meets and the Iranian complaint against the Russians comes up." He sniffed the brandy in a long breath. "We lead the attack and we haven't settled you yet. We must polish you off if we want to crack the Russians in council."

"Why me?"

"Here!" Asquith interrupted. "This is pre-war brandy."

"No thanks," MacGregor said impatiently.

"Go on. You are going to need it."

MacGregor drank unappreciatively and went on. "They don't have to settle me any further. What are they afraid of? They've finished me already."

"You and your opinions have to be thoroughly discredited and even dishonoured, if Harold is to have his effect in the Security Council. He has to be absolutely acceptable, unquestioned, authoritative, final, and nicely near perfect. Like that, he can deal the Russians a staggering blow. So long as you and your opinions can be taken seriously, Harold's position isn't worth a damn."

"Has someone explained that to the newspapers? Have they been instructed in New York as well?"

"Newspapers don't have to be instructed. They only have to know that you gave the Russians the benefit of the doubt. The rest is inspiration and instinct."

"I didn't write that letter to save the Russians."

"That is perhaps what makes it so dangerous." Asquith drank another brandy. Jane Asquith gave him coffee and did not complain about that second brandy. "Your letter was the sticky expression of an honest man, MacGregor, and I'm wondering if you were so stupid in writing it after all. Actually it was Kathy who was wondering this morning if it wasn't a good thing. That pellucid honesty of yours is easy to ridicule, but so hard to discredit."

"Honesty means nothing in this."

"It doesn't exactly settle it, and honesty is certainly not enough," Asquith agreed. "Weren't we trying to tell you so, time and time again? But it means something. It always means something."

"It may mean something to you and me, but it means nothing to a collection of newspapers and diplomats. They've been rending it like mad dogs since Essex started making statements."

"Essex had to act quickly and drastically," Asquith said. "Don't get mad with him. He had to turn the tables on you to save himself."

"He did it thoroughly."

"Don't imagine it's over yet. You have been made into something of a fool and a mountebank, but the loud voices will eventually insist on your own retraction. Essex was looking for you yesterday and again to-day, but I told him you had gone off to the country and couldn't be found. I'll tell him where you are when everyone has calmed down. Better for both of you that way. Better for you anyway. Better for me too. It's a queer tangle." Asquith rubbed one finger around his lower lip. "Can you see your way out of it?" he said.

"No I can't," MacGregor said. "Can you?"

Asquith shook his head. "You seem to be thoroughly hemmed in," he said.

Asquith's saying so made MacGregor realize his desperate position. Now another and more drastic decision was being forced on him, and the pressure was destroying him. He must face a compromise which he could not avoid, however much he detested it. This was his own worry and he could not take it any further with Asquith.

Asquith had to go out anyway, and MacGregor was left with Jane, seated silently before a gas fire in the living room. He spoke to Jane of other things, of the iron tracery in the Victoria and Albert Museum, of which she knew something. She had a book with a chapter about it. She sat in a large leather chair writing letters while MacGregor read the detailed analysis of the ironwork and understood little of it. He sat across from Jane, nursing a large grey cat which had found Mac-Gregor's legs instead of Asquith's. Into this, Katherine arrived rubbing her hands and arms. "I came here to get warm," she said. "That old barn of Uncle Paul's was not built for fuel shortages."

Jane Asquith put away her letters. "Why don't you live with your mother, Kathy?"

"She fills the house with those incredible people. She's got some Polish countess there now. All the petty nobility of Europe seem to have known her somewhere or other. Why don't all those Poles go back home and get what they deserve?"

MacGregor had given her his chair and he was now seated between the two of them, and Katherine glanced sideways at him and said, "Hullo."

"Hullo," he said.

Katherine went on talking to Jane Asquith, sighing the lack of the physical comforts they had enjoyed in the Moscow Embassy, and mentioning by the way that Sir Francis Drake had been shifted back to London and that Clark-Kerr had finished with Moscow and was going straight on to Indonesia to see what he could make of the shambles there, although it was always hopeless trying to work with those stupid Dutch.

"Are you going back to work, Kathy?" Jane asked her.

"I've been asked to go to Washington," Katherine said. "Odd, isn't it?"

"I don't think you would like it," Jane Asquith said. "If you don't like your mother's Poles I'm sure you wouldn't like Washington. It's a nice place, but these days it's full of that same type of people, and there is always that terrible American assumption hanging over you that we are there to beg, accusing us at the same time of being there to run their affairs. It's very discomforting and a little degrading."

"I can put up with that, and anyway I need some new clothes."

"That's hardly reason for going there," Jane Asquith replied. "People are always running away to America for something or other. That's not like you."

"Nothing is like me, Jane dear," Katherine said good-naturedly, "and I might as well be in America as here or anywhere else. Don't you think so, Mr. MacGregor?"

He nodded. "You might as well be in America," he agreed dispassionately.

Katherine looked disappointed with him, but she took the cat from him and threw back her lazy head and relaxed as he had not seen her relax for some time. "It's too nice here to argue with you," she said to him with her gentle eyes on the ceiling. "I'm rather disgusted with you for being so naïve, and for expecting angry men to forgive you your opinions. Only MacGregor would think of contradicting a whole world and expect to survive it. It would have been so much easier if you had been nice to Jack Bickford. He could have said all you had to say and more, and without the terrible identification of letter writing. Now I suppose you expect it to blow over?"

Katherine was half-pleasantly and half-provokingly putting herself into his affairs again, almost asking to be taken in. However much he needed her, he refused her out of contradiction and retaliation and anger. She had turned her head to look at him and he flushed with its intimacy. "I'll survive it," he told her. It implied that he would survive it with her or without her.

"Sorry," she said. "I shall say no more."

MacGregor immediately regretted his revenge and his stupidity, and he excused himself and went upstairs to sleep, to fail to sleep, to consider himself beaten before he had begun, to stir himself into a restless pacing which exaggerated his confusion; and finally to exhaust himself with an honest man's fear of dishonesty. He had decided that to-morrow he would see Professor White, one of the Government geologists at English-Persian. With a little luck he could get away from this whole affair; back to Iran.

Chapter 44

D<small>R.</small> W<small>HITE</small> was his former professor at London University and later one of his direct superiors in the English-Persian laboratories at Fields. MacGregor respected White as a scientist, and as a responsible human being, who would tell him his situation as an unspecific micro-paleontologist hoping to return to Iran. The Professor came out of his office to get MacGregor, having been told that the young man was waiting to see him. He greeted MacGregor with a curious and rather amused smile, and he apologized when MacGregor had to move a dozen books to sit on a chair. Professor White's office was not appropriate to its big-business surroundings of international oil; it was more of a University study, a very untidy study. Books and papers were stacked on the four or five small tables; maps and charts were on the walls and stacked on the floor; and there were rock and soil samples on the window sills, on the tables, desks, ledges, and in a neat glass case in a corner. With all its objects, it still had the rather bare and museum-like appearance of the geologist's work-room, and MacGregor sniffed it and tasted it and knew that he had finally come home.

"I see that you have become a principal figure in our latest political scandal," Professor White said. "That's not at all like you, MacGregor."

"I suppose not," MacGregor said ruefully. "But I didn't exactly plan it that way."

"No?" the Professor said. He seemed to be suggesting that political scandals were commonplace things and that MacGregor was usually better able to avoid them. "Silly business," he said about it and that was all. "How are you, MacGregor?"

"Very well, Professor. And you?"

"I am really rather short-tempered these days. I don't like aeroplanes, and suddenly all the effort on earth has become so urgent that we are all supposed to zip from one place to the other like demons. In a week I fly to Iran and in another week I come back, and then the week after that I go to Burma or Java or some other unearthly place. I am a slow-thinking man, MacGregor, and it isn't good for me. It is making me short-tempered, and I hate short-tempered people."

544

"You were always short-tempered," MacGregor said. "Don't let it worry you."

"It doesn't worry me, it annoys me," the Professor told him. "And what are you up to, MacGregor? Can't those India Office people let you go yet?"

"I'm not sure," MacGregor said. "Actually I wanted to ask you about the situation in Iran. If I can get out of this mess I think I would like to go back."

"As far as I'm concerned you can always come back to English-Persian, Ivre." Professor White was serious and he looked hard at MacGregor. "I'm not the head geologist, but as I say, I'm going out to Iran within a week, and if you can settle your affairs by then, you can come with me. We run our own cursed plane service now."

MacGregor hesitated. "I didn't exactly want to go back to English-Persian," he said. "That's all part of this thing to me."

Professor White nodded sympathetically. He had a sympathetic face, small, with large bulging eyes and calm erect ears. He looked toothless but his speech showed short square teeth, which were well divided. He was a short square man and he spoke rather slowly for a small man. "Nevertheless," he said, "if you want to come back it is quite easily arranged."

"I was wondering if anyone was doing research work in the north," MacGregor said. "Field work or laboratory work—it doesn't matter which. I heard of a Russian up there investigating the Khush plateau, and I thought you might know if any of the universities or foundations were sending out teams. I'd like to go back to the north if possible."

"I don't know of anybody. I'll look around and inquire, but times are difficult for the sort of work you want to do, MacGregor. Most field work is prospecting and heavy-handed petrology these days, but there is plenty of interesting work at Fields for a good man. You can work with me while I'm there, and I'll leave you with Sutton; you might even be able to spread out a little on your own. We are really desperate for men like you."

"When would you need to know definitely?" MacGregor asked him.

"By next Sunday."

"When would you be leaving?"

"On the Monday."

Monday was now reported to be the day on which the Security Council would discuss Azerbaijan.

"Will that give you time?" Professor White asked him.

"Yes. It's simply a matter of making up my mind whether I want to go back to English-Persian or not."

"Don't let this newspaper nonsense influence you." The Professor tapped a newspaper on his desk. "Newspaper tricks are the work of unintelligent men. They do it to alleviate their own ignorance."

"I think it's more than that this time," MacGregor said.

"Oh there are probably all sorts of plots going on, but you keep out of them. It's not a very good idea to get mixed up in politics," he said, "particularly if you don't know anything about them. Scientists are too imprudent for politics, MacGregor, too honest and too reasonable. But never mind; once bitten twice shy."

"I don't know much about politics," MacGregor said with more direction than he had first intended, "but I believe I know as much as the newspapers. As for Iran, they know nothing at all about what is happening there. You know what's going on there as well as I do, Professor."

"Perhaps not as well as you do," Professor White said carefully. "But I know enough."

"Don't you think it needs a little general explaining?"

"Not by you and me, MacGregor." Professor White hesitated a moment but went on. "There must be people better qualified than we are to throw light on these political affairs."

"Perhaps. But they don't seem to be doing it."

"True. But you ought to keep out of it, MacGregor. You are not really a man for politics. You are a young scientist, a very promising fellow if you have half a chance."

"I wonder about that," MacGregor said. "There doesn't seem to be much of the scientist left in me."

"I suppose you are a little behind, but aren't we all in view of the war. You get back to your work. Untangle yourself from these terrible disputes. This is the sort of thing that we are all being trapped into these days, political disputes and economic rivalries. It's dangerous encroachment on our work and we should resist it."

"How?"

"By ignoring petty politics," the Professor said.

"This isn't petty politics," MacGregor was still going farther than he had intended, but the thing itself demanded argument and discussion and he could not avoid it. "How can a man be still if he sees such a great wrong being instigated?"

"It's difficult, but it's necessary," Professor White insisted. "Science must go on unhindered, and if we bring politics into our work we will cease to be scientists."

"Will we cease being human?" MacGregor demanded with the rudeness of justifying himself. "Should we hand over our affairs to men we despise?"

"I suppose that is unanswerable." Professor White was as deep into

546

it now as MacGregor. "But when we dabble in politics we suffer what you are suffering now, and it isn't worth it. Is it?"

"I don't know," MacGregor said morosely.

"Then why destroy yourself?"

"I don't believe a man has much choice any more," MacGregor said. "There seems to be some kind of a battle going on for any existence, science and all."

"You may be right," the Professor said. "We are certainly facing a situation of terrible choice. Only yesterday the physicist chaps back from America brought in a petition to sign against control and secrecy of information and research in nuclear physics. Once they start on this secrecy business there is no telling where it will end. It was bad enough when we were working at Tennessee. We cannot have those ignorant politicians telling us what we must do."

"They are already telling us what we must do," MacGregor argued. "The military control so much research that the physicists are becoming straight-out weapon-makers and nothing else."

"It's not the physicists' fault, Ivre . . ."

"Then why don't they stop working for the military? Now they are talking about radio-active dust clouds and the biologists are producing concentrates of bacteria for wholesale disease-making. What's the matter with them? Have the generals got them so scared that they meekly do as they are told?"

"Weapons are part of life," the Professor commented sadly, "and since the politicians refuse to be peaceful, at least they ask for weapons and give us a chance we would not otherwise have of making enormous strides in costly research."

"Perhaps. But don't we care how the products of our research are used?"

"You are looking for logic where there isn't any," the Professor said. "It isn't science which shapes the world, young man."

"No sir, but we are part of it."

"Really a very small part of it. The ultimate decision on human affairs lies outside science. We may be part of it, but if you are looking for the deciding factor in the shape of existence then I don't know where you'll find it."

"I don't know either," MacGregor admitted with grim largesse, "but I'm beginning to think that the real decision of existence is in all these particles like Azerbaijan which eventually make up the whole."

The Professor smiled. "And where does science fit in?"

MacGregor was struggling to work this out as he went along, and he did not notice the Professor's brief smile. "I suppose it fits in everywhere. It's just as much a part of this Azerbaijanian dispute as it is of everything else. That protest by the nuclear physicists is part of it somehow."

"And your dislike for going back to English-Persian? Is that part of it?"

"In a way, yes. Incidentally — did you sign that protest?"

"Certainly I signed it. But I can't see that it is quite the same as your problem."

"I think it is," MacGregor said. "Yet the way things are now we are beaten before we begin."

"Are we?" Professor White shook his head and watched MacGregor's quiet face becoming bitter with this unusual confusion. It was something the Professor did not like to see happening to a sensible man like MacGregor. "I can see that you are set on this political question," he said. "Perhaps you are ahead of me. I hope you are, because we must have clear young minds fighting for the existence of science. But do not destroy yourself, Ivre. Do not forget that you are a good scientist, an excellent man in your own field. You should get back to your own work. Have the India Office finished with you yet? What's the matter with them?"

"I have resigned," MacGregor said, "but they won't accept it until they settle this fantastic situation."

"Get it over and done with Ivre and come along with me to Iran. I insist. If you don't, it will soon be too late for you, and I think you know it."

MacGregor nodded and stood up.

"I'll expect you on the Monday," Professor White said. "I'll let you know where to appear and all the details. Where can I get in touch with you?"

MacGregor gave him Asquith's phone number and also Mrs. Berry's.

"If you don't want to stay with us at Fields that's quite alright," the Professor told him as they shook hands. "You'll probably be able to find something out there that you want to do."

MacGregor said "Yes" to that, and took it as an argument to finally convince himself. He had known that Professor White would be as generous and as understanding as any man. MacGregor thanked him sufficiently and left. All he had to do now was to get himself out of the India Office and go with Professor White to Iran. That meant having his resignation accepted. That meant going to Essex.

MacGregor could not voluntarily go to Essex, and there was no use trying to do so. He could go to his Charing Cross bank and tell his friend the Chief Clerk that he might be leaving; he could telephone his mother and assure her that he was alright and that he would be down to see her in a day or two to explain everything; he could even make a feint at packing his books and buying a large suitcase to hold his excess possessions; but he could not go to Essex, not until another day of accusation and sensation had caught him.

Two men had discovered him at Asquith's and they had spent the afternoon bothering Jane who had treated them politely and nicely but without enough discouragement; she was incapable of being ruthless with anyone. Asquith's name was now brought into it, and the nation learned that its biggest sinner, MacGregor, was hiding out in the house of the Honourable John Anthony Ahab Asquith, who would assist Lord Essex at the Security Council discussion on Azerbaijan. It was too much for MacGregor, and he knew that it was nearly over for him. By morning his sin had become more terrible and the crisis worse. From newspapers and former Cabinet Ministers, from the Church and the Lords, from the great men and the small, from all people with the right kind of voice, there came a demand that the Government take a stand, that MacGregor be dealt with quickly and finally. They all ordered the Government to treat the situation as a crisis in British diplomacy, which in fact it was. Only a few days remained to the Security Council meeting and denials and statements were not enough; they were not nearly enough to meet this critical situation.

And now Asquith had been dragged into it.

If this didn't make up MacGregor's mind, then Essex decided the matter for him. Essex sent his own car and one of his newer, brighter, young men. MacGregor knew that he could avoid it no longer. It had to stop, and only a settlement between himself and Essex could finish it, because ironically it was as bad for Essex as it was for MacGregor. The outspoken critics of the Government's foreign policy, the back-benchers, the Left Wing columnists, the liberal newspapers, the Communists, and some of the wary men of the objective world were all suggesting that Essex's appointment to the Security Council be withdrawn in view of the scandal and the doubt about his accuracy in interpreting the situation in Azerbaijan. This was not new, but it was a stronger voice than before. It was the contradiction that had inevitably resulted from the increasing accusation against MacGregor. As one opinion gained momentum so did the other, and now it had to be settled. MacGregor went to see Essex.

"You've done John Asquith a terrible disservice, MacGregor, dragging him into this." Essex was wearing half-moon glasses. He wasted no time in conversational balance. "You knew that he was quixotic enough to fight your battles for you. Now he will be in trouble."

"Asquith was not fighting my battles," MacGregor said. "He was decent enough to give me a chance to escape the newspapers and to see a little sense in this affair."

549

"Do you see any sense in it?"

"No," MacGregor said. "It's gone too far."

"You brought it upon yourself," Essex told him, "and I can't sympathize with you. By now you undoubtedly realize what a mistake you have made, and what a damn fool you have been. Are you ready to call in that letter and apologize?"

"Is that the only way to settle this and end it?"

"Yes," Essex said. "What else did you expect?"

"I don't know," MacGregor said. "All I want to do is resign and get out of this; but it's still too much to expect me to betray myself like that."

"I don't know why I do this for you, MacGregor, but I'll put it clearly to you. If you retract that letter quickly I can save your skin. I believe I might even be able to save your job. Retract it now and I can look after you."

"I don't see why that letter is so important . . ."

"It's the root of the whole thing, MacGregor, and it must be withdrawn. As it is, I'm having the devil's own time restraining the Service Security people from throwing the book at you. I've waited patiently, MacGregor, but I won't wait much longer."

MacGregor needed this tangible attack to begin resistance. The unanswerable and intangible war upon him through the newspapers and the radio, plus the large voices, had put MacGregor in the dark and had given him little chance to directly fight back. Faced by Essex, MacGregor had to fight back, whatever he had originally intended doing. He could finally come to grips with a real opponent. "We've been over that," MacGregor said. "I came here because I thought we might be able to work out something that could settle it decently. It's no use talking about that letter any more. The more I hear about it the more I resist the idea of taking it back."

Essex took off his glasses and re-estimated his man. "If you can't understand one proposition," he said, "let me try another. I'm trying to settle this decently for you, but so long as you insist on maintaining your stubborn attitude it's hopeless. One last chance, MacGregor. You want to resign and get out. You want it clear-cut and easy. Alright, I'll see that your resignation is accepted without reservation if you withdraw that letter. It's got to be that letter."

It was finally simple: his complete freedom for the ignominious withdrawal of his opinions. MacGregor was being held for political ransom and he was surprised at the crudity of it, however much he had expected it. He said so to Essex. "I didn't think you would hold me for political ransom. So nakedly, anyway."

Essex held the edge of his desk with white strong knuckles. "It will be a damned sight more naked if you don't make up your mind," he said.

"This is serious now, and there is no time for niceties. Naked you want it, naked you'll have it."

"No pretence and no shame," MacGregor said cynically.

"Neither." Essex was white. "I'll give you an idea how serious this is. Your letter has already been handed in by the Russians for discussion. They are even suggesting that you be called to give evidence before the Security Council. You see how deep you have taken yourself."

"I simply wrote that letter," MacGregor said. "Nothing more."

"There's a great deal more." Essex's temper flared again. "There is a portion of disloyalty in what you have done, MacGregor, and you cannot dismiss it so easily. You have used your position to suggest serious breaches of conduct by your own Government. Remember: You are not any old Tom, Dick or Harry giving his opinion. You're a man who was sent as a representative of the British Government on a confidential mission to assist me in carrying out a government policy. You are committing a seditious act to set yourself against the Government. That is taking advantage of your special position. You are entitled to your opinion, MacGregor, but your position forbids you to embarrass the Government with it. To use it as you have amounts to betrayal."

"Betrayal of what?"

"Don't shout!" Essex said. "I'm not accusing you. I am stating the position as it is in very hard fact. Indisputable fact."

"That is not the position at all," MacGregor said. "I have betrayed no confidence and no trust. I simply wrote a letter in which I stated the truth — for the Government or anybody else."

"A letter in which you accuse the Government . . ."

"Of course I accuse. If the Government uses falsehood and the blind-eye to conduct its affairs, then shouldn't I accuse! If I am betraying a trust to reveal it, then I am still right and you cannot make me wrong."

"You're a wretched moralist," Essex shouted him down, "and this is a technical more than a moral question. Technically you can be accused of every sin under the political sun and it's going to happen unless you can see a little daylight through that moral fog of yours. Perhaps betrayal is a harsh word, MacGregor, but you've got to face it."

"I have betrayed nothing. Nothing!"

"Then call it disloyalty."

"No."

"Then call it what you damn well please, but realize what I'm talking about. You could be responsible for the failure of all my work, MacGregor, but I hardly intend to let that happen. If you want to resign and get out then go ahead. You can do it if you withdraw that letter as I've asked. Otherwise, there are ways and means of settling this and I'll use them."

"I know you will," MacGregor said, "but I think you're wasting your time. You failed a long time ago — in Moscow and in Azerbaijan. There is no failure left and I'm certainly not responsible for your predicament."

"There is no predicament for me, MacGregor. Only a choice of methods. You are a fool. Don't you know that when you went into the India Office you signed your life away? For publishing that letter you are liable to prosecution under the Civil Service Act and even under the Secrets Act."

"What for?"

"For violation of trust, for sedition, and a dozen other charges."

"Is that supposed to be my final choice?" MacGregor's voice rose again.

"It is only my restraint that is protecting you at this moment," Essex cried. "If I let go, MacGregor, you'll get the whole lot."

MacGregor almost closed his eyes. "What do you expect me to say to that?"

"There is only one thing you can say."

"Then I'll say it." MacGregor stood up. "You can go to the devil! I could never retract that letter. You convince me that I am right, absolutely right. I have always been right!"

There was stillness between them until Essex flung his glasses on the desk.

"Do not blame me for what you are about to suffer," Essex said grimly. "Blame yourself. Blame your blundering attempt to interfere in a policy so vital that it represents our national existence."

"Your national existence is not mine," MacGregor said, "and if I blundered it is because I did not know what an important thing I had done. Now I am as desperate as you are, and there's no end to it yet. I can take this as far as you can."

"Any more public announcements from you, MacGregor, and by God the very worst will happen. You know what to expect."

"Yessir. I expect your damn'dest."

"Are you mad!"

MacGregor was leaving him.

"Come back MacGregor," Essex said. "Come back and behave like a normal sensible objective loyal British human being. Come back here or the consequences will be more than any man can survive. Come back or you will suffer calamity for your dishonour and your disloyalty."

MacGregor had closed the door without replying.

Chapter 45

H<small>E</small> NEEDED Asquith now, but above all needs he must keep Asquith out of it. Any more incrimination for Asquith would be disastrous, and MacGregor was already placing guilt and curse on himself for allowing Asquith to be even touched by MacGregor's own contamination. Asquith would have enough explaining to do already, in fact it would be almost impossible for Asquith to give good reason why MacGregor was hiding in the house of Lord Essex's principal assistant. Nothing more must touch Asquith. Yet MacGregor needed him more desperately than ever before, because MacGregor knew he must face Essex with more exposure on Azerbaijan. On that, he had decided. If his letter to *The Times* had been so effective, then a complete *exposé* would meet all of Essex's arguments before they were presented. He knew the consequences of what he was doing; but the consequences did not worry him yet. He was more concerned in deciding if he was justified in taking this irrevocable step. He needed Asquith to tell him if he was right or wrong. He also needed Asquith to instruct him on how to proceed.

He could not go down on the street and whistle for a newspaperman and pour out his revelation. Nor was Dr. Ross the right method. What MacGregor must say had to be properly said, widely said, seriously said, importantly said, effectively said, and he knew that the right circumstances for it were too much for him to handle. He did not trust himself to do it effectively, and this was too vital for any risk or any doubt or any failure. He needed Asquith, and he couldn't have Asquith. He needed Asquith or Katherine, and there was only Katherine.

If it required a mental struggle for him to go to Katherine he didn't know it, because he had made up his mind in an instant. Not all a man's active choices are subjective and this one decision was bigger for him than another. His natural reason gave him no alternative. He was still angry with her, unsure of her, resentful, and even bitter; but he could at least face her with it, and he knew that Katherine's choice would be as vital as his own. It was more than a choice between himself and Essex, and it gave him one more desperate reason for facing her.

He did not know where she lived. He remembered her saying that she was now staying with her Uncle Paul, but he didn't know who her Uncle Paul was. He had to find Jane Asquith and ask her. Jane was in an empty room sitting beneath a dim window. The room wasn't quite empty. It had a long Windsor table in it, old and chipped. Jane Asquith was seated on one end of it oiling the leather covers of a stack of old books. She knew what she was doing and she looked up at MacGregor and smiled without saying anything. MacGregor watched her for a moment but he was too impatient now to have any interest in it.

"Jane," he said. "Where would I find Katherine?"

She turned her head slightly to look at him. "I think she would be at her Uncle Paul's," she said. "It's just across in Belgravia."

"Who is her Uncle Paul?"

"Eastminster." She wiped a book clean. "The Earl of Eastminster. He's very old and I think he's been ill. Do you want to see Kathy?"

"Yes."

"Do you want me to telephone and find out if she's there?"

"No. No," he said. "I'll just go over there."

"She may be here for dinner to-night," Jane said. "I had only mentioned it to her casually but if you like I will insist. Then you can be sure of seeing her."

MacGregor shook his head. "As a matter of fact I shan't be here," he said. "I think I'll go back home to-night, Jane."

"Why do you want to go home?" She was surprised.

"I can't stay here for ever," he said.

"But there is no hurry, Ivre. You must not rush away like that."

"I think it would be better," he said.

"It surely isn't because the newspapers found you here!"

"No," he said. "That's done now. I can't say how sorry I am that you were brought into this. Now I suppose they'll be at John."

"Oh don't let that worry you," she said. "They'll put it down to his craziness. The newspapers are always expecting him to do something peculiar. Please forget it. He would be very hurt if you left now."

"The truth is," MacGregor said with an unhappy face, "it's about to get worse. I think I'm about to have a rather public argument with Essex, and this time it will be more serious."

"Is that why you want to see Kathy?"

"Yes."

"It's quite right that you go to Kathy," Jane said. "I don't know what she'll say to you, Ivre, but please be careful with her. She can make a terrible mistake the way she is now. I'll send John over when he comes home and he can help you arrange whatever you want to arrange."

MacGregor said, "Don't do that. He can't have anything to do with this. I insist, Jane. It's really for my own sake, believe me."

"I think you might be mistaken, Ivre. He is deeply concerned about what is happening, and he would like to know what you are doing." She put down the book and folded her quiet hands. "John sees a lot of himself in you. I think your decisions now are those which he would also like to be making, but he believes that it is too late to do anything himself. That is why he is absolutely determined to see that you have a fair chance to do the right thing. He has always felt that he made the wrong turning himself in his early life, and he is afraid you might be forced to make the same mistake because of all the pressure on you. He is really very unhappy, being caught between his friends, and you can imagine how he feels when he is trying to work with Harold and at the same time watch over you like a father. In many ways I have never seen him quite so unhappy."

"That's why I'm better away from here."

"No," she said. "He wants you here. Perhaps he feels that your decision will be his decision again, so you must not feel that you are hurting him by remaining."

"I don't want to hurt him in any way, Jane. I just don't want him to protect me at his own expense. I think he must keep clear of my trouble. He must! I will do nothing if he is going to make trouble for himself."

Jane Asquith nodded slowly. "Alright," she said.

"Where is Katherine's house?" MacGregor asked quickly to end it.

"It's the big Georgian house . . . the corner of Belgrave and William Square." Jane Asquith came down to the front door to see him out. "I will expect you to stay with us for a few days longer, Ivre."

"I can't," he said, "but I'll be back later on to-night."

He went out without his coat and walked through the soft London rain in the twilight, through Cadogan Gardens and up Chesham Place until he came to the large Georgian house that occupied a deep corner of Belgrave Square. It was iron-railed and gated, and its porticoed entrance was heavily pillared and large and handsome. It looked dark and miserably cold and empty, and MacGregor pushed the wet bars of the gate and felt a moment of bad depression as he pulled the door-bell and waited. He decided then that if Katherine was out he would not come back.

A soft grey-haired and smooth-faced woman opened the door and turned on the inside light. She opened the door wide and politely, and MacGregor did not know if she were part of the family or part of the household. He supposed that only the proper people would open the door and he guessed that she was the housekeeper. He felt wet and dirty as the woman looked at him, but he cleaned his feet on the mat and stepped in and asked for Katherine. "Is she in?" he asked.

"I'm not sure," the housekeeper said. "Is she expecting you?"

"No."

"Oh! Whom shall I say is here?"

"MacGregor," he said. "My name is MacGregor."

The housekeeper nodded and asked him to wait on a satin-covered settee which was placed in the centre of the rotunda-like entrance hall. She left him, and MacGregor looked at this enormous round beginning to the house. It was a perfect circle of high marble wall on which there were white pillars rising to a glass dome. This white enclosure was broken by a black staircase. It curved gracefully to the upper balustrades which were lined with red velvet, hiding the housekeeper's journey into the upper interior of the house. Apart from the staircase, there were doors and passages to break the marble cylinder. Large paintings hung on the wall, and a life-size figure of some ancient Greek athlete stood dejectedly and rather forgotten in the shadow of the rising staircase. It was all exposed by sensitive light from a large teardrop chandelier, and MacGregor was momentarily flattered that this whole chandelier was alight for his presence in this museum-like house. Its parquet floor and its marble walls and its cared-for importance reminded him of the Kremlin. He had sat down as a gesture, and now he stood again and smoothed out his coat and straightened his tie and his waistcoat and pulled the flaps of his pocket out and wiped the rain from his eyebrows, and walked to the paintings and the large vases on pedestals, and finally to the athlete. He was intent upon identifying the motion of the athlete, running, walking, or hurling, when Katherine stood behind him.

"That is Phidius," she said flatly, "one of the four Athenian runners who followed Pheidippides with the news of the victory at Marathon. My grandfather stole it from the mountain where it had been erected two thousand years ago to bring it here and put it under that staircase. Do you like it?" This could be one Katherine or the other.

"I came to see you," he said.

"Then you had better come upstairs where it's warm," she said. "Im not dressed for shivering down here." She wore a pink and gold quilted dressing-gown which reached to her ankles. It became an ordinary article of clothing by the careless and rather quick way she turned around to lead him upstairs. She had obviously been lying down and she rubbed under her eyes with the flat of her hand as they walked up the marble staircase and through the red hangings. They walked along a dark hall, and off it MacGregor was taken into a small room furnished in gilt. It was only half-divided from a large bedroom by a light blue wall which was broken by an arch. Katherine turned on two lamps and threw a book off a damask armchair. There was a low coal fire and Katherine put her slipper out to it.

"Please put some coal on the fire," she said to him.

MacGregor took a large lump out of the scuttle and dropped it in the grate over her outstretched ankle. He broke up the coal with a poker and then straightened up and stood beside her, wiping off his hands. He had absolute confidence in his decision to ask for her final attitude, but he could not do it easily or clearly. "I came to see you because you are the only other person beside John Asquith who can do what I want done," he said. "As a matter of fact you are the only person, because I cannot drag Asquith into any more trouble."

"Can you drag me into your trouble?" she said.

556

He did not fight with her reply because he could not blame her for it. He had started rather badly but he would not retreat. "You couldn't be dragged into anything, and you're not exactly in Asquith's situation," he said. "But it is time that you had to make up your mind."

"What am I expected to make up my mind about?"

"Heaven only knows," he said. "I have never understood the sudden divisions which change you overnight from one person into another."

"Then what do you understand about me?"

"That's up to you."

"Is that why you came here?"

"No," he said impatiently.

She waited as if she had taken a grip on herself to be silent and let him speak.

He knew it and he did speak. "This afternoon," he said, "Essex and I had a bit of a row, in fact it was rather critical and unpleasant."

She nodded. "I know," she said. "I had tea with him."

"He didn't waste much time."

"No," she said. "Neither have you."

"Then I don't need to explain what happened." He was glad of that much.

She shrugged. They were standing side by side with their backs to the dull fire which was just beginning to burst into flame with the new coal. The grey smoke was racing up the chimney and MacGregor put his toe in the coal to break the top and make a draft. "If you know what happened between us," he said, "then you probably know what I came to ask you."

She said nothing.

"What did he tell you?" MacGregor asked.

"Enough to know that you are both intent on destroying each other."

"That's not quite right," he said. "I'm hanged if I care about Essex one way or the other. I simply disagree with all that he is doing, and if I can I will stop it."

"Will you?" she said on the razor's edge. "How?"

"By giving your newspaper friends a detailed account of what is actually happening in Azerbaijan. I would like to tell them exactly why we went there and what we did there."

"Why that?"

"Because it is the only argument to Essex," he said. "That is why I need you. To do it properly is beyond me; but you know these newspapermen and you could arrange it so that I could talk to the right men in the right circumstances. It will have to be done quickly because the Security Council meets to-morrow or the next day and all that I should say must be well said by then."

"Don't you know what Harold will do to you if you go to the Press?"

"It's too late to go into that."

"No it isn't," she said. "I don't think he'll let anybody take action against you if you keep quiet and let the devil lie in hell."

"I don't want to talk about that," he said. "It will make no difference."

"It should make a difference," she said and stepped away from the blazing fire. "There is no use being impulsive and dragging everybody down in a terrible crash."

"I am not being impulsive or stupid," he said. "If you do not want to have any part of it then say so and I shall go."

"Do you expect me to be impetuous about it?"

"No, but for once you must be straightforward, one way or the other."

"There's nothing very straightforward in it." She had taken a brush from a lacquered table and she began to brush her hair. "Anything you do could be simply a personal and bitter retaliation against Harold."

"If you think so, then I can't convince you otherwise."

"How do you know that talking this out all over the place will be effective? Don't you think Harold can cope with anything you could say?"

"No, I don't think so. Do you?"

"I wouldn't underestimate him, and I would think carefully about what you were doing. God only knows where this would end for you. In the long run it would be worse for you than it would be for Harold. Realize what you are doing, MacGregor. I know what Essex will do if you go to the newspapers, and I might as well make it clear to you. You are defying all the rules of the game: Government, State, Law, anything you like to name. I gather that Harold has promised to invoke them all if you go to the Press."

"Did he ask you to make that clear to me?"

"No. As a matter of fact he asked me to find you and persuade you to drop the whole silly idea of talking your head off. Would you drop it?"

"Would you persuade me!"

Katherine stopped brushing her hair and lifted her straight head to look at him. She smiled suddenly, and Katherine's impulsive smiles were rare gifts. "My dear MacGregor!" She faced him with her mind made up.

"Would you?" he said.

"No." She looked at him for a moment and then slowly resumed her brushing.

MacGregor could not accept her decision in that form. He had to have it direct. "Do you think that you might do what I ask?"

"I might," she said.

It was almost enough. "This time Kathy there can't be any sudden changes," he said. "This time it's too important."

She had walked away into the other room and she came back with

558

stockings and she sat down on the damask chair. "MacGregor," she said calmly. "It seems to be a rather drastic risk you're taking if you go to the Press. Wouldn't it be better if somebody else did it?"

"Who?" he said suspiciously.

"I suppose I could do something," she said.

"Would you?" He did not quite believe it.

"I might," she said again. "Do you want me to?"

"No." He moved away from the fire, flushed with it and hot. "This has to come from myself to be right, and I think you know it."

"I know that it's going to be a terrible business when it begins," she said. "Harold is not joking, and I wish you could find some other way of ending this bitter affair."

"There is no other way."

"No," she said slowly. "I suppose not. But I can't see how you're going to escape Harold's calamitous promise."

"Nor do I," he said unhappily. "I don't want to talk about that."

"You'll have to meet it somehow. You must."

"I don't want to talk about it."

"Alright," she said. She obviously had intentions of her own about it. "When can you get these men?" he asked her.

"To be effective," she said, "you'll have to have everything nicely planted and alive by morning, and to do that you will have to say what you want to say to-night. Can you?"

"Yes." He watched her pulling the mellow silk over her bare foot.

"Can you cope with men like Hamber?"

"I can cope with anyone," he said.

"Then go away and come back in about an hour and a half. At half-past seven. I'll have them here by then and I want them to be here before you. Fortunately a lot of the Moscow correspondents are in town. I can get you the right men, but you will have to convince them. Don't come any sooner than 7:30 and not much later."

"Is there anything I can do?"

"If you can find some coal you might bring it," she said. "This is the coldest house in London." She looked up at him quickly so that he blushed because he had been watching her. "Do you want to wait a little while?" she said without taking her normal eyes away from him.

"No Kathy," he said. "No, I had better go."

She turned her back to him for a moment and then put her stockinged feet in her slippers and walked ahead of him to the door. He went out and she reached up and pulled the back of his hair. "I've wanted to kick you so hard," she said.

"Not now," he said. "Not now."

"Why are you still so careful, so sure?"

559

"I'm not sure about anything," he said.

"Aren't you? I wish that your face could give you away a little more." She stopped at the top of the stairs. "If I confuse you, remember that you always leave me in doubt about myself. You're too careful with me. You are being too careful with me now."

He had walked a few steps down and he stopped when he saw that she was not following. "I never know what you're talking about," he said.

She shook her head and turned away and left him. MacGregor walked down the black stairs and out of the cold dark house.

When he came back, it was erect with light which came through the tall windows, over the heavy pillars of the entrance, from the basement, and in reflection of the rain upon the pavement. The light revived the mansion, and it now possessed some of its original, wonderful, life. Katherine was the life-giver.

MacGregor entered the house carrying a black scuttle containing a week's supply of coal. The housekeeper was not surprised by it, and MacGregor left it near the door as the quiet woman took his coat and led him along one of the bright passages to a large double door. She opened it and MacGregor stepped into a library full of men. In the moment that he stood there he was surprised, but in a few seconds Katherine was gripping the inside of his sleeve and walking with him to the fire-place and asking him quietly if he had brought the coal. When he nodded she smiled with some kind of relief or amusement, and she turned him around to face his judgment.

There were more than a dozen newspapermen in the room. They had already quietened down, and MacGregor knew that they were surprised by his arrival. They knew who he was, but they certainly had not expected him. That was obviously Katherine's clever intention. MacGregor saw in a moment all the men he knew: Hamber, Steele, Jeb Wills, Jack Bickford of *The Times,* and the grey-haired Welshman who had been in Moscow for the *Daily Worker,* Jack Tanner. Looking at them all, MacGregor sensed the disadvantage he suffered already by having these impatient men swept here so urgently by their common regard for one woman. Each seemed suspicious of the others, and MacGregor knew it and lost some of his confidence. There was no charm, no ease, no camaraderie, no great man, no Essex. Only MacGregor who stood by the fire, his hands straight beside him, his face showing some of the grip which the world now had on him. He needed its grip because there was no doubt that this was the last moment of one life. He did not like himself at this moment because he was too complicated. As for these newspapermen, they did not matter to him now except for their necessary use. He was glad of the familiar faces however, even Hamber's, and he looked at the men he knew rather than at those he did not know. They were all important men to their newspapers, American or English. They looked back at him with an important kind of scrutiny. Though Katherine had cleverly surprised them they were suspicious, because they were already thinking that they were being used, and they did not like being used. They held their quick drinks and waited for Katherine to explain it.

"If any of you fellows did not already know it," she said, still holding MacGregor's sleeve, "this is Ivre Angus MacGregor." She was well brushed and alert and slightly flushed, but unhurried and impersonal. "I don't quite know how MacGregor wants to begin this, but anyway you are about to hear a revealing account of that famous mission of his and Essex's. Everybody has been having his say about that mission but I suppose Essex and MacGregor are the only two that really know the full story of it. Harold will tell the Security Council about it the day after to-morrow, but MacGregor will tell you about it now. It may take a little time so why don't you sit down. I don't like to see you all standing, it's unnatural."

"Kathy," one of them said. "Is MacGregor talking for private or public information? He surely isn't allowed to be public about it."

Kathy smiled but it was only half a smile. "You're too close to the Foreign Office, Mr. Smythe," she said. Mr. Smythe wore morning coat and striped pants. "Surely a newspaperman shouldn't ask if a man is allowed to give information or not. I've never heard such a thing before."

"Well, is it printable or not?"

"Is it MacGregor?" she said.

"Of course," MacGregor said.

"There you are Michael," she said to Smythe.

"What about your part in this?" Hamber asked her. "What is it to you, Kathy?"

Katherine interrupted him. "You can ask me that when you have heard Ivre. It isn't important until then, and by that time you will not be interested in it."

"I'll bet Harold Essex will be interested in it," Steele said.

They laughed and Katherine looked bored and not at all impatient, although MacGregor could feel the grip of her fingers in his arm. These men had to be pleased and amused, and yet they must be made attentive. MacGregor waited confidently for Katherine to effect it.

"I don't know whether he intends telling you of the Moscow negotiations or not," Katherine said. "I suppose Molotov and Stalin are better left out of this."

"Oh no!" Hamber said quickly. "He might as well start at the beginning."

"On principle!" Steele said.

561

"Then go on, MacGregor," Jeb Wills said. "There's a principle involved."

"One thing more, MacGregor," Steele said. "Why are you so anxious to spill all this hot information? Are you trying to embarrass Essex?"

"No," MacGregor said. "I simply disagree with him."

"Surely that means that you agree with the Russians."

"It could mean that," MacGregor said, "but it's not important."

Steele was about to go on, but the others complained and even Jack Bickford told Steele to get-off-it-for-a-while so that they could hear what MacGregor had to say. "Let's hear it, MacGregor," Bickford said, "from the beginning, and you might as well start with why you went to Moscow. Did Essex really hope to talk the Russians into changing Azerbaijan to our requirements?"

"Essex didn't quite know what he should do with the Russians," MacGregor said as Katherine loosened her fingers to let him go on. "One way or another he had to restore Teheran's authority in Azerbaijan. That was about all the instruction he had, the rest was up to him. He knew nothing about Azerbaijan, but Azerbaijan was never the real concern in itself. On the first day, Essex remarked that we were fighting a traditional battle in Iran with the Russians, that our interests in the Middle East were threatened by Russian influence in Iran, that our only hope of survival there was to restore Teheran's authority in Azerbaijan and get the Russians out."

"Did you resist Essex at that stage?" Steele asked him.

The others quietened Steele again. "Let MacGregor tell it," Jeb Wills said. "For God's sake let him tell it the way he wants to tell it. We can ask the questions later."

"I don't suppose I did resist Essex then," MacGregor said. "I didn't know much about what was going on. I did know that all our information on Azerbaijan was bad. It came from the worst sources, from the most disreputable politicians, from the most corrupt men in the army and gendarmeries, and even from men we knew were German agents during the war. They were obviously our best informants in Iran because they were telling us what we wanted for our own political needs: that the Russians had set up the autonomous Azerbaijanian regime by force, that any revolt in Azerbaijan was Russian-inspired and Russian-made. This was wrong because Azerbaijan has always been in revolt. But I didn't take much notice of our intentions in Moscow until the negotiations had actually begun. From the outset, we were negotiating for a balance of influence in Iran. Azerbaijan and its actual situation never really interested us. We simply wanted the balance of power in Iran back in our favour, and that meant restoring the Teheran Government's authority in Azerbaijan. We controlled the Teheran Government; and

562

whenever we suggested a restoration of its rights we were talking about our own rights, and each time Essex met the Russians we had some new scheme for re-establishing the Teheran Government's authority in the north. At first we simply demanded a guarantee from the Russians that the Teheran Government could restore its authority in Azerbaijan, and we asked the Russians to sit down and negotiate the proper change. Essex felt that he could achieve something if he could get them negotiating. But Molotov wouldn't negotiate anything. He said that it was a local Iranian matter and not an international matter; it should be discussed by our ambassadors in Iran. So Essex made it an international matter by having Drake present the Russians with a Note accusing them of violating the British-Iranian-Soviet Treaty of 1942, saying that the Russians had interfered in Azerbaijan's affairs and had ignored Britain's vital interest in the matter."

"On what exact day was the Note delivered?" Steele asked.

"I don't remember."

"Haven't you kept a record of these things?"

"Yes. I can give it to you later on."

"Let him get on," the others said. "What happened about the Note, MacGregor?"

"Vishinsky rejected it and said that Britain's vital interest didn't enter into it. Vishinsky put us on to Suchkov of the Near Eastern Division, saying that Russia didn't mind discussing the substance of the Azerbaijanian situation, but they would not discuss any proposals or solutions. When Essex discussed it with Suchkov, it really became an argument about the validity of the Azerbaijanian regime. The Russians said it was a genuinely democratic regime and we said that it was Russian-made. It wasn't really an argument because we had no facts to prove our point and the Russians had plenty of facts to prove theirs. We weren't doing very well in that discussion, so Essex steered away from it and asked for a widening of the Azerbaijanian Government to include the representatives of all parties. To that Suchkov said he would not interfere in the affairs of Azerbaijan. It became another argument about who was really interfering in Iran, and it wasn't difficult for the Russians to prove that Britain had interfered in the affairs of Iran just as much as we said they were interfering."

"Surely Harry put forward some practical suggestions, MacGregor," Hamber said cleverly. "Didn't he offer them an investigation?"

"Yes he did. He suggested a Committee of Enquiry to investigate and report on the origins of the autonomous regime in Azerbaijan. It was to be a Committee of five, one each of the British, the Russians, the Azerbaijanians, the Teheran Government, and the Americans, who would obviously hold the balancing and decisive vote. The decisions of this committee were to be accepted unconditionally by all. The whole scheme for us depended on the Russians accepting the Americans as impartial, but we had worked it all out with an American Embassy chap beforehand. Their attitude was our attitude. The Russians rejected it anyway, although we talked about world suspicion and testing the Russian's faith and anything else that would put responsibility onto the Russians. The whole idea failed. It had to fail, and Essex had decided to go home when Stalin sent for him."

"Did Essex ask to see Stalin?" one of the unknown correspondents asked.

"No. He had hoped to see Stalin soon after our arrival but he had given up the idea. Stalin asked for Essex, and it was really Essex's last chance to achieve something. He told Stalin that the situation in Azerbaijan was a deterrent to British-Soviet relations and appealed to him to use his influence to effect a compromise. Essex said that our intent in Azerbaijan was not interference, but historical association. We had helped to make Iran and we were not strangers there. We also had to consider our rightful interests in the south, since most of our oil came from there. Essex said that the situation in the north was dangerous, and that the Azerbaijanian regime was not beneficial to Iran because it was one of revolt and plunder and terrorism. He wanted Stalin to consider the British attitude again and have faith in the good intentions of the British Government."

"Exactly what did Stalin say to it?" Hamber asked. "Word for word."

"I don't remember it word for word," MacGregor said, "but he told Essex that he was obviously misinformed about the situation in Azerbaijan and asked him if he was interested in making a personal study of the situation. Essex said he was interested, and Stalin told him that he would give us a plane and that we could go where we liked in Azerbaijan. That is how we got there," MacGregor said.

"That's a once-over-lightly," one of them said. "Can't you tell us the exact order of the negotiations and the dates, and at least a few quotes from Molotov and Stalin? A little more fact and not so much opinion."

"I have copies of all my reports," MacGregor said and touched his breast pocket. "I can tell you anything that you would like to know."

"Can we see your reports?"

"Yes," MacGregor said.

"We want to hear the rest of it first," Jeb Wills said above the noise. He was unusually impatient. "We haven't got as much time as you magazine writers. Go straight on MacGregor," he said. "Some of us have only got an hour to catch a deadline."

"I'll be as brief as I can," MacGregor told him.

"And give us a few more facts," Mr. Smythe said.

"I can't do both," MacGregor replied. "I'll give you a fair outline, and if you want more facts afterwards then you can see my reports. But facts are not enough," MacGregor said. "I know very little about your job, but I know that in this case the simple details will tell you nothing of our actual intentions in Moscow. Events will tell you nothing of our invisible plotting. We cheated from the first day we arrived in Moscow. We thought we could trick the Russians into agreeing with our schemes, and we were there to scheme for our own interests in Iran. Nobody we spoke to in the Embassy considered it otherwise when they talked in hard terms of political business. There were no nice considerations among ourselves about the sovereignty of small nations and 'free peoples'; it was one desperate plan after another to out-plot the Russians. The Russians were not quite so stupid as we thought, and that is why we failed. Our failure in Moscow had nothing to do with British regard and Russian disregard for the rights of small nations. It had nothing to do with the lack of Russian friendship and co-operation. We simply could not out-trick them and that was all."

"What about the Russians' intentions?" Steele asked.

"Whatever the Russian intention," MacGregor said, "it will not change our own. To-day we have no right to accuse the Russians in the United Nations of interfering in Iran's affairs. We have always interfered in Iran and we are at this moment interfering. That was our purpose in Moscow. Even our mission of so-called investigation to Azerbaijan was quickly turned into a scheme to buy and cajole political influence there; political influence against the Russians and for ourselves. Before we left Teheran we were briefed in an Embassy conference on the situation in Iran. We were told just how quickly we must stop the Tudeh and other political parties who were demanding free trade-unions and wide land reforms. It was made quite clear that our situation in Iran would be hopeless if the Democratic Party stayed in power in Azerbaijan and managed to put through its economic and social reforms. We were told that the effect on our oil-fields in the south and upon the political situation in the whole Middle East would be disastrous. We were told that our only British hope was to strengthen the rival parties, principally the religious party of Sayyed-el-Zil, whom we had exiled during the war because he was a German supporter. The Persians are not very religious, but our policy in Iran was to re-create Moslem influence because it opposed the reformists and the Russians. There was no concern about interference, our idea was to interfere as much as possible, and no bones were made about it. Even our route into Azerbaijan was decided by Embassy experts, and it was planned so that Essex could visit and impress some of our contacts and give them assurances of our support in whatever they wanted to do against the Azerbaijanian Government. A large part of our journey was routed through middle Kurdistan because we had sheikhs there who had to be impressed and urged on to more effort. For that matter we were depending on the Kurds for quick armed action against Azerbaijan; not only for the effect on Azerbaijan, but because we wanted to keep the Kurds and the Azerbaijani fighting. The Kurds are almost as much a problem to our future as the Azerbaijani because they surround our oil-fields in Iraq, but at that stage our hope of coping with the Kurds depended on keeping them fighting among themselves and against anybody else. Essex decided later that the Kurds could be the most useful force in the Middle East if they were taken over and welded together under our guidance; but that came after we had been there. When we set out, we were given a large sum of money with which to implement some of our influence, but as it turned out, we never really reached most of our contacts because we were diverted by the Mukri Kurds. We did see one man, however, the Governor of Zenjan. He was quite important to us, but when we got there he was besieged on his own estates by one of the Azerbaijanian Democrats, Javat Gochali."

"What about Kathy?" Hamber interrupted. "Since you seem to be talking for the lady, how is it that she got on that trip and we didn't? Was she an official or an unofficial attachment?"

MacGregor did not want to be reminded of his own suspicions about that; and he did not know if Hamber was provoking him about it. He looked at Katherine. She was unconcerned and silent, and MacGregor was antagonized for a moment. "I don't know anything about Katherine," he said. "All I know is that she came with us."

He was interrupted then by the quiet housekeeper bringing in the scuttle of coal and putting some of it on the fire and leaving again. Some of the correspondents made use of the moment to fill their glasses from the crystal decanters on the mahogany table, and MacGregor looked at Katherine again, this time to appeal for a restoration of attention. This time Katherine smiled because she knew MacGregor's thoughts with both his glances.

"I didn't have much difficulty in persuading Harold to take me," she said to them. "At that time he wasn't sure whether MacGregor was going or not; they had been fighting about something."

"About what?" Hamber asked her.

"MacGregor didn't like the idea of the trip, as far as I remember."

"Then why did you go?" MacGregor was asked.

"Because Katherine went," MacGregor said, and smiled a little with his own admission. Some of them laughed and some of them told him to get on with it, and MacGregor went on with it. He told them about the siege of the Governor, of Essex's attempt to save the Governor's situation, of the bastinadoing of Javat and the Captain, and finally of the brutality of the jack-booted officer.

566

Hamber interrupted. "What about that officer?" he asked.

MacGregor drew a breath and said, "He was directly responsible for the death of the Captain who had been bastinadoed with Javat. As we left the estate I managed to push him into the car, and I eventually turned him over to the Democrats."

Hamber persisted. "What happened to him, MacGregor?"

"They hanged him." MacGregor kept his eyes on Hamber and on all these men so that they would not see how the cold words affected him.

"Would you consider yourself responsible for his death?" Steele asked.

"Indirectly, yes."

"Do you think you have the moral right to deliver a man over for certain execution?" Steele asked. "Doesn't that bother you, MacGregor?"

"Yes," MacGregor admitted unhappily. "It bothers me, but I actually didn't know that they would hang him."

"Is that an excuse?"

"No. I am not trying to avoid the responsibility for it."

"You admit his death was mainly your fault."

"That is something I can't decide for myself," MacGregor said with his eyes glued to Steele now. "Killing was as much part of the Governor and Javat's war as it was in our own war. I suppose in the desert I was the indirect means of killing hundreds of innocent men. They were men who were the enemy."

"Did you consider this officer your enemy?"

"Yes," MacGregor said slowly. "I suppose I did."

"Oh let's forget this moral cross-examination," Jeb Wills said. "Get to the end of it MacGregor so that I can catch the morning papers in New York."

MacGregor did not like to avoid any issue of the officer, but he was glad that Wills had got him out of it. He went on to describe their detailed adventures with the Mukri, and the political arguments between himself and Essex in relation to Zada and Salim. He explained Zada's ambitions and said that this was the man Essex had decided to support because he opposed Kurdish independence. It was only later, when Essex realized that the Kurds were going to fight for their independence, that he had the better idea of taking over Kurdish independence and containing it within the limits which the British Government would set.

"What about that cash you said you were given in Teheran?" Jack Tanner asked. "I heard that Essex gave it to the Zada fellow."

"I don't know what happened to the money," MacGregor lied.

"Harry probably bought carpets in Tabriz with it," Hamber said, and they laughed and passed on to affairs in Tabriz, which was Hamber's intention.

MacGregor said they had very little time to do anything in Tabriz because Essex was in a hurry to get home and catch the Security Council meeting. "Katherine and I walked around the town," he said, "and though there were Russians in Tabriz, there were very few compared with the number of Azerbaijanian troops. It was a place in arms, but there was no terrorism and no looting as we had been told to expect. The Democrats we saw in the Government were all Azerbaijanians. A few of them had spent some years' exile in Russia and others had been here in England, but for the most part they were Tabriz revolutionists or educated reformists similar to the old Constitutionalists. In fact there were a few old men among them who had taken part in the Revolution in 1906. With one exception, none of them talked of separating Azerbaijan from Iran; and none of them talked of collectivizing all land and industry. Their ideas on reform sounded about the same as the Labour Party here, except that they intended breaking up the large estates to parcel out among the peasants. But in social reform and education and administration, they were asking for the bare necessities. The one man that talked of separating Azerbaijan from Iran was more Russian than the Russians. He was an army man but no one seemed to take much notice of him."

MacGregor felt his own eyes widen as he saw Asquith's head suddenly appear through the door. Asquith looked around, looked hard at MacGregor, and pulled in his head and closed the door. MacGregor did not know if any of the others had seen Asquith or recognized him but he went on quickly.

"That's about all there is to it," he said as he rubbed his dry hands together. "We came back to Teheran in a hurry and left Iran in a hurry. Even though we didn't investigate the situation in Azerbaijan very thoroughly, we saw enough to know what was going on there. We saw few Russians. We did not see any sign of Russian political or military interference. On the contrary, we saw enough to know that the Azerbaijanians were revolting by themselves and for themselves. Not all of them were revolting, but enough of them were taking part in it to make it effective. As far as I could see, the only Russian interference was in preventing the Teheran Government from dispatching an army into Azerbaijan to crush the revolt; but I don't believe the Russians took any part in the revolt itself. It was unnecessary. It was the first time that the Azerbaijanians had been given a chance to revolt, and they took it; and whatever they say in the United Nations they can't do away with that fact."

"What would have happened if the Russians had allowed the government's troops into Azerbaijan?" Steele asked. "Could the revolt have succeeded?"

"No," MacGregor said. "I don't suppose it could have succeeded. The Azerbaijani were not very well organized for fighting and they had very little equipment and no idea of how to use it. Any army could have broken them."

"Do you think that still applies?" Jeb Wills said.

"I don't know," MacGregor said. "I don't know enough about the changing situation. If Teheran could get things going I suppose they could still break the Democrats because most of the revolt was local. There isn't a large cohesive force among the Azerbaijanians, and there isn't likely to be for some time. I should think that anything could happen, but I can't see the Russians allowing anything to happen unless we force the situation. If we do, then we will be directly responsible for the destruction of Azerbaijan, for the end of their reforms, and any hope they had of breaking corrupt rule from Teheran."

"Is that all there is?" Hamber said.

"Unless you want these." MacGregor drew the reports out of his pocket. "They have fuller details and dates and all that I wrote to the India Office at the time. The last report is a summing-up of the whole mission, but I don't think anybody in the India Office or the Foreign Office read it."

Only a few of the newspapermen were interested in it, Bickford and the magazine writers. The remainder hurriedly shook MacGregor's hand and bantered with Katherine for a moment and swept off with what they had.

Jeb Wills was also in a hurry, but he paused long enough to depress his forbidding eyebrows and say "Kathy: here I am finally going to America and it looks as though you won't be there to see my tragic homecoming." He was looking first at Katherine and then at MacGregor, cynical as always. "Unless, of course, you still intend coming."

"I might," she said; "but you'll never go back, Jeb."

"Don't be too sure," he told her. "Anyway the rate you're going they'll never let you in. I doubt if they'll let me back in," he added almost sadly.

"You'll always be around somewhere Jeb," she said.

He did not reply and he walked away with a casual motion of farewell.

The only American remaining now was Hamber. MacGregor could hear him questioning Katherine about the validity of all that he had said. But Hamber was also in a hurry and he stood for a moment before MacGregor, running his hand over his close-cropped hair and smiling with his wide lips. "I think they've got you this time, MacGregor," he said. "I can almost see you in the Tower. You and Kathy both," he said and laughed and left them.

Jack Bickford of *The Times* was the last, and he asked MacGregor if he could borrow the reports, promising to return them in good order. "It's a pity you had to do it this way, MacGregor," he said, "but I suppose you couldn't do it any other way. Pity though," he said and shook his head a little and put on his hat. "Pity," he said again and followed the others.

MacGregor and Katherine waited silently until they had heard the front door close for the last time, and then they hurried to find Asquith. They discovered him in one of the large and brightly lit rooms. He was sitting gloomily in a Louis chair with his overcoat still on, and his legs stretched out. He was drinking brandy which the housekeeper had brought him on demand.

"When I saw that look on your face," he said to MacGregor without getting up, "I thought I had better keep out of it. Didn't want to spoil it all. Actually that is a simple lie. I did not want to meet your newspapermen. What did you do? Dispose of Essex?"

"They seemed to think I disposed of myself." MacGregor meant it.

"Perhaps they're right," Asquith said and blew on his cold hands. "You might as well know that to-morrow the Civil Service big-wigs will sit with the Service Security people to decide your legal fate. With this additional crime upon your head there is no doubt about their decision."

"What about Essex?" MacGregor said.

"He's pretty grim." Asquith straightened up a little. "I suppose he'll be a damn sight grimmer to-morrow when he sees what you've done. One more day to the Security Council, and you hurl another bombshell. Poor Harold. Heaven only knows what will happen now. He really didn't think you would go through with it, MacGregor, and I was doubtful about it myself. I wondered if you could muster more stomach than I've ever had. How are you my dear Kathy?"

"You shouldn't be here," she said. "MacGregor was trying to keep you away from this *Bolshoi scandál*. What did you come here for?"

"I came to get MacGregor." Asquith sounded definite about it and he looked up at both of them. "None of this stupid talk about keeping me out of this affair. A little of my insides are left, boy, and though your consideration is touching it could crush me." Asquith was on the light side of seriousness, and he pulled nervously at his moustache to discredit the real intention of anything he said.

"So far," MacGregor said and remembered Jane Asquith, "my presence at your place can be attributed to your craziness and your eccentricity; something like that is expected of you. But not a second time."

Asquith appeared struck by its cruelty, and he could not hide his unhappy eyes even by the sudden rise to his feet. "Eccentricity, eh? Is that the reason, MacGregor? Is that what you would say, MacGregor?"

MacGregor knew how much Asquith had been hurt by it, and apart

570

from being surprised he was made additionally aware of Asquith's own bitter conflict. "No," the Scot said quickly. "I wouldn't say that."

"Then what the devil are you up-and-away for!" Asquith said with too much recovery. "It's not the sensitive thing to do to me, my boy."

"Then I'll do the sensitive thing," MacGregor sighed, "and come back."

"Good," Asquith said flatly. "Kathy: Jane was expecting you for dinner."

Katherine looked at MacGregor, who was waiting for her. "No," she said. "I promised to see Tom Cromwell at the House of Commons. I must see him to-night."

"What for?" MacGregor asked.

"I'm not sure yet," she said. "Tell Jane I'll be there for lunch to-morrow."

MacGregor could not argue about it because he knew that he must not argue with her, whatever her intention. He waited while she found his coat, and at the door she helped him on with it and watched Asquith push open the iron gates.

"Don't talk about leaving there now," she said quietly to MacGregor.

"But you know he'll be in trouble if I stay."

"That's up to him," she said. "He's having one of those desperate bouts with himself. It must be damned uncomfortable tailing with Essex and hanging onto you so grimly."

"I know. I know." MacGregor did not want it spoken of.

"Then let him fight it out himself," she said. "Don't hinder him."

"He doesn't know what he's doing," MacGregor said.

"Then he'll have to find out," Katherine said impatiently. "Actually everything is evened out a little now, and even Harold must be having a desperate time. It will be so fascinating to see how Harold keeps his case intact."

"Can he?" MacGregor was trying to dispute any suggestion of its possibility.

"I don't know," she said with the same doubt. "He can still face the Security Council."

"MacGregor!" Asquith called.

"Perhaps John can tell you what to expect of Essex," she said.

"No," said MacGregor.

"Then ask him about yourself," she said. "If there is a Service Committee sitting to-morrow then he will know what to expect for you."

MacGregor shook his head. "He's better left out of it."

"MacGregor!" Asquith called again.

Katherine sighed and closed her lips as if to thin out her lipstick. She touched one side of his face and kissed the other and laughed at him because of his long wait and his long flush. "Good night," she said and he heard her close the door behind him even before he had reached the first step.

MacGregor joined Asquith in the Humber and sat intent upon the dangers of Asquith's driving, finding it better worry than the sudden danger he felt in his new situation. The moral sustenance of his aggressive defiance of Essex had already gone. Now he must wait again for official satisfaction to decide his future: official satisfaction, or government action, or the proper measures, or any other of the nice broad terms that meant quick retaliation in its legal loyal form. He knew that if he talked to Asquith about it now, he would get one of Asquith's philosophical answers, and he did not want that. He forgot about Asquith's own dispirit, and for a moment he did not need Asquith at all.

Asquith, however, needed MacGregor, and he wanted MacGregor to need him.

"MacGregor," he said fraternally. "Don't let the fear of your sin catch you now. I can see it worrying you already into vacillations. You have done the only thing that an honest man could do and you need never dispute it."

"I'm not disputing it," MacGregor said.

Asquith went on to convince himself. "What you must avoid now is the martyrdom which you were so carefully resisting. You are in a martyr's position at the moment, boy, and that is what you get for being a one-man revolt. Only anarchists and assassins believe in the value of one-man revolts, and I would like to save you from such unreal political philosophies. I think you might survive alright, eh?"

"I think so," MacGregor told him.

"However," Asquith said, "you will first have to survive the considerations of the State. In what you have just done, MacGregor, you have shown a grim, blind, amazing, honest, contempt for the Rule of Law, and you cannot escape the terrible consequences. You realize that?"

"What Rule of Law?" MacGregor said.

"The Rule of Law, the iron heel, the State, its authority, its legal existence, its moral existence, in fact the whole hog's-blood and witchcraft of State omnipotence."

"I doubt if I have interfered with the State's existence in any way," MacGregor said ruefully. "At the most I interfered with Essex and his policy."

"At the most!" Asquith repeated and echoed. "There is nothing more my boy. Essex is the State, his policy is the State. The State is simply the authority of the governing body, and in revolting against Essex you are revolting against the State itself. For that, MacGregor, there is no forgiveness, and the retaliation is desperately quick and legal and decisive."

"Then I suppose this committee to-morrow will charge me."

"It might," Asquith said. "It depends on other influences and I don't mean the moral or legal influences, I mean the political influences. No Service Committee will really worry about the legalities of what you've done. They'll worry about the political tug-o'-war, and they will decide your crime by the political situation you have created. To-morrow all political England will be taking sides for you or against you if they haven't already done so. If you can guess the decisive political side, then you can guess your own fate."

"It may depend on Essex's influence."

"It may," Asquith said and fought angrily to pass a taxi, shouting to the startled driver that he was a vicious menace. "Harold will have your blood if he can get it," he went on, "but on the other hand you may have his. You may have ruined his influence. I don't know," Asquith said. "Your satisfaction at the moment, MacGregor, must be in yourself. Did you realize that overnight you had become the perfect symbol of human choice?"

"No, I didn't realize it!"

"No. I suppose not," Asquith said dejectedly. "You wouldn't see it as clearly as I do, because you have done something that I might have done when I was your age, but didn't. In twenty years I have had time to think about it. I know exactly what you had to choose between. It's only the fool who has lost his choice who knows about it. You wouldn't know."

"I had no choice," MacGregor said. "I had no alternative. Essex made the situation for me, I had very little to do with it."

"In the last moment MacGregor, it could only be yourself. Your choice was there between all your known conception of human existence and a new conception of it. To defy Essex you had to decide that all your life had been a hoax, that the mumbo-jumbo of legality and loyalty and authority and statecraft were a hoax, that your own intelligence and understanding were more important than all other values and loyalties, however deeply ingrained. In a moment there, you had to break with all your past. You had to decide that society itself was false and you had to break its hold on you because your reason forced you to. There you have it! Every time a man acts like that for his reason and his intelligence, he is an instigator of revolution whether he knows it or not."

They had arrived in front of Asquith's house and they sat in the Humber for a moment.

"If you hadn't taken sides against Essex," Asquith said morosely, "you would henceforth be spending your life as I have spent it, cynically, foolishly, bitterly, and to no purpose whatsoever. I have known all my life that our organization of society is false, and yet I have spent a life-time working for its perpetuation. I have never been able to break its grip on me, and every year since I was twenty it has become more and more difficult to break away, until now it is impossible. I might be taking you in to-night, MacGregor, and I might be understanding and believing in what you have done; nevertheless to-morrow I will be with Essex as the Asquith he expects, a normal Asquith, an assistant Asquith, an undivided, unchanged, untouched, unalterable and eccentric Asquith, who will part-ner him on his great mission to the Security Council. To-morrow I will be Asquith, the bitter-end of a man, who will no doubt assist Essex in cancelling out your own valorous tilt at the windmill. Come on in, boy, and we shall drink a little brandy to break these terrible burdens."

Chapter 46

Essex first had to understand why MacGregor had really taken this fantastic step. "Didn't I warn him that another public pronouncement would bring Security charges against him? Didn't he understand that, John? Didn't he realize that I meant it, that it would mean more than his crazy Persian fixation was worth? Both he and Kathy must have been drunk last night! There is no other explanation. Dragging Kathy into it is a dastardly thing for MacGregor to have done and I hope that he has the decency to renounce publicly her part in this and take the responsibility on himself. By God there is no honour left when a man like MacGregor does this to me. The man deserves his pun-ishment. If MacGregor is allowed to escape with such dishonour and disloyalty, then anarchy stares us in the face. Overnight MacGregor has shaken a world confidence in an Englishman's loyalty. I can understand him being defiant, but why didn't his English sanity intervene at the last moment and jolt him into proper reason, into a sense of duty and loyalty and trust and service and honour? Why did he do it?"

Asquith picked up another newspaper. "Why don't you send for Mac-Gregor and ask him why he did it? He'll tell you."

"I never want to see the fellow again," Essex said.

"As for Kathy," Asquith went on from his reclining position on the leather couch, his pallid face showing headache and dizziness, "Kathy arranged it all for MacGregor."

"I don't believe it," Essex said.

"I know you don't, but you might as well face it. Why don't you get hold of Kathy? She'll explain it all to you very clearly, very simply."

"I insist on keeping Katherine out of this," Essex said. "We'll have to make sure that she is exonerated and untouched by it."

"Is Kathy also facing Security charges?" Asquith dropped his arm to the floor and let the paper slip out of it. He picked up another and tried to ease his aching head by covering his face with it.

"Certainly not."

"Is MacGregor?"

"It's out of my hands," Essex said. "You know that."

"Is he?" Asquith repeated.

"Of course they'll charge him now."

"I wonder!" Asquith took the newspaper off his face and folded his hands on his stomach and looked at the panelled ceiling of Essex's office. He touched his dry lips and closed his eyes again. "MacGregor has given you an awful crack, Harold. If the Government thinks that he has enough opinion on his side they won't hit him too hard. In fact you might be the victim, not MacGregor."

"MacGregor is too clumsy to achieve any effective support," Essex said. "Even his own statement has turned against him. He might have imagined that he was finally discrediting me last night, but as far as I can see he has discredited himself. To begin with, he didn't fool the Press because this morning they are all demanding disciplinary action against him for his rotten behaviour."

"Most of the Press is on your side, Harold." Asquith groaned and sat up. "There's no doubt about that. But you can't be too delighted about it because you know what you think of the Press. You're satisfied because you can see that they publish a few words of MacGregor's statement and take the rest of their print to quote large men demanding MacGregor's quick destruction. But it isn't all like that, and not everybody is demanding MacGregor's scalp. Some are after yours. Our most dignified paper publishes nearly all MacGregor's statement and suggests that in view of the scandal, the doubt, the controversy, the keen international eye upon our intentions, that you and your case against the Russians be dropped. Not that they are accusing you. As they point out, they simply want Britain's good name in the Security Council to be clear of our internal disputes. Of course they ask for an investigation of MacGregor's facts and motives, and suggest punishment if he has shown betrayal of trust; but that's a fair opinion for anyone. There are others that agree, including your old friend the *Daily Worker*."

"Naturally! But it will not be the *Daily Worker* that decides MacGregor's strength against mine, if you want to be so crude about it."

"Don't be too sure," Asquith said. "Whether you like it or not, you can't ignore the import. They too quote big men; and these men are asking for your dismissal. Sixty back-benchers have already petitioned the Prime Minister for your removal, among them some clerics and other such respectable God-fearing Labour men. Additionally, an Archbishop, a former Ambassador, two atom-bomb scientists, the Chancellor of a University, eleven professors, five important trade-union leaders, and plenty of other odd men think that your name in the Security Council can only damage British diplomatic prestige, whatever the right or wrong of MacGregor's attack. The trouble is you are branded, and that gives the politicians something to worry about."

"Branded be damned," Essex said and took a pinch of snuff from his Persian opium box. "Who is going to take any notice of that collection of political half-wits? Do you think that a government policy is dependent upon the opinion of men like that? And politicians be damned. There are bigger things in this world than labour governments, and we'll see where policy is really made." Essex straightened a picture of Mr. Churchill.

"Be that as it may," Asquith said wearily and with his eyes still closed, "and whoever decides policy, they won't let you go into the Security Council if they think that MacGregor has supplied your opponents with some real ammunition. That may not decide MacGregor's unhappy situation, but it can decide yours."

These two old friends had known each other all their lives and there was no pretence left between them because Asquith had killed it all.

Essex said indignantly, "What are you worrying about my situation for? I can tell you that I will attend the Security Council meeting to-morrow and there is no word worth-a-damn to the contrary. To-morrow Azerbaijan will be discussed. The Russians can't keep it off the agenda any longer. To-morrow I will go to Central Hall and give the Security Council all the facts and information which I have carefully prepared. My case is complete. I can prove conclusively that Russia's interference in Iran is serious enough for Security Council intervention. On my evidence I will demand and get Security Council action to stop Russia. If you think that MacGregor can halt me now you are underestimating my effort, John. Don't lie there and worry your thick unhappy head any farther. If MacGregor has created a difficulty, then I assure you that I intend meeting it."

"Yes. Yes." Asquith turned his head to watch Essex reading reports that had come in on the Reuters tape from New York and Washington. "The smartest thing you could do would be to make sure that MacGregor is not charged, accused, or punished for any disloyalty."

"Good God! What is smart about that?"

"If you get MacGregor in trouble, Harold, there is going to be increased support and admiration for MacGregor for taking the stand he did, knowing the consequences. Half the papers publish the fact that he was threatened with trouble if he said anything. If it becomes a truth then your name will be mud. There is plenty of conviction in what MacGregor has done. He has everything to lose, and that gives him support for his bravado. If you step in and save him now, Harold, you will wipe out half the political opposition to your personal behaviour."

"That's utter nonsense and crazy twisting," Essex said. "The only way to meet MacGregor is to prove that he has been disloyal and bedevilled. Make an example of him for it. The best answer is to show that he has committed a crime against the State itself and must therefore be punished for it. This will be made clear by the time I go into the Security Council meeting to-morrow, have no fear about that. There will be a question in the House of Commons at seven o'clock this evening about MacGregor, and if I know the answer, then MacGregor will no longer be a danger to anyone. Not even our desperate opponents in the Security Council would dare quote a man who is under charge of betrayal to his own country. They know a little about betrayal themselves and MacGregor will cease to be of any use to them."

"By Christ you're a stubborn man, Harold!" Asquith stood up and swayed a little and grasped the couch for support until his eyes straightened out.

"What do you expect me to do?" Essex said. "Betray my own trust and my own conviction to save MacGregor? I am not a cynic and an eccentric, John. I am a man who believes in what he is doing, in what he must do. I know that at this moment I must fight grimly and angrily for my country and my birthright; and for that matter so must you. To stop Russian interference in Azerbaijan is to stop it everywhere, including England itself. If we can't stop it alone then the Security Council must stop it. There is no future for this nation or for Europe if we allow Russia to dominate Europe with its false ideology and its threatening power. Wittingly or unwittingly, MacGregor has aided and supported them by his attack upon me. Without personal malice or revenge I must halt his desperate plunge so that no more damage can be done, so that our one chance of stopping the Russians is not lost. To say that I am stubborn is to say that I am loyal. But you are a fool to talk about stubbornness. Stick to your cynicism. MacGregor knew what he was doing, and there can't be any excuse for him. I am as sorry as you are to realize his tragic future, but I have had to steel myself against sentiment and friendship and all the demands that want to save him. If it depended on myself alone then there could be compassion for him, but now it is more than myself and more than MacGregor."

"A word from you," Asquith insisted, "would clear MacGregor."

"Nothing can clear MacGregor. He is on one side and we are on the other. I can't escape that sharp division between us now, and neither can you. It's too late."

"He may still be too much for you," Asquith said morosely and inadequately as he looked across the Park at Buckingham Palace.

"He can't do much more by to-night, and he can't run away. Where is he, incidentally?"

"With us," Asquith replied without turning around.

Essex almost lost his voice. "Didn't you get him away?"

"He left," Asquith said, "but I brought him back home."

"Then get him out of there," Essex shouted undiplomatically. "Send him away. Get rid of him. The first time he was found there by the newspapers didn't matter because you're crazy enough to do anything, but now it would be the final straw to break the back of this whole ridiculous situation. What credence can be given my word if you are harbouring the man that denies it! What is your attitude supposed to be if you are working with me and housing our betrayer! In fact I could ask — what is your attitude anyway?"

Asquith still did not turn around. "MacGregor is alright," he said. "Leave him where he is and no harm will be done."

"Harm? I won't have it, John. What sort of ridicule is this? You work with me and you have enough sympathy with MacGregor to give him the protection of your home after what he did last night? Compassion or not, he'll have to go. Immediately."

Asquith waited a moment. "I don't think so," he said.

"What are you doing?" Essex said to him. "You know that you can't have it both ways, particularly now. Having MacGregor with you gives him an authority that must be considered dangerous. You know that. You can't be personal and sentimental about it. This is a critical political situation and any hint of your support for MacGregor would make the both of us ridiculous. If I'm going to be fighting this case out in the Security Council I can't have this hanging over me. Telephone now and send him away. I don't care how you do it but do it quickly."

Asquith turned around and brushed his mouth as if he wished that it were not there. "Sorry Harold," he said like the shadow of a man. "It's more than I could do, so don't ask me."

"I must ask you."

"I know it."

"Then what are you talking about? What am I to think if you serve MacGregor as you cannot serve me? It's an odd choice, John, but you must take it."

Asquith smiled as a man would smile at his own death. "You might even call it a ridiculous choice," he said.

"Of course it's ridiculous, but it's necessary and you can't play with this situation as you play with others. I can't afford to let you play with it. MacGregor with you is a mockery of me, and MacGregor has to go. Get rid of him John, I'm really demanding it."

"Demand all you like," Asquith said with a voice that did not want to hurt Essex nor really deny him. "It's something I can't do, Harold."

"You must."

Asquith shook his head and his full heavy eyes hardly saw Essex.

"But this is ridiculous," Essex said. "John. Have some sense, man. You have obviously had a big night; why don't you go and sleep it off for a while and then do what you must do. You can't afford to be erratic now."

"Don't call me erratic and eccentric!" Asquith cried.

"What else can I call you? Dare I consider you sane at this moment?"

"Consider me tragically sane."

Essex held up his hands to quieten Asquith. "John," he said. "This isn't a thing we need fight about. Is something like this going to decide our whole lifetime of association and friendship? It's absurd. MacGregor isn't worth an angry word by either of us. Let him go, John. For God's sake let the man go and let's have no more of this bitter dispute. It's suddenly getting hold of us."

"Yes," Asquith said slowly. "Odd isn't it. Only last night I was telling MacGregor that a man doesn't know his choice until he makes it. I am a fool Harold, and I have to laugh away twenty years of avoiding a few moments like this. I know that you have to cut me free from MacGregor, but I know that I can't let you. MacGregor is the last shred of myself, my last moment of honesty or courage. What would be left if I gave him away?"

"Go and sleep it off," Essex told him angrily. "I won't press you now. You will be able to think a little better if you consider your own situation in what you are doing. I won't press you John, but . . ."

"Don't retreat now," Asquith said and shook his head. "Don't go back an inch Harold, for God's sake."

"I'm not retreating," Essex said. "I can't retreat, but I know that you are being foolish and crazy, and that a little thought on the matter would change your mind."

"No. No," Asquith said. "I want no more thought on the matter."

Essex was lost for a moment. "It isn't simply a choice between Mac-Gregor and myself," he said desperately. "It's a decision you are making for your whole person. I'm facing you with it because one way or another your grim support of MacGregor will wreck both of us if you allow it to continue. I'm not forcing a decision on you. Sooner or later you would have to decide it yourself. You know that it's impossible for you to carry on here if you give sustenance to MacGregor. You know it. If you walk out of that door with MacGregor as your star, there's little point in walking back under any circumstances."

Asquith picked up his raincoat and his ivory-headed stick, and he looked a sadder man than Essex. "There are all sorts of reasons why I am walking out on you, Harold, but none of them would have existed unless we had faced this sudden definition of myself. I hardly expected to have the opportunity again. For that, Harold, I shall always be grateful to you." He meant it. "It seems a providential accident more than a real moment in a man's life. It's not what I expected. Not at all what I expected."

"Is there nothing that I can say to you?" Essex would never accept his exit now. He stood before Asquith almost blocking his way.

"No."

"I'm sorry that you are such a blind dangerous fool."

Asquith shook his head to silence him. "If you apologize for it then so must I. Let me alone, Harold."

"I'm not taking this as final," Essex said. "I'll expect you back."

"At the price of MacGregor?"

"Damn MacGregor. It's so ridiculous. You can't walk out on me, John."

"Too late," Asquith said and he was at the door. "You don't need me anyway."

Essex held his arm. "Then if you have made up your mind I suppose I can count on you to be discreet. You must be discreet. Until to-night. To-morrow. A few days, John, until I have fought this out."

"I'm not sure!" Asquith said. "I really disagree with what you are doing."

"To MacGregor?"

"To MacGregor and to a whole political situation."

"Do you intend betraying me to rescue your friend MacGregor?" Essex's bitterness did not spare Asquith its real meaning. It stopped Asquith.

"I'll do what I can for MacGregor," Asquith said with no defiance, only a sorrow. "I will not damage you Harold, but I won't have MacGregor destroyed. Perhaps I can threaten a few people with a few more exposures and a few more facts. My own. But only if it's necessary."

"I'm sorry to hear you say that. I would sooner be struck down than hear it."

"I'm sorry that I had to say it."

"I think you're too late anyway," Essex said. "It will all be settled to-night in the House, and in the Security Council to-morrow. Don't be a madman, John. I tell you that you're too late anyway."

"Perhaps you're right," Asquith said. "Good-bye Harold."

Essex had almost exhausted his control but he did not stop Asquith again. "Good-bye," he said and then took a good grip of himself. "Give my love to Jane."

"Yes. You must come out to dinner one day next week."

"I'd like that," Essex said. "Good-bye."

"Adieu." Asquith passed through the large doorway of English oak which was hand-carved with the pattern of the tree, its branches, its leaves, and finally on the apex the acorn itself which started the cycle all over again down the other side of the door.

Chapter 47

As Asquith was leaving Essex, Katherine was insulting him in his absence for not coming home to lunch. "Where is he, Jane?" she said. "I wanted him to meet Tom Cromwell. John is an unreliable devil. What do you imagine he's doing?"

"I really don't know Kathy," Jane Asquith said. "I expected him home, but he telephoned about an hour ago and said that he was going to see Rowland Smith and some other important sort of people."

"I suppose he and Harold are having a busy morning," Katherine said. "It doesn't matter. Tom can eat his lunch. Do you really have enough to give him? I'm sorry to drop him into your lap Jane, but I had hoped to have MacGregor and John here. Do you really have enough?"

"Certainly," Jane said. "My sister sent me a ham last week from Vancouver."

"MacGregor," Katherine said. "Have you given Jane your ration book?"

"No." MacGregor was embarrassed. "My landlady still has it. I didn't think I would be staying here so long. Shall I go and get it?"

"Not now," Katherine said. "But get it some time. Jane is probably having a difficult time feeding you."

"Are you?" MacGregor asked her.

"Don't let Kathy embarrass you," Jane Asquith said. "The only thing we are short of is butter and we are always short of butter anyway, so let him alone Kathy. When will Mr. Cromwell be here?"

"Now," she said.

"Then I'd better go and see to the kitchen," Jane Asquith said. She stopped for a moment to glance at MacGregor. He was lying on a window-seat — as Asquith had reclined on Essex's leather couch. Jane took a cushion from one of the drawing-room chairs and lifted his head carefully and dropped the cushion under it, smiling at his need for as little head-movement as possible. Katherine clicked her tongue as Jane left them.

"I suppose you arranged that back-bench petition to the Prime Minister last night," MacGregor said to Katherine with a suggestion of accusation. "Is that why you were off seeing Cromwell in the middle of the night?"

"I didn't arrange it," Katherine said. "He did. That is why he wants to see you. To-night there is going to be a heated debate in the House between your friends and your enemies. Cromwell wants to know exactly what he can do."

MacGregor was not fully attentive. "I thought they were debating the Coal Bill," he said. "But what is there to debate about anyway?"

"The Coal Bill is finished," Katherine said and leaned over him to look at the black branches of an old elm which spread over the Mews below. "To-night they begin a debate on Foreign Affairs. Before that there will be question time and someone on the Opposition benches will ask a question about you: whether you have been punished and disciplined properly and adequately. Cromwell says that he and his back-bench Labour friends are going to ask the same question about Essex. That means that you are both about to be settled: one way or the other."

"What's the use of asking a question about Essex?" MacGregor started to sit up but changed his mind. "He'll be at the Security Council to-morrow going for his life. I thought I might have made enough impression by this morning to stop him, but there's hardly a man in England that could see through the mess the newspapers made of it."

"Don't be bitter," she said.

"What do you expect me to be?"

"Intelligent. Anyway the Russians will know what to say to Harold."

"That's not enough. They don't know all the details."

"The Security Council know the details. They have your report."

"How did they get it?"

"I made sure that they got it," she said.

"By now Essex will have changed his arguments and his facts, and my reports will mean absolutely nothing. The only hope I ever had was of stopping Essex before he started. Once he gets going nothing will stop him and no one will be able to pick him up on the details."

"Well there is nothing more that you can do about it, so lie still." She had pushed his feet over and was sitting on the window-seat still looking through the cold grey glass.

"As far as I can see," MacGregor said, "there was never anything I could do about it. I believe I've made the biggest mistake of my life,

Kathy. A man has no right to imagine that he can influence political decisions and the Government of his country. It's one thing to have a vote to make a Government, but what can a man do with the Government he elects? What can I do now that will change its attitude to Azerbaijan, which I know is putrid and dangerous and immoral? By Heavens — I know what Asquith was talking about when he was telling me that I had put myself against the Rule of Law. Government be damned. Government seems to be a masquerade for all that intangible authority that weaves and plots this nice political pattern. You can't get at it, Kathy. There is no way of affecting it or of damaging it. It takes little nuisances like me and eats them up, in the newspapers, in the legalities, in the disgrace that it can bring a man. What chance did I ever have of affecting the course of this large nation? Could I change an empire, could I decide history, could I make an honest policy where there never has been honesty to count for? What am I doing when I risk everything that makes my life livable — risk it for a stupid attempt to right a whole wrong? I must be a fool and I'm surprised that you didn't stop me in the first place and let me go back home to Iran and do what I should be doing. There is nothing that I could ever have done to defeat Essex. Even if I had defeated him, there would be other occasions and other men. But I could never have defeated him. I know that. I know it. Why, there was never a moment when I could feel that the forces opposing me were tangible or recognizable! Only Essex personally. For the rest there was some great blanket of opposition that covered everything I touched. All the shape of authority and information and decision were close-knit and impenetrable and ungettable. All so much in alliance and so carefully aligned. Now that I am really caught I'll be smothered in one quick act. I don't actually care because there is nothing more I can do about anything. I can't even get out and leave the mess I've made for myself. I have to wait for official satisfaction to be given to all who want my blood. Has ever a man made such a mistake as I have made, such a stupid mistake? Government and policy simply exist. You and I can't do anything about it. It's too big, too powerful, too organized, too set. It's something we just have to put up with and live with, taking its direction and its decisions like acts of God, indisputable and irrevocable. For those who defy it, let MacGregor be an example. I have wrecked myself for nothing. It was all a waste of endeavour, of yours of mine and Asquith's and of anybody else who felt that they could force a change in the state of affairs. No one can force a change in political affairs. We can't beat the combination opposing us. We might as well give it up. I have learned the lesson that I should have learned at the very beginning, and if I can ever get out of this mess then I'll keep out of it. Never again will I attack an authority; I know that one cannot defeat it. At best one can keep away, and if I get the chance I'll get out of the way of any more politics; I'll go back to Iran with White to-morrow and struggle with oil and let the rest go hang — if ever I get out of this mess, which is most unlikely now."

Katherine had arisen and she stood away from him. "I don't want to talk with you if you are like that," she said. "Are you defeated because the whole world did not suddenly change over for you? Did you imagine that stopping Essex and breaking a government policy would be easy? Did you think that you could do it with one blow, and is that why you are defeated?"

"You exaggerate," he complained. "If I had made some slight effect on the set course which Essex is taking, then I wouldn't feel that it was hopeless. But I know that Essex is going on as before, and his plan is exactly as before, and nothing I have done in all this fight has changed it one atom."

"That is silly despair," she said disgustedly. "I hardly expected to hear you give yourself over to dismay like a wretched French intellectual or a Danish farmer. You may be a condemned man but that is no excuse."

"That has nothing to do with it." He had to sit up, however much it cleaved his brow. "Whatever happens to me it will not change the hopelessness of trying to affect government and policy."

"You are one man," she said, "and one man can't effect a change. Nor is your way of doing things the only way. For the most part you've been clumsy and inadequate and unreal. Even your final decision to come out against Essex was an act of desperation rather than one of political sense."

"Are you denying it now?"

"No. And don't martyr yourself more than is necessary. For you, MacGregor, it was the only thing to do. It was an incredible thing to do. Now you are spoiling it — complaining that you didn't perform a miracle. It was always a slim hope that you would succeed, but I thought you knew it. I am sure you knew it last night. If the real result is a disillusionment, MacGregor, then you had better take a quick lesson in reality. Don't imagine that you are the only man who is fighting this battle. Don't imagine that all others are suddenly going to abandon their attitude because you couldn't stop Essex. Long before you knew a political word there were men fighting for your Azerbaijan; not only in Azerbaijan but here and everywhere for that matter. It isn't one day and it isn't one act. It's a steady desperate battle and each day one more person is taking part in it, not for the immediate decision that you expect, but for the total decision that encompasses all politics: Azerbaijan and Essex and the Security Council included. You have held on so grimly until now that you were something of an Horatio — almost unbeatable and unbreakable. To see you now is more than I can bear. I won't talk to you until you see that you are stupid and egotistical and without any hope at all."

"Hope in my case," he said, "became a folly. What did I achieve? You think I should take a quick lesson in reality? Why don't you? Look at the situation now and tell me that all our effort achieved anything."

"You don't know yet what it has achieved. Because the newspapers tore you to shreds doesn't mean that you have achieved nothing. Your side of it is just as intangible at times as the other side."

"A lot of good that will do. It will not stop Essex."

"There's more to it than that."

"What more?"

"Normally you could see the full extent of what you were doing, but you are too bitter and broken now to see a damn thing. This isn't over by any means. You really don't know yet what effect you've had on Essex. To-day is only the beginning."

"To-morrow Essex goes to the Security Council."

"I won't talk to you any more. Go and drink a lot of coffee and see if it will bring back a little sense into your fogged brain. If you are going to despair and die now, then you can jolly well do it alone. I shan't have anything to do with you." She left him, and MacGregor sat angrily and dejectedly and alone until Tom Cromwell came.

Cromwell was a small man with determined spring-like heels which left the Asquith carpets with a definite snap. Katherine had said that his name was originally Zimmerman, which everyone had thought as amusing as his political ideas, so he had changed his name to Cromwell and said, "Let's see them laugh at that." He came in holding a bundle of papers tight in his left fist while he shook hands with Jane and Mac-Gregor with his right. He obviously considered greetings something to be dispensed with quickly, and he immediately sat down in the nearest chair and talked with Jane and MacGregor as a man who had known them intimately for a long time. The top of Cromwell's head was bald but over his ears and the bump of his head there was a fuzzy crop of brown hair. He was obviously such an occupied man that Jane Asquith called for lunch, after Cromwell had refused a cocktail. He had stuffed his papers into his coat pocket and over lunch he explained the situation to MacGregor, who could only half-listen because he had his own thoughts. In fact MacGregor was lethargic and almost disinterested in anything that Cromwell could offer him.

"Nobody really knows which way the axe is going to fall," Cromwell said. "I think a quick estimate of the House late last night showed that a majority were in Essex's favour, but that means very little. What happens to you is really a Government decision or a Civil Service decision, and those are hidden forces, even for me. I am sure that the Government will not abandon its foreign policy on this Essex issue, but they may have to compromise on Essex himself, in view of your revelations."

"Isn't it too late for that?" MacGregor said and avoided Katherine's angry eye.

"Probably it is. But the Government knows that we will ask a question on Essex, and they have to estimate the situation as it is now, this morning, so that it is really hard to say whether it's too late or not. Essex has become an embarrassment to the Government, and there is a great deal of opposition in the Labour Party to our easy retention of Tory diplomats. Essex is a bad example and that will play some part. However, he has always been a fair man and they may let him have his say in the Security Council at least. No scandal can quite take away the respect he has built up in the last ten years, and he handles himself so well that personal conviction may influence many of the people who decide these things. On the other hand, MacGregor, your rather political honesty is hard to dispute and discredit. You didn't make a very good job of the Press last night, and not half of your story has been presented or understood. It's too late to get it out in detail in the House, but it's a pity that you left it so long. Of course on the diplomatic level the Foreign Office will have to estimate carefully just how much use the Russians can make of your statement. The Russians have all your reports by now from the Security Council, and that's a blow to Essex. The real trouble is, MacGregor, that you definitely have broken regulations by revealing the details of a confidential mission. There is no doubt at all that you can be caught by the Civil Service Act and probably by the Secrets Act. I think that you might face some charges, unless of course there is an element in this that we don't know about. That's hardly likely because I know everybody that can fight it out on higher levels for you. So don't be too hopeful. We handful in the Labour Party are in this because we see it as an example of the increasing desperation of our bad foreign policy, and you have shaken us up a bit. There is a great deal of admiration in the House for what you've done, MacGregor, and it urges us on because we realize that more people like yourself are willing to commit themselves politically, whatever the consequences. I am glad to see that you are a quiet and intent-looking fellow. I wanted to see you like that, and I must say I am not disappointed. We'll fight for you all the way, MacGregor, so take some heart in some support."

Tom Cromwell had eaten Asquith's lunch as quickly as he had snapped flashing words and judgments at MacGregor. After lunch he did not waste time in getting to the details that he needed. He sat with MacGregor on the window seat with his papers in his hand and a fountain-pen tight in his fingers. His questions were more like those of a newspaperman than of a politician and he knew exactly what he wanted of MacGregor; a disinterested MacGregor whom Kathy obviously hated.

"How old are you MacGregor?"

"Thirty," MacGregor said.

"Born in Iran weren't you? Lived most of your life there? Speak the languages don't you? Know its people and its geography?"

"Yes."

"Do you speak the Azerbaijanian dialect?"

"A little."

"How much? Enough to converse in it?"

"Yes."

"You've never had anything to do with the Russians have you? In Iran I mean, or even here in England. Never joined one of the Friendship Societies for instance?"

"No."

"What about a political party? Do you belong to any of them, here or in Iran, or have you had anything to do with a political party?"

"No."

"Who did you vote for in the last elections?"

"Labour."

"Why?"

"I couldn't tell you why." MacGregor didn't have his heart in it. "In the choice it seemed the sensible thing to do I suppose."

"You didn't ask to go with Essex to Moscow, did you?"

"No. I was trying to get out of the India Office and go back to my own work. They wouldn't release me under National Emergency."

"You applied to enter the India Office in the first place?"

"No."

"I won't ask you about your war record because I have that already. That's a great thing MacGregor and it's an argument in your favour. How did you learn Russian?"

"We lived with a Russian family for some time in Iran."

"Did you see them when you went to Azerbaijan?"

"No. They went back to Russia before the war. They were really half Armenian."

"Have the Russians ever approached you for information or support?"

"No," MacGregor said slowly. "Only Doctor Ross."

Cromwell laughed at the connection. "Did he? What for?"

"He wanted something for the *Daily Worker* about Azerbaijan."

"You refused?"

"Yes."

"Is there anything else I should know?"

"I don't know," MacGregor said.

"I haven't time to go any farther, and you don't seem very co-operative. I simply wanted to know the answers to the worst questions in case we have to refute some false statements about you in the House. The Opposition will fling everything at you to-night, MacGregor, because they are as desperate as Essex. The debate is certain to carry on where the questions leave off, but you can be sure that either you or Essex will go down in a heap to-night. Good-bye MacGregor! I will probably see you later at recess. Don't be too hopeful. Essex really has it all his way and I don't see anything that can give you the advantage. Good-bye."

Tom Cromwell left, and Katherine ignored MacGregor and went with him.

MacGregor stirred himself sufficiently to begin a difficult task: writing to his mother to explain the latest turn in events. His brief phone conversations with her had been unsatisfactory for both: she could not quite understand what he was doing, and he could not explain it. All the same, she accepted his side of it against all others, and she wanted to come to London to give him some support. He had asked her not to come. He was tangled up enough already, so he assured her that he would be down to Shipbourne as soon as he could get away. In the meantime she was not to go all the way into Tonbridge to ring him up. She had no phone of her own and she would not speak from the local post office, so she went six miles to Tonbridge and spoke from the more impersonal telephone box there. He told her not to do that. He would write to her each day. He sat down now to keep his promise, but he had not gone far when Professor White rang.

He told MacGregor that if he still wanted to make that trip to Iran he should be at the London Office with his luggage at midday to-morrow. The plane was leaving at two o'clock. MacGregor did not commit himself, but the Professor left it open for him and said that he would expect MacGregor to-morrow.

Then Asquith came home. He did not tell Jane or MacGregor about his partition from Essex. He said that he had come to take MacGregor to the House of Commons for Question Time and the Debate on Foreign Affairs. It was getting late and they had better go.

Chapter 48

Aᴌᴛʜᴏᴜɢʜ Asquith was a fast and reckless driver, they missed the Speaker's procession, and the House was already hearing prayers when they entered the long stone approach of St. Stephens Hall.

The Commons' own chamber had been burned down in the Battle of Britain, and until the new was built, government attended the nation from the House of Lords. MacGregor felt cold from the moment that he heard his feet clip-clopping on the flagstone corridor; perhaps it was the grey wet walls or the bad lighting or the certainty that this would be another farce, the last and worst of all; perhaps it was the obvious dejection and silence of Asquith whose dismay seemed equal to MacGregor's own. Embittered, MacGregor had no belief at all in this court — the highest court in the land — which he was now attending to hear himself condemned. He didn't think that Asquith felt any better about it either, because Asquith was not attempting to hide his solemnity, as if he too would be condemned. MacGregor for a moment looked for Katherine, expecting to see her somewhere, but there were only policemen and clerks and hurrying men in the open passages. He stood near the policeman, waiting with Asquith without knowing what they were waiting for.

They did not move about and did not talk. They both had their hands in their overcoat pockets, and MacGregor had reached the point where he was feeling sick with anticipation and defeat, when a tall man in striped pants and black coat came by the policeman and greeted Asquith. "Hullo John," he said. "You'll be in the Members' gallery. I'll hand you over to the usher and I'll see you at recess if you feel like some tea in the cafeteria." When Asquith introduced MacGregor to this young but greying Tory, the man seemed a little surprised, but he signed their passes. They were taken upstairs by an usher, and after signing a book they were let into a short gallery with two small carved pews upholstered in red. It was really a small carved pulpit for six or seven people, but entering it they were in the House, no longer a cold abbey, but a rich red chamber packed with men.

Katherine was there in the first small tier, and because John Asquith was ahead the usher put him near her. MacGregor sat above them and behind them in the short upper pew. His feet were almost at Katherine's neck but he could see over her silken head down into the House. As he looked down he eased out of his raincoat, trying not to disturb his neighbour who was an elderly woman, a duchess at least by appearance. He bundled the coat between his legs as quietly as he could, and felt like a man in church as he saw the stained windows and the Gothic arches and the carved wood panelling which encrusted the mellow walls. For a man seeing it for the first time, and for a man who could regain a moment of curiosity from bitter thoughts, he was not disappointed in what he saw.

The House was clearly divided by the opposing tiers of benches below him. The Government were seated on his left and the Opposition on his right, both easily identifiable by the familiar figures of each party. At the deep end of the Assembly was the Speaker, enthroned in his elaborate chair, a robe and wig and ceremony of a man. Beneath and before the Speaker were the clerks, and farther down was the long table which divided the front benches. It was stacked with books and papers, and the Mace lay at one end of it. A few feet across this table the Government and Opposition leaders were facing each other, Mr. Attlee, Mr. Churchill, Mr. Dalton, Mr. Eden, Mr. Strachey, Mr. Bracken, Mr. Morrison, Mr. Law. Sir Stafford Cripps's long legs stretched out so that his feet rested on the table's edge, and this informality shocked MacGregor's sense of respect and proportion. The soles of Cripps's shoes were face to face with Mr. Eden on the opposite bench. The Members' benches that mounted up in four tiers each side were filled with restless men and a few quiet women. Members were still coming in at an entrance hidden below Mac-Gregor, and he could see them bowing to the Chair as they entered. Around the top of the House on MacGregor's level was a single narrow balcony which had a few people at one end of it. Right at the opposite end to MacGregor there was a larger gallery, and by its appearance Mac-Gregor guessed it to be the Press gallery. Of the remaining people who were attending the session, MacGregor looked for Essex, but Essex was nowhere to be seen. Essex was not in the House at all.

MacGregor knew enough about Question Time to know that it opened every session of Parliament. Most questions were written and notified before the session, and the usher had given MacGregor a printed list. But before the written questions there were oral questions, questions without notice which were asked direct of Ministers. At this moment Mr. Dalton was giving some information on the importation of tobacco under the American loan agreement. Impatient as he was, MacGregor was interested in the questions. Some concerned goods and monies, but most of them dealt with the incidental but sorry injustices of administration. They came from both sides of the House and the Ministers involved were expected to give satisfaction. It educated MacGregor quickly in the forms and procedure and innate seriousness of elected assembly, but he only wanted one thing of this assembly. Himself. That was slow in coming. When it did come, there was a moment of real expectancy in the House. A stream of members came in as if warned that an expected moment had arrived. MacGregor understood the moment and looked down on Katherine's head, but she was hard against him and rigidly facing the scene before her.

The Speaker called upon a Right Honourable Member for Lombardy who had risen from the Opposition benches to ask his question. He was an old man and an important man, white-haired and wearing black glasses on a ribbon around his neck. He was tall and thin but he spoke with the low growl of a clever dog.

"Mr. Speaker. I direct a question to the Minister representing the Prime Minister." He took his time. He was deep and terse and he glared around the House for a moment. "A servant of the Crown, one I. A. MacGregor, has recently published his opinions of a government mission to Moscow and Azerbaijan, a mission which he attended. He has made serious accusations, not only against the Government, but against one of our most respected envoys, and against the British Commonwealth itself. He has cast terrible and disloyal and unwarranted suspicion upon our integrity in dealing with other nations. In view of the serious international dishonour we suffer, in view of the disservice which MacGregor has done the Commonwealth, I would like to ask the Government what real steps have been taken finally and drastically to disqualify MacGregor's statements. And further," he growled, "what steps have been taken to punish this man for a serious breach of Trust, Code, and Regulation."

There was nothing dramatic about it, yet no man could hear such calm words cast upon himself without having the blood drain from his wretched face. MacGregor leaned over to hear Mr. Attlee answer it, but he saw that Mr. Attlee had gone and so had a number of other Ministers. Instead of Mr. Attlee a short dark man with horn-rimmed glasses stood up and put a few sheets of paper on the table before him and cleared his throat.

John Asquith leaned his head back to talk up to MacGregor. "That's Butcher," he whispered, "One of the Parliamentary Under-secretaries; hanged if I remember which one."

Mr. Butcher took off his glasses and cleaned them, and MacGregor asked himself angrily if they all took so much time. "I have been asked to reply to this question," Mr. Butcher said, "because it concerns our department." He spoke disinterestedly, almost mumbling, but MacGregor could hear every word of it. "This isn't the sort of question for a quick reply, and I ask the Right Honourable Member's indulgence in the matter. MacGregor is really a complex problem, a problem which cuts right across the path of three or four different Ministries, including the Foreign Office and the India Office, as well as the Prime Minister's and our own. More than that, it is a Civil Service matter. It also is a very delicate and dangerous subject at this moment because it can influence the conduct of our affairs in the Security Council to-morrow. However, I will answer the Right Honourable Member's two questions as best I can. First, I think the House will agree that this man MacGregor's statements to the Press were in bad taste as well as in bad grace and bad liege."

"Hear! Hear!" MacGregor heard it from both sides.

"Bad liege and infamous!" a Member cried in addition. Others added similar comment to Mr. Butcher's condemnation, and the Speaker called for Order.

591

Mr. Butcher leaned on the table with his knuckles. "The House will also agree that adequate statements were made by the proper authorities disqualifying MacGregor's opinions from serious consideration. I refer principally to the statements of his superior, the man who conducted the mission to Moscow and Azerbaijan: Lord Essex. We believe that no better authority than Lord Essex could be offered in denying MacGregor's ridiculous accusations."

"Hear! Hear!"

Mr. Butcher drew a breath and raised his voice a little. "As for what steps will be taken concerning Mr. MacGregor himself: I had hoped to have the answer to that question by the time the House met this evening; but I haven't. If the Members will have a little patience and let me finish! I know that this situation around MacGregor is critical and concerns our international good name, nevertheless it is a Civil Service matter and the proper Service people are deciding action on MacGregor at this moment."

"How long must we wait?" asked the Right Honourable Member for Lombardy without rising from his bench.

"I hope to have an answer before the House adjourns to-night, in fact within a very short time. I will ask leave of the House to offer further information about MacGregor's situation when I have it."

The Member for Lombardy rose quickly and growled again. "In view of the unsatisfactory reply, and considering this in the proportions of a national crisis, I serve notice to the House that I intend referring to this matter again in the Foreign Affairs Debate which follows."

Mr. Butcher rose. "We have no objection," he said. "We will no doubt be able to settle this question of MacGregor to the Right Honourable Member's satisfaction when I receive word of the Service decision on him. I repeat: it shouldn't be long, within the hour."

Nobody appeared satisfied with Mr. Butcher's reply and the Speaker had to call for order again. MacGregor himself lost his last shred of patience with the body of men below him, with the Assembly itself and all it represented to him. He could not consider this a temporary reprieve. He looked at his white hands gripping his knees, and knew that it was another agonizing delay. There seemed to be no end to his sorrows. He must sit and wait a Minister's pleasure. For a moment he decided to rise and go away, but Asquith leaned back and grinned at him as if he had understood MacGregor's intention, and MacGregor nodded and stayed.

Tom Cromwell was on his feet. He appeared with agile suddenness just behind Mr. Butcher. He shook his handful of papers above his head and addressed his question to the whole House. "The Minister representing the Prime Minister," he announced quickly: "I would like to know if the Government has considered a certain petition asking for the immediate dismissal of Lord Essex from office and withdrawing him as soon as possible from his special assignment to the Security Council to-morrow." The Opposition were already crying *Withdraw!* and Cromwell had to shout above them. "I ask this because of the serious doubt and suspicion which MacGregor has put upon Lord Essex, particularly in view of the fact that Mr. MacGregor's accusations seemed to be accurate and unanswerable."

There were angry scenes and disorder and pandemonium and heated exchanges and all other forms of Parliamentary temper. MacGregor stood to hear what was going on, but half the House seemed to be on their feet shouting across the aisle. MacGregor could distinguish the Tory who had given Asquith their passes. MacGregor could hear him accusing Cromwell of sabotaging the finest diplomat that Britain ever had, of wrecking a mission which meant Britain's very existence; finally calling Cromwell a bigger traitor than MacGregor. Those ringing words seemed to be as far as an "unheard" Parliamentary accusation could go. It sobered the House enough for the Speaker to be heard cautioning Members and calling for Mr. Butcher. Mr. Butcher had been standing disinterested and bored while this tempest lapped around him, and he extracted full silence from the House before answering Tom Cromwell.

"This too is a serious matter," Butcher said solemnly. "It is impossible to make a statement on it at such short notice. Lord Essex and MacGregor are really part of the same problem requiring a measured and careful solution. When I have the answer to one of these questions I will have the answer to the other. Members will have to be patient. This is a delicate situation and we had hoped that Members would be more discreet. Gentlemen on both sides of the House are dangerously intent on getting their man, but I cannot say a word until other decisions are made. They are being made now, and at the end of Questions I will leave the House and return shortly with the solution to this extraordinary situation. Until then I hope that Members on both sides will be careful what they say about Lord Essex and Mr. MacGregor, and our diplomatic affairs."

Mr. Butcher sat down, and before there could be any further spontaneous out-of-order discussion the Speaker had warned Members that any more breaches of proper conduct would bring serious consequences; he did not want to name members but he would if necessary. This silenced the House and they went on with the remainder of Questions like dogs at a leash waiting for a later moment when they would be free to fight without restraint.

At recess Katherine and Asquith left their bench and MacGregor put his coat on his seat and followed them. They were given thirty minutes' freedom by the policeman and they went downstairs with Cromwell to the cafeteria, which seemed to be a cellar with more history than a cafeteria permitted. They sat at a table so that they could occupy a place before the rush of Members filled all seats. Cromwell asked them what they would have, and MacGregor said nothing and Asquith said coffee and Katherine said she would choose her own. MacGregor sat and watched her talking pleasantly with Cromwell as the two of them held trays and walked before the glass food counter and chose what they needed and returned. It was almost too much for MacGregor when he saw that Katherine had given herself a tomato salad. How the devil could she eat anything! She sickened him until he had to look away.

"Why don't you eat something?" she said to him.

"No thank you," he said.

"Tom believes you have a lot more support in the House than he expected," she said. MacGregor said nothing.

"You shouldn't feel quite so hopeless," she told him softly.

MacGregor could say nothing, no word.

Asquith and Cromwell had been talking intently so that Katherine could be gentle with MacGregor, but in its failure they immediately filled the unpleasant quiet with their own comment.

"There's some big talk going on somewhere," Cromwell said. "I haven't had time to find out much about it, but I think we really will hear the answer very quickly."

"You all seem unusually lurid in the House to-night," Asquith said, more for MacGregor than Cromwell. "I wonder what you fellows would do if you were refused the use of such full-blooded and royal adjectives. I thought you Labour politicians had changed all that."

"It's the royal red upholstery!" Cromwell said and thought it a good joke.

Asquith's Tory passed by, and seeing them he came over and greeted Cromwell by the name of Tom and leaned on his shoulder as he bowed to Katherine and nodded to MacGregor and asked Asquith how Jane was. "Tom," he said to Cromwell. "Are you going to Liverpool on Wednesday with the shipping delegation?"

"I think so Jeff," Cromwell told him.

"I'll travel up with you," the Tory said. "But for God's sake keep me a seat near the window and with my back to the engine. I'm about the only man in the world that gets trainsick. See you later old boy," he said to Asquith. "Good night," he said to the others.

When he had gone Katherine looked apprehensively at MacGregor's tight white face and went on eating her salad. Almost immediately MacGregor got up. "It's cold here," he said. "I think I'll go back to the House." He left so abruptly that even Katherine was surprised.

"Damned unpleasant to hear your name badly treated in the House,"

Cromwell said, watching him go. "If MacGregor is handed over to Security it will be a crime we will never quite live down as Socialists."

"What's the matter with him, Kathy?" Asquith asked. "I thought he would take it better."

Katherine had turned to watch MacGregor plunge through the swing doors. "I don't know," she said nervously. "I don't know."

"After all," Cromwell said. "He is taking an awful beating."

Asquith nodded. "More than that!" he said.

"I think he has given up his whole effort as a terrible waste," Katherine said. "He has lost confidence in all that he has done. Whatever they decide it will be just another bitter joke for him, the way he is now."

"Go on out with him," Asquith said.

Katherine shook her head. "I can't do anything."

They had little more to say to each other, and before their thirty minutes had expired they went back to their pew and found MacGregor sitting stiffly against the gilt railing next to the Duchess. They sat in front and waited silently for the debate on Foreign Affairs to begin.

The House filled, and when the end of recess had been rung the Speaker entered, the House rose, and the debate began. After the formalities another expected moment had arrived when the Right Honourable Member for Lombardy rose to address the House. He held his glasses in one hand and gripped his coat lapel with the other. He was a dramatic archaic Englishman and his thunder spread out on the House like a distant but approaching storm.

"It is appropriate," he grumbled, "that this MacGregor scandal is now to be settled in the House. It is a scandal that had to find its way here because it crystallizes the issue we face to-night in this debate on Foreign Affairs. The issue, Sir, of whether we are to allow the evil of Communism to decide our vital affairs.

"We, on this side of the House, are seriously disturbed with the Labour Government's inability to combat this menace at home and abroad. Now we have the astonishing spectacle of a Civil Servant of Communist inclination giving aid and comfort to a foreigner, and the Labour Government does little or nothing about it. In demanding disciplinary action on this man MacGregor we are demanding that the Government finally wake up to the menace which is threatening British Democracy. What is going to become of this nation if such men are allowed to sabotage our administration and our rôle in world affairs. What is going to become of this nation if the Kremlin is allowed to continue browbeating small neighbours and using its insidious influence in the affairs of other nations, including our own? It is high time that our Socialist friends stopped turning a weak and jaundiced eye to this evil. The British people did not give them mandate to hand over our affairs to recalcitrant Communists and their MacGregor ilk, nor have the Socialists a mandate to tolerate these wretches. With Socialist permission they have wormed their way into the very heart of our national affairs, into our political parties, our unions, our press, our universities, yea! and even our clergy. Worse! They have riddled the Public Services with their friends, even to the extent of attending important and vital missions which they sabotage for their masters by disloyal opinions. It ought to stop, I say. These traitors might cry free speech and democracy, but so did Hitler. It would not be an encroachment upon the free speech and democracy of this country if the Communists and their little friends were rooted out of our national institutions. In fact we must stamp them out if free speech and democracy are to continue. This internal evil cannot be separated from the international evil, because we here are the bulwark of Western Democracy, and the survival of the West depends upon British vigilance at home as well as abroad. And I am asking the Government to begin at home, so that our hand in international affairs can be strengthened. I am not asking for legislation to illegalize this Red influence; not yet anyway. The menace can be met if the Socialist Government sees its responsibility and begins a purge, yes a purge of government departments, rooting out and prosecuting all men with Communist intentions and Communist affiliations. They can begin with this man MacGregor. He may not be a Communist, but he is a good example of the evil I am talking about. We find men like MacGregor in every step of our daily lives, men who are directly or indirectly under the influence of Communistic ideas. There he is, on a government mission, the most important government mission since the end of the war. There he is, sabotaging the mission and attempting to discredit that premier and noble diplomat, Lord Essex, whose personal honour and integrity have been stamped in the dust by this vicious young man. If we give such men free rein, where will it end? We can't laugh at these MacGregors. They are not fools. They are dastardly clever and they use their important positions to further the interests of another State. Yes. Another State! Nor are they all little men like MacGregor. Some of them are big men, professors and scientists and engineers and editors and experts. We find them particularly in our institutions of learning and science, and that is where the real danger lies and where we must stamp them out. A man may have a right to criticize the Government, but I'm hanged if he has a right to brazenly use his free speech to attack our way of life. More and more we see men in science and profession and academy abusing their privileges of expression by crying that their real liberties are threatened by patriotism. Is patriotism above these men? Do they have a right to express their views, to carry on their work, to be free men unless they are patriotic to our society? I say no sir! Loyalty is one of the prerogatives of freedom, and these men who launch Communistic attacks upon our Nation and our Empire are disloyal. And it isn't only a Socialist Government that they betray, but the Crown itself. This takes the problem beyond the lines of party politics. We must unite in identifying and eliminating these men from about us. We must tear them out from their disguise as liberal, progressive, and rationalist. We Conservatives offer the Government full support in any measure taken against these monsters. We demand a purge, a purge of the Services to begin with. A purge of the MacGregors who sabotage our position at home and abroad. We are giving the Government this chance for co-operation before making it an issue for the English people. The Government attitude now, on MacGregor, will be our yardstick for their good intentions. Here is your chance. We will see if you can take it. The Government is facing a choice between Lord Essex and MacGregor, a choice between national trust and national betrayal. The eyes of the world are upon this House to-night, and the fate of this nation may depend upon the course which the Government takes in this matter. Choose, Gentlemen. Face history with your courage or your folly."

The Right Honourable Member for Lombardy growled at the House again before stepping back and sitting down, amid loud acclamation from both sides of the House.

"Such a wonderful man," the Duchess beside MacGregor said to him. "Such a magnificent man; histrionic, proud, aggressive, determined, noble."

MacGregor nodded politely and wondered if anything more could be stripped from his faith in a British institution and a British honour. Here was a man for whom MacGregor had the highest respect, "the Great Lombardian," the man whom all England respected above party and politics; here was this man making a mockery of honesty and fair play. To hear such inaccurate condemnation from this man hurt MacGregor more than the actual sense of it; and if this could happen in the House of Commons then anything could happen and the Duchess beside him might as well call the Great Lombardian magnificent and noble. What little belief in nobility or honour was left for MacGregor?

Already other men were on their feet but a small red-headed man from the Labour benches was already talking and the Speaker acknowledged him: the Member for Scottish Industries.

"Mr. Speaker," he cried with his tongue on the roof of his mouth like a good Glaswegian. "We have heard a chapter in Red-baiting to-night which is bad enough for America's famous Dies Committee, but unworthy of any member of this great House. See how easily the word Communist slips from the nimble tongue of our noble Friend opposite. He flings it callously at this MacGregor, seeking only to discredit an honest man who has had the courage to risk his social existence for the publication of a few terrible facts. He uses it as the Nazis used it, to damn every liberal idea, every progressive act, every needed political reform. This House should absorb his speech and hastily take stock of itself. Red-baiting similar to that of our Right Honourable friend's has become the aggressive weapon of universal reaction and war-mongering everywhere. The world over, these noble men have made a bogy of Communism so that they can label every man of free-thought a Communist or a Communist sympathizer. Any man who fights for the simplest liberty is a Communist, and Communism must-be-stamped-out-sir. Scientists who fight for freedom of research, teachers who fight for the right to teach, politicians who fight for the right to reform, workers who fight for the right to organize, and diplomats who fight for peace itself, they are all considered Reds by our Honourable friends. Reds or not, such men are the defenders of common liberty, and it is against our common liberties that our Right Honourable friend opposite has declared war with his Red-baiting. The fight is on, my friends, and in this House it not only concerns a man called MacGregor, it concerns every man. Start a witch-hunt for Reds in the Services and it will end where it did in Germany and Italy. Begin with MacGregor and it will end with every man on this side of the House. There is derisive laughter from the opposite benches, but Tory laughter deceives no one. Tories cannot hide their past and they cannot hide their intentions. Nor can we. If we allow this dispute about MacGregor to be turned into a precedent for dismissal and dishonour, then we Socialists are doomed men. It isn't MacGregor that we Socialists should be damning. It is Lord Essex who should receive our bitter words. It isn't MacGregor who is conducting a policy which amounts to betrayal of our Socialist principles. It is Lord Essex. From all aspects, Lord Essex has shown himself to be a ruthless follower of our imperial policy against every breath of social reform. We should not destroy MacGregor for exposing this man, we should save and preserve MacGregor as a courageous man, an honourable man; a good English contrast to that other plotter of cunning policy. And if there is diplomatic catastrophe in MacGregor's courageous behaviour, then we can only blame ourselves. It is we Socialists who have allowed a Tory Civil Service to remain and influence and conduct our foreign affairs. How does a man like Essex represent a Socialist Government? Is he a Socialist? Is he half-way a Socialist? Or is he a rabid Tory? Are our Ambassadors to other nations Socialists? Are our so-called advisers in the Foreign Office Socialists? No sir! They are all Tories. Tories by birth, by fortune, and by politics. If we must have a purge, let it be of these men. By their influence they are shaping our foreign policy to the perfect satisfaction of our Tory opponents. And it happens to be a policy of little-brotherism with America and terrible war with Russia. When a man like MacGregor comes along and exposes these intentions we are asked to destroy him; and some of our Labour Ministers have the infernal cheek to agree and condemn. What sort of Socialists are we? MacGregor is the man we should attend, not that premier and noble diplomat Lord Essex. Essex must go. Policy or no policy, it is easy to see that MacGregor is telling the truth. I know very little about MacGregor personally, but I know enough. I know that terrible pressure has been put on him to withdraw his statements, but he has refused like a man of positive conviction. Now he is threatened further with disgrace, made the symbol of Red terror, and called coward and traitor. Shame on that old tyrant opposite for such unscrupulous words. I shan't withdraw! This man MacGregor is not a plotter. He is not a traitor, not a coward, not a political opportunist like that Right Honourable gentleman who sits on the front bench opposite with his white head so proudly erect. MacGregor is not even an ambitious public servant. Ironically, he was released from the army and taken into the India Office by a Tory administration under the Coalition Government, an administration which was apparently satisfied that this was a brilliant young man who was better needed in the India Office than he was in the army; a man who could speak three or four languages, whose background was unimpeachable even by Tory standards. He was chosen by Lord Essex himself to go to Moscow because he was considered an expert on Iranian affairs, having lived most of his life in that country. MacGregor is no politician, no diplomat, and no Civil Servant; he is a geologist and a man of some expectancy in that field. More than that he is an honourable fellow, a man who fought in the war with great distinction, a man awarded the Military Cross, several times mentioned in dispatches, and twice wounded. He did not ask to be dragged into diplomatic missions to Moscow or to Azerbaijan. He has never had any political axe to grind one way or the other. I tell you that a man like MacGregor cannot be so easily dishonoured, my friends. You may be able to damn him and break him in this House, but to many of us he will always be something of a hero among silent men; a courageous man who has spoken out at a time when too many good voices are quiet because they fear disruption for their honesty. If we take honour away from this man because of his honest and expert opinion, we will be men without any shred of honesty ourselves. MacGregor may have broken regulations, and he may deserve punishment, but this is the highest court in the land and our verdict is a verdict for all men. We dare not dishonour this man. More than that we dare not sanction the beginning of a Red-baiting campaign by impinging MacGregor. If we do, it will be our admission that Tory policy is our policy. I say that this is our chance to be Socialists, to be courageous men for once. If we damn MacGregor, then history will damn us."

The Scot sat down in a moment of silence and there was no acclamation.

"That man is paid in Moscow gold," said the Duchess to MacGregor, "and he too should be tried as a traitor. To think that such men are elected to the House of Commons and breathe the same air as Mr. Churchill and Mr. Eden and the magnificent Lombardian."

"Yes," MacGregor said politely — a civilized man.

He was glad at least that there had been some reply to the great white statesman. In his one brief speech that histrionic figure had become infamous to MacGregor. This reply had been necessary. Nevertheless MacGregor knew that nothing the Scot had said for him would affect the decisions being made. Nothing that was said in here would decide MacGregor's fate. That decision was being made elsewhere. This was not the highest court in the land. The highest court in the land was somewhere else in some unknown building; in a room with locked doors, a room which MacGregor would never enter and never see. This was a great camouflage for the authority that stemmed from another unknown source.

There was anger now in the House and there were short arguments and accusations across the floor, and the Speaker had to shout above the growing uproar. He finally broke the disorder by sharp pronouncements, and in a moment the Right Honourable Member for Lombardy had arisen from the Opposition benches again. All others on both sides of the House sat down in awe and respect for this noble man who glared at them again, so that the Duchess next to MacGregor said "Bulldog breed! Grand old man!"

"Our Labour friends," said the grand old man, "have made an heroic attempt to confuse the issue of this debate, but despite their efforts the issue remains the same. It is still Communism. If they must have it abroad then call it Russia. It is time we came to it anyway. We seek only peace with that large Asiatic dictatorship, but what we want and what they want are two different desires. No nation has disregarded the moral code of international affairs with such terrible regularity as that Oriental colossus. Apart from their own hidden expanse, they have trapped half of Europe into their Communist net. They have heavy fingers on the heart of China. They stand astride the northern gates of India. Persia, Turkey, Afghanistan, Greece, are facing the frightening threat of envelopment. The very life-lines of the British Empire itself are menaced by the expanding tentacles of Red Imperialism. East and West, this Imperialism is extending its grip upon the world we live in. Our Labour idealists may be able to ignore the East, but they cannot ignore the West. The pestilence has even spread to the borders of our beloved isle, and it is time we put a stop to it. If Western Democracy is to survive then Western Democracy must organize itself. Already the great nations of Eastern Europe are lost. The iron curtain has descended upon them like a political guillotine. Finland, the Baltic countries, Poland, Czechoslovakia, Rumania, Bulgaria, Jugoslavia, Hungary and half of Germany are gone. So little of Europe remains that only a vigorous organization of Western nations will prevent further a complete envelopment by Red Fascism. If the Labour Government does not take steps immediately to organize a Western Bloc of nations for its vital defence, then the Labour Government must face the anger of the British people who demand it. They must take responsibility for betraying the good people of Europe. To survive — this nation must lead all others in a strong and forthright defence of cherished liberties and cultures. Together with our American partner across the sea, we must forge a body that cannot be opposed by any other nation or combination of nations. Our far-flung Empire must be organized into a political arsenal of democracy, always ready in council and field to follow the lead which Britain must give. With the peoples of the world on our side we cannot lose. With the unanswerable power of the atom at our disposal, we cannot be denied. The Labour Government faces the terrible choice of achieving these aims for Democracy, or of sinking in the swirl of a bloody Red whirlpool. Already Labour is facing its first decision in Iran. In Iran, Russia has used her privileged position to dissect that nation and create a false republic of its wealthiest province. It is the pattern they will use on all Europe if we allow them to succeed in Iran. It is no use our Labour friends confusing the issue of Iran by defending this man MacGregor. The Russians have interfered in Iran, whatever the MacGregors say. They are interfering everywhere, creating a fifth column of Communists ready to seize power at the first opportunity. We must expose them. We must come to the call of every nation already in such trouble. Iran is not the first and she will not be the last. Unless we act now to create our Western alignments, then France, the Low Countries, Scandinavia, Austria, Italy and Spain will go to the Red Devil. Germany too is our concern. We must save her for Western Democracy. Imagine Europe with a Red Germany; and that is certainly what our Soviet friends are aiming at. They have already created a police state in Germany behind that cordon of Red bayonets, and they are sending their spies, and saboteurs, and agitators into the Anglo-American zone to disturb our process of democratization. In the peace that we must give this defeated enemy, we cannot allow one terror to replace another. Furthermore: to complete our war tasks and our war aims, we must make sure that our international organizations for peace-making and security are in the proper hands. We in the West must act as a single unit in the United Nations. This way we can create a strong Democratic world organization which will cope with any threat from the East. And let there be no mistake about our intentions. We do not want war, but we will not be frightened by the grim threats and heavy hand of our Soviet friends. Perhaps we should remind ourselves that we share the secret of that remarkable and supernatural explosive which man has torn from the hands of the gods: the atom bomb. It is now part and parcel of our Western Democracy, and as such it should remain our secret until other nations are fit to enjoy our confidence and goodwill. God has given us this weapon to defend our Christianity and our Democracy; our Christian Democracy! And the world should not forget it. Our other first line of defence must be Iran. To-morrow in the Security Council the British representative must make it clear that Iran's fight is our fight. Nothing that one disgruntled Civil Servant has said must turn us away from our duty. We must disavow this man MacGregor and reiterate our confidence and trust in Lord Essex. Essex must be supported. Our Labour friends opposite must refrain from insulting Essex, and this House must not tolerate any further threat to that great diplomat. He must be given a full free hand to conduct his mission to-morrow as he sees fit. We must show the world to-night that this whole assembly is behind him, above party and above petty dispute, and our first act of confidence in Essex must be a repudiation of MacGregor. We must show the world that we consider him a traitor, and we must treat him as such. If we begin there, we can end wherever we wish. From this side of the House we demand that the Labour Government denounce Russia as an aggressor. We demand that the Government send an ultimatum to the Soviet Government insisting that her interference in other nations' affairs cease; that her diplomatic representatives be instructed to be polite and more respectful in their dealings with Great Britain. We demand that the British Government take immediate steps to form a close military and political alliance of Western Powers, beginning with America. And we demand that a Royal Commission be established to investigate the link of the British Communist Party and other similar organizations to the Kremlin. In all affairs, Sir, we demand a showdown with Russia. Now!"

MacGregor now watched the Government front benches for Butcher's arrival. MacGregor did not know how he remained here when every word that was said added so much to his defeat and his anger. He hardly cared what Butcher would announce, just so long as he would come and get it over and done with. This beating was more than MacGregor could stand. After the Great Lombardian there seemed to be little more damage that any man could do him, but when the Duchess thanked God for this great institution the House of Commons which enabled the Great Lombardian to remain the spiritual leader of the Nation, MacGregor turned upon her with unthought-of bitterness and said, "There is nothing great or spiritual in this institution, and if that man represents our national intelligence then we are fools and the gathering below is a collection of hypocrites."

Both Katherine and Asquith heard it and they looked around quickly, startled, as was the Duchess. MacGregor felt foolishly defiant and he was saved from bad embarrassment by Tom Cromwell, who was beginning a speech as if he were in the middle of it, his fists in his coat pockets in unusual restraint.

"It wasn't long ago," he said, "that Fascism destroyed every liberty in Europe in the name of anti-Communism. It destroyed every item of free existence, every life, mind, and voice that represented a glimmer of human right. Twenty million people or more were uprooted and destroyed by the war that Fascism launched against 'Communism,' the sort of 'Communism' that existed in France, Norway, Czechoslovakia, and Britain herself. To-night we are asked to carry on where the Fascist left off at Belsen and Buchenwald. It is no exaggeration. Those immeasurable instruments of human torture and destruction are the ally of this campaign against Russia and Communism. At this moment we are asked to join in, beginning with MacGregor. If we do, the men and women in this House are facing their own political destruction, and this House will go down in the dust with all other 'Communist' political institutions. Though this scheme begins with Russia and Communism, we all know where it ends. We have witnessed it before, and again it is being led by the same men. The anti-Communists are always the great crusaders or the great defenders: defenders of Democracy, defenders of the Faith, defenders of race, nation, a Way of Life, freedom, Constitution, grace, culture, law, order, family, home, Free-Enterprise, womanhood, and civilization itself. These great defenders live in every land, leading the campaign to-day against Red Imperialism. Here they begin with Mosley, and in Europe they begin with the fascist politicians and the vicious collaborators. They are your expected allies. They are all in it. Europe's shining example of anti-Communism is General Franco. He will be your friend and ally in this Western Bloc, he will defend Western culture and liberty and Democracy against Russian expansionism and Red Fascism. It will be his lead among others that we will follow in this political crusade, and once more Britain's international name will be linked with the wickedest forces in Europe. We will again be the nation of the finest words and quickest betrayal. We will again arrange the most shameful of political alignments in the name of British honour and British fair play."

There was a shout. "What does a Socialist know about British honour?"

"A lot more than the Honourable Member: you who once called Hitler the Galahad of Europe. It's a miracle that we have any honour left the way some men in this House have behaved. And if we do have any respect left we will never recover it in present or future history if we allow Lord Essex to begin these alignments in the Security Council to-morrow. Even more than that: if we desert men like MacGregor, who seek to determine our path with grim and unselfish honesty, then we will be formally rejecting the best in any Englishman, because this island is full of MacGregors, and we can never completely defeat or deceive them. MacGregor is among the careful men of England, perhaps the studious men or the thinking men or the scientific men, all of whom are watching our attempt at government with sharp scientific honesty. One by one and a hundred by a hundred, the MacGregors are taking part in political affairs, and they are too intelligent to be misled by the clever manœuvring of political fireflies like Essex. They are too intelligent to be taken in by any antics or pretence in this House about our so-called mission in the world or our holy crusade against Bolshevism. They know the game we are playing, and like MacGregor they will cry it out, whatever the consequences. They know that there is little hope for human existence if this nation throws itself upon a Russia branded evil by the great men on the Opposite benches.

"If our great men must talk about evil and imperialism and expansion-ism and threat, in another nation, then let them talk about America. There you have the real Tory collaborator in this new attack upon Russia. American capital has taken up this easy banner of world disorder and we are simply the poor willing fools that follow on behind. We are expected and asked to beat the Russians to death, and yet we are the ultimate vic-tims ourselves: we Socialists, we democrats, we progressives, we liberals, we republicans. Though it isn't the private crusade of America, American capital is conducting it, financing it, directing it, and using it, because America to-day is in the hands of violent expansionists, imperialists, cap-italists, fascists — call them what you like. They believe the world is theirs, with their atom bomb and their sickening dollars. They are men who have seized America from the feeble hands of a frightened man, and through him they are directing a brazen attack upon the common liberties of all men. With our imperialists they ask the world to stop Russia!"

"Hear, hear!" said the Lombardian.

"Stop Russia for what?" Cromwell demanded. "So that American capi-tal can extend its economic and political dominion over this entire uni-verse, even to the poles! Like our own — these American imperialists are terrified of any movement for social and economic freedom because their Imperialism cannot exist in a better world and they know it. It cannot exist while Russia remains an example in social ownership and social courage.

"If we ever looked to America for leadership in human affairs, we may

604

have looked to the late President Roosevelt, but these men are not Roosevelt men. Roosevelt's men have gone. Instead we have the new men of America. The men of capital representation, of military ambition, of political threat, of economic force. These are the men we are expected to follow in this great campaign against Russia. But it isn't only Russia that they attack. Their war is upon a world of resisting people who seek self-determination and some ultimate, simple, liberty. Their war is upon every progressive citizen, particularly those desperate partisans who fight for their liberty in America itself. Already the American schemers have the world by the throat. This very nation they have buttered with their silver dollars, saving us from the sins of all-out Socialism. Our entire economy to-day is primed and based on the American loan. What more dominion could one nation have over another?"

"Shame!"

The Lombardian stood and cried: "You impugn our greatest Ally. Withdraw it. Withdraw, I say!"

There were other cries for withdrawal.

Cromwell shouted back in reply. "I will withdraw word for word with that Right Honourable *Ally* opposite. Let him take back what he says of Russia, and I will withdraw what I say of America."

MacGregor could feel the touch of recklessness and danger in all these men. They were ready to abandon parliamentary limits as they shouted in disorder above the rulings of the Speaker. There was a moment when he could see them as anything but Englishmen. Yet this potential moment of abandon quickly turned them back, and he saw them Saxon again as a tall stately woman seized their restraint to call upon them in a strong clear voice of dignity. "Friends!"

There was a laugh.

"I know!" she said with a smile. "I know it's an odd word to use in addressing the House. But I use it to remind Honourable Members of their responsibility to each other."

There was silence.

"Now for some Liberal objectivity," Asquith said to MacGregor over his shoulder in a whisper that the whole House must have heard. "You know who that is!"

"Is that Miss Livingstone?"

"Yes, and she's going to sterilize this place with sanity."

"Shh!" said the Duchess.

"You see!" Asquith said.

Miss Livingstone was already talking, and MacGregor felt like every other man in the House; he could feel this woman turning them into schoolboys, commanding their attention, ridiculing their anger. She was the First Lady of the House, its great figure of British Liberalism;

Humanist, Pacifist, a woman whose sincerity no Member would question.

"I had no intention of joining in this argument," Miss Livingstone was saying, "but I must say I am morally bound to take a stand in defence of our American friends. And that doesn't mean I am attacking or criticizing Russia. I am merely suggesting that we be sensible and give America her due. I can't see why we should suspect American motives in the world. Why should we suddenly picture that great Liberal Democracy as a Moloch and a Mars? There is no sense to it! Surely it should be clear to everyone that America is now the largest world power; so why should we object when she takes on responsibility equal to her importance? It is no use complaining that she came out of the war industrially richer than when she went into it while all the rest of us went on the rocks. Industry was America's rôle in the war, and if it hadn't been for American production I ask you where would we be now!"

"Right where we are!" the Glaswegian claimed.

"That's not true. We owe an enormous debt to America; we owe a measure of our Liberty to America and we should not repay it in insults. All over the world to-day America is using her enormous wealth to sustain the thin thread of Democracy in the face of disorder and poverty. Why should we suspect her motives? Why should we consider her self-seeking? There is nothing to suggest that she is satisfying self-interest! The Americans are known the world over for their tolerance, their big hearts, their bluff goodwill. Let them help the world where they can. Let the spirit of Jefferson and Roosevelt show the backward countries of the world an idea in Democracy. Yes! And let them show us as well. The Americans are decent honest people, and they have worked hard for what they've got. So when they offer to share their abundance and give disinterested advice, let us treat them like brothers. Let us stop calling them pariahs from the floor of this House. Fortunately the majority of this House agree with me in this, but I appeal to the few exceptions to be tolerant. Learn that tolerance from America herself; and if you still doubt the good hearts of our Atlantic comrades, then at least wait until history makes its calm decision on American world policy before condemning it out of hand."

"Hear, hear!" said the Duchess.

The House accepted it in silence and MacGregor felt that the whole being of parliament had been poised in a neutral position. Even Tom Cromwell looked as if he had been suspended for a political moment, and he let out a breath as if he had held it too long.

"The Honourable Lady confuses the American people with American policy," he said wryly. "It is the very generosity of the American people which makes it possible for their policy-makers to confuse and trick them into believing that America is the Godfather of the world. That is nonsense, and the American people should know it. If they don't get to know it, then the continuation of their present policy will make them the most despised people on earth. I know the Americans are generous. I know American policy is generous. But there you have two different things. What the policy-makers expect in return for their dollar bounty is political co-operation against Russia and any other nation they like to call Red! I would remind the Honourable Lady that it is their anti-Red benevolence that is universal. In China, American capital is still spending more to create the military dictatorship of Chiang Kai-Shek than it did to assist China against Japan. With so many other nations in Europe and Asia broken by the war, American assistance with money and machinery almost means life itself. For national existence however, American policy has a price. It offers unconditional money, machinery, and arms to any nation that will denounce Russia and Communism and pronounce America as the God of all free nations. Even in defeated Italy, Germany, and Japan, American policy supports any sect that is anti-Red and anti-Russian. There is no end to this white American morality, it has its wide wide arms across the globe, its long fingers in every nation, and its loud voice in every ear, including this House of Commons."

"So has Russia!" The Opposition was on its feet and there was more commotion, but Cromwell shouted above it.

"Why talk about Russia!" he demanded. "If we must talk about interference by one nation in another's affairs let us talk of this American interference in every nation's affairs. Is there a nation on the face of the earth to-day except Russia and her so-called satellites which can hold up its head and say it is independent of the American dollar? We are all on our knees, and we won't admit it. Our American masters do not need arms and occupation; capital is enough. Capital is enough to strangle the earth if only it has the support of its victims. We are asked to support it — to bring others to their knees: France, Jugoslavia, Bulgaria, Czechoslovakia, Poland, all of Eastern Europe, Greece, Turkey and Iran. The world over, we are asked to replace so-called Communism with the dollar. That dollar means governorship by those who will sell themselves and their nation for a smell of wealth and a grip of power.

"Such men are international. America has no monopoly on evil and stupid men. America simply has the wealth for bigger evil. The rest of us follow her according to our own evil and our own stupidity. British policy to-day is as bad as America's despite our Socialist Government. I am a Socialist and a member of the government party, but every day I ask myself how a Socialist can conduct the affairs of this Nation by co-operating in international policies with the desperate and grim capitalists of America. It isn't by force, because we still have an alternative. It is apparently by choice, by our own fear of stepping up to our necks in Socialism. We prefer to be half-baked about it, to be respectable about it, to be careful instead of being daring. Our policy to-day is not to make Socialism work, but to make capitalism work. For that we conduct our foreign affairs with the same intentions as our Tory opponents. Because of our own fear of Socialism, our policy has become theirs. Theirs is the common anti-Russian front of American and British imperialisms struggling to survive in a world that is rejecting colonial domination and economic slavery. Yet we are not deep enough into it for our great friend opposite. Each step we take into this anti-Russian campaign he asks us to go one more, deeper and deeper, until we are finally committed to war. Our men of capital and imperialism ask us to follow the American crusade so that Britain can gather a few crumbs of Empire in the struggle; the few crumbs that we can get in Iran for instance. Ironically, we are expected at the same time to release our grip on the straggling Empire so that American capital can enter and take over."

A Minister stood. "You are going too far," he said.

"Too far!" Cromwell replied. "I'll go farther. There are men in Britain today who are willing to co-operate with expanding America, even on those terms. They would sink their British Empire for a share in the domination which their American friends expect. Yes, and for the most part they sit on the Opposite side of the House" (Uproar!), "men with Empire in their blood and bones, men whose families made it, held it, and finally lost it. Men by honour our greatest men, who now become our most miserable men. They demand this front against Russia. They demand blocs, alignments, show-downs, ultimatums, anything that will organize a world against this one Nation, or this one idea."

Cromwell waited for the noise to subside.

"If we do not stop these war-makers now," he went on, "it will soon be too late. We are the only nation that can halt this crusade. It might be too late in America, but it isn't too late here. Without British support the whole scheme would collapse. For that reason the future of all nations depends upon the policy which is decided in this House. More than that, the final position of Britain in the world is being decided. If we support these so-called anti-Communist crusades through the world as we have supported it in Greece, then our good name and existence will be threatened by the hatred of all free-thinking men. We cannot suppress all desire in Europe and Asia for social change by branding it Communism from Russia and persecuting its supporters. Social change doesn't have to come from Russia, whatever the Foreign Office or the Americans say. It is a product of the miserable conditions under which the majority of the earth's population exist. There are fighters for social change in every land, here as well as anywhere: MacGregor among them. We Socialists are among them. That is the reason for our predominance in this House today. The very men

608

that we try to suppress in other countries are asking for far less liberty than we enjoy here, far less social change than we Socialists hope to initiate in Great Britain. Are we going to betray these men by labelling them Communists and crushing them wherever we find them until we have launched ourselves at Russia herself in a war that will wipe this island off the face of the earth? The American imperialists say that this is the American Century. Are we to sacrifice ourselves for that great ideal, or are we to stand beside the people of Europe and Asia and other lands who seek independence, economic stability, self-determination, and the right to conduct their own affairs? Are we going to partake in an anti-Red campaign when we ourselves are Reds?"

There were cries of "*Oh Oh*" from the Labour benches.

Cromwell turned angrily upon his colleagues. "Yes," he said. "To our Tory opponents we have always been Red, and we are Reds. The red flag is the flag of office of the Labour Government, and we are not barbarians or monsters or devils or terrorists. We might be fools. If we are, that is our only virtue for the men Opposite. Actually we are honourable men, sincere men, great men like the common men of every land, like the MacGregors: the men we are asked to betray. We dare not betray them if this world is to survive. We dare not begin with MacGregor!

"Some among us might think that there is political expediency in following this anti-Russian crusade without really getting enmeshed in it, creating a Third Force in Europe of their friends, a balancing force for power politics. In that you have the real policy of our Government to-day. But how can we avoid final involvement? Our American vanguard will stop at nothing. They hold their atom bomb aloft with nervous fingers. It has become their talisman and their faith. It is their new weapon of anti-Communism, a more efficient Belsen and Maidenek. It's first usage was morally anti-Russian. It was used to end Japan quickly so that Russia would play no part in the final settlement with that country. No doubt they would have used it on Russia already if they could be certain that Russia did not have an equal or better atomic weapon. That terrible uncertainty goads them into fiercer political and economic activity against the world's grim defenders of great liberties. In that you have the heart of this American imperial desperation. They cannot defeat the people of Europe and Asia with the atom bomb alone. They cannot win unless we lend them our name and our support and our political cunning. To-day they have British support, in policy as well as in international councils where the decisions of peace and security are being made. With our support America is undermining every international conference with its anti-Russian politics. Perhaps we are even the leaders of this policy in international discussion: this Socialist England! This elective body of Labour men!"

"You ought to be proud of it," a Tory shouted.

"We should be ashamed," Cromwell said and he was now addressing both sides of the House in equal bitterness. "Think of it," he was saying. "We are being asked to lead this wonderful crusade by allowing Lord Essex to begin the attack on Russia in the Security Council to-morrow. We are to have the honour of striking the first blow, while our American partners put in a good word here and there for Democracy, Free Speech, Free Peoples, Free Religion, and Free Enterprise. More than that we are asked to begin upon ourselves by dishonouring this man called Mac-Gregor. MacGregor must be disgraced if the British case against Russia is to succeed. Our Socialist authority against Russia must be Lord Essex, a Tory diplomat whom we Socialists have disputed and despised for twenty years. What miserable fools we are! We hope to keep our economic hold on Iran by smashing a movement for self-expression and sovereignty. We are Socialists using capitalist methods to hold our imperial possessions not only in Iran but everywhere. We are Socialists using the political expediency of anti-Communism to cling desperately to our imperial heritage. There is no surer way of losing our heritage than by our present policies abroad. The Tories demand that we accelerate and arm those policies. Well, we Socialists demand that our leadership halt and disarm their present foreign policy. We demand an end to this silent pact in foreign affairs with our Tory enemy. We demand that our Foreign Minister publicly denounce and deny British association with anti-Russian alignments and Western Blocks. We demand that our Government support all movements the world over which seek social and economic reform. We demand that our Civil Service and our Foreign Service be socialized, given Socialist intentions and Socialist staffs, from top to bottom. We demand that our Colonial peoples be given a New Deal in the definition and decision of their own affairs. We demand that our policy in the United Nations be governed by Socialist British interests and world peace. We demand that our representatives in the Security Council to-morrow take no part in the anti-Russian attack. Above all we demand that here to-night the Government repudiate Lord Essex and his policies, withdraw him from the Security Council to-morrow, and give MacGregor freedom of his own opinion and the freedom of his existence. We demand MacGregor's exoneration. With these straightforward Labour policies Britain could champion a world of struggling people. We could begin the great social change which is the only way of bringing security and sovereignty and peace to ourselves as well as to the rest of the universe. It is up to us on this side of the House. We will have the support of the British people, of all people. We can have this new policy now: either that or the policy of the Anglo-American crusaders; a policy which begins with MacGregor and ends with the atom bomb. We have the choice. If we don't change our policy now, then the British people and the people of all nations will change it for us, violently. This is our last chance!"

That was the end of it for MacGregor.

Butcher had arrived in the House and he waved a piece of paper at the Speaker so that he was given the floor amid these suddenly quiet men who stopped fidgeting and waited as MacGregor waited for this confident man's solemn announcement.

"I have a short statement to make," Butcher said. He paused ruthlessly for that ultimate silence and then went on without ceremony. "It has been decided by the proper authority, Gentlemen, that Ivre Angus Mac-Gregor, a temporary servant of the Crown who recently made public vital and confidential information concerning a mission he attended, should be dismissed immediately from service with the India Office. Because of his war record, however, and upon the personal suggestion and appeal of Lord Essex's assistant (the Honourable John Anthony Asquith) no charges will be made against MacGregor under the Secrets Act or the Security Regulations. However, MacGregor is dismissed dishonourably, with the loss of all privileges and pension, and with a judgment that states he may never enter His Majesty's Services again, at home or abroad."

"Shame!" some cried, and others the long wail of the Parliamentary "Oh!"

Mr. Butcher silenced it himself by waving his paper again, and he went on. "As for Lord Essex. There is no taint or suggestion of doubt about the integrity of Lord Essex, whom we consider our greatest diplomat. His honour, his conduct, his loyalty, his policy are unimpeachable and correct in our Socialist estimation. Lord Essex's position and authority among our diplomats is higher to-day than at any time before, and we have nothing but honour and praise for this man. Nevertheless, in view of the distortions which have recently been put abroad concerning his mission, we feel that it would not be fair to ask him to carry on with his task as special delegate to the Security Council. Lord Essex will be withdrawn immediately and no part of his mission or evidence or fact or report will be offered to the Security Council when it discusses the Iranian case. We feel that this course is best because we do not wish to carry our private political affairs into the Security Council; and in the interests of wholeheartedly supporting the U.N. we are willing to withdraw all evidence that might be considered locally controversial. To-morrow the case on Iran will be conducted by our ordinary delegates upon the evidence offered by the two countries concerned. Lord Essex's work will not be referred to, and the decision of the Security Council on Iran will be accepted by us, whatever it is. In withdrawing Lord Essex we should like to repeat that this does not in any way withdraw our faith

611

in Lord Essex. He will be given another post or another mission immediately. It will be of greater importance than that which he has just completed, and we are most regretful that all his good work in Iran has been wasted by the petty act of a disloyal official. We hope that our Right Honourable friends Opposite are satisfied, and in the National Interests we suggest that no one raise the matter again to-night."

Mr. Butcher took off his glasses and listened to the uproar for a moment before sitting down. Like all others, he waited while the Members of the Opposition threw question lists and notes and papers into the aisle, shouting that the Nation and the British people and Lord Essex had been betrayed. It went on until the Great Lombardian rose again, silencing them all by his bulldog look.

"We are certainly not satisfied," the Lombardian announced angrily, "and I intend to raise the matter further right now. But first I would like to know why the Prime Minister and the Minister for Foreign Affairs are not in the House attending this vital debate. If it isn't their job to be here at this critical moment then it is their duty, and I suggest that they be called immediately."

Mr. Butcher rose. "The Prime Minister and Mr. Bevin are attending a reception at the Soviet Embassy, given by Mr. Vishinsky, the Soviet delegate to the United Nations. The Leader of the Opposition, Mr. Churchill, is also present at the reception." Butcher smiled. "I suppose it's hard to know these days where one's duty lies."

There was laughter and Katherine turned around for MacGregor.

MacGregor had gone.

Outside and about, Katherine and Asquith could not find him and Katherine would not take Asquith's assurances that he had simply gone home. "We'd better find him," she said. "I'm not sure how he took it; and this morning he was talking about running off to Iran to-morrow."

"He'll be alright," Asquith said. "He won't run off anywhere until he has at least heard what the Security Council has to say to-morrow about Iran. This may have been too much for him, but he'll be alright. He'll be alright, Kathy."

"He's not alright," Katherine said. "He will take Butcher's pronouncement very badly. He really could take it either way, despite Harold's equal defeat. It's a rotten thing to be dishonoured like that from the floor of the House, and I'm sure he has taken it badly! I don't think he cares a hang any more what happens to Essex or to Iran. He has lost all his perspective and a lot of his sense. We'd better find him," she said, "before he gets a chance to run away."

Katherine did not find him, even though she waited at Asquith's and went with John to Mrs. Berry's. He was not there, and she went to her own house and waited for him until she knew that it was hopeless. She went to bed, thinking that he might recover himself by the next day and behave sensibly instead of fleeing to Iran in terrible defeat. It was really a slim hope, and the last hopes of MacGregor faded when Asquith came in the morning to tell her that MacGregor had been to Mrs. Berry's. He had taken all his belongings and left in a hurry.

Chapter 49

KATHERINE could probably have found out quite easily what had happened to MacGregor, but she did not want to find out. In her sanity and in her anger with him for disappearing, she preferred to let the day go by and decide in itself whether MacGregor had gone away or not. Though her first impulse had been to stop him, she had now convinced herself that this last day was MacGregor's choice. If he chose to flee or if he chose to stay, it could only be MacGregor's decision. Yet finally it appeared to be a mistake, because the day passed and Mac-Gregor did not come, although she knew that he would have come if he had stayed in England.

She waited for him in the lovely Georgian emptiness of the spacious, regal house. She did not bother to dress. Most of the day she spent before the solitary fire in her own room, but she could not help leaving it to walk about in the long passages and the cold rooms, holding her golden robe tight about her. . . . There was so much in this house. Her unusual moment of waiting gave her the first chance she had ever had of seeing its treasures. She had been in and out of this house all her life, but there had never been a moment like this one, forcing her to look about her for the time it occupied. She saw the furnishings, the tapestries, the priceless Persian carpets from Shiraz and Isfahan, the masterpieces of Flemish and Italian and English art on the walls, the Greek vases and the Cretan bowls, the Chinese goblets and the Italian porcelain, the illuminated manuscripts and books, the statuary, and the huge carved oaken doors. It was all hers. This was her part of the old man who was rotten with age: the last remnant of a family who were already nobility when William the Conqueror came and created Eastminster from the small tax-holdings along the eastern banks of the Thames and gave it to this family to ensure their co-operation and their loyalty. Her Uncle Paul was the last bloody drop of the Eastminsters. She herself was among the next of them through her father, but so far removed from direct descent that there was no continuation at all. The only continuation was this large empty house which could hardly survive the fuel shortage and the housing shortage and the great social changes of England. Katherine wondered for the first time what she would do with it. She supposed that the lawyers or her father or someone had already decided what to do with it to avoid the debt of inheritance. It would all go, including the stolen monument to Phidius who had followed Pheidippides with the news of the victory of Marathon.

When it was too dark to see about her she went back to her fire because she did not want the house lit up in its emptiness. It was better dark and forgotten. The housekeeper, however, told her that there was a fire in the library, that her dinner was there waiting for her because it was warmer downstairs than in her own room. Katherine walked down the steps brushing her hair, and she sat in the library reading the evening papers and eating soup and a small lamb chop and drinking coffee. The newspapers were full of a giant Red plot which had just been discovered in Canada. This was all over their sensational front pages. Yet they were still full of MacGregor and shame and Essex and praise. They were also anticipating the Security Council decision to-night. The Security Council must be meeting now while she ate her lamb chop; but MacGregor had gone and all his short-lived belief in political action had gone. How much of Katherine herself had gone? She did not know and she might never know, and she drank a little rich red wine to see how much of MacGregor remained in her. She went to sleep until she heard the bell of the front door ringing in the basement below. The housekeeper had apparently gone out, and Katherine went herself, turning on the portico light as she opened the door.

It was not MacGregor. It was Essex.

"Hullo Kathy," he said. He was dressed in a tight double-breasted grey overcoat, grey felt hat, and he carried a silver-headed cane. He looked young, handsome, and expectant. "Are you getting dressed to go out?"

"No. Come in," she said. "I was sleeping by the fire. What time is it?"

"About twenty past eight."

"Have you had your dinner?" she asked him.

"Yes," he said.

"Good. I couldn't offer you any."

"That's alright," he said. "I wouldn't mind some of Paul's black brandy. Only man in England who still has liqueur that is black with age. It's really a mellow purple. Does he still have it?"

"There is some in the library," Katherine said as she took him there.

Essex took off his overcoat and unhesitatingly put some coal on the fire. He sat down in one of the bucket chairs while Katherine gave him brandy in a crystal goblet. Leaning back, he sighed and unbuttoned his blue coat. It was unusual for Essex to wear a blue suit, and its lines gave him a well-cut appearance right down to his white silk socks which were boyishly loose on his ankles.

"Where's MacGregor?" he asked Katherine.

"I don't know," she said.

"I half expected to find him here," he admitted.

"Did you want him?"

"No. I wanted you. Where's he gone?"

"I haven't the slightest idea," she said. "Probably back to Iran. I think he gave up the ghost after hearing all the nonsense put on him in the House last night." Katherine was not being sensitive about MacGregor or herself or Essex. That was the truth, and she had an idea that Essex knew about MacGregor's absence, although heaven only knew how he would find out. Now that John Asquith had left him, no one could tell Essex about MacGregor.

"I haven't had a chance to apologize for all this trouble, my dear," he said. "I tried to prevent your name being dragged in so scandalously, but the situation was out of my hands."

"That's noble, Harold," she said, "but I am entirely responsible for any part I played in it, so forget about it. I don't think we ought to talk about it. There is always too much recrimination in going over these things. We were simply on opposite sides and that's all there is to it."

"Of course," Essex said. "I didn't come here to talk about that."

"Didn't you?"

"No. We have all been torn asunder and I don't see much point in analyzing our relative parts in it. I don't want to put the blame on anyone and I don't want to probe the results. Also I am too English to acknowledge catastrophe."

"Then let's drop the whole subject," she told him.

"I'm surprised to hear you say that," he said with some of his old familiarity. "I didn't think that there could ever be a situation which you wouldn't torture with discussion and cynical analysis. Are you sparing me your tongue or have you changed your attitude?"

"Oh stop it," she said. "MacGregor was bad enough."

"Poor MacGregor," he said. "I really feel sorry for him, making a fool of himself and destroying himself and tumbling down in such a wretched heap." But Essex was angry and he could not hide it. He got up and re-filled his glass with brandy and sat down again. "Apart from my personal feelings for MacGregor, I'm rather glad that the fellow has gone."

"No doubt," Katherine said.

"Yes. It might bring you back to your senses," he said. "Oh, I can understand how you felt about him! I always liked MacGregor myself. I suppose I still do if I leave respect out of it. But you see Kathy there is a world of difference between MacGregor and us. His world and ours

615

were always irreconcilable, whatever idealistic hopes we had that our native differences could be forgotten. They can never be forgotten. That is what makes you and me different people from the MacGregors. Any relationship between you and me, Kathy, is natural. Any relationship you have with MacGregor is unnatural. I hope you see what I mean. I am not exactly a young man Kathy, but I know that you and I are about equal in all other considerations. I have known quite a few women in my time; some were beautiful and some were damned intelligent; but I never really encountered a woman who had my entire respect and admiration and affection. That is, except yourself. I know that you have decided against me in this dispute because of that intense belief you have in a changing world. But I don't think you really decided against me. I think you were trying to decide against yourself, and you failed. You cannot step out of your natural level in society, Kathy. If your own example hasn't convinced you then see what has happened to John Asquith, who has wrecked himself completely. Can't you see that you can never really change? Any attempt to disturb your proper place and responsibility in society ends in ruin like John's. Kathy!" he said. "We have deep understanding and regard for each other, and it's about time we put it to its real use. You must see now that I am the only person who can thoroughly satisfy you. We are rare people and we both know it. We may be different in some outlooks, but I am not beyond compromise. I understand the world as I see it, but I know that your perception and understanding is even better than mine. I am not without usefulness in that direction. Despite this set-back which MacGregor engineered so treacherously, I am more honoured and better considered in my field than ever before. I am the person you need for your passion and belief, Kathy, because I am the one man who can implement and appreciate your efforts. I am the one man Kathy. I am like you, incapable of ordinary stupid human failure. I can never know ignobility or indignity. We have that happy fusion of pre-eminence between us. These advantages you must see. I cannot let you ignore them Kathy. I cannot allow you to suppress our natural affinity. Forget all that has gone, and understand me now as I am, my dear. Among the men of England I have found my place. In the matter of history I have made and marked my name as much as any man. There is no nobler title than mine in England, none to have such honour endure. These things are important Kathy and you and I must consider them. More than that I have the right to you. You have given me that right in your own behaviour. I have demanded and received nothing of you Katherine, whatever I have expected; but this is a moment when we both must take the full measure of our devotion. It is the beginning to a relationship that had to be fulfilled. That is what I am asking of you now, Kathy. There is nothing for you but me. You must realize that." He drew a breath and stood up and faced her. "I think I am leaving for Washington almost immediately — in a day or two. We could make the arrangements there or here, whichever you wish. But I need you soon, Kathy. I need you soon."

Katherine was sorry that she had drunk the rich red wine and fallen asleep and awakened to find Essex at the front door. She was sorry that there was no MacGregor and no certainty of him and none of his presence at all, because she had forgotten what MacGregor could be like sitting there as pitifully as Essex. There was no one left but herself.

"What can I say?" she said to him. "How easy is this to decide Harold?"

"I can't wait until you decide," he said desperately. "I want it decided now, Kathy. To-night. I know that if it isn't decided to-night it will never be decided."

"I am really flattered, Harold. I know you well enough to appreciate it."

"I don't want you flattered. Nor do I want you to evade me."

"No. No," she said. "If I wanted to say No to you Harold I would do it without hesitating. But I don't know what I can say."

"Then I'll wait," he said.

Katherine stood up and tightened the belt of her robe and gave him more brandy. She poured a little of it into her wine glass and sipped at it, although she did not like brandy at all. She needed something bitter and distasteful to give her a moment of sense and life and living and continuity.

"What are you going to do in Washington?" It was not an important question, it was Katherine trying to hear her own voice to understand herself.

"It's rather delicate," he said, "but it begins with a plan the Americans have for financing European recovery." Essex also needed the sound of his practical voice to restore himself. "They supply the dollars and we supply the leadership. It's as big a thing as anything we have attempted Kathy. The most important diplomatic job I've ever had."

"How long will you be there?"

"Three or four months at least."

"I had a chance of going to Washington," she said and heard the long peal of the bell in the basement below. "I turned it down because Jane persuaded me that it was a rather disloyal thing to do."

"There will be nothing disloyal in coming with me."

"I suppose not," she said. "Excuse me a moment Harold, I'll just see who is at the door and if you don't mind waiting a little I'll also get dressed."

"Take your time," he said, and she left him to open the front door.

She turned on the portico light and turned the cold brass knob and opened the door. In the white and black atmosphere stood MacGregor, a rather shamefaced-looking MacGregor without hat or coat, a damp and solemn MacGregor. He did not approach until she stamped her foot and said, "I'm cold here. Come in, for Heaven's sake." MacGregor wiped his feet on the mat and came in.

"You always come too late," she said as she closed the door.

"Too late for what?"

"I don't know," she said. "Why were you so long?"

"It really doesn't matter."

"It does matter." They were standing in the dark of the temple-like hall. The soft marble was lit only by the shaft of light from the portico through the small panes of the door windows. It was really an elongated shadow right up to the foot of the stairs.

"I'm sorry," MacGregor said. He wiped the fog from his face with a used handkerchief which was rolled into a ball. He wiped his hands with it as an engineer wipes his hands with a piece of waste, and he put it in his coat pocket as she watched him critically.

"I thought you had gone to Iran," she said, trying to calm herself, trying to be sensible with him. Yet she could not be anything but angry. It was not deliberate anger. It was the contradictory anger which took such a dangerous and ungovernable hold on her against her will. "So you didn't go!" she said.

"No."

"Where were you?"

"I very nearly went with Professor White, but I didn't go."

She turned off the portico light and there was only the blue darkness which came in the glass dome above them, and Katherine walked to the stairs with the confidence of knowing her surroundings. MacGregor had to walk carefully, and he was tempted to put out his hands before him but he scraped his feet instead.

"You had better come up with me," she said.

"Can't you turn on a light?"

"There is nothing in your way," she said ahead of him.

MacGregor felt the same edge of panic which had accompanied his disgrace on the ice-rink at the Moscow Embassy. This was the same Katherine and he was the same victim, and he had to make sure that he could not fall or stumble. He felt the cold marble flatness of the bannister. He held it and walked up the stairs with dignity and care, dark as it was. She hardly waited for him at the top but there was a small light at the distant end of the passage. It supplied enough vision for MacGregor to see his way behind her, off the passage and into her rooms. He waited until she had turned on the golden lamps and he went straight to the fire. Though it was low he did not put any coal on it until Katherine told

618

him to. He wondered if this was the last of his own coal and he did not lavish the fire with it. He put on enough to keep the flame and to give quick warmth.

"Dry your hair," she said and gave him a towel. "And please turn your chair around. I want to dress before the fire."

MacGregor took the towel and turned the arm-chair about so that its back almost faced the fire. He had one half of the hearth and Katherine had the other as she dressed. He could hear her movements and he stared ahead.

"More than anything else," she said to him. "your moments of indecisiveness anger me. They don't come very often MacGregor, but when they do they seem to take complete hold of you. Did you have to disappear like that! Did you have to wait so long? The way you were last night I decided that you had given up in disgust and gone back hopelessly to Iran with Professor White. Why didn't you go with White anyway?"

"I changed my mind," he said moodily.

"What took you so long?"

"It had to take time," he said. "I had to know what I was doing."

"Are you still thinking that you have wasted all your effort?"

"Not altogether."

"Weren't you at least satisfied last night that you had stopped Essex?"

"No," he said. "I wasn't satisfied at all. It's not much use stopping Essex if the same men are going to make the same decisions anyway."

"You still think that nothing can be done, I suppose! That the Rule of Law is all too powerful, that no man can effect any changes in the affairs of a nation." She was repeating him with such cruelty that he blushed.

"Ah, I can see that some political changes have been effected," he admitted harshly. He stirred in his chair. "But they are so minute that they do not touch the real authority and the real purpose of government or the nation or the State, or whatever it is that decides our affairs. Perhaps we did stop Essex, and perhaps we did interfere with this particular scheme he had for hanging on to Iran. But they'll come again."

"Of course they'll come again."

"Yet I thought that if I stopped Essex it would stop — all the plotting and the scheming. I thought that this would be the end of it; that our diplomats would leave Azerbaijan alone and behave like gentlemen and take their defeat as final. There's the bitter part of it Kathy," he said wistfully. "There is nothing final about it at all. Essex may be out of the way, but there are other men with other schemes who pick up where Essex leaves off. It never stops, so how can I stop!"

"Has it taken you this long to find that out?"

"No. But this battle has just begun for me and I can see that I can never avoid it. I could do better if I understood the construction of what

I was doing politically: I would be less indecisive if I knew what I was doing. It is no use letting things happen and then deciding what can be done. There must be a method of understanding all the political forces at work, and a method of acting intelligently on that understanding. There must be a science to political occurrences — a natural and material science which can make a man's actions sensible and positive."

"You are not being scientifically careful again are you? I don't like that!" Katherine put her hands on the back of his chair but he did not see her.

"No, I am not being too careful at all! Perhaps I am being too scientific, but I must know what I am doing and why I should do it and what results to expect. So far, all the rules and reason that I thought governed political affairs have turned out to be worthless: diplomacies, policies, States, Rules of Law, and even the House of Commons itself. I have lost all the easy and unquestioned respect for these institutions. Now I must know what worth they really have. That's how far this has taken me, Kathy. In fighting Essex about Iran I suddenly find myself fighting a battle with the form of the State itself. I suddenly find that all of my life has become inseparably political — everything I do, even my work, even going back to Iran. That is the essence of this confusing situation I am in, Kathy, so don't expect easy decisiveness of me. Don't expect it yet."

Katherine said nothing but looked down on his sandy head and let him talk.

"I am so stupidly ignorant," he said impatiently, "and my ignorance always ends in the same place. If I knew the laws and the impulses governing political developments, then I could understand any situation and know my exact part in it. No principles that I've been taught are of any use, and until I can find a clear and proper analysis of society I will go on being ignorant. All I know now is this: I am right and Essex is wrong. I was right in Iran, and I was right to fight with him, and right in what I did. I know that Essex can never succeed in establishing his political ideas because he opposes all the natural rights which any man must claim for himself. He and the Lombardian can't do what they like by calling every man who opposes them a Communist; but not everybody will be defeated and shamed by accusations of disloyalty and betrayal. Perhaps that is what brought me back. I have betrayed nothing that did not need betraying, and I don't believe I owe any loyalty to bad politics, State or no State. If I am to be accused of disloyalty I had better start investigating what loyalty means. If loyalty means acknowledging the ideas of Essex and the Lombardian and even Butcher, then I am disloyal and I will go on being disloyal because I will never agree with those men; and what does it matter if they do call me Communist for it. I don't know anything about Communism. I only know that the men who accuse me

620

are frauds. Particularly that Great Lombardian. I wonder how I could have ever accepted or respected that man. He has suddenly become the real menace himself, misleading and dangerous and even treacherous. When he demands the loyalty of science to his political conceptions it is really serious, Kathy. It upsets me more than anything else. Men like that stupid bigoted Lombardian dare not touch science. It is inconceivable that they should be allowed to interfere by their ideas of political loyalty. If they are allowed to interfere there will be no science left. They will kill it."

Katherine was standing before him now, dressed in a skirt and jumper and wearing short socks with flat-heeled shoes. She looked younger than she had ever looked to MacGregor and he did not get up immediately but looked carefully at her and drew a long breath.

"I don't quite know how I got this far Kathy. I don't know how I became so deeply involved in such a political issue with such important decisions, but I am not sorry for it. I don't like what has happened to me and I doubt if I will ever feel normal and uncomplicated again; but I don't want to go back on any of it. I don't think I belong in big decisions and diplomacy and I've been kicked out ignominiously anyway. Nevertheless I haven't given up, if that is what you wanted to know. I could never give up now. I even feel that I haven't lived until now, and I know at least that I didn't waste my time and effort. I retract that for you. I did stop Essex, and the Security Council has decided not to interfere in Iran."

"What did the Security Council decide?" she interrupted.

He was surprised. "I thought you would know," he said.

"No."

"They rejected the Iranian complaint about interference," he told her. "They decided that no action would be taken; that the situation in Azerbaijan could be settled by direct negotiation between Iran and Russia."

"Is that what changed your mind and brought you back?"

"No." He stood up beside her. "I only found out about the Security Council when I went to Asquith's."

"Oh!" she said. "You went there before coming here?"

"Yes."

She took the towel from him. "I thought you had been wandering around in the fog," she said — disappointed that he could go anywhere before coming here.

"No," he said unimaginatively. "I walked here from the Asquiths'."

She nodded coldly. "You had better come downstairs with me." She waited while he moved a chair and put a brass screen before the fire. "How is John?" she asked him.

"He's alright," MacGregor said as she turned out the light.

"What did he have to say to you?"

"Nothing much."

"Was he disgusted with you for disappearing?"

"No. He knew I would be back."

"Did he?" she said. "That's more than I knew."

MacGregor was in the darkness again going down the stairs, and once more he felt the danger of Katherine's impersonality and he took great care with himself.

"Did you know that he had resigned?" she said.

"Yes."

"Well?" she demanded. "Didn't you talk about that?"

"No," he said. He was not going to parcel up Asquith for Katherine's sake. What existed between himself and Asquith could not be shared, even with Katherine. There had been no embarrassment for him in going back to the Asquiths', as there had been for him in coming back here. He had not stood shamefaced upon the door-mat and waited to be let in. He had opened the door and walked straight up the stairs and given himself back to the Asquiths as simply as a natural man could. There was little said between them although it seemed to MacGregor that Jane Asquith's blue eyes had been better to greet him than any English word. He thought that she had cried a little when she had left him with Asquith, and knowing it MacGregor had felt like a man coming home. Even John Asquith's unusual quiet had given MacGregor this man's absolute understanding, and MacGregor had been silenced by his own deep regard for Asquith. MacGregor could have told Katherine that Asquith — more than she herself — had brought him back by reason and example. MacGregor had said nothing to Asquith about the act of support against Essex which had cost him so much. Nothing need be said or could be said. Asquith had referred to himself by saying unimportantly that he was finally out of the mess he had made for himself all his life, and for that he could thank MacGregor. However, he was still the same Asquith, because he had sent MacGregor off to Katherine with shocking remarks about Katherine's ill-temper and inconsistency, telling him to hurry up before Essex got there. Asquith said that he had seen Essex at Central Hall. They had both been waiting for the Security Council decision on Iran. Even as MacGregor had crossed the street Asquith had walked a block with him to tell him about the Security Council and to bet his bottom dollar that Essex was in desperate defeat and off to Katherine. It was one of Asquith's acts of living to stir a man up like that, but MacGregor had known that Essex would not be here.

MacGregor followed Katherine through the library door. He entered the room as a man enters a room to himself, and it was not until he reached the hearth that he shook quite visibly to see Lord Essex standing there teetering with a glass of brandy. MacGregor faced Essex along the

622

rug which covered the hearth. They were at opposite ends of it and the rug shone softly from one man to the other. It was an Amritsar rug, so tightly woven that it looked like red velvet. The fire was bright between them, and each stood with his feet a little apart.

"Good evening, MacGregor," Essex said — too lazily.

MacGregor drew a breath. "I didn't expect to see you standing there," he said.

"I suppose not," Essex said. "We thought you had gone off to Iran." He held out his glass to MacGregor. "Just give me a little more brandy will you?"

Katherine got the brandy and poured it out.

"Why should I go off to Iran?" MacGregor said.

"Kathy said something about you giving up the ghost."

"Kathy didn't know what she was talking about," MacGregor said. He was watching Katherine as she gave him her own glass and poured brandy into it so that he could drink it quickly. He held his breath again so that he could drink it without spilling it. Katherine sat down a short distance away from both of them.

Essex yawned and took a little snuff. "I don't think I expected to see you again, MacGregor," he said. "Nor did Kathy. I doubt if she was expecting you to-night." It meant that Katherine was damn-well-not expecting MacGregor at all, that his presence was inconvenient and clumsy and that he would be better out of here.

MacGregor sat down.

"Why didn't you go to Iran?" Essex asked as a mildly curious man. "Under the circumstances, wouldn't you be better off there than in England?"

"Under what circumstances?" MacGregor said.

Essex could stand alone no longer and he too sat down. By their attitudes each man established his right to sit there. Each man planned to sit and outlast the other. One would remain when the other had gone, and the defiance of their comfort in the Victorian chairs indicated grim and final contest. Each was immovable in his leather fortress, each held a crystal goblet like a talisman of endurance, while Katherine supplied a sustenance of black brandy for their siege.

"Well I don't wish to hurt you with any reminder of your unpleasant situation," Essex said.

"I've survived it," MacGregor told him.

"No doubt you have!" Essex said nicely. "You can thank John Asquith's ruination for that."

MacGregor let it pass.

"I suppose you are going back to your true occupation," Essex said. "Chipping at rocks and drilling for oil and all that sort of thing."

"More or less," MacGregor said.

"Did Professor White's aeroplane leave, MacGregor?"

"This morning," MacGregor said.

"Won't they take you back at English-Persian, my boy?"

"I doubt it." MacGregor was not going to be evasive now.

"Perhaps I could help you," Essex said. "I could ring Lord Derring of English-Persian if you like. He's a good friend of mine and I could see what he might do about getting you your job back out there."

"Thank you!" MacGregor said. "But it's hardly worth while."

"Oh no trouble," Essex said.

"No, don't bother," MacGregor replied.

"I insist," Essex said.

"That's nice of you," MacGregor said politely, "but it's unnecessary."

"I feel a certain responsibility for taking you into political life, MacGregor, and I feel it my duty to see you return to your own understandable world." Essex leaned deep into his chair. "Your place is with your technology, my boy. England needs every man of science and technique. We need you at your work with full attention to the demands of production and defence. We need skilled men more than we need amateur diplomats, and there is no time for you fellows to be dabbling in politics. Each man must do his own job and stick at it. Forget the petty squabbles of diplomacy, MacGregor. Go back to your own work and leave politics to those that understand them."

MacGregor sat still and did not argue with Essex. Even now he knew that Essex would have the better of him in the delicately balanced situation which held the three of them here together. Katherine interrupted the silence.

"Harold," she said. "MacGregor says that the Security Council decided not to take any action about Azerbaijan. They threw out the Iranian complaint and decided that Azerbaijan was a matter for direct negotiations between Russia and Iran. Did you know?" Katherine might have added why-didn't-you-tell-me-before.

"Yes I knew, my dear," Essex admitted. "But they did not throw out the Iranian complaint at all. I can see that MacGregor is feeling victorious, but I wouldn't be too satisfied if I were you MacGregor. There's a little more to it than that."

"What more?" MacGregor said.

"The Security Council may have decided that Azerbaijan is a matter for direct settlement between Russia and Iran; but they kept the complaint on the Council agenda. That means that the dispute can be brought up again at any time if it isn't settled by direct negotiation, and I can assure you that it can never be settled by direct negotiation. I can tell you that no Iranian Government will ever settle anything with Russia, not while a British representative in Iran has any blood in his veins. Don't be so sure of your victory, MacGregor. The dispute will not be settled. It will be brought up again at the next Security Council meeting in New York, and this time there will be no hitch. This time your Russian friends will be properly dealt with, and Azerbaijan will be restored to normalcy."

Katherine rose and gave a little brandy to MacGregor.

MacGregor was provoked by Essex's illogic, and he stirred uneasily in the chair. "I don't know how you can feel so sure of what will happen in Iran," he said.

"It will be quite simple to decide Iran's future in New York," Essex said and relaxed.

"You may hope to decide what happens in the Security Council," MacGregor said, "but I know that you can never determine the course of events in Iran. Perhaps you can prevent direct settlement of the dispute about Azerbaijan, and you may succeed in New York where you failed in London. I don't know! But I do know that you can never finally succeed in keeping Iran the way you want it. You can do what you like. You can march the Teheran troops into Azerbaijan, and you can break the new Government and subdue the revolt, but you can never stop the Azerbaijanians or the Persians from eventually revolting again and again until they get rid of the corrupt governments, the landlords, the police, the army, and everything else that keeps them subjected, including ourselves. You can't stop it by making decisions in the Security Council. All your decisions discount the Persians themselves, and that is the mistake of your ignorance and your plotting. To you the Persian is a stupid peasant who can't decide his own affairs; an uncultured wretch who will take all manner of deceit and oppression and diplomatic twisting. If you do see any signs, any glimmer of revolt, you blame the Russians and take it to the Security Council. But it isn't the Russians. It's the peasant himself who is revolting. If any of you understood Iran you would know that. Dirty and wretched they may be, opium ridden and backward and dull, but they are really the people you should fear, not the Russians. It may take time, and there may be set-backs, but sooner or later the Persians are going to throw us out and throw out all our corrupt and friendly governments. They don't need any complicated political excuse to revolt, however much you cry Communism. There isn't a single man, woman or child in Iran who isn't landlord ridden; who isn't a slave by the way in which he works; who isn't preyed upon by corrupt officials; who isn't beaten and insulted and robbed by the police and the army. The peasants are impoverished by the tithes they must pay the Khans, and the mechanics are underpaid and underfed and overworked. There isn't an adult in Iran who isn't ridden with some chronic disease, there isn't a child who survives all the ravages of poverty and dirt and sickness. The whole government structure is rotten with bribery and extortion and petty cruelties, and there isn't a modicum of justice in the land. There are no real courts, no political rights, no representative government, no wage laws, no right to organize, no means of adjusting the bad conditions of life, except by revolting, as the Azerbaijanians and the Kurds are revolting. Thank heavens the Russians have given them a chance to revolt; and damn us for preventing it wherever we can. We will fail anyway, whatever the Security Council decides in New York. You can get the Russians out of Azerbaijan and you can give it back to your merchants and wazirs of Teheran, but after a little while it will all begin again because you cannot stop the Persian from deciding his own affairs. He is not ignorant and stupid about his political situation. He is not so wretched and afraid of revolt. He is not even uncultured: in the language he speaks and the use he makes of it there is more natural culture among the peasants of Iran than you can find among the world's diplomats at the Savoy Hotel. He is backward and poor and dirty, but that is largely due to the influence we have had on Iran for a hundred years or more. Now it is too late for us. These people have reached the breaking point, and they don't care about the wise men of the House of Commons and the clever men of the Security Council. These people are desperate, and for our reckless methods of holding our power and our oil it ought to be a warning. It will all go. The oil, the power, and the last drop of influence. Rather than let us have any of it the Persian will wreck Abadan and the wells and every other sign of our presence and our strength there. They are beginning to hate us and that is beginning a battle which we can't stop, which you can't stop in the Security Council. Unless we are determined to kill every man in the country we will lose. We cannot help but lose."

Katherine gave a little brandy to Essex now, so that this would be balanced. She did not sit down but stood near the fire, as if she were waiting impatiently for this duel or this siege to end. It could hardly go on much longer because there was more decision in the air than any of them could tolerate for long. The moments of silence seemed the moments of somebody's decision, some one of them, but Essex drank his brandy and retaliated.

"MacGregor," he said. "There is not going to be any more revolt in Iran, I assure you. We will restore the Teheran authority to Azerbaijan because we will carry our intentions much farther than the Russians dare. Already an Indian Division is being moved to Iraq and it will stay there ready for any emergency in Iran. The Americans are about to transfer ten million dollars' worth of arms to the Iranian Army, MacGregor. Think of it. Ten million dollars' worth of assistance, of equipment, guns, planes, tanks, transport, everything that an army needs to keep law and order in such a lawless country. What chance will your friends have, my boy? We will save democracy in Iran, and the Russian menace will be stamped out."

All the brandy had gone and Katherine was poised impatiently between them.

MacGregor was uncomfortable but he remained in his chair, on the edge of it. "If you are depending on ten million dollars to save Iran for you," he said, "you will certainly lose. Twenty and thirty million dollars would not make Iranian democracy better than it is. To begin with, half of your money will be taken by your best friends in Iran, the corrupt Ministers and the other good friends of Britain and America. What is left will not convince the rest of the population. It isn't American motor cars and refrigerators that the Persian wants, it is simple liberty that he needs. American money can never buy that off, and your American friends seem to realize it. I suppose that is why they provide for military equipment to save Iranian democracy. It's a revelation in the matter of democracy and its salvation when it can only be implemented by American dollars and American guns and British political plotting. Even so, I would bet on the ignorant stupid Persian defying you and defeating you, any day. You can pour out the money and you can pour out the guns, but you can't pour out the people to support you. Dollars and guns will only mean a new form of subjection, and it only adds another enemy for the simple man to fight. Perhaps almost too much for a simple man to fight!" MacGregor had become weary of it and he stopped suddenly. He watched Essex almost close his eyes in sleep and rest. MacGregor looked at Katherine, but she was hostile to both of them and she too had reached the last limit of her patience.

MacGregor stood up and they both watched him.

"It's getting late," MacGregor said.

"Yes," Katherine agreed pointedly.

"I suppose I had better be going," MacGregor told her.

She had not taken her eyes off him. "Perhaps you had better stay," she said to MacGregor.

They were quiet again and they looked at Essex.

Essex stirred. "How about some coffee, Katherine?" he said.

Katherine relaxed as if someone had snapped his fingers and awakened her from a nervous sleep. "It will have to be black," she said. "I had the last of the milk for dinner."

"Oh I never drink it white anyway," Essex said, and Katherine left them to make the coffee. She closed the door quietly as if she did not want to disturb them, and the room was very quiet without her presence.

They said nothing to each other. MacGregor was standing on the

Amritsar rug and Essex was deep in his chair with his blue suit neatly draped over his body and into the chair. He had folded his arms by holding his elbows, an old Essex habit. MacGregor watched him do it and realized that he too was holding his elbows like that. It was something that he had learned from Essex. It solved the problem of what to do with his hands, so MacGregor kept them as they were, even though Essex looked at him and smiled and dropped his own and felt for his pipe. He seemed to need his pipe but he did not straighten himself up. He went deeper and deeper into the leather chair, apparently determined never to leave it. When he had lit his pipe he threw back his head and blew a long cloud of smoke aloft and then settled back into his sunken position until Katherine arrived with the coffee.

Essex did not get up for his coffee. Katherine gave it to him and he drank it quietly. None of them said anything until they had finished. It seemed a long time, but Essex finally sighed and rose stiffly.

"I suppose I had better be going," he said.

Essex gave his coffee cup to Katherine and looked around for his grey coat.

"Have a lot to do for my Washington trip," he said.

MacGregor held his coat while he got into it.

"Can I drop you anywhere, MacGregor?"

"No thank you."

He held out his hand. "Then good night, my boy."

MacGregor felt his grip trail off. "Good night," MacGregor said.

"And good night Kathy," he said.

"Good night, Harold."

Katherine walked slowly with him to the library door. Essex did not turn around to see MacGregor standing on the hearth. He went out with Katherine, and MacGregor waited here for Katherine to come back.

When she came she was rubbing her bare arms. "It's getting cold," she said, and bent over the fire to have all its warmth and all its deep glowing colours. Then she stood up beside MacGregor, and they both looked straight ahead across the library waiting for the other to speak.

"Why did you say you were going?" she asked him briefly.

"I did that for Essex," he said.

"Oh?"

"I felt sorry for him," MacGregor said and still did not look at her.

For one reason or another she walked away, walked around the room, inspecting the books and the window and the two Etruscan vases, while MacGregor watched and wanted her to be still.

"What are your plans now?" she asked him. "Do you think you might stay in London?"

"No," he said.

628

"Well?" She finally confronted him. "What will you do?"

"I think I'll go back where I came from," he told her.

"Back to Iran?"

"Yes."

"Back to English-Persian?"

"No."

"Back to Azerbaijan?"

"If it's possible."

"What can you do there?"

"I don't know exactly."

She sat down to throw her head back and look at him. "You must have some idea," she said. "What about your work? Surely you have some plans. Are you a paleontologist again, MacGregor?"

"Not yet," he said, "but it will not take long. I'll pick up what I can at the Royal College, but once I get back home I'll be alright."

There was a moment of sharp delineation in her eyes, a demand for it. "You once said that micro-paleontology required the special conditions of a large oil-field. Will you find that anywhere in Iran but at English-Persian?"

"I doubt it."

"Then how will you do your work in Iran?"

"I'm not sure about that yet," he said and looked unsettled by this new problem. "In a way I'm not going back there just for my work."

"No?"

"This other thing has taken hold of me, Kathy. I've got to see how it comes out. I've got to be there. I can't quite explain it. I can't abandon my work, but even that means nothing unless I can see what is going on between one side and another in Iran. And don't imagine that I'm leaving here to run away."

She waited.

"If anything I am probably going deeper into this political mess."

"And your science?"

"I shan't know about that until I get there."

"You're not being indefinite about it are you?"

"No. No."

"Then how will you do your work?" she persisted. "Particularly if you go back to Azerbaijan. Are you thinking wildly of abandoning it?"

"I couldn't abandon it if I wanted to," he told her, irritated by her obsessive desire to clear this up. "I might have once; but I don't think anything else could have held me for long. I have to go on with my own work and even in Azerbaijan there are a hundred ways of picking it up where I have left off. There is more work there than any one man could do. Admittedly it's mostly field work, but even within the range of field

629

geology there is so much research for the micro-paleontologist that I'll be lost in it, Kathy. In some ways it will satisfy me more than the laboratory grind at Fields, and it will probably be more creative anyway."

"That's all very nice," she said. "But somebody has to give you this work."

"Javat Gochali was at me in Zenjan, and then again in Tabriz. They're desperate for geologists. They were all at me so often in Tabriz that I was tempted to stay even then."

"What if the Azerbaijanian regime is upset by Teheran?"

"There'll always be something going on there, Kathy."

"How will you live if that happens?"

"I have nine hundred pounds in the bank and the army owes me about three hundred pounds in terminal leave pay."

"But what can you do on your own?"

"I can be living there," he said and he was finally impatient, "and I can be doing whatever work I can until something else turns up. But I've just got to be in Iran."

She stood up slowly, facing him seriously. "Just so long as you are not going wildly off into some remote scheme, abandoning your work, and looking for the perfect answer to everything in an idealistic burst of home-coming."

"Are you suddenly acquiring an interest in my science, Kathy?"

"No, I'm not," she said. "I haven't the remotest part of a scientific brain in my head and I never will have. The most interest I have is in the simple answers it gives to the shape of the mountains, but beyond that I'll never be much interested in it. I'm only interested in making sure that you know what you're doing."

"For God's sake don't start that again."

"I shall always start it," she said. "And stop licking your lips as if you were in the middle of a desert."

He wiped his mouth dry with his handkerchief.

Katherine was still standing before him, looking at him with calm eyes, and waiting for something, some move on his part.

He bent down to put more coal on the fire.

"Don't do that," she said. "We shan't be needing the fire any longer."

He did not know what to do with himself for a moment, knowing that Katherine expected him to make some move in her direction. He turned casually instead to a small oil-painting of a vase of roses, his back almost to Katherine.

"What will John Asquith do, now that he has left the Foreign Office?" he asked. He was surprised by his own question because it came unintentionally.

"Well, he has an income of his own," she said.

"I don't mean that."

"I know you don't." She wanted to hear him talk of John Asquith, but he would not go farther. She had to answer the question for him. "You can be sure," she said, "that John will never sink into bitter retirement. Now that he has turned himself completely around he'll become a human dynamo of activity, trying to make up for the twenty years he considers lost."

MacGregor could say no adequate word of his feeling for John Asquith. He went on looking at the deep red picture of the roses. To change the subject Katherine asked him what sudden attraction the picture had.

"I was thinking of the roses in the barber's shop at Hajiabad."

"Those terrible things with collars on them," she said.

"What was terrible about them?"

"The paper frills spoiled them," she said.

"Perhaps they needed spoiling a little," he suggested mildly. "The Persians always look upon the rose as a conceited flower."

"Conceited?"

"Yes. You would probably like what they say of it," he said.

"Is it another of those exquisite extravagances?"

"Yes," he said.

"Then go on," she told him, but not impatiently.

He said slowly: "The Rose cried, 'I am Joseph in this Egypt-like garden, and I am also a priceless ruby with my mouth full of gold.' I replied, 'If thou art Joseph then show me a sign.' The Rose rejoined, 'Look at my bloody shirt!'"

She was smiling at him with her slight soft lips and her warm eyes and her long tender hands. "My dear MacGregor," she said softly. "Do you think we might ever go back to Hajiabad?"

He gave it elaborate thought. "I don't like those poppy villages," he said.

"Then do you think we might do anything but stand here?" she said.

"I don't know." He was almost laughing at her, but making no move, making no gesture, making no break with himself.

"Must I hit you on the head and drag you off?" she said quietly.

"My dear Kathy," he said with the smile still on his lips.

"Do you think you could try again?" she said.

It was slyly done, and while MacGregor felt the colour rising in his face, she slipped her hand very gently through his arm.